The virile, brilliant son, Father Thomas Kinsella—a priest whose rise to the presidency of Notre Dame could be a step toward a Cardinal's post, if he can put behind him a forbidden love for a beautiful movie star, his father's underworld connections and the bizarre conflicts of a Notre Dame football weekend that could shake the foundations of a powerful family, a city government and the very church itself!

"FULL OF COLORFUL CHARACTERS"
—*Milwaukee Journal*

**"HUMAN AND TOUCHING . . .
I LOVED IT!"**
—Ann Landers

FATHER'S DAY

A Novel by
Eugene Kennedy

PUBLISHED BY POCKET BOOKS NEW YORK

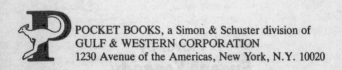

POCKET BOOKS, a Simon & Schuster division of
GULF & WESTERN CORPORATION
1230 Avenue of the Americas, New York, N.Y. 10020

Published by arrangement with Doubleday and Company, Inc.
Library of Congress Catalog Card Number: 80-2560

ISBN: 0-671-43242-7

First Pocket Books printing March, 1982

10 9 8 7 6 5 4 3 2 1

POCKET and colophon are trademarks of Simon & Schuster.

Printed in the U.S.A.

ACKNOWLEDGMENTS

My special thanks go to many people, to my brother, Bernard, who may be the most dedicated Notre Dame fan I have ever known, and to those at that university, particularly in the archives, who offered me assistance, and to Dick Conklin in the Public Relations Department. I am grateful to Jacqueline Kennedy Onassis and Lisa Drew, who edited this book. It was really fun to work with them. I want also to thank Tom Boodell and, especially, Dick Trezevant. And there were Kay Phelan and my wonderful secretary, Mary Louise Schniedwind.

FOR

SARA . . .
BILL MADDUX . . .
FIGHTING IRISH EVERYWHERE . . .

CONTENTS

PART I

PART II

PART III

PART IV

PART V

PART VI

PART VII

The bells of hell go ting-a-ling-ling
For you
But not for me . . .

Brendan Behan

PART I

PART 1

Introduction

Rockne, I always thought, was a noisy bastard, a brass band of a man forever crowding you and winking inside at his own tricks. You've heard that he had the faith of a child, dying with his beads in his hands and all, but he was cunning too, as cute as FDR, and he might have gotten to be President if he'd put his mind to it. There is no doubt that Rockne helped put us, Notre Dame that is, on the map and maybe you have to understand him to understand the whole thing.

Rock wasn't the spirit of Notre Dame, not all by himself, despite that Pat O'Brien movie. But he was like the men, a handful and a half of them, who made the spirit of Notre Dame. Tough and active, some vulgar and some pious, they all had one thing in common. Mind you, they didn't think the thing out at all. Such men don't have the time for grand introspective journeys. The world of action was the place for them because of what, to a man, they understood so well, which was how to get, keep, and use power.

I want to tell you about one of them, the lad who took over when Father Hesburgh left for that big international job. A tough act to follow, you say, and you are surely right. But Thomas Patrick Kinsella was a man in his own right, as was his father, old P.B. You've heard parts of the story already but let me fill you in. It was complicated. After all, it involved church, state, football, politics, power in all of them. And sex too, even though not everybody, not then and not now, was willing to call it that.

And I—Austin Kenna is my name—had a ringside seat.

Since Frank O'Malley died in 1974, I have been the sole surviving bachelor don, I truly am, and pretty old too, the last of a long line of professors who never married and who made the University their life, keeping rooms, as I've done for more than fifty years, in a hall on campus. Since Frank has gone—can it be ten years he's dead now?—there's nobody much to talk stories with over a drink anymore.

So, thinking about Tom Kinsella and his father, I decided to put it all down before I can't remember, or start making it up instead of telling it straight and clear. There wasn't much I didn't know first hand, seeing that, even though I'm not a priest, I was sort of father confessor to almost everybody involved. And the things I've learned just sitting at the bar in the University Club on campus, well, they'd fill the archives. Then there were the notes and Thomas Kinsella's own journals, not to mention his father's. But I'd seen most of it close up anyway.

I've gone eighty now and I interrupt myself for a drink now and then and sometimes I wonder if I dreamed parts of it. No matter. It will help you understand Notre Dame. I'm not sure it could ever have happened this way any place else.

1

Notre Dame
October 21, 1983
6:00 P.M.

It was the day before the Southern California game, just after dinner time, and the campus was like a golden dream. The turrets and shields of maples and oaks always took on richer and subtler tones in the autumn twilight. If you didn't notice the tangle of toilet paper draped across a bank of evergreens you would have thought the scene was idyllic, just right for the picture postcards. The campus was always quiet, in a special kind of way, even during a hectic football weekend. Always lots of people at work in their rooms and the library. Ambition was part of it but so too was the special brand of Catholic obsessiveness, as hard and true as the Protestant ethic, that had pervaded the place from the year one. Come along now. There are things you must see and important people you have to meet.

A mysterious quiet hung almost like a veil over the broad quadrant that stretched out in front of the administration building. A wonder of Victorian construction, that building, and thrown up in less than a year after a disastrous fire took the first one down in 1874. It is one of those buildings that is hard to get a really good look at no matter where you stand. A lime-colored mass set with churchlike windows, it was choked with columns, ramps of stairs, and a French village of gables and spires that spread out on the roof just below the outsized golden dome on which the statue of the Virgin stood. *Notre Dame,* Lady of the university's two lakes, icon of two thousand years of Catholic devotion, Holy Mother of learning and virtue, glowed on a burnished half-globe in the fading light.

Students were hurrying across the walks and lawns, past a century's worth of changing architecture, toward the tortoiselike shell of Stepan Center, in which the pep rally for the next day's game was to be held. Close up the band, so military at a distance, looked different. Its sweating members seemed astonishingly vulnerable to the miscarriages of life, here a homely girl wore a tuba and there a boy with acne played at the drums. But they bent to their tasks with great sincerity and were already filling the carapace of the hall with the spirited anthems of football.

The young man who had thrown the toilet paper into the trees was standing near the entrance watching the parade of Notre Dame coeds and girls from nearby St. Mary's College with a swelling heart and a painful sense that all he could ever long for or ever want was passing before him just beyond reach. His name was Timothy Duffy and he felt that he might die at the freshness and lightness of the young women who streamed past him.

Back across the sweep of the darkening campus at the main entrance, just down from the old cemetery, one could make out the Morris Inn, the conventional brick motel that looked out on the University golf course. Gifts, both of them, the

golf course from an alumnus in the twenties and the inn from
another one, a non-Catholic at that, who had been taken in
many years before by the school even though he had no
money. Inside another alumnus had just registered and gone
with his wife to their room. Patrick and Mae Kinsella were a
little different. Their son, "Father Tom," as she called him,
was now president of Notre Dame University, this splendid
shrine of a place for just such Irish couples, this altar of
religious devotion and symbol of Catholic determination and
achievement in American society. Patrick, old P.B., had
played on Rockne's last team and some said that he had never
recovered from it, that in his bull-like way he had continued
to live out the unquestioned virtues of football, hitting hard at
life, and turning suddenly quiet and calculating when it did
not give in to him.

Old P.B.—"Powerful Bastard," some said the initials stood
for—was still handsome as some Irish are, in a way that
seemed almost unfair to men less blessed by nature. His blue
eyes were clear and his face, always tanned, was only lightly
seamed by either age or regret. P.B. did not feel guilty about
his life. He was still too caught up in it to lay it freely on any
balance scale. He looked so good—politician, aging Hollywood star good—and, besides that, he gave little thought, if
any at all, to the times he had been so bad. I always wondered
whether he was aware of how he used his force and his tricks
or whether he even noticed much when he pushed others out
of the way. Patrick had no ear for the wailing of the wives and
children whose husbands he had ruined. He was pleased with
himself, comfortable with getting what he wanted, and generous in his benefactions. Mae kept a paneled room at home
filled with his awards and trophies along with those of the
children, including Father Tom. She held on to her men, this
shouldering tribe so different in many ways and so alike in
others, in this hideaway where the light blinked softly from
the medallions and frames. She could savor these men,
especially P.B. and Father Tom, around whom her life had
been built. I don't think she ever let herself ask how well she
knew them or where she really fit in their scheme of things.

"Have a drink, Mae?" Patrick Kinsella asked as he ran his
fingers through his white wavy hair and pulled his tie loose.

"Why not?" she answered in the phrase she had used so
many times before. "The sun has set and we're on holy
ground." Mae's voice had a smoky, crackling quality to it;

that larynx had been through a lot, regular washes of liquor and the exercise of shouting matches, not to mention the cigarettes. Well, you know the voice, it goes with women who get to be called "handsome," women standing in high style on the last slopes of middle age, the good looks a little stiff and pinched but still there if you don't look too closely. Mae had learned how to smile even in grim circumstances. It was a handy talent to have.

"Shall we call Tom?" she asked.

"Later," P.B. said as he unzipped a carrying case for a bottle of scotch and one of Bourbon. "Some important visitor's with him, some Italian Archbishop in from the Vatican." He threw the sentences away like an underplaying actor. Mae looked at him quizzically, wondering what he knew about the visit that he was treating with deliberate casualness.

"What is it about, Pat?" she asked dryly.

"Damned if I know," her husband answered, turning toward her with a sharklike smile. "I suppose it's some ginney who wants scholarships for all his sister's kids down in Sicily."

"Oh, Pat," she said in the tempering voice she had used to charm or calm him over the years. "He may be a very holy man, P.B. Back from darkest Africa, begging for the poor . . ."

"Not likely, Mae," Kinsella replied as he poured scotch into two plastic glasses. "Never know, of course. It's business, I think. Odds are, he has his hand out."

"Well," Mae responded, "here's to Tom then. May he not give away the Golden Dome tonight!" She looked for P.B.'s eyes, but he had moved to the window to peer through the falling darkness toward the administration building, where his son's offices were.

"Agreed," he said without looking around. "Maybe he can give the football coach to the ginney. Matt Finn would be a good human sacrifice to offer the Holy See."

The president of the University of Notre Dame, Thomas Patrick Kinsella, was a grand stand of a man, just past forty-three and put together from the best pieces of his mother and father. He had just toasted Archbishop Luigi Trafficante, an assistant to the Vatican Secretary of State, with a glass of the prelate's favorite wine. Tom's memory for just such details had always served him well; he was particu-

larly good at remembering the fancies of older and more
powerful men. He had always felt two ways about them,
liking their survivor's hardiness but wary of the doings in
their closed-off innards. Being with them was always like
being in a game. Tom decided to make a move.

"Excellency," he said in his almost musical voice, "welcome again to South Bend. A small city and yet there are
those who love her."

The Archbishop, a sallow indoors man with a face smooth
as a noodle, smiled thinly. "Thank you, Father Thomas," he
said in lightly accented tones. "But your South Bend is no
small city. It contains your great University."

"Yes," Father Kinsella replied, the music gone for the
moment from his voice. He had some idea of why the
Archbishop had insisted on coming to Notre Dame. He
sensed that there was something beyond sociability, yes, and
something beyond the delivery of some Vatican manuscripts
to the library, as phony a cover story as he had ever heard.
Kinsella had sensed it in the way the original letter had been
phrased and had even overheard it in the oily voice of the
Archbishop's secretary when the latter, all oohs and ahs, had
confirmed the visit by phone. And now he sensed it with great
clarity as the Archbishop sat without his secretary in Kinsella's office on the second floor of the administration building. Thomas Kinsella decided to wait Trafficante out; he was
very good at waiting people out.

"There are other great cities in your country, Father
Kinsella," the Archbishop said. He paused, this diplomat
who moved as gracefully and silently as a pendulum, because
he knew that one introduced every important subject gently,
almost diffidently. Shadings and nuances could mean everything in the language of papal inquiry that had been rubbed
to the subtlest of glows through hundreds of years of use. The
phrase was in itself almost enough to get his meaning across.
It suggested places beyond Notre Dame, dark but airy
openings and opportunities, a barrelful of possibilities to a
sophisticated listener like Tom Kinsella.

"Yes," Kinsella responded steadily. "There are great cities
throughout this country, in every direction." The Archbishop
had turned to inspect the wall of books on the west side of the
room. He suddenly turned back toward Tom, as though he
had decided to move more straightforwardly than it seemed
at first. A man of surprises, this Trafficante, Tom thought as

the Archbishop put his glass down on the president's desk and addressed him directly.

"Father Kinsella," he said almost sweetly. "You are a man of great experience. You have worked in education, you have served in the missions, you have, I believe, even carried out diplomatic assignments for the Holy See. I know that I can speak frankly and confidentially to you."

"Of course, Excellency."

"There is no need to observe all the niceties, as one would with other people. I am here to ask you if you would be interested in accepting new responsibilities from the Church."

Tom looked directly back at Trafficante, giving nothing away in his expression, and letting the Archbishop take responsibility for the conversation.

"As you know, Father Thomas," he continued, "the present Archbishop of Chicago is already past the retirement age. He is ready to accept an appointment in Rome. He is, I might say, quite willing for this to happen. We can discuss the reasons for that later. The important thing is the archdiocese, the largest in your country. The Holy See wants to have the right man take it over. It needs new leadership, a rejuvenation . . ." The Archbishop paused and walked toward the window.

Father Kinsella still had not changed his expression. This was a big offer, a sure Cardinal's hat, a chance to give strong leadership among a field of American bishops known best for their genial mediocrity. But it was a difficult job as well because the archdiocese had been demoralized for years with lay people who were rebellious or indifferent and bands of priests who were similarly divided. The loyal, unquestioning Catholics had all gotten old and lived under the sun in Florida or Arizona. Chicago was not what it once had been as a vital center of Catholic life. But Trafficante was implying something more; something Tom could not quite understand had been factored into what otherwise seemed a surprisingly clear presentation. He decided to listen further rather than to speak.

"First of all, Father," the Archbishop said as though he were beginning his explanations afresh, "there is a grave problem with authority in the Church, with spiritual authority and its acceptance through the teaching authority of the Pope and bishops. You are a man who could help greatly to

re-establish this authority in the United States. You have the
credentials, you already have a very significant position even
though you have been in it only a few years."

He paused again. "And, Father, I don't have to tell you
that there have been problems in Chicago, that it is now
urgent, for the good of the Church, to make the transition as
smoothly as possible. There can be no great delay or we will
witness an effort at popular voting for the present Cardinal
Archbishop's successor. We will see, in other words, more of
the trends that have eaten away at Church authority. That is
why there is some urgency about this. I am sure you
understand."

Kinsella understood well enough. He was being offered
one of the most influential positions in the American Church.
That did not surprise him. Such offers had been made to
previous presidents of the University. One of them, the
ascetic John O'Hara, who lay buried in the old Sacred Heart
Church not more than a good peg from the outfield away
from this office, had become Archbishop of Philadelphia and
a Cardinal. Kinsella looked directly at Trafficante, who had
once more picked up his glass of wine. "This is an unusual
and very great honor, Excellency," Kinsella said slowly.
"You must understand that I need time to think about this, I
need to pray about it . . ."

Back in Stepan Hall Coach Matt Finn, with one loss and a
couple of close shaves in the football season so far, looked
under pressure as he rose to speak to the pep rally gathering.
The band had stopped but the music, like heat waves on a
summer day, still hung in the charged air. A few signs
wobbled above the shifting crowd of students. "Coach Finn
Can't Win," ran one inscription while another proclaimed,
"Against Sin and Finn." A scattering of catcalls greeted the
football coach, who, as so many Notre Dame coaches before
him, found that a little bad luck in football could transform
students and alumni into a thumbs-down crowd out of the
lusty old Coliseum. Many coaches had gone down under
these and the other pressures connected with his job. Finn
also knew that he had the fundamental loyalty of the students
who were spread out before him. He looked vaguely
depressed—he always did, you remember—but he understood that he was at the center of one of the spectacles that

held the autumn together, that gave the students some sense of identity at least temporarily, and made them feel one with a vibrant tradition. Finn knew that he was dealing with the mythic element in University life and he was ready to summon up ghosts to generate a storm of spirit for the next day's game. He had taken a drink at two o'clock but its effects, mild as they were, had long since dissipated. "Students of Notre Dame," he thundered in an oratorical style that was ideal for such gatherings, "God may want us to be Number One . . ."

Cheers and applause exploded beneath the quilted aluminum ceiling of the hall. Finn, looking truculent and morose at the same time, waited for the noise to die away and then cut across the last murmurs with his powerful voice, "But we have to do the work to make ourselves Number One!" The students erupted again, enjoying letting themselves go in what seemed pure and innocent passion.

"Wait," Finn said, raising a hand to still the now rhythmically chanting crowd. "Listen to the voices of the past. You can hear them in the trees and in the wind . . ."

Now the place was silent, even the energy of the music suddenly evaporated. Finn knew how to lead an audience along; he had done it on the banquet circuit with great success, he had brought tears to the eyes of the alumni in many a crowded ballroom with his lost battalion reunion mixture of pathos and verve. "Listen and you can hear them in your hearts, the great coaches and priests and players who were here before you, the ones who built our traditions . . ." The students began to cheer again and to hold up their hands in the "We're Number One" symbol. Finn was waiting them out.

Back by the entrance door a young dark-haired girl in a raincoat with no makeup on her plain but open face, approached Timothy, who was standing near the wall. She touched him on the shoulder and lifted her face toward him so that he could see her dark, almost haunted eyes. He jumped a bit and felt a strange warm current flowing through his body. "Timothy," she said, "you are Timothy Duffy, aren't you?" "Yes," he said haltingly for his breath seemed to have escaped him. "Would you come with me, Timothy?" she asked against the background of Coach Finn's voice summoning the shade of Rockne to appear. "Where?" he asked

somewhat confusedly, but he was already being led away by
this fantasy come true, by this girl who seemed to float, a
vessel of bittersweet promise, just beyond him.

Halfway back across the campus to the west the lights were
on in the rooms of Father Jack Allen, whose great lined face
showed the wear of every one of his sixty years. "Come in,"
he yelled in a roughened voice, one of the accidental luxuries
of personality that made him seem fierce when in fact he was
not. A younger priest, Father Andrew Simmons, degreed
twice with doctorates in physics and philosophy, entered. He
was thirty-four years old and had once been a student of
Father Allen's. "Well, well, if it isn't Doctor Doctor," Allen
said as he entered. "Welcome to Professor Allen's Pep
Rally." Father Simmons took a chair as his host searched
around in a closet for a bottle. He emerged with two, one of
them an empty Chivas Regal bottle, and the other filled with
a brand of scotch that Simmons had never heard of.

"Watch this," Allen said, an impish and playful tone
invading his voice. "I went out to the liquor store this
afternoon, see, and I asked the guy behind the counter if he
had any cheap scotch. Well, smart little bastard, he says, 'We
don't have any cheap scotch but I can show you an excellent
inexpensive scotch.' Fine, I say, so he shows me this stuff,
four dollars the bottle." He began pouring it into the empty
Chivas Regal bottle.

"Jack, what are you doing?" Father Simmons asked, half in
surprise and half in amusement, for he had always taken
delight in the purposeful exaggerations that marked Father
Allen's style.

"Well, your great expert, Ronald Keating, will be dropping
in for a drink in a little while. You know he thinks he has a
great palate for the fine wines and liquors. Watch him head
for this Chivas when he comes in. The bastard'll smack his
lips and tell us how wonderful it is, how different from your
ordinary brand . . ."

"Are you really going to do that?" Father Simmons asked.
"I mean, he may taste that there's something wrong right
away . . ."

"Keating? Hell, he's been freeloading drinks for years.
Christ, he'd drink anything as long as it was free. His tongue
is like a stick of wood. You watch and see . . ."

"Do you have anything besides this?" Simmons asked, half

afraid that he might have to participate in the ruse more than he desired.

"No, no," Allen said, producing yet another bottle. "The real Chivas is in this, in your nice Black and White bottle. Stick with this. Gotta be ready for the big game tomorrow." Allen was speaking ironically, for he was not enthused about the football team or about the focus it had in the public view of the University. "Why, the buses are lining up back in Cicero and Berwyn right now. Waiting to take on your nice hogbutchers and sewerworkers ready with their knockwurst sandwiches and their flasks of rotgut, ready for their big day falling out of the stands at good old N.D." Allen ended with a flourish and poured himself a weak drink. He was always mindful of not irritating a now healed ulcer.

Father Simmons laughed. He knew that Allen was trying to entertain him and that there was no bite at all behind his bark. He also understood that Allen loved an appreciative audience for his sardonic pronouncements. "Jack," he said in the space that opened up while Allen sipped his drink, "I hope you have some time later for a talk. Just you and me."

Allen stiffened in his chair. Simmons had been one of the brightest apples of his eye, a young man ready to carry on the best traditions of dedicated Catholic education. Allen had been expecting that the young man would want to talk to him, had, in fact, feared it and wanted to wave it or pray it away. Too many of the young men he had encouraged had come to him in the last ten years, knowing they could talk to him freely about the decisions they were pondering. These had coalesced into a great weight on his own soul. He had always been willing to listen to people's troubles but it had never been such a burden in the old days. The good old days—he would often smile as he thought of them—the good old days when the Church was a great disciplined presence and there was no faltering, there were no conflicts in the young about doing their own thing, or finding their true selves. So many of them had come to him for counsel and he felt a loss each time one of them decided to leave the priesthood even though he knew it might be the right thing for them. He felt as though he had gradually been picked apart and there was a great longing and wonder about it in his soul. He knew that Simmons, the brilliant Simmons with so much promise, would bring him another problem like that. "Sure, Andy," he replied softly. "Any time."

There was a knock at the door and Father Ronald Keating, scholar extraordinaire but a man who never quite finished anything, including his doctoral dissertation, entered. He was handsome, with a streak of white running through his dark brown hair. "Aha!" he said. "Jack, you old devil, you're serving Chivas Regal. Nothing quite tastes like it." Allen and Simmons, their own serious business in abeyance for the moment, exchanged poker-faced glances as Keating poured himself half a glass of the substitute liquor. He sipped it and smacked his lips. "Ah, nothing like it," he said. "You can tell right away."

The young girl had led Timothy around the lake and across the campus to a far edge of the golf course. She had said little as they moved through the darkness. "You look like someone who will understand," she said. "I know that you do understand."

"But where are we going?" Timothy, growing apprehensive, asked as they hurried along under a moon that was just rising in the sky.

"We are doing the Lord's work, Timothy," she said, pulling him along more urgently. "There is so much the Lord wants us to understand." Timothy wondered about all this because he was still stirred by this girl's fresh and open qualities, by the almost overpowering sensuality that rose from her, and he was in conflict about her and about what he wanted or might expect from her on this surrealistic journey. He had not, however, expected Joan of Arc, and was confronting the terrible conflict of having indulged his lustful longings, of having committed an old Catholic sin, of having said yes to a proposition that was all in his imagination. It had not been offered and Timothy knew that it never would be.

"Timothy," she said as she stopped at a place about a hundred yards from Route 31, that edged along the campus as it bisected South Bend. "This is where we will celebrate, this is where we will remember. This is where the Lord wants us to call for repentance." Her voice had become quite intense as she pointed to an object that was lying on the ground just beyond where they stood.

Timothy stared down and could make out that it was a large wooden cross and that next to it lay a pick and shovel and some rope.

"Oh, Timothy, help me put this cross up here, this symbol

of salvation." She seemed far away from him now, in some other world, and, all his carnal musings having vanished, he began to be afraid.

"Please, Timothy," she said. "The world has been evil and impure. The world has forgotten the word of the Lord. The world has shamed the good."

Aware that he had come close to forgetting this completely himself, Timothy decided to acquiesce. "Okay, okay, but then I've got to go." He took up the pick and began to soften the ground at the point to which the young girl pointed.

About forty-five minutes later the cross was standing firmly in the fairway sod. Timothy was perspiring heavily and, feeling that with luck he might have made amends for whatever failures were his earlier in the evening, he said, "Well, I gotta get back . . ."

"One last thing, Timothy, one final request from the Lord," the girl said pleadingly. She unbuttoned her raincoat and let it fall to the ground. She was wearing a white gown, a flimsy one tied at the waist with a cord.

Timothy stood there, on the edge of being caught up once more in the plaguing desires of his young manhood. "Yeah?" he asked warily, unable, try as he would, to look away from her.

"You must help tie me to the cross now, Timothy," she said in a clear and commanding voice, as though she were now exactly sure of what she had to do.

"Oh, Jesus!" Timothy said involuntarily.

"It is for Jesus that I ask for your help," she replied.

"Look," Tim said in a shaking voice, "I don't even know who you are. I mean, what are we doing here anyway, what are we remembering and who are we calling to repentance? I can't tie you on that cross . . ."

"Oh, Timothy," she said. "There've always been doubters. You looked like a believer to me. That's why I trusted you . . ."

"Well, thanks and all, but it's late and, and . . ." Timothy turned and began to run as fast as he could, already resolving to say nothing to anyone about the incident, running swiftly back to his dormitory, which looked like a castle of saving lights in the distance.

Back at the Morris Inn Mr. P.B. Kinsella had just received a long-distance phone call from Chicago. It was the still reigning Cardinal Archbishop who wished to speak with him. P.B. smiled as he picked up the receiver. "Everything all right, Your Eminence?" he began, and his smile broadened out.

Across the lake in Moreau Seminary Coach Finn had seen to it that the football players had all retired for the night. He was thinking of having a drink but decided against it as he remembered the early rising when he and the team, mostly not Irish and some black and some brown, and half of them not Catholics at all, would all attend Mass together to pray for a great victory in the afternoon game.

Father Keating had stayed on for three of Jack Allen's scotches and had launched into a monologue about the book he was almost ready to write, the big one that would amaze all scholars, the one he would write, yes, when he wasn't quite as busy as he was now.

In the guest suite at the Priests' Residence Archbishop Trafficante was sitting at a desk writing a report in a fine spidery hand.

Father Thomas Patrick Kinsella was walking slowly through the darkness toward the Morris Inn for a visit with his parents and a late dinner.

On the golf course, under a now bright moon, a young woman had managed to climb up on a small pediment set on the upright of the cross and tie one arm to the crossbar.

In Zahm Hall the students, shifting into the night life rhythm that dominated their lives, talked of how much beer they could drink, of their fantasies about girls, and of the great football victory that lay on the other side of dawn. "Where have you been, Tim?" Joe Sclafani asked as his roommate, perspiring and agitated, stumbled through the door. "You look like you've seen a ghost."

2

October 21, 1983
9:30 P.M.

It was after nine, and me in my slippers and just the slightest bit unsteady from nothing more than a brandy—or was it two?—when a knock sounded on my door in Sorin Hall. Most of the bachelor dons had lived there, including old "Colonel" Hoynes, the great old dandy who taught law for forty years right on the first floor, right near the room with the piano where the Shea boys wrote the Notre Dame Victory March back in Teddy Roosevelt's time. A crusty old hall, with a handsome share of slate turrets and even an old-fashioned front porch, and my rooms were just fine, big doors and high ceilings, and since I was a bachelor, nobody to scold me for the piles of papers and books all over the place. Cozy I would call them, a man's rooms. And there was a man at the door, Thomas Patrick Kinsella himself.

"Austin," he said in a voice as soft as the shadows he stood in, "do you have a minute?"

"That's mostly what I have," I said, "if you don't mind the scholarly disarray. Come in and have a chair."

I must say I didn't know what to make of it, the president of the University at my door, a scene I had only imagined—and enjoyed imagining—as happening some morning when they found me stiff and dead, you know, like I was the Pope, so old and around so long they'd have to hit me on the head with a little hammer to make sure I was gone, an old man's fancies to be sure. But there he was, and both of us still alive, only he looked tired, as tired as I felt, as he walked into the light of the room.

"Would you have a brandy, Father Thomas?" I asked, still

17

using the formal address even though I had known him well for many years, going back to when he was a student, a quiet sort of fellow in class who never asked many questions but was good with the answers.

"Yes," he said, "I think I would." He sat down in a cracked brown leather chair where the lamp outlined his features, quite Irish they were, like those of a cop on a safety poster, and improving with early middle age. I poured him some brandy and, my head cleared by the surprise of his arrival, I added a dash and a little more in my own glass.

"Austin," he said calmly, turning the snifter in his hands, "I want to talk something over with you, the way a man might with his confessor. In fact, I was told that I might discuss this with a confessor, so, if you don't mind, I'm appointing you that for the evening."

"Well now, just as you say, just as you say. My experience, however, has been more with making confessions than hearing them."

"Well, you've kept many a confidence over all these years. That's what I want now, to talk with somebody who knows how to do that." He paused and looked directly across at me. I felt a little flustered, with no joke at hand to lessen the tension that strung out on a line between our eyes. Let me admit I was always better at the pat on the back, the "Buck up, lad," and a dash of bitters mixed in with some humor, the better to deflect the demands of intimacy, very Irish of me as you may have noticed. But Thomas Kinsella was not there for banter outside the pub, he was not there to swap stories, and his look sent a shiver through me.

"I know, Austin, that I haven't been in these rooms since I was a student here. You're an old friend and more. You are an institution, you know that, a genuine Notre Dame institution. You've lived through a lot of our history. I feel that, in many ways, you are a real link with our history, our experience, whatever you want to call it. I still like to think of it as a special spirit we've had here."

"Yes," I said. "An old-fashioned word, spirit, but a very good one."

"You have what I guess we could call a certain perspective that nobody else could even put a claim to. You know our ideals, you know our failings. That's why I decided to talk to you."

He had not sipped his brandy; he held it as though it were a stage prop and I, alert and mildly anxious, sloshed mine gently in the glass while the president continued.

"I've been offered a new position," he said, and my heart jumped for, ashamed though I am to confess it, my first reaction was to wonder how I would make out and who would take care of me if he left.

"It's an important job but it would mean leaving here, giving up educational work and becoming a bishop." He spoke matter-of-factly while I tried to calm myself.

"You may know, Austin, that I have a visitor from the Vatican, Trafficante by name. He wants go get it settled this weekend if possible. The job in question is the archbishopric of Chicago." Kinsella paused but not in the style of a man waiting for me to say something back to him. In fact, his mood, that of a confident man musing out loud, relieved me. It wasn't advice that he wanted; it was a safe place to talk and an open ear on the head of a man whose ambitions were only souvenirs from the past. And I think he wanted a believer, somebody who still had romantic faith in the glory of Notre Dame, and not some nitwit climber in a Roman collar ready to hop into his chair if he so much as got up to go to the washroom.

"It's a great challenge," he said, and I was glad not to hear any false modesty, not a temptation to unworthiness there.

"And it means a red hat within a year. Most of all it means a chance to take leadership in the Catholic Church in this country. You know that I have always been critical of most American bishops. Well, this would show whether I could do any better, whether I could try to get the Church going again the way John Kennedy talked of getting the country going again back in 1960." Kinsella put his glass down and frowned.

"The problem, as I see it, and I haven't really thought much about it, haven't really had time to, has at least two parts to it." Seeing as I was still not needed, I took a gulp of my brandy.

"The first problem would come up right here. A problem of succession would open up and the University doesn't need that trouble right now. We've come too far, particularly under Hesburgh, to risk having almost any of the possible candidates take over . . ."

"Well," I blurted out, "there's Father Green. I mean, many people think that he . . ." But I let the words fall of their own weight to the floor as Father Kinsella said nothing, just made a kind of steeple with his hands in front of his expressionless face. It wasn't advice, especially not advice about a possible successor, that he wanted.

"Austin," he said evenly, "there is no number two man here."

I sipped some more brandy as he finally took a bit of his before he spoke again.

"This is a great University and not just on football weekends. That is the least of it, in a way. Excellence is a rare commodity, especially in Catholic education, perhaps in education in general, and, Austin, to tell the truth, I am not sure whether it is more important to be the president of Notre Dame or the Cardinal Archbishop of Chicago."

What struck me, of course, was the easy flow of his words, as though no debate was needed, as though he was absolutely certain of his judgment, or, more accurately, that he did not even need to make a judgment about it. Here was a lad easy with power, I thought, as easy with it as his father, P.B., had always been, but different too. Oh, I had noted it before at the University. Hesburgh had been like that, no false protests of humility, no wondering what to do; so had others, including Rockne and Leahy. They all seemed to have an instinct for power. I'll tell you this, they never apologized for having it, and Thomas Kinsella, big as life in my cluttered sitting room, wasn't apologizing either.

"Well, Austin, there is more to it than even that. And this is what really concerns me. I have a funny feeling about this and I can't be sure of what it is . . ." His voice trailed off; if he was intellectually assured, he seemed to be searching his emotions, sorting them out, quietly enough but under some pressure too. He was bothered, I could see that, like a man befuddled by a compass that wouldn't give a true reading.

"All I can say," he began again, "is that it is a remarkable offer and yet there is something about it that makes me wary of it."

"Well," I intervened tentatively, "there does seem to be a lot of bait on the hook."

"Yes, yes," Father Kinsella said, "I think that too. But it's more than that. You know, Austin, I just had a bite of supper with my parents. I didn't mention this business, not at all, and yet it seemed to be in the air. Just hanging there, sort of a pressure of expectation . . ." He paused again, for we both knew that he was getting into close quarters, into the intimacy

that made me uneasy, into family reflections he might otherwise keep to himself. People had often speculated about the
Kinsella clan and old P.B., the patriarch, but not many,
maybe not any of those who speculated, really had any inside
information on how they lived or what they thought about
each other. They were in the magazines and the papers all the
time, old P.B. and Mae and the sons, the two lawyers, Martin
and Joe, and Father Thomas, the goddam fulfillment of every
Irish-American's dream, the president of Notre Dame, and
there he was staring intently at me, scaring me that I might
learn more about the Kinsellas than I wanted to.

"Austin," he said, "you've known my father a long time,
since before I was even born." He shifted in the old chair and
just barely tasted his brandy. "I'd like you to tell me about my
father, about old P.B., I'd like to hear you talk about him."

"Well," I said, trying to regain my balance after such an
unexpected request, "a great man, your father, a great man,
as you and your marvelous family must know. Always a
scrapper, P.B., one of the greats . . ."

"Austin," Father Kinsella interrupted me, "I know all that,
I've heard it a thousand times. That's not what I'm interested
in, the great flag-waving papal knight, the great industrialist
and benefactor. I've lived with that a long time. I just want to
hear what you think about him without the usual clichés.
That's why I came to you. I thought you were old and wise
enough to speak off the cuff to me. I don't expect any great
revelations, Austin, I just want to hear about him from
somebody who has known him from another angle. That's
you, Austin, from way back when he was a student here."

"Well, Father," I began, my head suddenly a slide show of
old P.B. and my chest filled out, like a sail in the wind, with
ambivalent feelings about him. "You must know that your
father is a most unusual man, not a man that leaves people
feeling indifferent about him. Love him or hate him, that's
mostly it. I think he makes weaker men afraid, that is, men
who don't have the self-confidence he's always had. Why,
Thomas"—I hardly noticed my own shift into more informal
address—"I remember the first time I saw him, oh, it must
have been 1928 or '29, at a football scrimmage. There was this
giant of a fellow and your father was just medium-sized
compared to him. And the fellow, right out of the steel mills
by the name of Flathead or Pinhead or some such name . . ."

My recollections, rising like an unsteady stream of smoke

out of the past, were interrupted by another knock on the door. What an evening, I thought to myself, it'll probably be old P.B. himself, roused from his sleep by a sense that someone was talking about him. It was instead Father Green, a vice-president, a slim, dark-eyed fellow, who still used Vaseline in a mane of hair that was the color of a cloudy sky.

"I'm sorry to disturb you, Professor," he said, trying to peer over my shoulder into the room. He was all unguent, I thought, as I looked at him in the half-light, a slight gleam to his skin, a sweaty look, you might say, and a slop of chrism in his voice. He was half an Arab and half an American, but he favored the Arab and I wondered if oil didn't run in his veins.

"I've been looking for Father Kinsella," he said, "and I was told that he was seen heading this way."

"Well, he's here, to be sure," I said, waving him in.

"What is it, Jeffrey?" Kinsella asked, looking more than a little annoyed that we had been interrupted, and maybe a little mad that Father Green, a snooper around the residence halls if ever there was one, had tracked him to my room.

"I'm sorry to disturb you, Tom," he said, "and I ordinarily wouldn't bother you with a thing like this. But I knew you had Archbishop Trafficante here and that we have a big game tomorrow and, well, I thought we ought to let you know."

"About what, for God's sake?" Father Kinsella asked in a voice that sounded like he had a sore throat.

"Well," Green, showing no upset at all, replied, "we had a call from the campus police about half an hour ago. Something's going on out on the golf course. There's a crowd gathering, some of them our students, some of them people from town, we're not sure how many, maybe a couple of hundred." He cleared his throat and went on.

"There's a young girl there. She's tied to a cross and she's proclaiming a time for repentance. She's singing and praying and she's got the crowd doing it too. She says Notre Dame is the place for an act of national repentance for all the country's sins . . ."

"That's not a police matter, Jeff," Kinsella answered. "That sounds like a medical matter, a girl who needs some help. Is she one of our students?"

"We're not sure, maybe St. Mary's."

"Well, Jeff, this isn't a thing to get out of proportion, not a disturbed girl calling for repentance."

"No," Green replied in a tone that left me uncertain as to

whether he was upset or glad that the incident was occurring. "I know we shouldn't disturb you. But the crowds won't let the campus police near her and the dean of students hasn't had any luck either. They're all just praying and singing around this cross and they won't let anybody get close."

"Jeffrey," Kinsella said, as though giving an order, "this is something that will go away if you don't blow it up. It needs gentle handling, not panic. You should take care of this quietly. And quickly."

"Well, I would," Father Green replied, "and I've called the public relations people. But cars are beginning to stop out on Route 31, and somebody phoned in a report about it to the all-news radio station in Chicago and they just went on the air about it."

"What the hell is the matter with you people? Don't you know how to handle anything?"

"The thing that convinced me I should find you is that ABC is moving its television van from the stadium over to the golf course. They've got all the equipment for national TV coverage of the game and they're moving it all to the girl on the cross right now."

Father Kinsella put down his brandy and stood up. That's all we needed, I thought to myself, some cheerleader calling for handstands for Jesus on the eighteenth fairway, and this dumb Arab has already done everything but sell tickets.

"Come on, Jeff, we'll go back to my office and see what we can do."

They both left, Kinsella in control but angry and Green like a man ready to join the crowd and roll on the ground if he had half a chance. Maybe it would dry the oil slick off him, I thought. It seemed very quiet after the door closed. I poured myself another brandy and began to think about old P.B.

PART II

PART II

1

Autumn 1929

Notre Dame was a scattering of spires and buildings on the
flat black Indiana farmland with great squeals and grunts
going up as Brother Donovan slaughtered the cattle and the
pigs, bloodying the ground where a seminary stands now, but
feeding the lot of us when, that is, he wasn't off winning grand
prizes at livestock shows in Chicago. Well, it was a close-to-
the-land time and the football stadium Rockne wangled out
of them with the money his teams brought in, half a million
dollars some years, not to mention the publicity, well, the
stadium was still no more than a big scoop out of the earth.

The lads played just north of it at Cartier Field, its
splintered old stands having room for only ten thousand, but
with sod as sacred as that of Ireland itself, so holy it was
thought, or maybe just lucky, that they transplanted it, every
blade of grass of it, into the new stadium before it opened in
1930. It was there, and just a year before that, that I first saw
P.B. Kinsella.

The football team was scrimmaging and P.B. was the kind
of fellow you always had to keep your eye on. Quick he was,
and a fair size, well built but no colossus, a player who liked
to fake you out and break the rules just to be doing
something, a finger in your eye in the pileup or a knee in the
groin maybe, and himself an innocent bystander helping to
pull you up afterward.

Well, this day he had picked on a big Polish lineman,
Pinhead by nickname, not that his head was small, just that it
seemed that way on top of his great body that looked like it
had been welded together in the steel mills back near Gary,

where he came from. Pinhead was no dummy, he was smart
enough and even good-natured about the jokes people told
about him, but that day he had half again enough of Kinsella's
extra gouges and kicks in the shins. As the practice broke up
he called out in his rough, deep voice, words that came out
slowly and carefully, like railroad cars easing around a bad
curve in the tracks.

"Kinsella, you mick bastard, you play dirty."

Kinsella was trotting away across the field making Pinhead
even madder by ignoring him.

"Kinsella," Pinhead shouted again. "You Irish son of a
bitch, I'll get you some day and break your Irish ass for you,
you play dirty like that any more."

By this time Pinhead was standing in mid field alone, sort
of an heroic figure but a little beleaguered, like a traffic cop
after the rush hour is over, shouting great involved Slavic
curses after Kinsella, kind of pathetic, like Goliath demanding a rematch from David. While Pinhead was still calling
after Kinsella, who, brassy as he was, had stopped to chat
nonchalantly with a couple of students on the sidelines, an
open car, one of those grand touring cars of the twenties, had
pulled up about half the field away, and in it, his bald head,
like the nub end of a torpedo, glinting in the sun, sat Rockne.
He had been down with phlebitis but he got out to the
practices, his leg bandaged up like the Baby Jesus, by car,
squinting and scowling and shouting orders through a mega-
phone horn like a movie director. His car slowed and you
could see that he was watching the scene, a little smile making
his mouth crooked, the breeze lifting a tuft of hair, like a
horn, from his forehead. He was enjoying the mischief of the
event, Kinsella feigning deafness as Pinhead shouted his
halting litany of vengeful oaths at his back. Finally Pinhead
stopped and turned to leave the field in the opposite direction
and you could sense how the Polish lad, full of his mother's
warnings about not losing his temper or hurting anybody with
his great strength, struggled to regain his self-control as he
moved away.

Then it happened, a classic Kinsella move, quick, fierce,
and decisive. In an instant he broke away from his conversation and darted about ten yards beyond to a small clump of
manure, fresh and hot from the bowels of one of Brother
Donovan's great farm horses that had pulled a wagon past a
short time before. With no hint of hesitation Kinsella dug into

the pile like a boy going after the first packable snow of winter, formed a ball of it in his hands and lofted it swiftly toward the retreating Pinhead. It arced slightly, a spew of tobaccolike juices trailing behind it, and exploded in spray and shreds and globs on the back of Pinhead's massive neck, as good a shot as Billy Mitchell dropping a bomb down the smokestack of a battleship.

"Fuck you, you yellow Polack!" Kinsella shouted just as the manure splattered, and the bystanders broke out in laughter. Pinhead turned, a webbing of dung sliding down his cheek, and regarded the taunting Kinsella for a split second, everything about him—eyes, veins, and muscles—bulging and twitching, before he charged toward his grinning tormentor. Kinsella, needless to say, was off like a man with his ass on fire toward the main part of the campus, sending another lad and his pile of books sailing like playing cards as he went. Well, as fate or luck or some strange power deep in the heart of dirty Irish tricks would have it, Pinhead, hot in pursuit of the fleeing Kinsella, stepped right into a bucket, not right into it exactly, it was more that he crushed it with his great paddle of a foot, caught himself on the handle and turned in a cartwheel to land, in a terrible melding of curses and crumpling metal, a fine shower of wet dark particles playing around his head, flat on his back. The spectators' laughter roller-coastered up to a peak and then dropped as they sensed that they might be in danger from Pinhead's wrath, but he just lay there, shaking and sobbing a little, muttering, "Son of a bitch, son of a bitch . . ."

Rockne had watched, had, as a matter of fact, enjoyed the whole thing, his gleaming head thrown back in laughter, and tears forming at the edges of his narrow eyes. But he was quick to compose himself, and he barked—yes, truly his voice was more a keen-edged bark at times than anything else—an order to his driver to go see if Pinhead was all right. The driver untangled Pinhead's foot from what was left of the pail, helped him to get up, and led him slowly back to Rockne's car. Sheepishly, the lineman, only smearing his face more as he tried to clean it, presented himself to the coach.

"Who started this, Krol?" Rockne snapped.

Pinhead just stood there, his face reddening in shame, unable to speak. Finally he said, "Kinsella started it."

"Well," Rockne said in a mixture of derision and sympathy, "you certainly didn't finish it. That what you're gonna do in the game Saturday, curse the other team like a sailor, and get covered with crap and flat on your ass for your pains?"

"I'm sorry, Coach," Pinhead said slowly. "I'm real sorry but he did things he shouldn't of done . . ."

"Listen, Krol," Rockne replied swiftly, "you let other players upset you like that and you're no good to the team, no good at all. You lose more than your temper. Then you're no good to yourself either." He said all this very quickly, out of the side of his mouth, like an auctioneer, but loud, yes, and clear too. "Well, we'll talk about it later. Go get washed up. And don't break any more equipment on your way in."

As Pinhead turned away, Rockne growled another order to his driver, "Get Kinsella and tell him he's to be in my office right away. Now, do you understand? Now."

Rock was already in his tiny office, his leg propped up, talking on the phone when they brought P.B. to the door. Kinsella was still in his uniform, sweaty and dirty as a war hero, at ease almost, like a man waiting to get a medal. Rockne ignored him, waved his assistant out of the room, and continued his phone conversation.

"Yeah, yeah," he said, reaching for an apple, "I know you're a great school, a great Catholic college. I appreciate all that but we have our schedule set for next year . . ."

There was a pause as Rockne listened to what must have been a last pleading argument.

"No, no. I don't think it's good for Notre Dame to play other Catholic colleges, that's right, not good for them, not good for the game." Rockne took a bite out of the apple while he listened some more. "Okay, okay," he said swiftly. "Write me a letter on it. Put it in writing." He said good-by, replaced the receiver, and, without glancing at Kinsella, began examining some papers on his desk.

Kinsella shifted from one foot to the other, pushed a lock of black hair back from his forehead, and cleared his throat. Rockne did not even look up.

"You wanted me, Coach?" Kinsella asked.

Rockne continued to shuffle papers, wrinkling his brow above his old club fighter's face. The phone jangled again and he answered it with an abrupt "Rockne here!"

Kinsella observed all this quietly. He knew he was going through one of the Rock's classic drills, that he might stand there ten or twenty more minutes before the coach even acknowledged his presence. A slight smile began to break on his face, for Kinsella had been through things like this before, the *Beau Geste* treatment, he called it. The nuns had been great for it in grade school back in Chicago, making him stand while they waited to lecture him properly for his latest mischief. He got it for a whole afternoon once when as a second grader he refused the role of a fairy in a school play. Early on he had gotten the sense of it and decided that he could play the game too. He smiled as he recalled the afternoon he had been standing in front of the principal, old Sister Monica, a great war-horse of a nun with a fine little moustache, who used to make him stand the way old Rock was making him stand now. Young Patrick had always been fascinated by the sprouts and whorls and springy stiff hairs that described the terrain of her face, the part that could be seen, that is, squeezed through the opening of the starched white headpiece of her habit. Patrick had been caught throwing snowballs at the convent door that lunch hour and Sister Monica, who had caught one in the breadbasket when she stepped outside to investigate, had not been amused. The truth was, as it was with Rockne, that she grudgingly liked Kinsella, partly because of the imp in him, and yet she knew he needed discipline before he took over the school entirely by making a charming shambles of the nuns' authority.

Well, Sister Monica was sitting there sternly when young Kinsella said softly, "Sister, Sister," only to be ignored by her. Again he spoke up, a little more urgently, his face like an angel's bringing a message to the holy family. "Begging your pardon, Sister," he finally blurted out as Sister Monica burrowed more deeply into her work. "There's a mouse been crawling up your cape!" With that, of course, Sister Monica shrieked, knocked over her inkwell, and bolted for the door, while little Patrick, controlling his laughter, cried out in his St. George's voice, "Don't worry, I'll get him!"

Now, Sister Monica was never sure whether that mouse ever existed, not to her dying day, when she was near ninety and P.B., wearing diamonds by then, would send her flowers on her feast day every year. But she knew she had lost the battle of nerves to a twelve-year-old that afternoon, knew in her heart that he had the upper hand in their relationship forever afterward, and never tried the silence treatment on him again. She would make him go to the library and copy great speeches out of a book, or send him on errands to the local stores; she disciplined him after that in ways that would set up no contest between them.

Young Patrick challenged every intimidation from then on; he had discovered something that would be important for the rest of his life about himself and others. If he remained in control of himself, he discovered that he had a lot of control in any situation and against any adversary. If he pushed ahead confidently, people with less self-confidence would pull back all around him. There was no theory to it; it was all action and the more he did it, the easier it got. He studied Rockne and imagined his battered face squeezed into a nun's wimple. Rockne, mind you, was no Sister Monica and very few people had the nerve to strike a match on his defenses in anything like a power struggle or even a practical joke. They still told the story of the day Rockne almost tore up the campus searching for the student who had filled his driving gloves with white paint. Kinsella studied the coach, a half smile still on his lips, as Rockne continued to lob sentences like mortar shells at the person on the other end of the phone.

"Well, I'm a little tired of professors who think they know everything. If they're so smart, why are they here teaching for four thousand a year telling their students how to make a fortune . . . ?" After these sharp bursts Rockne took a bite from his apple.

"Coach," Kinsella said softly, in almost the same tone he had used on Sister Monica on that snowy afternoon so long ago. "Coach," he said again, knowing that Rockne would continue to ignore him.

"Yes, and tell that guy on the *Trib* he's the greatest fiction writer I ever read," the coach snapped just before he hung up the phone and took the last bite of the apple.

"Oh, Coach," Kinsella said in more alarmed tones. "I was trying to tell you, there was a worm in that last hunk of apple!"

Rockne choked, coughed, and began to spit pieces of apple down his sweat shirt and onto the papers on his desk. Because of his leg he couldn't swivel to get at the wastebasket. Kinsella hurried over to his side. "Here, let me get the basket for you!" he said, and began pounding the coach on the back.

"Damn!" Rockne spluttered, leaning toward the basket held out to him by Kinsella. "Damn! Probably sent by Army's coach." But he coughed again, his face reddening, as he attempted to regain his composure. Kinsella stepped aside, as though some innate dignity had moved him back away to lessen the coach's embarrassment. In fact, it was the old Sister Monica strategy again, and, considering the risks involved, it had come off pretty well so far. Something had shifted in the balance of power in Rockne's office; if Kinsella was not in charge, he was at least not quite so firmly under the theatrical domination of Coach Rockne.

"Thanks, kid," Rockne said, probing his mouth with a finger for any last remnants of the offending apple. "A man could choke to death on one of these." He studied Kinsella for a moment. Rockne sensed that something had tipped inside of him, something had moved in the darkened fields of his emotions during the few seconds the incident with the apple had lasted. It made him uneasy because he realized that, in some way, he had been taken, that young Kinsella, this cute mick in front of him, had pulled the kind of stunt he enjoyed pulling himself. He laughed out loud.

"You're a wise guy, Kinsella," he said, conceding a point to the younger man and thereby regaining the advantage for himself, relaxing the tension for a moment and then tightening it again immediately. "And you take chances. I like that." Rockne's smile faded and his mouth twitched just a bit. "But, young man, you take another chance with me and you may not get any older. A worm in my apple, my eye. Think I'm another sucker like Krol?"

Kinsella stiffened a little. This was the time not to reveal his feelings, but the truth was that, although he was surprised by Rockne's quick recovery of the situation, he was still not afraid of him. In fact, he retained an edge of the observer's amusement at the scene in which he found himself.

"No, Coach," he answered evenly.

"Kinsella," Rockne said with a frown, "you're suspended for a week. You're off the list for the trip this weekend and I want you out doing calisthenics and wind sprints every afternoon. Understood?"

"Yes, sir," Kinsella responded. "May I go, sir?"

"No, not yet," Rockne answered, breaking the words off sharply and shifting himself to make his leg more comfortable. "Sit down, Mr. Kinsella, it's time we had a talk."

The young man moved to a straight-backed wooden chair,

his expression not changing, as the coach flicked a last shred of apple from his desk.

"Kinsella, you've got lots of drive, lots of spirit, lots of what it takes to go places, as far as you want in life." Rockne paused and pulled a long cigar out of his desk drawer. He mouthed it, struck a wooden match, and began to speak again, his phrases made even more jerky by this stage business. Rock was not a man unaware of the uses of a good pause; it was one of his oldest tricks and it never failed to settle any wandering attention back on him.

"Krol may be a little slow but you baited him. He's a good man. And you baited him, you made a fool out of him." Rockne paused again and puffed on his cigar. Kinsella watched him in return, still somewhat amused, thinking to himself that, in some way, he had also baited the great Rockne, that he had, improbably enough, ended up on something close to even terms with him.

"Now, if I punished Krol, it would break his spirit, break it, do you hear?" Rockne extracted the cigar from his mouth and exhaled a cloud of smoke. "But, Kinsella, if I punish you, I won't break your spirit at all. You'll eat it up just to show me you can take it. And, besides that, everybody else'll be glad to see you get the hook a little. Glad to see me whack you down a bit, they're always glad to see me do that to a smart aleck."

Kinsella looked straight across at the legendary coach, who suddenly seemed as smart as everybody said he was. He had been bluffing Rockne and now Rockne was showing him he could take it and raise the ante at the same time. It was as though the coach was acknowledging that he and Kinsella were going through a performance together, a necessary show that had to be played out for its effects on the rest of the troops, but a show nonetheless.

"So, Kinsella, you drag your ass out on that field and start running right after you leave here. Make it an hour, a half hour off, and another hour."

"Yes, sir," Kinsella responded, feeling somehow that he and the coach were tenuously joined in a conspiracy to support the appearance of discipline on the team.

"Kinsella," Rockne began again, "you and I know this is the way it has to be. No use kidding you. You're too street smart to be fooled, you've been on the South Side of Chicago too long. I can just see you stealing fruit off the pushcarts now. There's some of the con in you. I don't mind that. It gives you an advantage in a tough game, gives you an advantage in life too." The coach placed his cigar in an ashtray and folded his arms across his chest.

"I think you are going to go a long way in life. You've got the brass and the brains for it. My God, I see something of me in you. But I see the dangers too, if you don't keep yourself in balance. Play to win, that's fine, and use all your tricks. That's fine, too, manly, I'd say, in a world where the sissies are getting all the say. Pretty soon you'll have players asking for a time-out because they've got a run in their stocking. Play hard but play fair. I'll do the same with you. Try something like this again and I'll break you for good. Now clear out of here."

Kinsella stood up, said nothing, and trotted out toward the field. His head was filled with wonder as he jogged along. Rockne had disciplined him, yes, that would be clear to everyone. But he had done something more. He had spoken directly to that little boy who had thrown Sister Monica, bristly-faced old Sister Monica, permanently off balance. Rockne had seen right into him, right into his trickster's heart. And he had winked at what he saw.

2

Autumn 1929

The straight of it in those days was that undergraduate existence at Notre Dame was strictly supervised, maybe a little to the left of seminary life, but not too much. Mass every morning and none of the coed stuff they've gone gaga over in the last generation. All the girls right in their place at St. Mary's, which wasn't too different from a convent, except the president wrote poetry and I always felt soft toward them for that. There was grand poetry under the old strict Catholic

regime, a special poetry that was a mixture of demanding
ideals and a great feel for sinners, because, when all was said
and done, that was the true state of things. Now, of course,
the discipline of the old Church is gone and with it the poetry
too. How can you think human beings are tragically noble if
you've no way to feel guilty about anything?

P.B. was not one to feel very guilty, of course, and he went
along with his punishment, although Rockne sent him for the
weekend trip at the last minute. Fond of him, he was, couldn't
stay mad at him too long, and he often sparred with him, in
words that is, sometimes with the whole team watching.
There would be Rockne in his wheelchair, the big flop felt hat
on and the cigar in his mouth, giving the needle to Kinsella
while everybody enjoyed it. P.B. could take it and he had
learned when and when not to give it back. They knew how to
play off each other and Kinsella would act the straight man
for the coach sometimes.

"Say, Coach, what do you think of having a hockey team
here at Notre Dame?"

"Glad you asked that," Rock said, plucking the cigar out of
his mouth. "It doesn't seem like a good idea to me, putting
clubs into the hands of so many Irishmen."

But the Rock was not functioning too well, what with the
phlebitis and all, and he had to run the beginning of the
season by remote control, talking by phone into the locker
room, watching practice from a wooden stand they built
specially for him, and missing the first away games altogether.
That relaxed things just a little, the iron hand gone, and that
was all Kinsella needed to slip away when the team railroad
car had to be switched at Chicago on the way back to South
Bend. P.B.—the rest of the team said the initials stood for
"Pretty Brassy"—skipped the train and headed across the city
to meet a pal from his old neighborhood of Canaryville on the
South Side.

Well, this weekend P.B. was in a mood for some relaxation
and nothing would do but a show at one of the big theaters
and a visit to one of the gambling places. The latter were all
over the city in those days, common as gas stations now. Big
Bill Thompson was mayor and it was a toddlin' town all right.
The gambling was mostly in the horse parlors, handbooks
they called them then, but there were other places that
operated at night, mostly set up in office buildings, with an

occasional raid for decency's sake, places where they checked
your membership through a peephole.

The lot of it was controlled by the gangs who collected the
profits when they weren't shooting or dropping one another
in the Chicago River with the fast-drying cement shoes on.
Maybe the grimmest part, the smudge that won't wear out,
was the fact that the political organizations made a lot of their
money by franchising protection to the gamblers through the
police department. Great days, full of the smell of excess,
carnival days in the big city, with the merry-go-round going
all night long and everybody stepping fast, like they do in
old-fashioned newsreels. And the police commanders and
captains, eyes as true blue as their uniforms, fussy about
where the envelopes were slipped to them so they could
preserve their reputations for honesty, standing staunch and
tall as admirals all over the place. Even some of the reporters,
your great crusaders, were in with the gangs, fixing things, or
getting souvenir belts from Al Capone, the kind with diamonds on them he liked to give away, greasy fellow already a
little loony with the syph, taking the standing ovations at the
ball park and the racetrack for making beer available in dry
times.

P.B. had grown up in Canaryville, a place full of tough
Irish, the Pigshit Irish as they were called before they moved
on to lace curtains. So he wasn't innocent about the city; he
exulted in its blind energy and its dirty fingernails, its unre-
fined excitement and its crudeness; Chicago always seemed
like a con man in an evening suit or a whore with the Queen's
jewels on and he could only take so many weeks in South
Bend before his craving for its atmosphere overcame him.

So there he was, dressed to the nines, heading for the
Loop, where he would meet Jack Moran in front of the
Chicago Theater, one of those mock Moorish castle movie
houses on State Street. Jack was a few months older than
P.B., a hustler in a striped suit, a thin, twitchy fellow who had
grown a moustache to try to make himself look older. It made
him look just like a fellow who had grown a moustache to
make himself look older. But he did know his way around
Prohibition-bound Chicago, he had learned how to make a
few bucks, and spend them too, mostly working in the
handbooks during the day and doing some work for the
Democratic organization on the side. Public relations, they

called it, which meant that he got to deliver envelopes to worthy municipal employees from judges to janitors. "As good a game as football, Pat!" he'd say, flashing a big, old-fashioned ten-dollar bill like a wand filled with magic. "Yes," Pat would answer, "and no big apes trying to tackle you."

P.B. filled his lungs with the city air; there was nothing like the flavor of soot and cinders to revive his almost desperate longings to participate in the action that flashed its hints and promises from every marquee and electric sign in town.

"Patrick!" Jack Moran called as he came out of a little alley that ran by the side of the theater. "Did they let you play this week?"

"Yes," P.B. answered, his sense of excitement heightened at the sight of his friend, who, this fall evening, was wearing a felt hat turned down all round like an umbrella. "A little. Most of the game."

"I suppose you were grand, I mean, a hero again, knocking the shit out of some poor farm boys for a couple of hours."

"Those farm boys have hard heads, Jack, and they're used to killing pigs and cattle. Tough bastards, every one of them."

"Pat," Moran said, a strange wild light in his eyes, like that of a ghost ship making for shore, a signal of impetuosity I've often observed in the Irish, as indeed it was here, "let's skip the show. I've got an invitation to go to a lock-up joint up near Division Street, a place where lots of the swells are. They've got blackjack and a wheel, plenty to drink; it's the place to be."

Kinsella looked at him skeptically. "What the hell are you talking about, 'the place to be'? You forget you're just another boy from Canaryville? What are you up to anyway?"

"Look, Pat, there's a chance we can make some dough out of this. Meet some of the right people, make some connections. I been going there for a month and I've met some nice people and I've gotten some nice side jobs out of it. If you're not interested, Patrick . . ."

"I didn't say that. I just want to keep the signals straight. Sounds interesting to me. I could use some extra money right now."

"Okay. Save your dough and we'll walk up. It's only about a mile."

And with that, off they went, the steady Kinsella, watching

everything and everybody as they walked north across the
bridge, and the twitchy Moran, absorbed in himself and
talking endlessly about the fortune he was going to make. In
twenty minutes they were at the front of an apartment
building, one with big, bulging turrets of windows at the
corners of every floor. It looked quiet and respectable as they
passed into the foyer through a door which was ornately
decorated with ironwork. Wood all around inside, smooth
and polished like a coffin lid, and little lamps shaped like
candles that gave barely any light at all. Moran pushed a
button and an elevator door half clanked and half slid open.
They went to the fifth floor, where an even darker hallway led
past a door or two to a little open lobby, where they stood on
a patch of marble flooring in front of yet another door. Jack
pushed another button and a slide in the door opened.

"It's me, Moran, with my friend from Notre Dame."

The door opened and there, sprouting out of a tuxedo,
stood a bulky fellow with a face lumpy as a bag of potatoes
beneath a spreading of Rudolph Valentino hair. "Hello, kid,"
he said in a guttural accent. "Who's your friend?"

"This is Pat Kinsella, Tony, you know, the Kinsella who
plays football for Notre Dame. Played today out in the corn
country."

"Yeah, yeah," Tony answered in a tone of the mildest
interest. "He with you, it's okay by me." With that he turned,
sort of like a wind-up drummer boy, stiff, you could see that,
or muscle-bound, and opened yet another door. Kinsella and
Moran entered a long room in which thirty or forty people,
many of them in evening dress, were distributed around
gaming tables. Blackjack was catching a lot of attention, a
ripple of laughter lifting off the crowd there where the house
was giving them a streak of good luck, letting them taste
blood to draw them out even more. Smoke was heavy in the
air and there was another mug in a black tie serving drinks to
people. The roulette wheel was just slowing down, the crowd
around it looking grim and expectant like the best or worst
news they were ever going to hear was about to be announced
to them. The house was doing fine here and as the ball
clattered into its final slot, it had done just fine again. The
croupier, who might have looked honest except for his
marcelled hair and his timid little moustache, raked the chips
back swiftly and smoothly. In a far corner, in one of the

bulges where the windows were heavily draped, five men were playing cards at a circular table where the chips were stacked almost as high as the drinking glasses.

"Jack," Kinsella said, drawing his friend close to him, "this is big-time. We've got no money for a place like this." But as he said it and truthful as it was, he felt a pull in his gut toward it. He loved the atmosphere of excitement, the fact that chances were being taken in every moment, that it was fast, faster even than football, that it rang and tingled with a rawness he loved.

"Don't worry, Pat, don't worry."

No sooner had Jack assured him than Tony, who had let them in, clomped up stiffly, more now like a man who had collected a lot of smashed bones in his day, and said, "Mr. Lane'll see you now." They were led across the room, where a tide of enthusiastic noises now rose from the suckers at the wheel, like they were trying to put English on it, and presently another door opened into a room that had no windows at all. Behind a large mahogany desk sat a solid-looking man, beet red in the face like he just came from a steam room; he wore steel-rimmed glasses on his George Washington nose and had a spotty head of hair, all tufts and fuzziness, like a man getting over a sickness. He was examining some ledger sheets. "Good evening, Jack," he said in a smooth, cultured voice, a practiced kind of voice good for saying hello to strangers, a voice that floated on its own without an arch or support of sincerity. Kinsella disliked him right away.

"Mr. Lane, this is my friend, Patrick Kinsella, the one I told you about."

"Good evening, Patrick," he said, as mannered as a man taking his hat off in an elevator. "Won't you both sit down?"

Patrick eyed him even as he seated himself. There was something in this man's whole manner, even in his polished little fingernails, that made Kinsella feel that he was already being used, that he was being fitted into a slot as easily as the ball at the roulette wheel.

"I have followed your career at Notre Dame, Patrick. I have, as a matter of fact, won some money since Jack drew my attention to you. So I want you to feel welcome here, even though it's not the kind of place you usually go to."

"Yes, sir," Patrick replied. He felt even more manipulated,

as though he was the object of the older man's curiosity, interest, and disdain at the same time. He experienced an uneasy sense of oppression.

"You are very fast with your hands, Patrick, a great talent for a center on a championship football team."

"Mr. Lane was wondering, Pat, whether you'd like to make some money working on the side for him," Jack interjected. Patrick said nothing. He gazed intently back at Lane, like he was in a contest with him to see who would blink first.

"What would you want me to do, Mr. Lane?" he asked, controlling his sense of uneasiness.

"Well, Patrick, I thought you might like to work in one of my places. Learn the ropes. Start in a grind joint, that is, a handbook, as an assistant manager. I need some men like you, college age, clean-cut. I've got plenty of mugs, too many. What I need are fellows like you and Jack, fellows who will give the places a little tone. People would like the idea of a football player around."

Patrick remained silent.

"You think about it a little. I know you wonder how you could go to school and do this. Well, you could start off one day a week. That is, if you can make it back and forth on your own from South Bend. Then, when vacation comes or school lets out, you could take on more time. Fifty bucks a week to start. What do you say?"

Patrick's silence had made Jack uncomfortable. "It's a great deal, Pat, what do you say?" he asked in a jolly lodge member voice.

"Can I think about it?"

Mr. Lane looked away and sighed. "Well, I don't know, Patrick, I don't know. You won't get many offers like this. You're not a big star, you know, just another guy. Maybe the excitement is too much for you . . ." He continued to look away from Kinsella. "Maybe this would be too fast for you . . ."

"No, Mr. Lane, it's not that," Patrick answered. "You can't name a game that's too fast for me." He paused; he sensed that he had to make some kind of move to keep himself free, to get some breathing room. "It's you, Mr. Lane, it's you I don't like."

Lane turned slowly back toward Kinsella, a slight tic playing at the side of his mouth. Jack was half out of his seat.

"He doesn't mean that, Mr. Lane. What he means is, this is all kind of new for him, and, well, you know, he needs time to think about it . . ."

Mr. Lane was maintaining his self-control. "Well, Patrick, I can't understand that. You don't even know me." The oil was flowing freely now, like Lane was Moby Dick shaking off an unexpected harpoon. "My dear young man, I don't make generous offers like this every day."

"No," Patrick replied. "That's what bothers me, that, and the way you make me feel like a piece of meat you're buying at the butcher shop."

"Now, Pat," Jack said, but Lane raised a hand to silence him.

"I'm sorry if you feel uncomfortable. I realize that you're not accustomed to these surroundings, being from Canaryville and all." Patrick gritted his teeth but said nothing as Lane continued, "But my offer still stands. No one is trying to buy you like meat. This is a business matter, strictly a business matter. Take it or leave it."

"I'll take it," Kinsella answered softly. He felt a little better inside; he had made the relationship more equal in some way by his previous remark, he had touched a nerve in Lane and he breathed a little easier. "When can I start?"

Lane smiled ever so slightly, like an oriental ambassador, and removed a cigarette from a silver case. "Jack will let you know. You'll begin by helping to keep the accounts. Jack will tell you where and when. Now, gentlemen, if you'll excuse me . . ." He glanced up, like a man who was forever encapsulating hostile surges within himself, a man who let his hatred out slowly, like his soul was all looped with IV tubes that carried it round and round till it came out in little drops, diamond-hard little drops of hate.

Jack said their good nights and Patrick remained silent as they made their way through the doors and through the passage of laughter and light that was the gambling room and out past stiff old Tony and down the elevator and out into the night. Patrick had the feeling that something really new was beginning in his life.

3

Autumn 1929

Patrick was willing to go back to South Bend after the excitement of being inside the gambling house; he was full of dreams and wishes, ripe with plans, even though he didn't know quite what they would lead to, as he caught the South Shore train, a two-car Toonerville trolley if ever there was one, that stopped outside the LaSalle Hotel downtown a mile or two from the University. He took the streetcar to the end of the line by the statue of Notre Dame's founder, Father Sorin, a great bearded Frenchman who knew plenty about power, believe me, and how to use it. Anyway, Kinsella got back without much trouble. He had this way of not looking nervous, of always seeming to be where he belonged, so even when he was late or out of place something about his manner made him look innocent and proper. That's one of the reasons they liked lads like him to work in the handbooks and gaming rooms.

It was a fierce month, October of 1929, what with the stock market giving off ominous sounds, Rockne put to bed with the phlebitis pounding away like radiators in the winter, and a tough schedule of games coming up, Navy and Wisconsin and Carnegie Tech, the last crowd having humiliated Rockne's Ramblers, which they were called more than the Fighting Irish, just the year before, a terrible blow in Rock's worst football year, when he called the team the "Minute Men," telling the sportswriters, great downplayer that he was anyway, "Put them in for a minute and the other team scores, put them in another minute and they score again." Well, with a full schedule of practices and classes and the games on the

weekend—and bed and Mass checks too—Kinsella was hard
pressed to get back to Chicago. On the other hand, Rock was
laid up, trying to coach over the phone, and only the young
assistants were in charge, so it wasn't so difficult for someone
as nimble as Patrick to slip away from the campus and then
charm them into thinking he'd never been gone.

Patrick returned to Chicago in the middle of the week and
Mr. Lane, who seemed no more likable than the Saturday
before, sent him to work at a grind joint, a handbook where
anybody could come in off the street to make a bet. The place
was on Clark Street, just a couple of blocks from the Chicago
Avenue Police Station and the story was that the loudspeaker
carrying the track announcer's voice was so loud it could be
heard by the desk sergeant. Well, it mattered little, except for
decorum or to please the city's reformers who frowned on
such activities by the lower classes. Everybody else was
happy, that is everybody around the handbook, and there
was a good crowd, three or four hundred, all of them shuffling
around, talking and making bets and listening as the announcer, in flat dramatic tones, rattled endlessly about track
conditions, odds, the close of betting, and then the electric
"They're off!" which got everyone's attention pretty quickly.
It was a friendly atmosphere, with a fine edge of suspense to
it, and Kinsella thought it was close to heaven.

He met George Muldoon, a giant of a man in a checkered
suit, with a face that had all the colors of a crushed funeral
bouquet, kind of a sickly yellow, and patches of black under
the eyes, and as delicate a rose blossom as you'd find to his
nose. "Kinsella is it? I'm George Muldoon," he stated in a
voice that would have been perfect for "Asleep in the Deep."
He waved Patrick after him and they made their way through
the crowds as the loudspeaker crackled out the description of
a race from some place in Florida.

The handbook was a marvel. There were men at large
blackboards marking the names of horses and odds and
strange faraway places in chalk, and another set of men
working like bank tellers, only they were taking the bets.
"Those fellows are writing sheet," Muldoon declaimed.
"Some of them are policemen on their day off, some of them
are firemen. It's a big happy family here and no worry about
the law." Patrick was enthralled, every bit of that, by the
mood of the room, by the bettors who looked, as they lined
up at the windows, as determined as pilgrims on their way to

Lourdes, and the smoke and occasional laughter, yes, and the constant activity, and the loudspeaker going, now in a singsong manner, now with a clipped kind of tension to it, and money, basketsful he guessed, being exchanged constantly, money flowing back and forth across the counters as sweet and green as the river Shannon. He turned back toward it, like a boy who doesn't want to leave home, as Muldoon closed the door of his small office.

"Sit down, Kinsella," he said, pointing to a desk with a gooseneck lamp and a pile of ledger sheets. "This is where we want you to work. We trust you, we know you're honest, coming from a good Catholic school and all, and playing football with your name in the papers too. That's another thing. We figure you won't want the good fathers or that Swede football coach of yours knowing about your extra employment. That would put your name in the papers in a different way. You follow me?" He pronounced it "folly" and Patrick smiled inside at the appropriateness of it. "Well, do you?"

"Yes, Mr. Muldoon, yes, of course."

"That's good. We also want you because you're smart, a college boy, and we want somebody quick with the figures. We want you to go over these sheets, get them balanced, give us a picture of where we stand."

"Is this for taxes?" Patrick asked wryly.

Muldoon's eyes bulged and Patrick thought he was going to lay the back of his great fist against his jaw.

"Just a joke, Mr. Muldoon, just a joke between Irishmen."

Muldoon swallowed, then he began to laugh. "Yeah, yeah, a good joke, a good joke." He had never had anybody try humor with him in quite this way before and yet something about the way Kinsella did it attracted him. "Ah, you're full of blarney. Or maybe bullshit, I don't know which, Kinsella. But here's where you work and get to it." He paused. "You know, Kinsella, if you take to this, you can do very well, very well, indeed, for a little mick football player from the South Side."

"Thank you, Mr. Muldoon, I'll do my best." Then he decided to probe the giant again. "That's what the priests always tell us, do our best and we'll be a big success."

Muldoon rubbed his jaw, a man uncertain as to whether his leg was being pulled or not. "Do they now?" he replied sarcastically. "Well then, get your ass in the chair and let's see if you practice what they preach."

Kinsella was captivated with the long sheets spread out across the desk before him. They were filled with the story of the handbook operation, about how much had been bet every day so far that week, and about how much had been paid out and how much was profit. There were other entries as well, sums paid to a long column of individuals, only their last names and first initials showing. They were listed for amounts ranging from fifty to five dollars. There were other entries that were not so clear, with initials only, and for much larger sums. Just a quick inspection told him that almost ten thousand went out to this vague aggregate every week. What a business, indeed, thought Kinsella, who loved the way in which numbers popped and bounced and then came together again at the bottom of the rows; there was a dark mystery connected with any number preceded by a dollar sign, for its purity was gone but its attractiveness, its sensual power was immeasurably heightened.

What he had to do was not so much for a bright college boy and when Muldoon returned a couple of hours later Kinsella smiled and said, "All done, sir."

"Let's see, Kinsella, let's have a look." Muldoon studied the neat columns and totals, the clear tracings that lay bare the entrails of handbook commerce for the first three days of that week. The sport of kings, my eye, Kinsella thought to himself as Muldoon continued to study his entries.

"Looks okay, kid. Now I've got something else for you to do. Mr. Lane just called from up at the club, the Lake Terrace, the place you met him at. He wants you to deliver this satchel to him personally. Now, we know how long it takes to get there, so hop a cab and I'll call so's he can have the doors open when you arrive. Got that?"

"Sure," Kinsella answered as he took the leather traveling bag, hefted it, and smiled at the hulking Muldoon. "This got your secret plays in it?"

"Get out of here, you smartass Irishman," Muldoon growled as he set the accounts back on the desk. "And be back in half an hour. I'll have more paperwork for you then."

Kinsella passed through the smoky wonder of the handbook and out to Clark Street, where he hailed a cab and, holding the bag like a football, headed for the Lake Terrace Club.

He was readily admitted through the same doors by which he had made his first passage into the place. There were no customers in the afternoon; this was a late night operation and the club had the closed-in atmosphere of a restaurant, the tables all set and the air a little musty, waiting through a long afternoon for the first customers of evening. It seemed foreboding to Patrick as he knocked on Lane's office door.

The great black door seemed to swing open automatically, revealing Lane, who looked as oppressively self-contained as ever, seated at his desk, on the top of which were several stacks of paper currency.

"Come in, Kinsella. Let me have the package."

Kinsella placed the valise on his desk and Lane hurriedly unlatched it and, as swiftly as a miner going for a nugget, began removing thick brown envelopes. He paid no attention to Patrick, who stood there somewhat dumbly watching him check the contents, more wads of money in each, and place them along with the other cash on the desk.

"I better go, Mr. Lane. Mr. Muldoon wants me right back."

Lane looked up, as an impatient parent might at a child who persists in misunderstanding things. "I tell Mr. Muldoon what to do. I will also tell you what to do. You are about to get an education in business life in Chicago. I don't know why I bother or why I don't just let you go back. Maybe I don't want to see you spend the night in jail. Wouldn't look good on your record."

Patrick felt a sharp stab of uneasiness. Something was going on; he was in the midst of or on the edge of something he did not quite understand.

"What do you mean, sir?"

Lane ignored him for a moment and then he said almost unctuously, "Just stay where you are. I'll tell you what to do." The phone rang as he finished and he let it sound a few more times before he picked it up. "Yes?" he inquired smoothly. "All right. Now will be fine. Don't call back on this line." Then he turned his eyes, which glittered slightly under his heavy brows, back to Kinsella. "The police are just leaving to raid the handbook you worked in today. I could have had them wait until you got back. I'm telling you this because you think you're smart and I want you to understand perfectly clearly just who the boss is. You owe me, I don't owe you."

Kinsella experienced a novel sensation, one he had not known since he was a child; he felt that he was under someone else's control and that he, out of smartness or eagerness to be rich, had gotten himself into this uncomfortable situation. He flushed at the notion that he had done this to himself, that he had let himself get wrapped into a package by a man about whom his guts had given him fair warning.

"Why, Mr. Kinsella, I do believe you're blushing," Lane said in a rather self-satisfied tone. He scratched his ear, looked back to the money, and began, very deliberately, to speak. "You do what I tell you to do and when. Remember this is strictly business. That raid is being held to keep the newspapers happy. Muldoon knows how to take care of himself. We let, or arrange for these things to happen periodically. It's like a timber fire, very good in the long run for the forest. It makes it more healthy." Lane took out his silver cigarette case and held it in his hands for a moment.

"You are a man with a name and you want to get ahead. That is a fine combination. A Notre Dame football player running a club would be very good for business. And we can put you in the business. But we can also keep you out of it, ruin you right now. A night in jail might be good for your soul but it would get you expelled from Notre Dame. Let us say that we have to learn to cooperate. Do you understand?"

Kinsella, still smarting at finding himself dominated by the fastidious and oily Lane, could bring himself to say nothing. He nodded his head.

"That's fine, Patrick, just fine. Now take this and get back to school." He handed Patrick a fifty-dollar bill from one of the piles on the desk. "We will see you next week. And"—Lane struck a match to light his cigarette—"good luck against Navy on Saturday. We may be putting some money down on that game. Do your best, just like the good fathers told you."

Kinsella left as quickly as he could and headed for the station, where he would catch the next train back to South Bend. He could hear the sirens of police cars in the distance as he crossed Chicago Avenue. He still felt warm; he could not have felt worse if Lane had kissed him or made a grab for his fly. A new vow was forming in his consciousness: if he could help it he would never give himself into the power of another human being. Never.

4

Autumn 1929

Patrick was a chastened man as the South Shore rattled along through the autumn landscape of changing leaves toward South Bend. It had been easy enough to spar with old Sister Monica but the odds were always on the side of a mischievous boy in any contest with an old nun. Any jury would have let him off. He smiled. But maybe he was more smart ass than smart, maybe, after Rockne had let him get away with his few little tricks, he thought he could get by with just about anything. But Rockne could have crushed him—still could, for that matter—at any minute. Mr. Lane, swarthy and slick as a haggling merchant in a Mideastern bazaar, was another bowl of chowder altogether; he possessed no recesses of benevolence that Patrick could tap into with his charm, no secret store of sweetness that might ooze out of the barren hive of his soul. Patrick regretted that he had not followed his first instinctive reactions to the man, for these had been filled with warning; now he could feel the steady and unrelenting pressure of an assassin who was not quite an assassin, a manipulator who kept power by never pulling the garrote fully tight on Patrick's neck.

Was this evil, was this what the catechisms and sermons, and his mother especially, had warned him about so often? Well, he thought, evil has two faces, the one with the exhilarated look of excitement and the other with the sour grimace of death. The excitement was bewitching, a seductress with just the right spell for his soul; it seemed irresistible, this high pitch of living that went along with taking

chances, and he wondered if the flirtation with death, even
this dangerous game into which he had entered with Mr.
Lane, might not be worth it in the long run. What a bargain
to strike, he thought, to outwit the devil himself and so to be
free of sharing one's winnings with him. Still, he shivered as
the coaches jolted to a stop in South Bend, breaking his
reverie and returning him to the real world of the old and
homely shops and buildings of the city.

He decided to walk back to his residence hall; he could take
shortcuts across fields and enter the campus at a point where
he would not be noticed. He was still troubled as he walked
along. Patrick was sure of only two things: his desire to be
free of Mr. Lane and his determination to avoid giving
himself willingly into anybody else's power in the future. He
began to pray in the self-referent fashion that marked all his
prayers; that's the way, he thought, most people pray anyway, when they're down on their luck, or sick, or in a tight
spot. Patrick was Catholic enough to realize that prayer was
an available vehicle for any petition, large or small, and at
any hour. Why, a man even got credit for trying it even if he
was no good at it. One could be forgiven, on the promise of a
good resolution, and one could be approved through God's
hand bringing some deliverance into one's life. Patrick did
not think that he had done anything wrong in going to the
gambling house; wagering on the horses was not a great
Catholic sin, it was more a preferred scandal of the self-
righteous, for those Puritan souls who thought that the moral
governance of society had been placed in their hands. The
real sins, as Patrick had learned long ago, were those of
violating the flesh rather than the pocketbook, and, as he kept
himself guarded against these, he continued to count himself
virtuous. What he needed was a way to lead his double
life—bright-eyed football player and gambling house
accountant—without having his soul in hock to Mr. Lane. He
stopped by the Sacred Heart Church and knelt in the last row
and peered through the darkness toward the old wedding
cake altar beyond the banks of candles. He was about to
strike one of his many bargains with God; they would become
a habit throughout his life and they always ran along the same
general lines. If God were good to him, then he, Patrick
Bailey Kinsella, would always be good to God in return. He
urgently needed a blessing right now, some grace, some
divine intervention that would allow him to ride the eagle of

good fortune without being shredded by its talons at the same time.

When he opened his door, his roommate, Tom McGuire, seemed quite excited. McGuire was a slightly built Irishman from Pittsburgh, a wishbone of a man, clean of meat but full of tensile strength. "Did you hear, Pat, the news?"

"What news? What are you talking about, Tom?"

"Oh, God, Pat, there's a train full of Ku Kluxers that's headin' for town. They say they're comin' to teach the Papists a lesson. They're gonna burn their crosses here, hold a meeting right out in front of the main entrance, white sheets and all. We're all goin' down to meet them at the station."

"When, when is all this happening?"

"Tomorrow, tomorrow at noon their train is due, that's the truth of it. And hundreds more are coming by car from all over the state. Come along, Pat, we're havin' a meetin' downstairs to see what to do about it."

Jesus, thought Patrick, make God a promise and he takes you right up on it. A holy war, the next best thing to the Crusades, or at least to beating Southern Methodist, seemed in the offing and something in Patrick's soul made him feel that, if he committed himself to this wholeheartedly, salvation from Mr. Lane might be closer than he dared hope.

When he and McGuire arrived in the large basement area which was also used for recreation purposes, some thirty or forty students had already gathered together. A red-haired young man from New York had the floor.

"This is our chance to get them back. They helped defeat Al Smith last year for President, they've been shooting Catholics and coons down South for generations. We ought to be ready for them and beat hell out of them."

A chorus of cheers went up in the low-ceilinged room.

"That's right, Drew!" another voice called out. "Let's get the baseball bats and welcome them to town."

The mood of a lynching filled the air, rising like mist from the roiled emotions of Catholic boys who had heard stories from their infancy about the oppression of Catholics of all nationalities and of the special role the Klan had in it in America. Cries of revenge laced with the salty taste of blood rose from their throats, and in a moment a chant began to pound against the ceiling, in railroad track singsong, "Get the Klan, get the Klan."

That, I might tell you, was what I first heard up in my

rooms. It was like a battering ram rhythmically shaking the
hall and I went downstairs to see what was causing the noise.
As I made my way down the steps, Patrick Kinsella was
waving them into silence, standing in the center of the
students, who, arms locked together, were swaying as they
continued their chant. I didn't know then that Patrick believed he was sealing an agreement with the Lord as he sought
to gain the attention of the crowd. What I do remember was
that he looked handsome, as handsome as a man in a collar
ad, in the half-light that was splayed into sections by the
crisscross of steam pipes in the old room. Just behind me
Father Martin had descended the stairs and was observing the
scene over my shoulder. Patrick finally broke the chain of the
students' incantation and began to speak, softly at first, to get
their attention, natural actor that he was.

"This is a big challenge, a big challenge for us and for this
school dedicated to Our Lady."

Such unexpected piety, I thought, from Patrick Kinsella,
but the crowd had begun to quiet down.

"When we have to play a tough team, Coach Rockne
doesn't tell us to use bats or stones. He tells us, first of all, to
use our heads. Let's try to do that now."

"What do you want to do, Patty, throw horseballs at
them?" a student called out derisively. There was a quick
burst of laughter that died down as Patrick stood, raising his
hands again for quiet, and looking as solemn as a stone lion in
front of a library.

"We can beat some of them up and lose respect for our
school and our religion while we do it."

As he paused, Father Martin whispered in my ear, "Quite a
lad, quite a lad."

The basement was dead silent now as Kinsella continued.

"Rock tells us that first we've got to outsmart the other
team, that we have to beat them mentally, that we have to
show them we're smarter than they are. And that's what we
have to do with the KKK. Suppose we fight them and hurt
some of the football team and then we end up losing to Navy
on Saturday. Wouldn't that make nice headlines for your
folks to read back home?"

"What'll we do instead?" a voice called out.

"Simple," Kinsella replied. "We do just what Rock would
do. We mislead them. We get busy tonight painting signs,
directional signs, all of them with *University of Notre Dame*

on them, dozens of them, and we spread out and get them up all over the country leading in every direction but here. Then some of us can get the old school bus and we'll fix up a sign of welcome to the KKK. Meet them at the train and drive them straight out of town, pretend to break down, and leave them with their sheets but in the woods someplace. Then, some others'll put on armbands and lead whoever else is left all over town until their tongues are hanging out. Let's take the fight out of them rather than give them one."

"Oh, come on, Brassy," a bushy-haired classmate yelled. "This is crazy, crazy. You don't think this'll work, do you?"

Before Patrick could answer, Pinhead Krol broke through the edge of the crowd. Expressionless in a white sweater, he looked like the iceberg that had just taken the *Titanic* down. He gazed around as if in judgment; Patrick threw in a silent codicil of a prayer for good luck before Pinhead spoke.

"Listen, you guys, nobody here thinks Kinsella's more full of shit than I do." He paused a moment. "But I'm with him on this. Let's not get killed for a bunch of Ku Klux Klan bastards."

With that, of course, Kinsella's motion carried and there was great scurrying about for poster board and paint as well as gatherings for the more exact laying of plans for the morning's strategy. Patrick was at the center of it all. Father Martin backed up the stairs with me, shaking his head and smiling.

"Praised be Our Blessed Mother," he said in the soft brogue he slipped into when the occasion seemed to warrant it. "What good sense these Irishmen are showing for a change. Austin, let's get the word around not to mind bed check too much tonight." He winked at me. "The lads are doing the Lord's own work."

Well, that was one way of looking at it, I thought, and I must confess that I chuckled to myself at the mischief of it, quite as good, in its own way, as the mouse on Sister Monica's cape and the worm in Rockne's apple. All of the same genus, if not exactly the same species. Who could have known that Kinsella was laying heavy indebtedness on the Lord through this con man's crusade? Then I thought of Father Sorin, Notre Dame's old founder, stroking his beard and fooling the government into making him a postmaster, or sending some brothers off to California in a winter storm to find gold; he'd try anything, that man. And I thought of Rock himself, halfway across town with his leg propped up, and of how he would have winked and laughed out loud at the whole thing.

It was quite a night around South Bend with Notre Dame boys in a couple of old flivvers tacking up signs on fence posts and trees and at all the key crossroads, down on Route 6 and up on Route 12, and at dozens of intersections on the old country roads that twisted and split and joined again in north central Indiana. You would have thought they were knights on a joyous mission, so hard did they work and so eagerly and full of laughter did they return to tell their tales of bewildered and curious farmers. Patrick, as I've said, was at the center of the councils of war and had reserved for himself a role in meeting the Ku Kluxers' train with the old bus with the great box of a motor up front. The boys had painted a sign on oilcloth, "South Bend Welcomes KKK," and tied it to the side. They had it parked in front of the railroad station down on the south side of town, the one used by the New York Central, a half hour before the train was due to arrive. Inside the station, a couple of dozen Notre Dame students, with armbands reading "Guide" on them, waited on the platform.

Well, it was a sight as the Ku Kluxers, who were kind of squinty and mean-looking anyway, fell for the plan, nodding and surrendering their bags to the boys without a suspicion that they were being taken in. And there was Patrick by the side of the bus, helping the visitors aboard and whispering slogans like "Up the Pope" to make them smile a little and climb willingly into their seats. He got about forty of the Klan members on board, then closed the door and stood staring down the rows at them. He kept a solemn look on his face and then, pointing to his roommate, who stood at his side, he began to speak.

"This is Luther Calvin," he said, putting his hand on Tom McGuire's shoulder. "And he's here with me, Wesley Mather, to welcome you to South Bend. This is a day for judgment." A few of the Klansmen shouted out in evangelistic agreement. "And I'm sure that by nightfall, you'll agree that judgment has been made." More assents and a little applause followed this. Now Patrick had them taking the bait; it was time for them to bite on the hook.

"We have advance information of a most serious nature."

Throaty noises from the assembled Klan.

"It is our understanding that the Papists have armed themselves for your coming. They have even got special uniforms and are at this very moment conducting drills on their campus."

Sounds of patriotic alarm, of paranoia lanced like a boil, in the back of the bus.

"So," Patrick continued as McGuire struggled to maintain a poker face, "we must use strategy. Approach them by surprise. Use back roads and stealth, yes, stealth to get on their grounds." Patrick wondered if he had gone too far, using a word like "stealth" with this collection of mechanics and shoe salesmen. But there was no indication of puzzlement. The word had a satisfying conspiratorial sound and had only made them more attentive. "So let us keep our discipline and stick close together." Patrick paused and a phrase from his American history class slipped into his mind. "We stand at Armageddon and we battle for the Lord," he proclaimed. With that a cheer went up and Patrick slipped into the driver's seat, throttled the bus into motion, and headed it east toward the Culver Military Academy.

Culver was a high school complete with military trappings, flagpoles and ivy-colored buildings, banners and the sound of drums and a marching field for the students who, dressed up, resembled junior-scale West Point cadets. It was a proper place and that morning Superintendent Hagstrom was holding a full-dress parade drill, a practice for the visitors' weekend that was coming up. "We want everyone to look smart today, Captain," he said to his assistant as he watched the students march from their quarters to take their positions on the field. "We have some important people coming, some big donors, and I want everything perfect. Do you understand?"

"Yes, sir!" Captain James replied. "Would you like them to carry the new school flag?"

"Good idea, Captain," Hagstrom replied, and made a note on his clipboard pad. At the same moment on the far side of the drill grounds, just beyond a thick wall of evergreens an old school bus was pulling to a stop.

"Here we are," Patrick announced. "We'll need quiet." He opened the bus door and gestured for the men to step out, shushing them into silence as they did. Meanwhile McGuire was unloading their bags from the carrying bin that was just below the homemade welcoming sign.

"We want to thank you for your help, Wesley," a plump man with steel-rimmed glasses said to Patrick. "My name is

Lester Morton. I'm the Grand Giant of our county. And
these men," he said, pointing to two men nearby, "are my
Nighthawks. Shall we wear our robes?"

Patrick nodded and, with a dumb show, the plump man,
who resembled a druggist who knew every secret in town,
indicated that the Klansmen should open their bags, remove
their white garments and hoods, and put them on. In a few
moments it was done. Bags were sprung open or unstrapped
all along the dusty roadside and forty middle-aged men
removed their coats and shifted their suspenders or ties in
preparation for their transformation into ghostly knights.
There was something sad in that interim moment before these
clerks and tailors, these farmers and traveling salesmen,
donned their flowing raiment. Here were the true shapes of
the human condition, worse than if they had been naked,
because in that instant between doffing their coats and
wiggling into their sheets, there was an almost touching
revelation of distended bellies and sloped shoulders, subtle
gimps and hitches in their arms and legs as well as uncertain-
ties in their balance and vision; they were all men sliding
downhill out of fear and looking for courage in the absurd
phalanx of their communion. "Look kind of pathetic, don't
they?" McGuire, who had a poetic side, whispered to Kinsella. "Fuck them," Patrick replied hoarsely.

In a short while they were assembled at the edge of the
woods. They could hear the sounds of bugles and drums from
the field beyond and their blood began to race at the thought
of a confrontation with what they supposed were the Notre
Dame soldiers just out of their view. Kinsella signaled their
leader, who was about to put his pointed headpiece on, to
come with him through the trees. They made their ways to a
place where, hidden by evergreen branches, they could see
the marching columns of cadets.

"There they are!" Kinsella said softly. "Just waiting for
you. And look, look at that flag, that gold one. That's the
fucking papal flag!" That was all the plump druggist who was
the Grand Giant needed to form his resolve. He returned
quickly to the roadside, arranged his men into a column, and
began to lead them through the trees to the marching field.
Just before they broke out of the thickets at its edge the
druggist lighted a large cross that had been wrapped with
rags. Holding it aloft he stepped onto the grass and urged his
men, all now wearing their slitted hoods, to step forward.

From across the field, Commander Hagstrom noticed a bobbing flame and then a number of figures who seemed to be wearing white sheets coming out of the trees. The band was playing a Sousa march and his voice was almost drowned out as he turned to Captain James. "What in God's name is that?"

"I don't know, sir. But they're coming this way."

And so they were, a band of middle-aged Klansmen bearing a smoking cross as its standard was marching, slightly out of step, toward a group of uniformed high school students practicing their weekend drill. Back at the edge of the road McGuire and Kinsella had just climbed back in the bus, leaving the scattering of bags and coats along the edge of the road. Kinsella gunned the bus and almost stalled it in his haste to get away; he deliberately restrained his own urge to wait and watch the anticlimactic confrontation that was about to take place.

Back at the University that evening there were wild reports about Klansmen driving all over the county, half of them ending up at a Quaker settlement near the town of Nappanee. There were stories of women chasing them with brooms and small children peppering their ranks with stones. Father Walsh, the University president, had received a call from Commander Hagstrom at Culver Academy but professed to be at a loss as to how it happened that forty Ku Klux Klansmen had terrified Culver's student body during marching drill that morning. A dozen of the Klansmen, including one who took a wild swing at Hagstrom and gave him a black eye, had ended up in the local jail while the rest were still trying to find their way out of town. "No," Father Walsh said, "I'm sure no Notre Dame men were involved in that. No, I have no idea why they thought you were a Catholic school."

In the back of Sacred Heart Church Patrick Kinsella sat with a contented smile as he gazed up at the altar again. He wasn't praying this time; he looked more like a man waiting confidently for an answer.

5

Autumn 1929

Rockne was of two minds about the whole incident. He loved the fun of it, the psychological warfare, throwing the enemy off with a poker face and coming home without a casualty. On the other hand some of his football players, including Patrick, had taken big chances in a season in which, according to Rockne's strategy, the team could afford no risks at all. Rolling around in his bed trying to get his leg comfortable, he bit and chewed, and growled some too, like a hound in a snare. In a way, of course, Rock was in a snare, trapped in his own bed and unable to make the trip to Baltimore for the Navy game that weekend or even to Soldier Field in Chicago the next one for the Northwestern game. Notre Dame won them both but the coach was restless and not having any of the fun at all of being on the sidelines.

During these ten days Patrick made a few more cautious trips into Chicago. He wanted to keep some contact with Lane but he did not want to become too active in the gambling establishments. Fifty dollars extra was not bad every week so he gave Lane no more back talk and just did what he was told, which was to check the ledgers from several of the grind joints and to deliver satchels of money back to Lane's office. Lane did not say much either; he seemed pleased with himself, and Patrick thought that must have been the attitude of slave traders and pirates who enjoyed not only profit but a sense of emotional triumph from the subjugation of others. So Patrick swallowed his irritation and, although even he did not know it, he was laying the foundation for a principle that he would follow throughout his life:

let the other fellow make the first mistake, then hit him with
everything you have. It took considerable patience and, had
it been motivated differently, Patrick's attitude might have
seemed like that of the Christian saints under trial. Of course,
he was still laying down prayers to a whole collection of the
latter, asking for freedom and revenge or a chance to get
even, and never for a moment did he imagine these to be
unworthy sentiments.

There was plenty of football practice those days because a
grudge game was coming up against Carnegie Tech, a team
that had beaten Notre Dame two years in a row, losses that
rubbed Rock's soul raw, losses that he had not been able to
live down. He felt doubly trapped when old Judge Steffen on
the winter banquet circuit in Chicago had taken to describing
these games not as "upsets" but as "setups."

There were a few times Rock had been caught out by his
own strategy and one of them had been in 1927 when he was
off in Chicago in the press box at the Army–Navy game
while Notre Dame was losing to an underrated Carnegie
Tech squad. The writers and alumni still gave him the razz
about that and he cursed his phlebitis and, as he talked to
the team by a telephone hooked up to a loudspeaker on
the practice field, he longed for revenge and prayed as
fervently and as often as Patrick did and to just as many
saints.

Now, the other time Rock was caught had not been so long
before that. He was forever getting offers from other colleges
and teams, promising him big money and plenty of extras,
and he liked to use these as a lever with the fathers at Notre
Dame to pry out of them what he wanted for his football
squad. Well, he played it cleverly, leading the other teams on
but always throwing in a caution that their negotiations were
dependent on Notre Dame's willingness to free him from his
contract, something he knew they would never do. So, pusher
and shover that he was—not that that isn't a good idea when
you're dividing the money with the clergy—he could have it
both ways. He enjoyed the offers and applied pressures to
Notre Dame at the same time.

Now, you mustn't think the old Rock was starving to death,
even though his pay was not so grand under the Golden
Dome. But he wrote a newspaper column for the Christy
Walsh Syndicate, taught at summer football clinics, spoke all
over the country, and was on the payroll of the Studebaker

Automobile Company to go around and give pep talks in his locker room style to their sales people.

So when Rock was flirting with Columbia University it seemed like the same old thing. They offered him $25,000 a year to begin with and, as usual, he accepted, stating his escape clause sort of under his breath. But this time Father Walsh, the University president, decided to play the poker hand out with Rockne. He issued a statement, "If Mr. Rockne wishes to better himself, Notre Dame will not stand in his way." Well, there went Rock's bargaining chip for good and there was never any more talk of his negotiating with other schools. Of course, Notre Dame knew his value too or there wouldn't have been that big hole in the ground where they were building his football stadium.

So there it was, two men, each on the far edge of the other's consciousness, struggling with traps and frustrations they didn't seem able to overcome, Rockne laid up in bed and aching to beat Carnegie Tech, and Patrick badly in need of loosening the hold that Mr. Lane had on him. As it turned out, they were both to deal with their problems during the same week, beginning with the Thursday, October 24, before the Carnegie Tech game.

That was the day the market took its first major slide. It wasn't good news, to be sure, but hardly anybody realized that we all stood on the lip of the Depression. It was more like finding out you have a fatal disease but not feeling any of the symptoms and still seeming your old self. After all, J. P. Morgan and the other bankers were meeting and, despite the fact that thousands of investors were wiped out, they issued statements that the American economy was basically sound. And people had a tendency to believe bankers and senators back then. So the shadows were not quite as long as they would soon get and Rockne was thinking about Carnegie Tech, "Those Scots," as he called them in his complaining voice, the flat tinny notes of which sounded like the wail of a man who had never had a bit of good luck in all his life.

Depressions are not good for men with gambling debts, however, and with the first news of the rumblings on Wall Street, Mr. Lane tapped his little silver cigarette case and began calling in some of the big IOUs, a sheaf of which he kept in the top drawer of his desk. Young Patrick had no idea that gambling was as sensitive to economic shifts as it was.

Just the same, as he was boarding the train for Pittsburgh, he had a funny feeling in his gut, a strange message that was hard to decipher, a reaction that gave him a sense of foreboding.

Rockne was close to a fit that Thursday afternoon, throwing the bedclothes off and swinging himself gingerly down onto the carpet of his bedroom. His wife, Bonnie, was used to him; she knew by the look in his eye that he was determined to pull something off, even if it was the last time he would have a chance to do it in this world. "Knute," she said, "you know the doctor says you have to stay in bed."

"Yeah, yeah," he replied, groaning a little and perspiring from the effort of getting half to his feet. "But he hasn't lost the last two years to Carnegie Tech. Bonnie, get him on the phone. Come on, come on, sweetheart, call him and tell him I want to catch that train to Pittsburgh."

Back in Chicago there was a frown on Mr. Lane's face; he was badly in need of a completely trustworthy person to move satchels around town for him. "Operator," he said in his softly modulated voice, "I'd like to place a long-lines call to South Bend, Indiana. That's right, South Bend, Indiana . . ."

The short of it was that Rockne's doctor, not sure of whether his patient was being overcome by showmanship or infection, agreed to let him go to Pittsburgh but only on the condition that he go along to keep an eye on him. The coach seemed to relax after this agreement was struck and the doctor was never quite sure afterward whether Rockne had winked at him at that moment or not. It was a dramatic enough exit with the wheelchair to the station and Rockne's sealing himself in his compartment with no comment, like he was Lenin heading back to Russia.

As for Mr. Lane's call, I myself ended up getting it, since I was the only person about that afternoon in Sorin Hall who was willing to answer the phone. It was a call for Patrick Kinsella and to this day I remember the man's tone very well. He seemed very controlled, as though he were doing me the favor in asking me to find Kinsella or give him a message.

"Well, sir," I said, "you're out of luck today. Patrick has left for the station to go with the football team to Pittsburgh. And I'm leaving shortly myself. We don't look to be back until Sunday. Is this to do with his family? Is someone ill?"

"No, no one is ill. If you will, Professor, please tell him that I called. Lane. *L-A-N-E*. He knows how to reach me."

"Can I give him any message, sir?"

"No message is necessary."

And he clicked off. I remember feeling uncomfortable as I hung up the phone and went back to my rooms to get my bag.

Rock seemed in high spirits when the team arrived at their hotel in Pittsburgh. It was big news that he was out of bed and all the reporters, especially from the eastern papers, flocked to his suite as they always had before games in the past. As to the papers, if the WASPs wrote editorials, Irishmen wrote the sports pages back in the twenties, and Rock knew how to play on their emotional ties to Notre Dame, knew just how to play them like they were violins. And here, of course, was one of his greatest scenes, as he received them all around his hotel bed with his crooked smile and his leg propped up for all to see. It was a sweet sight, I'll tell you, and the genius of it was that none of them was sure just how sick Rockne was. They knew him and they enjoyed their banter with him. They wanted to believe in him and they were chilled, like children hearing their father is sick, when the doctor said, "Gentlemen, Mr. Rockne must not exert himself too much. It is possible that a blood clot might break loose and travel to his heart." So they left the room, still exchanging wisecracks with the coach they had helped make into a legend. When the last one left, Rockne got out of bed and had himself taken to the Pittsburgh Athletic Club where he watched, very nervously it seemed to me, as the team walked through their plays on the handball court.

Everyone was expecting the usual gathering in Rockne's hotel room that night. He always hosted the press and an assortment of sportsmen, actors, and politicians who liked to travel with Rockne to all of his away games. But Rock's suite was closed off; he was not receiving visitors, the doctor said, and the word began to spread that the coach had suffered a relapse. "A goddam shame!" an alumnus said outside Rock's door as he steadied himself for the journey back to his own room.

Nothing more was seen of Rockne until the next afternoon, with the stands jammed, the bands playing, and the teams in their locker rooms waiting for the last minutes to pass before the game was to begin. Patrick was anxious on two counts. He was half worried about Rockne and half again as much as that worried about Mr. Lane and how he would work things out

back in Chicago. His face looked funny when I told him of the
phone call. As to Rockne, however, Patrick felt that, because
he shared some of his instincts, he knew the coach better than
most of the other players. He felt that Rockne was sick all
right but he also felt that Rockne was not past using even his
own sickness to goad the team on to victory. Hadn't he done
it before, once with a fake telegram about his own kid being
sick and wanting the boys to win the game to get him well?
And there was the Gipper speech. Rock had to be careful
how many times he used it and where, especially since
everybody knew that the Gip had not exactly been the
all-American boy, what with the gambling and the whoring
around town for which he was so famous. Ah, Patrick
thought, timing is everything.

Patrick was thinking about these things when the team
members suddenly heard a loud roar from the stands. Even in
its muffled form it was a message that Rockne had arrived, as,
indeed, he had, in a long touring car that was moving slowly
down the field, Rock in the back, white fedora bobbing in the
window and himself tucked in a blanket. The car stopped near
the entrance to the Notre Dame locker room and the young
coach who had been subbing for Rockne, Tom Lieb, opened
the door. Then he and a couple of other fellows fussed around
like customs agents—just putting an edge on the suspense—
when the next thing anyone knew, Lieb was carrying Rockne
like a baby, the coach's black overshoes hanging down below
the trailing blanket. There was a sight, I'll tell you, and the
fans, even the Carnegie Tech fans, loved it, cheering and
stomping as though they were at the Roman Arena.

Well, into the locker room they came, the players solemn
and uncertain as they saw Rockne looking kind of crumpled,
like a Norseman who might not make it through the winter.

Lieb settled Rockne onto the training table, where he
leaned his head back against the wall and said nothing for
several moments while the tension built up among the
players, who, shifting from one foot to the other and aware
that the game was to begin shortly, did not know what to do.
Well, there were the fighting Irish, not that all of them were
Irish; for Savoldi and Krol stood next to Moynihan, and
Metzger and Carideo were on either side of Frank Leahy,
while Patrick stood next to Vezic and Schwartz. Finally Rock
stirred, pulling his features together in concentration.

"Everybody up!" he snapped in his familiar manner.

He looked around at the faces of his players. Nobody stirred in the room that seemed far away from the rising and falling sound of the stadium crowd. Rockne had found his moment and he began to speak softly.

"There's been a lot of water under the bridge since I first came to Notre Dame." He paused and then continued in a louder tone, "But I don't know when I've ever wanted to win a game as badly as this one. I don't care what happens after today." He glanced around again from face to face and gestured toward his outstretched leg. "Why do you think I'm taking a chance like this? To see you lose?" He leaned back again, as if for breath, and then began to bite off and then spit out his words like they were food he didn't like.

"They'll be primed. They'll be tough. They think they have your number." Then the grand pause once more. "Are you going to let it happen again?" Silence all around.

"You can win if you want to." He said that sharply, hesitated a few seconds, and, timing himself to hit the climax just as the team would flood out onto the field, he let go with everything he had.

"Go out there and crack 'em. Crack 'em. Crack 'em. Fight to live. Fight to win. Fight to live. Fight to win, win, win!" Then he let his head fall back, as if he were exhausted just as the team members erupted in a great roar and practically fought with each other to get out to the field.

A masterly performance. Even Patrick was caught up in it; it was, in fact, a scene he would never forget, because if there was calculated drama in it, there was also genuine risk. Rockne had made a bet with himself. If he won it, the stories about his missing the game two years before and the tale of Father Walsh's besting him in the poker draw about the move to Columbia, all of these would be forgotten; he would have all his power back again without a claim against him.

The game was as tough a one as anybody had ever seen. Clean, mind you, with hardly a penalty called, but hard going, man-to-man combat, the stuff of dreams and of life for Rockne, who watched it all from his wheelchair on the sidelines. Kinsella was hurt in the third quarter and hobbled back to the bench on a painfully twisted leg. "What's the matter, kid?" Rockne chided him. "Can't you take a little leg trouble? Maybe we'll have to get another wheelchair for the little mick." But the coach was absorbed in the game, carried away by the contest he had forged in his own image and likeness, busy pumping Notre Dame spirit, as though it were a cottage industry of which he was the sole owner. Kinsella watched him carefully as Joe Savoldi scored the game's only touchdown, giving Notre Dame a 7–0 victory. He knew he was observing a real leader, but what was it he was learning from him, what was it that was resonating so truly in his own soul? It was something about power, something about the way a man could risk everything in order to get everything back in return. But you had to have something to risk to begin with.

There was elation on the train ride back to South Bend but Patrick's leg bothered him a lot, although not quite as much as the idea of contacting Mr. Lane after he returned to Notre Dame.

The next week the stock market continued to go to pieces and, although nobody was still quite clear about what it meant, there was plenty of worry around. Patrick decided that he would try to get into Chicago by the middle of the week. It had been in the papers that he had been injured so, when he called Lane, he told him the doctors were concerned about his condition and that he could only travel with the utmost caution. Lane sounded a little suspicious but agreed that Wednesday and not a day later would be acceptable.

Tuesday, of course, the market went down like an old hotel being dynamited and Mr. Lane was more anxious than ever to call in all the paper he had out in the Chicago area.

"You see, Patrick," he said in words smooth and cool as ice cubes, "when something like this happens, you have to get your cash as quickly as possible."

Patrick, who had brought a cane along, partly out of need and partly out of a dramatic sense, looked wide-eyed across the desk at Lane, who had scooped a handful of IOUs from the top drawer.

"A lot of people owe me a lot of money. If things continue as they have in the market, they won't be able to pay. That would be unfortunate. That is one reason that I want a strong young man like you to visit some of them. Your job is to collect, even if, as you are so used to doing in football, you have to be very aggressive about it. You do understand, don't you?"

Patrick understood very well. He was being transformed from a ledger keeper and bag man into a strong-arm man. But he knew that God had not given him his wits in order to do that kind of work.

"Well, it's too bad, isn't it, that I've got this bad leg then, Mr. Lane. I couldn't even catch my own mother in a blind alley what with the pain and all."

Lane surveyed him with mannered disdain.

"Patrick, I have an idea that you are not quite as bad off as you make it sound. This is not child's play. I want you around this town this afternoon picking up as much of what is owed to me as possible." He was losing some of the unpleasant calmness that ordinarily masked his irritation. Lane gripped the edges of the desk as he said in rising tones, "This is not a fucking football game."

"That's true, as you say, sir, that it's no game. And I understand you want your money back. Why do you think I'm taking a chance like this?" He pointed to his leg just as Rockne had done on the training table. "To see you lose?"

Lane struggled to regain his composure.

"Look, Patrick, I want you out in a cab and I expect you to get this money this afternoon, as much as you can of it, and with whatever force you have to use. These people will be stuffing it in mattresses and teapots and won't cough up any of it. We're in for a bad time in this country. Any fool could see that there was too much speculation, too much gambling on the market. It's not a place for gamblers. I want as much of this cash in as possible. I've got others out working on this. But you're special. Anybody can collect from the shopkeepers. But I want you to visit some bankers, some city officials, some people who need to be dealt with smoothly but firmly. You've got the brains and the muscle for that."

Lane spread a sheaf of papers out across the desk.

"Most of these are in the Loop. You won't have to travel far. Some of them are right in City Hall. You should have no trouble."

Patrick looked through the IOUs. He recognized some of the names and almost whistled out loud at the size of the gambling debts he was expected to collect.

"Only cash, Patrick," Mr. Lane said evenly. "Only cash."

At that moment the phone rang and Lane answered it in his familiar smooth tones. Patrick looked at him and remembered something that his father used to say of some people: "Slick as shit and twice as nasty."

At this moment, however, Lane was becoming annoyed again.

"What do you mean, calling me here? I don't care what your troubles are." There was a long pause as Lane listened carefully, fishing in his pocket with one hand for his cigarette case.

"Commander, a lot of people have lost money this week. You are not the only one. And you have been paid well and regularly by me for your services. What do you expect me to do, cover for your dumb judgment?"

There was another pause and Patrick could hear the crackle of an angry voice coming out of the earpiece which Lane had begun to hold a little distance from his head as though to avoid infection from it. Lane spoke again in angry tones.

"Please don't make any threats to me . . . No, that's outrageous, outrageous." The other party had obviously hung up and Lane was left looking a little shaken, still holding the earpiece. He didn't say anything for a moment, then he pulled open a side drawer and removed a black pistol with a long barrel, checked to see that it was loaded, and placed it on the top of the desk.

"Now, listen, Patrick, very carefully. You and I are leaving here together right now. We'll go down through this back door. You'll have to stick with me, perhaps for several days. Forget about going back to school. There's a goddam fool of a police commander coming up here in a few minutes. He's been giving us protection and now he wants me to bail him out of his stock market losses this week."

Patrick said nothing, although his heart had begun to beat faster, as Lane methodically removed papers from his desk and began putting them into one of the satchels that were so familiar in the gambling world. Lane then rose, pushed a picture aside, dialed open a wall safe, removed several packets of money and what looked like small leather sacks with drawstrings at their necks. These too went into the satchel. Lane's forehead began to perspire and his hands trembled slightly.

"We simply have to take some precautions for a while. These people, your own people, Patrick, sometimes panic easily and lose their tempers. There, that about does it for now."

Just as Lane spoke, however, his door was thrown open

and a big man, football player size if ever Patrick saw one, came in. He was wearing a camel hair topcoat and a dark fedora. He had a gun that looked just like Lane's in one hand and the keys he had used to open the door in the other.

"What the hell are you doing here?" Lane snapped.

"Who the hell is this?" the visitor said, pointing his gun at Patrick. It was clear that he was desperate, that this was no game, no place for theatrics.

"This is Kinsella, a kid from Notre Dame," Lane replied. "He's a friend of your nephew, Jack."

"You from Canaryville?" the big man asked Patrick in a hoarse, dry voice.

"Yes, sir," Patrick said, a little surprised that he felt as calm as he did. My God, Patrick thought, Jack's uncle on the take. No wonder Jack got in this business. The room was filled with more tension than even the locker room had contained back in Pittsburgh on the previous Saturday.

"Listen, Lane," the visitor said, "I've saved your ass a dozen times. Maybe more. I need money, fifty grand, and I don't need it tonight or tomorrow. I need it now."

"Everybody needs money now," Lane replied in a voice whose control cracked only slightly. "But perhaps we might accommodate you." He seemed to realize that Commander Moran was more dangerous, dangerous the way wounded animals were, yes, far more dangerous than he had first supposed.

"You'd better arrange something, you son of a bitch. You owe me. Now, get fifty grand into an envelope." He held the gun pointed directly at Lane's chest. "You son of a bitch, maybe you'd like me to let it around that your real name is Lutz and what business you were in during the war. And the other businesses you been in. And the boys you've played with, funny games. How would that be? Nice, huh? Hurry up."

Lane was placing bills into a manila envelope and keeping a nervous eye on Commander Moran at the same time.

"You were always so pleasant to deal with, Commander," Lane said sarcastically. "There may be some things I know about you that your little red-haired wife would be interested in too, so don't give me any more of that."

Jesus, Mary, and Joseph, Patrick thought, here I am with a bum leg in the middle of two stiffs who might start shooting the lights out any minute.

"Here, Commander, count this," Lane said, and, with a swift gesture, he tossed the package at Moran, who shifted his balance and, in an unconscious reaction, tilted his gun away from Lane's chest in order to catch it. It was all the time Lane needed to sweep his own gun up off the desk and get the drop on Commander Moran.

"Just raise your hands and let the package drop," he said, his voice getting some of the oil back into it. "Just keep your gun pointed at the ceiling until Patrick takes it from you."

Patrick didn't know what to do. Wait for the other fellow to make a mistake, yes, he remembered that strategy, but how the hell was that going to happen here? He was in deeper than he ever thought he could get. Now he had to take the gun away from his old friend's uncle, an Irishman at that. He wanted to pray but he was so excited that nothing came to him.

"You seem to be a little slow, Patrick," Lane said as he pointed toward Moran, whose hoarse breathing was the only other sound in the room. "It is too bad, Patrick, if you moved quicker you might have had a great future. They'll be surprised back at Notre Dame to hear you were killed in a shoot-out with Commander Moran at a gambling hall. No, the fathers won't like that at all. But what can we do?" He began to edge around the desk to retrieve the money. "On the other hand, Patrick, it's probably better that I get the gun. Never trust Irishmen together. You just stay where you are."

He began to move past Patrick, who suddenly realized that Lane, the enemy, was in the process of making his mistake.

"There's a mouse on your cape," Patrick yelled as he slipped his cane between Lane's legs, jerked it, and threw him stumbling off balance.

There were two quick explosions as Lane began to fall. Moran had immediately lowered his gun and fired into Lane's chest and Lane had shot back at almost the same moment. Moran had careened back against the still open door, a trajectory of blood spouting out of his neck, while Lane, on whose shirt front a red stain was spreading like ink on a blotter, tried to steady himself with one hand at the desk. His eyes were wide open and he was gasping for breath, a little dribble coming off the corner of his mouth. Moran fired once more and Lane's face sucked in on itself—like something being carried down a swirling drain—as he fell backward, his hand, still gripping his gun, prescribing a wild arc past the side

of Patrick's head. He went right over the desk and onto the
floor, so that all that could be seen was a gartered leg with an
expensive black shoe on it sticking straight up above its edge
like a flagpole. Across the room, which was filled with the
smoke and smell of gunfire, Moran was sliding down the
door, which had closed behind him as he fell against it, his
blue eyes glazed over and an expression on his face that was
silly with surprise. He finally fell sideways, just missing the
package of money Lane had given him a minute before,
making a gurgling sound as his head hit the floor.

There was absolute silence now, although the room still
seemed to be shuddering from the gunshots. Patrick remained in his chair, holding his cane, whispering, "Jesus,
Mary, and Joseph," softly to himself. He felt stunned and yet
strangely delivered in this moment that seemed so out of
joint, this interval in which the souls of the dead men were
still pulling themselves loose from their wrecked bodies.
There must be devils or angels all around, thought Patrick as
he stood up and gazed at the dead men. He had a Catholic's
instinct to want to do something for them, call the priest, say
a prayer, do something that would make the final acts of their
lives seem less mean. "God forgive them," he murmured.

Then he saw the money, the still open satchel and the
manila envelope. And he also realized that nobody else was
in the club, that nobody else in the world even knew where he
was, and that if he could do nothing for the grotesquely dead
Lane and Moran, he did not have to leave their money
behind. He picked up the package by the side of Commander
Moran. It was flecked with red. Blood money, Patrick
thought as he started to put it into the satchel. Then he
paused and began to sort through the packages of bills.
"There must be three hundred grand here," he said out loud.
He undid one of the small leather bags and shook a dozen
diamonds onto the top of the desk. Jesus, he thought, I'm
rich. He collected the diamonds, put everything in the
satchel, and gazed back down at the dead men. They still had
their guns in their hands.

Well, thought Patrick, maybe there is something I can do.
After he riffled through the IOUs, he decided to take those
too. Who knew what value they might have? He took the
satchel, went carefully out the back door and down three dark
stairways and half another one to an alley door and out into
the brisk autumn air. He walked, satchel in hand, down to

Division Street. It seemed odd to him that people were passing him casually, as though the mystery of violent death were not hovering just a few floors above them. He had an impulse to stop one and to shout, "Hey, you know what just happened to me? You know what I've got in this bag?" He did not do this, however, but sought out a phone booth in a drugstore instead. First he called Police Headquarters and then he called one of the Chicago newspapers. He gave the same message at each place.

"Here's a tip. Listen carefully. Commander Arthur Moran has just been shot and killed in the line of duty while singlehandedly trying to break the gambling operation of Mr. Gilbert Lane at the Lake Terrace Club." Then he hung up and headed for the train station.

As it happened, Commander Moran, much to the surprise of his associates, his wife, and especially his nephew Jack, became the hero of the newspapers, which ground out extra editions with banner headlines about the brave police commander who had died doing his duty. The mayor, Big Bill Thompson, that is, got a great laugh out of it, seeing he knew both Moran and Lane so well, but he composed himself and made a solemn public statement. The department gave Moran a posthumous citation and there was a grand funeral at Holy Name Cathedral with cranky old Cardinal Mundelein throwing holy water over the big mahogany casket, and four cars of flowers. All in all, Commander Moran came off well, and his wife got a mysterious package a few days later with ten thousand dollars in cash in it. Nobody missed Mr. Lane much. In fact, it was a week before a brother, Harry Lutz, a butcher from Cleveland, claimed his body.

And back at Notre Dame, Patrick Kinsella sat at the rear of Sacred Heart Church and thanked God for his good fortune. Nobody ever connected him with the incident and when I asked him if the Lane that was killed was the same one who had called him, he smiled that grand Irish smile, and said no, it had been someone else offering him a job.

Patrick studied the papers, however, and decided that he had to find a way to invest his new fortune, because it was obvious that he could not start spending it while he was still in school. Self-discipline was needed, he thought, and biding one's time. He made a few more trips into Chicago and, after calculating that Samuel Insull's corporation could not suffer

much from the bad times, he put almost all of the cash into
that utility stock. He also started a savings account and got a
safe-deposit box for the diamonds and the IOUs. Then Patrick
went back to school and back to football. He slept well and
his dreams were filled with light.

6
Autumn–Winter 1929–30

Patrick slept well but there were moments when he had to
hold his breath as the last weeks of 1929 fluttered down on the
country like cards from a bad poker hand. Remember, of
course, that nobody knew quite how bad things were going to
get and in many ways life went on as close to usual as
possible. Samuel Insull, the bantam industrialist, in whose
companies Patrick was about to invest part of his fortune,
which still seemed as miraculous as deliverance by angels to
him, well, Insull went right ahead and opened the Opera
House in the first week of November in his great throne-
shaped building at the corner of Wacker and Madison. And
the lady he was sweet on, Rosa Raisa, sang Carmen for the
full-dress opening night crowd, pulling it off well despite the
fact that parties unknown had made off with a backdrop,
worth four thousand dollars they said, a day or so before. At
a distance of ninety miles Chicago remained all magic for
Patrick, who felt reassured about his money when he read of
Insull and his sweetheart opera singer, and his insides, from
which he mainly took his advice, told him he had better show
up in the big city because a number of people, the formidable
Muldoon among them, knew he had worked for Lane and
they might think it was funny if he didn't put in an appearance
in one of the grind joints.

He could still claim injury to his leg, the wound of Lancelot that he shared with Rockne, but he was traveling with the team for the Saturday game with Drake at Soldier Field, a great concrete amphitheater practically on the shore of Lake Michigan. He decided he would slip away afterward and check in with Muldoon, who was doing business as usual at his old stand on Clark Street. Notre Dame won the game 19–7, and, under the pretext of a quick trip to see his dear mother on the South Side, Patrick, still carrying a cane, took the streetcar northward toward the smoky, ragtime gambling room that excited him as much as football.

The place had lost none of its wonder and Patrick stood just inside the door for a few moments breathing in the atmosphere; the room radiated the squared-off sensation of a boxing ring overflowing with has-beens and hopefuls helping each other through the ropes for introductions before a championship bout, along with the smell of a crowd trying to hustle one more lucky day out of life. What wonderful danger, he thought, as he made his way toward the office that he had used when he checked accounts for Muldoon.

He knocked on the door and entered after Muldoon inspected him through a sliding peephole.

"Well, if it isn't the little mick smartass. Come in, young Patrick, and tell me about the game."

"Good evening, Mr. Muldoon," Patrick answered, tossing his cane from one hand to the other like a vaudevillian. Actually, he wanted to make sure that Muldoon saw the cane, then he threw in a wince as he went over to a chair.

"Still got the bum peg, eh, kid?"

"Yeah, they still won't let me play."

Muldoon looked at him suspiciously but Patrick was all apple-cheeked sincerity as he spoke. "I read about Mr. Lane and the policeman. What a terrible thing!"

"Did you now?" Muldoon scowled, lowering his weight into his squeaking swivel chair. "Too bad is right. Lane was a bastard but he kept his word. And what a laugh about Moran. A hero! Jesus, his wife must have been surprised." Muldoon had the week's accounts spread out on the desk and he riffled through the sheets as he fixed his eyes back on Kinsella. "Ready to get back to your work?"

"Yes, sir," Patrick answered, fearing to add more since he was not sure whether Muldoon was testing him, setting up a trap for him, or what.

"Well, get to work, kid, we've got the CPA coming in next week and I'd like to make sure everything's in order."

"The CPA?" Patrick asked in surprise.

"Sure, the Certified Public Accountant. We pay taxes, you know, just like any other business." Muldoon began gathering the papers together, handing them in packets across the desk to Patrick.

"It's a laugh, you think, you and your college boy jokes about it. Well, we do pay taxes and the funny part is that Uncle Sam takes the money. He don't care as long as it's money."

Patrick was amazed that a handbook operation paid taxes. He was certainly learning a lot, he thought, as he looked over the figures on the sheets Muldoon handed him.

"Don't you know how we get extra profit, Kinsella? Well, let me tell you. There's always a certain number of payoff slips written where we don't pay off. You got to be careful how often you use that but, with a little moxie, it can be profitable as hell."

Patrick limped his way over to a desk at the corner of the room, snapped on the gooseneck lamp, and set to his work. He didn't know what to think. Muldoon seemed suspicious but, then, he always seemed that way; it was a feature of people in the horse parlor business. Let Muldoon do the talking, he thought to himself as he worked over the accounts. The bad news from Wall Street had not hurt business too much, he thought as he lost himself in the rising and falling curves of the sums before him. Muldoon finally broke the silence that had settled over the room.

"Funny thing about Lane and Moran."

"What's that, Mr. Muldoon?"

Silence from Muldoon, who was examining a ledger. Patrick turned back to his own columns of figures.

"The funny thing, goddam funny, was the police didn't report finding any money. That's the goddam funny thing about it."

"That does seem strange," Patrick said as naturally as he could. "Didn't Lane always have a lot of cash there?"

"A shithouse full of cash, that's how much, but the boys in blue say they didn't find any."

"Do you think they took it?"

"No, we'd have heard if they had. We've got guys to find out about those things for us. No, it wasn't that. Besides, with a commander involved, they'd be scared to pull anything. I've got my own theory."

"What's that, Mr. Muldoon?" Patrick asked, forcing himself to be calm.

Silence again after a noncommittal grunt from Muldoon, who was bent over the ledger and making a notation with a yellow wooden pencil.

"Big Al," he said in a hoarse whisper that startled Patrick. "Big Al." Muldoon spoke as though he were afraid that he might be overheard. "That's my guess, so you're lucky your ass wasn't there when it happened, or you'd be looking up through the shamrocks now yourself."

"Big Al?" Patrick responded, the humor of Muldoon's theory tempering his anxiety. He felt like a little boy who has just discovered that the ice is thick enough to skate on. "You mean Capone?"

Muldoon nodded his head but held his finger to his lips as he rose and sidled over to Patrick's desk. He bent down close to Patrick's face and, whispering a garlic-tinged spray of words, Muldoon began to explain his theory. "Now, keep this quiet, kid. But when a copper and a guy like Lane get taken away like that and there's not a fucking cent, not so much as an IOU on the fucking floor, there's only one man could have pulled it off. Big Al don't fool around. He heard Lane was calling in his paper with the market taking a dive and it was his chance to settle an old score. Nobody could have set Moran up like that but Big Al, probably promised him the world. Got rid of two for the price of one, cleaned out the cash and the chits, and can take over Lane's stake of the gambling business all at one time. Makes it look like a shoot-out, gets the commander a fucking citation and a big funeral. I'm telling you, nobody could have done it but Big Al."

"Wouldn't somebody have seen him?"

"Quiet, kid, keep your voice down." Muldoon looked around the office. Some muffled sounds drifted in from the main room. "When Al goes to work, nobody admits to seeing anything. You know what I mean?"

Patrick, looking up at the check-suited bulk of Muldoon, suddenly had the feeling that the shadow of a very crazy man had fallen across him and his work. Muldoon had worked out an insane explanation of Lane's death which took suspicion off Patrick but at the price of involvement in paranoid fantasy that seemed more immediately dangerous than the reality of what had actually happened.

"Do you follow me?" He still pronounced it "folly," and Patrick thought to himself, It still is. "I think so, Mr. Muldoon, but where does that leave us?"

"Quiet, kid, quiet." He looked around again. "I expect we'll be hearing from Big Al any day now. A new business arrangement. You could go right to the top if you're nice to Big Al."

Muldoon bent even closer to Patrick, who was getting a fair shower with every whisper from his boss; he resisted his urgent need to wipe his face with his handkerchief.

"I'm glad you're back, kid. You've got some brains. Not like them shitheads outside, you and Jack Moran, you got a little class. Now, listen to me. This is a big chance, the best fucking chance you'll ever have in your life. The wop gangs under Capone run this town and any mick that's smart'll sign on with him if the chance comes along. The fucking Irish haven't been the same since O'Banion went out of the flower business five years ago. Al's got it all, and after last St. Valentine's Day, when Bugs Moran's mob went down, there's nobody gonna fight him. Now he's taught Lane his lesson, it's our chance. I expect we'll hear from Al any time now. The way I figure it, me along with a couple of smart kids like you and Jack, well, we'll get the green light to take over the Lake Terrace business. Hell, you can tell the fathers to shove the Golden Dome then, quit the fucking place, and become a millionaire. I expect we'll hear from Big Al any day now."

Something in Muldoon's tone sent a chill through Patrick. This was like discovering that the captain of a Lake Michigan steamer thinks he's Columbus and he's going to discover America all over again. Patrick did reach for his handkerchief as Muldoon lifted up and away from him like a balloon at a country fair. Muldoon turned away to go back to his own desk and, as he wiped the juices of their conspiratorial intimacy from his forehead, Patrick thought, Jesus, this guy is as crazy as a loon.

"Kid, I been waiting for a chance like this for a long time. But you don't pick out Al and sign up. You wait until Al picks you. Can you imagine? Big Al's got it all set." He paused and opened the top drawer of his desk, drew out a black pistol like the one he had seen in Lane's office, shoved it somewhere inside his coat, and said, "I expect we'll be hearing from Big Al any day now." Then he left the office to observe the activities in the betting room; before the door closed behind Muldoon, Patrick could hear the announcer intoning a race from a California track. He wished he were there.

Patrick kept working, wondering all the while where Muldoon, now that he had this crazy light in his eye for Big Al, would lead him. He felt relieved that he was not under suspicion but something ominous hung in the air and the throbbing in his leg and the discomfort in his stomach told him to be careful. Just as he finished his calculations, Muldoon came through the door, this time with Jack Moran in tow.

"Here we are, Patrick," Muldoon whispered happily, "the beginning of something big. Say hello to Jack darlin', nephew of the great hero, Commander Moran. Heroism runs in the family, don't it, Jack?"

Jack smiled thinly at Muldoon's remarks but was happy to see Patrick and they exchanged warm greetings.

"Now, you two," Muldoon intoned, "you're a bright pair." He took Patrick's account sheets, glanced over them, and put them back in the drawer of his own desk. "As fucking bright a pair as you'd find. So I've got a little treat for you. We're going out on the town for a little celebration. Now that Lane is gone, we've got the whole of it to ourselves, us and The Big Fellow, that is. So let's go out and have a few drinks to our new . . ." He paused. "Shall we call it an arrangement? Come on now, lads, the car's out back."

In a few moments Muldoon, the gleam in his bloodshot eyes growing brighter every moment, had led them through a series of doors to an alley where an old-fashioned sedan looked as big as a caboose in the shadows. They all piled in and, before he started the engine, Muldoon removed a leather-covered flask, gulped a mouthful, and passed it to Jack and Patrick, who sat on the back seats that were upholstered in a rich but stiff fabric. Jack took a swig but Patrick only pretended to as Muldoon, laughing now to himself, roared down the alley, scattering a pair of garbage cans and an old cat that had been feeding from one of them. Patrick looked back under the fringed shade that hung down over the oval-shaped rear window. He was relieved to see that the cat had survived and, as far as he could see, was not black.

In about half an hour they pulled up in front of a building
from which an archway awning, its canvas sides flapping in
the cool night wind, stretched out to the street. Muldoon led
them up to the door, which bore the legend "The Friendship
Club" in letters as formal as those on a lawyer's office door.
Again the peephole, the whispered exchange, the door opening silently, and a greeter in a tuxedo. Muldoon was made to
feel welcome and they were escorted into a surprisingly large
speakeasy, not quite as noisy or smoky as Patrick had
expected, but maybe the bad times were catching up with
things after all. He still felt uneasy as they walked over to the
bar, at which a dozen or so men stood drinking like they were
professionals at it, or so it seemed to Patrick. A small band
was playing from the stand against the opposite wall and a few
couples were dancing in a space not half as large as a boxing
ring.

"A quiet night, Mickey?" Muldoon inquired of the thin,
tight-lipped bartender who looked like he'd been through the
autopsy room and survived.

"A little early," he murmured as he served up three
foaming beers to them without Muldoon's having to give an
order. The beer tasted good to Patrick and he felt a little
better as he and Jack exchanged glances while Muldoon
greeted a friend.

"Muldoon's right, Patrick," Jack said, a fringe of foam
crusting his moustache as he took a drink of his beer. "We
could go places now."

"Jack," Patrick said quietly, "I'm not sure I want any part
of this. The more for you and Muldoon."

"Come, Pat, think about it, think of the grand, grand times
we could have. And hardly any work to it at all."

A loud discussion had broken out at the end of the bar and
Muldoon tugged on Patrick's sleeve.

"Watch this, micko."

A short man of about fifty was addressing a younger man
with a bowl haircut who looked like he had recently arrived
from the corn country. The older man's handlebar moustache
twitched in unison with his eyebrows and his center-parted
hairline as he spoke; it had a disarming, an almost hypnotic
effect, on any viewer.

"What are you saying, man?" he asked in tones of practiced outrage. "What are you trying to tell me?"

Muldoon whispered to his young companions, "That's

Garry Mahoney; he's a state senator and a cigar maker. He's going to take this rube for fifty bucks."

The rube, as Muldoon characterized him, had enjoyed a few drinks and in slow tones, the way he sounded buying a cow at the market, he said to Mahoney, "I think I'm as strong as you. I think I can take anything you can take."

"You do, do you?" Mahoney said. "Well, we will just see about that. Mickey! Get me a bucket of boiling water." The interest of the other drinkers was now focused on the state senator, who had removed his suit coat and tossed it over on the bar. "Fifty dollars, young man," he said to the sight-seeing farmer. "Fifty dollars says I can stand more pain than you. Put up now, or shut up!"

"Watch the rube now," Muldoon said. "Watch him take the bait."

"You're on, mister," the unwary visitor said, extracting some large bills from his pocket and laying them on the bar. Side bets were being made by the onlookers with Mahoney, whose various endowments of hair kept going up and down like a window shade as Mickey came around the side of the bar, his toweled hands holding a steaming bucket of water. The crowd moved in closer to Mahoney and a few people came over from nearby tables to find out what was going on. Patrick already felt a little sorry for the younger man who had delivered himself so naïvely to the city slicker. He's as bad as Pinhead Krol, he thought as he watched the drama continue to unfold. The con, he mused, the con is all of life to these people.

Mahoney moved his arms like a magician about to do a card trick as he circled around the tin bucket, which sputtered and popped like a cauldron out of hell. "Are we ready, gentlemen?" he asked in his smooth and practiced way. Then, without further ado, he plunged his right leg, shoe, sock, and pants leg into the steaming water, which sloshed hissing drops over the floor around the pail. Mahoney did not flinch, he just stood there and reached over to get a cigar out of his coat. As he lighted it, sucking it to make it flame, he said, steam rising up to blend with the cigar smoke, "Are you ready for your turn, my good man?"

The younger man looked down at the pail, Mahoney's foot still stuck firmly in its boiling contents, and scratched his head. Mahoney pulled his foot out of the bucket, shook it vigorously, and leaned back on the bar, puffing his cigar contentedly. A small round of applause broke out. The fellow with the looks of the farmer hesitated, swallowed once as he looked at the pail that was now only about half filled with hot water, and then he began to blush. "The money's yours, mister," he said slowly, pointing to the cash he had placed on the bar.

"Rightfully so," said Mahoney, working the moustache again. "And I hope you've learned a lesson." With that he pocketed the money as he accepted the congratulations of the onlookers and took their cash for the side bets he had covered. The poor young fellow who had lost the bet walked forlornly away when Mahoney, winking back at the rest of the onlookers, called to him, "Come back. No hard feelings. I'll buy you a drink."

"Son of a bitch," Muldoon said, downing half of his glass of beer. "That son of a bitch hooks a hayseed with that every night. The bastard's got a leg that's as wooden as this barstool. A great little con, Garry is." He began to splutter as he laughed at the event which he had witnessed so many times before. "Jesus, kids," he said to Patrick and Jack, "can't you see? Even in bad times, there's always going to be a lineup of suckers ready to hand you their life savings." He ordered another beer and Patrick noticed that the light, O light of golden ambition just within his grasp, now burned brighter than ever in Muldoon's eyes.

Patrick was about to say that his own leg hurt too and that he would like to go home when the greeter in the tuxedo suddenly backed down the entrance steps, two beefy fellows in overcoats and big gray fedoras pushing him along in front of them. A hush came over the room and the lighthearted jazz music of the band disintegrated in silence as two other large men, as unsmiling as embalmers, came down the steps after them. Two more fellows the size of halfbacks lumbered through the door, their hands in their pockets, followed by one blue-chinned man who came in, looked around, removed his homburg, and said gruffly, "Tell the band to start playing again."

"Holy Mother," Muldoon said. "He's here."

Who was not clear until, to the reinstated syncopation of the Charleston, another bulky man entered. He was wearing an expensive overcoat with a velvet collar and he carried a pair of gloves in his right hand. Beneath his outsized white fedora his sallow features seemed puffy but benign. A long cigar jutted out between his lips, which were thick and wet looking. As he turned his head, you could see a fishhook of a scar, shiny pink against his sallow skin, like it had been embroidered there, on his left cheek. His small brown eyes, a little glaze to them, swept the room slowly as he made his way toward a table against the wall that had been hurriedly cleared of its previous customers by the torpedoes who were riding point for him.

"It's him," Muldoon said excitedly. "It's Big Al. Jesus, he's here." He could barely contain his excitement as the room settled down after Capone's guards seated themselves at tables around their leader. Patrick could see him clearly across the room. Capone looked younger than he had expected as he watched him gesture to an aide, his diamond ring, as big as a bottle top, flashing in the half-light. So that's the Big Fellow, Patrick thought, feeling a certain fascination for the greatest American celebrity of crime since Jesse James. And dear enough Big Al had been to the hearts of millions for getting them beer during the dry years, except in the last few months, what with the Valentine's Day murders and other troubles piling up, and the merry days of the twenties crash diving all around, his romantic image had begun to fade. Patrick studied him carefully as he sipped his beer and listened to Muldoon's ravings about the way things were going to be. Jack Moran was hanging on Muldoon's every word, watching Capone and his entourage, and beginning to believe he was about to become part of it. Patrick thought Capone looked a little foggy, like the syph that was eating his brain had taken a big bite of important cells that day, or maybe business wasn't so good, or maybe he hadn't gotten over being put in the slammer in Philadelphia that year for carrying a concealed weapon. Patrick wondered if he wasn't watching the great comet of gangdom just before it lighted up the skies with its last plunge.

Capone was a little woozy, there was no doubt of that, and his cigar kept going out, not that he lacked for fellows to hop up with their lighters to set their boss smoking again. His musclemen had moved their tables closer to his so that now, looking a little disoriented, he sat in the middle of a splayed horseshoe of aides, all of them looking toward him like he was Jesus at the Last Supper.

The evening dragged on for, truth to tell, Big Al didn't do anything but sit there and have a few drinks and let his pals

relight his cigar. Muldoon watched the scene across the
smoky, music-filled room with undiminished excitement. It all
led up to what you might call a meeting of the minds. Then,
again, you might not. Big Al, the drinks not having helped his
own already flawed perception, suddenly wanted a waiter,
even though a drink had just been placed before him. He
raised his right hand, the ring flickering a beam of light
through the smoky atmosphere, as a signal for service.
Muldoon, need having worked him up to a terrible state, saw
the flash of the ring on Al's hand and, for just a second, their
glassy eyes locked on each other across the murky and noisy
room.

"He wants me," Muldoon said loud enough for everyone at
the bar to hear. "Al wants me."

With that, and before Patrick could restrain him or hook
him with his cane, which he was tempted to do, Muldoon had
slid off his stool, knocking it with a crash to the floor, and
begun to take his heavy steps toward Capone, who, for his
part, was still looking blankly at the big man in the checked
suit who was stumbling across the room toward him.

The sharp crack of the chair's fall to the floor, so like a
pistol shot, had attracted everyone's attention, and a sudden
appalled silence trailed after the advancing Muldoon, who,
mouth open, was moving like a nobleman across the court to
pledge his loyalty to an appreciative king. It was sight enough
to take your breath away as Capone's guards became alarmed
at the colossus of the red-faced Muldoon, who, hands now
stretched out like a family reunion was about to take place,
pushed on toward the throne. The place was deadly quiet, the
band members having quit and moved out of range. Capone's
torpedoes glanced nervously at him, feeling their guns in their
pockets, but Al just sat there, a kind of silly-ass smile, as they
say, on his face, watching Muldoon make his way toward him.
Lucky it was for Muldoon that his arms were outstretched,
because it was easy to see that he had no gun in his hand. Still
the tension had built to a high pitch as he lurched the last few
feet to Capone's table. Some of Big Al's men had drawn their
pistols and Patrick was almost paralyzed wondering what
would happen next.

In a few seconds, Muldoon, oblivious of the several guns
already aimed at his bulky frame, was standing above Capone, who, still smiling vaguely, placed his cigar in an ashtray
and looked up expectantly. There they were, the King of the

Underworld and the two-bit grind house operator, grinning at each other in a removed way, in the room where there was no sound at all, except for the scraping of chairs and tables as other patrons moved farther away.

"Al!" Muldoon croaked affectionately, like a fellow visiting his old man at the country home. "Al, I knew I'd hear from you."

Capone gazed up, his face half hidden by Muldoon's shadow. He pushed his chair back, his aides shifting their positions as he did so. Somewhat unsteadily Capone rose until his eyes looked directly into Muldoon's.

"Who the fuck are you anyway?" he said, pleasantly enough, considering the circumstances.

With that Muldoon reached his arms out and, before Capone knew what was happening, he embraced him and kissed him, a slobbery kiss but the best he could manage at the moment. Al did not resist but threw his arms around Muldoon and kissed him in return. "Who the fuck are you?" he asked again as they fell against each other for all the world like a couple of French generals passing out the kisses and the medals on the parade ground.

"It's me, Al," Muldoon said almost sweetly as, after an ominous sway, the two men toppled over onto the floor, overturning the table, the glasses and ashtrays making a great shattering noise as they hit the floor. Al's guards were now on their feet, their guns in full view, not sure what to do since Big Al and Muldoon, a tablecloth draped half over them, were still tangled in each other's arms on the floor. Patrick held his breath as the two men, helping each other awkwardly, began to get up. As Capone smoothed down his thin, greasy hair, he reached out his other hand to Muldoon, who, tears in his eyes, bent down to kiss it like Al was a saint or an Archbishop or something. The moment of danger seemed to pass as Capone, smiling that same distracted smile, kept looking intently across at Muldoon. "Who the fuck are you?" he asked again in puzzled tones. Then he half turned to one of his aides, steadied himself on his arm, and said, "Get him out of here."

With that, Muldoon, who had the look of a man expecting a grand inheritance, was grabbed suddenly by two of Capone's men and marched backward up and out of the door. Capone looked around the room, straightened his tie, pulled a one-hundred-dollar bill from his pocket, dropped it into the

broken glass at his feet, and, his entourage closing in around
him on all sides, headed for the exit. Patrick just stood by the
bar watching the whole thing, not knowing what else he could
do. Jack Moran was breathing heavily. "Jesus, Mary, and
Joseph," he said, "be with him on his way."

The short of it was that Muldoon survived, although the
two broken legs were no good for his posture and they
bothered him so much after he got out of the hospital the
following winter that he moved to Florida. Capone never
remembered anything about the evening and it was only years
later, when Al was out of the penitentiary and living down in
Miami, wacky as a bedbug, that he ran into Muldoon, who by
that time was wacky too, heaving himself around on two
canes, and never sure whether the sun was out or not. Funny
thing, one evening Capone thought he knew him and gave
him a big hello and a cigar at the dog track. The whole thing
was enough to let Muldoon die a happy man, vindicated in
front of his friends for all the years he had yapped about Big
Al and him in the old days. Muldoon and Capone both died,
innocent as babes to the world around them, in 1947, and
were brought back to Chicago for burial in a grand Catholic
cemetery, where they lie today about as far apart as they were
that night Muldoon began his fateful trip across the speakeasy.

There was a lesson in all this but the only thing that Patrick
cared about was the fact that he never had to go back to the
grind house. Hard days were coming for them anyway. Jack
Moran learned a different lesson, the glamour of it all
infecting him for good. With Muldoon all broken up and
living in a dreamland, Patrick, who thought often of the con's
way of life, knew that his last connection with the gambling
life was severed for good.

7

Winter–Spring 1929–30

It was at this time, having rattled home to Notre Dame safely on the last train out that night, that Patrick got religion again. The close scrapes in the big city where the con was a way of life set him to thinking, if not exactly to saying his rosary all the way through, and by the time he was in bed he had promised God several times over that he would stay away from the gamblers and the mobsters for good. It was the next day that he was poking around Sorin Hall, looking for Father John O'Hara, the rail-thin chaplain of the University who used to say Mass for the football team and give out little religious medals to Catholics and Protestants, the latter being some of the best players we ever had, before each game. He would pick out medals to match the opposite team, like Joan of Arc against Army. And he would bless players' injuries, too, although once he made the sign of the cross over a cheekful of chewing tobacco, taking it for a swollen jaw. Well, he was a grand fellow, who rapped out a religious bulletin on his typewriter for the boys five days a week, and later on was made a Cardinal as the Archbishop of Philadelphia.

As it happened, Father O'Hara was out but Patrick bumped into me, and I wasn't so much older than he, but he wanted to talk and that's when I learned about his adventures in Chicago, promising, as I did, that I would not tell anything to a soul. Keeping confidences has always kept me in good with the students. Not that I became intimate friends with many of them the way some of the other professors did. That's probably why I got on well with them, always leaving a

little space, a little distance, or maybe inserting a little
old-fashioned formality between me and them. And so young
Patrick got on with me, and so he continued to over the years,
and me never once sucking up to him after he got so rich and
all. Perspective, that's what it is, but there's not much of it left
in this world where people who would never talk to a priest
behind the curtain now confess their worst sins on television
every night.

To Patrick, Notre Dame and everything connected with it
suddenly seemed pure and lustrous, like alabaster lit from
within, for it gave him an education, a faith to interpret his
life, and a chance to play football under the Rock, who
seemed pleased that Kinsella's energies were better controlled and his mischief-making almost a thing of the past.
Patrick buckled down, not that he was fundamentally
changed, it was more that he was holding his breath, trying to
avoid mistakes, all the while thinking of his treasures, the
money and the diamonds, tucked away, protected by God
more securely because Patrick himself was so ardently pursuing the virtuous life. And Notre Dame was a good place to do
it, with hardworking priests demanding a lot and enforcing
the rules even on the prize football players.

1929 had been a great year for Notre Dame football since
they were named National Champs, but it was a bad one for
the country. By its end we knew we were in trouble, what
with the unemployment and the businesses closing, and Her-
bert Hoover, with his squinty eyes and his plump cheeks
above his high, stiff collars, acting just the way you would
expect from a Republican, and soon finding his name given to
the shantytowns, Hoovervilles they called them, that sprang
up around all the big cities. A cold and dark time, indeed,
but, of course, Patrick had his nest egg and as he got through
the rest of the school year he seemed almost like one of those
pure-hearted lads they were always writing pamphlets about,
and telling you about on retreat, the grand boys that were so
good the Angel of Death would whisk them away before they
lost their virginity. It was late in the spring that Father
O'Hara, sunning himself in his bathing suit down by the lake,
as was his custom every warm afternoon—it did no good, I
might add, seeing how he suffered from the arthritis later on
anyway—well, he saw Patrick sauntering along and called out
to him.

"Patrick, Patrick Kinsella."

"Yes, Father," called Patrick, who had an armful of books, and looked like the ideal Notre Dame student as he walked along the lake's edge. Father O'Hara, like a bony stork in his swimming trunks, stood up, threw a towel over his shoulders, and smiled his pastor-at-the-church-door smile. "Patrick, I've been meaning to speak with you. And we're getting to the end of the year, so I didn't want to miss you."

"Yes, Father," Patrick replied, shifting his books as he reached out to shake hands with the priest.

"I'll go along with you," Father O'Hara responded, picking up his breviary, the gold-edged book that priests were forever reading. The "office," they called it. "How is your leg now?"

"That last blessing must have done the trick, Father. It's much better." They began to walk along the shore of the lake together.

"Patrick, you have much to thank God for. You know that, I'm sure."

"Yes, Father."

"And you seem to have worked hard this past semester. You've settled down a lot since you've come here."

"Yes, Father."

"College is a very maturing experience for a young man. Notre Dame seems to have helped you a great deal."

"I, I"—Patrick hesitated—"I think you're right, Father. I've had remarkable experiences since I've been here."

"No doubt, no doubt." Father O'Hara nodded his head solemnly. "The grace of God is given to young men who are generous."

They walked along in silence for a while, Patrick wondering what this inquiry about his spiritual life meant. He had thought a great deal about life during the months that followed the great kissing match between Muldoon and Capone, trying to sort out the flimflam from the substance, but he was not too sure about anybody's motives anymore, not even the gentle Father O'Hara, who looked, with only his shorts on and a towel over his shoulders, the way Mahatma Gandhi did in the newsreels. Father O'Hara stopped, turned his gaze toward the trees massed along the far shore of the small lake, and, without so much as a glance in Patrick's direction, began to speak in measured and serious tones.

"Patrick, have you ever thought that God might be calling you to the priesthood?"

Patrick stiffened at this invitation which, truth to tell, he had never considered at all. The nuns in grammar school had thought him too much of a threat to ask him to take the cloth, and so had the brothers in high school, who cuffed him around for his mischief, but displayed no signs of wanting him to join their ranks.

"I know it's hard for you to speak about this, Patrick," the priest said. "But it is something you should think about. Remember the invitation in the Gospel, the invitation of Our Lord to the young man, 'Go, sell what you have and give it to the poor. And come follow me.'"

Jesus, Patrick thought, then he immediately tried to erase the blasphemy from his mind. What does this guy know about me with this "sell what you have" stuff? He calmed himself, however, and answered as truthfully as he could, "Father, I really never have thought of being a priest."

"Many have said that, Patrick, many have said that before you. The great Apostle Paul was unaware of his vocation before he was knocked off his horse on the road to Damascus."

What the hell does he know, Patrick asked himself, wondering if I, Professor Kenna, had blabbed about his adventures after one too many drinks one night. Which, of course, I had not, but, naturally, Patrick could not be sure.

"Patrick, it is from those to whom the Lord gives great gifts that he expects great things in response."

This did not comfort Patrick. Was Father O'Hara indirectly hinting that he knew about his windfall? He began to perspire slightly but managed to keep himself under control.

"I know that's true, Father, but, you see, I'm just not worthy, not worthy of the priesthood."

"Now, Patrick, no one is worthy. Even men who had been great sinners, like St. Augustine, have received God's call."

Great sinners? What was he driving at?

"Well, I'm not even a great sinner, Father, just an average one."

"Only God can read our hearts, Patrick."

Well, by now Patrick was quite uneasy, not that he let on. He was tempted to pull a trick, like his old mouse on the cape line, but he felt he could hardly do that to a holy man in a bathing suit. Besides, he didn't think it would work with Father O'Hara anyway.

"Well, Father, it's a great honor, your talking to me this way. And I'll think about it, I will. But my interest is your field, commerce and business."

"I have combined my teaching with the priesthood, Patrick. It isn't so hard."

A bell sounded from the Sacred Heart Church. It was a reprieve for Patrick. "Oh, Father, I've got to run." He began to move off.

"But you will think about it, Patrick?"

"You bet, Father." He looked at Father O'Hara, who, standing all by himself by the lakeside against the trees and skies, his holy book tucked under his arm, summed up all that seemed lonely about the priesthood and the clergy to him.

"I'll pray for you, Patrick, every day."

Patrick headed across the campus, still favoring his leg a little but mostly concerned with Father O'Hara's efforts to interest him in the priesthood. He liked the priests, mainly that is, and they were still nice to him even though he had spent so much time conning them in his first few years at the University. He had changed, he knew that, and he must have seemed different to the good fathers, who kept an eye on the students even when they were supposed to be praying away from their holy books. Great for that, they were, and Patrick suddenly felt that he had been under their eyes from all directions, from the priest peering down at him when he said *Dominus Vobiscum* at Mass, and from windows where the curtains masked the appraising gaze of some chaplain patting his stomach and feeling good that the Church had such fine candidates as young Kinsella there, you know, the football player, the lad who hurt his knee last fall. Patrick felt that his pressured virtue had gained him exactly the attention he did not want. Jesus, he thought again, this time not revising his casual blasphemy in his mind, is this what a guy gets for lying low and minding his own business? He imagined the gates of a seminary opening wide and some hulking archangel of a rector telling him to turn out his pockets and give it all to the poor. Like hell, he thought to himself as he decided to make a short visit at the Sacred Heart Church, just to make his intentions clear to God, just so they knew where they stood with each other. He bobbed a genuflection and sat in the back pew, looking down the cool, dark space to the great bakery box of an altar beyond the sea of lighted devotional candles, and confessed his distress at the idea that some great hand was reaching out to slap a Roman collar on him. God, Patrick prayed silently, I've tried to be good but not that good. He did not feel that it was fair for him to be misunderstood as pious when, in fact, he was only being careful. He sat a few moments, felt no reverberation of displeasure from the Almighty, got up, and, with a feeling that he had re-established reasonable relationships with his Maker, he went back into the sunshine. Two of the priests, their birettas clapped firmly on their heads and their black cassocks billowing behind them, smiled at Patrick as he emerged, the way farmers might look at a prize animal that was just getting fat enough for the slaughter. He smiled back a greeting to them but thought to himself, I've got to get the hell out of here for a while.

Patrick decided he needed some of the antidote of the big city, some of the raucous wonder at the end of the rail line, and the next morning he slipped away, turning over in his mind as he went the wonder of his young life, that the priests, gentle and good as they were, could so mistake his intentions and his aspirations. He was glad that he had made a visit to the Church to straighten things out. God understood. He was not so hard to do business with, and Patrick sensed that he was called to a life far different from that of the priest. Mr. Lane's money was not the Mammon of iniquity but a sacrament of deliverance, and Patrick would carefully post his spiritual accounts over the years, rendering to Caesar here and to God there, and preserving himself from excessive guilt at the same time. After all, he and God were in this together.

Patrick went first to his home on the South Side, where his mother, a light, bright-eyed woman of fifty, her wavy brown hair hardly flecked with gray, was cleaning the windows.

"Patty, what are you doing out of school? Don't you have class today?"

"Yes, Ma," he answered, smiling broadly. "But I was sent to Chicago on business. And I thought I should visit my dear, sweet mother before I leave for life in the monastery."

She paused, wrinkling her brow as she held her rag in midair. "Now, Patty, don't be joshing your mother that way. You were born to be rich and famous, not to hide away beating your breast as though you hadn't been raised by decent people. Why are you here?"

They embraced each other and Mrs. Kinsella tossed her rag into a pail. "Come now, we'll have a cup of tea together."

They sat on the wooden chairs of the small kitchen at the back of the one-story frame house and Patrick made up a fanciful story about needing to visit the bank downtown for the University president, a tale his mother accepted without comment, since she had every expectation that her only son and child would be chosen for just such important tasks.

"School will be out in a few weeks, Ma, and I thought I'd look for work downtown. My leg isn't quite better and I've dug enough ditches for a while."

"You're right, Patty, it's time you worked in a nice cool office instead of out on the hot, dusty street. Work where you can wear a nice blue suit and go out to lunch with the high muckity mucks. You're just as good as they are." That had been a constant theme from his mother as long as he could remember. He felt that he was beginning to appreciate it even more now that he had his secret treasure to manage and only one more year of college left.

"Here, Ma," he said, fishing some bills out of his pocket, "here's something extra for the house. I earned it at school."

Mrs. Kinsella looked in rapturous disbelief at the two twenty-dollar bills, as much as Patrick dared leave her without arousing too much suspicion. "Grand, Patty, and what did you do, rob a bank?"

"No, you might say this was a Providential gift."

"Are you sure now?" she asked, fingering the large bills. "Well, praise be to Jesus Christ, I have good use for these." She leaned over and kissed Patrick lightly on the cheek. "You've always been a good boy."

There was a knock at the back door and, after Mrs. Kinsella peered through the curtains, she unfastened the latch. "Come in, Mary, come in. Patrick's here from school."

The open door had blocked Patrick's view so he could not see Mary Fagan until she had stepped fully into the room. He had remembered her as still mostly a girl but as she came into view it was clear that she was a young woman.

"Well, Mary," he said, almost in astonishment, "you've grown up."

"Our family never did believe in growing down," she said with a smile. She was absolutely beautiful, Patrick thought as he looked at her fresh and open face, as Irish a face as one was likely to find, with a small nose and eyes a lovely watery blue, twinkling the way the lake did when the sun hit it just so. He looked her up and down quickly; her dress, a straight-lined plain white dress, was modest and she seemed as pure as the ideal woman the priests had preached so much to the boys about, the one the lads were to "save themselves for," the one who was a cross between the Blessed Mother and their own, the lovely fulfillment of a man's dreams, the woman who would bear their children, clean their house, and love them forever as purely as if they were living a legend.

"Don't be staring," his mother said sharply, breaking the spell. "Is that the manners they teach you at Notre Dame?"

"Oh, pardon me," Patrick said, using words that he hardly ever pronounced. "It's just that you were a little girl the last time I saw you."

"Well, you've become a big football player, Mr. Kinsella," Mary answered. "That's probably why you haven't noticed what's going on in your old neighborhood." Mary placed a dish on the table. "My mother thanks you for the use of the serving dish, Mrs. Kinsella."

"Well, Mary," Patrick said, "you have changed and I'm sorry I didn't notice. Are you out of high school?"

"Since February. I'm working downtown, a secretary in the health commissioner's office. My uncle Joe got me the job."

"Well, isn't that grand," Patrick laughed. "The health commissioner? Sounds interesting."

"Well, it's mostly typing and filing and answering the phone. As a matter of fact, I've got to go now. It's my day off but I'm taking another girl's place this afternoon."

"Well"—Patrick smiled—"I'm going down to the Loop myself. Shall we go together?"

Mrs. Kinsella looked at Patrick, clucking softly as she patted the twenties in her apron pocket. She knew that her son, her dear and only son, had suddenly become interested in a woman other than herself. "Well, get on," she said with an edge of sharpness in her tone. "Get on, the two of you."

Mary smiled, lowering her glance away from Patrick's. "I'd be pleased to go with you, Mr. Kinsella."

8

Spring–Summer 1930

Patrick found that even his leg felt better as he escorted Mary Fagan to the streetcar stop, talking all the way about Notre Dame and football, and listening as she spoke about herself and her work downtown.

"I could introduce you to my uncle Joe," she said as they climbed aboard the car and fell onto a straw seat together as it jolted into motion. Patrick pulled himself back from the unexpected stimulation of touching against her young, firm body. He began to blush, although he did not; she lowered her eyes and remained silent for a moment.

"I didn't mean to throw a tackle at you, Mary," he said in his most charming voice. Mary laughed and he felt relieved. There was just this wee voice from the back of his mind warning him about putting himself in the power of any other person, for that, of course, was the nature of love, or even of its second cousin, infatuation. But Patrick was enjoying himself and he pushed the thought away.

"Your uncle Joe, what does he do?"

"He's an alderman. And, I don't know, something else in the Democratic Party. But I know he loves football, and Notre Dame especially, so I'm sure he'll help you."

The motorman, a wizened man by the name of Houlihan, applied the brakes and the car came to a halting stop. This time Patrick braced himself and smiled shyly at Mary as he avoided bodily contact. "There, Mary," he said, "I never dreamed a streetcar might be an occasion of sin. How would I confess it? 'Bless me, Father, for I have sinned. I spent the

93

day falling against beautiful girls on the Chicago Electric Line.'" She laughed again at this man who seemed so masculine and quick-witted. At the front of the car, Houlihan called the name of the stop in a garbled whisper.

"What did he say?" Patrick asked.

"Oh, that's old Tim," Mary replied. "He won't pronounce any German or Slovak streets out loud. Wait till the next stop."

They fell into a sweet kind of silence, a communion that is very well known to the enamored, as the car moved along.

"Parnell Street!" Houlihan cried out in a loud and clear voice and Patrick and Mary smiled at the wonderful, typically Irish mischief in the motorman's small daily victory over what he perceived as an alien and undeserving world.

In another twenty minutes they were in the heart of the Loop, in the great granite building that was half City Hall and half Cook County offices. They mounted a broad marble staircase at one end of the building and went down the second-floor corridor to a door with the inscription "Alderman Joseph Keenan" lettered in gold across it. Mary spoke briefly to the secretary in the outer office as Patrick surveyed the men and women, separate even though clustered together on wooden chairs along either side of the wall.

"Patrick, I have to go now but Mrs. McGee there will call you when Uncle Joe can see you." She smiled as she pulled back half a step. Patrick grinned but they both let the interval of time and the space between them go without any effort to fill them. "I'll see you, Patrick," she said, leaving a trail of sweetness, or so Patrick thought, as she headed out of the door.

Patrick had barely seated himself next to an ancient man who was sound asleep, his straw hat on his knees, when the secretary called out, "Mr. Kinsella, Mr. Patrick Kinsella!" In another moment, and with his back to the stares of the constituents who had been waiting longer than he, he was escorted into the office of the Honorable Joseph Keenan.

It was a large and airy room, with wide windows that opened on the urban circus of La Salle Street. The walls were covered with autographed pictures of politicians, baseball players, and boxers. There was even one of Rudolph Valentino as the Sheik just to the right of a citation from the Elks. A large, uncluttered desk was set against the windows and standing behind it was a thin leprechaun of a man, no taller than a few inches above five feet. He was wearing a pinstriped suit, a blue tie with a bright diamond's eye winking out of its silken folds, and a black derby. Two rings blinked the unmistakable semaphore of political achievement from his fingers, in which he held a pair of pearl gray gloves. He was inspecting Kinsella with eyes as blue as his tie.

"You're the Kinsella then," he said in bemused tones. "The football player from Notre Dame. Come in, my good man, and take a seat. Take that one there, yes, that one." He pointed to a straight chair next to his own desk. Patrick seated himself but Keenan remained standing with his hat on, pumping his legs up and down like a man walking in place.

"You must recognize the value of exercise, young man. Sharpens the mind, and keeps the bowels open. Let me give you some advice. Keep your bowels open and very little can stop you in life. It was the death of my brother Ned, Father Ned, that is. More constipated than Martin Luther. I'll tell you, Kinsella, all his energy went into his bowel movement. He wouldn't do anything until he'd had it for the day. And, oh, the suffering of it. We went to Europe once and he spent his time in the greatest collection of marble bathrooms on the Continent. And me in the sitting room trying to read the goddam papers in French or Italian, while he groaned away. The pity of it. Here he was a good priest, and he missed his audience with the Pope because he couldn't move his bowels. Broke his heart, if you ask me. And what did the Pope care, I ask you? Well, Ned never got over it, I'll tell you, and he went into a decline. But he's at rest at last, the good man, and hardly a chance to enjoy life, as you might say."

Keenan began to increase his walking in place, puffing enough so that he stopped talking.

"I'm sorry to hear about your brother, Mr. Keenan," Patrick said solemnly.

"Not a bit of it!" Keenan snorted, stopping his exercise. "He's better off, always dreaming they'd make him a monsignor some day. A dreamer, he was, God be good to him." With that he dropped his gloves on his desk but did not remove his derby. "Now, lad, what can I do for you today?"

"Well, I hoped I could get some work for the summer. You know, until we go back in September. It'll be my senior year."

"Exactly," Keenan said. "The very thing. Employment for the summer. And who could be a better sponsor for you than

Joseph Keenan? Always glad to have a bright young man with a little education. And a strong lad like you that's played football. Well, there'll be no trouble at all. What was it you wanted, water tester was it, or maybe sidewalk inspector? I've got a couple of those."

"I was hoping for office work. I hurt my knee last season and . . ."

"Of course, of course, something behind a desk, and a fresh shirt every day, ironed by your dear mother. I know her, a lovely lady your ma, and your dad too. A good union man he was. Well now, let me think, let me think."

Patrick marveled at the process. Keenan did not care about his qualifications, only his connections.

"I've just come from a funeral, lad. Five hundred cars, a small one for a fellow so well known. But grand flowers for little Joey Magro, a slimy bastard if ever there was one. I always wear my gray gloves to the funerals. They give tone to a man. Them and spats can carry a fellow a long way. Well, we carried Joey a very short way today. Used to be a cop, God rest him if He can find it in His infinite mercy to do so. Did I ever tell you Joey's mistake? They got a new chief in, Honest John Dooley, and the first thing he did, he called in all the captains and he said, 'Put your hands flat out on the table.' And they did, and there was Joey's with three, mind you, three diamond rings shining up for all to see. 'You're fired,' says Dooley. 'You can't fire me, you mick son of a bitch,' says Joey, and with that, Dooley lays the slug on the side of his head that puts him cold, not to say out of work. Joey was never the same, never at all. Then he went full time into the rackets. Poor bastard. They shot him the other night in a whorehouse on the South Side. Not a thread of clothing on him. They had the sense that he would die happy, or happy enough anyway."

"Well," Patrick surprised himself by asking, "why did you go to the funeral?"

"Oh, a good question, young Patrick, a good question. Why did I go to the funeral? And why were there twenty other aldermen, five judges, fourteen uniformed officers from the police department, and as many from the fire department? And why was there a great heart of flowers from the sanitation department? Grand, it was, with red roses that spelled out 'Good Luck, Joey' on it. A little late for that, you might say, since Joey used up his luck a long time ago. Well, why does anybody go to a funeral?"

He paused but it was clear that he did not expect Patrick to answer.

"Loyalty, my good man. Loyalty. The lifeblood of politics. Loyalty in life and to a short distance beyond. It's all built on loyalty, more that than principle or your goddam political science. You build strength through loyalty and never forget it." He paused, out of breath it seemed from his impassioned statements. He wiped his mouth with the edge of his clawlike hand.

"Loyalty is the thing. What do you look for from your fans down at Notre Dame in good seasons and bad? Ask Mr. Rockne and he'll tell you the same I'm telling you. Loyalty. What keeps a marriage together when the old man's been sticking the poker in somebody else's wife, or when the old lady's dropped her pants for the delivery boy? Loyalty, finally, yes, that's the thing we've got, and the only thing to hold us together. That's politics, young Kinsella, and it doesn't cost you a goddam cent. The man who can't be loyal can't be in politics. So you go to funerals, and wakes, and weddings, and bar mitzvahs, and any other goddam thing that's a sign of people sticking together. Where's the life, if we can't get people to stick together?"

Patrick remained silent, although Keenan's words seeded his heart in a way that he did not expect. The crafty old man understood people, Patrick thought, and that's what he's telling me is important.

Keenan had gotten his breath back.

"Now, as to a job. We have an opening as a clerk in the City Council. You'd do some paper work and run some errands for the aldermen. A young man with a keen eye could learn a lot there."

"That sounds fine to me," Patrick said, the idea of being on the inside of municipal power appealing strongly to him.

"Now, we'll have to get some information and fill out some papers. Mabel, Mrs. McGee that is, can help you with that. It's a good job but let me give you some advice."

"Yes, sir?" Patrick said expectantly.

"Mind yourself there. And remember there's two kinds of Irish, the Pigshit Irish like you and the Bicycle Irish that have moved uptown and bought fancy curtains and think they shit ice cream. The Bicycle Irish give you a sore ass. And they're mean. Nobody meaner. Or smaller. Watch for them. They're the kind that like to become undertakers, smiling the big smile as they usher you into the hereafter picking your pockets as they do. Or the women. They like their sons to be priests. Makes them special, always talking about 'Father Tim' or 'Father Jack' and how they gained a plenary indulgence the day before yesterday. Loyalty doesn't mean a goddam thing to the Bicycle Irish."

Keenan took another breath.

"How do you think we can do business with a Republican mayor like Bill Thompson except that we can reach an understanding, as it were, with him. You couldn't do that with the Bicycle Irish. No, watch out for them, as it were, and fuck them before they can fuck you. Do you understand?"

"You've made it very clear, Mr. Keenan," Patrick answered. "I've always thought the same myself."

"Regular talker, aren't you, young Kinsella? Well, I'm glad to hear that. Now, what else can I do for you?"

Patrick thought for a moment, still marveling at the spry old man, for Keenan must have been sixty-five if he were a day, and the way he stood there, derby in place, passing judgments and granting or denying favors all day long. He began to understand why there were no papers on his desk. He did no business on paper, not of this kind anyway, or at least not in this office. Patrick would come to appreciate the old Irish political wisdom of not leaving any papers or records around. He suddenly thought of a question which he considered quite important.

"I wonder, Mr. Keenan, if you can tell me if it's a sound idea to keep money in the stock of Mr. Samuel Insull's corporations."

"That's a strange question for a football player."

"Well, you see, my mother has a small investment in the utilities and the way things are, well, I wanted to be sure it was safe."

"Safe? Yes, I'd say so. He's got half the city on his preferred list, which means selling them stock at below the market prices, as it were. And his stock has remained in good condition, not mint condition, of course, but better than most."

"You think it's okay to leave the investment. She doesn't have much and I want to be sure."

"I'll tell you, young Kinsella, old Sam Insull is a shrewd bastard. And he's tough. Of course, he's got so goddam many companies, I'm not sure that even he can keep them straight. And energy, great energy, still running the business and running around with the opera stars. Friend of mine told me old Sam told him once that as long as a man has his sexual powers, he's okay. But if he loses his punch, well, he's finished. So, from what I know, Sam is doing fine, as it were."

"Well, thank you very much, Mr. Keenan. I guess her investment is safe. And I guess I'll be seeing you soon."

"Fair enough, my boy. A pleasure to meet a fine young man. See Mrs. McGee on your way out." He slapped his gloves down on the desk. "I've got to start giving out the loaves and fishes to the beggars outside."

9

Summer 1930

School closed for the year, Patrick moved back to the South Side to live with his mother, to court Mary Fagan, and to go downtown, frequently with motorman Houlihan, whose pronunciation never did improve, to work as an assistant clerk to four of the city's aldermen. Not that the work was so heavy, consisting some days of getting them coffee and sandwiches or smokes of one kind or another. The clerks did typing and research and some of them seemed quite diligent, but as an assistant to clerk Joe Forrest, Patrick was not called upon to do much but be around, the handsome Notre Dame football player whose brawn seemed more important than his brains to the city councilmen.

The place he worked was lively enough, seeing that some aldermen kept a dice game going in the anteroom, and the atmosphere was colorful, brass spittoons still handy for the tobacco chewers or, as Patrick sometimes thought, for those aldermen who salivated for riches so openly. It was generally free and easy, as indeed the wood-paneled City Council Chamber was. Patrick enjoyed running errands in there so he could watch the aldermen, books, papers, and hats piled on the semicircular rows of places just below Mayor Thompson's bar-length desk, which rose like a judge's just below the embossed seal of the City of Chicago. Thompson, the fellow who had threatened to punch the King of England in the snoot if he ever came to Chicago, was a bear of a man who shuffled around in good suits that looked baggy on him, wearing a Stetson and mouthing more than smoking big cigars, making many a deal as he winked at the wide-open conditions of his city. Well, Patrick loved the look and feel of the whole thing, and, except for the excitement caused when Chicago *Tribune* reporter Jake Lingle, a fellow to whom Capone had given one of his diamond-studded belts, was shot to death in a railroad tunnel under Michigan Avenue halfway through June, things were fairly quiet. A number of the aldermen even seemed to take their work seriously.

Joe Forrest was a compact young man of about thirty with springy blond hair. He wore blue suits and a boater and he seemed more than a little distant, like he was afraid he was going to catch something from you. Patrick was surprised one summer morning when Joe suddenly proposed an outing together.

"You've been here a few weeks, Kinsella, and I wondered if you'd like to play cards tonight."

"Well, I'm not a gambling man, Mr. Forrest," Patrick answered in his shining knight's voice.

"Oh, you won't have to play to enjoy this. It's kind of a party. Joe Keenan thought you might find it educational."

"Educational?"

"Yes, seeing you're a college boy and all, and interested in learning. You'll learn a lot, I promise you that." Forrest leaned down to flick something off the toe of his gleaming shoe. "And I think you'll enjoy it. You might just be asked to tend bar, or change the ashtrays now and then. What do you say?"

So that was it, Patrick thought, his education would consist in serving as a waiter, and maybe a kind of bouncer, at some big card game. It seemed harmless enough.

"I'll go. Where do we meet?"

"Ten o'clock tonight. Come to room eight-sixty, the Beach Hotel. Know where it is?"

"Sure," Patrick answered, his stomach flashing a minor warning signal to him, "I'll see you there."

Patrick had promised to take Mary to dinner, which he did, breaking away after he escorted her home by saying that he had some work to do for her uncle Joe.

"What in heaven's name does he want with you at this hour?"

"Well, he's having a meeting with some important people and I guess I'm supposed to take the minutes, or something."

Mary leaned forward suddenly and kissed Patrick on the mouth. He put his arms around her and they fell into a dark but exciting void, the two of them as steamy as the languid summer evening. They pushed and pulled around a little, edging away from the light on the Fagans' porch until they were leaning together against the side railing, which creaked and groaned under their weight.

"My God, we'll be down in the bushes next," said Patrick, disengaging himself and straightening his tie. Mr. Fagan's voice could be heard booming from within, "Who is it? Is there somebody there?"

Mary touched her hand to her hair, smiled at Patrick, and whispered, "Be careful."

"I think I just was," Patrick said, vaulting over the front railing onto the lawn as he heard the door open and then Mr. Fagan's voice again, "Oh, Mary, it's you. Are you trying to tear your poor old daddy's house down?"

Patrick made the Beach Hotel at five minutes to the hour. It was a little north of downtown, a modest place that looked across Lincoln Park to the moonlit lake. Another hotel, the Shore, almost a twin of the Beach, rose next door; they were separated by an alley hardly wide enough for a milkman's wagon to ride through.

When Patrick got to the room, Joe Forrest greeted him and pointed to a bar that had been set up in the corner. Joe was wearing the classic greeter's tuxedo.

"There's one for you in the bedroom. Get changed and just keep the glasses filled. Understand?"

As Patrick moved toward the bedroom he surveyed the parlor that had been turned into a gaming room for the night. He thought fleetingly of the Lake Terrace Club as he glimpsed the large round table, the chips stacked in a special wooden

holder next to the score sheets and pencils that would be used
by the banker. The table was spread with a green felt cloth,
on which were ashtrays, a bowl of peanuts, and a round tin of
expensive cigars. It wasn't exactly a pang that Patrick felt but
he did sense the expectant mood in the air, the same feeling
that lay across Lane's old club in the afternoon before the
gambling started. It resembled the atmosphere of the City
Council Chambers, not only for its raffishness, but because it
was a setting in which power could ignite, it was like power's
natural setting. He could not help smiling as he quickly
changed his clothes; he was anxious to be a witness to the
action.

Uncle Joe was there, his derby still on, when Patrick
re-entered the room. There were two other men, both of
whom Patrick had seen occasionally around City Hall, at the
dice game as he remembered it. One was short, an inch or
two shorter than Alderman Keenan; his name was Tony
Panetta. The other one had the grayish look of a man either
just going into or coming out of bad health, or maybe bad
luck, Patrick thought, an otherwise good-looking fellow of
forty or so with brown hair parted in the middle; his name
was Alfred Childs. Keenan looked full of ginger, jabbering
away as he pumped his legs up and down in place.

"Clear the mind before the game, that's my motto, Alfred.
Clear the mind for the contest ahead. Hello, young Kinsella,
don't you look grand in your black tie! Bring me a glass of
soda water, if you please."

As Patrick poured the drink, he heard Alfred ask a
question that told him all he needed to know about the
forthcoming card game.

"Who's the mark tonight?"

"A banker in from Ohio. And the lady with him is not his
wife, as it were," Keenan answered. "Fellow by the name of
Coleman, regular pack rat of a banker, got money hidden
everywhere, and foreclosing more homes and farms every
day, the bastard." Keenan stopped his exercising as Patrick
handed him his soda water. "Thank you, Kinsella."

"Ever play with him before?" Childs asked as he took a
cigar from the can on the table.

"I have not, but he's been looking for a big game, as I
understand it, nibbling around here and there every time he
comes here. A cheater, they say, if you let him. Once a month
or so, he comes to town, always with some young dame,

playing a fast one on the old lady back home. George
Wharton told me about him. We've been bringing him along
nicely the last few days. He's in heat for a big game, the son of
a bitch." Keenan sipped his drink, taking a pill from his vest
pocket and washing it down before he turned to the shorter
man.

"Are you ready, Tony?"

"Always r,r,r . . . ready, your honor," Tony replied in a
husky voice.

There was a knock at the door and Joe Forrest opened it to
welcome the guest sheep for the con artists who had planned
to fleece him. A paunchy man with graying brown hair
combed straight back entered the room. He was about fifty,
as far as Patrick could tell, but he had a slender blonde of
about twenty, who looked dumb even across the room, on his
arm.

"Is this Mr. Coleman, then?" asked Keenan in a piping
voice of welcome, as, for the only time Patrick ever saw him,
he removed his derby briefly and made a sweeping gesture of
welcome to the young lady.

Coleman, his eyes darting about the room, shook everyone's hand, referred to the young woman as "my niece," and,
smiling rather covetously, as it struck Patrick, he took a chair
at the table, grabbing a handful of peanuts as he did so. "Shall
we begin?" he asked between chomps, a thread of moisture,
that is to say, spittle, stretching up and down between his lips
as he spoke.

"A fresh deck," Keenan said solemnly as he broke the seal
on a package of Bicycle playing cards and handed them to
Childs to shuffle. "Mr. Forrest, you're the banker I believe?"
Keenan had replaced his derby and sat quietly as Forrest
explained the betting requirements for this high stakes game.

"Is that satisfactory, Mr. Coleman?" Keenan asked.

"Perfectly," said the banker, the string of spit still running
up and down. "I'd like to start."

"Of course, of course, my good man," Keenan said. "Deal
the cards, Mr. Childs."

The young blonde drifted over toward Patrick but he
ignored her, thinking instead of Mary, thinking of virtue in
the midst of the chicanery, as he prepared drinks and watched
the game as closely as he could. The room was soon thick with
cigar smoke and there was little conversation, just the sound
of flipping cards and scattering chips. Mr. Coleman was doing

very well and within an hour was several thousand dollars
ahead. They certainly have let him cheat, Patrick thought.
Coleman looked pleased with himself as he studied his hand,
made his discards, and rearranged the cards in a tight little
arrangement, a bookkeeper's arrangement, Patrick judged as
he observed from across the room.

"Yours again, Mr. Coleman," sighed Alderman Keenan.
"You're teaching us Big City fellows how to play poker after
all."

"I would just as soon not have any conversation, Mr.
Keenan," Coleman replied with the kind of warmth he
probably used, Patrick fancied, on widows and orphans. The
blonde had settled into an easy chair in the corner and was
doing her nails.

Patrick grew anxious and more than a little angry as, in the
cold smoky silence, the chips continued to pile up in front of
the porcine Mr. Coleman. At about midnight Keenan, pushing his derby back slightly as he scratched his forehead, said,
"I propose a ten-minute break, as it were, to cleanse the
kidneys and to get the blood flowing." Coleman looked a
little sullen, but he nodded, rearranged his stacks of chips,
then stood up and went to the bathroom. Patrick wondered if
something had gone wrong with Keenan's plan.

The others milled around, Keenan pumping away for
several minutes before retaking his seat at the poker table. As
Coleman sat down again the blonde called out, "Oh, Willie,
ain't we ever going home?" He paid no attention to her but
merely picked up a fresh deck of cards from Forrest and
intoned, "Gentlemen?" in a condescending voice.

Patrick watched, a towel over his arm, as another tense
hour passed. At 1 A.M. Coleman, having taken another hand
with four aces, said, "I think that's about enough. Cash me
out."

Dead silence at the table. Childs spoke first. "That's not
very friendly of you, Mr. Coleman, to quit so early."

"Cash me out," he said coldly.

Panetta spoke up. "Listen, C,Coleman, you're in Chicago,
not Sandusky or C,Cleveland or wherever the hell you're
from. Y,Y,You gotta keep playing."

"I'm perfectly within my rights," Coleman said, handing
the stacks of chips to the banker, "and I think you all know
it."

Tony pounded on the table and stood up. "This is the

ch,ch,cheapest goddam thing I ever heard of, for C,Chris-sake, I never heard of such a thing."

"I agree with Tony," Childs said to Keenan, who had remained strangely silent. "What do you say, Alderman? I thought this was a friendly game." With that he removed a revolver, another of those long-barreled black ones that Patrick had seen so often, and placed it on the table.

"Now, now," Keenan said in conciliatory tones, "there's no need for that, no need at all. Put your gun away, Al."

Coleman was fidgeting and his mouth fell open a little, the dribble sort of poised there, like a diver on a high board. He kept handing chips to Forrest but his eyes were fixed on Childs's revolver.

"I want my money," he said, like a disliked kid wanting to take his bat and ball home in mid-game.

"Yes," Keenan said. "And you'll get your money. How much is it, Mr. Forrest?"

Forrest looked anxious as he totaled up the figures on his pad. He cleared his throat. "It comes to fifty-two thousand even, your honor," he said in a forced voice.

"Gentlemen, we have no choice but to pay up," Keenan said, removing a large wallet from his breast pocket. He peeled off several bills. "There we are, eighteen thousand. Now the two of you."

Panetta and Childs began to count out their money, grousing and complaining as they did. After the money was all on the table, Childs picked up his gun again, pointed it at Coleman, and said, "You son of a bitch. Here's our money on the table and you, you haven't shown us a dollar bill. What the hell is this? How the hell do we know if he has any money? Suppose we had won? Would this son of a bitch have paid us off the way we've paid, right here, right on the table?"

Coleman was frightened now, his lips working away at the spittle, but his voice unable to make any sound.

Keenan, like a wise magistrate, turned toward him. "Now, now, Mr. Coleman, I must say that Mr. Childs has raised a good point. How do we know whether you would have paid us? We've no proof you've any money. We granted you credit for this game, hearing you had a reputation as a cardplayer. But I don't know."

"I, I," Coleman began, "I have money. But not on me. I've got ten thousand on me. But I've got the rest in my hotel room." The blonde had pulled herself back in her chair as though she were trying to hide from the drama that was unfolding.

"Now, that's very interesting," Keenan said. "You came with only ten thousand. You couldn't have paid us at that. What do you think, gentlemen?"

In the silence that followed, Patrick searched each face for some clue to understand what was happening but he could read no message clearly. Finally the alderman, sighing deeply like a man about to perform an arduous duty, spoke again. "Now, I'll tell you, Mr. Coleman. Fair's fair. And we've no idea, not a bit of proof, that you have more cash in your hotel room. So I would suggest that, seeing we're all honorable men, that you should offer proof of that before we pay you off. That seems fair to me. Does it to you, Mr. Childs?"

"He can have his money if he shows us he had the dough to pay us."

"And you, Tony?"

"Okay," Tony growled. "J,J,Just put that g,gun away, Al. I d,d,don't like it when you pull the gun out."

Coleman was perspiring by now. "I'll go and get the money and show it to you. Would that be all right?"

"The girl stays here until your return, do you understand?" Keenan clipped the words out rapidly. "And leave the ten grand too."

"Understood," Coleman replied, rising somewhat clumsily, dropping his wallet on the table, and heading for the door.

Patrick breathed a sigh of relief as the door closed, but the room was not yet drained of its tension.

"You and your dumbass card games," Childs said sneeringly to Keenan as he put his gun back in his coat.

"W,Watch what you say to his honor," Panetta said in an offended voice.

"Shut up, you little wop," Childs retorted. "You never were good luck anyway." With that he moved toward the blonde, who, like a hostage with the robbers, had decided to be friendly.

"Say," she said in a Betty Boop voice, "you're pretty smooth, aren't you?" Childs sat on the arm of her chair and put his hand on her shoulder.

"None of that now," the alderman said quietly. "None of that, Mr. Childs, this is a gentlemen's evening."

With that, Childs got up, growling a little to himself, and

walked over to a window that opened on the alley that lay
between the Beach and the neighboring Shore Hotel. He
opened it all the way, stuck his head out, inhaled, and said,
"The fresh air feels good after this rotten night."

"Knock it off, Al," Panetta said, studying his hands at his
place at the card table. "Y,Y,You make too much noise
anyway."

Childs bristled and took a few paces toward Panetta,
reached down and grabbed the back of his suit collar. "I told
you to shut up, you little wop." The blonde looked terrified as
the alderman raised his hands and spoke sharply. "Now, stop
it, the two of you . . ."

At that moment there was a knock at the door. It was
Coleman carrying a briefcase, which he quickly placed on the
card table, snapping it open to reveal neat packages of bills.

"Here, I told you I was good for it," he said, wiping his
brow with a handkerchief.

"And so you were," the alderman said. "So you were."

Childs still had a grip on Panetta's collar. "I don't give a
shit about this hayseed from Ohio. It's this dago that's giving
me the trouble. He's been at me all day. Make him apologize,
Mr. Keenan, or I'll shoot his brains all over Mr. Coleman's
money."

Keenan looked alarmed. "Al, stop that talk. Leave Tony
alone, for Chrissake. We've got business to finish here."

"The hell with that. First I want this greaseball to apologize." He pulled Tony's jacket so that Panetta's head jerked
up toward his. "Apologize, you son of a bitch."

Patrick held his breath as everyone in the room remained
frozen in place.

"F,F,Fuck you!" Panetta said gruffly. With that Childs
exploded in a string of curses, pulled Tony up out of his chair,
and dragged him toward the open window. Tony was squirm-
ing and yelling half in English and half in Italian but he was
too small to battle successfully with Childs. All he could do
was sputter some curses as Keenan, his derby tumbling from
his head, rose in an ineffective effort to stop the fight.
"Please, boys, please . . ." Coleman was gasping, holding on
to the back of the chair in which he had previously sat.

"Now, you yellow wop," Childs snarled, picking the flailing
Tony off the floor. "See how you like this!" And with that,
and to a chorus of horrified gasps from the onlookers, he
pitched the screaming Tony out the window, the latter's foot

catching the shade, snaring and ripping it down and out the window as his body plunged headfirst into the night.

Coleman was heaving, perspiring like a horse that just ran the Derby, and the blonde just fainted away in her chair.

"Al," the alderman yelled in a shaming kind of voice. "You've killed little Tony. You damned fool!"

Coleman began to sag, as though he were about to collapse. Childs, his whole body in a spasm, turned, his gun in his hand, toward Coleman. Patrick wondered what the quickest way out might be.

Coleman gasped, "What'll we do? This is murder."

Keenan looked at him, taking him by the arm. "Get out, get out as fast as you can. Don't admit you were here. The police'll be all over this place in a few minutes. Here, Kinsella, throw some water on Mr. Coleman's friend there." Patrick dashed a glass of soda water on the blonde, who spluttered back into consciousness. She struggled up and Keenan pressed her into Coleman's shaking arms. "Not a word. You can't afford to have your name attached to this. It would ruin you. Did I hear a siren?" Coleman's trembling increased as he hurried out the door, dragging his blonde friend along with him. The door closed again and everyone remained still, staring at the window where the remnants of the shade flapped gently. Then Keenan began to laugh as he extended his arm toward Coleman's briefcase and wallet on the table.

"Beautiful, as it were," he said, breaking into laughter again. "Good work, Al. How's Tony?"

Childs was laughing now himself as he leaned out the window, extended his arm, and hauled Tony back through it and into the room. Patrick was so startled he remained rigidly still until he saw that all of them, Forrest included, were embracing and laughing like a team that had just won the World Series.

"A drink for everyone, young Kinsella, and one for yourself too!" called Keenan as he examined the money in the wallet and the abandoned briefcase. "Not bad, boys, not bad. Shall we cut it now or later?"

"Now is fine," said Childs, reaching out for the Bourbon which Patrick had poured for him.

"Don't throw me so hard the next time," Tony said, smiling broadly. "I'll miss the m,m,mattress some night and we'll all be sorry."

"Do you wonder at it, Kinsella?" the alderman asked, his eyes twinkling. "Here, look down out the window with me, right there."

Patrick walked over to the window and gazed down into the darkness. There was a ledge that protruded out several feet from the adjacent hotel about three feet below the level of the windowsill. Stretched out on it was an old mattress. Childs had merely tossed Tony out onto it and in the confusion it had seemed that Tony had passed to another world. The con was only possible because of the way the hotels had been built so close together.

Keenan put his derby back on his head as he snapped the briefcase shut. "We won't hear from the big banker very soon, of that you can be sure. I wonder now how he will explain where all that nice clean money went."

"He's so scared he'll never come back to Chicago," Childs said, and they all broke into laughter again.

"Well, that's it, Patrick," Joe Forrest said. "We can change now. Then we'll see the alderman home and call it a night."

"There's no need for that, Joe," the old man said. "Go on along. And, Kinsella, remember what you've learned tonight. Few things are what they seem." He was standing by the door as he winked back at Patrick. "And Coleman was Bicycle Irish."

It was a treat and a thrill for Patrick, who felt, as he walked through the night, that Chicago was a great Christmas tree of a city, with candy and sugarplums hanging all about, and that Santa Claus himself was a con man. He began to whistle and then to hum the Notre Dame fight song as he first skipped and then trotted toward the lights of an approaching streetcar.

Nobody mentioned anything the next morning and he began to wonder if he had dreamed the whole episode. He was still not sure what to make of it, this example of what seemed to be a well-established way of life for many of his associates. He found some paper work to do and he settled down to it, undisturbed by the occasional noises that drifted into the office from the nearby dice game. He glanced up and noticed a dark-haired man with heavy eyebrows looking steadily at him from across the room. He had seen the man before, another Irishman from the South Side, he was told, but the fellow always kept to himself and did not seem to do anything but work. It made Patrick a little uneasy. Was he an

undercover agent posing as secretary to some of the aldermen? Just as Patrick was leaving for lunch the man stood up
and put his hand out in greeting. "You're Pat Kinsella, aren't
you?" he asked in a deep voice that was heavy with the tones
of the South Side of the city.

"Yes," Patrick replied. The other man, whose clear blue
eyes seemed to look deeply into Kinsella's, said softly to him,
"I've read about you." Then the man took him by the arm.
"Let's take a walk," he said, again very softly. They descended to the street and its noontime noises and his companion moved along so swiftly that Patrick had to pick up speed
to stay abreast of him. The other man said little, although he
smiled greetings to several people who passed them. When
they were well down La Salle Street in the financial district
and its milling lunchtime crowds, his companion stopped and
began to speak without looking directly at Patrick.

"You're a fine young man. You've got a great future. A
fellow like you who's a good Catholic and has a good mother
at home should think about the friends he makes. There's
nothing as important as friends in life. Nobody goes through
life alone, that's what my mother has always told me. But the
kind of friends we have, you know, they can take us in the
right direction or the wrong direction. You ought to think
about the direction you're going in."

"What do you mean?" Patrick asked the man, who was
staring gravely ahead and still not looking directly at him.

"You're smart, a fellow who's smart could figure this out."
Then the man turned toward him and began to laugh, a
merry, infectious kind of laugh that was hard to resist. "Your
mother didn't raise a dunce, did she?" he asked. "Well,
neither did mine. My name's Dick Daley. Remember what I
told you."

10

Summer 1930

For Patrick the work was like having first crack at a box of chocolate creams, especially with the Committee on Public Utilities, which, as June faded away, was concerned with Samuel Insull and his empire. Patrick mentioned his holdings to no one as he took an inside peek at his investment, especially since Insull, high collars, black wire glasses, and white walrus moustache, was in the papers every day. A referendum was to be held on the first of July about the establishment of the Chicago Traction Company, which would provide for the reorganization and integration of the complex array of rail and elevated lines that served the city as well as for some rebuilding and new subway construction. All of it would come under Mr. Samuel Insull, not that he would make so much money off it; the money was to be made in the refinancing, a river of gold for a banker with a keen eye. And there was a pack of reformers, headed by a professor from the University of Chicago named Paul Douglas, who called themselves the Peoples Traction League, and they, of course, wanted to kill the whole thing. Patrick found the project as complicated as the interlaced pipes in the City Hall boiler room and he was fond of listening to Uncle Joe Keenan talk about it.

"Razor-sharp the old man," Keenan said as he leaned back in his swivel chair and tossed a crumpled sheaf of papers into his wastebasket. "Isn't that so, George?" He was addressing an old crony, George Wharton, the Wise Man of the Loop as he was called, a seventyish fellow who managed theaters but enjoyed nothing more than propping his feet up in Keenan's office and talking the news and rumors of the day, one of the great diversions of City Hall life. Patrick felt as he had when he was a small boy and his father let him sit up to listen to the deep-voiced union men when they hunched around the kitchen table at home. Wide-eyed he was as he listened to those big-fisted battlers tell of their struggles with life, always with an edge of the con, or at least a wink of the eye in it. It was the same with Keenan and Wharton.

The latter had a great mane of white hair and a theatrical style when he spoke, like an old leading man making the most of the character parts he was now offered.

"I couldn't agree more, Joe," he said in a voice that was as rich and mellow as lager beer. "Insull will get what he wants this time. And have you heard that he's made the bankers spread half a million dollars around to make sure the voting goes properly?"

"I heard that, George, I did, and cheap enough, I say, considering that this is such an inconvenient time for a vote to be taken, as it were."

"Damned inconvenient. There'd be no trouble if it was just another issue on a regular election day. Of course, these damned reformers have caused all the trouble. What hell there'd be if you let them loose to run the city."

"Why is that?" Patrick asked. He knew Keenan liked to have such questions proposed to him.

"Let me tell you, young Pat," Joe Keenan said as he unwrapped a cigar and bit off its end. "It's important for you to understand. These reformers are great for beautiful thoughts but they forget you have to collect the garbage. They draw great goddam plans but they forget you have to pay for them. They'd like the city to be fit for them and theirs, with carpets for them to step on when they get out of their cars and the flowers giving off nice high-class odors, and no privileges granted to the lower classes. I know them like a book, lad, and I doubt they could run the city anywhere but into the ground. All pure and holy they act. But life ain't Sunday School, lad, and we don't all sit around with our best clothes on singing hymns. Not at all." He lighted the cigar, tossed the wooden match at the wastebasket, and went on.

"Politics is simple. It means knowing how to get things done. And it means getting along with people. You can't have one without the other. It's not so complicated and it ain't fancy and there's no way you can get anything done or get along with people unless you understand that everybody wants something. What's wrong with that? Everybody deserves something. Something for you today and something for me tomorrow. That's the way the world works."

"Yes," Wharton interjected, "and that's why you Irish are such a success, with all your palaver. You get along very well. Whether you always mean it or not, I don't know, but you get along. And I'll tell you one other thing."

"What's that now?"

"You're on to something with that religion of yours. Do you understand why?" He paused, tossing his head a little and clearing his throat. "Because it says you can confess and be forgiven all your sins, that the blackest of them can be made white as snow. Sheer genius that, the very thing no other faith can guarantee. So you have a certain freedom. You can do something about guilt. Why, that's the greatest discovery in the history of the race. You complain about guilt but you have a way of getting rid of it in your confessional box. Isn't that right, Joe?"

"Well, I don't talk religion, no, I don't talk of sacred things like that."

"Exactly, exactly," Wharton exclaimed. "It's so much a part of you, you don't notice it. I envy you, I do, you're Catholic through and through. You expect men to be sinners, that is to say, it doesn't surprise you that they are sinners. It's all part of the business, that's why you Irish Catholics are so good at politics. You take the world as it is, the very thing the reformers don't understand, and you don't try to remake it, which is their fatal mistake. You just live with people as they are and sin is something that can always be taken care of on Saturday night with Father Gilhooley."

"Now, them's sacred things you're talking of, George," Keenan said, holding his cigar as if it were a dart he was about to hurl.

"Wonderful, wonderful. Don't you see? You're very Catholic all right, because religion is something you treat very nobly. And you take good care of your priests. But you don't see how well being Irish and Catholic serves you in your daily work! The Protestants can't hold a candle to you. They expect people to be good and they're appalled when they find out they're not. You don't expect them to be good, at least not all the time, and you've got a way of swinging them into heaven at the last minute anyway. Gives you great leverage in the day-to-day game of politics."

Keenan looked out the window and puffed on his cigar. "It may be you have something there, George." And then he winked at Patrick, the way only Irish Catholics might share a secret together. "But then again you may not. I was never much for the theology. I just say the prayers my dear mother taught me."

The conversation fell away from the subject but Patrick thought about it for a while as Keenan shifted the topic to racehorses. It was certainly true that Irish Catholics dominated political life in Chicago. And the Church was very important in the whole picture. The people might talk among themselves about their priests or the bishop, the sharp-eyed George Cardinal Mundelein, but they were bound to them with a strong loyalty and would vehemently defend them against criticism by outsiders. They forgave their priests their faults, maybe because priests absolved them from theirs. The Church had power in the great city by the lake; it lived closely with sin all the time, campaigning against it, of course, the way Mundelein forbade the burial of gangsters in holy ground, but living with it nonetheless, and didn't some priest like the famous P. J. Malloy from St. Thomas of Canterbury, manage to say a few prayers over the deceased at the graveyard, as he had for Dion O'Banion and many others? It was a mystery, that's what the catechism said about the Church, but Patrick understood this much about it: it was deeply involved in the way the city of Chicago was managed, as deeply as either political party.

He heard the name Insull mentioned and turned his attention back to the conversation between the two old friends. "The thing is," Keenan said, "Insull's got a preferred list. You get stock at a discount, at a bargain price. Well, even the reformers fight to get on that list, goddam hypocrites that they are. I must get ten calls a day from fellows who want me to get them on the list. Well, I wouldn't touch it, and I'm not on it myself." He could afford not to be, thought Patrick, as he remembered Keenan's skill at cards.

"But isn't the company going good, even in these bad times?" Wharton asked.

"Yes, it seems to be. But I'd be careful, George, I'd watch it very closely. I say no more."

Patrick felt a pang in his stomach because a warning signal, even the smallest one, from old Joe Keenan was worth listening to. Joe had gotten up and walked over to the window. He dared not ask him further questions about it but he was anxious to discover why the alderman, who only a few minutes before had praised Insull, was suddenly expressing such reservations. He restrained his urge to question Keenan and decided to listen carefully for any other hints that he might drop. Then again, he might ask his new friend, Dick Daley, his opinion of Insull. The dark-browed Daley said little but when he did it usually made good sense.

Wharton had risen from his chair and was preparing to leave.

"Back to the theater is it, George? How's business these days?"

Wharton smiled. "It's terrible, Joe. At the Princess the winos come in and climb up in the gallery and a couple of them die there in the dark every week. The cleaning ladies just scrub around them. Why, I'm taking in more money selling stiffs to Northwestern Medical School than I am at the box office."

"Grand, George, grand," Keenan said with an appreciative smile. It was just the kind of story he relished, an oddment about existence that redeemed it of its everyday dullness. That's why he liked the con so much, Patrick thought; it was more the excitement of the adventure than anything else. Rubbing some shine into the jewels of the commonplace, that was fun, if not all of culture, for the alderman. It was a way of life, there was no doubt of that.

As it happened, the traction referendum passed, 325,468 to 58,212, much to the chagrin of the reformers and to mild delight on the part of Uncle Joe, who would talk about Insull but not about his preferred list or of why he had urged caution on his old friend, George Wharton. Patrick asked Dick Daley about the matter but Daley just listened intently, his blue eyes never blinking and his expression never changing. Then Daley had laughed, in that merry but distracting way of his, and, punching Patrick on the arm, he said, "A young fellow like you should be bringing his paycheck home to his mother every week!" Then Daley laughed again and asked him how the Notre Dame team would be in the fall of 1930 and wasn't there a new stadium opening, and how was Rock's phlebitis, and, before he knew it, the notion of Insull's preferred list had fled from Patrick's mind.

The summer passed pleasantly enough. There was Mary
Fagan to court and interesting work to do every day despite
the worsening conditions of the Depression. Dick Daley had
invited him to a meeting of the Hamburg Club on Emerald
Avenue in Bridgeport. Daley was the president of this
athletic and social club which seemed to be filled with Irish
Catholics. He even substituted on the baseball team Daley
managed one evening but he came up lame after sliding into
home and Daley, worried about his knee, wouldn't let him
play any more. This Dick Daley, Patrick thought as the days
of summer slipped swiftly off the calendar, was an interesting
fellow, a young man who knew how to get along with people.
He promised to get Daley tickets for the Navy game that
would open the stadium on Columbus Day and then he
packed up and headed back to South Bend for football
practice and the beginning of school.

11

Autumn 1930

It was a grand autumn at the University not only because
Coach Rockne was feeling better, having been to Mayo's for
the phlebitis, and hopping around wearing rubber stockings,
telling the reporters, "They say I'm ninety per cent a new
man and I say to hell with the other ten per cent," but also
because Notre Dame was coming into its own as an educational institution, not yet Harvard by any means, but a place
the country's Catholics could be proud of for something more
than football. It was Patrick's last year and, although he still
worried a little about Insull and longed at times for the
dappled festival of Chicago, he threw himself into his studies,
especially since his knee kept him sidelined more than he

liked from football practice. That gave him more time to spend near Rockne, however, because the tough Swede liked the Irishman, the more so since they were both frustrated by leg problems that seemed the work of the devil himself. Patrick would sit with Rock in his office, taking care of odd jobs and helping him sort out ticket requests from alumni and admirers of the Ramblers, which, as I've told you, was a more common nickname than the Fighting Irish in those days. And Patrick liked to observe Rock's style, which had the flavor of the con but a core that seemed bright and pure when compared to what he had seen in Chicago.

Patrick wasn't surprised one afternoon in the locker room when Rockne, a pair of battered football shoes in his right hand, hobbled over to a reserve player he wanted to try out that day, dropped them on the bench in front of him, and said, "Here, kid, these belonged to the Gipper. See if you can fill them this afternoon." Well, let me tell you, the effect was electric but not surprising, seeing that Rock had learned so much about the human personality over his many years of coaching, and since he had a pile of old shoes to pick from anyway. Patrick asked him about it later in the coach's office.

"No, that's not a trick, not at all," Rock barked out, "just a way of bringing out the best in a man, that's all. Same thing when you have a fellow who's too easygoing, too phlegmatic. Just tell him he's yellow in front of the whole team." Rockne smiled, his eyes, which were a little squinty to begin with, narrowing even more. "That's how you motivate men. Appeal to their pride. If they don't have that, there's nothing I can do for them. Nothing they'll do for themselves either."

Kinsella and Rockne fell to having these chats once or twice a week. Later on, Patrick realized that they had been the coach's way of keeping his spirits up, of helping him to learn something about leadership, or the use of power, which came to pretty much the same thing. But Rockne was restraining Patrick a little as well, as though he realized that young Kinsella was filled with energy and the possibility of ruthlessness. "Remember, Kinsella, you can't be an actor. People are never thoroughly fond of actors on a full-time basis." Then, as he often did, he winked at Patrick, like Kinsella was some kind of accomplice, and turned back to the pile of mail on his desk.

There was great excitement about the official opening of the new stadium, a long oval field with brick sides that was

almost a half a mile walk just to get around it. There was a
torchlight parade and fireworks and the band pumping away
through the streets of South Bend with the Victory March, a
very American event, you might say, and one that amazed
Mr. Gilbert Keith Chesterton, the mountainous English
Catholic writer who had come to give thirty-six lectures on
Victorian literature during October and November. Chesterton wore a flat hat and a cape and, what with his flowing
moustache and his nose glasses, he looked like a fictional
character. He thought the boys were angry when they were
only winding up for the big Navy game with their noisy
festivities the night before—but the English never did quite
understand the Irish spirit anyway. Besides, he came to Sorin
Hall after lights-out and drank a bunch of us professors out of
our whiskey, not once getting his bulk out of his easy chair to
go to the bathroom while his cigarette ashes mantled his great
stomach like the first snow on a good-sized hill. "Massed
Catholicity," that's how he described what he saw at Notre
Dame and he seemed to relish it, drawing cartoons and
writing poems for the student magazine, but, I'll tell you, his
wife gave us what for when we delivered him back home, like
a great smuggled cargo, at an early hour that next morning.

The stadium opened and Rock let Patrick play a few
minutes, just so he could say he was in the game, and part of
the great victory, 26–2, over Navy, the second win of the
season which, although nobody knew it at the time, would be
Rock's last. It was a sideshow and a circus with the battered-
looking coach in his torn jersey thinking through the season
to the game he really wanted to win against Southern
California in December. Other players, like Moon Mullins,
were also hurt and then, scandal of scandals for the most
famous Catholic University in the country, Joe Savoldi,
maybe Rock's most reliable man, the fellow who once said to
him, "Send me in and I'll win the goddam ball game for you,"
well, it was revealed in mid-season that Joe had not only been
secretly married but that he was also getting divorced. He had
to be let go, of course, and Rock gave him a check to help him
start a new life, and didn't the big Italian turn to professional
wrestling and make $80,000 his first year out? None of this
helped Rock's composure or his still throbbing legs as the
season ground down, with Notre Dame undefeated but with a
couple of close calls, and all his concentration focused on

Southern California, a team that had been snowing under its opposition by half a dozen touchdowns and more in every game.

When he could, Patrick would get into the city to see Mary Fagan, who continued to work in the health commissioner's office. And he would visit Uncle Joe, who kept his derby on and invited him once or twice to card games and told him great tales about politics in Chicago. It was from Uncle Joe that he learned that Father P. J. Malloy, the priest who was so good at burying the gangsters, had been in some mix-up trying to make peace between two mobs and had been forced to take an unexpected boat ride to safe exile in South America. Patrick remained intrigued with the relationship between the Catholic Church and political life in Chicago and he felt, in a strange but accurate way, that as a Notre Dame football player he could do well in both worlds, that he had the right name and the right religion to get along fine after graduation. The priests at Notre Dame kept emphasizing an ideal of service, and he felt that Joe Keenan, in his own way, had that too, and he puzzled at the great striving being of Irish Catholicism of which Chicago and Notre Dame were inseparable elements. It was real, this entity of Catholics on the climb in society, and Notre Dame was the shining symbol of their faith and their aspirations just as Chicago, glowing red, was the hearth of their practical achievement. It was all one thing, Patrick mused, whether it was the con or the confessional. Steady belief or a wink of the eye, all part of a wondrous heritage that was breathing deeply and flexing its muscles like a greased-up strong man.

Rock was a great churchgoer, not showy but regular, a convert to Catholicism back in 1925, and he seemed to have no difficulty combining his faith and drive with an unerring sense of how to use power, including an almost holy employment of the con, since it was always in the name of glory. It was almost Thanksgiving time and Rock had the plumbing all over the University loose, making the players do the "washbowl shiver," through which these brawny fellows would grab and shake the washbowls as hard as they could, one of Rock's conditioning tricks, like the time he hired the magician to help the boys learn sleight of hand in passing the ball. Rockne was thinking deeply about the Southern California game, preoccupied, so Patrick thought, but he was curious, so he

asked the coach about the Church and football one afternoon. Rockne looked up, raising his eyebrows and showing
how lined his face looked after the stress of illness. "Why,
outside the Church the best thing we've got is good clean
football," he answered in the manner of a man pointing to a
self-evident statement. "The whole idea is to make men out
of youths, make 'em fight clean and hard, make 'em true to
themselves." But the phone rang and when Rock had finished
the call, the subject, like a buoy on the tide, had drifted just
enough to make it impossible to bring it up in quite the same
way again. Rock started to talk about how great Notre Dame
was and about other Catholic universities and why he kept
them off Notre Dame's schedule. "This is Catholic loyalty
we've built on. Play another Catholic school and you're
bound to divide that loyalty. Only a fool would do that. But
just let us play Southern Methodist and who are they going to
root for? Remember that, Kinsella. Divide the opposition,
not your own forces."

Well, it was an education all right and as the end of
November approached Patrick sensed the excitement, as
invigorating as the colder air, that settled over the team. They
were undefeated, the defending national champs, and they
were headed for California for the game that would make or
break their claim to that title. The papers were filled with it
and with speculations on how Notre Dame, riddled with
injuries and worn down by a difficult schedule, would be
lucky to get a tie with the vaunted Trojans. Good newspaper
stuff, of course, and, as Patrick observed, Rock seemed to
encourage it, putting on a poor mouth, as my father used to
say, when any reporter asked him about the game, like he was
some playground instructor who hadn't mastered the rule
book yet. The Los Angeles papers, naturally, were trumpet-
ing the chances of Southern California to grab the championship by crushing the Ramblers from the Indiana flatlands.

Rock was laying a spell, Patrick sensed, and hatching a plot
at the same time. On November 30, a Tuesday night as I
remember well, Patrick was sure of it as the Notre Dame
Special pulled out of the La Salle Street Station in Chicago,
making its way with a handful of stops for practice, to the
West Coast. Rock had little to say as he entered his compartment, propped his leg up, and pressed his bald head against
the window, like a man lost in thought. Patrick knew that the

less Rockne spoke the more he was thinking, and he slept well as the train swayed along the roadbed that led south out of Chicago.

On Wednesday the train pulled into Tucson, one of the places Rockne liked to have the team work out, a way of showing itself on the road, and getting publicity for the game at the same time. It was the first piece in a complex jigsaw puzzle that the coach had pondered ever since leaving South Bend. He also knew, of course, that the Los Angeles reporters would be waiting for him. "Two years ago these writers reported our practices in such detail," he muttered to an assistant coach, "that I've always held them responsible for our losing 27–14." As he eased down off the train Rockne put on his sad face again as the reporters, their notebooks flipped open and their pencils ready, followed him down the platform. He finally stopped and looked around at the circle of newsmen. "It doesn't look too good. I'm afraid Dan Hanley just isn't up to it." Now, Dan Hanley was a fullback and the writers knew he had been injured. That was the first story they sent humming back to the West Coast.

That afternoon Rockne put phase one of his plan into operation. He called on a third-stringer, Bucky O'Connor, and had him switch jerseys with Hanley. "You'll never get away with this," one of the assistants said. Rockne just moved forward, his face not showing a sign of reaction, like a man who had committed himself too far to make any changes now. Well, O'Connor didn't give much of a showing in Hanley's jersey and the writers ate it up, firing off stories that made Notre Dame sound like a team that was dragging itself to the executioners. One of them asked Rockne for his prediction of the outcome of the game. He took a sharp breath and said stoically, "We'll lose by two touchdowns."

When Patrick got out to the grounds of the Arizona Fieldhouse the next morning he found a group of the players standing around talking. He asked Nordy Hoffman what was going on. "The dressing room's locked up," Nordy replied, "so we're just waiting to see what happens." Soon the rest of the team arrived and everyone was standing around swapping stories and small talk when Rockne's car pulled up and the coach, his little eyes sparking and his fists clenched, marched into the crowd of players. The tone of his voice got attention quicker than a finger scratched on a blackboard.

"What's the idea? Nobody dressed and on the field?"

"The door's locked," one of the players responded a little weakly.

"It is not!" Rockne fumed, and, hunched down like a fellow making his way across No Man's Land, he headed down the tunnel toward the door, grabbed it by the handle, and flung it open. He turned back and stepped aside. "Now get moving. Everybody up in five minutes."

Well, you never saw such a scramble, with the chagrined athletes, the suspicious Patrick among them, slinging their pants and their shoes in every direction in hopes that they could forestall any further wrath from Rockne. Out they clambered, like men getting out of the engine room of the *Titanic,* and there, on the edge of the field, stood Rockne, his arms crossed and his head down. The players quickly formed a circle around him.

"Forget it," he said brusquely. "Forget it."

Deathly silence from the big hulks, some of them still tucking in their shirttails.

"I'm out here against doctor's orders," Rockne began, looking from one player to the other as he spoke. "I'm risking my life with the phlebitis, and you numbskulls can't even get to practice on time. It's obvious you don't care about a thing. You don't care about yourselves or the team. So forget it." He paused a moment and began to speak more softly, so that they had to strain to hear him.

"I'm taking the next train back to Chicago. Coach yourselves. Or get somebody else to do it. I'm a sick man and I've had it."

Stunned silence from the group. Patrick decided to take the bait.

"Give us another chance, Rock," he said as plaintively as he could.

"We'll beat hell out of Southern Cal," Pinhead Krol called hoarsely.

Rockne frowned and peered into the crowd of tense players, like he was Diogenes on the lookout for an honest man.

"One last chance," he barked. "Maybe I'll be back here at one o'clock to quiz you on your assignments. I won't be associated with anyone who doesn't know exactly what to do when the ball is snapped." And with that he was off in his car and hardly out of sight before the team members, desperately anxious to please the coach, were scrambling for the play-books and cramming like it was final exam time.

Rockne was back at one o'clock, looking grim, and he popped questions at them for two hours, until they were almost dizzy, about every possible combination of circumstances that might occur on the playing field. "Who'd cover? . . . Where would you be? . . . What would you do?" The players were in a high state of excitement when Rockne finished his questions but they weren't ready for the next act in the coach's little play. "Now listen to this," he called out. "This is from an interview in the Los Angeles *Times* with your old line coach Tom Lieb. He says you haven't got a chance against SC, that you're soft and worn out, and he's sorry you're making the trip." Then Rockne threw the paper down contemptuously and strode away while the team, their anger at a boil, began to shout and yell like they were at the Dublin Post Office at the Easter Rebellion. Well, of course Rock had put Lieb up to the whole thing beforehand, just as he had fixed the dressing room door, but he had what he wanted, a team that could hardly wait to get to California. He experienced a little trouble managing things in the hotel lobby that night when a reporter asked for an interview with Hanley and, with some winks and hand signals, he got Bucky O'Connor to play the part again, and quite successfully too.

The team was bubbling like bootleg champagne when it boarded the train out of Tucson the next morning. Their arrival in Los Angeles was dramatic in yet another way. Rock put the cork on them, forbidding them to talk to reporters, then there was a police escort, with sirens wailing all the way down Sixth Street to the Ambassador Hotel. "No one speaks," Rock growled as he led the team across the lobby to the elevators. He wasn't through orchestrating the day, not by any means, and he called a succession of secret meetings in various hotel rooms throughout the afternoon, feeding the boys new information and new plays, keeping them busy and at a fine edge of excitement. The centerpiece of his arrangements came that evening, when he accepted an invitation to speak at the great rally and banquet that were held at the University of Southern California. The evening papers were filled with dire predictions about Notre Dame's fate and Rockne acted like he took them seriously as he glumly rose to speak. The band music and the cheering had died down as Rockne, hitching a finger in the armhole of his vest, looked directly at the members of the Southern California football team spread out in seats just before him.

"It will be no disgrace," he said slowly, "to lose to a team with such spirit. I have warned my boys against overambition. We are not overambitious in this game." The California players hung on every word, tense but proud of themselves, as he concluded, "No, we are not overambitious in this game. There is room at the top for only one great team." Then, as he sat down in the silence, he looked to one side, a twinkle in his eyes, and added, "But maybe this is just another funny story." Rock had thrown a stinger in at the last minute, but the Californians, their chests swelling up, broke out into applause at what they thought had been a graceful concession speech from the great Notre Dame coach. How could they lose if even Rockne said they would win?

Well, they found out the next day, in front of almost 100,000 fans at the Coliseum. Just before the game Rockne had come into the locker room and scratched a pass play on the blackboard. The music that had been drifting in stopped as the USC band left the field and it was quiet again, except for the muffled sound of the crowd waiting for the game to begin.

"Boys, you are going up against a great football team. How great we don't know. But I don't think they're a bit better than you are. I know what shape you're in physically and I know how much football you know mentally. But there's one thing I don't know." Rock went into one of his celebrated pauses. "I don't know what's in your hearts. What *is* in your hearts?" He looked from player to player, laying down, as Patrick thought, the last card in a hand of poker that Uncle Joe would have relished. "You're going out there this afternoon and show what's in your hearts." Then he was off, the words crackling out like bullets from a Gatling gun. "Now, if we win the toss and kick off, I want you to go down that field with everything you have. Hit 'em hard right at the start and take the heart out of them. And I want you men in the backfield to be alert, play heads-up football. Watch for passes and when the ball is in the air, go and get it!" He had a full head of steam now as he headed toward his conclusion and the image most of the players would carry of him for the rest of their lives.

"And when we get the ball, that's when we go, that's when

we lift our knees high and go inside of 'em and outside of 'em. That's when we charge down the field. That's when we Go, Go, Go.'' The last shouted loudly and causing the players to erupt in a frenzy, crowding to get out the door. And a grand day it was, with the Ramblers scoring almost immediately on the pass play Rockne had just given them. Bucky O'Connor, still disguised as Hanley, went eighty yards for a touchdown shortly after that. The Southern California players, conned by Rockne's dour predictions, were thrown off their timing and with Rockne slipping in one trick after the other, like having the players march deliberately and slowly from the huddle to their positions, they were kept off balance all afternoon.

Patrick played for a while and had tears in his eyes when Rockne hugged him as he left the field, just as the coach did all the other players. It was a high moment of emotion and a great 27–0 victory. Patrick dreamed about the game even into his old age, just as he dreamed about Rockne's way with the con, with his crooked little smile and his big felt hat, looming up out of the darkness as Patrick fell asleep, still enjoying the zest of the challenge, talking a blue streak, but always winking and adding, just before he disappeared into the night, "Or is that just another funny story?"

12

Winter–Spring 1931

1931 began brightly. Patrick had been on a National Championship team and he had learned lessons that he could never have mastered except for his associations with Uncle Joe and the Rock, two mellow tricksters who had some Catholic sense that their games were not all of life, and that even existence itself needed seasoning or it would be totally indigestible. It was a theology of life, Patrick thought later on, but, whatever he called it, he knew he would live by it throughout the years ahead.

During midterm break he came to Chicago to visit his mother and to see Mary. The city was in the midst of a campaign as bitter as the weather for the mayoralty, with Anton Cermak, the Bohemian president of the Cook County Board, challenging Big Bill Thompson, who, by that time, was living in the Sherman Hotel with a police lieutenant cooking for him in order to stay off the public scene. Great days in the bawdy house of a city and Patrick went down to see old Joe Keenan at the first opportunity.

"Thompson'll make no friends by calling Cermak them names. People will sympathize more than anything else. Imagine, calling him 'Pushcart Tony,' and Thompson pretending he was once a cowboy. Cermak's a cunning fellow." Uncle Joe seemed only mildly amused by the campaign. He knew that he would remain in office no matter who was mayor. He was the perennial politician, secure in his ward's affections, and a permanent fixture around City Hall. Uncle Joe had seen them come and go for years.

Patrick was also pleased to note that the stock of the Insull

Utilities was rising nicely despite the winter whose winds carried no hope to the jobless and discouraged families who were the new poor of the Depression. Patrick stopped to see his old friend Dick Daley, who turned down his dinner invitation because he had to take an exam at law school that night. But Patrick found Mary in the health commissioner's office and took her to lunch in a restaurant not far from City Hall.

"How pretty you look," Patrick said as they settled into a booth together.

"Oh, Pat, you're getting more Irish blarney every day," she replied as he leaned over and kissed her on the cheek. There was a simplicity and innocence about her that Patrick found almost overwhelmingly attractive. They chatted, laughing a lot, as they enjoyed a lunch of salad and chicken, and then Mary's face became serious.

"Pat," she said softly, as though she were afraid someone would overhear. "There's something I want to tell you, something I overheard in the office. But you must promise not to laugh at me. And you must promise not to tell."

"By the shield of St. Patrick!" he said in mock solemnity.

"I couldn't help but hear but I wasn't sure what it all meant."

"Yes, yes, Mary, what are you trying to tell me?"

"Well, I know you said your mother had some stock in Insull, so when I heard the commissioner mention his name I paid attention. I was in his office taking dictation and a phone call came through."

"Yes, yes," Patrick said, trying to conceal the anxiety he felt at hearing the name Insull.

"Well, the commissioner seemed concerned and he told the man that he had been trying to reach him. I think he called him his broker, would that be the word?"

"Yes, yes."

"Well, very confidentially he told this man on the other end of the line that he had been treating some lady who knew Insull well and that she had been very upset because . . ." Mary blushed as she hesitated. "Well, that he couldn't do it anymore . . ."

"Couldn't do what, Mae?"

"You know . . ."

"I do not but has this got something to do with sex?"

"Patrick!"

"Well, Mae, is that what you mean? What exactly did you hear him say?" Patrick could hardly disguise his interest in Mae's information.

She looked down and then whispered, "He couldn't get it up, that's what he said, but I wasn't sure what he meant. Honestly, Patrick, I don't know whether it's got to do with sex or not."

"Never mind. Go on."

"Well, the commissioner said to the other man that he thought this was a bad sign and that he wanted him to sell all his stock in Insull Utilities."

Patrick swallowed hard, remembering Joe Keenan's story about Insull's adage that when a man was no longer sexually potent, he was finished in business too. So that's what old Joe had hinted at, that was something Joe had picked up somewhere and referred to when he told old George Wharton to stay away from the utility stocks.

"Mae, darlin', did he say anything else?"

"He said something about a preferred list or something like that. And he seemed very anxious to have the man sell his stock. Was it all right for me to tell you?"

"Yes, yes, of course, I have to be on the lookout for Ma's stocks. It was right for you to tell me. But I wouldn't tell anyone else if I were you."

Mary promised not to do that and Patrick could hardly wait to walk her back to her office so that he could get in touch with his own broker.

"That's a rather large block of stock, Mr. Kinsella," the round-faced man with the bow tie said after Patrick told him what he wanted to do. "Insull stock is doing very well now. I'd advise you to keep it."

"No," Patrick replied, "I'm grateful for your advice, Mr. Wills, but my mind is made up. There's nothing more certain than an Irish mind that's made up."

"Well, as you say, Mr. Kinsella. You will make a large profit even now."

"Yes, I believe so," Patrick replied. "I want it in a cashier's check so that I can put it in the bank."

And so, following his tip from Mary, Patrick sold out. She had saved his fortune, although he wasn't sure of it until later in the year, in September, when England went off the gold standard and there was a panic among the bankers. Then the House of Morgan went after Insull in earnest and in a few months, don't you know, old Insull was on the high seas fleeing to Greece while his empire fell into ruins, preferred list and all, back in Chicago.

But before that Patrick had to graduate, which he did, with honors, in June. It was a sad occasion, Rockne having been killed in a plane crash at the end of March, when he was on his way to Los Angeles in connection with some movie deal. Patrick missed him terribly and carried him, as I've said, in his dreams all through his life. But that day, in the old field house with his mother and Mae in the audience, Patrick was happy and filled with expectations. Great expectations. He barely concealed a smile as the commencement speaker, an unctuous bishop, talked of the years the graduates had spent at Notre Dame. "Great changes have taken place in your lives during these four years. You have learned things that you never imagined before. You have been in touch with good and inspiring men. You have learned of your place in God's plan for all mankind. You owe much of this to your dear alma mater, Notre Dame."

A smattering of applause followed the conclusion of the bishop's talk, and Patrick winked at the fellow next to him and whispered, "Or maybe that's just another funny story."

PART III

1

October 21, 1983
10:00 P.M.

My reverie about P.B. ended abruptly when I heard loud voices below my windows. Students were jogging along in the moonlight toward the golf course. And, despite the hour and my age, there was something out there calling to me too. That's the best way I can describe it even now. And there seemed to be something signaling through the night to students and priests and even the campus police, for many of them were making their way, some quietly as though under a spell and others boisterously as if they were going to a party, toward the place where the girl hung on the cross. I was curious, in a mixed-up kind of way, feeling that I was being drawn to a dark and forbidden experience, that there was something enticing on the wind and I didn't want to miss it. It reminded me of one of those old DeMille biblical movies, something buzzing at the core of it, something that warmed more than the heart but what harm was there, seeing that it was all about Moses, or St. Peter, or something else religious? Yes, I thought, religious the way Renaissance Cardinals were, their robes and chains covering many a lecher's heart. No mind, I slipped on my high-top shoes and down the stairs, like a boy on the way to the peep show.

A spectacle it was. The big television bus had just lumbered onto the fairway and the technicians had managed to turn on one floodlight. It was playing across the crowd, which numbered in the hundreds, and all shapes and sizes too, and occasionally, like a lighthouse beacon, it would swing past the cross and illumine the girl for just a second or two, then the glare would pass and she was a delicate tracing with just the sheerest outline of her body touched by the moonlight. The people were swaying a little, holding hands many of them, keeping time as they sang softly "If We Only Have Love," a song, you understand, that has become more popular in the Catholic Church than the *Ave Maria*. I stood on a little rise to get my breath and my bearings; it was like falling into a dream. Then Jack Allen's voice, rough and real as an old piece of wood, awakened me again.

"Out here to watch the tart on the cross, Austin? I'm surprised at you, you old billy goat."

He was standing with Father Andrew Simmons just a few feet away, the latter quiet and a little goggle-eyed at it all, but Jack, as I could see, was puffing on his cigarette with a Humphrey Bogart smile on his face.

"Well, Jack, I don't know that I'd call her that."

"Come on, Austin, you're like the rest of them here. Nothing like a girl on a cross to get the fathers and the old dons out. Does them good, makes the blood run faster. I'm surprised they haven't wet her down. That's always been a crowd pleaser."

"Jack," I said, feeling he had thrown too much bitters into his observations, "it's a shocking thing, positively shocking, but there are lots of good people here. Just look around."

"Yeah," he responded, flipping his cigarette away. "The same crowd that goes to accidents or public hangings. The madness of crowds, Austin, the madness of crowds. Who the hell let it get this far?"

I had no answer, of course, as the whole thing seemed to have a life of its own. It was as if the people there needed something like this, as though they had been waiting for such an occasion, poised fully dressed behind their doors and ready to go when the trumpet of assembly sounded; it seemed the most natural thing in the world.

Allen was shaking his head slowly, as though, sadly enough, he too had expected something like this, that it was a flowering of seeds that had been germinating for some time. He seemed to be grieving over it all, the way a statesman whose warnings had gone unheeded might look as the capital was overrun by the enemy.

"Well," he said dryly, "I suppose something like this was bound to happen somewhere. Just a little puberty coming out of the box. Long overdue." He shook his head slowly as

Father Simmons, who would have been handsome except for his broken nose and thick glasses, turned toward him quizzically. He opened his mouth to say something but Allen had already turned and begun to walk into the darkness and back to his rooms. Simmons hesitated a moment and then followed after him.

They were still having trouble adjusting the television lights and their alternate flashing on and off, peeling the darkness away from the crowd in one moment and then rolling up toward the bright moon in the next, intensified the theatricality of the event. People were popping pictures, firefly fashion, and other media representatives were gathering with notebooks and microphones, the lot of them making quite a stir with their random shouts and exchanges about sound levels and camera angles. Nobody was in charge, and the University's public relations director, Dick Cummings, had all he could do to respond to reporters' questions, much less do anything to disperse the crowd. Some of the priests were mixed in with the crowd, singing away like the Pope was next on the program. Others stood rather tentatively at its edge, trapped in the same ambivalence in which some of them led most of their lives, not sure whether to be part of the crowd or not, unsure as to how to lead it and uncertain as to whether they should follow it. Dick Cummings was in the middle of a circle of journalists.

"Is it true the girl is a student here?"

"We do not believe that she is a student here or at St. Mary's," Cummings responded.

"You got a name? Anything about her?"

"We need confirmation. We really don't want to give out any names just yet."

"Is it true she's done this before? I mean, we heard she went up and laid herself out on the altar of one of the chapels last week, asking for repentance, that she's hung around by the river . . ."

"Yeah, and that she was washing people's sins away there the other night."

Cummings sighed. "I really don't know anything about those incidents. They sound like rumors to me."

"Then you've heard of them?"

"I didn't say that."

"How about the story that she was in the convent and got

the heave-ho a year ago for this same sort of thing. On the altar at midnight, scaring the shit out of some old nun who came down to pray?"

"I hear she's a relative of Princess Grace. Know anything about that, Dick?"

Cummings was waving his hands and shaking his head. "No, I don't know any more than you. You'll have to wait to get more information. We don't want to blow this out of proportion. We would like to get her down."

As he said that the girl let out a loud groan and the singing fell to pieces in a scattering of unfinished notes. The floodlights were turned toward her and even the media people grew quiet, as though they were expecting a message, maybe a couple of envelopes like Fatima, or that a spring would burst out of the golf course sod. She groaned again and twisted her body, throwing her hair back half sensuously, like an all-American girl in a shampoo commercial.

An older man, a brother from a nearby religious monastery and a familiar character around town, called out to her from up near the front of the crowd.

"Do you have a message for us?"

The girl groaned again but this time she opened her eyes and looked down at the brother who had spoken to her. Her chest was heaving, you could see that clearly now that the lights were on her, and she began to speak, softly at first, but quite clearly.

"Our Lady asks for something . . ."

Shouts from the reporters, "What was that, what did she say?"

Shushing from the crowd which was now bending expectantly toward her.

"Our Lady asks for repentance for all sins of the flesh. Our Lady asks us to do penance for a sinful age. God asks the world to become pure again, to wash away the filth of the last generation . . ."

Her words trailed off but people here and there in the crowd began to shout, "Amen," like the wild-eyed at a revival, while others called out, "Bless the Lord," and one foreign student priest near me who was dressed like Fidel Castro yelled, "Right on!" Then, by God, cheers broke out and a nice round of applause. Heaving and straining against the ties she was not exactly your ordinary holy card saint but she went right on and repeated the whole message, almost word for word. Well, the cameras were whirring away this time, and some reporter was poking a microphone up out of the crowd to try to pick up her voice more clearly. Then she closed her eyes again and seemed to drift into a trance. A moment later the television crews killed their lights and the cameraman, swinging out behind his camera like a man on the back of a hook and ladder, called to an assistant, "Hold it until Garbo talks again."

Big clouds were beginning to move across the moon, so now the light was fragmented and patchy. As my eyes adapted to the darkness I could see the size of the crowd as well as several clusters of people standing at various distances from it. They were, I thought, all looking for and seeing something different. I wasn't sure, mind you, exactly what it meant, or whether it was good or bad, or where it might fit in between those two extremes. I just knew that there was need abroad that night inhaling and exhaling like the monster who always mooned about in fairy stories for the touch of beauty and gentleness. It was as though a ravening spirit inhabited the crowd and, however it happened, the girl was an offering for the discontents of its flesh as well as a symbol of the longing in its soul. It did not make me tremble but it made me think about the event and what it was telling of the lives of all those who had gathered at this cross. The forbidden fruit was there, the virginal offering, the sacrifice to the gods, yes, all of that even as Jack Allen had observed. But there was something more, and I think Allen knew that too, something basic, a common denominator for this assemblage of townspeople and university personnel, so different they seemed, and yet so alike in the filament that had been ignited in them by this bizarre occurrence.

The crowd had just launched into "Amazing Grace," another big number on the Vatican II Hit Parade, when a disturbance broke out near the cross. There was shouting and yelling and the hymn wavered and broke off. Somebody, an assistant dean of students it turned out, was trying to address the crowd over a portable bullhorn.

"We are asking you to leave now," he said in the same tone the cops use when they say, "The place is surrounded." "We are asking you to leave now."

Members of the crowd began to shout back, "Go home yourself," and, "Leave us alone," and then they began to sing again so that the announcements were first muted and then

overwhelmed by a swelling chorus of the old spiritual. Well,
they sang a couple of rounds of that and moved right on to
"Let There Be Peace on Earth." You could tell that the
crowd, under the in- and out-again harvest moon, was having
a good time of it, and they weren't going to be ushered off the
golf course easily.

After that song ended there was a scuffle and the bullhorn
was passed to someone else. It turned out to be the brother
monk who had asked the girl for the message earlier. His
name was Brother Chrysostym, a gaunt-looking man with
silver-rimmed spectacles and a crew haircut. He was a master
carpenter back at the monastery, happy banging away in his
workshop but quiet otherwise, "very spiritual," they called
him. Better the monastery than the funny farm, I had always
thought, especially after I learned how he used to make and
fly giant kites on his days off. He would only make them out
of Catholic newspapers and he was forever building little
devices that were fixed with timers or burning string, or some
other such contraption, to drop little statues of the Blessed
Mother, rigged up in tiny parachutes, over downtown South
Bend or into some farmer's yard. Leaflets too, about the
Communist menace, and once a shower of rose petals, oh, he
was a number, I thought, and now he, who hardly spoke at
all, had the bullhorn.

"We are all here lawfully," he started out in a high-pitched
voice that sounded pinched from lack of use. "We are here to
honor Our Lady, Our Lady of Notre Dame." Shouts of
"Amen!" again from the crowd. "We are here to hold a vigil
for purity and to make reparation for all the foul deeds of the
flesh, for all the wicked thoughts and desires, for the terrible
passions that have burned away like maggots inside us."
Brother was just warming to his subject as all the pent-up
fantasies he had formerly worked out through kite flying
began to tumble out. "For lewd women standing on the
corners to tempt men everywhere," he intoned, "let us pray
to the Lord!" "Lord, hear our prayer!" came rolling back
from about half the crowd. Many others were getting uneasy
at the way Brother was transforming the night into his own
personal essay of daffiness. "For women who are unclean . . . " He was sailing right along, of course, dividing the crowd as he went into the hard-core enthusiasts and
the disenchanted. A number of the priests and students
pulled back and away from the gathering but there was still

a good group chanting along after Brother Chrysostym's invocations. "For young men breaking the sixth and ninth commandments with no firm purpose of amendment . . . for those who give in to the sensuality of rock music . . ." Brother was, naturally, an embarrassment and then suddenly a black-robed man as big as a football player collared him and led him away. His keeper from the monastery, I guessed, but he had come too late to prevent the television cameras from recording most of the good Brother's prayers. I could just imagine how he would be described, probably as "a member of the Notre Dame faculty," or "a scholar in the theology department," or some other looniness to connect Brother Kiteflyer with the Golden Dome.

I thought that would be the end of it but the girl was still up there and the lights were back on her after the cameras had gotten some good shots of Brother being hustled away in the night. A younger man, a graduate student I learned later, had taken the bullhorn. He had a calm and cultured voice and the crowd, what was left of it, that is, quieted down as he began to speak.

"We are not here for sensationalism, my friends. We are here as a community of the night and, if we want to hear the Lord, we must keep vigil with him." He paused, consolidating his hold on the people standing around. "We should do this in silence." He paused again. "And on our knees." Some of those who had begun to drift away turned back toward the direction of the crowd. Others in the crowd who had warmed to Brother's prayers began to move away. The group was breaking up and reforming itself like an amoeba. "Now, let us all kneel together," the young man said in reverent and measured phrasing. "Let us kneel and pray for the world together."

Here was a fellow who knew how to control a crowd, because, without complaint, its members did exactly what he asked of them. Now the television lights panned across the suddenly quiet assembly, which, like a knowing old dog, was settling itself in limblike sections onto the ground. It was one thing, I thought, to haul off Brother Dingbat praying for women having the menstrual flow but it would be quite another to break up an orderly crowd that wasn't making any noise at all; in fact, it would be impossible, for on television it would be the worst kind of vision, something like police whacking away at civil rights demonstrators, to have Notre

Dame forcing silent people off their knees in the name of law and order.

"The only thing we will allow," the young man said, "is for individuals to come forward to make their own personal witness in silence before the cross, to kneel before it with their own private prayers and intentions." A woman in a pants suit, the kind of woman you see shopping in the supermarket every day, arose and made her way forward. She knelt down beneath the cross and stretched out her arms in prayer. The girl above her was off in one of her trances again but the scene below her was as peaceful as a cloistered chapel. She twisted a little and turned her head up toward the moon.

When the woman had finished praying silently, a young man, obviously a student, took her place, stretching out his arms in the same cruciform gesture. I watched three or four people follow and then I noticed a figure that looked familiar moving forward in the darkness. As he knelt down I could make out that it was Matt Finn, the football coach. The television people didn't recognize him until he had risen to make his way back through the crowd. Then they turned the lights on once more, just in time to catch the Notre Dame quarterback moving up to take Finn's place. Good God, I thought, he's got the whole team out here, he's breaking their training rules, to have them pray for the game. After midnight but there they were, big hulking fellows, Protestant and Catholic, black, brown, and white, the lot of them moving in succession to give witness behind their coach. Well, the television people and the reporters loved it; what more could they have wanted than the Fighting Irish kneeling here like they were looking to be cured at Lourdes? I sighed to myself and turned to go back to my rooms. "What a long night this will be," I thought. "What a long, long night."

October 21, 1983
10:30 P.M.

Thomas Patrick Kinsella was not amused by the summary of events which he received when he returned to his office. It was as if someone had purposely poured sand into the mechanism of self-control that had been central to Notre Dame for generations. Self-control, the perennial virtue that had survived and even flourished under the Golden Dome when it was to be found on hardly any other campus in the country. Through Kinsella's memory flashed a picture of Father Hesburgh, awash in the tumult of the sixties, but instinctively knowing his students and his alumni as well as the Catholic tradition that bound them together at unconscious levels. Hesburgh, the master of anticipation and delivery, taking the demonstrators on, daring them to cross the invisible line he drew for them, and giving them fifteen minutes to break up or to lose their identity cards. He had won everything because he knew just how to risk everything, which, of course, was by knowing all the cards in your own hand and in everyone else's. The only thing that ever bothered Hesburgh about that was the letter of congratulations he got from Spiro Agnew afterward. But more of that later.

That was what people wanted from Notre Dame, discipline and self-control when the rest of the colleges were making themselves into candy stores for all the sweet tooths on campus. Catholics liked self-control, despite the newfangled theology that had taken over. Hesburgh had understood that and so did Kinsella. But now someone had pulled on a thread in the ancient doublet and the whole thing might unravel.

What should have been a simple matter to handle had become difficult even to approach. And glory be to God, it was a sickly sweet mix of religion, sex, and downright nuttiness.

"Jeffrey," Kinsella said, his eyes sparkling in the soft light, "now that we have this May crowning, with our own football coach and the team in the procession, just what do you plan to do about it?"

"Well, Tom," Green answered with the gravity that went with his unexamined liberal philosophy, "I think we have to let these people use our property. They're not doing any harm. Certainly the publicity can't hurt us. After all, what does it come to but a group of people praying? And Notre Dame football teams have been saying their prayers before games for years. I think the public will understand . . ."

"Understand?" Kinsella said sharply. "I'll say they'll understand. They'll think we've gone out of our minds, letting a poor disturbed girl tie herself to a cross and be the center of a nationwide television show."

"Now, Tom, I wouldn't be so sure. We would look bad driving them off in the middle of the night too."

"Let them stay here and there'll be five thousand more by breakfast time. And ten thousand more by lunch. What do you think we're running here, a circus?" Kinsella paused in order to get a grip on his own irritation. He had always known that Green was immature, that he could be found in the forefront of any fad, standing on his head for Yoga, fasting to free some Iranian bomb thrower, or carrying banners to save the baby seals, but he was intelligent, a fine teacher, and up until now, a competent administrator.

"Not a circus, Tom, but certainly a Christian community where people can meet together and share . . ."

"Share, my ass, as my father says. Now, Jeffrey, I am going to tell you a few things that I want you to do. I expect that they will be done within the next hour." Kinsella paused again as he regarded Father Green; he wondered whether he was asking a carrier of the disease to bring the serum through. Green stood as impassively as a martyr who did not expect the emperor to understand his faith.

"First of all, in order to resolve this situation, the girl must be brought down from the cross. Gently, with all the understanding in the world. And not by the campus police. I want you to get some of the chaplains together and have them approach her in a group. Make sure they wear their collars and have them talk to her nicely, and then escort her away to where she can get some psychiatric help. St. Joseph's will take her, I'm sure. But call them first. I don't want them throwing holy water or saying prayers or talking to reporters. This is a pastoral activity. We want to take care of the girl and if we do, the demonstration will fall apart."

"Yes, Tom," Green answered, "if that's what you really want."

"That's what I really want. Secondly, get hold of Matt Finn and tell him, if he's still out there, to get back to the seminary with the team. Quietly. No interviews. Tell him that comes from me and I don't want any questions or arguments about it. There's a chapel at the seminary if he wants to say any more prayers."

"Okay, Tom, but you may have misread this whole thing. The country's looking for something like this, for a rallying point, for some event that symbolizes its spiritual needs. There were shrines for that in times past but no more. We could be in, right here, right now, for a modern, a contemporary religious revival . . ."

"Jeffrey, we can discuss this later, but what is taking place on the golf course is neither religious nor much of a revival. Now, get this last part straight. I don't want anyone talking to the press except Dick Cummings. No interviews, no interpretations, no explanations. We want this over and done with and we want to go on tomorrow as though this never happened. This can be healed quickly but it won't be if we keep scratching it. Do you understand that?"

Green nodded but said nothing. He was withholding something, Kinsella understood that, but he was not sure whether it was motivated by the Arab haggler in Green's genes or his incurable addiction to whatever was religiously romantic.

"Now I'm going to be unavailable for interviews or comment. I want this all handled on a lower level and finished before the sun comes up tomorrow."

Green turned to leave but stopped just at the door. "Tom, may I say something?"

Kinsella looked up from his desk and raised his eyebrows expectantly.

"Tom, we can't live in the past forever. We can't handle things as if they had no meaning for our times. That's what you want to do with this."

"Jeffrey," Kinsella answered calmly, "I know that you are naturally sympathetic to whatever is new and different. This is neither new nor different and I want it attended to now, right now, and I want a report back in half an hour on your progress. That's all."

The door closed behind Father Green and Thomas Kinsella stretched, shook his head as if to rid it of the gritty residue that Green's logic had deposited there, and drew a thin cigar from a box on his desk. As he struck a match and held it just below its tip he wondered about the priest who had just departed. Green was up to something, something to do with his camel driver's ambition. Green wanted to be president of the University, Kinsella had known that when he took over himself. It was not so bad having ambitious people around; you could tease a lot of work out of their ambition but you had to keep them on a short lead and not let them have any real power. Kinsella sighed at the possibility of Green's accession to his job.

"By God!" he said aloud, squashing his barely smoked cigar in an ashtray. "That's it!" Kinsella surprised himself by speaking out loud in the quiet of his own office. He shook his head again, smiling grimly, the way a surgeon might after discovering something inoperable. The private phone, the one his Arab vice-president had once wanted to paint green in honor of the Fighting Irish, rang.

"Hello, Tom, what's going on down there in the cornfields?"

It was the bright, clear voice of Maria Moore, the words articulated with the theatrical diction that went with being a star of Broadway and Hollywood, the voice that rode firmly but lightly on the night air, the voice of the one woman Thomas Kinsella had ever truly loved.

"Maria, where are you?"

"In Chicago. At the Drake. What is going on down there? Can I get the part when they make a movie of it?" She laughed as she asked the question and Thomas, for the first time that evening, laughed as well.

"Now, the girl is not Joan of Arc. She's a little young too, a little young for you."

"Thomas, how can you say that?"

"You're my age, that's why, and I'm too old to be chasing crazy girls across the golf course."

"Well, I just saw something about it on television, the ten o'clock news, just a brief clip, but it doesn't sound like Notre Dame to me."

"It isn't Notre Dame. It's some craziness in the air and some of our people seem to be infected with it. Never mind that, tell me how you've been. You're still coming down for the game tomorrow, aren't you?"

"Well, if it's safe to come, I mean you're not going to have somebody out selling indulgences or pieces of her cross, are you?" There was a pause but her tone, which always had a hint of celebration in it, softened slightly, as though the footlights had gone out and she could be herself. "Tom, it would be good to see you, even in a big crowd."

"Well, you'll come to the luncheon, of course." Now Kinsella paused, like a man taking a deep breath. "I'd love to see you too, Maria. There's lots to talk about."

"Yes, Tom, we need a good talk."

"It's been like a zoo down here tonight, Maria."

"You mean the girl?"

"No, more than that. The Vatican has asked me about a new job and I think Greenie is already plotting to take my present one."

She interrupted him in the aggrieved voice of a woman whose husband is always being transferred to another city.

"A new job? What do you mean?"

"Well, I wanted to talk to you about it. I need to really. So I'm glad you'll be here later."

"Tom, what is this job? It sounds like you've already said yes."

"No, no, as a matter of fact, I haven't. It's an offer to become a bishop, Archbishop of Chicago. Probably a Cardinal . . ."

There was silence for a moment and then Maria spoke again. "Tom, haven't you done enough, I mean . . ." But she did not finish the sentence; she had never been able to finish that sentence in any of the versions in which she had tried it.

She shifted her approach and her tone at the same time. "Tom, you can't take a new job and let Greenie take over.

He'd turn the place into an oriental bazaar with tents and snake charmers and God knows what."

"Yes, it's pretty ridiculous. But he's after it, I think he's really after it." Thomas laughed dryly. "He might bring a lot of oil money in. Who knows? Maybe he fits things in the Church these days."

The conversation bogged down; they both edged away from the subject of the new assignment. They talked about the football game but they both understood what they were doing.

"Oh, Tom, what the hell are we talking about football for? You may become a Cardinal, for God's sake. That's even worse than being a University president. They'll put a red skirt on you . . ." There was another pause, a tender one filled with the intimation of tears held back Then Maria spoke again.

"I don't know what to think any more. I used to think I was making a noble sacrifice." There was just the hint of a quiver, a blip that flashed and disappeared quickly, but Kinsella had heard it, he always heard it. It was one of the few things he did not know how to handle; it was a signal about their relationship and the fact that it could not be handled, that it could only be lived through one day at a time. Sometimes he thought it was more like climbing in the dark, because so much energy went into just keeping going that you couldn't think too much about where it would finally lead.

"But, Tom, when I look around at what has happened in the Church. When I hear about this sideshow you're having, and all the work you've done, well, I wonder if the fruitcakes aren't inheriting the earth . . ."

"Now, now," Kinsella replied softly. "We've tried to do the right thing. We've always lived by faith . . ." But he paused too, for he had said these things so often that they were almost automatic now and he wondered if he fully believed them anymore. He felt that every time he spoke them he was asking her for more sacrifice, that it was she who kept giving in the special love they shared, and he just hoped that he could get by with reassurance one more time. He didn't want to deal with this problem—this problem of all problems—not tonight, not with a girl rigged up on a cross, a crazy, heavy-breathing girl who seemed to be the symbol of everything that was distorted and adolescent about the Roman Catholic Church, and who, like the moon, was bringing out something different in everybody.

"We can't let the inmates take over the institution . . ."

There was only silence between them. Somehow the deluded young woman on the cross had begun to pull at the delicate balance of his long friendship with Maria. Suddenly, here in his own office, filled with the symbols and souvenirs and the musty paraphernalia of almost twenty years in the priesthood, in this quiet of midnight Thomas Kinsella wondered at the pull of the full moon and the pull of the girl, intermingled in the darkness, the strangeness touching people without their awareness, drawing them toward secret places in themselves. And he was caught in its revealing light, in a painful moment with the woman who had meant more to him than anyone else in the world, the woman he had always put off because he was so sure that his work as a priest and an educator had to come first, and they were both facing off the edge of their lives again, into the shadows where they had looked so many times before.

"Tom," Maria said very softly, "I sometimes think they already have taken it over. I can't help it, I simply can't help it. You've spent your life making the Church look good, the same Church that has hurt so many good people, that's always put itself into everybody's private business, the Church that preaches love but doesn't love, not much anyway. Tom, I wonder if it's worth it any more . . ."

But Thomas did not know what to answer. It was a question he could not afford to ask himself, not tonight especially, not with all the other questions that had to be settled, all of which necessarily involved Maria. He was uncomfortable with not answering, with using a dodge, but he did it anyway.

"Maria, I know how hard these years have been on you. Let's talk tomorrow. We'll have a chance, I'll arrange it. There are other things I have to talk to you about. Important things . . ."

"Tom, I'm sorry. I just get so filled up sometimes and it has to come out. I'll be all right, you know that. I'll see you at the luncheon." She paused again.

"I love you still," she said, and hung up. Kinsella replaced the phone in its cradle and sat for several moments without moving at all. Then he walked toward the windows and looked up at the moon, pale bride, mother, or mistress of the night, but always she, he thought, always she.

3

October 21, 1983
10:45 P.M.

Well, I was just crossing the edge of the golf course to get back to my digs at Sorin Hall when I saw Father Green, solemn as a gravedigger, double-timing it toward the scene I had just left. With him was Monsignor Jack Egan, a grand old character around Notre Dame, spry as a jockey and good in any emergency. He had been assistant to the president under Hesburgh, the latter a great fellow for taking in good priests, and former priests too, scholars and the like, who had been treated badly by bishops. Jack was from Chicago, and his crime there as far as anyone was ever able to figure out was doing good, something that made the old Cardinal distinctly uneasy. No matter, there was Jack, in black suit and Roman collar, and a couple of the other chaplains, younger fellows you would more often see in safari jackets or wearing ten-gallon hats, like they had just driven the cattle in from Montana, but there they were with collars on as well.

I decided I had better not miss the next act in the little drama, so I fell in with them and in a few minutes we were back at the cross, about fifty yards of kneeling people away, that is. The television van was still there but the floodlights were out, at least for the moment. People were still making their way up to give their witness, all very quietly with no speeches, for which I was glad, since some prize campus ninnies were throwing themselves down in front of the cross.

Ida Twitchell was one of them, a former professor who had been canned years before mostly for nuttiness, but who still showed up at campus gatherings and who loved to attack the University at every opportunity, as, for example, when the priest asked the people to state their own intentions for the day's Mass. "To overturn the fascistic regime of the administration," she would shout out. "Let us pray to the Lord." Or, "That the fund drive may fall short of its oppressive goal," or some such nonsense as that.

Anyway I could see that Monsignor Egan had made his way over to where Matt Finn was standing with a group of the football players. I couldn't make out exactly what Jack was saying but I could see that he had reached a fatherly hand up to Finn's shoulder and was punching out sharp little gestures with the other. Egan's head, smooth as Rockne's, was nodding up and down and he was about as much in a mood for dialogue as an Irish traffic cop on a busy day in Chicago. Jack was pointing toward Moreau Seminary, where the team was supposed to be, still speaking emphatically, the whole of it like a scene on a disco floor, what with the strobe lights of the photographers flashing intermittently, and Egan looking like a bantam bouncer giving marching orders. Finally Finn nodded his head and gestured toward the team, a few of whom, mesmerized by the girl, who was still twisting a little in the moonlight, didn't want to tear themselves away. Off they went anyway, photographers trailing, floodlights from the television switched on again, and a fellow hunchbacked with a portable camera hurrying after them.

The crowd stirred during this and, rising to its feet, started to growl a little, the way such an organism does when it feels some injustice is being worked on one of its parts. It seemed to want to stay together and a line of its members stretched out, like a trickle off a river, after the departing team. I could see, however, that Egan still had Finn collared at the head of the procession and was moving faster despite the groans and wails that were beginning to go up. The separation was soon complete, with only a few stragglers collapsing back into the crowd as Monsignor Egan turned and headed toward Green and the other chaplains who had gathered below the cross; they looked a little embarrassed, like they had been caught in front of the dirty book stand and didn't want to be seen sneaking a glance at it. As Egan approached, the crowd closed in behind him and pressed forward. Egan paid no

attention to them but went right up to the cross, as easy as a
gas man going to read a meter, and spoke directly to the girl,
not like some fag priest in the movies but in the tones of a
father telling his daughter that he was putting a hold on her
allowance for the week.

"It's time to come down now, Mary Ann."

"Mary Ann who?" a reporter asked loudly while another
called out hoarsely, "What's that name? Did you get a
name?"

Egan ignored them and kept looking up to the girl, who
had opened her eyes, like somebody waking up in the
morning, trying to get the monsignor into focus.

"What, Father?" she asked softly, swelling herself up a
little and rolling to one side.

"I said it's time for you to come down now. I'm Father
Egan and it's time you had some rest."

The girl said nothing for a moment. She was just staring
down, eyes a little glazed. Then she said, sort of trancelike,
"Bless us, Father, for we have sinned . . . We have all sinned
so much. Bless us, Father, for our sins of the flesh . . ."

Egan ran a finger around the inside of his collar, like a man
not sure whether to use a hammer or a screwdriver next, but
he kept his eyes fixed on the girl.

"Now, Mary Ann, we can talk about that later. Right now,
if you want God's blessing for all of us, you'll come down."

The crowd was very quiet now, even the reporters. The
television camera was whirring away and the floodlights
buzzed and popped a little and then the girl let out a groan
that was like a finger scratched on a blackboard in its effect on
everyone standing around. Then, looking beyond Egan, she
began to speak in a louder voice.

"I will descend only that I may rise again."

Nutty as a fruitcake, I thought to myself as she went on
spouting lines that were one part Bible to one part Bram
Stoker. Egan stood his ground, like a cop the Puerto Ricans
are dumping garbage on from the tenement roof, but many of
the people in the crowd, most of them from town, seemed to
be listening intently.

"I will come down but only to raise the cross again. Will the
believers here help me?"

"We'll help you," called the graduate student who had
organized the quiet vigil earlier. "We'll move across the
road."

Shouts of agreement from the crowd.

"Now," she said. "Now"—twisting away again, as if the idea was exciting her. "Now is the time."

Egan had always been a man to know when to accept the best bargain offered, even if it was not much of a compromise. He looked around at the other chaplains, who seemed as uncertain as they had before, and said, "Fine. You come down, leave the campus, and you can go wherever you want." Then he stepped back as the graduate student moved forward with about half a dozen other men out of the crowd. They didn't exactly take the girl down, what they did was to start twisting the cross up out of the earth very slowly, bumping her around a little, but not too much, in the process.

In a few moments they had the cross, the girl still on it, flat out on their shoulders. The girl was moaning and she looked like she had slipped into another trance. The graduate student was exchanging words with two other men, making a plan, it seemed to me, while the cameramen, yelling and talking all the while, jostled each other for better positions. Egan had stepped aside with the other chaplains and, against the noise of the crowd and the reporters, was talking earnestly to Father Green. Greenie's eyes were half closed, the eyes of a bargainer who is always selling things he doesn't own yet.

"We shall overcome," the graduate student called out in his clear and commanding voice. Well, the crowd had disintegrated somewhat during the lowering of the cross, maybe half of it had broken from the group and drifted away like clouds going downwind. There was still about a hundred and fifty, however, hot for the next act, and they took up the phrase right away. A little wobbly at first but soon they were booming away enthusiastically, righteous marchers for the Lord, "We shall overcome some day . . ."

Well, it was a scene if ever I saw one, as the pack of them, some of them carrying the cross, others reaching up to keep the girl from rolling off, began to move out toward the road that ran by the side of the golf course toward Route 31. The television people clambered back into their bus, dragging wires and cameras and lights as fast as they could, while the other reporters and photographers hurried like outriders to keep up with the strange procession. In the moonlight I could see the cross moving along like a choice morsel on a receding tide of ants. And all the while the strains of "We shall overcome some day" were drifting back to the few of us from the University who remained standing near the hole where the cross had been set.

Egan came by me and called out, "Austin, you'd better make notes on this one." Well, he prophesied better than he knew, I must say, but I responded, "Well, Jack, you did a good job, a good job. Maybe not everything you wanted, but a good job."

"Yes, Austin," he said, putting his arm on my shoulder, "I learned long ago in Chicago a very basic principle."

"What was that, Jack?"

"It's better to take the ass than lose the whole cow."

4

October 21, 1983
11:00 P.M.

Thomas Kinsella was still gazing at the moon when his private phone rang again. It was his brother Martin, four years his junior, and, as he always began his telephone greetings, he was singing a chorus of the Notre Dame fight song. He sounded a little flat and a little drunk.

"Well, Tommy lad, how are you now?"

Thomas winced slightly at Martin's brogue, an affectation that blossomed like a failed hybrid under the influence of alcohol.

"Lad, do you hear me, Tommy lad, do you hear me?"

"I was waiting for the English subtitles," Kinsella responded dryly.

"Ah, what's the harm, boyo, in glorying in our national heritage a bit?"

"Well, Martin, part of the heritage is a hundred proof. I hope you're not smoking. You're liable to blow yourself up."

"All right, Tom, all right," Martin answered, smoothing the brogue out as he did.

"Martin, if you're calling about what's going on down here, the answer is nothing. Just a sick girl and she should be taken care of by now. Nothing to it, except that we were a little slow to handle it."

"Well, Thomas, I was curious about it. And the old man called me a little while ago. Has he talked to you?"

"I saw him earlier, with Mother, but I haven't talked to him since our, shall we call it, 'incident' occurred."

"He was trying to get you, said your private line was busy."

Thomas hesitated. What, he wondered, was this all about? He felt something shift inside him just slightly, a familiar signal of caution.

"Well, Martin, I'll see him in the morning anyway." He left it at that. There was a pause on the other side of the line as well. It was not the first time in their lives that they had stepped carefully with each other, two sons of an old brawler using their Irish radar on each other, in a clinch now on the long-distance line between Chicago and South Bend.

"I'm sure you know what P.B. wants to talk to you about," Martin offered tentatively.

"Probably about getting me to fire Matt Finn," Thomas countered.

"Well, maybe that."

"Now, Martin, it's getting late and I wouldn't have to be a genius to know that you had something on your mind."

"Ah, Thomas, you were always one for getting to the point."

"Was I, now?" Kinsella answered, mocking his brother's efforts at a brogue.

"Tom, the old man is worried that this girl on the cross will ruin everything. You know, the bad publicity, the talk . . . will ruin your chances . . . ."

Thomas interrupted his brother, "My chances for what?"

All quiet on the other end of the phone. Then Martin lapsed into his brogue again.

"Tommy, don't be pulling my leg now. We all know that ginney Archbishop isn't down there to take the waters. Don't pretend now that you're not the man of the hour at the

Vatican. Come now, my boy, this is your family that knew you when you still shit in your drawers."

"Martin, whatever you think you know, I can't talk about with you or with P.B. Do you understand that? It's a matter that affects me, not you."

"Tommy, it was only that we were going to get a purse up for you, yes, a nice purse for Father dear and a cruise, yes, the fathers love the cruise ships, saying Mass on the high seas and getting old widows to sign over their money to the Church. It's . . ."

Thomas broke in harshly, "Cut it out, Martin! Stop the palaver and your stage Irishman act. I don't think you're funny. And what's happening between me and the Vatican is a personal matter. I don't want your advice. Do you understand that?"

"No need for temper, no, no, Tommy. Actually this is a family matter. It involves all the Kinsellas, not just our fair-haired favorite. This is the run for the roses, Tommy, you're just the horse we're betting on."

Thomas furrowed his brow and held his tongue. He did not understand what his brother meant but he felt deeply uneasy, not the shivers exactly, but a sudden sense that influences were operating on him that he did not fully comprehend, that he was in the center of vectors of force that he could not make out clearly in the dark.

"Anyway, Tommy, this filly on the cross isn't helping things for good old ND or for you. Or for us, your family. The Kinsellas." Martin spoke of the family as though it were a great bank or a foreign power, an institution whose presence and influence had to be acknowledged. "The family is very much involved in all this."

"Don't be ridiculous, Martin, and, besides, I'm not sure that we are even speaking about the same thing."

"Don't try any of your diplomatic horseshit on me, brother dear. We know very well you may be the next Cardinal Archbishop of Chicago. Jimmy the Greek makes you the odds-on favorite. You think we don't know that?"

"Whatever you know, it is still really my business."

"Not when you've got some two-dollar item wiggling her ass on a cross on the late news. Bad publicity, makes you look bad, gets all the people upset. Don't want something to blow the deal now. Why, for Christ's sake, you could be the Pope some day. Once you've got a Polack, you can have anything, a Chinaman, a spic, maybe a smart harp like you."

"There's little chance of that, whatever I decide. But whatever that is, you'll have to let me do it as I see best."

"Best for what? You? Notre Dame?"

"How about the people of Chicago? How about the Church? Still go to church I understand, Martin. You remember the Church?"

"Yes, Tommy, and you've done very well for it. And by it. But you're a Kinsella, and you're like all the Kinsellas. They like power. Jesus, Tommy, you love it, you just don't know how much you love it. Don't give me that shit they print in *People* about how you sleep on an iron bed. You're smoking a two-dollar cigar right now, probably. So don't talk to me like we weren't brothers, like we didn't understand things."

"Power has many meanings and many uses, Martin."

"Yes, Professor, but let's not talk philosophy. And let's not talk religion. We want you, P.B. wants you to take the Chicago job."

Thomas did not answer. He decided he would drop out of the conversation, which had begun to sound like so many of his father's that he had overheard when he was growing up. Martin knew just how to apply pressure to him, and he knew that he was not speaking for himself but was, in fact, preparing him for the breakfast meeting he was to have with his father. Martin always did what his father told him to do.

"Martin, there's really nothing more for us to discuss. But I want you to know something, since I fully expect you to talk to the old man before I see him."

"Yes?" Martin replied in a flat, inquiring tone.

"I may not accept the offer."

Martin did not reply immediately but Thomas could feel a swelling combination of exasperation and disbelief on the other end of the line. They were in another clinch but Martin, as Thomas understood, might kick you in the groin or stick a finger in your eye to gain the advantage.

"Have you gone daffy, Tommy? I only called you to tell you the babe on the cross looked bad in national headlines. Don't blow that out of proportion. Don't turn down something just to spite us. Be Irish but don't be that Irish. I mean, lad, you have to be joking, kidding your dear little brother Martin to say such a thing."

"As Mayor Daley used to say, 'That's my statement, it speaks for itself.'"

"Tommy, Tommy, what's going on, this girl strike a spell on you like the rest of the rubes down there?" Martin paused a moment and then went on, "I know what it is. It's Maria, isn't it? Maria Moore? You never have gotten over that, have you? She still trying to get you out of the collar? That's it, isn't it? Jesus, how romantic. What do you want to do, Tommy, kill the old man, not to mention the old lady? Skip town with the endowment and the great actress, is that it?"

"That's enough, Martin, quite enough. In fact, we've talked quite enough, quite enough for a long time, as far as I'm concerned." Thomas was mad and he sounded it; he could hear his own anger, his own defensiveness against this attack on the innermost chamber of his soul. He could hear himself breathing heavily in the silence and he thought, yes, the phone call is becoming obscene and the breathing fits very well. He thought again of the moon and of the girl on the cross and of the madness that seemed to have fallen across the land and he wondered a moment about Irish curses and the superstitions that he had always thought of as the negative image of faith. And he thought of Maria and the tone in her voice earlier, the almost defeated tone of a woman who wondered whether her sacrifices for love had ever really meant anything.

Then Martin's voice came through the earpiece again.

"Tommy, I'm sorry, I really am. I shouldn't have said that."

How Irish, Thomas thought, for brothers to fight until one was half dead and then to find them embracing with tears in their eyes.

"It's all right, Martin. Let's just forget it," he said softly, almost wearily.

"But, Tommy, you know we have to stick together. That's been all of us, always, no matter what. That's why we're interested, that's why we're concerned. Lad, you know we're proud of you, we'd do anything for you. But let me tell you something, we need you too."

Thomas sensed that there was something else coming, perhaps not so bluntly put as the questions about Maria, but something that might give him a key to what Martin and his father really had on their minds.

"Tommy, let's imagine something, you know, like when we played games as kids. You were good at it. Suppose your family was in danger and needed your help. Not to do anything bad, mind you, just to do something that's your duty anyway. And all you have to do is your duty in order to help your own kin."

"What kind of trouble are you talking about, Martin?"

"Just imagination, Tommy, just imagination. Suppose in that big bad world out there somebody had ambitions, political ambitions, a federal attorney, and what he needed was a big case, the front pages, St. George and the dragon all over again."

"Martin, are you talking about Murphy, Finbar Murphy? The prosecutor in northern Illinois, that one?" Thomas felt a pang of concern, for if Murphy were St. George, Patrick B. Kinsella could certainly pass for the dragon. "Martin, they haven't got anything on the old man, have they?"

"I'm just giving you an exercise in imagination, Tommy, I'm not mentioning any names. This is all 'perhaps,' as they say in Ireland. Suppose the fellow, an eye on the White House maybe, wanted to make trouble, say, for a family with many business interests and political connections. Who would he pick on? Now that Daley is gone, the target would have to be a big one."

"Are you saying that he's going to investigate the family?"

"Imagine it, Tommy, just imagine it. Even if there was nothing to it, the grief it would cause, the publicity, the uproar. And what for? So this bastard can get a reputation, that's all, just to get a reputation. Using all the tricks, giving immunity out like it was lemonade, you know the way Thompson did it to the Daley machine? Well, Murphy would make that look like a prayer meeting."

"Well, I'm genuinely sorry to hear this. But how likely is this? After all, the Kinsellas are supposed to be clean. And they're not without influence . . ."

"Well, let me go on with my story, Thomas, my little imaginative exercise. Where, I would ask, is the biggest Catholic population in the country? Chicago, of course. Now suppose, just suppose that a member of the family that was to be investigated became the Archbishop, the spiritual leader, the great religious leader of the city. Well, the family doesn't look like the dragon any more. In fact, anybody who tried to prosecute the Archbishop's own mother and father would ruin himself politically in a town full of Catholic voters. Wouldn't dare make a move, he'd be so checkmated."

Thomas did not know what to say but at least he knew where he stood. Becoming Archbishop of Chicago was a family affair, after all. How like a medieval family filled with kings and popes, dreaming every night of power—and this, what a finesse of power! The kind of move his father loved the way Patton loved battle and, if the truth were told, Thomas was good at such moves himself, although he did not let himself think about it much; power came naturally out of the fingertips of those who had a feel for it. It was in the blood, yes, the every night fever of the Kinsellas, a fine family affair after all.

"That's quite a lot you've asked me to imagine, Martin."

"Yes, Tommy, but you see, there are some things in which all a man has to do is his duty, accept his call, and he'll do his whole clan more than proud."

Thomas felt the pressure of the clan, all right, and all his wild Celtic ancestors stripped naked and painted blue for the pagan festivals in the times before St. Patrick came, warriors and farmers and God knew what, gathered invisibly about him on this night of the full moon and the crucified girl, on this October eve on which he had suddenly been forced to re-examine two things he had for so long taken for granted, love and power.

5

October 21, 1983
11:55 P.M.

Father Green called Father Kinsella at five minutes to twelve and reported that the crowd had left the golf course after the girl on the cross had been carried away in the night. Thomas had seemed satisfied and Green said little more, although he did add one observation before he hung up.

"It's all very symbolic, Tom. You can see that, can't you?"

Thomas was in no mood for metaphysical inquiry.

"Jeffrey, it was symbolic of illness and that's all. Thanks for giving me the report. Good night, good morning, that is."

Well, Greenie rang off, of course, but he was not finished, for he wanted to meet with two of his classmates with whom he shared a penchant for the peculiar. Overinflated, that's how I always thought of them, and overeducated, but without too much to show for it in the way of production after they graduated. Great planners and talkers, these lads, heavy with dreams of what they called "building community," in which the lions and the lambs would frolic together and there would be neither lust nor war. Golden boys, that's the way others referred to them, meaning, of course, that they had grown up in the sixties with a fine sense of themselves as the chosen generation, thinking themselves far wiser than their elders ever were, and favored by destiny to remake Notre Dame today and the world tomorrow. Well, as I've said, they were great for talk and that's what they were doing with Green later on that long night. There was Father Harold Maxwell, the fellow who was "into" film, writing the theology of the cinema with crazy theories that in heaven we would find ourselves playing parts in our favorite movies like *Casablanca* and *A Night at the Opera,* great for that stuff he was, lecturing on "Cinema, the Shadow of the Heavenly City," which the students, God forgive them, loved, since they spent so much time watching old movies anyway, and he made them think it was better than praying.

And there was Frederick Morgan, another bright light that never lived up to its wattage, who was a theologian, supposedly a pastoral expert, but he seldom saw the inside of a church. Off to Tibet he was, at the drop of a hat, to find some guru to have a staring contest with, or off to a conference about tub soaking as spiritual healing, but not much for work, hard everyday work, that is. If his old man had not been a great benefactor of the University, I wondered if he wouldn't have been out on his ass a long time before. And he could talk too, always about getting out into "the real world," which certainly was some place different from where he was.

Well, there the three of them were in Green's rooms, having a drink and talking about the girl on the cross.

"The difficulty," Green said, "is that most major events are hardly understood as such at the time they occur. They are perceived that way only after the passage of time. To understand the moment itself, that is the work of genius."

"I think I hear you saying," Morgan began, as he did practically every observation he made, "I think I hear you saying that this event may be a major turning point." He spoke softly, as though he were saying something very important, which he seldom did, although he had the inflection of significance down very well.

Green nodded and went on, "Exactly. This is the moment for a crusade, a new kind of crusade, a great peaceful crusade that begins at the foot of that girl's cross. We have to take advantage of it, we have to lead because, as I sense it, the people are ready to follow."

"Yes, spiritually starved," Maxwell interjected. "Spiritually starved, the very thing Bergman has been trying to tell the world for years."

Green continued, in the manner of a man who has finally grasped his real mission in life. "This could be it, the time for a great revival. A call to all Americans, yes, it's clear, the symbolism is clear."

"Perfectly clear, Jeff, perfectly clear," Maxwell said enthusiastically. "Antonioni has been developing this theme cinematically for years."

Green's eyes were burning brightly as he stood up and began to pace the room.

"The symbolism is perfect. It's perfect. Think of it, the girl crucified, the jeering crowd, and her faithful ones carrying her away to a safe place in the dark of night."

He started to gesture sharply with his right arm, sawing the air with it.

"And Pontius Pilate washing his hands of it, skeptical of its truth, washing his hands and thinking it is over and done with. Tom Kinsella, the Pilate of our time, missing the meaning of it and turning back to his precious fund drive."

"I hear you saying we're having a passion play here," Morgan said solemnly.

"Yes, Fred, a passion play with a woman in the place of Christ, can't you see it? Notre Dame, Our Lady taking the place of Christ, taking the role of the priest because the priests reject her and her message."

"It's very cinematic, Jeff, I mean it's the passion myth, very contemporary, very real, I think, very much speaking to us."

"Of course it is. It's what we've been waiting for, to break into a new age of religious awareness, calling us back to purity and yet calling us forward to community together."

"Well, Jeff," Morgan observed as he poured himself another drink, "it's very pastoral. It cuts across all lines. There's only one thing missing."

"What's that?" Green replied, stopping his pacing to look down at Morgan.

"You need a resurrection. I mean from what I hear you saying, there's been the passion, the symbolic death and burial, and now we need a resurrection to make the symbol complete."

"Dead right," Maxwell interjected enthusiastically. "Aesthetics and theology meet here. Resurrection, the great mystery, the mystery of film itself, I might add."

Green was not listening too carefully. He was caught up in thought. "Resurrection," he said slowly. "Yes, we'll have to see about that."

At the same time Jack Allen, smoking a cigarette and making himself another weak scotch and water, was talking to Father Andrew Simmons.

"Well," he said, stretching the word out as he spoke, "it's been quite an evening."

"Jack," Simmons replied earnestly, "the whole thing has just made me think more. More about my own life, what I'm doing, where I'm going."

Allen sat down, balancing drink, cigarette, and glass case carefully, and, like a man steeling himself for bad news, said simply, "I guess it's time you got settled, Andy."

"It's hard to talk about, Jack, I mean I feel bad because I think this hurts you."

"Well," Jack said philosophically, but his voice trailed off.

"But, Jack, no matter what I do in this, somebody is going to be hurt. Me, my family, my friends. There's no way out of that. I think . . ." And Simmons paused, averting his eyes from Allen's. "I think I've got to leave, Jack. I can't go on living this way."

Allen felt a pang but he didn't speak; he sat looking straight across at the younger priest.

"I was over at the retirement place visiting the other day. And, Jack, I was never so depressed in my life. Here are all these priests. Oh, they're getting good care and all, it's not that. But it's very quiet over there. They're just passing time, sitting in the sun, talking, when they do, about the old days. I saw old Father McCormick there in his wheelchair and I spoke to him and he looked up kind of puzzled. I think I frightened him and he couldn't figure out who I was. So I put my arm on his shoulder and big tears came into his eyes and rolled down his face. I've never seen anybody who looked so alone."

"Oh, Andy," Allen replied, "the world is filled with lonely people. Lots of them are married. They're still lonely. Jesus, we've all got to face that."

"I know that, Jack, but I can't grow old that way. I mean, knowing you're going to be put in the sun every afternoon and nobody really to care. Old priests aren't persons, Jack, they're problems. They don't fit any more. They won't let them work and they really don't have a family, not really. We do the best we can but it's not like having your own family. Didn't you ever think of that?"

"Oh, yes," Allen answered with verve. "They'll never put me in one of those places. They can just forward the checks to me, wherever I am. My brother's got a place for me to move into any time I want. No, I don't want to be caught with the old fathers wetting their beds and fighting over what television program to watch."

There was silence as they both sipped their drinks. Then Allen spoke again.

"But, shit, Andy, you don't plan your life on what you're going to avoid at the end of it. You can't plan anything that way. The thing is, what are you going to do with your life now? That's what you've got to be straight on."

The younger priest shook his head slowly. "Yes, I know, I know that. And, Jack, I'm fine when I'm at work. It's going to the priests' recreation room now that kills me. It's going back to my own room at the end of the day with nothing to look forward to but another day that will be just the same. Jack, I'm at the point where it's just too painful, I mean, it hurts all through me. And I've tried not to see Laurie. We've tried everything. We've been apart, we've said our prayers, I've made retreats, I've told myself a thousand times that I should stick to the priesthood." His voice began to crack. "But, Jack, I can't go on just working and offering everything up. And she can't either."

Allen nodded wearily. "Andy, don't you think I know what you're going through?"

The younger priest wiped his eyes on the sleeve of his coat. "I don't know, Jack, it doesn't make any difference. You've always been strong. I don't know, maybe the times were different for you. Maybe you did what was right for you." He paused and cleared his throat. "But I can't hack it this way any more."

Allen looked at him compassionately. He didn't know what to say. He had encouraged the young man in every way he knew. And he wondered if the young man was not right, he wondered at the struggles he had experienced over the years and whether his decisions to stay on and make the best of it were correct after all.

"Well, Andy," he said gruffly, deciding on self-deprecation to relieve the tension of the moment, "it's too late for me to make any changes. We all do what we have to. The world's changed a lot since I was your age. We were sure of things then. And you had great friendships in the priesthood, great times." He tried to smile as he went on. "Now you have girls on crosses, for Christ's sake, and a pack of fags ready to follow her. I don't know, I really don't know. Shit, this used to be a profession for real men. You could count on each other." He shook his head and sipped his drink again.

"Jack, I'm sorry to burden you with all this. I just don't

know who else I can talk to. They all say the same thing. Say your prayers, take cold showers, give her up. I mean, Jack, do you think half these guys have any idea of what life is all about?"

Allen smiled. "Hell, the ones who know what life is all about never talk about it. The rest of them live in a fucking dream world. They think the people love them. Jesus, how they lap it up. Nothing too good for the fathers. No, Andy, I don't think they know much about real life. No, the poor bastards are playing a game, front and center at mealtime, right there for the viands every time. That's the tip-off. They like being fed. They're not so good at feeding others. That's why I hate to see you go. Oh, I hate to see you leave for selfish reasons. Who the hell will laugh at my jokes? But I hate like hell to see somebody like you, somebody who's a good priest, the kind we need, I hate like hell to see us lose you. Too damned few of them to start with."

"Well, Jack, you won't exactly lose me. I mean, I'll go on teaching. Tom's open to that. And I have tenure. I'll see you plenty."

"No, Andy, if you're going to lead another life. If you're going to get married, you can't hang around the priests' house. Jesus, if you're going to make a break, make a break. Don't do it like some of these guys who want it both ways."

"But, Jack, we'll be friends . . ."

"Sure, Andy, I know that. But you can't, I mean it's got to be different too." Allen went into his gruff act more intensely, the better to cover his own mixed feelings of confusion and disappointment. "Why, hell, Andy, once you and Laurie get settled, I'll be over to dinner all the time."

"One more thing, Jack. Laurie and I would like you to marry us, once we get the permissions and everything."

That seemed final to Allen, and, although he smiled and said he would be glad to do it, the notion cast a shadow over his spirit, as though the sun of his best hopes had slipped below the horizon for good. He felt that he had lost something that he had really had no right to try to hang onto, that something he had valued more than he knew had drifted just out of his grasp, and that he would never get hold of it again.

6

October 22, 1983
12:30 A.M.

Thomas Kinsella walked very slowly from his office back down the corridor of the administration building. From the walls, already dimly lit at the early morning hour, gazed the oil-painted features of his predecessors as president of Notre Dame. They were dark enough in daylight, their somber hues glazed with varnish, but they seemed more remote, all those pairs of eyes, as though their possessors had taken a step back into the canvas the better to see what was going on at their University. Thomas shook his head at the notion that these men were watching him and descended the wide wooden staircase to the ground floor of the now palpably quiet old hall. The night air felt good after the surreal evening but he could still see the moon over the roof of the nearby church. It seemed scrubbed and pale now, drained of its power to draw the madness out of men and women. Kinsella hurried along toward his living quarters and as he climbed the stairs past Jack Allen's rooms, he noticed that his light was still on. He tapped softly on the door.

"Enter!" Allen called from within.

Kinsella opened the door to find Jack alone, still seated in his easy chair and still sipping the drink he had poured with Andrew Simmons an hour before. His clerical shirt was open and his Roman collar sagged down across his shirt front. He was watching an old movie, a war film in which guns flashed and shells burst silently because the sound was turned so low.

"Excuse me, Jack, I hope I'm not disturbing you."

"No, not at all, just winding down, that's all. How about a

drink? You've had quite a night with the loonies here and all."

"Thanks, Jack, I think I could use a nightcap."

Allen stood up and poured a scotch for the president, adding some chips of ice from a bowl on a table by the television set. Allen moved slowly, as though his joints were stiff. He handed the glass to Kinsella and smiled wryly.

"Well, Tom, little did you know what you were getting into when you took the job."

"No, I must say I have had quite a few surprises. Makes you yearn a little for the old days, when things were simpler in the world and in the Church."

"Gone, Tom, they're gone for good. Well, here's to you." He reached his glass, as if toasting Kinsella. "You ought to begin keeping a log, Tom, the way they do on a ship. The last journey of His Holiness's good ship, *The Roman Catholic Church*. Jesus, Tom, it's in the ice fields already and it's taking water."

Kinsella smiled, for there was a tonic quality in Allen's characteristic exaggeration.

"Things are not that bad, Jack. Notre Dame is still afloat."

"Yes, but the crew is full of the scurvy. Tom, this whole incident tonight came goddam close to breaking the place wide open. I mean, let the trumpet sound and you don't know who will rise up to answer it. Jesus Christ, Tom, people who haven't been out of their rooms in years stirred to life tonight. These guys sleep with their eyes open waiting for the fucking moon to rise every month."

Kinsella smiled because he knew that there was always some truth at the core of Allen's colorful analysis of events.

"Do you still think Father Bagby sleeps hanging from the steam pipes?"

"Oh, hell, yes. Hasn't been in his bed in years. Part tree sloth, that's what he is, hangs right above the washbowl. But I saw him out there on the golf course tonight, front and center. I can hardly wait to hear the fathers talk about it at breakfast tomorrow. All the big experts, talking about mystical experience and states of prayer. Why, for Christ's sake, not one of them will admit that it was sex, looking for the old nooky, that routed them out." He shook his head and sipped from his drink.

"It's over now. Greenie was a little slow getting this thing under control."

"Of course he was. Fucking Arab, just his cup of tea. Thinks it's the new religion where we're all going to hold hands and dance around the garden together. You know, Tom, sometimes I'm glad I'm getting older. I hate to think of what the future will be when guys like Greenie are all that we have left."

"It does give one pause, Jack, but the clergy has had many ups and downs during history."

"Well, we're heading for a down now. I don't know." Allen began to shake his head. "Do you remember when this used to be fun?"

"We had a lot of good times years ago. Yes, I remember. That's one of the reasons I'm worried about who will take my place. If anything happened to me, that is."

"Hell, Tom, you're young yet. But you'd better begin thinking about it. Frankly, I think Greenie is campaigning already. If he had his way, we'd be having something like the girl on the cross before every football weekend. I don't know, Tom, I don't know if these guys believe in the school for the sake of the school, or whether they believe in the University because of what they can screw out of it."

"That's exactly how I feel, Jack. Too many people ready to use the place. That's always been a danger."

"Yes, but we've never had perverts out to run the place. It would be goddam odd after all these years of sports being the thing we are known for, it would be goddam odd if the fairies took over."

Kinsella laughed at Allen's scenario. "Well, they'd have the Board of Trustees to deal with first, Jack. But, seriously, I've been thinking a lot about this. What would you think—and this is just speculation, mind you—what would you think if a layman were to become president here?"

Allen's face went solemn. Here, from yet another angle in this long night, was a battering ram against the priesthood which, as a rough and masculine occupation, he had loved so much. He rubbed his jaw but not in the manner of a man in doubt. He knew the right answer, even if he regretted it.

"We've got little choice," he said slowly. "It's the future, there's no doubt of that. I never thought we'd come to it but I suppose we have to face it."

Kinsella made no reply. He sensed that Allen was sharing a truth that was wrung from his depths, that he had said out loud something that was, in effect, a judgment on the leadership quality of the clergy. Allen shifted in his chair. He had known Kinsella long enough to realize that he would go no further in the discussion and that he would not even explain why he had sought Allen's opinion. All that it meant to Allen was that change was to continue, that the Church in which he had been born would be totally transformed by the time he died. He also knew that being a close friend of the president's required him to offer support and not to push him when there were things on his mind. Well, he could still entertain him.

"Jesus, Tom, we're getting awfully serious here just because some screwy girl climbed up on a cross tonight. This isn't the craziest thing I ever saw. Say, do you remember old Father McCoy up in the coal country where we used to teach? Now, there was a priest of the old school."

Kinsella smiled. He knew that Jack was not going to ask him any unnecessary questions, that he was, on the contrary, going to recount some old-fashioned stories. Kinsella nodded his head and sipped his drink as Allen continued.

"Used the title Doctor instead of Father. Remember? Shit, the bishop sent him to Rome to get his degree and poor McCoy came home thinking that he was going to teach at the University and, before he knows it, he's up with the shit-kickers in Lowville, Pa. Poor bastard. First Sunday he was there he put on his alb and cope and marched down the main street challenging the Protestant ministers to come out and debate him!"

Tom had heard the story many times but Allen's tales were always balm for the soul. He sat back and relaxed as Allen continued the familiar story.

"Well, Doctor McCoy hated that bishop, oh, Jesus, did he hate him. When the bishop'd make a pack of monsignors, old McCoy would say to him, right to his face, 'You're like God. You've made something out of nothing . . .'"

Down across Route 31 the graduate student, whose name was David Weber, and about one hundred of the persons who had moved off campus with the cross had propped it up against a parked automobile that had been driven into a vacant area off the road. The graduate student had been trying to talk to the girl but she had remained silent, her eyes closed as though she was asleep. About a dozen people in the crowd had begun to recite the rosary in classic singsong fashion while the others seemed to be waiting for some direction about what to do next.

Out of the darkness Father Green suddenly appeared. He had changed into a turtleneck sweater and had obviously been running. He called to the graduate student, whom he knew from having him in class.

"Dave, Dave! I want to talk to you."

"Yes, Father," Dave replied, turning away from the silent girl.

"I want to thank you, Dave, for helping to lead this group away in such orderly fashion tonight."

David said nothing. Green moved closer to him and began to speak in confidential tones.

"David, I cannot invite you officially, I want you to understand that, but I also want you to know that there are those on campus who sympathize with your religious spirit." He put his arm around David's shoulders.

"David, there are those who understand, who see the vision."

Weber nodded solemnly.

"Yes, Father, the spirit of the Lord is in this."

"Well, David, what we want you to know is that, even without an official invitation, the Notre Dame campus should be big enough for you and this group. We have to welcome all worshipers, all those who want to respond to the Lord. You understand?"

"Yes, Father," David said blankly.

"Well then, I think you are responsible enough to handle this. Why don't you reassemble at dawn, and raise this sign of belief to the world again?"

"Oh, we plan to stay with her all night, Father."

"Yes, yes, of course, but at dawn why not raise the sign on campus again?"

"How would we do that?"

"Well, David, I'm sure you could come quietly to the church or to some other quiet place. The grotto of Lourdes, yes, the grotto. Our Lady would certainly welcome you there, if you came quietly and prayed again in silence."

David did not speak right away. He looked back toward the girl, who seemed to be in a deep sleep, and then, in a trancelike voice, he said, "Yes, Father. Thank you, Father.

Yes, the grotto, the shrine of the Blessed Mother. Yes, how right it would be."

It was almost 2 A.M. when Thomas Kinsella left Jack Allen's rooms. He was still smiling as he thought of the outrageous stories that Allen had told him and of how much better he had made him feel. As he put the key in his door he heard steps behind him. It was Jeffrey Green on his way to his quarters down the hall.

"Jeff, is that you?"

"Yes," Green replied calmly. "I was just out to see that everything was quiet."

"Thanks, Jeff. I'll see you in the morning."

"Yes," Jeffrey replied. "In the morning."

PART IV

1
February 1969

It was a time of upset, as you well remember, what with Nixon, almost sincere-looking, taking the oath of office just the month before and the memory of Hubert Humphrey's campaign—a great occasion gone all to pieces, like Christmas Eve with your father coming home drunk—still heavy upon us. Campuses all over the country were going up for grabs the way Chicago had during the Democratic Convention the summer before, and some fellows even tried to sponsor a pornographic film festival practically in the shadow of the Golden Dome.

They were hustled away quickly, of course, tumbling out of the science building like gangsters that had been tear-gassed, and the whole thing came to naught, although such an idea was surely unexpected, not to say shocking, for old-time Notre Damers. The peace movement was holding meetings of one kind or another all the time and there had been a big protest against the recruiters from the Dow Chemical Company, the fellows that made the napalm. Nothing, however, attracted as much attention as the Sunday night rally at Stepan Center that featured one of the Berrigan brothers—I forget which, since one or the other of them was always in jail or at large in those days—as well as a shaggy-looking bunch of folk singers and the star attraction, the famous actress, Maria Moore herself.

She drew a great crowd and, curious as I was about seeing a real star and sympathetic in my own fashion to the peace movement, I got there early for an aisle seat and a good look at the show. Not that I hadn't heard the same kind of

173

speeches before, but Father Berrigan was moving in a wild-eyed kind of way, the singing was grand, and Maria Moore, in a proper-looking gray suit with a high-cut neck, was as fair a sight as I had ever seen. It took a little adjusting to seeing her life-sized instead of twenty feet tall on a movie screen but you couldn't mistake those famous cheekbones and those perfectly even white teeth. Why, I was like a kid myself, applauding and stamping and leaning forward in my chair.

She had the commanding presence of an actress and she talked very briefly, her eyes flashing as she tossed her red hair back, about how she felt she had to speak out for peace and she hoped the Notre Dame students would too. All very nice with the students hanging on every word and asking her questions afterward, mostly to keep her there so they could look at her. Then one of the lads, a sophomore from Pittsburgh with a playful glint in his eye, suggested that she come back to his dormitory, you know, so the boys could develop a deeper interpersonal relationship with her, those being all the rage at the time. That brought the house down and they trotted out the folk singers for another go at "We Shall Overcome," and Miss Moore, moving swiftly, the way celebrities get to do, hurried out of the hall. That was the beginning of her long and complicated relationship with Father Thomas Kinsella.

Of course, it wasn't much of a relationship at the start, just a little sparring by a couple of professionals who knew how to protect themselves. Father Thomas was a young priest, with a strong chin and no gray hair at all, just a few years out of graduate school with his doctorate in philosophy, but well thought of around the University. You didn't have to be a weatherman, as the saying went then, to know which way the wind was blowing for him; he was the classic golden boy of the clerical world, the handsome fellow with brains they mark down early in the promotion book, and it didn't hurt that his father was a millionaire in Chicago with a switchboard full of political and business connections.

As it turned out that night, the car that was to take Miss Moore back to Chicago, where she was appearing in a musical play, broke down and Father Berrigan and the folk singers were heading in another direction, so Father Thomas got called to see what could be done. He wasn't enthusiastic about it—polite, of course, but definitely restrained—and kind of backed into it when they couldn't figure out anything

better at ten o'clock at night. He would drive her into the
city—a quick run on the Indiana Tollway of about ninety
miles—and, when he spotted me, Father Thomas asked if I
would go along to ride in the front of the car with him while
Miss Moore sat in the back.

Thomas was handsome but he had always seemed impervi-
ous to the influences of women, as though his emotions had
been Scotch-guarded to protect his holy motivations for the
priesthood. No mind, he was proper and diffident and quite
accustomed to lots of attention himself, so I had grown used
to seeing him smile politely as he eased his way smoothly out
of parties and other gatherings where women always found
reasons to ask him was it all right to take the pill or did he
know so and so had her tubes tied and by a Catholic doctor
and what did he think of that? Anything, you might say, to
have a chat with him. Thomas had not attended the rally, not
that he was against the peace movement exactly but, as with
women, he kept a certain distance, maintaining a neutrality
that kept him free of marching, signing petitions, or striking
the matches for the draft card burnings. It was a delicate
balance, as they say, but he pulled it off well, being part of the
establishment while keeping lines open to the bubbling world
of protest.

"Miss Moore?" Thomas inquired politely as we met her
back at the lobby of the Morris Inn, where she had gone while
arrangements for transportation were being made. "I'm
Father Kinsella and this is Professor Austin Kenna. We're
going to take you back to Chicago."

Miss Moore smiled and nodded to both of us, not saying a
word as she followed us out to the car. She was good at
keeping a little distance too, not that she treated us like
footmen, but you could see that she was used to having men
take care of her. Well, we got settled in the car and were just
passing the old cemetery when the headlights picked up the
first flakes of snow. Now, as you may know, if snow is falling
anywhere it's on South Bend, lying as it does just southeast of
Lake Michigan, and in the path of the winds that pick up its
moisture and spread it in a frosty cloud that lasts into spring
across northwest Indiana.

"Oh my," Miss Moore said enthusiastically, "I love the
snow. How beautiful for someone who lives in California
most of the year."

"We've lots of snow here," I volunteered somewhat flatly,

turning my head halfway toward our celebrated passenger in the back seat.

"I saw you at the rally tonight, Professor," she said out of the darkness. "Have you been working in the peace movement?"

"Well," I said, clearing my throat, "in my own way, don't you know, in my own way."

"Professor Kenna went there to see you," Thomas said, and I wished he hadn't. We stopped at the tollgate plaza to pick up our ticket and as Thomas lowered the window a rush of crystal-like snow billowed in on us.

"And you, Father?" Miss Moore asked in a controlled voice. "Were you there tonight?"

"No, Miss Moore," Thomas answered, turning his head to check the traffic as we entered the toll road proper. "I was busy. But I understand you had a good crowd."

"Why wouldn't you find time for a peace rally?" It was strange, hearing that well-known voice in the otherwise muffled tunnel of the night.

"Like Professor Kenna, I have my own way of supporting the peace movement."

"Draft counseling? Is that what you do?"

"No, I don't do that. But I've referred kids to priests who do."

"How brave of you," Maria Moore said sardonically. Then there was a long silence, at least it seemed long to me since Thomas said nothing in his own defense. It was beginning to snow more heavily and a great orange truck trailing a path of blue highway salt lumbered onto the road a hundred yards ahead of us.

"What do you do at the University exactly?" the actress asked as we passed the truck and a shower of the tumbling salt pellets peppered the side of the car.

"Well, right now I'm running what they call a renewal institute. It's for priests. Nuns and brothers too. To update them on what's been going on in the Church, to give them some refueling, I guess you'd call it."

"And that's the way you support the peace movement? By supporting the peace movers?"

"Yes," Thomas said somewhat cautiously. "That's the idea anyway, to help them in all their pastoral work, including peace and everything else."

"Well, Father, I feel a little better about you. You sounded like you just played things safe before." Miss Moore's voice was more relaxed.

"I don't play things at all," Thomas replied as he switched the wipers to a higher speed against the accumulating snow. "That's your profession, isn't it?" There was a twist of lemon in his voice, as though he was evening the score.

"Yes," the actress answered without skipping a beat, "my profession but not my whole life."

It was getting a bit heavy for me, I must say, since we were at such close quarters and I didn't want to get hit by any of the shell fragments from the exchange that was taking place, so I tried to throw a distraction in. "The snow's getting worse," I said feebly just as a discomforting, slapping noise started near the back of the car and we began to heave up and down on the tire that had gone flat. Thomas pulled the car onto the shoulder of the road.

"I'm sorry, Miss Moore, I really hadn't planned on this. I'll get out and fix it." He opened the driver's door and heavy flakes of snow swept through the opening out to the night. He closed the door and moved around to the trunk of the car. I shifted in my seat and looked at Miss Moore. She was already opening the back door behind me as I said, "I'm afraid we'd best get out."

"I'm out," she called to me, sounding as if she were enjoying it. There was, I could see, by the last light that beamed out of the car before the door closed, a big kid's smile on her face. The snow was beginning to catch in her red hair.

"Are you warm enough?" I asked, pulling my scarf loose. "Here, put this around your head." But she had turned and stepped back by the trunk of the car, which Thomas was just opening. The wind howled on the dark and lonely roadway and great galaxies of snow rose and fell around us.

"What wonderful air!" the actress said. "So clean and healthy."

Thomas said nothing as he searched in the darkened trunk for the automobile jack. A semitrailer truck rumbled by in the outer lane like a ghost ship, great billows of snow rising in its wake.

"You'd think they'd stop and give us a hand," I said as Maria moved to Thomas's side. "Here, Father," she said, "let me give you a hand. I had to do this in a picture last year."

"I don't want you to get dirty or hurt out here, Miss Moore," Thomas answered, a little put upon, it seemed to me, that she had even offered to help.

"Come on, Father," she said, her voice still a musical sound in the soft silent night. "You've got your best black suit on too. It's no problem. Let's do it together."

With that, they pitched in and, with Thomas doing most of the heavy work and me stamping my feet in the cold, they changed the tire in a few minutes. There was a reluctant smile on Father Thomas's face as he heaved the shredded remnants of the blown tire into the trunk.

"Thanks," he said softly. "You're pretty good at that."

"Correction, Father, I'm very good at it. I had to do it twenty times for that one scene. I could probably do it with my eyes shut." She paused and then began to laugh. "Well, I mean, I don't mean that you weren't good. I mean, for somebody who doesn't do it often, you were pretty good yourself."

Thomas closed the trunk with a slam and I could see that, perhaps for the first time in his life, a woman had gotten inside the perimeter of his defenses. He was mildly irritated but he seemed to enjoy it; he didn't really quite know what to do about that feeling. Maria was still laughing, half at him and half at the situation, when a car sped by in the outer lane, just a few feet from us, peeling up a ribbon of slush seeded with blue salt and depositing it like a sash of decoration diagonally across the front of Father Kinsella's coat. Well, that made Maria laugh all the more as she asked, "What was it you were going to say, Father?"

"Peace!" Thomas said, making the famous V signal with his gloved fingers. He was smiling broadly as he began to brush the mess off his coat. "Did you make movies with the Keystone Cops?" he asked, in much better humor than I expected he would be.

"No, no," Maria answered, catching her breath from laughing. "Here, let me help clean you off." She reached toward him but he stepped back a little, waving her off in a friendly kind of way.

"You've brought me enough bad luck tonight," Thomas said as he shook the last heavy clots of slush free. "Let's get into the car before something else happens."

So we climbed back in, our humor turned several degrees warmer because of the adventure, and settled down for the rest of the drive into Chicago. I felt ever so much better and Thomas and Maria, having laughed out loud at the predicament they had shared, fell into an easier discussion. The snow continued to dance in gigantic pirouettes across the almost empty highway before us.

"Have you been to the play yet, Father?" Maria asked quickly. "Or you, Professor Kenna?"

"No," Thomas replied. "I'm afraid I haven't. But I've always liked the story."

There was neither time nor opportunity for me to reply before the actress spoke again.

"Yes, a wonderful story, and very good with the music added. *The Bridge of San Luis Rey*. Wonderful old Thornton Wilder stuff. I play La Perichole, a famous actress. Does that sound right for me?" She laughed again. "Of course, she was a real character, the mistress of a Viceroy in Lima."

"That doesn't sound like you," Thomas said with no bitters in his tone this time.

"No, heavens no! But she's a woman of character. And it's a play filled with mystery." She leaned forward, placing her hands on the back of the seat behind me to support herself. I jumped a bit at the touch of her fingertips in the darkness.

"I'm captivated by the story. Almost did the movie once, so I jumped at the chance to do this. It's thought to be a little old-fashioned, you know, with its idea of Providence leading us along."

"Do you believe in Providence, Miss Moore?" Thomas asked suddenly.

"Yes," she said slowly. "I suppose I do."

"That's why you're doing the play, isn't it?"

I thought it a pretty straightforward question for Thomas to put, full of interpretation as it was. But Maria didn't hesitate, not a bit.

"Why do you think that?"

"There's just something about the way you talk about it, something in your voice that says you believe it, that you were meant to do it. You believe the five people were all led onto that swaying bridge by God's hand, that their lives were complete when they started to cross. You think about the play that way."

"Yes, I guess I do." She paused. "But it's a great part, one of the great characters of all drama."

"And opera too," Thomas added. "The name means

'half-caste bitch' if I recall correctly." Then he began to laugh. "Now, that doesn't sound like you."

"Oh, you'd be surprised. Besides, it became a name of affection for all her followers down in Peru."

"It's too bad you can't be at Notre Dame this week, Miss Moore. We're having a bishop from Peru visit our pastoral institute. Quite famous down there. His nickname is 'The Red Shepherd,' and he's got quite a reputation. Some people have accused him of being a Communist. And others say he wears a pair of pistols, empty, but a symbol of his fight for his people." Thomas paused momentarily before adding, "Sounds like a fellow you'd love to march with."

Maria pulled back from the rear of my seat. "I'll bet he knows how to change a tire," she said quickly. "He does sound like somebody I'd like. How about you, Father, what's your relationship to this institute? It sounds a little subversive."

"My job," Thomas said, pausing a moment to adjust the heating controls, "my job is to manage it and to keep it on an even keel. I guess I'm the one who's supposed to referee things, keep everybody from getting carried away while they're learning new things. Sometimes, in their zeal, these people go to excess."

"Amen," I thought silently to myself, thinking of some of the loony Masses I'd been to, with balloons and African drums, and people hugging and kissing like they were in a marathon contest. However, neither Thomas nor Maria was much interested in me; I had become more an observer than a participant in the conversation.

"Excess," Maria said with a sigh. "Excess is a peculiar word, Father Kinsella. Have you ever noticed how often it's used to describe people who want to do good?"

"You mean people like the peace workers?"

"Yes, when war is the excess, the unimaginable excess of hate and death. Burning draft cards and protesting are thought to be an excess when anybody can see where the real excess is."

Father Thomas was silent for the space it took us to pass a tank truck, braced with red and green lights, that was rumbling along through the snowstorm.

"Have you had any opposition to these public appearances you've been making for the peace movement?"

"Well, Richard Nixon certainly won't invite me to the

White House, which must mean I'm on the right side of this. There are plenty of protests, lots of hate mail, lots of people who say I'm a Communist. They've got people picketing the theater in Chicago." She paused for a moment. "I may be out of work soon." Then she laughed and leaned back in the rear seat and I could tell that Father Thomas wasn't quite sure what to say.

In a few moments we came to the end of the snow; it's like passing through a curtain when you get by a certain point of Lake Michigan, and Chicago often has a night full of stars when the snowplows are out in South Bend.

"What is it you teach, Father?" Maria asked after we all remarked on the relief we felt at leaving the snow behind.

"Philosophy," Thomas replied as he turned off the windshield wipers. In the distance the sky glowed with the lights of the city.

"Yes, that makes sense," Maria said almost to herself. "Philosophers are good at theory." Then her voice trailed off. Thomas opened his mouth but thought better of it and did not speak. Then she asked me what I taught, out of politeness more than anything else, it seemed to me, and I explained that I was an old professor of Church history and had been around so long they didn't know what to do with me anymore. She leaned forward, resting her arm on the back of my seat again.

"Do you two have to drive back to South Bend tonight? I mean it's such a bad night."

"It's no problem, Miss Moore," Thomas said smoothly. "We do it all the time." I thought he was being a little macho about it all, especially since it was almost midnight, but it seemed he had to do it to prove something, although I wasn't exactly sure what. And besides, Father Thomas's parents had a large apartment near the Drake Hotel and we could easily have stayed there without forfeiting our manhood.

"Remember, Father," she said in bemused tones, "you won't have a spare tire for the ride back." Short pause with no reply from Father Thomas. "Or me to help you if you have any trouble." Then she laughed and Thomas laughed a little, but not too much.

"We'll just have to try to do our best, won't we, Austin?" he asked me, again not expecting an answer.

We were on Lake Shore Drive, climbing up toward the main part of the city, with the darkened lake on our right and

we fell to talking about the sights of Chicago. It was not long
before we turned onto Walton Street and pulled up at the
canopied entrance of the hotel. Father Thomas got out, came
around and opened the door behind me, and extended a hand
to the actress as she climbed out onto the curb.

"I want to thank both of you," she said as a late night
passerby paused to watch this famous woman talking to a
priest, and me too, of course, the old duffer in the front seat.
"I really enjoyed the ride."

"It had its moments," Thomas said, "if a philosopher is
allowed an opinion."

"Yes, yes, of course, you mustn't be hurt by what I said."

"I wasn't . . ." Thomas began to say, but Maria interrupted him.

"Now, it's cold out and you have a long way to go. Would
you two be able to come to see the show? I'll have my
secretary, Helen Barnes, get you tickets. How about next
Saturday?" And with that she turned and vanished into the
hotel through the revolving doors.

Father Thomas got back into the car and we headed off on
our long journey home.

"An interesting woman, Austin" was all he said about her
before he switched to small talk about university life, that
automatic conversation we could have carried on in our sleep.
At least the snow had stopped and we got home without
further incident. But I couldn't help thinking that Father
Thomas, strong-willed son of a strong-willed man, had met
his match that night—and had liked it.

2

February 1969

We got back to the campus in the middle of the night, tired but pleased with ourselves, the way Catholics were when they had done their duty in adversity. That was typical of Thomas, that's what I think even now, since he always drove himself so hard, and me too on this occasion, but, of course, I didn't have to get up quite as early as he did. The next day proved to be a long one indeed. It wasn't only the rumbling on the campus, dissent blowing through the air like the snowflakes the night before, and every now and then some sign, like the attempt at the pornographic film festival, that the famous discipline of Notre Dame might be coming unstuck. There was great talk about it anyway, in the student paper, *The Observer,* and in every gathering on the campus. And, in the background, students were occupying deans' offices from coast to coast, burning and scattering their records like the Huns on the warpath, not that I didn't think many a file deserved to go on the bonfire someplace.

In any case, Father Kinsella, having risen at six after the short night, was breakfasting with a group of the priests who had gathered for the institute he was running, the fifty-thousand-mile pastoral checkup as the wags among them called it. There was treasonable talk at that table too, not for bloody revolution of course, but it was the heyday for Church "reform," as they called it, and all the old rules and regulations were being questioned. I was steaming along, my lungs feeling full of hoarfrost, when Father Jack Allen, dressed like a general on the Russian front, hailed me, wanting to know if I had seen Father Thomas.

183

"I wouldn't be surprised if he were at the dining hall, where I'm headed this very minute," I told him, and he fell into step with me.

"Got another little clean-up operation for him, Austin, just something to keep his hand in."

"What is it now? He had a late night, you know."

"So I've heard, so I've heard. And I hear you went along with the great actress, is that right?"

"I did, indeed I did," I said a little defensively. "Now what's up today?"

"There's some pastor loose in the dorms preaching to the kids about sex and sin. Last I heard he was in the chapel at Lewis Hall telling the nuns their habits were impure. One for the funny farm. And Tom and I are elected, as usual, to ship him out."

We were at the dining hall and, within a few minutes, we had summoned Thomas to a quiet corner, where Father Allen outlined the problem to him.

"You got anybody enrolled in your institute who fits the description?" Allen asked in that wonderfully gruff and world-weary way he had.

"We'd better take a look at him but, offhand, I don't think we have anybody with that MO," Thomas said, smiling—for what else could he do?—at the news. "We'd better get over to Lewis Hall. Luckily, it's near Psychological Services. They've got a smart lady psychiatrist there now. They say she's very good. Better give them a call and tell them we may be delivering somebody for her attention." He turned to me. "Would you do that, Austin, while Jack and I get over there?"

I nodded, but I didn't want to miss the show myself, such disturbances being rare on the well-controlled campus. But with student revolt the talk all over the place, I supposed anything could happen. I made the call and hurried after them.

By the time I got to the hall, which had been made a residence for nuns and some laywomen who were taking courses at the University, Fathers Kinsella and Allen were standing about halfway down the chapel aisle, inching toward a late middle-aged man in a long hooded black robe who was preaching away to the mostly empty pews, most of the nuns having left for class.

"And I tell you," he was saying in a high-pitched and agitated voice, "these new habits violate all modesty. For shame on all of you, for shame." A real owl, I thought to myself as I took a place, half kneeling, half sitting, in the last row. I didn't recognize him but that didn't mean too much, seeing as priests and religious brothers and sisters lighted down all the time at Notre Dame like migrating birds that were there one day and gone the next.

Father Kinsella was within a few feet of him now and Father Allen had split their formation, dropping to the side of the preacher, who had pulled a crumpled sheet of yellow paper from his sleeve.

"For shame, you lewd women, for shame. The Sacred Congregation on January 12, 1930, reaffirmed the prescriptions of September 24, 1928, 'a dress cannot be called decent which is cut deeper than two fingers' breadth under the pit of the throat, which does not cover the arms at least to the elbows, and scarcely reaches a bit beyond the knees' . . .'"

It was then, when he was at a keening pitch, that Father Allen moved right next to him, putting his arm around his shoulder like a cop making a collar. Father Thomas stepped up and spoke softly to him, taking the crumpled paper as though it were a message meant for him, and holding the man's hand, like that of an old friend, in his own. The monkish-looking fellow stopped preaching immediately, his mouth falling open, and his eyes widening like a child's as he surrendered himself, quite willingly, it seemed to me, into the priests' care. They came back down the aisle, the preacher asking weakly, "You will tell Father Hesburgh my message, won't you?" and Father Allen, still keeping a good grip on him, saying, "Sure, sure," as they all passed me on their way out of the door and over to Psychological Services.

All in a day's work, I thought to myself as I gave a bobbing genuflection and followed after them, a movie star one night and some lost soul the next morning. I wondered when Father Thomas ever got any work done, since he was so often called when an emergency, major or minor, came up. But he was the sort of fellow the place could count on, the kind of good man who gave great strength to any institution. It was one of the things that made Notre Dame and the Church work, this full devotion of key people at certain levels. You could stand a lot of dreamers and even some downright boobs in the ranks if you had a couple of people with common sense in the right places.

I found later that the preacher who had made his little crusade across campus wasn't a priest at all, but rather a character well known in churches around Chicago who had half a dozen religious getups and was forever showing up to take an extra collection, beg for alms at the church door, or ask Sister Principal if he could interview the eighth-grade boys about vocations, making a few passes at them when he wasn't passing bad checks to various pastors, that is. It was a wonder, the whole shooting match, and Thomas didn't know whether to laugh or cry about the poor man once they had him packed off to some sister of his they located by phone during the morning. Thomas smiled, nonetheless, after everything had settled down and he was back in his office, a place I took to dropping into, especially since I was to give a lecture to his group of pastoral workers later in the week.

"Well, Austin, the next thing on the schedule is a student revolt. Have you heard about that?"

"I doubt it," I said, sounding more self-assured than I actually was. "Our lads are not for the barricades. None of that for them."

"I hope you're right. In any case"—and he paused and wrinkled his brow—"Father Hesburgh has had about enough of the protest movement. I think he's going to make a statement on it."

"A bold man," I said with no discernible inflection. "And great for timing."

"The question is whether a statement by him will settle things down or stir them up. We'll know soon enough."

Then Father Thomas shifted back to talking about the priests and nuns who were in his refresher course. He had a variety of specialists speaking to them on everything from psychological counseling to biblical theology. He picked up a folder and handed it to me.

"Here's a roster and a little background information on the group. They're first-rate people, most of them. Worn out by working too hard, that's their general condition." He paused again, framing the suggestion he was about to make so that it wouldn't sound like one. "Austin, I'm sure a talk from you will help their perspective. Let them see some of the ups and downs of the Church, that periods of turmoil have occurred

before and we've all survived. It's not good if they get their
hopes up too high. 'The revolution of rising expectations,'
and all that. Some of them seem to think that we're about to
change the Church into a constitutional democracy."

I nodded benignly as I took the folder from him.

"By the way, Father Thomas, have you made any plans
about seeing the play?"

"What play? What are you talking about?"

"Why, *The Bridge of San Luis Rey*," I said in surprised
tones.

"Oh," he said, smiling as he stood up. "How could I forget
that? No, Austin, no plans yet. Too busy this morning. You
seem quite anxious to see your favorite star again soon." The
last, good-naturedly as he touched me on the arm and began
to lead me out of the room. "Some of the priests are in
discussion groups now. How about visiting some of them with
me?"

In a few moments we were in a classroom where six priests
and three nuns had drawn chairs into a circle and were busily
talking to each other. There was some scraping of chairs and a
few murmured greetings as they made room for us.

"The whole thing," said a stocky, dark-haired priest,
whose name I later learned was Father Ralph Traglia, and
who gestured as he spoke, "was fish on Friday. Once we let go
of that, the balloon went up on everything else. That was the
best symbol we had going, especially since my family's in the
fish business."

Everyone laughed and the talk went on about parish
problems and the need these good, hardworking people felt
for more freedom and more closeness with their parishioners.
Shop talk, most of it, but very moving, especially as one of
the nuns described the work she had been doing with the poor
in South America. After about fifteen minutes, we moved on,
leaving as quietly as we could while one of the priests recited
his complaints about his bishop. We went down to another
classroom, where another group was clustered together,
talking animatedly about the problems of pastoral life. A thin
man with a patrician face and Buffalo Bill style brown hair
drooping on his shoulders, was speaking. I had met him
before; his name was Frederick Peters and Thomas had
known him for many years. He looked and sounded very
intense—too intense for his own good—as he spoke.

"It's the system that needs change. Get out of the rectories, break down the clerical caste." Father Peters did not even glance at us as we pulled up our chairs. "The Church is like a big corporation, that's why it's unconsciously racist. It can't help itself. What's wrong with it is that it is an institution. Maybe Christ never meant it to be that way, maybe He meant it to be a movement but not an institution. Did you ever think of that?" He turned toward Father Thomas as he said that, as though he was baiting him with the remark.

"If the Church weren't an institution," Thomas replied evenly, "it wouldn't be able to help people. It's just human to institutionalize good things, just as natural as anything could be." He glanced at Father Peters and smiled. "Why, try to keep Christianity a movement and some of you would say in a few years, 'You know we ought to get this thing organized.'"

The priests in the group laughed, all of them but Father Peters, that is. He was a revolutionary not to be put off by Thomas's wry sense of humor, an angry fellow, as some of these lads who had been in the midst of the Church battles too long seemed to be.

"Bullshit, Tom!" This from Father Peters in a voice that injected tension like a paralyzing drug into the group. "That's the party line. I don't buy any of that crap, all that crap about the institution. It's a blind bully of an institution, that's what it is, and you always want to make it sound like the Hardy Family Says Its Prayers, something sweet like that." The gentle priests sitting earnestly together in the classroom weren't accustomed to violent confrontations and the silence was electric. Thomas remained calm, but he stopped smiling. Father Peters raised his hand to keep Thomas from speaking. "I work in the goddam ghetto, that's the institution I know best and there's nothing organized about it at all. Nothing well-ordered, like the bishops like it, nothing at all. It's chaos, social disaster, poverty that can only get worse. The fires in the cities last year were just a hint of what can happen in this country. It's the system, Tom, for Chrissake, it's the organization of things—and the Church is part of that—that's the problem. And you, with your big Irish smile, you want us to say, 'Okay, the system isn't so bad. Live with it, work on it from the inside.' The hell with that." He turned his head to survey the other members of the group. "You know goddam well that lots of the bishops have bought into the system. We need less of the system, and less of them." He paused, breathing heavily from his rapid-fire indictment. The chime of the tower bell could be heard even through the closed windows of the classroom. Father Peters looked down at his shoes while the other priests glanced at each other uneasily. One of them spoke up, in an effort to bridge the gap of silence. "That means time for coffee break. What do you say, Fathers?" With that the meeting broke up, although Father Thomas remained behind, waiting while Father Peters finally pulled himself out of his chair and looked directly at us again.

"I mean that, Tom," he said, his voice crackling with nervous strain. "I don't know what the answer is where I work but the old ones aren't any good." The three of us moved out of the classroom and down the hall to the stairs that led to a room where coffee was being served. Everybody was relaxed in that atmosphere and the incident, like so many others, seemed to have been obscured by the already crazy design of the day. After the break, which was filled mostly with small talk about how Notre Dame's football team would be in the Fall, we began to break up. Father Thomas and I were climbing the stairs when Father Peters caught up with us. "Tom," he said plaintively, "I'd like to talk to you a little more." He seemed more relaxed, although his face looked pale by the flame of the match he held beneath his cigarette in the half light of the stairwell.

"Sure, Fred," Tom said in an easy tone, "Austin and I just have to go over a few things for his talk, and I'll be free."

Father Peters followed us up the stairs and down the hallway to Father Kinsella's office. As we were about to enter, Jack Allen rounded the corner and gave us a wave and a signal to wait for him.

"Ted's coming out with a statement on protests, Tom," Father Allen said as he reached us by the office door. "I thought you'd like to know. It's going to be pretty strong stuff, the way I hear it. On-the-spot expulsions for students or teachers if they don't pack their banners in after fifteen minutes."

Father Peters grew even more pale as Father Allen summarized the strong stand that Father Hesburgh, the University president, was about to take, a symbol for the washed-out Peters, I supposed, of authority oppressing the innocent again.

"He can't get away with that," Peters growled half to himself as he took a long drag on his cigarette. "Not in this day and age."

"Just watch him," Allen answered as we entered Thomas's office and he continued on down the hall.

"Father Hesburgh gives a lot of thought to these things, Fred," Father Thomas said as he sat behind his desk, gesturing to us to be seated. "I think he knows what he's doing."

Peters quashed a cigarette out in the ashtray on Thomas's desk and immediately shook another one out of the pack he removed from the breast pocket of his coat. Father Thomas handed a folder over to me but before I could open it, Father Peters spoke again. "I want to speak to you, Tom." He struck another match and held it just below the fresh cigarette. I began to get up. "You stay, Professor, I don't mind." I raised my eyebrows inquiringly as I glanced at Thomas and then sat down again. The truth was that I didn't want to miss anything.

The match in Father Peters's hand went out and Thomas leaned forward and struck another light for him.

"You're under terrific stress here, aren't you?" Thomas asked as he shook the match out and let it fall in the ashtray.

Father Peters inhaled, let the smoke float lazily out of his mouth, and looked, sadly I thought, at Thomas. "I'm sorry I blew up before. I didn't want to do that."

"It wasn't that," Thomas answered. "That was understandable. I do represent the establishment. I know that. But it's more than that, something that's been building up. You seem different than I remember you. We've known each other a long time."

"I'm not really different, Tom." He paused as he puffed his cigarette. "Maybe in some ways I'm more of myself." He was twisting a little in his chair, however, and he quashed the cigarette quickly, clearing his throat as he went on.

"Tom, this is a long way from my parish in Chicago. Makes you see things more clearly. I used to think we were number one, the biggest diocese, lots of money, lots of clout. Then it all started going bad after the Council. I guess it showed how old-fashioned we were and didn't know it. Then all the fights with the Archbishop. Well, you know it as well as I do. Hell, he would have been swell back in the thirties but he didn't understand the sixties."

"Who does?" Father Thomas asked, like a man joining himself to the doubts of his friend.

"Well, you know that's when I decided to get out of the work I was in and try something different. I got out of the big suburban parish and volunteered for the inner city. I didn't have to think of the Archbishop and how to please him every day. But, Tom, I was running, really running from something. Hell of a place to run to, wasn't it?"

"You're a little hard on yourself, aren't you?"

"What do you expect? I'm a cradle Catholic, born to make amends. The funny thing, not really funny, was I found the same thing there that I knew in the suburbs. Same problems. I guess because they were in me. Thought a lot about the Archbishop even though I didn't have to deal with him. Just wanted him to be nice to us, to like us, to let us alone. I made the whole thing worse by making so much of the situation. I wanted a good daddy, but a Big Daddy, that's what I learned there. I'd brought my problem with the Archbishop along with me."

"You're still hard on yourself."

"Well, I've come to admit some things about myself, some things I never looked at until I lived with people you couldn't get anything out of, these poor bastards in the ghetto, they didn't have anything to give. They made me an honest man."

"You've always been honest with me, Fred."

"Yes, in a way, but of course you had a Big Daddy of your own. Old P.B. He's still a Big Daddy. If I'm honest, I think that's one of the reasons I got friendly with you, not that I didn't like you, but your old man and all that dough, they had an undeniable attraction to them. Hell, you must have that happen all the time."

Thomas said nothing; he just looked across at his friend, who was fussing with a fresh cigarette. Thomas handed him a book of matches.

"Tom, I, I . . ." Father Peters broke off again as his match burned down to his fingers and he dropped it into the ashtray.

"Hell, Tom, I, I . . ." He paused again and pulled forward in his chair. "I've learned a lot in the inner city. I've learned it isn't just the Archbishop, although he drives me bananas. It really is something about me. You know those people are so good and they've been murdered by Whitey for so long. Oh hell, I get all out of breath when I think about it." Indeed, Father Peters was sighing and heaving like a fellow who had just dropped out of a race. "I felt for those people, I really did. And the Archbishop hasn't done half what he could for them. Hell, he had some Cardinal from the Vatican here for a visit and they're out for a drive and the Archbishop says to his driver, 'Show Cardinal So and So a ghetto.'" Father Peters shook his head at the bad memory of it.

"I really love the black people. I caught 'ghetto fever' like the other guys who've burned themselves out there. And the worst part, the really bad part, was the realization that I was white and always would be. No matter how hard I worked, no matter how much I tried, I'd never be anything but Whitey, never anything but an outsider." Tears began to form in Father Peters's eyes as his voice cracked. "Nothing but Whitey. That's the problem, Tom, that's it. I can never be what I want to be, never." He snuffed and threw his head back as he struggled to keep himself under control.

"But that just made me face something else about myself." He bit his lip and pushed back a lock of hair that had fallen across his forehead. Then he looked straight at Father Kinsella and took a deep breath.

"The real problem, Tom, is that I'm gay. Surprised? I'm surprised to hear myself say this out loud. I'm gay. And I've been gay as long as I can remember but, until I went to the inner city, until I realized I'd always be white no matter how much I wanted to be otherwise, I could never admit it at all, not even to myself. Now, don't worry, Tom, I haven't been molesting children or been shacked up with some lover. Not like that, not exactly." All this in a rush and me not knowing what to say or which way to look.

He sighed deeply. "Things go back a long way. Things that scared me, things that confused me. I didn't know what the hell was going on. I mean, I thought I was the only one with those feelings, the only guy more interested in the boys than in the girls on the beach. You couldn't talk to anybody, not in the seminary. God, they were always hinting about what a demon you were if you liked other men, and how you should report it if anybody made a pass at you. And all the talk about avoiding particular friendships when guys had crushes on each other all over the place. 'Spiritual friendships' we called it, it had to be spiritual, things were so repressed." Father Peters was visibly upset, his hands shaking as he talked, and a little tic playing in his cheek. He paused, like a man badly in need of fresh air.

"Nobody knew what was going on inside them or what their feelings meant. I certainly didn't even want to find out. And all the lectures about celibacy and being on your guard with women. I never knew what they were talking about. And they kept us busy, busy work mostly, and camp in the summer. Jesus, I can feel it now, the strain, yeah, the strain of it all, feeling I had this terrible brand on my soul, that I was damned . . ." He paused again and ran his hand through his hair. "Things were just beginning to be liberalized when I was in the seminary, they just began talking about changing things, we had a little more freedom and I suppose we let go a little. That's what really bothered me afterward, that made me feel I was possessed or something. There was another guy, his name doesn't make any difference, and we had this thing, this crush, whatever you want to call it, and one night he embraced me and kissed me. And I reacted, I mean I really got excited. Then I felt I had to confess it but I didn't know what to say. We used to go to old Father Hugo. He was half deaf and half in dreamland and he'd just nod his head and tell you to say three Hail Marys. Maybe it would have been better if I'd have gone to old McEvoy, who would have choked and yelled and made me leave on the spot."

Father Peters was shaking his head again and Father Thomas just sat there looking at him intently. I must confess sex has always been a puzzle to me and I was a little uncomfortable listening to all this, wondering about myself and the little wisps of feelings I'd had for some of the lads over the years. But then I'd had them for the girls, too, and still had some for both of them. Well, needless to say, I kept my mouth shut.

"Well," Father Peters said, gulping air like a swimmer halfway through his stroke, "there were plenty of embraces and kisses, and talks about spiritual friendship and lifelong devotion to each other. I'd go to old Hugo, confess everything, and feel relieved immediately. Then it would all start up again. One night I was sick in the infirmary, nobody else there. And my friend came to see me late at night. Gradually he put his hand under the covers. He reached in and held me, just held me while I got big as a house, and finally let go. God, I loved it and then I was miserable too. I went to see McFarland, the theology teacher, and I told him as much as I could. I felt like I was in a vise, wanting sex and feeling I couldn't have it, feeling I had to be a priest whether I wanted to or not. And McFarland said I should stay, that my problems were no different than a heterosexual's, that the celibate life was the same challenge for both, and I should pray and do penance.

"Well, I stayed. And I did a little better, felt a little less guilty, and, then a year or so after ordination, it all began again. I was working with teen-agers and I'd find ways to fool around. I'd get them in wrestling contests, then I'd hold them next to me. God, what a life, I'd think when people would tell me how wonderful I was. I was living off cheap thrills from feeling up teen-age boys who didn't have a clue that I was using them. I used to think, Jesus, if some man in the parish had any idea what I was doing with his kids, he'd come in and kick the shit out of me. And I'd still see my old friend on our days off. Well, it got to the point where I was pretty frantic. Then the whole Black thing came up, the inner city, the place to forget myself for a change. It looked like salvation to me, and, by God, everybody thought I was heroic. I was on the run, for God's sake." He broke off, out of breath again, and it looked like he wasn't going to say anything else. Deathly quiet, it became, and then Thomas said to him, sort of half softly, "I take it, it's never gotten any easier for you."

"No," Father Peters answered, "but at least I became honest. That goddam ghetto would make anybody honest. I'm just queer, that's all, queer, gay, a fag, whatever you want to call it. That's me, the queen of the inner city." But then he began to sob, and he rubbed his eyes with his sleeve, and we were all quiet again.

"I've done my damndest, Tom," he said between sobs, lowering his head and waving Thomas's extended hand away. "I'm all right. I'm all right." He drew his breath and turned his face toward Thomas again.

"That's why I throw myself into everything, why I don't trust Big Daddies any more. I think the Church got me into this; I'm just beginning to realize how angry I am about it and what it's done to people's sex lives. That's why I'm against the government, too. But I'm filled with guilt, sweet Jesus, am I filled with guilt! And all this stuff about coming out of the closet hasn't helped me any. It's made me go farther in. There's no place for a homosexual who admits it in the priesthood. Look what they've done to guys who've written or talked about it. Scares hell out of them, doesn't it? They don't want that one out of the box. No, there's no place for me, as I am, only as I pretend to be, only as I keep running. Tom"—and he paused, letting ashes fall from his long-dead cigarette onto the floor. "I'm worn out. I don't fit. I am a homosexual and yet I can't become one. And I can't leave the priesthood, not now. But I don't know where to go or what to do. I'm tired, Tom, tired."

Father Thomas put his hand out and touched Father Peters's shoulder. "You're my friend, Fred," he said softly. "I think I understand."

"How the hell could you?" Father Peters snapped before he caught himself. "I'm sorry, Tom, but I'm not sure anybody could understand. And you can't tell anybody. I mean, if you told the Archbishop that Father Peters was gay, the old boy would smile and say, 'Of course, that's what's wrong with him.' He'd take it as a victory, whatever sex he is, or if he has any sex. Being gay is being queer, it's being wrong, morally and spiritually, and if the Archbishop could believe that of me, he could write off everything I've said and done, no matter how good it's really been. I've seen him do it before, to other men. Queer is the great pigeonhole. They'll put up with you, they'll even use you. But they keep you on the discard pile. I'm a great threat, didn't you know? And whatever I've done, whatever I've suffered, or however much I've atoned for my thoughts and feelings; none of that makes any difference to Big Daddy. Hell, they don't care about the gay problem among the people and they sure as hell don't want to find out about it among the clergy. Better not to have any sex at all, right, Tom? Better to be neutral, better to have power the way the Archbishop has. Then you don't have to worry about sex at all." He lighted another cigarette with a still trembling hand.

"The Church doesn't think you're a sinner, Fred."

"That's easy to say. What would you really know about it anyway? You've been a fair-haired boy all your life, picked for this job and that, front and center all the time. Say, Tom"—and his voice became sarcastic—"did you ever think your looks got you where you are, that you made the juices run in some old fag monsignor and he put you at the top of his list?" He broke off, shook his head, and said, "I'm sorry. I truly am sorry."

Now, Thomas was calm enough under all this. He had wondered about such things before but, self-confident as he was, he never let them bother him much. "I know you don't mean to hurt me. I know that. And I want to help you, Fred, and anything I can do, well, you know you can count on me."

"What can you do? Can a man be born again? It's a funny question at that." Father Peters laughed in a self-mocking way.

"Well, I'm not sure that staying in the inner city with all the added stress is going to help you. We could arrange for you to stay here awhile. You have a degree. I'm sure they could find a place for you at the University; Ted Hesburgh has helped a lot of men who have been in trouble. He's wonderful about it. I could talk to him about it, if you like, and maybe you could get some psychological help at the same time . . ."

Father Peters was shaking his head slowly. "This is my purgatory, that's how I look on it. I may be here for neurotic reasons, maybe most people are where they are for neurotic reasons, I don't know. Next to all that poverty and misery in the inner city my little problem doesn't seem so important. That's what I wonder about. Who cares if Father is married or gay or whatever in the midst of that? What difference does it make when there's so much that needs to be done? What difference does your sex make if there's no love around anyway?" He sighed again, then managed a smile. "I'll have to think about it, Tom, I'll have to think about it."

They sat together for a while in silence and when he got up to leave, I thought Peters looked more relaxed. But Father Thomas was frowning and he seemed very quiet.

3

February 1969

Father Hesburgh's statement was issued the next day, a tough one, as Father Allen had predicted, since it gave protesters fifteen minutes to think about their options before surrendering their identity cards and making themselves ex-members of the "Notre Dame Community," as the president of the University called it. Well, it was all over Walter Cronkite and Huntley and Brinkley that night, not to mention the front page of the New York *Times* the next morning. I remember they made the "Quotation of the Day" from it: "Without the law the university is a sitting duck for any small group from outside or inside that wishes to destroy it, to incapacitate it, to terrorize it at whim. Somewhere a stand may be made."

Grand stuff and as noble and brave as a thing could be, considering the way universities were backing up all around the country for fear of offending their students. Mind you now, such student protests were nothing new in history but Notre Dame's stand surely was in that dark and cold winter. Thomas's father, old P.B., called him from Chicago to tell how he thought it was a good idea.

"You've got to hand it to Father Hesburgh," the elder Kinsella said, his lively voice booming through the receiver so that I could get the drift even though I was seated across the desk from Father Thomas. "It's great public relations for you people. Just what the country's looking for, a little backbone somewhere."

"I'll tell Father Hesburgh you're pleased about it," Thomas said, a half smile on his face.

"And tell him something else for me, will you?"

"What's that?"

"His timing was terrific."

"He's good at that."

"Damned right he is. The thing is, Tom, he knew very well that he wasn't taking as big a gamble as the papers make it sound. That's the genius of it."

"What do you mean?" Thomas asked, reaching for one of the thin dark cigars he loved to smoke. I could hear his father's laughter crackling over the phone.

"Father Hesburgh knew he couldn't lose. That's because he understood the students who go there—and their parents— very well. The parents would back him up, he was sure of that, and your students aren't as rebellious as they'd like to make themselves sound. They're not going to buck him, or not for long. So Ted wasn't risking anything but he gained a tremendous amount in the process. Goddam! That's a man who knows something about power. You sure he wouldn't like a job with Kinsella Industries?"

"When was the last time you got invited for the 'Today' show?" Thomas asked, his smile returning. "Ted'll be on that tomorrow or the next day."

I could hear P.B.'s infectious laugh again and had to smile myself, especially since I agreed with his analysis of the state of things.

"Say, when are you coming up to Chicago? Your mother says you're going to a play or something. You want to stay with us?"

"Well," Thomas said, finally getting a chance to light his cigar, "Austin Kenna and I are going up this weekend, Saturday night as a matter of fact. *The Bridge of San Luis Rey*. Would you and mother like to go?"

"Oh, hell no, we're going to the country for the weekend. But make yourselves comfortable here. Martin or Joe, or maybe both'll be here."

After a little concluding small talk, Thomas hung up but he was still smiling as he looked up at me.

"You know, my father's right, I think. The students are going right along with Ted. They feel a need for a little leadership too." He puffed on his cigar. "Well, Austin, are you ready for your talk this afternoon?"

I nodded. "Say, Father Thomas, when is the bishop coming in from South America, the one they say wears the gun?"

"The Red Shepherd? He'll be here late this afternoon. He's going to meet with our groups this evening. Are you coming?"

My own talk to the forty or so priests and nuns went well enough. People are always surprised to discover that so much of what seems new is really old, as these good souls were when I explained that America's first bishop, John Carroll, asked Rome to put the Mass into English back in 1797. So much for your contemporary liturgical movements. Two things distracted me during it. One was Father Peters sitting alone, a few rows away from everyone else. The other was a kind of low-grade infection of curiosity about Bishop Muñoz, and, after I finished with the question period, it was still perking away in me as I walked back to Father Thomas's office.

"Will it be Marx or Jesus tonight?" I asked with what I presumed was a twinkle of good humor.

"Is that a disjunctive question?" Father Thomas replied, using the old Irish trick of making another question out of what was supposed to be an answer. But there was a twinkle in his eyes as he stood up and put his arm around my shoulder. "You'll soon find out. I'm going out to the airport to meet him. Why don't you come along?"

Which, of course, I did, having discovered that the leisure of retirement from full-time teaching allowed me such adventures. We drove out to the South Bend Airport, a neat, red brick building with no aspirations to anything but utility. The plane from Chicago had just pulled up to the gate and a crowd of salesmen trickled out of the door and down the flight stairs. There was no mistaking Bishop Henrique Muñoz when he appeared in the door, even though he was wearing a black tie instead of a white collar under his gray overcoat. He was tall, a big fellow the size of Thomas himself, and beneath his Indian black hair he had the face of a grandee, his bronze coloring a contrast to the background of the slag-gray winter sky. He looked around as he descended the steps and, when he spotted Father Thomas's Roman collar, his face crinkled around a big smile and he waved in friendly fashion as he made his way toward us. I inspected him carefully but found no bulges of a suspicious nature. He was carrying a scarred black suitcase in his hand and as he drew near to us his smile, set off by teeth as white as Maria Moore's, grew even larger.

"I am Henrique Muñoz," he said with just enough of an accent to add both charm and mystery to his voice. "And you must be Father Kinsella."

Father Thomas bent down to kiss the bishop's ring, one of those plain cigar-band-style rings that had become popular with some bishops, although not all, mind you, since some of them still fancied the flash of the big stone. In any case Bishop Muñoz would have none of it, raising his hand out of range, and laughing as he spoke.

"No, no, Father, it is not a sanitary practice . . ."

"For you or for me?" Thomas asked, and we all laughed as Thomas introduced me and we turned to head back to the car. The bishop was dressed in a gray suit and as far as I could see, there was no sign of a shoulder holster. Since he only had the one bag we were soon on our way back to the University.

"It seems strange," Muñoz said as he scanned what he could see of South Bend in the late afternoon light, "to be away from the mountains. Natividad, my diocese, is in the highlands, mostly on a great plain, and the mountains watch us silently all the time."

"It's pretty flat around here," Thomas said as we came within sight of the Golden Dome, which looked dull against the darkening eastern sky. "But the soil is rich, the richest in the world." Well, it was mostly small talk like that, although we all seemed comfortable with each other right from the start, and the pressure that often came along with an interesting or important guest was absent entirely. We took the bishop to the suite of rooms Thomas had reserved for him and he asked us to wait in the sitting room while he cleaned up. As he removed his overcoat I took another close look for signs of a sidearm.

Muñoz smiled as he caught me looking him over.

"Professor, you are looking for my pistol, is that not right?" And he laughed. "Do not be embarrassed. Many people look for it." He opened his suit coat so I could have a better look. "But people still want to believe I carry a gun, some say with an ivory handle, like General Patton. They are disappointed that I do not do it." Then he went into the bedroom part of the suite, still laughing softly with the kind of merriment granted only to men who have lived very deeply.

In a few moments he returned in his shirt sleeves, a towel thrown over his shoulder.

"I have brought you a little present." He fished in his bag and brought out a bottle with a label I did not recognize. "It is pisco, a favorite drink in Peru. Perhaps we could have a drink together. I see there are glasses here. I have been visiting in New York and in Chicago before this and this is the last of the few souvenirs I brought along."

It was near to six o'clock by now and, since I had usually had at least one good stiff whiskey by that time on an ordinary night, the idea appealed to me, although it was hard to get the stuff down once it had been poured and I had a glass in my hand.

"Welcome, Bishop," Thomas said in genuinely warm tones. "On behalf of everyone at Notre Dame, you are welcome, with or without your guns."

We raised glasses and sipped a little of the drink. Thomas spoke again.

"There are plenty of legends about you besides the pistol. Haven't I heard that you run the hills like a wolf at night?"

"Probably," Muñoz said, smiling again. "The legend makers are forever busy. What will they think of when I get back from the United States!" It was more an exclamation than a question. He sipped his pisco again. "No, I have no pistol and I most certainly cannot run the hills. But people like to believe such things. Perhaps they simply want to. Or perhaps they need to. It is all mixed up, much of religion, especially where I come from. It is one part faith, one part animism, another part a belief that bishops want to lead revolutions. It is no easy life, living up to the legends of the Red Shepherd." He smiled, a little ruefully this time.

"How did all this start?" Father Thomas asked. "I mean the stories about the pistol and so forth?"

"So many things start inside when people have great need," Muñoz replied, a touch of the actor's deliberation in his voice. "Who knows where so many things start? Where did the great spirit of Notre Dame come from that even I, the Bishop of Nowhere, have heard of it? Such things all start in the same place, in the hearts of people." Muñoz shrugged his broad shoulders. "For you the spirit of Notre Dame was born in the hearts of poor American Catholics who needed a symbol of unity, of identity when they felt oppressed. Yes, yes, I think very much Notre Dame was in the right place at the right time, so all the hopes and dreams of Catholics were invested in it. Is that not so?" Muñoz walked over to the window and gazed out at the campus that was just sinking under the spreading wave of the evening darkness.

"There is something in what you say," Father Thomas replied, "but we have tried to keep faith with the people too."

"Of course, of course," Muñoz answered, making a sweeping gesture with his arm as he turned back toward us. "There are always two parts to a myth, whether it is about the Fighting Irish or the Red Shepherd. Yes, of course. But the need for a myth so often exceeds what we actually do to deserve one! That is where legends are born, in the needs of the people that cannot be met in any other way. We have a saying in my country, *'Vale un Peru,'* It's worth a Peru, meaning it's worthless. So the need is so great that I am not surprised that the people believe that I carry an empty pistol."

"You've told them that you don't carry one?" Thomas asked.

"I gave up telling them long ago," Muñoz said, running his fingers through his thick, dark hair. "The people say I only wear it when it cannot be seen, when, for example, I have vestments on for Mass. That is part of the wonder of the legend, perhaps of all legends. When I walk among them in my ordinary clothes, they say I have left the pistol at home. They do not believe in the pistol because they actually see it. On the contrary, they believe all the more firmly precisely because they never see it." Muñoz sighed and took a sip of his drink.

"It is strange that something that does not exist has so much power. The lawyers in town, and the landowners, they all believe I go about armed, that I am a dangerous man." He smiled again as he looked first at me and then at Thomas. "In many ways I do not mind. It is helpful to have an air of mystery about oneself, something that may be this way or that, but about which no one is sure. And running the hills, well, that arose when I used to travel so much. But" —and he winked as he spoke—"perhaps that is not entirely bad either. The people then think that I know everything." Then he laughed and so did we as we finished our drinks and headed off to dinner before the bishop's evening talk.

I explained to him that the main course was what the students called "pavement chicken," a dinner of fowl that they claimed had been prepared by running over it with a truck. But Muñoz just laughed in that *Viva Zapata* way of his and cleaned his plate, talking, in between bites, about the unspeakable problems of poverty and ignorance that were the chief enemies of his work. "It is not the little sins the people commit," he said, patting his mouth with his napkin, "it is the big sins that have been committed against them." But it was time for us to go to the hall where he was to speak, so we didn't have any time to follow up on these matters. As we trudged through the crisp night air, with the snow squeaking and crunching beneath our feet, I wondered if Thomas was disturbed by the bishop's approach to things and whether he thought Muñoz would just stir up the priests, making them even more discontent with the plodding bureaucracy of the Catholic Church. Thomas did seem cautious as he introduced the bishop to the group, making the point of how different things were in South America. All to no avail, I'm afraid, since Muñoz proved to be so appealing, charismatic as they say, and, as with his own people and his pistols and running the hills, the priests and nuns seemed to think he had talked about things dear to their hearts even when he hadn't mentioned them.

What he did do was tell them about his work and the conditions of life on the Altiplano of Peru. "It is like climbing up the back of a great dead whale," he said, "to travel from one end to the other. And the people in some places have not yet learned to use the wheel. You pass through many centuries in one afternoon of travel. They live mostly on potatoes, they are riddled with TB, and they chew coca to lighten the pain of life. And the progress we have made is small, so small. Listen, my friends, we did establish a credit union with the help of some American missionaries so the people might begin to own a share of the land they work. But you have to outsmart the great Catholic landowners, yes, and the great Catholic lawyers too, to do it. After we established the credit union, one of these Catholic lawyers from Natividad, he said to me, 'We will have all that land you bought back within five years.' That is why I do not mind some mystery about my work. It gives me the edge with the lawyers."

He really didn't give a talk as such. After he explained his work for about fifteen minutes, he just asked for questions, and one of the first was whether he believed that priests should fight for changing the law of celibacy.

"I will tell you something," Muñoz answered, seating himself on the edge of the table behind which he had been standing. "I do not think that priests and nuns and brothers should fight for anything but justice and peace. These are the only things worth fighting for. But you should not waste your time in this world fighting against rules either for them or against them. Justice and peace are the issues on which we will all be judged. If we fight for these everything else will take care of itself."

This was not exactly the reply they were expecting and I don't think Father Kinsella expected it either but it sounded sensible to me. Father Thomas did raise his hand, however, and ask the bishop whether he supported the regulations of the Church about priests and members of religious orders. Muñoz smiled and said simply, "Yes, but they are not the issue in a world that needs justice and peace. I do not worry as much as some bishops do about them." That drew a round of applause. Then a young priest sitting in the front row cleared his throat and asked, "What about the theology of liberation? What about talk of priests being revolutionary leaders?"

Muñoz smiled again. "Ah yes, a favorite pastime for theologians, for teachers at universities." He glanced, a bright boyish grin on his face, toward Father Kinsella as if to remove any sting his remark might contain. "Excuse me, but I am sure you have your dreamers here at Notre Dame. They are, after all, everywhere." More laughter from the members of the crowd who were caught up by the bishop's manner. "And there is no doubt that these people—my people—need liberation. But we are a long way from revolution. We should always be a long way from violence. It is one thing to write a learned paper on it. It is something else to lead a revolution. Do you know, my friends, not one in three hundred of these Indians can read or write? Do you know that they are still their own worst enemy, families always leaving their little land, a few furrows to this son and a few to that, so that in the end not one of them has a scrap of it, so they always end up hopelessly dependent? Do you know that we are years away from helping them learn how to farm efficiently, or even save money . . . ?" His voice trailed off momentarily and was just above a whisper when he began to speak again. "And very few priests, very few of mine, are ready to lead a revolution. How many bishops are there who can give even a good sermon much less issue a call for revolution? We have bargaining power when the police or the army or the land-owners are afraid the people might rise. But it comes from a mixture of their fear and the people's needs. That is what my supposed empty pistol stands for. The idea of potential force. But we are far from force. We are very far from that." There were more questions and a great round of applause for the man who struck the assembled priests and nuns as a dedicated shepherd, red or not. I noticed that Father Peters slipped out the back door while the others were still applauding.

Father Allen joined us as we walked the bishop to the University Club to give him a sample of an American drink and to talk some more. Jack Allen kept chuckling about Muñoz's remarks about dreamers on university faculties. "By Jeez," he said, raising his glass to the bishop in the quiet club, "you hit it on the head about the dreamers. Great for the big picture, they are, but a little slow on the everyday practical work." The bishop laughed and the talk was pleasant. Father Thomas seemed as captivated by the bishop as everyone else had been, although he was not ready to give up on the need for rules and regulations. He mentioned Father Hesburgh's edict about protests as an example of what the world needed.

"Yes, yes," Muñoz answered. "Of course, in running a university, yes, but that is not what the university exists for. The university exists for justice and peace." Well, there was good-natured give and take on this until Father Allen cut through the seriousness. Raising the drink he had sipped carefully during this conversation, he looked at the bishop in mock seriousness.

"I tell you, Bishop, there's only one way to put an end to all this celibacy talk and all this mooning about over having deep interpersonals."

"What is that?" the bishop asked, taking the straight man role effortlessly.

"The Nebraska Plan. I've been pushing it the last couple of

years but, so far, it's no go. Maybe you can talk some other bishops into backing it."

"The Nebraska Plan?"

"Yeah, as I see it, all we have to do is buy up one of those big rambling resort hotels out in Nebraska that have been closed for years and fix it up as a treatment center for priests who spend too much time daydreaming about sex. You know, your crusader against celibacy and all that. Great talkers, most of them. Well, this would put an end to the talk for good. You see, we'd staff the place with the finest madams we could find, maybe hire 'em from Las Vegas. Then we'd fly priests in from all all over the country, by the planeload. We'd give them each a free week at the place to have his go at the whole thing, get it out of his system, then fly 'em back to work. Why, half of them would be so scared of a real woman, they'd flee immediately, and half of the rest wouldn't be able to get it up. By Jeez, you'd clear up all this talk in no time. Here's to the Nebraska Plan!"

"To the Nebraska Plan," Muñoz said, struggling to control his laughter.

It had been quite a day and when I went to bed I could not help but wonder at these two extraordinary people Father Thomas and I had met in the last few days, one in a play about Peru and the other from the country itself. It was too much for me to ponder and, thinking of the Nebraska Plan, I fell into an old man's heaven of a sleep with a smile on my face.

4

Chicago
February–March 1969

True enough, we went to the theater the next Saturday. We were met by Miss Moore's secretary, Helen Barnes, a businesslike lady in her fifties, who gave us our tickets, front and center, grand seats indeed. And the show was enjoyable, leaving out the interlude of ballet, that is, which revealed more of the male dancers and less of the plot than I was interested in. Maria, however, did look radiant, even in her dark makeup and a costume as cumbersome in some scenes as an old-fashioned nun's habit. Her voice was not for opera but it was sweet and clear and the wonderful old plot was handled with respect. They even had a bridge that seemed to lead off into the mists, wonderful magic the whole of it, and I didn't doze at all.

After the curtain calls we were welcomed backstage, where we could see the other side of the mysteries that had beguiled us for the previous two hours. It was like life itself, I thought, as Thomas and I glanced around at the rather dingy walls, the ropes and pulleys, and the real face of the stage sets, scratched and tacky-looking when the transforming lights were not playing on them. Maria came out of her dressing room, pulling back the voluminous sleeves of her costume as she approached us. You could see the greasy cast of the makeup on her beautiful features and the black wig, which looked so brilliant under the stage lights, seemed dull and stiff.

"Well, how are the fighting Irish?" she asked with just the slightest touch of acid in her tones.

"Oh, we're all for peace these days," Father Thomas answered, flashing a V sign with his hand. "You've made converts of us all."

"Oh, I thought that was your business." She leaned forward and gave me a kiss, well, more of a peck, the way she might have kissed her grandfather, but I was happy to settle for that. She shook Thomas's hand and said, "You two wait here, or take a look at the stage if you like. I have to change, then I'll have to meet some people. So wait for me, I'd like to have a visit with you." And with that, she turned, her garments making a great rustle, and made her way through the darting stagehands and cast members to her dressing room.

Nobody paid any attention to us. They were all busy closing up shop for the night. We wandered around some ropes and curtains to the stage proper, which was still dimly lighted. The bridge of the title, which looked like thonged leather from the audience, was actually made out of plastic, and was being folded back in sections by stagehands. When they had finished, it still protruded like the beginning of an arch just above our heads. The make-believe of it all, I thought, as I realized how well the illusion had been carried off.

"Sometimes, Austin," Thomas said as he turned toward me, shifting his overcoat from one arm to the other, "I wonder if we don't deal in make-believe too." There was a wry smile on his face and I wasn't sure exactly what he was thinking. Perhaps it was the effect of Bishop Muñoz, who had continued on his travels down to St. Louis and Houston but was expected back at Notre Dame in another week or so. Well, I had no time to inquire as Helen Barnes, a warm smile on her face this time, came through the semidarkness of the stage area to tell us that "Miss Moore would like you to come in now."

The dressing room was not nearly as large or grand as I supposed it would be. Functional, yes, that's the word, functional the way an old-time confessional was, with just enough room in it for the business that had to be carried out. Maria was in dark slacks and a black turtleneck sweater. A small gold cross suspended from a thin chain was her only decoration.

"Why, you look like a bishop," Thomas said good-naturedly.

"Oh, God, no." She smiled as she reached to the back of her hair to remove a pin that had gone astray. "That's your line too, Father. This is a cross I got when I marched with Cesar Chavez once."

"I should have known," Thomas replied resignedly, as though he expected she would tell him she also ran a secret bomb factory. Then he shifted his tone and his focus.

"The show was wonderful. And you were marvelous."

"Yes, indeed," I echoed. "A grand bit of theater."

"Well, thank you," Maria said, obviously pleased by our genuine reactions. "It's a wonderful story and I think the treatment is very good. Besides, it has something to say."

"There's no doubt of that. It's probably doing more good than my sermons."

"How nice of you to say that," Maria said, looking directly up at Thomas. "Although I'm sure you are well prepared. You're not the kind of man who doesn't prepare for things." Then it was her turn to shift mood and focus. "Helen has arranged for a light dinner back at the hotel. Can you two join us for a drink and a visit? I have to eat after these performances and it takes a long time to settle down so I can sleep."

I looked tentatively at Thomas and was mildly surprised when he said, "Yes, that sounds like a wonderful idea. We're staying in town tonight anyway."

"Fine," Maria said in a businesslike tone. "Let's go." She rose from her chair and pulled on a trench coat that Helen handed to her. Then she tied a silk kerchief around her head. Helen opened the door and we made our way down a narrow corridor to the stage entrance. A crowd had gathered in the cold, dark night to see Maria. A voice yelled, "Commie lover!" and somebody else booed but most of the greetings were warm and effusive as we hurried toward the car that was waiting for us.

It was not a long trip back to the Drake and, since Maria moved so swiftly through the crowds of people whose mouths were just opening in recognition of her, it seemed no time at all before we were in her suite. Helen Barnes disappeared into another room as we settled on a divan that faced north to the curve of lights that was Lake Shore Drive. Maria was businesslike as she opened a cabinet that contained liquor and glasses, asking for our orders over her shoulder as she bent down to remove some bottles. As she was pouring what I

might say were generous and welcome drinks, Helen Barnes
returned bearing a tray of cheese and fruit.

"Oh, thank you, Helen, just put them over there," Maria
said, pointing to a coffee table. Then she handed a drink to
her secretary and they both sat down across from us.

"Some sandwiches are coming up in a few minutes," Maria
said, raising her glass. "Happy St. Patrick's Day, a little in
advance!"

"Slainte," said I, and we all sipped our whiskeys.

"By the way, Miss Moore, since you are Irish . . ."

"Yes," she said with a smile, "although there were French-
men in the family tree somewhere too . . ."

"Well, Irish enough, then," Thomas went on. "My parents
are holding a St. Patrick's Day party a week from tomorrow
night. It's before St. Patrick's Day but they always do that
because the Irish Fellowship dinner is on St. Patrick's night.
They would like you and Miss Barnes to come. If you're free,
that is." Father Thomas seemed enthusiastic but tentative,
like a boy talking to a teacher he liked. "They only live up the
street a few blocks." He held out his drink toward the
windows as a pointer. "Right up there."

Maria looked at Helen Barnes, who, of course, gave no
indication of preference.

"Why not? It sounds like fun, although I must warn you
that we may not stay long. We try to rest as much as we can on
weekends in order to keep our energy up . . ."

"For the marches?" Thomas interposed with a smile.

"Well, partly, partly," Maria said with medium good
humor. "Now, tell me, Father, I understand your father is a
big man in this town. He doesn't have a gun collection and
want to bomb Hanoi, does he?"

"My father is a more subtle man than you'd think. And he
doesn't have a gun collection. Fishing is his game. And, as far
as the war is concerned, he's against it, believe it or not. Says
it's tearing the country apart."

"Next thing you'll tell me is that Mayor Daley's against it."

"As a matter of fact, he is. My father says Daley's against it
for the same reason. You know, here's something about
Daley you may not realize. He lives in a neighborhood where
boys have gone off to war and come home to tell him about it.
That's what turned him against it, the stories he heard about
Vietnam from the kids who grew up with his own children."

"But not publicly, certainly," Maria said, sipping her

drink. "Father, I don't know whether to believe your stories or not. People like your father and the mayor are not the big heroes of the peace movement in this country."

Blessedly, the light dinner of steak sandwiches arrived at this point and the conversation shifted again as we sat and munched. It had been a long time since I had eaten anything so late at night but it went down very well. Maria told story after story of how the play had been put together and how many struggles there had been to get the story and the characters right. After we finished eating, Maria got up and prepared another round of drinks. Then she picked out some fruit and curled up in the easy chair next to the couch where Thomas and I were sitting.

"I haven't talked to a priest, except on a picket line, in a long time." Maria's voice was suddenly more personal and it made me feel a little uneasy. I glanced at Father Thomas, who just sat there, as if he were listening to some lady tell him her troubles in a rectory parlor. It wasn't so much that she was telling her troubles—she didn't sound troubled—it was more that she wanted to talk about something that had meaning for her, the way people talk about old wounds that are now healed, or losses once the mourning is done with.

"You don't know much about me, Father, but I'm a Catholic, or however you say that these days. I was scared to death of priests when I was growing up. And they seemed to be all over the place where I was brought up in Boston." She paused again and looked at me. "Professor, how's your drink?"

"I'll help myself if it gets too washy," I answered, staking a claim on the scotch in case the conversation went on too long.

"Did you know I was married once, Father?"

"I think I read that someplace," Thomas answered.

"Not in the *Enquirer,* I hope. They get everything wrong. I was nineteen and still in college. He was a writer. We had dreams, artistic dreams, I guess." She sipped her drink and looked directly at Father Thomas. "But we didn't strike it off, we seemed to be pulling in opposite directions. It was more like being in an accident with someone than having a marriage. I was too young. Neither of us really knew what we were doing. I wasn't well known then, of course, and we didn't have any children, thank God. We might have passed on our streak of bad luck."

Maria gazed into the half distance, like somebody looking into a fireplace where embers of the past still glowed.

"I had a hell of a time with the Church when we tried to get an annulment. All kinds of questions, things that were none of their business. And they never granted it anyway. Did you know that?"

"No," Thomas replied simply. "I'm sorry to hear of it."

"It doesn't matter now anyway. Poor David drove off the Pacific Coast Highway one late night about a year after that." She broke her reverie and looked directly into Thomas's eyes. "That was almost as painful as the marriage and the divorce. But then I was all right with the Church again. Because he was dead, that's why, because this poor sensitive man smashed himself into jelly, I was 'free,' as the priest told me, 'free to marry again.'" A sad smile crossed her face.

"So, I've been wary of your—I suppose I can say our—Church, except when it's been fighting for the poor or for peace. And the people who do that in the Church don't get any thanks for it. Did you know that J. Edgar Hoover thinks priests in the peace movement are a threat to the country's security?" She laughed. "And he's been sending their dossiers back to the bishops! It's a crazy world we live in."

"Why are you so active for peace? Isn't that part of your Catholicism?" I thought Thomas sounded a little too serious as he said this, as though he was sticking up for the Church, which, of course, he saw as part of his job.

"I think it was the first time I marched with Chavez," Maria answered. "Maybe being a Catholic had something to do with it, but I'm a kind of fugitive Catholic at best. And when I first marched for Chavez, I was very nervous. Oh, I was established and all, but the people who run studios are like bishops in some ways. They don't want you to go against the established order. Then I heard Chavez speak. So simple, so pure, what a beautiful man! And he said that people's lives can be ruled by fear, the fear of losing what they have, whether it's money or fame or whatever. And he said that was the first fear and if you could get past that, nothing could hurt you, because nobody else could have power over you. Because you didn't let them have it. And I realized that's what I was afraid of, and that I was letting somebody else have power over me because of it."

"And you've gotten over it?" Thomas asked.

"Mostly." Maria smiled. "I don't even worry about critics

much anymore." She suddenly uncoiled and bounded out of
her chair. "This has gotten far too serious . . ."

"Yes," Thomas said with his best smile. "I'll be giving you
three Hail Marys and telling you to make a good Act of
Contrition next." And we all laughed and went back to
talking of other things, of Notre Dame and Thomas's work,
and even a few stanzas about me, the aging professor
emeritus. Well, it was an unusual evening and it did not end
until almost 1 A.M. We all parted with genuine warmth and
with a happy anticipation of meeting at the Kinsellas' St.
Patrick's Day party.

I had been to the Kinsella apartment—a great rambling
one with mellow woods and fireplaces in a stately old building
on Lake Shore Drive—but never for the annual St. Patrick's
Day party, an affair which, when I came to think of it,
Thomas himself was often too busy to attend. I'm not even
sure how much Mae Kinsella enjoyed it, seeing as old P.B.
held a sort of an open house that evening for all his old
friends, Irish or not. Mayor Daley and his wife always made a
brief visit along with many another local politician, not to
mention the assortment of business and union leaders, and
the Archbishop himself, Leo Williams. It was a night for
singing and dancing and sometimes P.B. would even have the
Irish pipers there, a grand evening indeed to kick off the week
of St. Patrick's Day itself.

We arrived at about eight and there was already a fine glow
on the evening. Mae Kinsella, holding a martini—I always
seem to remember her that way—was smiling at the doorway
and gave me a kiss as she welcomed us. She had a special
feeling of possession for her eldest son, for fair Thomas, who
had always been so good and had always made her so proud
of him. Well, there's been many an Irish mother like that,
whether their sons were priests or not. It wasn't that Mae was
so protective of him, exactly, but you could see that she had
invested a lot in him, that he was special and that in the midst
of a life with P.B. that was as unpredictable and exciting as
the St. Patrick's Eve party, Thomas had been a source of
peace, a kind of a mixture of a four-leaf clover and a
sacrament whose priesthood somehow guaranteed that the
Kinsellas would all land on their feet, not to mention being
forgiven their transgressions and saved too.

"Father Tom," she called him, putting her hand on his arm.

"You must tell me all the news. I haven't seen you for weeks. And"—turning to me with a gracious smile—"make yourself at home, Professor, and happy Saint Patrick's Day to you!"

Well, Thomas and his mother chatted for a little while at the edge of the milling guests, who were obviously ready for a good time. There were people in evening clothes and a few in what you might, if you were kindly, call Irish costumes, half a dozen priests and more than one military uniform, but mostly business suits with big fellows busting out of them, the lads from the banks, the union halls, and the construction business. A grand parade and all of them having a good time. As I made my way to the bar, P.B., Patrick Bailey Kinsella himself, hailed me, breaking away from a group of beefy, blue-suited associates to do so. He looked like the lord of the manor, which indeed he was, expansive and intimidating at the same time, but charming and hospitable nonetheless as he extended his manicured hand in greeting. P.B. was wearing one of his favorite outfits, gray slacks and a blue wool jacket. The tie, of course, was green.

"Austin," he said heartily, "I'm sure you'd like a drink to start the vigil of St. Patrick's Day properly." With his arm around my shoulder, we started to move toward the bar, a real one, mind you, in the paneled library.

"Have you seen the other Kinsellas?" he asked as guests made way for us. "I mean Joe and Martin and their wives. I'm a grandfather, and more than once, would you believe that?" He began looking around for his other sons.

"Joe! Joe," he called, heedless of the interruption he was causing in the normal social flow of the evening. "Bring Deirdre over here. I want you to meet a friend of mine."

The guests across whose bows he had launched this cannonball of an invitation pulled back a little as Joe, holding his red-haired wife's hand, broke away from a conversation and headed in our direction. P.B. was looking the other way by this time and signaling with his hand, not unlike a cop directing traffic, for Martin and his wife, Meg, to join us as well. That's the way it was with old P.B. and I wasn't surprised that Thomas didn't come to such gatherings on a regular basis. P.B. summoned his sons as though he was calling them out of the backyard when they were five or six. That's what their lives were like, I thought to myself, as Thomas's younger brothers joined their father and me, like biblical sons leaving the fields of harvest at the bidding of the patriarch.

"You remember Joe and Deirdre, Professor," P.B. said as he leaned over and kissed his daughter-in-law. "Joe's twenty-five now and they've got a nice start on a family. Isn't that right, DeDe?" P.B. smiled expectantly as though he was placing an order for another grandson.

Joe bore an amazing resemblance to his father as I remembered him years before. He had some of his father's presence too, I could see that, as he shook my hand and smiled, with just enough of a conspiratorial glint in his eye to let me know that his father's commands did not really bother him.

"And Martin and Meg," P.B. said as the middle son, a more heavyset man with straight black hair—the Kinsella good looks pressed slightly out of shape—joined us. "Martin and Meg have made me a grandfather too," P.B. said as I greeted them. Martin seemed anxious to please and there was no suggestion in his manner that he would ever do anything but exactly what his father told him to do.

"Get the professor a drink," P.B. said as he caught sight of the police superintendent just making his entrance.

"Well, you have wives that would both win the beauty contest," I said, wheezing some old-fashioned charm into the awkward meeting that P.B. had set up and abandoned when the head of the police arrived.

"What would you like to drink?" Martin asked, departing immediately when I said scotch and water.

"Well, Professor," Joe said, turning slightly toward his beautiful red-haired wife, "Deirdre was the Queen of the St. Patrick's Day Parade a few years ago."

"Come on, Joe, Professor Kenna doesn't care about that." There was something in her tone that attracted me to her, a little spunk, and I thought to myself that these two might be a good match for old P.B. and Mae one of these years. Martin's wife was also lovely but, like her husband, looking for cues as to how to please one of her father-in-law's old associates.

"Did you teach P.B. in college?" she asked pleasantly.

"I did, I did," I answered, but, before I could say more, a big fellow wearing a green tam above his business suit called out for attention.

"It's time for a song!" he shouted in a voice that hushed at least a part of the buzzing crowd.

"That's Muggsie Hoolahan," Joe said to me. "He's worked for my father for years. Kind of a mascot. P.B. loves to hear him sing."

"Now, now, Joey." Hoolahan was shaking a finger at P.B.'s youngest son. "We need quiet if we're to sing properly. What'll it be, folks, what'll we start with tonight?" This in a voice that had grown slightly thick with drink but choked with an urgent need to perform and please at the same time.

"What'll it be now?" he asked again.

"How about 'The Wind that Shakes the Corn'?" somebody called out.

"Just so," Hoolahan replied, a smile spreading across his face. "Just so. And a terrible sad song, as you may know. In 1798, good men from all over Ireland rose against the Crown and its troops. Now, the young man in this song, well, his sweetheart was shot by a British bullet. So he joined the rebels."

And with that, and on an uncertain note at first, Muggsie Hoolahan intoned the ballad for the crowd.

> "I sat within the valley green,
> I sat with my true love.
> My sad heart had to choose between
> Old Ireland and my love.

> "I looked at her and
> Then I thought
> Oh, Ireland was torn
> While soft the wind blew
> Down the Glen
> And shook the golden corn . . . ."

Well, on and on it went, growing sadder with every verse, and the smile on P.B.'s face getting bigger as he listened at the far end of the room. I drifted away once Martin had delivered my drink, sidling between couples and other guests, some of whom had begun to talk again even though Hoolahan was singing away like a mick Caruso.

I saw Father Thomas, his mother still at his side, near the entrance and decided to station myself with him and to survey the party, which was beginning to achieve a certain uncheckable momentum, from a safe distance. I did not want to be

asked to get up and tell stories about Rockne or great
Fighting Irish teams of the past.

A man taller and wider than Thomas had just approached
him, clutching a drink in one hand and lightly punching
Father Kinsella on the right shoulder. "How's the passing
arm, Father Tom? Your dad tells me you're keeping it in good
shape. Always wise to keep the passing arm in shape."

"Fine, Judge, fine," Father Thomas said as the big man
stumbled past him.

"How's the passing arm?" I asked as I drew close to him
but Thomas merely arched his eyebrows as a response and a
comment.

Muggsie had switched to some other mournful song when
the apartment door opened, and there, as though waiting for
an entrance cue, stood Maria Moore in a tweed cape. Helen
Barnes was just behind her. Well, it was a showstopper and it
even stopped Muggsie for a while as the guests, even those
whose moorings had been loosened by the freely flowing
whiskey, turned as though a spotlight had swept across the
crowd to direct its attention to the place where, for a
well-timed moment, Maria paused before moving toward
Thomas and his mother. Then the party started up again,
with Muggsie moving on to something called "Black Velvet
Band."

Father Thomas introduced Maria and Helen Barnes to Mae
and nodded toward me, a signal that I was to look after the
actress's secretary while he escorted Maria around the edges
of the gathering. I cleared my throat and, with as much charm
as I could muster, accompanied Helen as we trailed behind,
smiling and chatting, mostly with perfect strangers, one of
whom pressed IRA literature into my hands. We caught up
with Maria and Thomas just as they encountered P.B.

"Welcome to the Kinsellas'." P.B. beamed. "But be
advised, there are plenty of actors around here tonight." P.B.
made a deft move and Maria was on his own arm moving
through the crowd, meeting commissioners and presidents of
banks as well as a whole roster of politicians.

"Is Mayor Daley coming tonight?" Maria asked as she
accepted a glass of wine from Martin Kinsella, who had
brought Meg across the room to meet her.

"He'll probably be here a little later," P.B. answered. "But
you have to look sharp for him. Sometimes he's in and out

before you know it. I've known him to spend more time at a good wake than he does at some parties." P.B. looked directly into Maria's eyes. "You don't plan any demonstrations here, do you?" he asked in the tones of a man who was not against her, no matter what she had heard about him. Still, he did not want any unexpected interruptions in the party. He was using every bit of his charm to keep her under control.

"No," she answered, holding his eyes with her own. "No speeches on your home turf, Mr. Kinsella. I always play by local rules."

Muggsie's voice went dry and somebody else started to play the grand piano. Thomas made his way to the other side of Maria and, after a few minutes, Mae elbowed her way up to P.B.

"Ray, the doorman, just called. The mayor is on his way up." P.B. nodded and, making a quick excuse to Maria, took his wife's arm and headed for the front door of the apartment.

"Well, Father, this is quite a gathering. My mother had a name for all these Americans who make so much of being Irish."

"What was that?" Thomas asked, bending his head close to hers as a chorus of "The Minstrel Boy" swelled through the large living room.

"Shamrockery, that's what she called it, shamrockery." Maria smiled impishly.

"Well, I wouldn't say that too loud, not tonight anyway." Thomas smiled. "How would you like to see the view? There's a closed-in balcony over there."

"Fine," Maria said just as Mayor and Mrs. Daley, their faces beaming, arrived to almost as much attention as the actress herself had received.

"Unless you want to meet the mayor first," Thomas said. "My father's not exaggerating about how quickly he gets in and out of these affairs."

"All right," Maria answered. "As long as you're sure he won't throw me in jail."

"Oh, he wouldn't do that, not at an Irish party. Well, not at this Irish party anyway." Thomas escorted us around the perimeter of the crowd to a point where it was easy for P.B. to make the introductions, not forgetting to include me and Helen Barnes at the same time. Mayor Daley and his wife,

Eleanor, smiled and shook our hands, moving smoothly along as they had done at thousands of similar gatherings over the years. I wondered was it all a blur to them after a while as Helen Barnes and I followed Maria and Thomas out onto the balcony, a large, comfortable area which, after the sliding doors were shut, was relatively quiet. We stood looking down at the lights and the great swath of concrete walkway that stretched up from the Drake Hotel along the edge of Lake Michigan.

"I'm glad you could come, Miss Moore. These are really good people, just trying to enjoy themselves," Thomas said.

"Do you like parties like this?" Maria asked.

"Not much. I guess I've grown to like the quiet life."

"You're an interesting man, Father," Maria said without changing her gaze from the shore's edge, where dark wind-driven waves, their edges illumined by the streetlights, broke and smeared across the walkways. "How did you ever break away from your family? They must have had a strong hold on you."

"I'm not completely separated, I mean I didn't enter the cloister or anything when I joined the priesthood. But I am in another line of work."

"That must kill that handsome father of yours."

"We've had a few differences about it."

Helen and I were talking about the weather while this was going on, with me trying to overhear Maria and Thomas and missing half of it anyway. I could tell, however, that Thomas and Maria were getting friendly, that they were more at ease with each other, and were enjoying this quiet moment high above the city while the St. Patrick's Day party raged behind the doors a few feet away. Not that they were lovey-dovey, far from that. They were both on their guard against that, for different reasons, of course, but they seemed to intrigue each other, the great peace-marching actress and the handsome priest who was a bulwark of the established order.

"May I ask why you never married again?" Thomas inquired in a way that drained the boldness out of the question.

"It hurt too much the first time," Maria said, still gazing down toward the shore, "although I've had lots of proposals. For marriage and lots of other arrangements." Then she laughed, a soft, self-observing laugh. "I never accepted any of them." A muffled chorus of "Dear Old Donegal" came through the doors of the apartment, and from the streets below rose the filtered sound of the evening traffic.

"Besides, after David died," she said as though in a reverie, "I decided to put everything into my career. You can't get married and do justice to a family. I've seen it over and over again. Too many kids who know the nurse better than they know their mother and too many husbands competing with their wives. Not for me." She stopped and smiled as she turned toward Thomas. "Well, this is getting to be a serious conversation. Isn't this supposed to be a party?"

"The Irish always leave room for sorrow," Thomas replied. "Haven't you listened to some of those songs in there?"

"Why did you become a priest?" Maria asked suddenly. Thomas took his turn gazing down at the lake's edge.

"I guess it seemed that's what God wanted me to do . . ."

"You felt a call, then, is that it, a call from Christ?"

"Well, in a way, yes. I mean I didn't hear Him speak and I didn't have any visions. It just seemed the thing for me to do."

"Any regrets?"

"No," Thomas answered slowly, turning back to her, "no regrets. In fact, I like it a lot."

"Wouldn't you know it?" Maria asked, tossing her head back and laughing. "The first priest I've liked in my life and he has no regrets about his job."

Thomas blushed and didn't seem to know what to say for a moment.

"I'm only teasing, Father," Maria said, touching his arm playfully.

"We can be friends, you know," Thomas said, regaining his composure. "That's what life is all about, having friends."

"You sound like a banner, Thomas," she said, using his first name quite easily. "Or do you prefer Tom?"

"Tom is fine," he answered, and then he glanced over at me and Helen. "And I'm sure the professor emeritus would prefer to be called Austin."

We all smiled as I shook my head and confessed that I'd always disliked the name. However, I allowed that Maria could call me by it any time. We went back into the party after Father Thomas said, smoothly, I thought, "Maria, shall we rejoin the Irish?"

Pat O'Brien, who had come to town for the big parade later in the week, had arrived and was giving his Rockne locker room imitation. And not bad, I might say. The Daleys had gone but Archbishop Williams had arrived and was standing next to P.B. while the actor clipped off Rock's instructions to go "inside" and "outside them," and to "crack 'em, crack 'em," famous words out of the past. There was great applause, of course, and Maria went over to say hello to Pat O'Brien, who had once played her father in a movie, and to say hello to the Archbishop, who, in his usual way, asked, "And what line of work is it that you're in, Miss Moore?"

P.B. started to smile, then he took Maria by the hand and walked her back toward me and Helen.

"You mustn't take the Archbishop too seriously. He's very busy with his tireless work for souls." Then he laughed out loud and so did Maria.

In the background Muggsie was announcing the next song, a carol the Catholic children were alleged to sing in Belfast. Against the shouts back and forth between him and the guests Maria and Helen made their good-bys to the Kinsellas. Father Thomas suggested that we see them down to their car. As we stood in the foyer waiting for the elevator we could hear Muggsie rapidly chanting rather than singing back in the living room.

> "Up the long ladder
> and down the short rope
> To hell with King Billy
> and God bless the Pope
> If that doesn't do
> We'll tear him in two
> We'll send him to hell
> with the red, white and blue . . ."

As we stood waiting for the elevator, the big judge who had spoken to Thomas earlier came out to say good-by. He was now listing slightly although still clutching a drink as though it were an antitoxin as he ignored the rest of us and stepped close to Thomas. "Keep the old passing arm in shape, Father Tom. Remember that." Then he turned, sort of like a sailboat does, and headed back into the party. Our eyes followed him and in the half distance, above the bobbing heads and the raised glasses, we could see that P.B. had climbed up on a chair to lead a song for the crowd. It was a favorite of his, Thomas told me, not an old song but one that Brendan Behan

had scribbled off while sipping a pint one day. P.B. had made
it his song, however, and I can't help thinking of him to this
very day when I hear it.

The elevator doors opened as he pitched into it. We stood
listening as P.B. began to sing,

> "The bells of hell go ting-a-ling-ling
>   For you but not for me.
>   Oh, death where is thy sting-a-ling-ling,
>   Oh, grave thy victory? . . ."

The elevator doors were just closing as he hit the refrain
again.

> "The bells of hell go ting-a-ling-ling
>   For you but not for me . . ."

Needless to say, we drove back to South Bend, arriving in
the middle of the night again, but there was no snow and
there was an undeniable lightness in Father Kinsella's manner
the whole way. It had to do with Maria more than St. Patrick,
for he talked about her—and it was unusual for him to talk
much about women, except his own mother, and the Blessed
Mother, of course—and over the weeks that followed he kept
in touch with her. He went to the play again, with P.B. and
Mae, and he got notes from her and sent back notes of his
own. They had, tentatively but surely, become friends. But it
was a long time before they admitted just what good friends
they had become.

5
March 1969

The thing of it was that Thomas didn't know that he was falling in love, or he didn't let himself know, which, you might say, was a surprise in somebody so intelligent. But he was also guarded, as only the Irish can be when they hide the secrets of their own hearts from themselves, and he was a very dedicated priest who liked his work even when it involved hauling lost souls out of campus chapels or, on the quiet, delivering some important Church figure—I doubt that he was asked to handle anything less than monsignors—to the rest home to get dried out. So having a good woman friend was one thing but falling in love and getting married was an idea he didn't let himself think about.

But, on the other hand, he recognized that Maria was coming to mean something in his life, something very important since she was separate from his frankly possessive family, and separate from other priests and professors, somebody just as unusual and just as intelligent as he was and he could talk with her, not just about important things, but the little things as well. It was love all right, and Maria knew it, patient though she was and understanding too. She didn't want to complicate her own life any more than she had to and she didn't want to disrupt Thomas's life. But she loved him and she knew it. And she understood that he loved her even when he didn't let himself know it.

I could tell this, not because I was such an expert on love, but because there was no hiding the way his voice changed when he spoke about Maria, or the way he would sort swiftly through his mail until he found the letter from her that he was

223

looking for. Or how he would slip away to make a long-distance call, not saying to whom, and not needing to as far as I was concerned. And it had other effects on him—deepened him, I don't know—whatever it was, his spirits and his outlook were different, and only a blind man could have missed it.

A bittersweet situation, you might say, and you could sense that whenever they were together. They were getting close, not that they saw each other so much, but they were in regular communication even after the play's run ended at Easter time and Maria and her secretary and the wondrous fold-up bridge moved on to St. Louis for the next stop in the tour. Meanwhile Bishop Muñoz returned from his travels and spent a week on the campus, visiting Thomas and the priests at the Pastoral Institute regularly.

Bishop Muñoz decided that he would make a brief retreat before going back to his beloved highlands and Thomas agreed to go with him. He wanted some quiet time to think, that's the way I saw it, and besides he enjoyed the bishop's company, and I was delighted when he invited me to go along for the ride. Then Jack Allen, a man ordinarily wary of monasteries, said that he wouldn't mind going along either. We were an interesting crew as we drove the two hours down into Indiana to the old abbey whose father superior had issued a standing invitation to Thomas to come anytime, especially since Thomas had been so helpful in taking care of one of the monks who went around the bend the year before while studying at Notre Dame.

The drive was a lark in itself, Muñoz being so interesting and Allen adding ironic counterpoint now and again. Father Kinsella, as I saw it, was being influenced by the Peruvian bishop almost as much as he was by Maria, in a different way, mind you, but with a similar result in a softening of some of his hard edges and a modification of some of his more rigid views. The trip down into the Indiana hills, where the limestone monastery lay on a rise just above a river, was no exception. Father Thomas had asked the bishop about some of the problems he had to face on the Altiplano.

"They are not exactly like yours, Tomás, not like the ones the priests in your institute speak about. We would count it a blessing to have the problems of a well-ordered Church. No, we do not have those problems." He flashed that toothy smile, as infectious as Franklin D. Roosevelt's, as he looked at Father Kinsella in the driver's seat next to him.

"What do you mean, 'problems of a well-ordered Church'? I'm not sure I understand . . ."

"Well, my friend," Muñoz answered, pulling at his seat belt to make it more comfortable, "things run more or less according to plan. There are problems, yes, but there is a basic foundation in which they are set. There is a certain reasonableness to them. That would be a luxury in my diocese." He laughed, half to himself. "My bishop's motto should be 'We do the best we can.' "

"How do you mean?" Father Allen asked from the back seat, where the two of us were perched like a couple of old trophies.

"Perhaps you have to live in and with it as long as I have. When visitors come from the States they are, shall we say, surprised. Shocked perhaps, yes, at how we have to deal with things. Like this Archbishop from Chicago. Williams, Leo Williams. He came down because he supports a church in the barriada of Lima, the tar paper town the squatters from the country live in. He is a man I do not understand . . ."

"Hell, you'd need a team of psychiatrists to understand him . . ." Allen interjected.

"On the one hand," Muñoz said, letting Allen's remark go by with a smile, "he is concerned and he can be generous. On the other hand, he seems on the outside of things, a man who cares mostly about form . . ."

"I suppose you could put it that way," Father Thomas said with a grin. "My father says the Archbishop's trouble is that he doesn't believe in God."

"Oh, I don't know, I don't know," Muñoz said. "But he was concerned about our problems and our approach to them, I can tell you that. It was a typical day, the day he arrived with his secretary, Monsignor Mulcahy, and they were dusty and tired from the trip. And the altitude, that too. But he wanted to visit some of our parishes and see the work in the highlands." Muñoz paused. "What he did not understand, you see, and what many people do not understand is that we are literally on the top of the world and at the end of the world too. There is nothing we can do for many of the ills of the region, nothing that we can do to undo history, nothing to change the hard truths." The bishop turned halfway toward us and put his arm up over the seat behind Father Kinsella's back. "First, I drove the Archbishop in my jeep to visit an old man who was very ill. I did not think he would live out the day. And a woman was there and two children, small boys hanging onto their mother's skirts. And I went into the hut where the dying man lay and the Archbishop crouched in behind me. And I talked to the man for a while and said a prayer and we left. The Archbishop wanted to know about the couple, were they husband and wife and why had I not given him the last sacraments? Those were logical questions, you see, from a well-ordered United States Church. And I told him, no, they were not married. And he asked, what of the children? Could I not fix the marriage on the man's deathbed and give them a real father? And I said nothing as we drove along through the poor villages, hoping Father Fernando would not be in when we stopped by the next church. But it was bad luck that day, for Fernando was there, in the square, in a dirty old cassock, holding one of his bastard children in his arms and talking to the woman he has lived with for years. I don't think the Archbishop understood exactly what the situation was, although he seemed quiet, like a man in shock almost, as we drove back later toward Natividad. He began to ask about the dying man and was I going to stop and see him again. I said that I was and the Archbishop began to talk again about fixing up the marriage and he would do it, if I wanted, because he had special faculties from Rome. He seemed very nervous about it, very concerned about the man's soul and the marriage. And as we came close to the hut again I thought he would suffer an attack, he was so excited and upset at what he thought was my indifference. And when I visited the dying man and did not anoint him or attempt to marry him, the Archbishop was almost speechless. So I finally told him, as we got back in the jeep, 'Archbishop, that man is the woman's father. He is also the father of her children. Not even special faculties can make a marriage there. There is nothing we can do but be with them and comfort him and bury him when he dies. But we cannot fix his marriage, no matter how much we would like to.' The Archbishop turned a little pale and said no more about my pastoral problems. They are not, you see, from a well-ordered world. They are the real world and filled with pain. So we do what we can but it is not much . . ."

The story of the man dying high in the Peruvian mountains

quieted down our spirits, turning us thoughtful for the
remainder of the ride. I understood then why Muñoz just told
people to work for justice and peace and not to worry about
other things so much. Well, it wasn't long before we were
driving up the gravel road that led to the monastery, a
building out of another age with a grand bell tower and a
cloister walk too.

Guests were housed in what they called the "new wing,"
new when Harding was in the White House maybe, and the
high ceilings and dark wood trim in the rooms reminded me
of Notre Dame. We had basins to be filled by pitcher from the
washroom down the corridor, where the tile floor was like
that in an old barbershop. Father Superior—his name was
Flavian—saw us to our rooms, gliding along in his long black
mantled cassock like he was on rollers. He nodded a farewell
after getting us situated, and then, his arms folded under the
front layer of his habit, drifted away as silently as smoke.

"Jesus," Father Allen said, "these places never change.
Look at these old porcelain doorknobs. They must be in
every religious house in the country."

"I think I'll just take a walk," Thomas said after he joined
me and the bishop and Father Allen in the hallway. "I'll go
with you, Tomás," Bishop Muñoz said. "There is time before
dinner."

After they left, Father Allen took my arm and asked, "Is
there anything interesting in your room?"

"Not much," I answered. "Unless you want a Papal
Blessing from Benedict XV."

Father Allen went by me into my room, glanced at the
faded Papal Blessing with a piece of withered palm sticking
out from behind it, and began to open the drawers of the
bureau. I watched him from the doorway.

"Never can tell what you'll find in these old places," Allen
said, half muttering to himself as he worked through the
largely empty drawers. He tossed some old prayer books and
another elaborately entwined piece of Easter palm on top of
my bed. "Junk! Nothing but junk."

"What did you expect to find exactly?"

"You never know. I found a whole set of silver plate in one
of these places once. They leave the damndest things around
these old monasteries."

He slammed the last drawer closed and looked up at me.

"Austin, what do you think is on Tom's mind these days?"

I paused, for it was clear that Father Allen knew the answer.

"Well, I think he's trying to sort some things out. You know, he's still a very young man . . ."

"Hell, I know that," Allen said, frowning as he searched for a package of cigarettes. "It's this actress, that's it, isn't it?" He placed a cigarette in his mouth.

"Has he talked to you about it?"

"Hell, no. Just a guess. He's been different, preoccupied. I figure that he's got to be thinking about this Maria Moore."

"Yes, I daresay you're correct. Is that why you came along?"

Allen did not answer right away. He took a long drag on his cigarette and blew the smoke in a rolling cloud across the old room. "Well, Austin, I'm not much for these nuthouses otherwise. I thought I'd just tag along for the fun."

"Well, I doubt that he'll talk much about it. I'm not sure he knows what to make of it. I believe he looks on his relationship as a good friendship, nothing more than that."

Allen nodded his head as though he understood. "Well, Austin, shall we take a walk too? Or would you prefer a little drink before they sound the supper bell? Like I say, you never know what you'll get in these places."

Well, there was no choice there, as far as I could see, none at all, so Father Allen got a bottle out of his bag while I went down to the washroom for some water. We were sitting with our drinks when Bishop Muñoz and Thomas returned.

"What's this? Drinking on retreat?" Thomas asked with a smile.

"Retreating while drinking, that's how I see it," Allen replied. "Will you join us?"

Thomas shook his head but the bishop accepted. I looked over and I could see that Jack was about to say something and then thought better of it.

"I think I'll go down to the chapel for a while," Thomas said. "But I might have a drink with you tonight." He started to leave and then turned around. "It's peaceful and quiet here, isn't it?" he asked, and was gone.

We sat sipping our drinks in silence, and it was in silence that Thomas was dealing with whatever his feelings were about Maria, a silence which neither the bishop nor I nor Jack was free to enter. I wondered again at the whole thing, since I was there when the two of them met, and it was clear that

Thomas was resisting the truth, although I thought it would have to catch up with him someday. And Jack Allen was mildly worried about him, afraid he would turn in "his book and cup," as Allen said, and leave the priesthood and the promising career that lay before him. The bishop said little and, considering his normal work, it probably seemed a less than momentous problem.

We saw Thomas again at the dinner, if you want to call it that, which was served in the refectory at long tables, with the monks chomping away energetically at the stew, mostly vegetables, that finally got passed down to us. A young monk, standing at a lectern above the heads of the community members, was reading aloud from the works of Blessed Hugo, the founder of their order, all about wrestling with the flesh and such like. Not to my taste any more than the meal was. But the monks had a clean-the-plate club going, as far as I could see, and didn't seem to pay any attention to the reader anyway.

After supper we were making our way out of the hall when Father Flavian floated across the tiles toward us, smooth as a hockey puck sliding toward the net.

"Father Kinsella," he called. "May I talk to you?"

We stopped and Thomas nodded.

"Come up to my office, if you don't mind. I want to ask your advice on something." We looked expectantly toward Father Flavian and he waved us all along as well. We followed him up the stairs, down a corridor, and into a large office with big, old-fashioned windows that looked out on the river. On the abbot's large desk stood a pair of wine bottles and a sheaf of papers with colored designs on them.

"I know you're here for retreat but I also know you've had experience with some of these problems. I know you helped us out when Father Anthony got sick last year."

"What's the trouble?" Thomas asked, looking reluctantly destined to get involved in the life of the monastery even when he was trying to escape it for a few days to think about his own life.

"Well, Father Anthony's been acting up again. Ever since he had his trouble in grad school at Notre Dame, we've had him working on the farm. The doctor said it would be good for him." The Superior leaned forward on his desk, pushing some of the papers out of the way as he did. "Well, as you know, we keep silence during the workday. Now, Father

Anthony hasn't been saying anything but he's been working on the hayrick." He paused again. "And he's been tossing these bales of hay down and hitting the other brothers with them, knocking them flat all over the place. Never says a word, just shoves a bale of hay off the rick as it goes by. Last week, he knocked Brother Adelbert cold. He has a concussion and he's still in the infirmary. And today he knocked Father Jason over and broke his shoulder . . ."

Well, it was hard to keep from the giggles and I dared not look at Father Allen, who was covering his face with his hands, as though he had a headache. Bishop Muñoz merely looked bemused and I wondered whether he would put this in the well-ordered problem category. Father Thomas looked relieved, although he fought off a smile as he listened to the story of the hostile hay baler.

"Has Father been taking his medicine regularly?" Thomas asked as a prelude to a brief discussion of the case, which, it seemed to me, only needed the application of common sense. Which is what Thomas gave Father Flavian, seconded by Father Allen along with a smiling nod from Bishop Muñoz. The abbot seemed relieved and grateful, promising to get Father back to his doctor before he killed somebody in the barnyard, and we got up to go. Then he pointed to the bottles on his desk.

"These are our new wine bottles. We make some excellent wines, as you may know. And we are getting a good market share, for monastery wines, that is. But we need a new image, something more, well . . ."

"Monkish?" Thomas asked, a smile beginning to break out on his handsome face.

"Exactly," the abbot answered. "And here are the designs for our new label. Would you care to look through them?"

"Some other time, perhaps," Father Kinsella replied, and we made our good nights to the abbot, who was still shuffling through the batch of label designs when we closed the door to his office and headed back toward our rooms. Something about the incongruity of the abbot's problems had braced our spirits and, like the bishop's story of life in the Peruvian highlands, made our own concerns, even our concern about Father Thomas and Maria, seem less important than before. We decided on a good-night drink in Bishop Muñoz's room, which was larger and better furnished than ours.

"A privilege of rank," Muñoz said. "They always save the best room for the bishop."

"Yes," Allen said, twisting the knobs of the old floor-model radio that stood against the wall. "Let's see if we can pull in the A and P Gypsies on this." Father Kinsella brought in a bottle that he had tucked in his bag and I went to get the water again. We laughed at more stories about the strange quirky condition of things within the Church, which, to me, had come to seem a great, sometimes heroic, sometimes ragtag parade of people, men and women, sinners all, but most of them trying to do their best. "To justice and peace," Thomas toasted, raising his glass toward Bishop Muñoz. A fine toast at that as we settled down to more good talk about the characters we had all known across the years.

Well, an hour or so slipped by and the conversation drifted, by some unconscious pull, to the subject of priests and women. We were getting close to the bone, it seemed to me, but Thomas seemed eager to talk about it.

"We should talk of men and women," Bishop Muñoz said, "not just priests and women. We should not make ourselves too special a case."

"Have you had any woman influence you?" Thomas asked directly. "Besides your mother, of course?"

The bishop smiled good-naturedly and sipped his drink, letting the twinkle play in his eyes as he did.

"That is an American's question, Tomás. We cannot help but have women influence us. It is normal if we do not hide away from the world. When men hide they begin to throw bales of hay at each other and keep their vows of silence at the same time."

"Seriously, seriously," Father Thomas said. "They say Teilhard de Chardin was strongly influenced by women all his life."

"Yes," Allen said. "And they practically buried him without a funeral."

"He could not have been in touch with the universe," the bishop said, "if he had not been in touch with women, real women, that is."

The conversation went on along this line, a little theoretical, it seemed to me, and even Bishop Muñoz wasn't telling everything he knew. Then Thomas turned to Father Allen and asked, "Jack, have you ever been in love?"

The mood of the room shifted from merriment to a tense thoughtfulness as Allen lifted his lion's head up slowly, as a man would to make sure that a question had not been asked in jest. He smiled and looked intently at Thomas, hunching his shoulders as he leaned slightly forward, a cigarette in one hand and a drink in the other.

"Yes, Tom, I've been in love." He drew on his cigarette. "I don't know about Chardin, I don't know much about the theory of it all. I just know I was in love . . ." He looked at the bishop. "And I'll bet you have been too. It happens to good men all the time."

Muñoz said nothing; he just looked at Jack seriously and attentively, as though Allen had struck a chord finally on a problem that was never well-ordered.

"It's the toughest thing in the world, Tom, the toughest thing for a priest," Allen said, speaking softly. "I was in love years ago but I broke it up. Maybe I'm still in love, I don't know. It was the biggest battle of my life to give her up. She was a nurse. This was years ago; I met her after I had my stomach operation, the time I nearly died. There was no acceptance of the idea then, none at all . . ."

Allen broke off, shaking his massive head slowly. "Well, that was a while ago. It was hard to face it. It was like having a fifteen-round championship fight with yourself. That's where the battle was . . ." He did not sigh but Thomas wondered whether, as Allen looked back on this victory, this having kept faith, he was free of regret.

"So I've done what was expected of me. Jesus, that's gone out of style altogether now." He sipped his drink again. "But one thing I know. It's better to have known what real love was than to imagine it the way so many poor bastards do. It's better to feel sexual attraction than to have crazy notions of what it's all about."

"Are you still in touch with her?"

"Cards, mostly. Christmas and things like that. She's married and has kids. I even married them when she asked me to. It's a funny thing. It goddam near broke me, believe it or not, but I'm glad it happened. And I think the fact that we loved each other helped her too, helped her in her marriage."

"Do you think she still loves you?"

"I can't afford to let myself think about that. Hell, you've got to be realistic, you've got to take things as they are."

Thomas was grateful that Allen did not press him for

details of his own friendship with Maria. Allen's way of being sympathetic was to reveal some of the scars on his own roughhewn heart and to pretend they didn't hurt any more. Jack was a man who understood suffering, however, and the complex situations into which people so easily got themselves. He was a realist, that's why he kept his guard up, seeming almost cynical sometimes in order to protect himself from any more hurt. Thomas looked across at his old friend and saw something new in the man with the deeply lined face who had always seemed so settled and secure, the victor in many battles with himself and life.

Allen suddenly looked undefended, not shamefully so, more noble than that, for he was a man getting older who had triumphed over what used to be called temptation in a Church where it was no longer the fiery and hidden demon that it once was, a man who had closed a door on a great love and turned back to duty. All at a far higher price than any of us suspected. The bishop was very quiet, as though he recognized the depth of Father Allen's unexpected confession. Allen seemed to be still in love with the long since married nurse, their impossible passion tamed and domesticated in a distant house with children and a dog and a husband she liked but might never love the way she had loved Allen. That love and a hundred wonders about it were all quite alive just below the surface of Allen's craggy face as he looked at us with no funny remark to cover up his deep feelings.

"Tom," Allen finally said, watching the line of smoke that rose up from his cigarette, "you're at the age where you have to be settled about these things. You know that, don't you?"

"I think I'm settled, Jack." Thomas sighed. "But maybe it's better to have problems like this than problems like Father Anthony."

"Such problems are the only ones worth having," the bishop said gently.

We all smiled and I poured myself another drink.

"Yes, I suppose so," Allen said quietly. "Life gives us surprising combinations. I mean, they surprise us all the time. Hell, the four of us are a surprising combination, especially to be found in this place. But I mean the people who get together and why." He drew on his cigarette again. "I sometimes think that half the marriages I know are held together because there's some other love just off stage, just out of view. Hell, there are all kinds of priests who are keeping marriages and families together because the wives are in love with them. They provide things the husbands don't, tenderness and understanding mostly. Sometimes there's sex and sometimes there isn't." He puffed on his cigarette again. "Surprising combinations, that's what I mean. People who can't get married for one reason or another but who help keep the world going in some way, like it was a big computer that works because some secretary kicks it once a day or fixes it with a hairpin."

We sat in a comfortable and settled kind of silence, like the one that comes after you find out somebody is going to make it after a bad sickness. There was no embarrassment at Father Allen's very human revelations. They had power in them, especially his vision of a universe patched together and held in a wobbly orbit by impossible loves, a bittersweet notion if ever there was one.

"You are a good man," Muñoz said softly to Allen. "A brave man. It is hard to speak of the love one finds in life. And it is always surprising, always surprising."

I wasn't too sure what Father Thomas was thinking about all this or whether he was thinking of the man who fathered his own daughter's sons in the Peruvian highlands, or of the daft fellow giving the purity speech in the Lewis Hall chapel back at Notre Dame, or of the half sad, half comical figure of Father Anthony felling the monks with the bales of hay, like a silent movie the whole thing. But he was thinking of Maria, and that friendship with her, especially against the patchwork background of life inside the Catholic Church, wasn't such a bad thing after all. Thomas looked at his watch.

"Strange combinations, that's right, Jack," he said as he stood up. "If you gentlemen will excuse me, I've got a call I want to make."

6

Spring 1970

Father Peters went back to Chicago and hung on in the inner city work, keeping in touch with Father Thomas in the meanwhile, while efforts were made to arrange some teaching position for him at the University. Not much was open but finally an opportunity arose for an assistantship in the liturgy program and the Archbishop gave him permission to come to Notre Dame. It was not much of a job really, but he had a degree in the subject, and he had a roof over his head as well as the encouragement and support of friends. Since I had known him at the Pastoral Institute, Father Thomas invited me to come for breakfast after I attended Father Peters's early morning Mass.

I had been a little worried about the Mass, since with these liturgy experts you never knew whether they would arrive in Army fatigues or a top hat and tails, or whether they might talk you to death before they ever got to the consecration of the Bread and Wine. Father Peters was a pleasant surprise, saying Mass straightforwardly and no sermon at all; fine, except he seemed to twitch a lot. No matter, we were out in the sunshine and on the way to the priests' breakfast room on good time, the latter being the yardstick by which we old-fashioned Catholics rate our priests, four stars going to the man who can turn you out of Sunday Mass, sermon and all, within forty-five minutes.

I had been to the breakfast room a few times before, although the laity were not generally invited, seeing as it was a clerical domain, one of the last places that the priests had been able to keep to themselves, what with women storming

the altar and ready to take over in the rectories if you gave
them half a chance. Father Peters seemed a little unsure of
himself as we walked along.

"I think you'll like it here, Fred, there's plenty to do all the
time. In fact, as Austin can tell you, it's almost a way of life,
teaching here at Notre Dame."

I nodded professorially.

"Feels good already, Tom," Father Peters replied, scanning
the campus and the passersby, students mostly, all of whom
gave us a friendly greeting. "I feel like I've found a home
here."

"It is a lot like a home," Father Thomas replied, "with all
the discomfort and consolation which that implies."

As we arrived at the breakfast room we couldn't miss the
large sign that had been Scotch-taped to the door: "Toaster
Broken." We entered anyway. There were a dozen or so
priests seated at the tables, which were covered with white
cloths and the litter of the waves of breakfast eaters who had
come and gone already. Jack Allen was still there, spinning
yarns and smoking cigarettes, and he waved to us as we
entered and took our places.

There was mostly small talk after we ordered some eggs
and coffee, the mood of the room subdued, like an undertaker's outer office, with an occasional burst of laughter from
Father Allen's table. Young Father Simmons was there,
enjoying the older priest's stories, while two other priests
looked uncertain about what to make of him. Father Peters
glanced around a good bit, like a coal miner blinking his way
back into the daylight. Occasionally he would sigh, the way
you do after you've just survived a near accident, while
Father Thomas went along telling him about events of the
day, such as the meetings he had to go to, one with a pack of
fund raisers, Cunningham and Cunningham, and another
with the representatives of a devotional group, the White
Army, who wanted to have a holy whoop-de-doo at the
Athletic and Convocation Center, the twin domes, which the
students, in their usual mischievous way, called "The Big
Bra."

While we waited for our breakfast another priest, silver-
haired and carrying a prayer book—and not many did that
any more—came through the doors and headed straight for
the toaster, dropped in two pieces of whole wheat, and stood

there for a little while before he announced, "The toaster's broken." Well, even I knew that, and nobody paid him much mind at first. Then he came over and tapped Father Thomas on the shoulder.

"Tom," he said, as irritated as a fellow who had found a fly baked into his blueberry muffin, "the toaster's broken."

"Yes, Gerry, there's a sign on the door about it," Father Thomas said calmly as his breakfast was placed before him.

"Nobody told me about it," the priest remarked. "Why doesn't somebody tell us about these things?"

It wasn't much of a storm, of course, but it was the kind of thing that drove the devotees of the well-ordered life up the beanstalk. That was part of the life of the clergy, I thought to myself, and any alteration in the expected lineup of the day, any brush with the uncertain schedule most people followed was very disruptive to the people, like these priests, whose existences were lived in and through a big institution. Well, old Gerry sat down next to a fellow who was reading the morning paper and he got a grunt and a snap of the front page for his pains in telling him the toaster was out of order.

"Things don't change in these places," Father Peters said morosely as he picked at his scrambled eggs.

"We clerics," Father Thomas replied, "are an example of the immutability of a species." The priests at Jack Allen's table had left and he and Father Simmons moved over to the empty seats at our table.

"Say, Tom," Allen began in mock serious tones, "did you know the toaster's broken? Could you call maintenance and have them send a couple of fellows over right away? Or wire Ted Hesburgh to come back from visiting the White House with a new one?"

It was sardonic antidote, the craggy Allen's specialty, and even Father Peters laughed freely. Then there were introductions all around and Father Thomas, sensing that Allen was in a story-telling mood, laid some bait on the water for him.

"Jack, that table of yours was pretty raucous this morning. Have you been telling stories again?"

"No, Tom," Allen said, lighting a fresh cigarette. "Nothing like that. I was trying to help the good fathers we were sitting with. Isn't that so, Andy? I feel that the time has come for them to get thinking about the big changes that are coming, the ones when they're going to be off the dole and out in the world of work. No more money falling out of the sky like manna, they're going to have to get off their asses and work for a living. Comes as a terrible shock to them."

"And just what did you have in mind?" Father Thomas asked, straight-man fashion.

"Well," Allen began, "I've been trying to think of jobs that will preserve something of what they had when they were in the clergy. Something with a uniform, I figure, so that everybody'll recognize them, something to keep up their dignity, and they're used to special clothes. A doorman, for example. Now, your average doorman looks good, has everybody saying hello to him, and is helping people find their way. Very priestly, as I see it. You would rule out your ticket taker as not being dignified enough. But your toll booth operator can be very presentable. Meeting people all the time, a kind of a mediator of life's journeys, and taking up a sort of a collection all day long. Very suitable. So I was telling the fathers to get their bids in early and maybe to practice a little to get used to the idea."

This exaggeration, marvelously acted out by Father Allen, seemed to cheer Father Peters considerably. It reassured him that he had not signed on for ten thousand breakfasts of broken toasters. It was the kind of cheer Allen was good at dispensing, for what sounded cynical was soft deep down. He was a man with a great eye for the foibles of clerical life and humor was obviously a means of survival for him.

We all had second cups of coffee as Father Allen continued to regale us with stories about eccentric clergymen he had known. As the laughter died down Father Peters, taking a cigarette Allen offered to him, asked, "Are there any really normal guys functioning?"

"Normal is a broad range," Father Thomas interjected, offering Father Peters a little support, as I saw it, and trying to ward off some example from Allen that might strike too close to the problems Peters had struggled with so long. I held my breath a second or two as well, feeling the wrong story might discourage Father Peters just as he was getting his feet on the ground. Father Allen knew nothing of the reasons that Peters had come to the University, as far as I knew at least, although, grizzled old dog that he was, he could sniff out the truth in every garbage pail on campus.

"Oh, yes, yes," Allen was saying, nodding his head. "Those here present, for example. But you know what

Satchel Paige says. Don't look back. The bastards may be gaining on us."

"I'm afraid you and I have to go meet Cunningham and Cunningham, Jack," Father Thomas said. "Are you ready for the latest fund-raising scheme?"

"Hell, Tom," Allen replied, beginning to rise from his chair, "I was inoculated against these guys long ago. What do you think they'll propose today, selling cemetery plots to the fans in the football field? Jesus, I can see it now: 'Spend eternity where you spent your life, with the Fighting Irish pounding over you every Saturday afternoon.' Why, that would be a money-maker, wouldn't it?"

"Well," Father Thomas said, folding his napkin carefully and taking a glance at Father Peters as he did so, "I hope they don't show us a movie, 'The Wonderful World of Jesus,' the way that last group did. We'll have to hear them out, in any case. Austin, would you mind showing Fred around? If you have time."

"Not a'tall," I said in my best fake brogue, seeing that I was long on time and felt bad for Father Peters, who from the look on his face wasn't in from the storm yet. "Have you seen the library, Father?"

And, with that, we were up and off, letting Kinsella and Allen, with Simmons trotting alongside like an affectionate setter, go to their meeting with the fund raisers. Not that Notre Dame ever had much to do with professional fund raisers, seeing they were so good at it themselves, what with their well-known name and slick fellows running finances over the years. They weren't quick to let the name of Notre Dame be used by anybody else, even if they promised real gold for the dome. That's part of how these presidents, going all the way back to that clever Frenchman, Father Sorin, developed their instincts for power, the power of the purse being the key to the whole thing.

Father Peters and I strolled in fairly leisurely fashion back across the wooded quadrants to the library, the one with the big mosaic of Jesus, "Touchdown Jesus" running down its side. Father Peters wanted to see Monsignor Jack Egan, an old friend from Chicago, who kept his offices in the library.

"How do you like it so far?" I asked as we made our way across the marble lobby to the elevators.

"It's fine," Peters answered. "Different, but fine. I hung around Chicago too long. I'm going to start seeing a doctor here in town. I want you to know that, Austin. And I'll feel a lot better when I can start teaching."

Well, I had no inclination to ask about, or even hear from him about his treatment, so I just backed off a bit, wishing him well and leaving him at Jack Egan's door. He did seem a different man than he was when I had first heard his sad story but I still felt just the slightest bit uneasy. I knew I felt sorry for him but I also felt concerned for him, the way you might as you let your little boy cross the boulevard on his own for the first time. Enough, I said to myself, and departed, knowing he was in good hands, and wanting to catch some of the fund raisers' presentation if I could.

7

Autumn 1973

Things seemed to flow along as smoothly as the St. Joseph River snaking its way through downtown South Bend. Father Peters was making the best of it but, of course, I didn't see him that much, just now and then, at the University Club or on the campus, and he had appeared, on those intermittent occasions, to have a livelier step and a brighter eye. The fund raisers, turned down quickly by Father Thomas, had departed only to be replaced by squads of others who lined up at Notre Dame like the cripples at Lourdes, all of them wanting the same cure, a slice of the revenue. And the White Army had to look for other camping grounds too, not that they hadn't been willing to pay and not that Notre Dame wasn't always ready to accept, since they rented the space regularly to ice shows, Airstream camper reunions, and God knows what. It was the White Army's idea of swathing the Athletic and Convocation Center in blue muslin, one of those outdoor art events, blue

muslin, mind you, in honor of the Blessed Mother, that put
them off. I marveled at the ideas people came up with and
was grateful that Notre Dame had the good sense to turn
them away. That was one of the jobs Father Thomas had and
enjoyed doing, especially if Jack Allen was there to add a
dash of bitters to the brew.

I was in Thomas's office, years later, on the afternoon the
call came. He and Jack Allen were listening to a fellow named
Andrew Rans, a fast talker if ever I heard one, kind of
angular and thin with the lean and hungry look Shakespeare
warned about, and representing Brother George's Bee Farm,
some offshoot of a monastery out on the plains, where they
were making honey by the ton and wanted to name some of it
Notre Dame Nectar. Jack Allen just sat in a corner, chewing
on a piece of paper, something he did when he was cutting
down on cigarettes and trying to hold his temper at the same
time.

"Just think, Father Kinsella," Rans was saying, "Notre
Dame Nectar. We'll have a label with the Golden Dome on it.
It'll be big, the dome on every grocery shelf in America, the
biggest trademark identification since the NBC peacock."

I thought I heard Allen groan a bit but Father Thomas just
sat there, his arms folded, a look of bemusement on his face.

"The honey of the Fighting Irish. You know, Father, I
don't have to remind you that people are looking for spiritual
nourishment these days. And here's the tie-in, honey made by
Brother George, a holy monk, the purest honey with the
strength of Notre Dame to back it up. And you get ten cents
on every jar sold. That's two forty a case and multiply that by
the thousands and what have you got? Let me tell you, a very
sweet profit." He laughed at his own joke, which didn't help,
and went on, apparently oblivious of the reception he was
getting.

"Why, Father," he said, ignoring me, "do you know that
just thirteen days before he died Pope Pius XII gave an
inspiring address to an international congress of beekeepers?
Think of that, we can put the papal seal on the back, a nice
tie-in, that associates yourselves in loyalty to the Holy See.
Let me read you what the Pope said. 'Some day we will
experience and see in heaven that the ocean of His light and
His eternal love is infinitely sweeter than honey.' Think of it,
Notre Dame and the Holy Father and the sweet holy nectar of
Brother George. A natural food, I might add. And what's

better than that? The Lord didn't promise a land flowing with
milk and yogurt, you know . . ."

It was here that the phone rang on Father Thomas's desk, a
sign, during an interview, that something important was up.
Otherwise, Thomas would have had his secretary hold his
calls.

"Yes?" he said softly into the phone. "Look, can I call you
back in a few minutes?"

Father Allen took over as Thomas continued to field the
call in rather subdued tones. Apparently the caller didn't
want to hang up.

"Well, Mr. Rans," Allen said, tossing his chewed wad of
paper into an ashtray, "this has all been very interesting,
Brother George and his little bees and all, but we would
never lend the University's name to a commercial product. It
just wouldn't be the right thing to do."

"But think of it, Father," Rans replied, his enthusiasm
undiminished by Allen's words, which had been spoken
gently but firmly. "Think of it, Notre Dame joining with the
Pope in bringing a healthy and holy food to Americans. A
food, I might add, that's strong on energy, oh yes, a great
source of physical and spiritual energy. Think of the tie-in."

"No, no, Mr. Rans. We appreciate all that. It's just we're
not the ones to do it. I'm sure you and Brother George will do
just fine without us. There must be plenty of other Catholic
places that would be interested."

All the while Father Thomas was listening intently on the
phone, now and then making a brief remark which I couldn't
make out. By this time, Allen had his hand on Rans's
shoulder and was moving him toward the door. The last thing
I heard Rans say before it closed on him was, "You wouldn't
want Southern Methodist to beat you to this . . ."

Allen came back and sat down, this time shaking a cigarette
out of a rather crumpled package he found in his side pocket.
Father Thomas was just concluding his conversation. "All
right. We'll see you here at three this afternoon. Fine, fine."
And with that he slowly replaced the receiver and looked
over at Father Allen.

"Jack, that was Maurice Ryan calling from Indianapolis."
Ryan was head of a big paint company there, an alumnus of
Notre Dame, and a benefactor as well. "His son Philip is a
freshman. He says that one of the priests here has been
making passes at him, has been giving him lots of presents,

and has asked him to take a vacation, all expenses paid, with him. He's very upset and is coming here this afternoon to find out about it." Thomas said this all matter-of-factly, distressed, to be sure, but ready to handle it.

"Who is it? Did he say?"

"Fred Peters," Thomas said, a little sadly. "But, of course, we haven't heard his side."

Allen just raised his eyebrows as he lighted his cigarette, and grunted noncommittally. Men who had been around any institution for a while were never surprised by such news. Their big problem was always how to handle it for the good of the institution and the good of the man. For my part, I didn't know what to say, since a vision of Father Peters's life collapsing like the bridge of San Luis Rey flashed through my mind. "God help him," I finally said to nobody in particular.

"Austin," Thomas said, like a man who knew he had to get on with an unpleasant task, "have you seen Father Peters lately?"

"No, not today anyway. Now and then I have. He's seemed more cheerful lately."

"Well, he won't be very cheerful today. Would you mind going over to his rooms and asking him to come and see me after lunch? He likes you and a visit from you won't draw as much attention as one from me or Jack. And I'd just as soon not call him. Do you mind?"

"No," I said, my heart fluttering just a bit. "No, I could do that. I mean, I think I can anyway."

"Good. Don't upset him. Just tell him to come by at about two-thirty or so. Can you be here, Jack?"

Allen nodded, exhaling a great billow of smoke as he did.

It was almost noon as I made my way to Father Peters's rooms, which were not so far from my own. I hesitated just before I knocked and felt relieved when there was no answer. Then I knocked again but this time a voice called a muffled question from inside.

"It's me, Austin Kenna," I piped, and the door opened to reveal a man who had obviously been sleeping, sheet crease marks on the side of his face, his hair sprayed out on one side, and a puffy look to his eyes.

"I won't disturb you, Father," I said softly, seeing that he had not opened the door all the way. "It's just that I was with Father Kinsella for a bit and he asked me to inquire if you would go to his office this afternoon."

"Oh, Christ," Father Peters groaned, lowering his eyes and tightening the grip he had on the side of the door. I thought he was going to throw up but he just swallowed hard and looked up again at me, his eyes like those of a dog the vet is just about to put to sleep.

"Now, now," I said, trying to buck him up. "No need to worry. Just wants to see you. Two-thirty, he said."

"Is that all he said?"

"Why, yes, that's all. Do you feel all right, Father?"

"I've had a little flu," he said, looking past me like a man watching a friend disappearing down a corridor. Then he fixed his eyes on me again and reached his hand out and grabbed mine. "Will you come with me, Austin?" My wrist hurt from the pressure he was putting on it.

"If you'd like me to," I answered fairly firmly, considering the ambivalence I felt inside. "Maybe you should have some lunch first. What do you say to a drink and a little food?"

"Okay," he said. "Okay. Just give me a minute to wash my face."

Then he disappeared while I stood in the corridor thinking of the poor man on the other side of the door. There wasn't much I could do for him, I thought with a sigh, and feeling, as I did, that I was just a coat holder at most events anyway. But I felt wretchedly bad for him, imagining his splashing his face with water and combing his hair and bound to emerge resembling a fellow whose life was put together, like his looks, late every day and fooling nobody anyway.

We stopped at the Morris Inn and he seemed a little calmer as he had some black coffee and a sandwich. He talked about football and Chicago and how much he had been enjoying his classes and about a dozen other things that weren't really on his mind. Or mine, for that matter, but I was a good listener and managed to throw in a few patriarchal comments between bites of my hamburger.

"It's gone two o'clock," I finally said, and we paid our bill and made our way out and northward toward Father Thomas's office in the administration building. Father Thomas and Father Allen were sitting where I had last seen them before lunch. Thomas seemed composed and at ease as he greeted us and waved us into our chairs.

"Tom," Father Peters blurted right out, "I think I know why you want to see me. It's the Ryan boy, isn't it?"

"Yes, it has to do with Philip Ryan."

"Well, I don't know what you've heard or where, but things aren't the way you think. I mean, nothing has happened, nothing." His voice was cracking a little, like his throat was dry, but he sounded convincing to me. Thomas's expression was that of a man who was straining to understand, a kind of receptive expression like that of a fellow who had heard too much bad news ever to expect it might be good once in a while.

"Fred," he said gently, "that's why I asked you over here, to hear your side of the story. What has been reported to us is that you have made some advances to young Ryan and that you have been giving him presents and have invited him to take a vacation trip with you, all expenses paid. That's all we have heard and, before anything else develops, we want to hear from you."

"This isn't a courtroom," Jack Allen threw in. "Just a discussion."

Father Peters hesitated, looked down at his hands, took a deep breath, and began to speak again. "It's not the way you think. I mean, I'm grateful to you for this chance to tell you my side, I really am, but the way you described it just isn't the way it is at all. I mean, do you know Philip Ryan?"

"I've met him. A quiet, gentle boy," Thomas replied.

"Yes, yes, a good boy. And he came to me one day to talk. Kids do that all the time, you know that. Well, he picked me out since I was an outsider, teaching here but no direct connection with the campus. He's got lots of problems. I ought to know. I've got plenty myself. But I've been working on them, seeing the doctor a couple of times a week downtown. And I've been working hard. You know that."

Thomas nodded, drawing a thin cigar from a box on his desk and lighting it.

"Well." Father Peters cleared his throat as he shifted in his chair and began to gesture with his hands. "I'll bet you heard this from his father. That's right, isn't it? His old man, the guy used to play football here, the big strong man in the paint business. Well, he's Phil's main problem. That's what we talked about. I mean, I can't go into any details but, you want to know Phil's problems, you've got to know his father. A hard driver, doesn't understand a son who wants to get into the theater. Calls him a fairy, compares him with his brothers, runs him down, tells him he's not sending him to Notre Dame to study interior decorating." There was a measure of anger in Father Peters's voice as he plunged along like a ship making for port through a heavy sea.

"Fred," Father Thomas interrupted, "we aren't really here to get Maurice Ryan's biography, or a critique of his role as a father. What about this other business that supposedly involves you?"

That stiffened Father Peters up a bit but didn't slow him down.

"Tom, you've got to understand something about his old man to understand the whole thing. Phil is sensitive and his father just can't understand that, can't accept him for that. So naturally I became a kind of father figure for him because I encouraged him to be himself, to become what he wanted to be in life, and not to feel guilty just because he didn't want to be in the paint business all his life."

There was a pause as Peters looked from Kinsella to Allen and then to me, who, after all, had no official part in any of this. I was hoping, however, that his explanation was a good one and that it would hold up.

"He'd come to see me often. And one night he told me he just couldn't take the idea of going home to Indianapolis for the long weekend that's coming up. So I told him he could come to Chicago with me, that I was driving anyway, and I'd get him a place to stay. That's not exactly like going to Bermuda together, you know. And I know I'm on my good behavior, for God's sake. You've given me a chance. You think I want to throw that away?"

"Is that all there is to it?" Thomas asked gently.

"That's the part you have to understand first. That I was trying to help this kid who had a hell of a problem with his father."

Father Peters paused again, rubbing at his chin with his hand, a nervous kind of gesture, I thought, like a fellow who can't get rid of a gnat that's bothering him.

"No, no, there's some more. But I swear it was innocent. I asked him out to dinner one night when he seemed to be feeling a little better about himself. And I had bought him a book on modern art that I thought he'd like, one of those coffee table books that cost about fifty bucks when they come out. I got it for nineteen ninety-five from a clearing house. It wasn't a big deal. But we had some wine, maybe too much wine. I got a little high, something I never do. You know that. I guess you could say I was drunk. And when we got in the car I told him he was a beautiful boy and a good boy. And he leaned over and kissed me, put his arms around me and kissed me and started to cry. So help me, he kissed me and I was so surprised I just held him in my arms while he cried and cried about how happy he was after all the rejection he'd had to find a friend like me. Well, I didn't try anything funny. I was a little drunk, I know that, but nothing like that had ever happened to me before. It was like finding I had a son, somebody who loved me and somebody I loved. Purely. I didn't want to hurt him and I didn't. I got him home and even though I was a little drunk I respected him too much to, to . . . to use him."

There was silence in the room and Father Peters began to sob a little, sniffling and wiping his nose with his handkerchief. "So help me God, that's it." I was ready to vote for acquittal but neither Kinsella nor Allen seemed as moved as I.

Father Thomas was frowning slightly and Father Allen just looked impassive. Thomas waited until Father Peters looked up at him before he spoke.

"Well, if that's the story, would you mind meeting with Philip's father to speak for yourself?"

"No, no, I'd like to do that."

"He'll be here in a few minutes. I think it would be best if we could resolve this matter within the walls of this office. If we can do that, there won't be any need for reports or records or administrative action. But I don't want you to go after his father. I already know that you don't like Big Daddies, so you can stay away from that. Do you understand?"

Father Peters nodded his head slowly, breathing deeply as he did so. "Marquis of Queensberry rules?" he asked with a half smile.

"Marquis of Queensberry rules," Thomas replied dryly, half ready, I thought, to let his old friend off the hook, but half not ready to either and, as I thought of Father Peters's looks when he opened his door, those looks that not even the influenza epidemic of 1918 could explain, I felt a catch, just a slight one, mind you, in my own feelings as well. Father Allen, the old war-horse, had said nothing and, for the life of me, I couldn't be sure of what he was thinking at all. Then there was a ring on the phone and we all knew that Maurice Ryan, on the very dot of three, was at the door.

Ryan, a squat sort of man, moved all of a piece, like a statue that hadn't quite made it all the way out of the block of marble, as he entered the room scowling beneath his perfectly bald head and not saying a word but seeming to give off steam engine sounds, the hisses and wheezes of a great force slowing down as it came into the station.

"Father Kinsella," he said abruptly, shooting a hand out. Then a nod to Father Allen, a half of a nod to me, and none at all to Father Peters as he settled into a chair by Thomas's desk.

"Father Peters has been here explaining his relationship with your son, Philip. He has agreed to go over it with you. And I'm sure that he will answer any questions you might have."

Ryan grunted and shifted in his chair. "I'd like to hear some explanation of this relationship with my son. I sure as hell can't think of any." He was angry and struggling to keep himself under control.

Father Peters told his story again, leaving out the parts that were too harsh on the elder Ryan and using the opportunity to explain the boy's artistic temperament to his father. Maurice Ryan was irritated but I could see that he was also reasonable and he gave Father Peters plenty of leeway and never interrupted. When Peters finished, Ryan just sat there, like a big muscle slowly flexing itself, before he spoke.

"That all there is to it?" he asked in clipped tones.

"That's all there is to it," Father Peters responded, somewhat relieved for having had the chance to speak his piece.

"Sounds goddam funny to me," Ryan said, "my kid crying and hugging you because he's found a true friend. Ever had a friend like that, I'd deck the son of a bitch." He shook his head as though he were trying to get the sour images out of his imagination.

"Now, Maurice," Father Thomas interjected, "Father Peters has been open and honest. I think we ought to be as fair as we can. The story isn't exactly the same one that you had, is it?"

"No," Ryan said, a little grudgingly. "No, but it isn't the Boy Scout Manual either. I'm sorry but I'm old-fashioned and it takes me some time to understand things like this. It's a different world for me." He looked directly at Father Peters and spoke very slowly and deliberately to him.

"Father, I don't know when I've been so mad as I've been today. I don't understand everything but I'm glad you tried to help my son. I don't want you to take him to Chicago and I don't want you taking him out to dinner or buying him books any more. But, if you agree to that, I'll go back to the paint business and forget about this."

"What do you say, Fred?" Father Thomas asked evenly. Father Peters closed his eyes for a moment and seemed to be gritting his teeth. Then, with a rush of breath, he said, "Okay, okay."

Well, the tension in the room diminished considerably, and, after good-bys, Maurice Ryan left the office, the great chunk of him moving out without any noise. Then Father Peters, smiling uneasily, left after thanking Thomas for the chance to tell his story. Thomas stood up, looked out the window and across the campus. "What do you think, Jack?" he asked quietly.

Allen stretched as he rose from his chair. Then he lighted a cigarette, took a puff, and said in a weary voice, "I wish I felt better than I do."

Thomas turned toward him and said, "So do I. So do I."

8

Spring 1974

It wasn't as if Father Thomas didn't have plenty to occupy his time. There are many other things besides the beekeepers and the fund raisers, things that involved him in academic affairs on campus and in doings for the bishops and such off campus. And there was Father Peters, who, after the go-around with Maurice Ryan, seemed quieter for a while, up early and working hard on his classes, and a long period when everything seemed okay. Then I began to run into him around twelve noon, when I often went to the Mass at the Sacred Heart Church. He'd be hurrying in at the same time to join the other priests in concelebration or just to sit in one of the back pews, and I could see that he was getting that slightly puffy, wild-haired look once more. It was about this time that he went to see Father Thomas again.

"Fred, how've you been? I'm sorry I haven't been in better touch with you." Father Kinsella was looking at him over a new set of half glasses he had taken to wearing; they gave his face character and he enjoyed peering over them, the same way he liked lighting a cigar slowly while he talked to you.

"Tom, there's something I want to talk about."

Expectant silence from Kinsella, who removed his glasses and slipped them into a leather case. No need for effects in this conversation.

"Tom, I've been here almost four years now. And I've been doing pretty well. Been seeing the doctor, doing a lot of reading, even some writing. I feel better, truly I do. I'm grateful to all of you here." He propped his elbows on the sides of the chair but his hands trembled slightly as he pointed them together in front of his chest.

"But you've come to tell me something," Thomas said directly. "What is it?"

"Well, I want to level with you. I'm still in love, I guess I can call it that, with Philip Ryan. We are friends in a way I can't express to you. That's why I've been doing some writing."

"When you say you're 'in love' with him, what do you mean?"

"Just that. I've told myself maybe I shouldn't be, I know what his old man said, and I think I know how you'll react. But it seems a good thing to me, a true and beautiful thing. And Phil feels something for me. I mean, I've had some relationships before, but I was never in love with anyone, not like this anyway. And I've never felt that somebody else, one person, that is, could love me in a special way. I can't believe God would condemn us for being in love. This sounds very modern and very romantic maybe. But it's true."

"Yes," Thomas said in that even way of his that indicated that he understood, not that he agreed.

"I want to go public. Come out of the closet. Call it whatever you want. I want to announce it on campus at a Mass for students. I want to put it all up front. And I want to work with the gay students here . . ."

Thomas just wrinkled his forehead, and Father Peters, like a fellow playing a high card, added, in a confidential tone, "There are gay students here. You know that, don't you?"

"Fred, whether there are, and however many there may be, I'm not sure you're the priest to be working with them as a counselor."

"Oh, for Christ's sake, Tom, am I going to get that from you too? Where the hell can a priest be honest about being gay in this Church? They'd like to pretend it only exists out there. The bishops would like you to think we only accepted virile men into the priesthood, that they had blood tests to prove it. You know as well as I there are gays everywhere. I'd expect some honesty from you." Father Peters's voice was angry and he squirmed in his chair as he spoke.

"Fred, we're not discussing my honesty. We're not even discussing whether there are gays in the priesthood. We're talking about a work you say you want to undertake here at the University. That's an administrative matter and I'll settle it right now by telling you that you won't have my approval or support for this project. If there are gays here, we'll minister to them like we minister to everyone else. Making them come out of the closet may be the worst kind of pressure to put on a kid at college age. You ought to know that. That's not the right work for you either, not now, not when you have the chance to build a life you can lead within the priesthood."

"Tom, I'm going to do this. I've got to."

"Not here, you won't. Your needs are one thing. University policy and the rights of the students to be left alone: they're something different. I can understand why you feel the way you do, but you might as well understand my position clearly right from the start. We've supported you and stood by you. I expect that you'll give us a little co-operation in return."

Father Peters remained silent. He had not expected Father Kinsella to be so firm so quickly. He was seeing the instinctively powerful Kinsella, who, having resisted Peters so strongly, now spoke more gently.

"Fred, as far as telling me you're in love with a student, what do you expect me to do? I'm a university official. I have to think of its welfare, of its good name. If you're speaking to me only as a friend, that may be something else. But Notre Dame is not prepared to have its teachers and its students announce their engagement on the chapel steps. That's a romantic fantasy. You cannot expect us to accept that. You must know that. As a friend I'll do anything to help you; I want to be a good friend but I have to be a realistic one."

Father Peters remained silent for a few moments but he was clearly angry. You could sense it in the way he grabbed the arms of the chair, his knuckles drained white by the tightness of his grasp, and in the way he stiffened and bit out his words; it was an old and well-simmered anger directed at fate and Providence and the angels that had not protected him from pain. It was the anger of a man who felt trapped even after he had found a relationship whose beauty floated just beyond his grasp, tantalizing him the way a vision of freedom frustrates a man in chains. Thomas Kinsella was the immediate target for this displaced hostility, which coiled across the desk like a gaucho's whip.

"Tom, you sound just like a bishop. That's what you want, isn't it? To be a bishop, Bishop Kinsella, the watchdog of orthodoxy, or President Kinsella, the president of Notre

Dame, the greatest Fighting Irishman of them all. Jesus, your old man'll be proud of his little Tommy . . ."

"Are you finished with me and my family?"

"No, God damn it, no. You've got everything, you always have, and I'm damned if I'm finished with you. You, thinking you've done me a big favor by changing prisons for me. That's all this has been, a fucking change of cells." Then he stopped and put his head in his hands, rocking back and forth and breathing heavily, but not crying. His voice was slightly muffled as he spoke through his hands.

"For Christ's sake, Tom, I'm not at home any place."

Thomas had risen and walked around his desk to stand in front of Father Peters. "Fred," he said quietly, "I know how much hell this has all been for you. But I can't let you put your neck out now. You're not ready to go public. That's something you ought to talk over with your doctor. You've got to get some peace inside before you can find it outside."

Father Peters looked up through his parted fingers. "Tom, you don't know how I feel. How could you?" His voice trailed off.

Father Thomas stood there, gazing down at his old friend, determined to block him from announcing his gay status on campus, but not quite sure what else he could do to help him.

"Tom, it isn't that I don't appreciate what you've done. It's just that I'm not sure I can take this any longer. And I don't know what to do about Philip Ryan."

"You don't want to hurt him, I'm sure of that."

"No, no."

"You can't really think that you can live with him, or have a sexual relationship with him, and not hurt him, can you?"

"I don't want to hurt him. He doesn't want to hurt me. We seem to need each other in a way that doesn't seem wrong, not wrong at all. I want him with all my heart. Can you understand that, Tom? I want him for good, to take care of him, to have somebody . . ." He broke off, shook his head, and sighed deeply.

"Fred, you have to take care not to hurt him. A lot of people hurt each other trying to love each other. It happens all the time. I'm not talking as an administrator now, Fred, I'm talking as a friend. Painful as this is, there'd be no future in it, no place for you to go with it. Maybe the fact that you have a friend in this young man is God's blessing, I don't know for certain. But it's something you have to deal with in your present context, as a priest trying to make a go of it. You can't forget that or the guilt you've had so much trouble with will come back with a vengeance. Perhaps you need to approach this spiritually."

Father Peters bristled and turned his face up to look directly at Thomas.

"Approach this spiritually? Tom, what do you mean by that? That's one of the prize clichés of all time. And what do you know about whether I approach this spiritually or not?" His voice had grown indignant again and this time he had Father Kinsella off balance, because he sensed that Thomas had vulnerabilities of his own. "It's all very well for you to talk about spirituality, you with good looks, money, and your own way most of the time. That's true, isn't it, Tom? You pretty much get what you want and it hasn't got anything to do with saying your prayers. Having what you want is what makes it easy for you to say your prayers, or like Archbishop Williams with his ass in a tub of butter in Chicago. It's easy to pray when you've got food and friends . . ." At some level Peters understood that the balance had tilted slightly in his favor even though Thomas betrayed no reaction as he stood unblinkingly above him.

"Tom, do you have any idea what spirituality is all about? The well-ordered life of the seminarian, is that what you think it is? Time for reading the Scripture and time for visiting the chapel and marching around in a chain gang saying the rosary together? Is that it? Then you don't have to let your right hand know what your left hand is doing. Very convenient, very reassuring for the soul. Come on, Tom, you know better than that. What the hell have you learned if you haven't learned that in all your travels?"

"We're not discussing my spiritual life or my work," Thomas broke in, but Father Peters was not to be put off, not now that he had tasted blood, a few drops of it anyway. It was not often that he had the advantage with anyone, especially Thomas Kinsella, but there was power in his own impoverishment and discomfort that challenged the fully armored confidence, the wealth of spirit and accomplishment of Father Thomas.

"Blessed are the poor in spirit, Tom. Do you remember that one? Blessed are those who mourn. Yes, and that one too?" Father Peters spoke in rapid, almost passionate phrases, like an evangelist finally sure of his subject and audience. "Well, Tom, you haven't had to worry about any of those things, except in sermons. I'll tell you what I think. Spirituality is what all the poor bastards like me have to come to. Do you think I enjoy feeling the way I do? We know something about being poor and persecuted. And you, well you know something about applause and being loved by everybody." Then, knowing he had a supreme chance to vanquish his benefactor, or at least to take one fall in the match, he rose from his chair and stepped close to Father Kinsella. "Why, you've even got the most famous actress in America on the string. Don't you think we know about that? All proper, sure, just a friend. Well, what are you getting out of it? And what's the spirituality of it? Sacrifice, I know, sacrifice, giving up marrying her so you can do the Lord's work, or your work. Come on, Tom, the woman makes most of the sacrifices in these relationships. Do you ever admit that to yourself?"

Thomas did not know what to say, for he recognized truth that stung him in the savage comments of his friend, who, as Thomas fleetingly thought, might, with bloodshot eyes and uncombed hair, turn up on the day of judgment as the world's greatest saint, the broken man who had battled his demons heroically even as the world smugly judged him, while he, Kinsella, might stand, earthly rewards as faded as Caesar's laurel wreath, in the cold shadows with the well-fed and powerful. Thomas felt a surge of warmth rise through his body but he resisted the temptation to strike back. He felt chastened, as though truth like a handful of lime had burned through his rectitude and eaten a fiery wound into a corner of his soul. Peters had made him angry but he had also forced him to examine himself in a way that made him uneasy. He was not going to let Father Peters know exactly how he felt; he was not, in fact, completely sure of how he felt himself. He turned away from Peters and walked toward one of the tall windows at the side of his office.

"The trouble with you, Tom," Peters said to Kinsella's back, "is that you haven't been in the street enough. You haven't got the street smarts. You live the way hardly anybody can when it comes to your emotions and getting your own way in life. That's not the way the world lives. It's all fucked up and it's full of sinners like me. That's when you learn about spirituality, when you're so fucking poor in spirit you have to depend on God, you have to admit the truth about yourself. That's what I've been talking about, not the good fucking order of the University and what's an administrative decision and what isn't."

Father Thomas was in control of himself, although he could still feel the glowing coals of Peters's comments settling in his own spirit. "Fred," he said firmly as he turned back toward him, "I do understand that you have suffered more than most men. I also know that I have my faults. But, taking all that into account, I'm still not going to approve of your using this campus to confess the anguish of your soul. I don't want to see you get into a relationship that may destroy you and Philip Ryan, even though you have as much right to love as anyone. You're asking me, you're trying to get me to give an implicit okay to your plans. Well, whether you think I'm spiritual or not, I'm not going to do it."

Father Peters watched Thomas coldly as he spoke these words. He felt that he had won something even though he had not changed Thomas's mind. He had never thought he could do that anyway. Peters had come off the battlefield with the flag of self-respect, howsoever tattered, in his own hands, and he felt better because he had drawn more even with Thomas, even though he had struck at him viciously with his remarks about Maria Moore and his family and his generally favored way of life. These had been blows against the benign forces that had treated him so poorly, that had reserved blessings for the already rich. Even though he had not gained Thomas's approval for a ministry to gay students or for his relationship with Philip Ryan, he felt avenged, at least in a minor way, as he moved toward the door.

"You're a grown man, Fred," Thomas said. "You have to come to terms with your problem before you can make any decisions that affect other people's welfare. I hope you'll remember that."

"I'll remember," Father Peters said in the tone of a man who didn't need to be told. "Thanks for your time." With that he left the office, letting go of the door so that it slammed shut behind him.

Thomas sat down at his desk and then leaned back in his chair. He was not happy with the way the interview had gone and he still smarted from Peters's onslaught. The worst part was that he knew there was something to it.

9

Autumn 1974

Patrick B. Kinsella owned five acres along the bluff-lined shore of Lake Michigan about forty-five minutes northwest of Notre Dame. A rambling white brick house, shaded by oaks and black locust trees, crowned a lushly overgrown brow almost one hundred feet above the green-blue waters. P.B. had built a separate house for sports equipment and tools with another section in which bathers could change and shower; it was in the shape of an Irish cottage, with white-washed walls and a thatched roof. The main house was filled with passageways and bedrooms, all of which sprouted out like pipes off a furnace from the oversize living room, whose large windows opened on the lake. Directly above was the master bedroom, almost as spacious as the living room, which had a porch along its full length facing the sky and water. P.B. and Mae had just arrived from a Notre Dame football game, a victory for the Fighting Irish over Northwestern that had turned out to be one-sided and, therefore, not completely satisfying to the elder Kinsella.

"Mae, there was more fight in that Northwestern team today than in the Irish."

"They won, didn't they, Patrick?"

"Yes, but, hell, anybody could have beaten the poor bastards. Notre Dame didn't really try. They're strong, but they took it easy, if you ask me. Hate to see that."

Mae was applying some lipstick as P.B. emerged from their bathroom, drying his tanned face with a yellow towel.

"Mae, ever since I've known you, you've been putting lipstick on. That's the way I'm going to remember you always, stopping by a mirror to fix up your beautiful face. You'll be doing it just before the Last Judgment, holding the whole thing up."

"You wouldn't want me to look bad there, would you? I mean, everybody'll be coming to that." She turned away from the mirror and smiled at her husband. "You do quite a bit of fixing yourself. A spray for this, and a gargle for that."

Patrick tossed the towel on a chair and walked toward Mae, a broad smile on his face. "Mae, did I ever tell you you're still my favorite girl friend? Would you like to close the doors and go to bed before dinner?"

"Patrick!" Mae said. "We've got guests!"

"The hell with them," Patrick said, embracing and kissing his wife. She loved this part of him, this romantic and tender part that the world hardly ever viewed. And she was not sure that he was not serious. It would be just like him, she thought, to want to make love with the sons and daughters-in-law and even Father Thomas and his guest, that actress Maria Moore, having drinks and waiting for them in the living room right below. Old P.B. really did not care what they thought, even if they could hear the bed squeaking; it was part of his self-confident exuberance and, although he was a gracious and generous host, he would not hesitate to let his guests wait for him if he suddenly decided to pursue some other absorbing goal. Mae, however, having been through such scenes with him all around the world, was not ready to go along with his sudden proposal.

"Patrick dear," she said sweetly, "your sons will think you've gone daft or something if we come down all red-faced and a half hour late. You always did have these ideas at the damndest times."

"All right, Mae, but you're missing a good thing." Patrick had not had to read the Kinsey Report to know that older people could still enjoy sexual relationships. He had never forgotten Samuel Insull and the fall of his kingdom after the failure of his sexual potency and he was determined that no such fate would strike him down. He had always smiled at the priests and bishops when they talked about sex. Patrick always felt, as he did about many subjects, that if you knew anything about sex you never talked about it. And he and Mae were still in love more than thirty years after their marriage. Mae had taken to drinking when he had to be away a lot, and she was a little too taken with a prayer life that found her making the rounds of churches all some afternoons to find those that were having Forty Hours Devotion or Exposition of the Blessed Sacrament or Father Paul's Novena for Birdwatchers or some other thing. But they had been through a lot together and there was unmistakable tenderness and devotion between them.

"Will you let me sign your dance card for the night?" Patrick asked as he offered her his arm and they descended to the living room. They looked good, the way handsome people in understated expensive clothing always look, as they came into the room where two of their sons, Martin and Joe, with their wives, Meg and Deirdre, were talking in the easy way people have after an afternoon in the sun with the prospect of a good meal just ahead. Martin, a heavyset man with a face that had barely overcome the pink and wide-eyed look it had as a baby, was lighting some kindling by the fireplace.

"Have you opened the flue, Martin my boy?" P.B. asked genially but purposefully. He couldn't help checking on Martin, even in such simple matters as this. Martin just arched an eyebrow in irritation and said, "No, Daddy, I'm planning to burn your house down for the insurance."

Joe, jet black of hair and almost an exact replica of his father, was almost thirty, and, in many people's judgment, the one most like P.B. himself. Joe was quiet, however, and not the singer of songs that Martin was, or the gracious and politically astute man that Thomas, the priest, was. P.B. liked having a son a priest well enough but he often wondered what Thomas might have become if he had not gone to the seminary. He looked out the windows to the sweep of lawn where Father Thomas, wearing plaid pants and a windbreaker, was pointing to something on the lake for his guest, Maria Moore.

"Tom sure knows how to pick 'em," Martin said, straightening up from the now crackling fire.

"Now, Martin, what kind of a thing is that to say?" Mae interjected. "Father Tom and Miss Moore are good friends. I think she comes to him for spiritual advice. She's never remarried since her husband died. But she's in good standing in the Church."

Martin's wife, Meg, a blonde with good manners and plenty of ambition, seconded her mother-in-law's appraisal. "Marty, you shouldn't say things when you don't know what you're talking about."

"What do you think, Joe?" Martin said, turning to his younger brother, who was just giving a drink to his wife Deirdre, the redhead who had once been Queen of Chicago's St. Patrick's Day Parade. "Do you think Tom should be making friends with movie stars?"

"I think it's Tom's business. I think it's good for him to have a woman's influence in his life."

"You're right, Joe," P.B. interjected swiftly. "Tom lives in a closed world in lots of ways." He sipped his scotch. "But he does seem to be sweet on her."

"Patrick," Mae said with some irritation. "Father Tom might hear you. You don't want to say things like that and embarrass him. Now, where are the children?"

"Out in the cottage, playing with the tools," Deirdre answered. "Maybe we had better go take a look at them."

"They won't hurt themselves," P.B. said, for he was a firm believer that risk and danger encountered early were wonderful builders of character.

"Well, I'll just go look anyway."

"I had no idea Michigan was so lovely, Tom, and the lake looks as big as an ocean from here."

"This is the nicest time of day here, just as the sun is beginning to set. It turns the lake into a twinkling silver sea. There's nothing more beautiful anywhere in the world."

"Do you get to spend much time here?"

"Oh, I come up from the University overnight quite often, especially when I need a quiet place to get some work done." Thomas picked up a small stone and scaled it far out over the bluff.

"I can tell you've been working hard. You look so tired. And it's obvious that something's on your mind."

"Would you like to take a walk on the shore?" Thomas asked, changing the subject more obviously than he usually did. He pointed toward a platform about twenty yards away. "That's our lift. Very English-sounding, isn't it? It's like a little railroad car that runs down the side of the bluff. You have to have them around here to get to the beach."

Maria smiled and climbed down the few steps to the redwood decking and into the small car, something like those that hung from Ferris wheels, and, as it jolted into movement, she reached out her arm and grabbed Thomas's shoulder to steady herself.

"Whoa, there, you'll be all right. These are perfectly safe."
Thomas took her hand and held it for a moment. "I'm sure
you'll be all right," he said in a voice that was almost drowned
out by the sound of the car clanking down the rusty rails
toward the shore below. Then he let go of her hand and
looked out at the lake beyond.

"Tom," Maria said firmly, "why did you let go of my hand?
Are you afraid of me?"

"I'm sorry," Thomas replied, straightening up slightly.
"I'm not afraid of you, no. I guess I just don't feel very free."
He paused. "Sometimes I don't know just what I feel."

Maria ducked slightly as the car passed under the drooping
branch of a weeping willow. She was biting her lip and
looking out over Thomas's shoulder toward the lake that was
patterned with light and dark patches beneath the swiftly
moving autumn clouds.

"Tom, we've got to talk about this. I can't go on wondering
what or how you feel. My life has been complicated enough."
She was silent for a moment as they climbed out of the car
and made their way across a hillock of beach grass to the
sandy shore.

"I know, I know," Thomas said, looking down at the
glacial pebbles and stones that were strewn in heaps and
mounds along the water's edge.

"Maria, I should never have gotten you into this, should
never have asked for your friendship. I've gotten you involved in my life, and there's no future in that."

"What exactly are you saying, Tom?"

Thomas hesitated for a moment, averting his eyes from
hers. "I'm saying that we've been good friends, that it's
worked out okay. You've had your life and I've been busy
and we kept our distance. I've thought a lot about it, prayed
about it . . ."

"Tom, you worry a subject to death. Are you like this in
class?"

"I'm serious, Maria. I love to be with you, I love to hear
from you, but I'm not sure I understand our friendship. There
isn't any future in it, you know that as well as I do." He
leaned down and picked up a smooth flat stone about twice as
big as a silver dollar and scaled it over the lake, where it
skipped three times on the surface before it disappeared into
the water. He looked into Maria's eyes.

"I think we ought to keep our distance."

Maria leaned down and picked up another flat stone. "Tom, you are afraid of me. Admit it, Tom, you're asking me not to put any pressure on you. That's it, isn't it? You don't want me to ask you to put up or shut up." She scaled the stone so that it made five steplike splashes to a farther point than the one Father Kinsella's stone had reached.

"There," she said, her eyes flashing. "Maybe I'm too much for you."

"That's not it, Maria. I've been trying to think about this from your viewpoint. I know you care about me and you don't push me, I know that. But I have to face it, I mean I'm not really a prospect for marriage. And you're still young, you could still have children. We have to face these facts."

"What do you think I'm going to do, enter a convent?" They walked together along the beach. "Tom, did you ever hear that people, if they are lucky, may have one great love in their lives?"

Thomas continued to walk, his head down, not saying anything, because he wanted to deal with their relationship in terms of friendship and Maria wanted to speak of it in terms of love.

"Oh, Tom, you get this great hangdog look on your face whenever you're having a spiritual crisis. You'd be disappointed to know you're not the only thing in my life."

Thomas turned and looked at her, unsure of how to take her remark. Maria knew how to lay a hook into him, there was no doubt of that.

"What do you mean by that?" he asked in tones that could have signified hurt had he not spoken them in such a measured way.

"You forget, I'm a star." Then she laughed and took his arm. "For God's sake, Tom, I'm teasing you. Can't you tell that?"

Thomas did not seem convinced. "Is there somebody I don't know about? Has something been going on I don't know about?"

"Tom, Tom," she said, letting him take her arm as they stepped over a pile of driftwood. "We've known each other a long while now. I've never known anyone like you, so gentle, so strong, so . . . good, I guess, just plain good. I love that about you."

"You've been good yourself," Thomas replied. "Maybe

that's the problem. For me, anyway. I deal with so many different things, sometimes I think the only sane person I know is you. You've been an anchor for me. But I can't handle anything more than the friendship we have. If I did, or if I tried to see you more often, well . . ."

Maria smiled gently in the manner of someone who understands another person's conflict and who makes allowances for it.

"I'm not demanding anything more. You know that. That's my fate in this Catholic Church of ours: the only things I've ever wanted, I haven't been able to have." Then she laughed and began to jog ahead of Thomas down the beach. "But the one thing I can't stand is your mooning about it." Her hair lifted lightly in the breeze as she moved ahead of Thomas, who had started to jog behind her.

"Besides," she called back as she stepped up her pace, "if I really wanted you, do you think I couldn't get you?" Then she laughed aloud, a good-natured one-upmanship laugh.

Thomas caught up with her by a clutch of birch trees that had taken root and flourished at the foot of a bluff about half a mile from the lift platform. He took her by the arms and turned her toward him. "You're trying to get my Irish up, aren't you, Miss Moore? Trying to get me off guard."

"You, off guard?" Maria laughed. "Fat chance of that."

"Well," Thomas said, doing a little teasing of his own, "see how you like this." And he pulled her close to him, touching her lips tentatively and then firmly. Then they just held each other a moment until Thomas pulled slowly away.

"Not bad," Maria said with a grin. "We might make great music together."

"Sorry," Thomas said, caught between remorse and enjoyment, half triumphant at his response to her teasing, and half distressed too. "But I'll bet Burt Reynolds couldn't do any better."

"Well, when he's wearing a moustache . . ." Then Maria laughed again. In some way she didn't know what else to do. They had used humor to release the building tension of their relationship. Things would be better for a while. Besides, she was leaving for location work in Europe the next day. Work was always the best treatment for the longings of the heart. But nothing had been resolved, although they had come closer to realizing what they meant to each other.

A bell clanged from the bluff of the Kinsella compound. "That's my father," Thomas said. "It's a signal that he's going to put the meat on the fire."

"Quite a fellow, your father," Maria said. "And handsome too."

They walked slowly back toward the lift, not saying much, although they held hands part of the way, not as controlled as a boy scout's leading an old lady across the street but romantic in the powerful way that chaste things can be. Maria put one foot on the step leading up to the lift platform.

"Tom, you and your father aren't really alike, are you?"

"Some people think so. In a lot of ways we are, I guess. In some other ways, we're not alike at all. Must be some of my mother's blood in me, a touch of the Fagan, as she used to say."

"Your father respects you, though. He seems to let you free."

"What do you mean?"

"Well, it's clear that he dominates Martin and Joseph. And their wives and children too."

"Yes, I suppose that's so. Joe's the one like my father. Not just his looks. He's got real killer instincts."

Maria laughed as they leaned against the railing and looked together toward the sun, split horizontally by distant clouds, as it seemed to flatten out before melting into the lake.

"Well, not killer instincts, exactly. But he doesn't let sentiment stand in the way of a deal."

"Why does your father leave you off the hook?"

"Oh, I'm not sure he does. He may not have figured out just how he can use me yet. Maybe if I ever become president of the University he'll think of something . . ."

"You're kidding."

"Maybe I'm hard on the old man. P.B. is quite a character."

"But you won freedom from him in some way. I sense that." Maria began to fix her hair as they climbed into the lift car.

"Becoming a priest was a big part of it. He wasn't for that at all. Wanted me to wait, wanted me to go into business for a while." Thomas pressed the button and the car began clanking up toward the rim of the bluff. He talked more loudly in order to be heard as they passed through the trees and bushes that clotted the hillside with green.

"One summer, I worked at a plant that my father owned. Worked with a bunch of Mexicans. They didn't know who I was and, despite my name, neither did the foreman. He abused them something awful. Max Collier was his name. I'll never forget him, bullnecked and mean. The Mexicans couldn't speak English, they didn't have papers, Max'd shortchange them on their pay." Thomas pressed the button again and the car stopped halfway up the bluff just beneath the weeping willow whose branches bent down over them.

"I started to teach them English on my lunch hour. They didn't know I was a seminarian and they were always inviting me to meet their sisters." Thomas laughed, the first laugh of the evening, and Maria patted his hand as he continued.

"Well, in about three weeks, they had made a lot of progress. They talked it all day, they were so anxious to learn. Then Max, poor old Max, couldn't buffalo them anymore. They could speak up for their rights and they checked up on their pay and figured out when he had cheated them in the past. Well, Max was very disturbed, I'll tell you. They were turning the tables on him and they contacted a lot of other Latins who were working there—menial labor mostly, lugging packing cases on and off freight cars—and damned if they didn't start talking of unionizing . . ."

"What happened, Tom?"

"Well"—and he smiled broadly—"I got fired. Max blamed me for the whole thing and to save face and try to regain control he fired me. Well, things were too far gone by then. They didn't get their union for a year or more but they got better working conditions and fair pay. They even got Max fired. I always thought I might have had a great future in the labor movement."

"And your father, did he know about this?"

"It took some time and since it was near the end of the summer I didn't look for another job. He hit the roof, however, when he heard his own son had been organizing workers at one of his own plants. He called me down to his office in the Loop and he was livid. I can still see him, his fists clenched, standing behind his big desk, yelling at me. 'Thomas, my oldest son, organizing workers! For God's sake, Tom, did you know what you were doing? First of all, it wasn't your business. Second of all, they're not ready to be organized, not at all. They'll get an appetite that can't be satisfied. That's how revolutions start.' Oh, he was mad all right, and he went on about how would it look if it got in the papers that P. B. Kinsella's son was organizing the lowest ranks of unskilled laborers. Is that what I wanted, he asked, to start something I couldn't finish? I remember how he said that: 'Don't ever start something you can't finish. You've given those Mexicans a taste of champagne and they can't afford beer.'

"Then I started quoting some papal encyclical on justice for the workingman and he came around his desk fuming, 'What the hell have I raised, a Father Coughlin for the Latinos? Why don't you quit the seminary and join Ralph Nader if you really want to do some harm thinking that you're doing good?'

"And with that he raised his arm. I don't think he was really going to hit me. It was just that he was so mad. Well, I reached out and grabbed his arm and held it and we stood there, like two fellows Indian wrestling. He had a powerful arm but, luckily, so did I, and it was a standoff. We were both straining, perspiration on our foreheads, and finally I whispered, 'Don't ever start something you can't finish.' And he began to laugh and we both let go, and we both laughed until we had tears in our eyes. Then P.B. surprised me. He kissed me on the forehead and said, 'I guess I might have done the same thing.' But as I left, he called to me, 'But don't do it again.' I think maybe that's when I won a little more freedom from the old man. Martin and Joe never had the grip I had anyway."

Thomas pushed the lift button and it moved the remaining twenty yards up to the top platform. "That's quite a story, Tom," Maria said. "My hero!" And she laughed and the spell of their previous tension seemed broken as they stepped out of the car.

"Well, here we are," Tom said. "Maybe you'll have to handwrestle P.B. tonight. Actually, he's very nice in many ways. And he and mother have made you feel welcome. They haven't even asked you much about Hollywood or what it's like to be kissed by Burt Reynolds."

"Maybe I'll tell them what it's like to be kissed by you."

"I'd rather you tell them about Burt Reynolds," Thomas said with a smile as they stepped onto the lawn. The bittersweet mood of their walk was reinstated in a muted way by the smell of the smoke from the applewood fire that rose like a signal from the main chimney of the house.

Maria put on her best smile, the smile behind which she could hide all her feelings, as they walked across the lawn. Mrs. Kinsella appeared on the porch, a martini in her hand, to greet them.

10

Autumn 1974

"I hope my son behaved himself," P.B. said, grinning across a scotch on the rocks which he held in a toastlike greeting. "Not that he isn't trustworthy, of course."

"You can be proud of him, Mr. Kinsella," Maria replied with a smile as big as the elder Kinsella's. "He did warn me about you."

"Touché, Miss Moore, but I'm nothing but a harmless old financier these days," P.B. said as he moved closer to her.

"Now, Pat," Mae intervened, "don't try any of your old Irish charm on Maria. And, Maria, pay no attention. He's been flirting for years. It makes him feel young again."

"Now, Mae, don't spoil things. How often do we have a glamorous movie star for a visit?" This against the clatter of the other sons, their wives and their unscathed children returning to the main house.

"Put the steaks on, Patrick," Mae replied with a gesture toward the patio, where smoke rose thickly from an outdoor grill. "Everybody must be starved. Oh, Thomas, there was a phone call for you while you were out walking."

Father Thomas, who had been observing the scene as he slipped off his windbreaker, took a slip of paper from his mother's hand and turned to Maria. "I'll have to return this right now. Would you excuse me a minute?"

"I'll entertain her while I cook," P.B. declared, taking

Maria by the arm. "Would you like to see the master chef in action?"

"That's his 'gallant' act. Irresistible," Thomas said as he moved away.

"You have a lovely place here, Mr. Kinsella," Maria said as she walked along to the patio with old P.B., like a girl having the world pointed out to her by a magical father. He was charming her and, what was more, he knew that he had intrigued her and was inwardly delighted with the opportunity to talk with her without his priest son's being present. Maria walked to the edge of the flagstoned area as P.B. stripped a foil covering off a platter of sirloin steaks.

"No drink, Miss Moore?"

"No drink, Mr. Kinsella." She turned back toward him as he tumbled the steaks in an explosion of smoke onto the grill.

"You and Tom have become good friends."

"Yes."

"How good?" P.B. always believed in getting to the heart of the matter. Maria smiled, as though she had been expecting something like that, a salvo worthy of this sleek old battleship of a man.

"Oh, we're good friends," she said in perfectly turned tones of ambiguity, catching and holding P.B.'s eyes as she did. Being an actress, she knew, had its advantages. P.B. sipped his drink and, sweeping his glance down over the sizzling steaks, said in throwaway tones, "Well, that's what I get for asking a personal question. Let me, as the lawyers say, rephrase that." He began flipping the steaks, looking at them instead of Maria as he spoke.

"You don't have to be told that you're two very unusual people. You also have a very unusual relationship for a priest and an actress. I mean ordinarily priests aren't supposed to have women friends at all. I could tell you a few stories about that, however. And movie stars are famous for having different friends every night." He put down his spatula and turned back toward Maria, who had a half smile in the style of Mona Lisa on her face.

"Why, Mr. Kinsella, you don't want to believe all those stories about either priests or movie actresses."

"I've seen a lot in my day. Mostly people trying to get something out of each other, even people in love. Sometimes, they're the worst. What do you get out of this relationship, Miss Moore?"

"I don't think about friendship that way, Mr. Kinsella. Giving seems more important than taking."

"Very idealistic, very idealistic," P.B. said in musing tones. Maria did not answer and did not move either.

"Well, Miss Moore, you've had quite an effect on Tom. You'd have to be blind not to notice it. He's opened up more, doesn't seem to be so, what'll I say? Clerical? Yeah, that's it. He's different. And that's a surprising thing to see in an ambitious man."

"You think Tom is ambitious?"

"We don't raise them any other way. You know damned well he's ambitious. So are you or you wouldn't be where you are." P.B. folded his arms and looked out at the afterglow of pink that softly touched the western sky.

"I've always been determined to succeed."

"Call it what you want. You're both unusual. That's why I wonder about your relationship and how you can remain just good friends. It's either dumb or a great love story, I'm not sure which. And Tom's a little naïve, an idealist. And I think you're an idealist, that's why you were in the peace movement. But I don't think you are naïve. And I am concerned for both of you. I've seen a hell of a lot of people hurt, some of them killed, by love over the years."

"That's the nature of love, isn't it?" Maria said softly. Then, as their eyes met, she added, with a twinkle of triumph in her eye, "But it seems to me Tom once told me a story about not starting something if you couldn't finish it. I think the story had something to do with you . . ." She let her voice trail off.

"Oh, he did, did he? Smart little bastard, isn't he?" P.B. looked at Maria again, taking another measure of her, deciding she could take good care of herself in any fight. "Well," he said more gently, "no harm in asking. I do care, as I say, and, for what it's worth . . ." He bent toward her and kissed her lightly on the forehead. "I'm for it." Now he had thrown Maria off balance again, this handsome man smiling at her in the half light of the autumn evening, this old Irishman with a sack filled with charm who had just transformed a touchy conversation into an affectionate exchange. She leaned forward and kissed him on the cheek.

"You're an old darling at that."

"Call me P.B., or Pat."

"P.B. has the right ring to it. Yes. P.B."

Thomas was just opening the door as P.B. called out, "Five minutes, Mae." He was frowning slightly as he walked toward Maria.

"Maria and I have just been having a nice avuncular chat. Wouldn't you say so, Maria?"

"Yes, yes, you might say that. Tom, is there anything wrong?"

"That call. I've got to go into Chicago after dinner. A problem's come up and I have to handle it."

"Oh, Tom," Maria sighed.

P.B. appraised his son's expression, decided to stay out of the conversation, and began collecting the steaks off the glowing fire. Thomas was distressed for two reasons: the call, which concerned Father Peters, and the disruption of this rare evening when he had a chance to visit with Maria. He felt confused. The call had caused him to feel an unanticipated pressure about his relationship with Maria.

"Sometimes I'd like to quit this business and get honest work," Thomas said rather grimly. "I'm sorry about this, Maria, I really am."

"Duty has a way of calling you, doesn't it?" Maria said resignedly. "I should have known that the day was too beautiful. Things that are too beautiful can get away from you."

"Damn!" Tom said. "Damn! I wish I didn't have to go."

"We're very good at saying good-by to each other." They turned and walked back to the patio.

"Oh, I'll be back in the morning. I'm going to say Mass for everyone. My father here likes to go to church at home and miss the collection plate. Isn't that right, P.B.?"

P.B. merely winked solemnly as he hefted the platter of sweet-smelling meat and, bowing slightly to Maria, indicated that they should go back into the house.

P.B. loved suppers at his lake home, loved to talk about Rockne, and many, but not all, of the other adventures he had enjoyed through the years. It was a command performance for the family and only young Joe would occasionally spoil a story by giving the punch line before his father could deliver it. Martin never tired of the tales and Mae still smiled, although she was frequently reciting prayers to herself during the more familiar passages. The daughters-in-law remained eager to please and the grandchildren, all five of them, hung on his every word as P.B., knowing he was head of the clan, thought they should.

"Did I ever tell you about the fellow we called Michelangelo? Grand lad, still alive, I think, and he was an artist at copying records, diplomas, birth certificates. You name it and he could do it. He gave out more diplomas than the University of Chicago . . ."

"Why didn't he just draw his own money?" eight-year-old Kevin, a freckle-faced grandson, asked in a piping voice.

"He got two to five years for that once," his grandfather answered gravely as the children squealed with delight.

Thomas rose, excused himself, and headed toward the car which he had left parked on the drive that curved across the front lawn to the house. Maria walked with him. They could still hear bursts of laughter from inside as they stood looking at the harvest moon that seemed to be climbing up through the clusters of tall trees that filled the property.

"More trouble, Tom?"

"Yes, Maria, and not pleasant. Matt Finn, the coach, got a call about an hour after the game from Maurice Ryan, an old alumnus. It seems one of the priests has been arrested up in Chicago with Ryan's son. Matt's known the Ryans and he's gone in to find out what's happened. I don't know exactly what's wrong. The boy, the Ryan boy, was apparently hurt in some way. It's a mess."

"We always get separated by messes somebody else makes."

"It seems that way, doesn't it?" Tom leaned back against his car.

"Heavy thoughts, Tom. Try to think of something better on the drive in. Think about me. I'll be thinking about you. Hurry back. You know I leave tomorrow night for location in France."

"Okay," Thomas said, taking Maria in his arms gently, and kissing her on the mouth. She wrapped her arms around him and put her head on his shoulder.

"Let me hold you, Tom. Just for a minute."

They embraced in the quiet darkness and then Thomas inched away, putting his hand under her chin and turning her face up toward his.

"Who the hell ever said, 'Parting is such sweet sorrow'?"

"Somebody who didn't know what he was talking about," she answered as he climbed into the car and drove through the huddled trees toward the road to Chicago.

11

Autumn 1974

It was not quite two hours' drive from P.B.'s country place to the police station north of the Loop where Father Peters was being held along with a group of other people, half of them in garish costumes, one of them, a slender young man, half naked and his torso painted shiny silver. It was a yeasty roomful when Thomas arrived and the sight of the group, its members talking in affected tones to each other, bewildered and disturbed him. Frederick Peters looked up at him; he was in casual dress and he said nothing as Thomas approached. He shook Father Peters's hand and somebody whistled and everyone in the room laughed. That put an end, for the moment, to the thoughts that had obsessed him as he drove down around the edge of Lake Michigan, past the steel plants, and into Chicago. He forgot Maria and his own wondering heart as he followed an exasperated-looking police lieutenant with pale red hair down a corridor to a room where Maurice Ryan and Matt Finn were waiting to see him.

"Father, you shouldn't let that priest hang around with that crowd," the police officer said without even looking at Thomas. "I mean, Jesus Christ, that's no place for a priest, hanging around fag parties."

"What about the student?" Thomas interrupted.

"That's the point. The kid got stabbed. Not bad, but that's the risk with some of these fags. He's in Northwestern, mostly superficial wounds. They treated him in the emergency room but they wanted to keep him overnight."

"I'm very grateful for your concern, Lieutenant. How's the father?"

"Mad as a son of a bitch. What did you expect?"

"Do the papers know about this?"

"Well, you can't keep a thing like this secret forever, you know. I mean, Jesus Christ, Father, they're in this dive, one of the worst dives in the city. Excuse my language, Father, but, Jesus Christ, you've got to be looking for trouble to go into one of these places."

"I don't think Father Peters wanted any real trouble."

"The hell he didn't. Look, Father, this one was lucky. And we'll do what we can to keep his name out of the papers. But who knows what Ryan will do? And it's pretty hard to keep things quiet these days."

"Well," Thomas said, with a sigh that took half its energy from the afternoon stroll on the beach with Maria and half from the current bizarre act in Fred Peters's life, "I know you'll do what you can."

The officer opened the door on a small room where Maurice Ryan and Matt Finn sat in straight-back wooden chairs at a scarred round table.

"Well, Father," Maurice Ryan began somberly, "our bargain didn't work out, did it?"

Thomas reached out his hand and placed it on Ryan's shoulder. As he looked down at his face Thomas could see that Ryan had been crying.

"Maurice, there's nothing I can say to defend what's happened. We all only want to help your boy and see that the right thing is done."

Matt Finn ran his hand through his hair and spoke softly. "Yes, Morry, you know that. We all want to help."

"Well," Ryan said very deliberately, "you can begin by getting that man off your campus." He pointed in the general direction of the room where Father Peters and the others were being detained. "Because, if you don't, I'll come after him. I swear to God I will."

"We've had enough violence already," Thomas said as he pulled up a chair and sat at the table. The lieutenant moved around to a chair by the wall.

"Father Kinsella," Ryan began again, "my boy's in the hospital. He could be dead. Don't talk to me about enough violence. I'll kill that son of a bitch, with my own hands, I'll kill him if he's ever near me again."

"I'm not even sure what happened," Thomas said in the quiet that had been generated by Ryan's anger.

"I can tell you," Matt Finn said. "I had a call from Father Peters after today's game. He used to come and see me once in a while. He'd talk a little about his troubles, I guess because I was a coach and not directly involved with anything he was doing on the campus. And I had known him back in Chicago when I played for the Bears. He was our parish priest. He had lots of troubles and I'd encourage him to hang in there. You know, the same thing you'd say to anyone. And he knew I knew Maurice here. I guess he hoped I'd tell Maurice he was being a good boy."

Ryan shifted in his chair and then leaned his arms on the table. He drew an audible breath and stared blankly as the coach continued to talk.

"Well, I knew I was in over my head. I mean, I didn't know what he was talking about. He'd speak of being in love with young Phil and I thought, Geez, this guy has got to be kidding. But, I figured, what the hell, a lot of priests have listened to me in my time. I guess I can listen too. And I actually thought he was doing better. I mean, he really tried, he really did. If a man ever tried, Father Peters did. But there was pressure, I could see that. Then I got to feeling that I was being used in a way, used as a buffer sort of, between himself and Morry here. I didn't like that feeling at all."

"You were right, too," Ryan said mournfully.

"So I got this call. And it was a difficult time for me, right after a game. I had made arrangements to meet various reporters. And I had to make a television segment, analyzing the game. But Father Peters says he needs my help, that Phil Ryan's been stabbed, and could I come right into Chicago? The police hadn't come yet, and they were treating Philip, as best they could, at this place, the Green Necktie. I said to him, get the boy to a hospital, and he said it's not that easy and he gave me the address on Clark Street, and he hung up."

As it happened, Finn got a ride with a television crew that had flown out to the game in a small jet and was able to land at Meigs Field, Chicago's lakefront airport, a little less than an hour after he received the call. He climbed into a cab to go

e medics, who were just placing the stretcher into the
nbulance.

Maurice Ryan was wiping the tears from his eyes as he
ished his story. "A freak house, that's what it was. Playing
nes, cutting people up. A priest wanting to set up house-
eping with my son." He cleared his throat and slammed a
nched fist on the table. "What's happened anyway? What
hell has happened?"

I'm not sure anybody can tell you the answer to that,"
omas said. "But we'll do everything we can to help you
your family."

Get rid of that son of a bitch Peters," Ryan said coldly.
t rid of him before I do."

homas looked up at the lieutenant.

'd like to talk to Father Peters alone, if that's possible."
'll see what I can do. Mr. Ryan, have you made up your
about pressing charges? Do you want to make out a
laint?"

an looked up at him with glassy eyes. "No, no. No
laint. Just have them get this priest away from my son,
all. I don't want any more publicity for my boy. Can
o that?"

e can let them all go now, if that's what you mean. Can't
em from talking, of course, but it's not likely they'll say
As to the publicity, I'm not sure, like I told Father
But we'll do what we can. I mean, Mr. Ryan, I know
u feel, I mean, I know how I'd feel . . ."

anks, Lieutenant," Ryan said. Then he turned to Matt
'I wish to hell I was the one who hit Dracula. Would
me to the hospital with me?"

e," Finn replied.

join you as soon as I've talked to Father Peters,"
said, reaching his hand out to Ryan. "I guarantee
t we'll see that Father Peters stays away from Philip.
s more help than he's getting now." They all stood up
omas asked, "Where can I see Father Peters?"
here," the lieutenant said as Finn and Ryan left the
'll bring him back."

e," Thomas added. "Bring him back alive."

to the address Peters had given him just before six o'clock.
Finn felt uneasy as he opened the door onto a dark, tunnel-
like hall that led to a staircase near the back. He could hear
opposing charges of rock music exploding against each other
the way they often did back in the dormitories when the
students were playing their stereos at the same time. He
jumped as a veil of fringe and beads fell across his face in the
darkness. He could hear other sounds as he made his way up
the stairs, a toilet flushing and a muffled shout from behind a
closed door. Light pulsed in flashes through an opening on
the second floor and, steadying himself and wishing he had a
drink, Matt Finn entered the large room. A strobe light
device glared in his eyes and went dark as he heard a voice.

"Matt! Is that you?"

"Put some lights on, I can't see a thing."

Somebody switched on a lamp and Matt stopped dead still
as he looked around the large room, whose walls were hung
with curtains of a color he would not put on a football team.
People seemed to be everywhere in the dim glow, many of
them in costume. He could make out a man dressed as an
Indian brave, his body colored with war paint, a white feather
hanging from the ridge of black hair that bristled from his
otherwise completely shaven scalp. A woman dressed as an
Indian princess, her nakedness covered with cascades of
feathers and beads, stood numbly next to him. Satyrs and
nymphs, their faces colored green and blue, grinned as they
pulled back against the walls. A man in a high hat and a
flowing cape, his face painted in exaggerated Dracula-like
makeup, bowed to him and said, "You're some hunk," as
Matt brushed him aside to move toward a couch on which
Philip Ryan lay, his shirt off and his shoulder and right arm
covered with wet compresses through which red stains were
rising. Kneeling on the floor next to him was Father Peters,
dressed in a black turtleneck sweater and black pants. He was
wringing a washcloth into a basin as Finn approached.

"What the hell is going on here?" Finn boomed.

"Thank God, you're here, Matt. I knew I could count on
you, I was sure of it. We need some help, we need to take
care of Philip. He got hurt at the party."

"Party? What the hell do you mean, party?" He pushed
Father Peters aside and sat on the edge of the couch, taking
Philip's wrist to feel his pulse as he did so.

"Phil, Phil! It's me, Matt Finn. Are you all right?"

Father Peters began to apply the washcloth to the young man's head but Finn shouldered him out of the way.

"Let it go, Father, let it go. We've got to get a doctor. Let me look at these cuts." He lifted the compresses away from Philip's shoulder and winced. "This boy needs medical help. He's lost blood. He's got to have more than compresses, for God's sake. Do you want to kill him?"

Father Peters, at first angry that he had been pushed aside and then anxious as he heard the tone of Finn's voice, pulled back.

"Jesus, Father, this is serious. Get on the phone and get the fire department ambulance."

The onlookers began to chatter and one girl in white robes fell against the far wall and slowly slumped down until, her eyes as vacant as her head was filled with drugs, she was sitting in a kind of dancer's split on the floor. The Indian tittered and one of the guests, a young man in a green silken vest and pants, said in what Finn thought was a surprisingly normal voice, "There's a phone down the hall. I'll call. But then I'm splitting." Three or four others, blurs of felt and feathers in the weak light, hurried out after him.

"Phil, are you okay? We'll get you to a doctor soon. Don't worry."

Philip opened his eyes and looked dazedly into Finn's face.

"Where's Fred?" he asked softly. "Where's Fred?"

"I'm here, Philip. Don't worry. We just had a little bad luck, a little mistake at the party, that's all. Nobody meant to hurt you. You know that, don't you?"

"I'm hurt, Fred," he answered, and closed his eyes again.

By now Peters had edged up against the couch again. He reached out a hand and touched the young man's forehead.

"This is the hour of suffering and sacrifice," the Dracula-like character said in falsely deep tones. "Is the virginal offering ready?"

"Come on, come on," Father Peters said. "Haven't you caused enough harm already?"

The man in the black cape lurched forward. It was clear that he, like almost everyone else in the room, had been on drugs. "I must have blood from a beautiful boy," he said. "I am Fagula, the king of the Vampires." Then he broke into laughter and staggered across the room toward the door.

"Is that the son of a bitch who cut Philip?" Finn asked

angrily. He rose, overtook him in a stride, spun h
to see that he was holding a long-bladed knife i
hand, and, cocking his arm only a little more th
struck the Vampire, who dropped like a game
the floor. Shrieks from the costumed guests, tw
knelt down in attention beside the fallen Dr
Matt Finn kicked the knife under the couch jus
licemen and a medic from the fire department
room.

"I got there about twenty minutes later," I
said. "They were bundling some of the woo
Indians and God knows what into paddy wag
guys who don't think the newspapers will be
crazy. What a dump, full of rooms where pe
on the floors, and God knows what else. A
Philip bandaged up and on a stretcher and th
down the stairs, with Father Peters, mind y
bitch Peters, walking alongside. I said hello
says to me, 'Don't do anything to Fred,' and
he goes. Well, I grabbed Peters by the arm
to talk to you.'"

Father Peters was standing on the
looking up at Maurice Ryan, who had s
arm.

"Let go of me, Ryan! Your son wante
didn't take him against his will. He's
before. He's the one who brought me he

"You son of a bitch, if you weren't a
"What? Just what would you do?"

Ryan calmed down and relaxed his
you hanging around with my son anym

"Your son wants to live with me."

"Don't be crazy."

"And do you want to know why?
louder in the stairway's cramped s
around the two men as they stared at e
why. Because of what you made hir
one that deserves the credit for mak

Ryan's hand flicked out and slappe
Then Ryan turned and stomped dow

12

Autumn 1974

Father Thomas found the next few days very painful. He was
not sure what to think about Fred but he knew what he had to
do. "He's suffered enough for several lifetimes already,"
Thomas said to me. "But there's no point in punishing him,
even though things can't go on as they have." Thomas was in
a reflective mood; he had to talk it out. "His troubles started
a long time ago with his own father. And he's had trouble
with fathers, good and bad and in-between ones ever since.
There's the Archbishop, Fred's boss, who must be as bewildered as anybody to discover that priests and people are
reacting to things that happened a long time before when they
rebel against or over-flatter him." Thomas got up and walked
across his office. "He must be astounded when people treat
him normally, hard as that might be for the healthiest of
them. Something strange in him complicated the whole
problem Fred had, that's clear. In any case, Fred's going to
have to leave here, even though, considering the circus-like
nature of what happened, we've been able to keep things
pretty quiet." How was young Ryan? I asked.

"He'll be okay," Thomas replied, "but he's going to take a
leave to work out his own problems."

Thomas returned to his desk, searched for and found a thin
cigar, which he lighted as he began to talk again.

"I'll never forget speaking to him in the police station that
night. At first I was put off by the strange costumes and
behavior of the other people in the detention room with him.
But the police turned them loose and a few of them said

good-by to Fred with real concern for him. They seemed to care, that strange kid painted half silver and the spaced-out girl who hugged him and handed him her cigarette as she left. Poor Fred, like the next sheep on the ramp at the slaughterhouse. Looking at him all my disgust and irritation melted away. All I could think of was something my father always says about a man who has brought about his own ruin. 'The poor bastard, leave him alone.' Fred was a broken man last Saturday night. There's no question that he brought it about, in some way or other. Even he seemed to know that. 'I've used up my three wishes,' he said in that wistful voice of his. 'Is the firing squad ready?' "

Thomas put his cigar in an ashtray.

"I told him not to talk like that, that we would work something out, but that he had to stop seeing Philip Ryan, and that he would have to get more intensive help. I felt bad for him and, then, as he looked away from me, I suddenly felt in a vise, that he had me just where he wanted me. I can't quite explain it; it was as though he had stained me with his disgrace or infected me with his shame. I had come to the rescue again. And there I was in the middle of the night in a police station filled with strange people on one of the few weekends I had free. He was down but I had leaned so close to him that he had been able to pull me down too; he had me doing all the work, trying to think up a new plan to save him."

"Come, Thomas, you're too hard on yourself," I said.

"No, not at all," he answered. "I had two feelings. I had felt that way many times about Fred. There he was dragging on a misshapen cigarette, a last blessing from the merry pranksters he had made friends with; he looked almost hungrily at me, as though if I came closer, he would chew me up and show me that he could still destroy my efforts to help, that he could use the hatred in him to wound me and, in some strange way, to take the day for himself. I pulled back. I remember feeling that.

" 'Fred,' I said firmly, 'I want you to go into a hospital. There's a good Catholic one near here and they've got a psychiatric unit. I want you to get some rest for a few days. You're in no shape to go back with me.' " Thomas picked up his cigar and had to light it again.

"Fred said nothing for a moment. He just took a last puff on his cigarette, dropped it on the floor, and, like a man finally surrendering to overwhelming fatigue, said, 'Okay, Tom. You win.'

"I ordinarily would have explained to him that I wasn't trying to win anything but I suddenly realized that I really was, and that I wanted to win very badly, that, in fact, I had to win for his good and mine too. God knows I've been in on a number of emergency cases during my troubleshooting career. You know that." Thomas looked at his cigar. It was out again. He dropped it in the wastebasket. "I've seen people get themselves into incredible, almost indescribable, problems. You know at some point I seemed always to be driving or flying by night to rescue somebody, or bail somebody else out, or put Monsignor So and So into the asylum for a while. Most of them were just poor, confused people who hadn't wanted to cause trouble but who just couldn't cope with life. Their problems were the only distress signals they knew how to fly, the only way they knew they would get some attention. I never felt in a contest with any of them; I never felt I had to win. They always seemed relieved when I arrived on the scene.

"It was different with Fred. From the first day he told his troubles to us, Austin, I felt that he had given me an unequal share of his burden, that it wasn't accidental that he let me take the responsibility of getting him out of Chicago and into Notre Dame. And it wasn't accidental that he drew you into it. He just piled pressure on me by doing that. I had to show you I was in charge." I raised my eyebrows but said nothing. "And he had tried me over and over again during his months on campus too. Fred was always throwing down a gauntlet at my feet, especially after times when I had enjoyed some success or recognition. That's how he was when he wanted to go public and when he started the trouble with Philip. I wanted to win, I had to win. So help me God, I had to get him under control." Thomas got up and walked to the windows again. "That has always been a goal for me, I can see that now. You must know that about me." I nodded but said nothing. "Fred kept prodding me, getting my attention when it slipped away for a few weeks, forcing me to make the treatment I had decided on for him work. Whatever has been going on has involved something he has been trying to do to me as much as anything else."

Thomas wasn't waiting for me to reply. What could I say in view of the whole situation?

"I don't regret getting him under control. That was the right thing to do. But I'm not entirely pleased with myself, or perhaps I should say Fred has made me feel bad because I've done what I knew had to be done." Thomas paused and closed his eyes. "He's coming back to the campus today. He'll be here for an appointment with me at five o'clock. These few days at the hospital have calmed him down but we'll have to get him to a private hospital this week for extended treatment, no doubt about it. I'm not going to let him manipulate me into feeling bad again. And I won't let him make me angry either. The Archbishop, who is his boss, has approved plans for further treatment, so it's all settled, as long as it's someplace far away from Chicago or here."

As it turned out, Thomas's meeting with Fred Peters went reasonably well. Fred seemed chastened and a little frightened, something like a child who knows that he has finally gone too far. But he agreed to go to St. Catherine's, a private Catholic psychiatric hospital near Washington where the doctors had a lot of experience with priests. Thomas was firm with him but still friendly and he detailed Jack Allen to go with him. He didn't want Fred disappearing somewhere along the way.

Jack was in Father Thomas's office the next afternoon after all the arrangements had been made.

"You know, Tom," Father Allen said quietly, "I wonder about Fred. Not that I can understand homosexuals. But maybe it was just another case of surprising combinations, and of something being set off in him that he never understood or never had a taste of before. Love, I mean. Maybe, in the midst of that mess, he was reaching for love, or trying to give it. I don't know, I really don't. I'm just not surprised too much, not after I've had a chance to think things over anyway."

It was then that the phone rang and, as soon as Thomas picked it up, it was clear that it was bad news. His face clouded as he asked a few brief questions. Then he replaced the telephone and, visibly shaken, began to stand up. Allen held the match he had just struck expectantly in midair.

"There's been an accident, Jack. Fred Peters is dead."

13

Autumn 1974

It was kept very quiet, of course, and, as far as I know, not a word of Father Peters's sad end was hinted about, much less printed in the papers. It was I, you see, who discovered the body. I had been over to St. Mary's to visit an old friend, Sister Claudia, almost as old as myself and around the campus about as many years. She was ill and, after I left the infirmary, I took a stroll back toward the river. St. Mary's Chapel backs up to the St. Joseph on a bluff about fifty feet high and, although the water rushes swiftly in some seasons, that afternoon it was only a placid stream flowing between the banks of rocks. That's where I saw this figure, face up, arms and legs thrown at angles, in a jumbled and terrible crucifixion on the rocks. I wasn't sure who it was from that distance and I felt a little weak and came close to pitching over the side myself but I hurried back to the college, where the nuns called the emergency squad. Then I climbed into their car with them to drive down and around to the other side of the river from where the body lay.

The ambulance and a police car, their lights circling eerily, were there when we arrived. In a few moments Father Thomas and Father Allen, both of them looking grim, pulled up. The medics had forded the shallow river in their hip boots and Thomas went over to the squad ambulance to see if they had an extra pair. He put them on and made his way to the other side while Father Allen stood with me and the gathering onlookers. I could see Thomas kneel down next to the body and make a sign of the cross over it. Then he bowed his head for a few moments in prayer and stood up to let the emergency workers put the body on a stretcher and bring it back across the river. As they lifted the limp figure I could see who it was, just as I could see that the back of his head was smashed badly as they placed him on the stretcher and then covered him with a sheet. Father Allen made the sign of the cross too as they brought Father Peters, as tenderly as they could, back to our side of the river and placed him in the ambulance. Thomas stepped carefully across the rock-filled water; he looked very grave as he walked toward us.

"I'll ride with the ambulance. Will you meet me at the hospital?" he asked as he pulled off the borrowed boots.

So Father Allen and I climbed into the car the two of them had come in and made the sad journey behind the ambulance and the police car, their lights flashing and their sirens going, although to what use now I was not sure. In about five minutes we were at the emergency room of St. Joseph's Hospital, sitting on uncomfortable little chairs and waiting for Thomas to come out of a room he had gone into with a doctor and a policeman. It might have been a half hour before he emerged, a bulky brown envelope in his hands and a very subdued and uncomfortable look on his face.

"There's nothing more we can do here," he said softly. "Let's go back. There will be plenty to do there."

I went along, depressed but strangely excited by the awful event, and I sat in Father Thomas's office as he and Father Allen made a number of phone calls to notify Father Peters's relatives and others, like his Archbishop, who had to know what happened.

"An accident," Father Thomas was saying. "Apparently Father went for a walk over by St. Mary's, lost his footing, and fell. He was killed instantly. We'll handle things here if you let us know any special instructions about a funeral home in Chicago. Thanks, Your Excellency. Yes, thanks very much."

Thomas replaced the telephone on its cradle, let his swivel chair turn a quarter of an arc, and sat as if in contemplation for perhaps half a minute. He seemed suddenly to pull himself forcibly out of his reflective mood and, hard edges sounding through his soft tones, spoke to Father Allen and me.

"This envelope contains Fred's personal effects. These things have to go to his family, his sisters. His parents are both dead, as I think you know. I looked these things over at the hospital. The police officer was very understanding and co-operative. There's not much here but there are a couple of letters, one for me and one for Philip Ryan. This is what is in mine:

Tom,
     I will be gone when you read this. I am very peaceful about my decision. I'm going to get out of the last corner I've painted myself into.
     I can't live no matter what I do. Philip has gone back to his father. Funny how those tough guys keep on winning, isn't it? Philip was the only person I ever truly loved and the only one who ever truly loved me.
     I won't miss the pain. You can't imagine how much pain I suffered. I know I've caused you pain too, you and Notre Dame and a lot of other people who wanted to be reasonable with me.
     That's why I'm doing this. I don't want to be reasonable. I can't be reasonable. Why be reasonable about life? It's never been reasonable with me.
     I can't live with guilt any more. I've tried to get rid of it, tried to drown it out, tried to find some relief with Philip's friends in Chicago. They all wanted me to be reasonable too, they all wanted me to stay a priest and not end up, as a girl told me one night, "dying all the time." That was what it was like for me, dying all the time, nothing but death. Life has all been time on the cross.
     You're going to have to take care of things. You must be used to that by now. I'm sorry but I can't help doing these things to you.
     I'll make it look like an accident. You do the rest.
     May God have mercy on my soul.
                                             Fred

Thomas placed the letter carefully on his desk and looked across at Father Allen and me.

"Fred killed himself, God have mercy on him."

"We've been telling everybody it was an accident," Jack Allen said in surprised tones. "This will be upsetting for his family, I mean, for everybody."

"We're not going to tell anybody," Thomas said firmly.

"Truths like this come out, Tom."

"I don't think so. He's let me know. That's what he wanted to do and that's done. There's no point in telling his Archbishop. He's liable to deny him Christian burial and turn the body over to the Unitarians or something. He doesn't have any feelings, not real ones, for a problem like this."

"That's a little harsh, Tom. The Archbishop would cooperate, you know that."

"He might. But he'd talk, he can't help himself. He's a gossip, it's about the only recreation he has. Can't you hear him now? 'Did you hear about the suicide down at Notre Dame? That's what comes of modern Catholic education.' He'd blame it on the University, you can be sure of that. He'd send a report to Rome, saying a priest of his lost his faith and killed himself at Notre Dame."

I had never heard Thomas speak in quite this way. He sounded as shrewd and unsentimental as old P.B. It was as though Father Peters's death had set off something in him, a previously hidden or muted instinct to get right to the heart of things, to act powerfully and swiftly and to show the Kinsella colors as he did it. Even Jack Allen, who was used to everything, seemed surprised at Thomas's forcefulness, the way a parent might when recognizing unsuspected powers in his own child.

"Notre Dame is not known for suicides. We have a remarkable record especially since suicides at universities are almost routine these days."

"But . . ." Jack Allen broke off before he said anything.

"I'm not just trying to keep the notoriety away from our name. But that is part of what I'm doing. Fred was not from here, he didn't go to school here."

"He died here," Jack said quietly.

"That's right, Jack. In an accident. He fell while walking by the river."

"Has anybody else seen that letter?"

"It was unopened when the police gave it to me. They didn't ask any questions."

"Well, perhaps it's for the best," I said, rather weakly.

"Can't you understand that this will be for the best for Fred and for his family too? What good will there be in adding to their grief by telling them their brother committed suicide because he was so guilty about being gay? Do you think there would be much comfort for anybody in that? People get enough bad news every day. They'd never get over it. They'd be sobbing and having Masses said for him for the rest of their lives. The way it is, they don't even know we were going to ship him off to St. Catherine's Institute. What do they lose, not knowing all the truth? They save a lot more by having a memory of a brother who worked hard in Chicago, and the inner city at that, and at Notre Dame."

"Yes, yes," I said. "Much better for them." Jack Allen said nothing, although he seemed less tense than he had been a moment before.

"We've kept the incident in Chicago quiet. Maurice Ryan has no reason to bring it up. In fact, he'll probably be relieved to hear that Fred is dead. What do you think he would say, and where, if he found out Fred killed himself?"

"What about Philip?"

"Philip has had enough troubles without thinking that he was responsible, even in a small way, for Fred's death." Thomas picked up the other sealed envelope. "This is addressed to Philip. I'm not going to read it. But neither is he." Thomas began, very carefully, to tear it into shreds and to drop them into his wastebasket. Neither Father Allen nor I spoke.

"If this letter is anything like mine, Phil doesn't need it. Whether it's a beautiful love letter or one putting the hook into him from beyond the grave doesn't matter. Philip and Fred parted as friends. And lovers, I guess. I don't know. But this letter won't make those memories any better. It might only spoil them. And I don't believe in spoiling people's memories or their dreams. That's all a lot of them have."

He dropped the last shred of letter into the basket. Then he took his own and did the same to that.

"Fred Peters died a tragic death. In an accident. He ought to be remembered without all the complications that being called a suicide brings on a person's name."

We were all quiet for a while. Everything had been settled without ambiguity. That's what Thomas was doing, I thought, removing the ambiguity that had always clung to Father Peters's life, performing his own spiritual autopsy, fighting him right over the threshold of death, under control at last.

"We'll have work to do tonight. We had better get some dinner." And with that, and in a settled but somber mood, we headed for the Morris Inn.

14

Autumn 1976

You have to know about Rome, for that's where I saw all the principal players in place and felt the engagement of forces, old and new, of this long story. It was in that fall that the aging Pope named both Leo Williams and Henrique Muñoz to be Cardinals, along with a baker's dozen and a few more besides from all over the world with every slant of eye and color of skin represented. A strange roll of the dice to have Williams and Muñoz on the same roster but long before that I had given up trying to understand Providential ways. I was happy, however, when Bishop Muñoz, who had also been named Archbishop of Lima at the same time, sent invitations to the Consistory at which he would get his red hat to Father Thomas, Father Allen, and, finally, as St. Paul says, to one born out of due time, myself. And I was even more delighted when Thomas bought me a ticket to go along to see the great city of Rome and the ceremony that would transform the humble Muñoz and the proud Williams into Princes of the Church.

TWA had rechristened the jumbo jet as *The Spirit of Chicago* just for the occasion. It wasn't every day, after all, that the city's Archbishop was made a Cardinal, and a special chartered flight had been arranged for the faithful who could afford it. Since Archbishop Williams had been a friend of old P.B.'s since the thirties, P.B. took his whole family along, Mae, the sons and their wives and the oldest grandchild, to see Williams receive his red hat. The new Cardinal was up in the first-class section with the Kinsellas and Mayor Daley and a crowd of micky-looking Irish whose boisterous good spirits could have burst the swinging doors off the corner bar.

There were other fellows, as I've said, from all over, some brown and some yellow and a few blacks. Father Allen said that the College of Cardinals was getting more like the Notre Dame football team all the time, except, of course, that you still had to be a Catholic to be a Cardinal. Just to add to the relationships that were to be underscored by the event, Maria Moore was in Rome working on a film with Fellini and Thomas was sure to see her. They had wrestled with their relationship over the years since they had met, with thousands of priests dropping out to get married in the background, but Thomas, resolute and determined—and ambitious, don't forget that—kept enough distance to survive quite well. He was a good priest, as you know, but I felt that he still never let himself know just how much Maria loved him. As for Maria, she had plunged even more energetically into her career, especially since the peace movement had tapered off, Nixon had left the White House, and demonstrations were almost a thing of the past. But she loved him, mostly from afar, I feared, and at what cost I didn't know. Not that I should sound so hard on Thomas, since he did care for her, he did love her even if he wasn't quite able to say it, and—they say it's a woman's gift—she was good at waiting. But she was waiting, of that I'm sure.

Anyway, there we were, like one great cocktail party flying across the Atlantic with Jack Allen entertaining everybody with his stories of clerical life. Thomas stood a foot or so away, in the space near the galley where they were serving drinks, laughing with the rest of them as Allen issued a warning for the new Cardinal Muñoz.

"Well, the thing is, Tom," Allen said with affected grimness, "you better warn him not to sign anything. That's where they get these fellows who just come in from the hills. Tell him to read the fine print. And tell him not to accept any of that papal jelly they send around. Many's the good man who sampled that on his morning toast and never saw evening again. Favorite trick of these wops. They even kill their own. Look what they did to John XXIII. Why, he was a healthy old gentleman, ate everything without a complaint all his life. Then he becomes Pope and calls a Council. First thing you know he's got stomach trouble and the next thing he's being given the big funeral. Very swift piece of work. Now, you warn Muñoz. He's not the kind they like hanging around, especially not in the Third World."

Laughter all around the galley, but it died away as Archbishop Williams, in a black suit with a chain that could have handled the anchor of the U.S.S. *Constitution* draped across his vest, edged through the curtain that separated the sections of the plane. P.B. was smiling like a satisfied political boss as he accompanied the Archbishop on his rounds of the big 747 that was filled with well-wishers eager for a handshake or a few words before they got to Rome. P.B. angled around by the side of Archbishop Williams.

"Here's the Notre Dame contingent," P.B. said, introducing all of us, not that the Archbishop didn't know Thomas anyway.

"I'm glad you could all make the trip," the Archbishop said in his slightly nasal voice. He was not great for small talk and, as Thomas thought, he did not really care, not down deep he didn't, about all the proffered hands and good wishes. He was great for the thin little smile, of course, and the "God bless you" that slipped off his tongue like a gumdrop, but as Thomas once heard his father say, all things being equal, there was not a lot of proof that Williams had a soul. Thomas was pleasant, as polished as the knob on a colonial door, but he was never comfortable with the man from Chicago who would, within a few days, become a Cardinal. And, despite all the business they had done over the years, he was not sure that old P.B. liked him very much either. The Archbishop and P.B. knew how to use each other; they had been doing it, for mutual profit, for decades, but they were not close to each other. P.B. did not want to be and Archbishop Williams did not really know how. It seemed a little sad, in this plane filled with good feelings, to watch P.B., smooth as the flight itself, escorting the Archbishop, who, while pleasant, might have given off a hollow sound if anybody bumped him too hard.

Thomas was thinking about his friend Muñoz, the poor and earthy pastor who was so different from Williams.

"It's the wonder of the Church," Thomas said to Father Allen and me, "that men as different as Muñoz and Williams should become Cardinals at the same time." He smiled and sipped a drink of scotch that he had been nursing for a thousand or so miles above the sea. We all turned slightly to watch the Cardinal Designate and P.B. make their way down the side aisle, where some people rose from their seats and leaned over to kiss Williams's ring while others gushed or asked him to autograph some souvenir of the trip.

"Well, there was a good thief and a bad one," Allen said with a smile. "That's been about average all through the history of this organization. Hell, if all the Cardinals were honest men, God might think the prophecy about the conversion of the world had been fulfilled and it might come to an end." We all smiled, and then decided to sit down and try for some rest before the plane, then at the high point of its arch above the Atlantic, began to curve down toward Rome.

We landed in Rome. Despite the queasiness the time zone change tripped off in me after we landed, I was excited to see the Eternal City for the first time. Except for the Archbishop, who went to Villa Stritch, a place maintained by the American hierarchy, the Chicago contingent was taken by chartered bus to the Cavalieri Hilton, a grand place spread across Monte Mario with rooms that opened on a panorama of the city. After a refreshing sleep I cranked up the slatted metal shade to see the view. Rome looked like a rising sea beyond the balcony outside my room, a coffee-colored sea frozen against the thin line of the distant hills. It was early October and smoke drifted up in a hundred places from the first burning of the leaves. I stood on the balcony and looked to the right at the dome of St. Peter's knuckling up out of the mass of Vatican City, a line of cypresses rising like a hooded choir above the great thrust of the church itself. The noise of the traffic, the tinny counterpoint of all the timeless grandeur of Rome, rose up from the city below. I was on the point of having lofty thoughts when my phone rang. It was Father Thomas.

"Austin, Maria's at the Excelsior with her secretary. Would you like to go over there with me in an hour or so?"

I sensed that he did not want to go calling in public on a famous movie star, that he wanted me to be a sort of chaperone. I agreed, of course, and we decided to meet in the lobby after we had breakfast. A number of the Chicagoans were up and about, cameras slung over their shoulders for their tours of the city before the big day of Cardinal making, the Consistory, as it was called, that was half a week off. P.B. and Mae were just going out onto the broad balcony on the city side of the hotel with Mayor Daley and his wife, Sis, a solid and settled-looking quartet, I thought to myself as

Thomas came out of the elevator to greet me. He was unusually light of step, a condition that arose whenever he was going to see Maria, and we headed immediately toward the cabstand at the main entrance.

"Jack is going to visit an old friend of his who's a prior of some religious order today. Otherwise he'd come with us."

No need to explain, I thought, smiling to myself at the eagerness of a heart that had been puzzled by love and its mysterious imperatives of separation and longing. Not that he didn't seem his usual highly disciplined and confident self. But that morning, I thought, he was leaving the powerful behind for a while; he was moved not by ambition but by another force that he did not fully understand. Not that I did either, mind you, but it seemed right somehow and I was a benign old uncle who granted some permission for it.

We entered the great opulent bulge of the Excelsior but I didn't see any of the Via Veneto Jet Set, just members of the hotel staff jabbering exuberantly with each other, sawing the air with their hands, shrugging their shoulders, coming together in groups and dividing like an erratically graceful organism, all the while giving the impression that they were actually doing something. Thomas had no eyes for such sidelights, however, as we marched to the elevator and up to Maria's suite of rooms. Her secretary, Helen Barnes, received us with the tempered warmth of the professionally discreet and in a moment Maria, in a green silk dress, came in to greet us. With all her control and theatrical discipline, she couldn't stage an entrance when Thomas was in the room. She just embraced him and as they looked into each other's eyes I just crossed my legs and looked away. The secretary had already left the room.

"Austin," she said, "forgive me." Maria stepped away from Thomas as I fumbled my way to a standing position and gave her a peck on the cheek.

"It's grand to see you, Miss Moore," I said, suddenly realizing that neither she nor Thomas had said anything, nothing out loud anyway. But they then fell quickly to talking and, as on so many previous occasions when I had seen them together, I was touched by the way they seemed so close even though they spent most of their time away from each other. I realized how hard it must be and yet, for all the sacrifice involved, wondered if such a demanding relationship could survive if they were less extraordinary than they were, or if they had a house filled with kids, bills to pay, and a pile of dirty dishes in the sink.

I'm not sure exactly how it happened but in a few minutes I found myself dispatched along with Helen Barnes to do some errands. Well, Helen was pleasant and all, but I felt excluded, no doubt of that, and Helen just kept her poker face, as though she had been sent on make-believe errands before. Back in the hotel room Thomas and Maria were sitting alone. I thought about that for a moment and immediately dismissed the images that came to my mind.

"It's been a long time, Tom," Maria said softly.

"Too long," Thomas replied. "I'm still at the same old store."

"But I understand you may be running it some day."

"Don't believe those stories. Father Hesburgh is still a young man."

"And a handsome one. It doesn't seem fair, Notre Dame cornering all you handsome priests."

"Put a Roman collar on anybody and they immediately look better."

Maria paused a moment and bit her lip before she spoke.

"Tom, we've got to settle a few things. I've thought about this ever since you called to tell me that you were coming for this Cardinal-making business. When I heard from you and knew you'd be here, it set something loose in me."

Thomas stirred uneasily in his chair. He had been troubled about things ever since Fred Peters had killed himself, troubled about the twisted and unadmitted side of Church life, the side he had seen so closely, the side he had helped to tidy up so often to make it look like nothing had happened, to smooth out the surface and obscure the fact that human fault arched through all its foundation stones. When he thought about Maria, he thought about sunshine and fresh air, about the good things, the simply human good things that seemed always just beyond his grasp. And he felt the conflict between loving her and loving his work. Was it, he wondered at times, a clash between love and power? Could any man have both?

"Tom," Maria said, standing up and moving toward his chair, "I've loved you since the first night we met . . ."

Thomas looked up at her, unsure of whether he wanted to defend himself against the tide of longing that rose in him. He had resisted for so many years, giving his best energy, it seemed, to the broken and the corrupt, and saving himself from what, like spring rain, was fresh and pure. And right, he thought to himself, not only good but right.

"You mean the snowstorm . . . the flat tire . . . ?"

"And you with the slush all over your coat." Maria spoke very softly. "How wonderful you looked, like a boy who'd been playing out in the cold." She sat down on the edge of his chair and put her hand on his arm. He looked up into her face and neither of them said anything at all. They just looked at each other, as though they could not inhabit this moment of presence fully enough after all the times they had said good-by and been away from each other.

Maria did not feel troubled. She felt, in fact, at peace with herself, as though she had let some restraints fall away within her and the world had not ended, that she had let go and felt that it was the right thing to do, yes, no matter what, it was the right thing to do . . .

Thomas gazed up at her and he knew that something was loosening within himself as well. If this was temptation, then he had misunderstood it all these years and he did not really understand the way people lived. Thomas was also calm, sensing that whatever was to take place was inevitable, that it had to happen despite twinges in his spirit that seemed like warnings and the death throes of misplaced discipline at the same time.

Maria bent down and kissed him, first on the forehead, then on the eyes, and accepting his embrace, fully on the mouth. He held her in his arms as they both finally accepted the simple imperative of their love. They had checked a fundamental demand for years but a moment had come, like the urgent time for love or death or the waiting harvest, that could be neither denied nor postponed. Now that it had arrived, it was not filled with the anguish of conflict but with a mood of peace and rightness. All the feelings that had been withheld for so long, or pumped into other channels, into hard work or peace marches, or into binding up the wounds of the clergy, now these had to be expressed just to each other.

They did not speak or struggle; they simply understood that they could not express themselves to each other except in this way. This was the truth for them, running strong and pure as rushing water, and all the piled-up dams of the years had fallen away. They rose and began to walk across the room.

Thomas looked again at Maria, who seemed transformed and almost luminous to him. He could still hear the canons of caution echoing within him and he hesitated for just a moment.

But this had a life of its own by now and they moved silently into the suite's bedroom and closed and locked the door.

Thomas stood there like a man in a spell as he took off his coat and began to loosen his clerical collar. He watched Maria, who looked infinitely delicate as she undressed, like a bloom of a fine and timeless structure that was opening for him alone. They did not speak, because their embrace bore the weight of what, at one level of awareness or another, they had wanted to express for years.

It was only later that Thomas began to feel uncertain, it was only as they were dressing, still half caught by the power of the consummation they had shared, and still without a name for what was so simple and wordless despite all the words that had been spoken and written about it, it was only then that he began to feel uneasy, that he shouldered again the burden of the righteous and dutiful role that was his life.

Thomas wondered if Fred Peters, in some shimmering vale of eternity, had thrown his head back in laughter at what could be described by those who did not understand these moments as the most ancient and vulgar pantomime, the desecration of goodness, the fall in the garden acted out again with a new set of players. Fred would feel righteous now, because Thomas had lost his innocence and a right to judgment on this day in, of all places, the heart of Rome, where the shadow of the all too human Church fell across everything. Thomas was subdued, like a man who had made a long and necessary journey, and, now that it was done, was not sure what to make of it. He wondered if death would be like this too, different than everyone supposed when it finally came.

Maria was quiet too, although she seemed peaceful, as though she had done what she had to do and would not regret it. But she was concerned about Thomas because she thought he would not remain comfortable with himself and that all the tiny ogres of guilt would soon be scaling the walls of his spirit in order to pull it down. And just as she knew that they had to give themselves to each other, so she now felt that she must allow him to go away. She was not sure if Thomas would come back, or when, but she had understood the mystery of waiting for a long time. She had passed through the hardest part and, for a while at least, she could give him back to the work in which he was involved.

"I know you won't be seeing me for a while," she said softly.

Thomas nodded. "I need some time to think."

"No, Tom," Maria said, drawing close to him as he adjusted his collar. "Don't think. Just let it be. Let's both just let it be for a while."

Thomas nodded again as though he understood that letting things be was the right course but he was at a loss to know why.

They were sitting in the living room of the suite, pretty much the same as they had been when we left. The same, except for the quiet. They said little and, truth to tell, they seemed peaceful enough to me. In fact, the tension that sometimes built up when they were together had drained away. Helen and I gave our report and, after we all had some sandwiches and coffee, Thomas and I got up to leave.

"Would you come to the Consistory?" Thomas asked. "Archbishop Muñoz would like that."

"We'd be delighted," Maria answered. "Can you make the arrangements?"

"I'd like to see our new Cardinal," Thomas said as we turned toward the Pincian Gate at the top of the street. "Muñoz, I mean. He's staying with the Maryknoll Fathers just a few blocks away."

We turned down the Via Sardegna and, after we entered the Maryknoll House, I found myself handed off again while Thomas went up to his old friend's room.

Thomas was kneeling by the Cardinal-Designate's chair. Although he was making a traditional Catholic confession, he did not accuse himself so much of sin as of confusion, saying that he was not sure that he had done anything wrong, but that he wanted to admit it all anyway. A very Catholic notion, I might add, since people often mentioned things in confession more to be reassured rather than absolved.

"My failing," he said as simply as a child, "is that I am so concerned with my own life, that I haven't asked myself what I really want or what I should do now . . ."

"My friend," Muñoz said, his hand touching his forehead and his eyes closed, the classic position for a Catholic confessor, "you feel you have failed but you do not know how. And now you are confessing something God already knows, that you are not perfect, that you have doubts, that you are confused . . ."

Muñoz's voice was very gentle as he spoke. "Perhaps you have discovered the best part of yourself, your humanness. That is what love lays bare in us. We are all sinners. Why else would God love us? No one can love anything or anybody who is perfect. There is no broken place for the light to shine through."

The Cardinal-Designate reached his hand over and placed it on Thomas's shoulder, his deep brown eyes locking on the bright blue eyes of Father Kinsella. "My friend, Tomás, you have found out that you are human, that you can love and be loved by someone else. This is not a wicked discovery, this is the truth you must know about yourself. Love is always confusing but, as you know, love is not the worst problem a man—even a priest—can have. What you want to do is to understand it, for your sake and for that of your friend. You must pray, yes, but you must never think you are condemned for loving, not if the love is true."

"I don't want to be easy on myself," Thomas interjected earnestly.

"Yes, yes, of course," Muñoz said softly. "God is not worried about that. He knows it is hard enough to be truthful with ourselves. And he wants you to face that truth for the sake of both of you. To have discovered that you are human is a blessing, my friend, and it will keep you from ever being too hard on anyone else. Perhaps that is what you are to learn from this."

Thomas lowered his eyes and began to recite the Act of Contrition as the Cardinal-Designate raised his right hand and, tracing a sign of the cross in the air, spoke the words of absolution.

Back at the Hilton another scene was just unfolding.

P.B. watched Archbishop Williams's face as he slipped into his Cardinal's cassock for the first time, his life's ambitions fulfilled. There he was in Rome, a laborer's son who used to play at being a priest when he was a little boy by cutting the newspaper so that it looked like a chasuble and pretending to say Mass at the kitchen table. Yes, a long and prosperous journey for this man who had grown as bulky as Santa Claus with little of his merriment, and held a bag that might be filled but was not easily opened for anyone else's benefit. There was something about those eyes, those narrow gray eyes into which Patrick had looked on so many occasions over forty years, something about their reserve that made P.B. think of the remark his mother used to make that "Still water lies deep with the divil at the bottom."

Williams, Leo Cardinal Williams, looked at himself in the glass as he adjusted his bright crimson sash. How often, Patrick thought, he had seen him preen himself before; no man had ever enjoyed the various shades of red that marked his rise from Monsignor through Auxiliary Bishop to Archbishop of Chicago more than Leo Williams. Well, P.B. used to think, what the hell, he knew what he wanted and has sucked the sweetness out of every upward move like a kid with a bag of candy at the Saturday matinee. Williams had never lost that look; he had it as he tried on the cassock he had just picked up at the ecclesiastical tailors in Rome.

"How does it look, Pat?" the Cardinal-Designate asked, turning slightly to check his profile, not as sleek as it once was, and to reach into a box overflowing with tissues to pluck out a bright red skullcap. He fingered its watered silk for a moment.

"This is the zucchetto, Mae," he said without looking across the room to where she sat sipping an afternoon glass of sherry. "How do you think it looks?"

"Heavenly," Mae answered wryly enough to cause P.B. to glare momentarily at her. Williams plopped the skullcap on his crown of graying hair and then fiddled with it until he was pleased with the image that came back to him from the mirror.

"You look great," P.B. said, although he was secretly amused at Williams's cardinalatial style show. He wanted to get down to business. "Now what's the schedule tomorrow?"

Williams removed the zucchetto and dropped it into its tissued box. He unsnapped the crimson sash and draped it over an arm of the couch in the sitting room of the Kinsella suite, in which they were gathered.

"The new cardinals will be with the Holy Father in the Private Consistory while all of you gather at the new audience hall to wait for us to come in for the Public Consistory, when the Pope gives us our red hats. You'll have good seats, but you ought to be there by eight-thirty. And you know the Roman traffic." All of this in a bored nasal tone that was familiar to all of Chicago. Williams unbuttoned the black cassock with the scarlet trim and, shaking it loose from his shoulders, more or less stepped out of it and caught it as it fell behind his back with a gesture that was second nature for a man who had been putting on and taking off ecclesiastical garments all his life. Mae stood up and walked toward him.

"Let me fold that for you, Your Eminence," she said with a smile. Williams did not protest her use of what would soon be his official title.

"Now, if you two old friends have a moment, I'd like to try on the red cassock too." He fished among the tissues in another cardboard box on the couch and pulled out a completely crimson garment.

"What's that made of, wool?" Mae asked as P.B. fought off a yawn that was growing like a tumor inside him.

"Yes, Mae," Archbishop Williams said. "Can you imagine that? Pope Paul VI changed many things that shouldn't have been changed. The Mass, for one thing. And the watered silk in the Cardinal's cassock, that's another. You need a touch of splendor in the College of Cardinals. But he clipped everything away, the red shoes, the *galero* . . ."

"What the hell was the *galero?*" P.B. asked. "I don't remember seeing any of those when I was an altar boy."

"The flat red hat with the tassels, Pat, the great hat they would hang up in the Cardinal's Cathedral after he died. You've seen them at Holy Name . . ."

P.B. nodded. "I don't know, Leo, a little simplicity is good. That's the taste of the modern world. Why, Tom's spic friend Muñoz'll probably show up in somebody's red flannel nightshirt that's been fixed up for the occasion."

"Yes," Williams said, buttoning the red cassock. "Archbishop Muñoz is all for that sort of thing. My thinking, however, is that, if you're a Prince of the Church, you ought to look like one. Isn't Muñoz a revolutionary? I mean, I've heard such talk in the past, that he's worn pistols and so forth." The Cardinal-Designate looked at himself in the mirror, trying to accept the red wool that was so dull in comparison to the possibilities of red watered silk.

"I suppose it's okay. You know my old friend, Archbishop Micolajczyk, the fellow who's the Nuncio in the Balkans, he was at the tailor's the other day and he ordered a watered silk cassock anyway, for use outside Rome. Not a bad idea."

"You don't want to do that in Chicago," Mae said. "Somebody might write to the Pope about you."

Williams was not sure of how to take her, but the idea of being reported for not wearing regulation vestments was upsetting to him. He knew about letters to the Holy See to cite infractions and abuses; he had written enough of them himself over the years. Besides, he was still ambitious. Williams might yet end up as the head of a Roman congregation with a hand in the most intimate affairs of the Holy See. Nothing was beyond the realm of possibility for the new Cardinal. Back in Chicago the priests had a classic clerical joke about their archbishop. Raising a glass, a frustrated curate would say, "Here's to the Archbishop, the only man who looks on the Papacy as a steppingstone." And the priests, familiar with the cud of ambition that Williams habitually chewed on, would laugh bitterly.

The next morning was symbolic in many ways, now that I look back on it. Not that anyone wanted it to be that way exactly. It was one of those things that just worked itself out. Archbishop Williams and his retinue were driven to the Apostolic Palace of the Vatican in a limousine, and Pat and Mae, along with the Daleys, had their own big car to take them to the Pier Luigi Nervi Audience Hall, a modernistic low-slung building off to the left of St. Peter's. And the rest of the Chicago crowd came in pretty good style too, tickets in hand, to wait for the ceremonies of the Public Consistory. Cardinal-Designate Muñoz, along with some new cardinals from Africa and the South Pacific, were bundled into tiny little Italian cars. Father Thomas, Father Allen, and I were crammed into a Fiat that didn't seem much bigger than an American refrigerator. We followed Archbishop Muñoz, who was in another Fiat along with two priests from Peru and one of the Maryknollers with whom he was staying.

"Jesus," Jack Allen said as we entered a traffic circle like a pellet dropping into a roulette wheel, "we're lucky we didn't have to ride on Vespas."

Father Thomas just smiled. He had been unusually quiet since our visit to Maria's, but he seemed at peace and he was very happy for his friend Henrique Muñoz, as, indeed, were we all. We were in the van of the Cardinal from the wrong side of the tracks, or at least the bottom side of the hemi-sphere, but he seemed like the right kind of shepherd to me, red or not. Thomas looked composed, even though he and Maria had decided, once the Consistory was over, to break off their contact for a while. They needed to think, Thomas told me later, to think about the future.

Maria and Helen Barnes had been given seats near us and we all fidgeted in the vast, low hall with the great star burst design spread across the wall where the Pope sat for his audiences. It seemed more like a railroad station than a place you could use as a church, but red- and purple-robed aides alternately darted and oozed around the edges of things, gesturing and whispering behind their hands to each other. There was an almost oppressive sense of expectation, with everybody wondering what went on at the secret part of the Consistory where the Pope had the cardinals officially notified of their promotions. Was it like the Masons, I wondered, or the initiation into the Fourth Degree Knights of Columbus? All these ceremonies, I thought to myself, were second cousins to each other. I glanced across the crowd and saw P.B. and Mae on the aisle across from us directly behind Mayor and Mrs. Daley and surrounded by a collage of ruddy faces, like the Communion Breakfast for all the officers of the police station and their wives. And there were clusters of blacks, some in native-like costumes with plumes and the like; and there were delegations of Orientals and Malaysians, and a pack of stiff-upper-lipped Englishmen not too far from us. A grand show altogether, and then suddenly there was the sound of trumpets and a choir burst into song and the Pope himself, smiling and blessing people as though he was at a fiesta, came into the hall and went straight up, convoyed by touchy-looking monsignors, to his chair, modest as thrones went, at the front of the great space where we were gathered.

Then came the new cardinals, smaller looking than I expected, the way movie stars are when you see them on the street. They filed in, seventeen of them, some of them very solemn looking, and a few even holy looking. Then, by some juxtaposition that astounded me, along came Archbishop Williams of Chicago and Archbishop Muñoz of Lima. I glanced down the row toward the center aisle where they were passing us as they headed toward the front of the hall. As it happened I had to look past the profiles of Thomas and Maria. Their heads were turned a little away from me, but there was something particularly striking about their fine features, quite reserved that morning, as I panned down to see Muñoz, in what turned out to be a secondhand cassock, moving with the simple nobility of the ancient Indian kings of his beloved highlands, his cheeks accented the way the Peruvian hills were by the thin sunlight of the Altiplano. There was something immensely attractive about him, something sensuous and something spiritual at the same time.

Just across the aisle, their faces turned toward us the better to view the procession, were the Kinsellas, P.B. looking as bold and pleased with himself as an Irish King, but a little withheld from it all too, and Mae, a diamond flickering on her upheld hand, looking sad, almost a mother of sorrows, as Williams, complacent in his achievement, like the fat boy who has seen the test beforehand, marched down the aisle, looking now to the left and now to the right but, try as he might, he remained incapable of generating even a stray beam of spiritual depth. They all froze in my imagination for just a moment, Maria and Thomas obliquely facing Mae and P.B., with the two cardinals passing down the aisle between them. It was an image for the television age, or the cover of the old *Life* magazine, the unplanned discovery of truth by a lens poking down a corridor or an unself-conscious line of people. "Murderers' Row," Jack Allen whispered in my ear as the chant once again swelled and my surreal vision of the principal players, the young and the old, the proud and the powerful, pulled itself out of shape and fragmented as the cardinals, with everyone shifting to follow them, passed down the aisle toward the waiting Pope.

PART V

1

October 22, 1983
1:30 A.M.

The thing of it was that Father Green didn't go to bed at all but, only a little more wild-eyed than usual, slipped back out into the moonlight and hotfooted toward the student dormitories, sort of a spiritual Paul Revere, as he fancied himself, or a Pied Piper, as others saw him, out to rally a brigade or two of students to welcome the religious renewal. He picked up his pals, Fathers Maxwell and Morgan, and there was no trouble finding students still up and about in the middle of the night. Greenie knew a few he could count on. They seemed mesmerized when he cranked out one of his whacko ideas and ready to follow him without question or complaint. You must understand that most of the students couldn't be roused by Greenie's rhetoric, which, once he got going, didn't make much sense even when it sounded good. However, many a lad has made his reputation with just such malarkey. What with his having been restrained so long, he was fairly bursting with a sense of rightness about his cause and, in semi-messianic tones, he would speak for a moment at this door and then at that, inviting a select group to a meeting in the basement of Sorin Hall, which was where I caught up with them.

I was past sleep by then myself and, when I heard the stirrings downstairs I descended, just as I had so many years before when old P.B. had taken over the meeting about the Ku Klux Klan, only now to find a different kind of a crowd and certainly a different kind of a leader. There might have been thirty students there as I peered over the staircase railing at the basement room that had not really changed very much over the years. And there was Father Green, who paid

305

no attention to me, standing in the middle of them and talking
very animatedly. Father Maxwell and Father Morgan had
flattened themselves back along the side wall with the look of
men who had been dragged into something they didn't want
to do by the dominant personality of a friend they didn't want
to lose.

"I'm glad you could come," Greenie was saying. "You
have always been the faithful core, the saving remnant of the
Notre Dame spirit." He turned around slowly so that he
could look into their eyes individually as he spoke.

"Yours has been the lost generation. You missed all the
great causes. You never marched against lettuce, you never
campaigned for Gene McCarthy, you never burned a draft
card, or went limp so the Pigs had to drag you away from the
peace march . . ."

He had their attention, that I must admit, but, as I recalled,
there were few, if any, of these things that he had done either.
It didn't matter, because he had found a way to work on the
guilt of these young men. He made them feel bad that they
had missed the action, which, of course, was no fault of their
own, seeing they were little more than babies during the
Vietnam War. But they felt bad, there was no doubt of that,
and Greenie knew just how to play on it.

"You weren't here when we organized protests to unionize
the University grounds-workers. And you missed it when we
boycotted the job recruiters from Dow Chemical. And the
Nukes, where were you for the big push against the Nukes?"
He stopped and closed his eyes for a moment, like he was
praying or getting a direct message from Headquarters; then
he shook his head, a little tremble like some angel had given
him a fix of inspiration, and he took up the litany of their
absences again.

"You missed the Chicago Seven and the Harrisburg Seven.
And what did you do for Angela Davis or Patty Hearst? And
when we marched against the University's anti-feminist
stand, you weren't here either. Then there were the demonstrations against Tenure. And when we tried to save the snail
darter and the whale . . ." Well, I almost let out a snicker,
seeing that all this was being taken in such a solemn manner,
but I managed to restrain myself even though the railing I was
leaning against creaked loudly during Greenie's dramatic
pause. He looked up at me and addressed me as though I
were to be his Greek chorus.

"Isn't that so, Dr. Kenna? You've seen it all, haven't you?"

Well, I blushed a little as all eyes turned up toward me, and I just smiled a little and fumbled a shy peace sign without uttering a word.

"Right on," a student with long curly blond hair shouted, flashing a thumbs-up sign of approval in my direction. "Right on!" the other students echoed, making the same gesture. Then they all turned back to Green.

"But tonight, this day, this morning you are here. And you can join in a spiritual movement which I believe God has sent to us. God had chosen our campus and you men to initiate a genuine renewal of belief in this country. This is not the moment for scoffers or for the weak. If you wish you had been part of the great movements of the past, then this is your chance to redeem yourselves."

I was all but forgotten as he warmed to his finale, like Rasputin dropping a spell on the Tsarina.

"God has chosen a young girl to bring us together in true worship and for a new effort to build community. We were witnesses in the events of last evening to the resurrection of the flesh as the necessary prelude to a new era of the Spirit."

He's hit the nail on the head there, I thought to myself, but I remained quiet lest I be called on to give my testimony again. Greenie rolled along, like a tidal wave in a disaster movie, sweeping up whatever lay before him.

"This is your chance to demonstrate that you care. This is your chance to stand up for a cause! Stand up and be counted with the Lord."

Another chorus of "Right on!" with a couple of "Amens" sprinkled in.

"What can we do, Jeff?" a husky lad in a sweat shirt called out. Green had a fancy for the students' calling him by his first name, as did his friends by the wall; it made it all more intimate, they said, but who, I often wondered, wanted to be intimate with them? No matter, the crowd there, small but determined, was ready for the cause, no matter how vague it seemed. You could draw onlookers any day with talk of the Lord, the Spirit, and building a new community, and these lads, with the trust and generosity of youth, were anxious to make their sign or give their witness.

"There's plenty for each of us to do. But probably the most important thing is to be the reception committee when they bring the girl to the Lourdes Grotto just before dawn. We

have to make it clear that there are those in the Notre Dame
Family who welcome this message from the Lord, that there
are those who can hear and understand it." Greenie was at
fever pitch now and I had half a mind to call for the men
with the nets. Then I decided that would only make things
worse.

"And we need signs. Each one of you can get a
friend, I'm sure of that, and you must try to have each one
of them recruit another friend for the cause. Can you do
that?"

Another chorus of enthusiastic agreement.

"Now, the signs will be picked up by the media. That's
what they'll focus on. So they have to be short and simple to
carry our message. And the message is part welcome to the
religious renewal and part protest against the administration's
refusal to accept its validity."

More happy yells, most of them from good young men
trapped in the last stages of their adolescent need for
protest, any kind of protest, by the persuasions of Father
Green.

"How about 'N.D. Welcomes the Cross'?"

"Or 'Carry the Cross with Us!'"

"'Prayer, Not Football, This Weekend!'"

"'Pray, Not Play Today!'"

All these being yelled from the group members, who were
catching the spirit like a gang of salesmen at one of those
"Make Yourself Great" meetings.

"'Pray for Tom Kinsella.' How about that? 'For He Knows
Not What He Does.'"

Father Green hushed them into silence.

"Those are fine. Keep them short, that's good. But I want a
banner, a big one. And on it in big letters: 'This Is My
Body.'"

There were a few gasps at Greenie's grabbing the sacred
words of the Consecration of the Mass but there was no
stopping him now.

"And on another one: 'Do This in Memory of Me.' It's
perfect because we're saying that this is a Eucharistic event,
that we will all consecrate our bodies to the Lord, as God has
asked us to do through this message."

Well, that seemed to convince the doubters in the crowd
and in a few minutes they were swarming up the stairs past me

to carry out their assigned tasks. I smiled, as benignly as I could, for this seemed like recess at the loony bin but the kids kept flashing the peace sign at me as they hurried by, like I was some wizened old trophy of the anti-war movement. There wasn't anybody left but me and the three priests. Fathers Maxwell and Morgan had come over next to Greenie, who looked out of breath from his evangelizing.

"It's very visual," Maxwell said, "and I like its flow."

"Yes," Green said. "It's right, I know it. After all these years of trying to be like Harvard or Princeton we have the chance to come into our own again as an authentic spiritual center for the country. Think of it! Nationwide television, dozens of newsmen, and thousands and thousands of people. And the emphasis will be on the Lord Jesus instead of Touchdown Jesus!"

Touchdown Jesus was the name given, as I've said, to the mosaic of Christ with his arms raised like a downfield referee that ran ten stories up the side of the library in full view of the stadium. I never fancied it myself but I fancied Greenie's plans even less. From the look on his face, I thought Father Morgan was uneasy too. He was looking at Green the way you might look at a friend who's just been hit by a bus, concerned but a little too late to be helpful.

"Jeff," he said soothingly, "I'm not sure it's good for you to get so stirred up."

"Why?" Green responded sharply. "What's the matter with you? Can't you read the signs of the times?"

"Well, it isn't that, Jeff, it's that I don't want to see you get sick or get hurt in this."

"Fred's got a point," Father Maxwell said. "Remember our commitment to each other, that we'd always look out for each other?"

Green stared from one to the other in disbelief. "What's wrong with you two? Don't you see the chance we have for leadership? Don't you know that our time has come at last, that this is the sign of it?"

"Oh, I think you're right," Morgan said, putting his arm around Green's shoulder. "But if you're going to see this through, you have to keep calm."

"Do you think St. Paul kept calm? Do you think Mao kept calm?"

Morgan looked at Maxwell, whose face was kind of

screwed up, the way it got when he was gestating intellectually.

"Passion. You're right, Jeff, passion is the key. There is no
art without passion. And this is to be a work of art, am I
right?"

Green beamed. "That's it exactly. Now let's pray on it, let's
pray together on this."

They all knelt down in a half circle, extending their arms so
that they could grasp each other's hands, and then Greenie
cut loose with an "Alleluia" that caught me by surprise and
almost caused me to pitch over the railing. The other two,
Morgan still looking skeptical but Maxwell deep into it again,
sang out another Alleluia in response, and then Father Green
started praying away.

"Father in heaven, help us to raise a great sign of faith to all
the country and to all its people . . ."

I turned to mount the stairs, feeling a little uneasy, as
though I had been in the locker room of French Foreign
Legionnaires when they were snapping towels at each other.
As I climbed back toward my room I knew that long pent-up
forces were engaged that I could do nothing about, that things
would sort themselves out explosively after daybreak, and I
certainly didn't want to miss any of it. I snapped open my
watch in the feeble light of the main hallway. It was ten past
three. Well, I thought, I've seen everything so far. There's no
use going to bed now.

2

October 22, 1983
3:30 A.M.

I washed up and picked up a golfing cap in my rooms—the shambles of which never looked more inviting—and slipped down and out the back way by the old loading dock. Curiosity overcoming fatigue, I began a north-by-northwest journey toward Route 31. I looped up around Corby Hall, where Thomas Kinsella lived. There was no telling whether his lights were on, since he had inherited blackout curtains from Father Hesburgh, who, arriving from some such place as Afghanistan at midnight for him but midday in South Bend, might close them to catch an hour's sleep. I thought Jack Allen's lamp was still burning and I was tempted to go up and share a good grumble with him about the goings-on. But I was making slow progress and I wanted to check things out before my legs gave out or knotted up with the cramps.

I dropped down by the Lourdes Grotto, a fair reproduction of that edge of the Pyrenees where the Virgin appeared to Bernadette. People still lighted candles there, not that they believed in the efficacy of melting wax; it was more a sweet and peaceful old devotion and it fit, don't you know, what with the University's being dedicated to Mary and all. Well, it was dead quiet there, serene almost with the moon that was sliding down the sky still coating everything with a soft edge of light. Just down and across from the shrine a road bisected Notre Dame's two lakes and made a slow breaking curve out to the highway. It was my guess that the loony birds would bring the girl on the cross in by this route but there was nobody on it and only a few lights from Columbia Hall on the right and the Moreau Seminary, where the football team was supposed to be, on the left. And there wasn't much noise, just the fallen leaves scuttling like beetles across the walks and roads, and an occasional wheeze from myself. All's quiet, I thought, all's quiet on the western front.

I could hear an occasional car whiz by as I got closer to Route 31 but it wasn't until I was right there gazing across it that I could hear the singing and make out flickering lights in a field across the way. They were still at it, so I crossed the road, careful as a schoolboy remembering his mother's warnings to look both ways first, and edged into what I could see was still a fair crowd. They were humming and singing "Rock of Ages," and I wondered what my mother would have thought about how popular that old Protestant hymn had become among Catholics, seeing as she wouldn't even let orange lilies grow in the backyard. The bitter old days were over and here in this Indiana meadow the lions and the lambs were kneeling down together in a semicircle around an area lighted by torches. In the middle I could make out the figure of the young woman, still on the cross, which was propped at about a thirty-degree angle against the hood of a car. David Weber, the graduate student who was in charge, was standing next to the girl, his hand on her forehead like he was checking to see if she had a fever or not.

The bizarreness seemed to have been contained a little, the way a boil loses its angry look after it is lanced, especially since the lights and cameras were gone and most of the reporters too, as far as I could see. But the elements were still in place and there was a powerful perverse attractiveness to the whole thing.

Just as I was surveying the crowd, a bicycle bumped off the road and into the grass. It was Brother Dingbat again. He had slipped his leash, I thought, but they would put the dragnet out again at dawn. His bike was fitted with a powerful light and as he trundled it past me, not so much as giving me a nod, I could see that he had it fitted out with instruments so that the handlebars looked like a cockpit dashboard. There was a radio, a coil of wire looping up to Brother's ear, an illuminated compass and speedometer, and a couple of other devices that had been bolted on for shortwave or police calls or maybe just the music of the spheres. Well, I thought, things are picking up again.

No one tried to stop me, so I made my way over toward the

cross, where young Weber, handsome and intense-looking like a knight pledged to a demented cause, was still playing pattyfingers with the girl's face. As I got closer I could see that her eyes were open and that she was speaking with her guardian. The torches, swiped from somebody's garden, I guessed, cast an uncertain light on the scene and the gentle singing drowned out what they were saying, so, God forgive me, I decided to get closer even if I had to appear to be giving witness to do it. I pulled my cap down a little and I stepped gingerly through a gap in the ring of pilgrims and knelt down just a foot or so behind Weber. Nobody paid any attention to me as I cocked an ear to what was being said. The girl must have been uncomfortable but she lay there peacefully enough, her breasts rising and falling in a regular rhythm of breathing.

"Can you understand me, Mary Ann?" This from Weber, whose face, all tightened up, I could see clearly in profile.

"Yes," the girl answered, turning her eyes up toward him. "Yes, but I am waiting for someone, for my master." Her face, with her hair spread out and sort of hanging down off the sides of the cross, looked like that of a very beautiful woman who was in some far-off land, the way people look when they've had an injection before going down to surgery.

"The Lord is your master," Weber replied in a preacher's tones.

"Yes, but my true master also lives."

"The Lord lives in all of us," Weber said, but I thought he was missing the point of whatever she was saying. He pulled his hand back from her forehead and bent down toward her, about six inches from her face.

"I think I should massage your arms, Mary Ann, so that the circulation will keep going." Sly fellow, I thought, as he turned slightly and took her right arm in his hands and began to rub it in one long gesture from her wrist to her shoulder, the way Groucho Marx used to kiss Margaret Dumont up to her diamonds in the old movies.

She groaned a little and turned her head up toward him.

"That feels good, that feels good."

Well, I didn't know what she meant exactly, seeing that she contorted a little as though he was hurting her instead of helping her but, by then, I thought you'd have to be up on your Krafft-Ebing to figure this whole thing out anyway.

"There, there, Mary Ann," Weber was intoning. "The Lord needs you to be strong for the dawn."

"Where is my sweet master?" she asked again, rolling her head back.

At that moment, who should slip down next to me but Brother Dingbat, the unplugged radio wire still hanging out of his ear and making me jump as it drew across my shoulder like a spider. He got right down to business, folding his hands and praying away, silently, I was relieved to note, his eyes fixed on the girl, who was twisting like somebody not wanting to get out of a comfortable bed. She groaned again, kind of animal-like, and Brother jolted against me, murmuring in his tinny voice, "Praised be!"

"When will my master come?" she asked in a dazed kind of way, enjoying the massage that Weber had switched now to her other arm.

"Shall I loosen the bonds for a while?" he asked.

"No, no. Only my master can do that, only my sweet master."

Weber just went on with his work, trying to look as pious and unconcerned as possible, although my suspicions were not lessened about who was enjoying the massage and why.

Then Brother bolted upright, the plug falling out of his ear as he did so, and took a step toward the girl. Well, young Weber was lost in contemplation and paid no attention to him and I, pulling the coil away from the beak of my cap, where it had draped itself, wasn't prepared to question or interfere with him at all.

Brother stepped close to the cross and began to inspect Mary Ann's hands, leaning down and squinting in the shadowy light of the torches. He opened her hand and peered into its palm like a Dickensian bookkeeper.

"You can see the sign starting," he said, a note of glee creeping into the keening sound of that voice that was just getting accustomed to being used again. "It's starting."

Now, none of this was too loud, thank God, and the crowd had shifted over to a rerun of "Amazing Grace," and seeing as it seemed to have about a thousand verses, the people were humming when they didn't know the words. I decided that I had better do something, Brother Dingbat's keeper not being in sight, so I hoisted myself up and, handing him the earplug and wire, I said, "Here, Brother darlin', I think you've lost something."

He looked balefully at me, grabbed the wire as though I had stolen it from him, and shoved it into his pants pocket. He didn't speak to me but went back to examining her palm like a regular Gypsy.

"Do you see something there?" I asked as gently as I could.

"Yes," he said, turning his head warily back to me. "Yes, I have." Then he paused and regarded me sternly. "Are you a believer?"

"And why wouldn't I be?" I answered, drawing on my Irish heritage for a reply that wasn't quite the truth and wasn't quite a falsehood either. Old Brother took it in a sense he approved of and beckoned to me to come closer.

"Look, look here, in her palms. It's the stigmata coming." He began to shake as I moved forward and gazed down into the girl's open palm. There was a pinkish welt, a kind of irregular wedge of red marks maybe an inch and a half long.

"Now, Brother," I said, suddenly feeling that Weber had turned his eyes toward me, "those are the marks from her fingernails, from when she clenched her fist. That's all they are." I put my hand on his shoulder, for I could see that he was upset, if not exactly shattered, by my explanation. Then he turned toward me, his eyes blazing. "No, no, no." He bayed almost like a coyote. But the wind was gone from him, I could see that and I half led him back to the place where he had been kneeling. He looked desperately at me, as though he wanted me to revoke my words, but I just said, "Why don't you say some prayers for the poor souls, Brother?" and he got down on his knees again.

Just then another figure broke through the edge of the crowd. It was Matt Finn wearing a windbreaker that made him an even more hulking figure as the flickering torches revealed his image, broken by the light the way the moon is fragmented on a ruffled lake. By this time Weber had abandoned the massaging and came around the foot of the cross to stand between Finn and the girl. It struck me that Weber didn't know who Finn was, and neither did the humming crowd, which was just fine as I saw it.

"What do you want?" Weber asked, a little defensively for a fellow who was all piety.

"I want to speak to Mary Ann," Finn responded.

"She should not be disturbed. You can pray but . . ."

Finn took him by the arm. "Listen, son, I understand that. What I want to do is talk to her. Understand?" He released

Weber's arm and stepped closer to the girl, who looked up and seemed to recognize him.

"Sweet master," she said dreamily, "you're here. I knew you would come." Needless to say, that got our attention, Weber's and mine at least. Brother Dingbat was still twitching away with his eyes closed. He had stuck the plug back in his ear, and I judged that he was reconnected with his own world again. Finn bent down over the girl.

"Mary Ann. Do you hear me?"

"Oh, yes, yes," she said expectantly.

"I'm not your master, do you understand? But I do want to help you."

The girl looked a little sullen, her lips pouting out and her body stiffening under the white tuniclike gown she was wearing. "Yes, I know you. But you are my master. Do you want me to come down now?"

"Listen, Mary Ann, this whole thing is a big mistake. I'm not your master but it is time for you to come down. I'm going to loosen these bonds and take you home."

"My home is in heaven," she replied. "My home is in heaven." And then her voice trailed off again.

Young Weber didn't like the sound of any of this, of course, and he certainly didn't want anybody to take Mary Ann down for any reason, not with the big show set to start just before dawn.

"I'll have to ask you to stop bothering her," he said in the tones of a nobleman taking a stand.

"Stay out of my way," Finn answered. "This girl should be home."

"My sweet master," she groaned again as Weber turned to the crowd and called in loud tones, "This man is trying to take Mary Ann away from us!"

"Who? Who?" Brother piped up, sounding like the proper cuckoo he was, while struggling to his feet again.

The crowd broke off the humming and a few of its members stood up and began to call out at the coach, "Leave us alone," and "Go away," mild enough as shouts went but with a fine edge of determination in them. Meanwhile Finn had leaned over and untied the bonds around the girl's right wrist.

"Come on, Mary Ann, it's time to go."

"No! No!" and other such shouts from the crowd.

"I can't go yet, sweet master," Mary Ann suddenly cried out, reaching her freed arm up and pulling Finn down toward her, throwing him off balance for a second, and planting a kiss on his cheek as it lowered toward her face. "I can't go, oh, not now. Sweet master will tell me again later," and with that she rolled her eyes back, let her arm fall back to the crosspiece and took a high dive into one of her comalike states.

Finn looked around, shook his head, and turned to Weber. "What you're doing here is wrong. I'll be back." And with that he turned and moved swiftly off into the night, letting the catcalls of the crowd fall on his broad back. He hadn't even noticed me, I thought, as he shouldered past, looking the way he did when he came charging out of the locker room with the team just before a big game. Sweet master, my arse, I thought, watching him bolt away and wondering what his connection was with this girl and why she had greeted him in that strange, sick way.

Weber, our knight in shining armor, tied her arm back to the crosspiece and turned back to the crowd. "Let us all pray quietly and sing to the Lord again," he said like a fellow who just managed to get the fire door closed in time. "Let us pray for those who do not understand us." The crowd settled down and somebody launched into "If We Only Have Love," which must have been having its fiftieth reprise of the long moonlit night.

Time to go, I thought, or at least to get to safer ground. I moved away and took one last backward glance. Brother Dingbat was up again, examining her feet this time, and Weber was directing the crowd's singing like he was Fred Waring. As I trudged toward the road, about a half dozen students were just crossing the highway, bearing signs on long poles. "Pray for Purity" was the only one I could make out as they went by me. Maybe the Klan hadn't been so bad after all, I thought as I stepped back onto the campus again.

3

October 22, 1983
4 A.M.

It was after four in the morning and, with a little imagination, you could make out the first feeble light in the eastern sky. Across the road in the field it looked like a revival meeting at the crackerjack bin. About forty students had arrived, some of them with signs on poles and others with bed sheets spray-painted with various messages like "Death Rather Than Sin" and "Repent, O Sinful Nation." The peacefulness of the night hours had given way to feverish activity, the way it is in the trenches before somebody shouts, "Over the top!" This crowd was ready to go, believe me.

The singing had stopped although a young man and woman, almost twins in their jeans and long brown hair, were tuning their guitars in the midst of the circulating crowd that numbered about two hundred. David Weber, handsome and noble-looking as an archangel, was stooped over the cross massaging the comatose girl's arms, alternately freeing and resecuring them to the crossbars. Someone brought a damp-ened cloth and he used that to wipe her face, patting her forehead gently, stopping to lower his head toward her mouth when he thought he heard her say something.

"What is it?" Brother Dingbat asked, jumping to his feet from the kneeling position he had maintained for the past hour.

"Come now," Brother insisted. "Don't keep any messages just for yourself. This girl may have important statements for the whole world to hear." Brother stepped closer, wrinkling his brow as he squinted down at her hands.

"Do you think the blood is coming?"

"I'm not sure," Weber replied, taking her palm and turning it upward.

"Listen to me. Those welts are the sign. They just need to be helped along a little. God wants us to do our part." Brother Dingbat's eyes were bright and flashing as they met with Weber's, which, although dark, seemed to be rolling a little loosely in their sockets. It was a meeting of minds in spiritual heat, a conspiracy formed without a further exchange of words, a plan joined just as the moon, which might have provided the last pull either needed to go over the edge, broke out of a cloud bank. It was spiritual lunacy as Weber and the Brother drew closer than either ever usually got to another human being and, exchanging nods, bent closer to examine the girl's hand.

"There," said Brother as calmly as a surgeon, as a thin line of blood plumped up behind the blade of the penknife which he drew swiftly across the girl's palm. She stirred, and attempted to pull away from them, but Weber had a strong grip on her arm.

"Now, the other one," he murmured as he closed the bleeding hand into a fist and moved quickly to the other side of the cross to pull the fingers of her hand open for Brother's next deft incision. They were superficial wounds but the blood was real and the girl twisted again, jerking her body and giving a little yipe. The conspirators closed that hand and, so swiftly had they performed their strange rite, nobody seemed to notice what they had done. Weber had been fussing around with the girl for hours anyway, so his movements with Brother did not seem unusual to the members of the crowd who were watching them.

"Now, Brother, don't say anything. Let someone else discover the sign."

"Yes, yes," Brother said eagerly as he replaced his knife in his pocket and threw himself back down on his knees, the high point of his demented quest for spiritual fulfillment having been achieved beyond his wildest fantasies. He would, in fact, ever after believe himself when he said he had nothing to do with it. Weber slipped back into the all-American boy shell of his paranoia, looking as virtuous as an early Christian refusing to burn incense before a pagan idol. He stepped back and knelt down a few feet from the cross. The moon disappeared behind a cloud rack and the girl's form was obscured once more by the darkness.

People were getting up, stretching, and talking to each other as though it were half time at the Coliseum and nobody paid any attention to the crimson droplets that began to fall irregularly, like water off a pipe on a humid day, from the girl's clenched fists onto the crossbars. The people sensed that they would be moving out soon, that their moment of procession and their opportunity for religious witness was fast approaching. There was an air of festivity that only the assuredly saved can experience as the students and the people mixed together, the standards stuck temporarily into the ground, so that the group resembled a confused delegation on the floor of a political convention.

It was at this point that Timothy Duffy, who had been chosen by the girl as her first accomplice, made his way across Route 31, drawn almost against his will to inspect what had so disturbed and distressed him the evening before. His roommate, Joe Sclafani, still tucking his shirt into his pants, hurried along behind him.

"Jesus, Tim, are you sure you want to do this?"

"Come on, Joe, I've got to see what's going on."

Not twenty yards behind, Father Green, dressed now in a black shirt and Roman collar and carrying a broad white stole over his arm, was also approaching the highway to make his passage to the encampment that flickered like a bank of vigil lights at the edge of the campus. If he could just blow a little more life into it, he would have a flaming spearhead for the religious revival for America in the eighties. And besides, if this demonstration galvanized the country, he would be standing in the right place when the Board of Trustees looked around for the right man to lead the University toward the nineties. It was all within reach now, he thought as he waited for a truck to rumble past before he crossed over to the field where the girl lay.

Timothy Duffy and Joe Sclafani circled wide-eyed around the edge of the crowd, like kids watching a yard party at a neighbor's house.

"Joe," Timothy said slowly.

"Yeah?"

"I think I could have stopped all this."

"You're crazy, Tim. Nobody could have stopped this. Hey, there comes Father Green."

Timothy just stared in wonder, catching glimpses through the crowd of the girl lying as if asleep on the tilted cross as

Father Green, obviously anxious to pitch right in, hurried through the group, greeting students, pointing to the signs with a smile, and finally climbing up on the hood of the car on which the cross rested. He gestured for silence.

"Fellow believers," he intoned in a voice infected with crazy zeal and excitement. "Thank you all for keeping vigil. God bless you for preserving this sign of our Father's concern for us."

"Amens" and "Alleluias" from the crowd as it formed itself into a semicircle around the auto which was a prop for the cross and a platform for Green.

"In a few moments we will move together back to the campus. I will leave first. You must lead yourselves. But I will welcome you at the shrine when you arrive."

The moon appeared again to outline Greenie in its soft light as he draped the stole over his shoulders.

"Let us pray now together that this country may heed the sign which we raise here today."

"Lord, hear our prayer!" rumbled back from the crowd.

"Let us pray that we may be heard as we preach faith in a country of unbelief."

"Lord, hear our prayer!" A little firmer this time.

Green was just about to launch into another invocation when a woman at the edge of the crowd let out a shriek.

"Look!" she yelled in such a sharp way that Greenie almost lost his footing on the car hood. "She's bleeding!"

Cries and exclamations, mostly oohs and ahs from the crowd which surged in closer to the cross, pitching Brother Dingbat forward so that he bashed his head on the crossbar and fell unconscious, twisting slightly and landing on his back. The blood from the girl's hands began to drop onto his upturned face. Nobody paid any attention to him.

"It's the stigmata!" cried the lady who had first observed the blood and who had now stepped forward, steadying herself by placing a hand on the kneeling David Weber's shoulder. "Lord, save us!" she cried, and sank to her knees. There was some screeching and hollering, and a lot of good old-fashioned elbowing others to get a better view. Father Green looked down, his mouth agape, at the blood which had accumulated enough on the side of the girl's hands and on the edge of the crossbar to be visible in the moonlight.

Timothy blinked across the heads of the shifting crowd but could not make anything out very clearly.

"Can you see anything, Joe?"

"Yeah, yeah. She's bleeding from the hands." Joe was getting excited if not enthused about the incident and he pulled at the sleeve of Timothy's shirt. "Come on, Tim, let's get a better look." But Tim just stood there, trying to make some sense out of what had happened over the last several hours.

Meanwhile Father Green was trying to make sense out of what had happened in the last few minutes. Even he had not expected such a spectacular signal of divine approval. His prayer service collapsed under the pressure of this new discovery and he slipped down off the hood for a better look at things.

"My God!" he muttered in the tones of a man who had not really believed in the girl until now. "My God, she's the real thing!" He bent over the cross for a better look, his stole slipping off one shoulder and trailing across the wet blood on the edge of the crosspiece.

"Sit down!" someone called from the crowd. "We can't see."

"Yeah, down in front!" Others, irritated at the way Greenie was blocking their view, joined in the chorus of yells.

But the priest was staring almost dumbfounded at the girl's left hand.

He pried the fingers open and saw the wound and the blood. The girl groaned and rolled slightly on the upright, closing her hand and whimpering as she did. Greenie remained staring, as though he was not sure what to do or what to make of this singular development. It threw him off balance because, up until that moment, he had felt that he was the master or at least the organizing genius of the demonstration. Now he shuddered at the thought that God Himself might have a direct hand in it and he stepped back, pulling his stole up around his shoulders and noticing the stain of blood that had soaked down on the side of it. He turned to the crowd members who had closed in on him, a crazed chorus for his mystical intonations.

"God is here!" he said. "Let us march together to Our Lady's shrine!" There was no mistaking the wild light in his eye now.

The logistics of it were complicated but he finally got the people in order, the cross rising on the shoulders of willing bearers, placards and banners waving unsteadily, and the guitarists striking a few chords of "All That I Am," another winner in the Catholic top forty. Somebody rolled Brother Dingbat under the car and David Weber took his place just behind Father Green.

The darkness in the eastern sky was lifting away from the horizon as slowly as an ancient drawbridge as Father Green, looking as demonically convinced as a Middle East terrorist, looked back at the crowd he had fashioned into an out-of-step legion. "Forward!" he called above the singing and, like a strange expeditionary force, the group began to move out and across Route 31, causing the few cars and trucks on the road to slow and stop. The singing swelled as the group flooded across the asphalt and disappeared into the trees on the other side. Joe had joined them and Timothy Duffy stood in the field staring across the traffic that began to move again as the last figure vanished from view.

He heard a moan and turned to see Brother Dingbat, his forehead swollen and stained with blood, pulling himself out from beneath the car. Brother put his hand to his head, regarded it through his cracked glasses, and shouted, "Alleluia! I've been washed in the blood of the lamb!" Then he seemed to grow dizzy, slumped against the car, and fell back into the grass.

4

October 22, 1983
5 A.M.

At about twenty to five I knew I had to do more than worry away what was left of the night, and headed for Corby Hall, where Father Kinsella lived, determined to rouse him as surely as if I were Paul Revere and the Redcoats were marching down Notre Dame Avenue. The campus was very quiet as I padded along. I could make out faint singing in the distance but it was periodically drowned out by the noise of the traffic carried on the wind. As I approached the building I could see another figure near the side door. Whoever he was paused, one hand on the knob, waiting for me to approach.

"Hello, Professor," Matt Finn called when I was about twenty paces away. I could distinguish his voice but he was still in the shadows, so I could not read the expression on his face.

"Is that the coach?" I asked, letting a little blarney slip into my voice.

"Nobody else," he said in a whisper as I stepped close to him. I could then make out the distinct odor of alcohol on his breath. Not that he was tipsy, but he did seem well fortified against the October morning air.

"What are you doing here?" I asked, realizing that he had not seen me when he had made his visit to Mary Ann on the cross a few hours before. He was in no hurry to answer, so I played such cards as I had.

"As for me, Coach, I intend to wake the president up to tell him there's a parade of ninnies bringing the girl on the cross onto the campus at this very hour."

"Where are the campus police?" he asked, truly surprised that I knew so much of what was going on.

"They can't be everywhere at once," I answered. "Besides, the loonies are cutting across country toward the Lourdes Shrine."

"Well, do you think you ought to disturb Father Kinsella? Shouldn't someone else handle this?"

"That's what I've thought the whole night but I'm the only one's been on the job as far as I can see."

I wondered if he would tell me of his own involvement, or whether I should question him about it directly. I was beginning to feel that I was in charge of things as much as anybody else but I held my tongue.

"I, I . . ." Finn hesitated. "I want to see Father Kinsella too." That was all he said, then he pulled the door open, swept his hand before me like a fancy greeter at a hotel, and followed me into the hall.

We climbed to the second floor, made our way past Jack Allen's room, where a faint light still seemed to be burning, and knocked softly on Father Thomas's door. We could hear some stirring about, then light showed at the transom, and the old-fashioned door opened. Father Kinsella, a lock of wavy hair hanging down over his forehead, was standing there wearing only pajama bottoms. He looked sleepy as he waved us into his room and went to a closet to get a bathrobe.

"What's going on that I have such a distinguished pair of visitors? Matt, are you naming Austin your new line coach, or is he going to ghost your autobiography for you?" He secured the bathrobe sash and pointed to chairs for us. Then he sat down on his barely mussed bed.

"Well, what is it?"

"Father Thomas," I began, only to discover that I was somewhat breathless. "Father Thomas, the girl on the cross is back. And headed for the grotto. Due to arrive any minute."

He arched his eyebrows and, before I could say more, he rose and went to the phone. "Get me the campus police," he said to the operator. "Have them call me here right away."

He hung up and turned back toward me. "How many?" He sounded like a general estimating an enemy force.

"A few hundred, I would say. But you know how the crowd grew last night. Very swiftly, as I remember."

"There won't be any problem if we can keep them from

settling in at the Lourdes Shrine. And if we can do it before the reporters get wind of this."

Finn remained quiet, so I took the floor again. "A number of students have joined their ranks."

"Yes?" Thomas said in the questioning manner of a man who knows that you are going to say more.

"And I think Father Green has become their Pied Piper," I added, taking delight in turning him in at last.

"I should have expected that. Now we've got a University official mixed up in this. Just what we needed." Thomas sighed.

The phone rang and Thomas picked it up and listened to what was apparently a status report from the campus police. Then he hung up and said flatly, "Greenie's got the advance guard to the shrine. They got there before the police could do anything. He's reassured them that he has welcomed a private devotional group to the shrine and the cops are not to bother them."

"What about the girl on the cross?" Finn asked.

"Nowhere in sight," Thomas replied, "not that the cops could see anyway. Just a lot of people dribbling into the shrine area singing and praying. They have us over a barrel there, all right. How the hell can we throw them out when they're praying at a shrine to Our Lady, to Notre Dame herself?" He frowned. "You can bet the girl isn't far away." He shook his head, then added, "Won't the papers love it though? 'Fighting Irish Drive Out Prayer Group. Girl on Cross Disappears.'"

Father Kinsella stood up. "I'm getting dressed. We've got to get some people on deck who can handle this thing." He went to his closet and took a pair of crisply creased black pants off a wooden hanger. He glanced at Finn, who was standing near the door, far enough away, as I thought, to keep Kinsella from smelling his breath.

"And you, Matt? Weren't you out in the moonlight last night with the whole football team making a pilgrimage to the cross?"

Finn blushed. "I can explain that . . ."

"Never mind," Kinsella said, buttoning his clerical shirt and inserting a Roman collar. "I want to get Jack Allen on this."

He shooed us out into the hallway before Finn could speak again and then walked the few steps to Allen's door. He tapped but there was no answer. He waited a moment, glanced up at the light that shone softly through the transom and called in a hoarse whisper, "Jack! It's Tom. Are you up?" He leaned on the door and it opened.

Father Allen was sitting in his chair, the small lamp on the side table illumining the right side of his face. The television projected the frenzied blank stare of a channel gone off the air.

"Jack," Father Kinsella called again, moving closer to him. Father Allen's eyes were open but they were as vacant as the television set. Father Thomas, not yet comprehending, touched him, and he sagged sideways, knocking the drink he had never finished off the arm of the chair and onto the floor.

"He's dead," Thomas said in a hollow voice. "My God, he's dead."

PART VI

PART VI

1

Summer 1931

Young Patrick still had an open door with Mae's Uncle Joe at City Hall and it was not long after he received his diploma that he once again made the journey to the alderman's office. He was ushered in ahead of the two dozen suppliants who crowded Uncle Joe's waiting room like Ellis Island immigrants. The alderman's secretary had taken to Patrick, who, of course, was not above winking his eye at her and lathering her up with so much flattery that she was slick enough to swim the English Channel.

"The alderman is expecting you," she said sweetly as Patrick, bowing ever so slightly and smiling broadly, passed through the hinged gate in the railing that separated the secretary's desk from the waiting room proper.

"Don't you look grand now, for a lady just old enough to vote?"

She waved a blarney-repelling hand at him as he passed. But she liked it. Patrick knew that everyone liked flattery and birthday parties, no matter how much they protested about both.

"Come in, Patrick," Uncle Joe called. "And congratulations to the new Bachelor of Arts. Ah, you must be terrible smart now. I hope you've not taken on airs like the Bicycle Irish. You haven't, have you?" Joe tipped his derby to Patrick and waved him toward a chair at the side of his desk.

"It's good to see you, Alderman," Patrick said after shaking the old man's hand. "You're looking very fit. And I haven't joined the Bicycle Irish as yet. My temptation is Lace Curtain . . ."

"Go'wan," Uncle Joe said, offering Patrick a cigar. "They're all the same. Just be yourself, Patrick, and the world will sing you Christmas carols the year 'round." He struck a wooden match between his thumb and his forefinger and held it just beneath the tip of Patrick's cigar. "Now, is there anything I can do for you? Do you want a job around here?"

Patrick drew on the cigar, exhaled a stream of smoke, and fixed his best blue-eyed and innocent look on the alderman, who was studying him in return.

"No, not a job here, not that I don't thank you for it. What I need is your advice about what line of work I should get into."

Uncle Joe narrowed his eyes for a closer appraisal of the athletic young man before him; he sensed something different about Patrick, and wanted to be sure of what it was before he proceeded.

"You could do any number of things, couldn't you?" he asked, putting the ball back in Patrick's court. "I mean, you could study law. Many's the young man has done well with that. Or you could study business, another very helpful thing."

"No, Alderman," Patrick said, "I don't want to go to school anymore. I want to get to work, in business of some kind. I've saved some money . . ."

"Have you now? These are hard times to save money."

"Well, I've won a few good bets. And you taught me how to play cards. I've been lucky." Patrick did not want to hint at the pile of money he had acquired from the late Gilbert Lane. He had to suggest that he had a stake to invest but did not want Uncle Joe to know too much. The old man seemed to have a sixth sense about such things anyway.

"And I'm hoping to marry as soon as I'm settled."

"Now you're talkin'," Joe replied. "Grand girl, my niece, grand."

He tapped the ash of his cigar into his wastebasket and leaned toward Patrick.

"Now, tell me of this money you've made. Having money makes a difference." He spoke carefully, the way a merchant does when he knows the customer wants diamonds rather than rhinestones. "What about this money? Where did you get it?"

"Betting on the games. Playing cards. I put it all together and made quite a winning on the Southern Cal game last year." Patrick spoke matter-of-factly, almost diffidently, about his good fortune.

"And you have a nice bit of savings. None of it reported to the government, I suppose."

"No."

"All of it in cash?"

"Most of it."

"Ah, Patrick, there are advantages and disadvantages to cash. You must be careful how much you spend. And where. You could get in trouble with the G. Cash is not all a blessing. Is it more than ten thou?"

"Yes, sir." Patrick kept his earnest look on his face.

"Quite a bit of money for a young man these days. Unusual, as it were." He tapped his cigar over the wastebasket. "Have you thought of politics? Cermak is mayor now, tough little bastard too, and he's a Democrat. Cash is very helpful when you want to make an entrance into politics."

"I'd really like to get into business. I hope to keep up my contacts in city government even if I don't get into it myself."

"You'd goddam better keep up your contacts if you want to make a success, a big one, that is, in this city. Do I take it you want to put your money to work? I mean, you're not interested in night school, sharpening pencils, and being somebody's secretary, as it were."

"That's right. I think I've got enough money and enough ability to get in on the ground floor of something."

"Not too quick, now, not too quick. You mustn't be impatient, even though you've got your diploma and all." The alderman took a long draw on his cigar and then rolled his chair back, blowing out the smoke as he did. He stood up and moved toward one of the tall windows that looked down on La Salle Street. Without looking back at Patrick, he began to speak, gesturing with his cigar as he did so.

"This city is a store in some ways, my young man, a candy store, as it were. Full of sweets and a man like you can have his fill. But you may have the wrong idea of how you get ahead. You don't barge in, like you were playing football, no matter how much money you've got. And, since you're asking me for advice, I'd say that you shouldn't make too little of politics." He turned and started to walk in a wide circle around the office. Patrick tried to look as attentive as possible. He had not, however, expected Uncle Joe to be so serious.

"Patrick, as I've told you before, politics is the whole thing. It isn't just running the government, though that's harder than you think. Politics is what makes anything work from your Catholic Church and the Pope right down to the cigar store on the corner. My mother, God be good to her, used to tell me there's politics in hell. Getting along with people is what makes it all hum. Don't ever forget it. So there's many a thing you might do but damn few you will do if you don't get along with people. Do you understand?"

"Yes, sir."

"Like my poor brother Ned, Father Ned, God rest him, the one who couldn't shit. Well, he couldn't get along with anyone either, not the bishop, not the parishioners, nobody, despite the nice friendly line of work he was in. And I'm damned if he would have gotten along with me except he spent so much time in the bathroom that I hardly ever saw him. I heard him, mind you, and that's what comes to mind when I think of him. Groans and farts. The pity of it. As I see it, he held everything in. That's why he never got along with anybody." Uncle Joe paused behind Patrick's chair so that the young man could not easily turn around to look up at him.

"Patrick," he said in a tone as solemn as a judge's, "you're not holding anything back on me, are you? I mean about this money you say you have?"

Patrick was unsure of how to answer. He could not be certain of what wily old Uncle Joe knew or suspected about the source of his fortune.

"I'm telling as much as I can," he answered, not wanting to offend the alderman but not wanting to commit his secret to him. "My money's mostly from gambling, that's the God honest truth."

"You worked at some gambling places a couple of years ago, didn't you?"

"That's right." Patrick wished that he could flash his blue eyes at Uncle Joe during the interrogation the way he used to at the questioning priests at Notre Dame. Uncle Joe put a hand on his shoulder.

"Patrick, Lane was a crooked son of a bitch, the fellow ran the Lake Terrace Club. He got what was coming to him, as it were. But I've always wondered about his passing. No money ever showed up, not a cent."

Patrick tried to remain casual but he could not completely

control his uneasiness as the old man talked down from behind him like a district attorney.

"And there's Crazy Muldoon, all busted up down in Florida. Out of his head half the time. But he has mentioned your name to visitors from time to time . . ."

Patrick did not know what to do but he felt that the time for action—any kind of action—had arrived. He reached up and took Uncle Joe's hand and, in the same motion, lifted himself lightly out of the chair, turning deftly so that he was facing and looking down at the alderman at extremely close quarters.

"What is this, the third degree?" Patrick asked, letting a friendly smile break across his face as he pressed his grip more firmly on Uncle Joe's hand. "You remind me of a school principal I had once. She used to suspect me of everything."

The alderman gazed up unblinkingly at Patrick. He was not afraid but he sensed the power in the young man. Keenan knew that he would learn no more from him. Besides, he felt he had chipped free the truth he had wanted anyway. Patrick released Uncle Joe's hand, laughing and stepping aside so that the alderman could move back behind his desk. "You know," Patrick said softly, "if a man doesn't know something, he never has to lie about it. Never has to testify about it. Didn't you tell me that once?"

"Quite so. Quite so," the alderman said as he eased himself back into his chair. He puffed on his cigar.

"Patrick, you're a grown man, I can see that. And a strong one. You must learn, however, not to let a few little questions upset you. I was testing you a bit. I admit it. I do it all the time to people in here, same as I did with you. You'd be surprised what I've learned, and how I've been able to parlay a little bit of information into very valuable knowledge."

Patrick felt that he had reached a standoff with Keenan, that a message had passed between them that had somehow equalized their relationship. The old man had not given in; he had only backed away to regroup his forces.

"Now, Patrick, there's a lesson in all this. You want to get ahead and you want my advice as well. The first thing you ought to learn is to keep your mouth shut about money. I'm not the only one who's wondered about you. Don't you know that? Jack Moran, that kid who worked with you, the inspector's nephew, he's had his questions too, especially when his aunt got ten Gs in the mail very mysteriously a few days after the killing. That means the money is somewhere. And I think I know where. But you have to be clever. You can't go throwing money around free and easy now. Do you understand what I mean?"

Patrick nodded, noticing that his cigar had gone out since Uncle Joe had started the inquisition. He leaned forward and took the box of matches off the alderman's desk.

"You've a lot to learn. The first thing is not to make any mistakes you don't have to. You'll make enough as it is. We all do. And keep your mouth closed. The second is to get into business but have a political connection first. You've got to get to know Cermak. He's got the high cards in town right now. And live modestly for a while, until you're established. But listen more than you talk and remember that there's always somebody watching you and somebody else who'll be delighted if you get into trouble and fall on your ass. They're not playing beanbag down here, as Mr. Dooley says."

Patrick relighted his cigar as Uncle Joe went on.

"Keep living with your mother for a while. That looks good in a young man. And stay away from the mob. There's plenty of money to be made without getting tied up with any hoodlums. Your old pal Jack Moran's been running with them, did you know that? Into the bootlegging, prostitution, protection, the whole thing. You don't need that. And, since you plan to marry my darlin' niece, I'd be very concerned if I thought you were palsy with the wrong fellows."

"I understand," Patrick said quietly.

"Remember to keep your ears open. Knowledge is power, as it were. You'd be surprised how much you can learn if you're not talking all the time. So don't be entertaining them with your fancy stories about Rockne and what a great player you were. There's plenty of guys who never get over playing football in college. They're in bars every night replaying some goddam game or other. It's not a thing to be overdone. A good thing but in its place. Do you understand?"

Patrick had developed a new appreciation for the alderman. He was tough and shrewd and he had not survived so long in the bull ring of Chicago politics by being just a colorful character. He suspected that Uncle Joe's affectations—the hat and the exercises—were all touches that threw people off and kept them at just the right distance for the alderman to examine them.

"I'm afraid some of the college boys underestimate politics. There's a lot they don't understand about what makes the world run. It ain't high-and-mighty reformers, I'll tell you that. The thing the professors don't understand is that lots of people, maybe most, are in politics because they have an ideal. A good number—more than you'd think—want to help people and there's no surer way to do it than through old-fashioned precinct politics. They want to make money maybe, but the ideal is there too. Lots of fellows in this city came from somewhere else, or their folks did, Catholics from Ireland and Jews from Russia and Protestants from Germany or some place where they didn't have freedom of opportunity. By Jesus, they've got it here and they're grateful and they want to help others. Never forget that. Anton Cermak started as a wood peddler, a Bohemian wood peddler, after he got out of the coal mines down in Braidwood. Now he's mayor and a big man. Never forget what I just said . . ."

"But what do I do to make a political connection?" Patrick asked, fearing that Uncle Joe's advice might be getting as long as one of his late brother Ned's sermons. Uncle Joe paused, drew on his cigar until it glowed to life, and then began to speak softly again.

"You need to get known independent of me. Directly with Cermak. The best way is to draw his attention to yourself for your hard work or for your support of him. Stand up for him, let people know in some way that it will get back to him. You can be sure people will talk about you. But don't show your money, not yet. The time'll come for wise use of it. Plenty of opportunities, but to get into a prosperous business, you need the political connection."

"What's a profitable business these days?"

"A fair question, as it were. Construction, lad, construction's the thing. The city'll be building something all the time. Sewers, schools, sidewalks. A grand business. Pat Nash, the county chairman, him and his brother never lack for sewer contracts. Good business for a strong young fellow like you. And the government'll be building too. And the Church, oh, this Cardinal's great for building. But you have to ease into it, you have to have the right pedigree, as it were. Do you understand?"

"I think I do," Patrick answered, flashing his ingratiating smile once more.

"Now, there's many another good business. The junk

business, for example. Why, the Taylor brothers from the twenty-fourth ward have turned many a good dollar in the junk business."

A smile began to play on the lips of the alderman. "It's wondrous, positively wondrous. The Sanitary District buys all this equipment, steam shovels and what not. Well, by God, sometimes it's only there a short while and it's declared rusty or busted. Not that it is, mind you. Then the Taylors pick the stuff up cheap and sell it again. The junk business. Not glamorous, but very profitable." The alderman sighed. "We'll be talking all morning and I've got to do my good turns for the day for my constituents outside. Very important work, helping them, each one a voter. Remember, Patrick, votes come one at a time. It's a retail not a wholesale business."

Patrick walked back toward the door. He was not exactly chastened but he had a new respect for Uncle Joe and a firm resolve about seizing some of the power which lay like humid weather across political Chicago.

2

Autumn 1931

It didn't take too long for an opportunity to arise. Patrick had arranged a double date with his friend Dick Daley, who was going with a girl from Canaryville named Eleanor Guilfoyle. They were to meet after Daley finished his evening law school classes at DePaul University. Patrick picked up Mae at her home and journeyed into Chicago on the trolley with the old Irish conductor to a Friendship Club not far from City Hall. They were to meet Daley and Miss Guilfoyle there a little after eight, so Patrick suggested that they have a beer and visit until their friends arrived. The club was a place you could get a drink in still dry times. He loved the atmosphere generated by the crowd of municipal workers and politicians from City Hall, "the Hall," as it was called. "Just listen to the talk," he said to Mae as they took two glasses of beer and sat at a table near the bar. "There's nothing like it. It's better than food."

"Well, maybe," Mae answered, "but we'll get some of that too, I hope."

"Don't worry about that. Has Patrick Kinsella ever failed to feed you?"

"Well, you do get carried away listening to stories sometimes . . ."

"Listen, listen, Mae, to what they're saying!" Patrick was like a boy eavesdropping on the conversation of elders. "Listen!"

A tall, thin man in a dark suit was standing a few feet away from them. He was a reporter named Jim Hennessy. Patrick had gotten to know him around the Hall and always enjoyed exchanging a few words with him. Hennessy was in the midst of a story.

"I met him on a golf course. And he said to me, 'You fellows are supposed to be reporters and you never get my name right. It's Nitto, with an *O*, not Nitti with an *I*.'"

"Patrick," Mae interjected to draw his attention back to her, "is that the gangster, Frank Nitti, he's talking about?" But Patrick smiled, squeezed her hand, and turned back to listen to Hennessy, who had shifted his attention to a Tong War that had been going on in Chicago's Chinatown.

"They killed the wrong Chinaman. Can you believe it? So Keith Preston wrote a poem in his column:

> 'They wanted Jim Moy
> But they got Willie Wong
> A slight but regrettable
> Slip of the Tong.'"

There was general laughter at this and Hennessy, catching Patrick's eye, walked over to say hello and to meet Mae.

"This is Jim Hennessy, Mae. We call him Spike."

"Pleased to meet you, Mae," the smiling Hennessy said. "You're as pretty as Pat here said you were." Patrick tried to get the reporter to sit with them but Hennessy said that he had to join his friends and went back to the men who were swapping stories by the bar.

"Do you remember Nails Morton, Spike?" one of them called to him good-naturedly. "The gangster that got thrown by his horse in Lincoln Park and killed. And his friends went out the next week, kidnapped the horse, and shot it on the spot where Nails was thrown. Then they called the stable owner and said, 'This is just a warning!'" The laughter exploded again as Mae, sipping as little as she could of her beer, tried to attract Patrick's attention back to her.

"Have you decided what you're going to do yet, Pat? Have you thought of going to law school like Dick is doing?"

"No, Mae, the law isn't right for me. I've been talking to your Uncle Joe and he's given me some good advice." He recited an expurgated account of his meeting with the alderman. Then they talked about the everyday things to which people so regularly turn not only to fill out their conversations but to secure their hold on their daily lives. It was about a quarter to eight when a loud argument started near the bar.

A stocky man in a straw hat was speaking very loudly. "I say this Cermak is nothing but a Bohunk, nothing but a peddler."

Patrick turned in his chair to get a closer look at what was going on. He did not know the man who was complaining about the mayor but he sensed that trouble was brewing. The man's bitter tones had soured the friendly atmosphere that had prevailed when his friend Spike and the others had been telling stories. There was a bristly edge of tension in the air as the man in the straw hat grabbed a middle-aged man by the lapel of his coat and began to berate him.

"You've sold out, for Christ's sake, sold out to this bum in City Hall, this shithead Bohemian who thinks he knows everything."

Mae reached a restraining hand across to Patrick's arm as the yelling continued.

"Let's call things by their right names, you son of a bitch. You're as bad as Cermak, every bit as bad. He's taking over the goddam city like he was king and you're all putting up with it." The middle-aged man tried to pull away. "Just a minute, I'm not finished. Admit it. You know damn well Cermak's nothing but a Bohunk who got lucky."

The other man remained silent.

"Leave him alone," Spike called out.

"Stay out of this, Hennessy," the stocky man said as he pushed the man who had been the subject of his harangue against the bar. He turned toward the grouping of tables and shouted another challenge to the customers, who sat stiffly and silently, each one hoping the man would get tired of bragging and walk out without causing further trouble.

"Anybody here doesn't think Cermak's a shithead?" he called loudly.

Patrick shook off Mae's hand and rose slowly, sizing up the man's size and weight as he did so.

"I don't think so," he said evenly as he moved clear of his chair.

"Who the hell are you?" The man spat the words at Patrick as if they were tobacco juice.

"I'm Bohemian," Patrick said, smiling like a gambler at his lie.

"You've got a mick face," the other man said, taking a step forward.

"That's why they named me Pat," Kinsella said as he threw a flying tackle at his antagonist, wrapping his arms around the man's waist, and hurling him against the bar as glasses, chairs, and people scattered all around them. The man's breath had been knocked out of him and, as he gulped for air, Patrick straightened him up, put a hand on either side of his straw hat and pulled it down over the man's forehead until the crown flared away, the stitching broke, and what was left of it came down around the taunter's neck.

"That's what you get for bad-mouthing the mayor," Patrick said, twisting the gagging man's right arm behind his back and forcing his face down toward some shattered remnants of beer glass on the surface of the bar.

"Say you're sorry," Patrick said to the man, who was totally under his domination. "I'm sorry," the man gasped.

"Louder," Patrick intoned, twisting his arm again.

"Nice work, Kinsella," Spike called as he took out his pad to make notes on the event.

"No story, Spike," Kinsella said in reply. "Just make sure the mayor knows about it."

Spike winked and put his notebook away. Patrick suddenly felt the pressure of another hand on his arm. It was Dick Daley, who had arrived just as Patrick tackled the man. Daley's dark eyebrows were knitted together in a frown of concern. "Pat, what's going on here?" He spoke very softly. "Let him go, Pat. Let him go."

Patrick released the man's arm and let him straighten up. Then he gave him a shove and the wreckage of the man's straw hat tumbled away in fragments as he stumbled through the front door. A round of cheers went up from the patrons.

"Come on, Pat," Daley said. "You don't want to waste your time on a bum like that."

But, as Patrick straightened his tie, and took Mae's arm to accompany Daley and Eleanor Guilfoyle out the door, he knew he had not wasted his time at all.

Anton Cermak adjusted his wire spectacles and studied the strong young man before him. Patrick's defense of the mayor had been reported promptly and the stocky Bohemian had sent for him about a week later. Cermak looked like a shopkeeper who maintained a neat establishment, its ledgers up to date, and the smells of bacon, coffee, and sawdust in the air. Patrick gazed down at Cermak, who still had said nothing to him.

"Kinsella your name?"

"Yes, Mr. Mayor."

"Good." Then Cermak picked up some papers, which he examined while Patrick remained at attention. Without looking up, the mayor began to speak again.

"Kinsella. That's Irish, right?"

"Yes, sir."

"I've had lots of trouble with the Irishmen in Chicago. Brennan and Sullivan and all them fellows. You know what I told them once?" He looked up expectantly. Patrick did not feel he was waiting for an answer.

"I told them someday I will fuck you Irishmen."

Cermak went back to reading the papers in front of him.

"And I have. I have fucked them because I'm the mayor and they have to work with me. Pat Nash, he's a gentleman, but he has to work with me even though he's Democratic chairman. I fucked the Irish. At their own game." He put down the papers and pointed to a chair.

"Sit down, young man. Even the Irish have to sit down."

Patrick did so, aware that Cermak was appraising him as he might pass judgment on a side of beef being delivered to the idyllic store Patrick had imagined as his domain.

"I hear you defended me the other night."

"I only did what was right, sir."

"Yeah, yeah." Cermak chuckled. "That fellow, that Snider you threw out, he's a pain in the ass. I want to thank you. Now, what can I do for you?" Cermak said with the ease of a man who did business on a *quid pro quo* basis every day.

"Nothing, Mr. Mayor, nothing at all."

"Come now, young man. I'm grateful, I'd like to do you a favor even though you're Irish."

"No. Sir," Patrick said in the earnest tones with which he had practiced this anticipated response, "I did the right thing, sticking up for you. I didn't do it to get a favor in return."

Cermak's eyebrows arched up above his glasses. "You're a nice young fellow. You're entitled to a favor. Don't go around turning them down. Damn few people will do them for you."

Patrick shifted in his seat in simulation of a shyness breaking down. The mayor spoke more softly.

"Don't be dumb, young man. What do you need, a job?"

"Well, sir, I could use some advice."

"Yes?"

"I've always wanted to get into the construction business. It seems like a good business to me. And I've saved a little money . . ."

Cermak raised his hand to interrupt him.

"Construction? Building? Very smart Irishman, ain't you? Good business. Maybe I can help you. Let me think about it. Meanwhile I've got a proposition I want you to think about. How about working for me for a while? You're young and strong, I could use you as a kind of assistant. You could learn a lot. I need somebody I can depend on, somebody smart and loyal. Somebody like you, Kinsella, an Irishman. I need an Irisher I can count on. Some men need a good Jew around. I need an Irisher. What do you say?"

"Well . . ." Patrick feigned inner debate for a moment, then offered full and effusive surrender. "Okay. It's fine. You can count on me."

Cermak stood up and walked around his desk to place an arm on Patrick's shoulder. "Good, good. How about you start today?"

Patrick asked God, with whom he still felt a special relationship, to forgive him for the lies he told Mayor Cermak that day. It was all to the good, as he saw it, to take care of

Ma and Mae. God understood, after all, that a man had to fight his own way to success.

Patrick took the job as a kind of administrative assistant. Dick Daley didn't say a word when he told him about it. He just shook Patrick's hand and wished him luck. That afternoon the mayor had him deliver a message to Alderman Mason, something he didn't want written on paper. Patrick could see that the alderman thought he knew everything about the deal, something about landfill in the World's Fair that was coming. Patrick kept a straight face. Seeming to know was almost the same as knowing. It ended up that the alderman asked Patrick to talk to the mayor about a favor connected with it. Patrick didn't do it but Mason would never know. That way, Kinsella thought, he would still have power with him, because the alderman could do things for him. Patrick smiled. What a hell of a funny life, he thought to himself.

3

Winter 1931

The wonder of it, Patrick thought a week or so later, when Alderman Mason, rubbing the Elk's tooth that normally bumped along on his bulging vest, stopped him in one of the spacious marbled corridors of City Hall.

"Say, Kinsella, I want to thank you for mentioning that matter to the mayor." Mason looked coyly pleased about whatever had happened. Patrick merely smiled, deciding to bluff out another hand of municipal poker, and, chucking the alderman on the shoulder, said in a low voice:

"Any time, George. You know that." Patrick decided it

was time to use the alderman's first name, to hoist himself up
to an equal standing with Mason on the transparent but
sturdy structure of the unperformed favor. Then, smiling
broadly as he continued down the corridor with the alderman,
he added, "Call me Pat. And call me any time."

Standing next to power, Patrick realized, constituted a
special possession of power. As Cermak's "Window Dressing
Irisher," as the mayor called him, he was perceived by every
politician in the city as having influence with the stocky
Bohemian who ran Chicago. Patrick smiled inwardly. It was
like discovering a hole in the line, it was the kind of weakness
in the opponent, as Rock used to say, that you had to
capitalize on or you could only blame yourself for losing. The
word about Patrick Kinsella's being a good man to know
spread swiftly and the young Notre Dame graduate had to
master a card player's face in order not to laugh out loud as
politicians of all ages and persuasions eagerly spilled their
dignity on the ground by asking him to talk to the mayor
about various matters that affected their interests or well-
being. He seldom mentioned any of the matters to Cermak,
who seemed to know everything that was going on anyway,
and relied instead on the percentages to work most of these
requests out favorably. When they did not turn out, Patrick
would merely shrug his shoulders, blink his innocent blue
eyes, and, more or less truthfully add, "I did the best I
could." The funny thing was that the suppliants were delighted with him for doing only that much. Besides, he had
asked for no favors in return. He was saving up those
opportunities as he became more deeply involved with Cermak. The mayor had a sweet side, Patrick thought, although
he knew that he was totally unsentimental in politics. "Politics," Cermak would say as he made a decision that adversely
affected one of his own old friends, "politics is a business of
the head, not the heart."

The only problem with his new job was that it demanded
most of his time and his opportunities to court Mae Fagan
diminished considerably. He was surprised to discover that he
did not miss this as much as she did. It was not that he did not
love her, it was that he loved even more the excitement of his
new work, this combination of politics, business dealings, and
the con, the con that seemed to be a glorious antidote to the
otherwise dull and routine possibilities of life. The country

was depressed but Patrick was not. Mae tried to be understanding but she keened for her handsome knight like an Irishwoman longing for her sailor husband gone too many weeks at sea. She would know the feeling often in the years that lay ahead.

Patrick was not totally surprised to receive a phone call one afternoon from his old friend Jack Moran. He proposed that they meet for a drink in Izzy Lazarus' speakeasy in the block just north of City Hall. Patrick was unsure of how to proceed. Jack had become deeply involved with the gangs and Patrick had stayed as far away from him as he could. Was he, Patrick wondered, the whoremaster and the blackmailer he was reputed to be? Could Patrick afford to meet with him now that he was an administrative aide to Mayor Cermak? He decided to ask Cermak himself.

The mayor adjusted his glasses and pushed the papers he was studying aside as Patrick described the invitation he had received from Moran.

"You know Moran?"

"We've known each other all our lives."

"You trust him?"

"No."

"Good." Cermak leaned back in his chair as though he was turning something over in his mind.

"You know, Moran is scum now. In with the worst, into everything. That's been one of the problems in Chicago. It's hard to have political control of the city when the gangs have so much control. Too much, that's why I've had the police department cracking down so hard on them. We have to break their power."

Patrick was not sure whether Cermak was pursuing the gangs because of civic-mindedness or because, as a shrewd political broker, he wanted to increase his power by breaking theirs. Just a short time before, two policemen had arrested a gang figure named Schemer Drucci and, claiming that he had made an effort to escape, had killed him in a car on Wacker Drive. The mobs had not liked the treatment and even the newspapers were demanding an investigation. Patrick remained silent while Cermak looked up at the ceiling.

"I'll tell you what, Irisher, you go and meet with him. But make it look like you bumped into him by accident. You understand? Hear him out. It may be important to know what he's got on his mind. The message may be for me, not for you. Okay?" Cermak picked up his papers again and Patrick turned without a word and left the office.

Izzy Lazarus ran a well-known speakeasy and, since it was so close to City Hall, it was frequently filled with politicians and newspapermen. Everyone knew that Izzy's protection was guaranteed by a reporter who covered the Federal Building and who regularly paid off prohibition enforcement officers to keep this and a number of other drinking places from being inspected. It was a nice sideline, a typical Chicago arrangement, Patrick thought, and, once again, everyone was happy but the reformers.

Jack was seated at a piano in the corner when Patrick entered. "The Singing Pimp" was one of Jack's nicknames, although it was seldom mentioned to his face. He loved nothing more than a good songfest, Irish airs preferably, and he sometimes even sang at weddings, showing up in the choir loft without the pastor's permission and soloing with *Ave Maria* during a nuptial Mass. He sometimes did it at ceremonies to which he was not invited, for churches filled with people whom he did not know. Many pastors had been astounded to hear a strange but pleasant tenor voice flowing sweetly down from their choir lofts. On one occasion a Monsignor Ramsey climbed up to investigate. Jack was halfway through the *Ave Maria* and he never missed a note as the obviously irate priest moved toward him. Moran just took the monsignor's hand and pressed it against the gun that he wore in a shoulder holster. The monsignor descended the loft stairs without a word as Jack came to a lingering end of his sacred song.

He looked pretty much the same as always, except that his moustache had filled out and looked more authentic now. Patrick ordered a beer and sat a few tables away from Moran, who was singing a parody of "Ireland Must Be Heaven."

"Ireland can't be heaven
'Cause the coppers came from there.
I never knew a copper that was ever on the square.
They will take your dough and pinch you
And they'll frame you to the chair.

Ireland can't be heaven, 'cause the coppers came
     from there."

He ended with a flourish, leaned over and kissed a blonde
who sat down beside him, and then played and sang "Danny
Boy," changing the words to "Patty Boy" as he caught a
glimpse of Kinsella sipping his beer at a nearby table.

He concluded the song, handed the blonde off casually to a
man who had been standing by the piano, and headed for
Patrick's table.

"Pat, my old friend, what a surprise to find you here!"

"A lot of the City Hall beasts water at this hole, Jack. You
still sing like an angel. But there's no halo in sight."

"Still full of the blarney, aren't you?" Jack signaled the
waiter for a drink and for a few moments the young men
exchanged stories about old times.

"Will you ever forget the look on Muldoon's face when
Capone's torpedoes hauled him out of that joint?" Jack
slapped the table in laughter. Patrick did not think any talk
about Muldoon was humorous. How much did Jack know
about the money from the Lake Terrace Club? Was Patrick
going to have to keep it hidden forever?

He waited until Moran had wiped his eyes with his sleeve
and then asked calmly, "You really didn't just want to talk
about old times, did you?"

"Getting to be very businesslike, aren't you, Pat? Just like
your boss." The smile faded slowly from Jack's face, which
suddenly looked old or hardened, Patrick was not sure which.

"You're right, Pat, I want to talk to you about business
matters. My business matters and yours, the mayor's, that
is."

"What can I do for you?"

"I want you to get a message to Cermak. I told the boys
that I had a friend could speak to the little Bohemian on a real
friendly basis. We want him to lay off. Who the hell does he
think he is? This is a big town and there's plenty of room for
business for everybody. Your boss wants to be boss of
everything."

Patrick looked steadily at his friend but did not speak, even
though Jack left him room to respond. Patrick knew that, if
he did speak, he would have to choose his words carefully. He
could not afford to be quoted about Cermak. Besides, his
power lay in what he did not say, in the needs and hopes, in

the grand and squalid expectations of others. Patrick's power rested in the dreams other people confessed to him as though he were the parish priest on Saturday night. He waited Jack out, knowing that Moran had asked for the meeting and that he wanted Patrick to deliver a message to Cermak. Well, Patrick thought, let him deliver it. But Jack sipped his beer, foam clinging to the bristles of his moustache, before he twisted in his chair to speak more confidentially to Patrick.

"You know, Pat, there's gonna be a lot of money to be made out of the World's Fair, the Century of Progress they're starting to build. I hear you helped Mason out on the landfill deal. You ought to be in a good position to help an old pal like me out."

Patrick regarded his friend critically, watching the remembered mischievous boy break through the hardened features of his face. Even though he was running with the wrong crowd and doing terrible things, Patrick loved that boy of long ago, that antic Irish tenor with the sparkling eyes.

"I didn't have much to do with that," he said without emotional adornment.

"Come on, Pat, you think I don't remember the old Kinsella lad, the football player and gambler? You'd take a good chance any time. That's why I want to talk to you. Chicago'll be filled with visitors for the Fair. We need a chance to provide them with good times. That's my business, Pat, did you know that? Good times, great times. But we're a business organization just like any other and we have to make plans. We have to know what co-operation we can count on. And what it's going to cost. Do you folly me?" He said the last in imitation of old Muldoon, smiling as he did so, as though he were good-naturedly soliciting nothing but permission to sell tea and lemon and distribute Bibles to the visitors.

"So, Pat, we have to know where we stand with the mayor. You know killing Schemer Drucci didn't go down so well. We don't want war with the city, we want to co-operate. So we have to make a deal now, we have to know where we stand. Can you find out for us? Or get the word to us where we stand with the police and crackdowns and whatever else that Bohunk has got in mind about taking the city over for himself."

"The mayor is an honest man, Jack."

"Come on, Pat, what about that Criminal Court Building went up on the West Side when he was president of the

County Board? He made a bundle on that, so I hear. That's one of the reasons we want to talk to him. He seems to have a very businesslike mind for a kid who worked in the coal mines once."

"I understand what you're saying, Jack, but I'm not sure I can do anything for you. I'm only an assistant."

"Sure, sure, and innocent as a babe, I can see that. Jeez, the fathers at Notre Dame'd be proud of you." Jack ordered another beer but Patrick said he had to get back to work. "Just see what you can do, Pat, just see what you can do."

4

Summer–Winter 1932

Patrick delivered Jack's message to the mayor, who listened without blinking and grunted more than replied. Cermak went on to other business and never mentioned the matter again over the months ahead. He continued, however, to use Patrick as a confidential messenger with various aldermen and, at times, with police officers. Pat would hear about Jack Moran from time to time but he never received another request for a meeting and, on the few occasions when he saw Moran at Izzy Lazarus' speakeasy, they just nodded and smiled but did not speak to each other. Business seemed to be going on as usual. In fact, Patrick had begun to use some of the information he acquired in the course of his work to his own advantage. He did not even have to touch his fortune to take a five-hundred-dollar option on a piece of property scheduled for demolition so that a new police station could be built, and his profit turned out to be more than the biblical hundredfold. That money went into another deal connected with building the Century of Progress Exposition and, before he knew it, his cash had multiplied many times over.

It was time for him to make his move into the construction business. He had come to know many of the aldermen whose votes were essential for both building projects and the permits necessary to undertake them. He became the intermediary between the aldermen who were willing to involve themselves in such arrangements and the builders who were ready to make political and other contributions in return for contracts and permissions. The only thing that surprised Patrick was the number of aldermen who refused to do business that way; he had thought that Chicago ran on the energies of corruption and admired those men who steadfastly maintained their innocence in the midst of so many cynical and lucrative opportunities to better themselves. So Patrick was friendly and helpful to these men as well, never asking for anything or giving any suggestion that he was willing to use his influence on their behalf.

The 1932 Democratic Convention was under way at the Chicago Stadium when Patrick's chance to become a partner in a construction company arose. The city lay under a spell of moist hot early summer weather and the sweating conventioneers had just nominated the governor of New York, Franklin D. Roosevelt, to be their candidate for President of the United States. He was flying across the country from Albany to give his acceptance speech and the Democrats were enthusiastically looking forward to a victory over the Depression-beleaguered Hoover administration. A mood of sweet anticipation had settled in by the time Roosevelt arrived and, with his patrician features outlined against the rafters and windows of the sweltering indoor stadium, promised a "new deal" for America. It had not yet come for Chicago, however, where only about fifty of its more than two hundred banks were open and where three quarters of a million men were unemployed.

Patrick felt, nonetheless, that something new had begun with the nomination of Roosevelt and he enjoyed the bawdy excitement of the convention, which he attended with Cermak. He even got to meet Roosevelt, smiling and joking and full of life, barrel-chested and big-armed above the wasted legs that showed through his pants when he was seated. "The Irish are very good at politics!" Roosevelt had said to him, delivering the line in sharply accentuated tones, and throwing his head back in laughter as Cermak interjected, "Sometimes, Governor, sometimes." It was a glorious, milling crowd of delegates, politicians, and reporters and Patrick was almost deliriously happy when he met Uncle Joe Keenan in a corridor of the Congress Hotel.

"Well, Patrick, you've been quite the busy lad," Uncle Joe said. "Have you met Monsignor Williams, my friend here?" The alderman bowed slightly toward a handsome, dark-haired young man in a black suit and a high Roman collar who was standing next to him.

"Good evening, Monsignor. You must be the youngest monsignor I've ever met. You're not going to play cards with the alderman, are you?"

"No, no, I can't risk the collection money on that," the priest said with a smile.

"Go on now, both of you," Uncle Joe said. "I hardly play at all any more, although, as it happens, I've a game this very night. Just a friendly game, for the fun of it, as it were."

"I thought you always played for the fun of it," Patrick said with a big smile.

"Now, Patrick," Uncle Joe said in change-the-subject tones, "I thought you might look after the good monsignor for me. He's been put in charge of building for the archdiocese and he has some problems he needs to talk over with someone. I could think of nobody better qualified than you."

"I'd be glad to talk to you, Monsignor," Patrick said, wondering why Uncle Joe had not dealt with the problems himself. He was suspicious of Keenan's motives. Perhaps the old alderman did not feel there was going to be any money in it.

"And how is my dear niece?" Uncle Joe asked as he began to turn away from Patrick and the priest.

"She's fine. I've been busy, so I haven't seen so much of her lately."

"Ah," Uncle Joe added as he moved away. "You mustn't let the bloom wither from lack of attention, as it were." With that he moved swiftly away and down the corridor, leaving the monsignor standing awkwardly next to Patrick.

"I guess you're nominated, Mr. Kinsella. I didn't mean to take your time tonight, but Alderman Keenan said you'd be around here someplace."

"Call me Pat," Kinsella said good-naturedly. "Shall we go have a cup of coffee?" They went down to the lobby, found a dining room still serving, and took a table together. It was the beginning of a relationship that would last many years and prove to be profitable for both of them.

As it turned out, the archdiocese had a plan for the continued building of churches and schools but, because of the Depression, as the priest explained it, there were complications. The Church had always been close to the Democratic Party. It needed a reliable go-between for ordinances and easements and other permissions and licenses that would be involved. Some politicians had made exorbitant demands and the archdiocese simply could not meet them. It was prepared, however, to co-operate in other ways with someone who could guarantee them help.

"What do you mean?" Patrick asked with a smile. "A spiritual bouquet, or a Mass on All Souls Day?"

The priest laughed but Patrick noted that his eyes were steady and unglinting. "I think we might be able to see that certain builders and subcontractors, say ones recommended by you, might get preference by us. We'd leave the rest to you."

It was just the link that Patrick had been looking for, the opportunity to represent a major prospective client to the host of suppliant contractors and builders who were always after the aldermen for business recommendations. Now he might have something above and beyond that, and with it the chance to become more independent himself.

"It's too bad we can't get a drink in this place, Monsignor," Patrick said with his best smile.

"Yes," Monsignor Williams replied in a mildly sardonic tone. "I think this may be the beginning of a very satisfactory relationship."

By the next winter, after Roosevelt had been elected and all, Patrick was launched in the contracting business, having squeezed a partnership out of one Francis X. Maher on the strength of a long list of favors he had done for him and Kinsella's own readiness to invest the fifty thousand and more that he had recently made into the firm. Maher and Kinsella, as its name became, had already started on a school and convent and were busy with plans for two more as Christmas, as dreary as a frost-deadened wreath for so many Chicagoans, dawned full of cheer for Patrick. He threw a big dinner for his mother and for Mary and her family. He even invited Uncle Joe Keenan, who took off his derby for the occasion, and Monsignor Williams, who said grace and told funny stories about the two years he had studied in Rome after he had been ordained a priest. It was that very evening that Patrick, after getting her father's permission, asked Mae if she would marry him. He gave her a ring and she cried and said, "I thought you'd never ask," and they planned a wedding for the next June, Monsignor Williams officiating, of course.

"Mae," Patrick said as he held her close, "we'll have a football team of boys and send them all to Notre Dame."

"How about a basketball team?" Mae said, laughing and holding her hand up to watch the ring catch fire in the lamplight.

5

February 1933

"What's the matter with the mayor?" Uncle Joe asked when he met Patrick on the great, hanger-on-laden main floor of City Hall.

"It's nothing much, Uncle Joe, he's got dysentery. Bad water in the hotel he lives in on South Michigan."

"The sewage, is it? And him having worked to get the Drainage Canal!" Uncle Joe shook his head. "He's off to Florida, I understand."

"You do hear everything, don't you? He's going down to Paddy Bauler's place to recuperate for a while."

"And meeting with Jim Farley too?"

Patrick merely smiled. It was true that the mayor was going to meet with Roosevelt's Postmaster General-designate to discuss federal payments to Chicago, but that was not a subject Patrick would comment on, not even to Uncle Joe. Instead he merely asked Joe how he had been feeling.

"Fine, Patrick, fine, as it were. And yourself? I see you've started building things already. You've done well indeed. It will be nice to become your real uncle. I'll have someone to play cards with in my old age." With that Uncle Joe laughed heartily and turned to greet an old friend while Patrick stepped into the elevator that took him to his office near the mayor's on the fifth floor.

When he arrived he learned that Jack Moran had called and left a message: "See you at Izzy's at two." Patrick crumpled the paper as he thought about the prospect of seeing Jack again. It could not hurt, he decided, as he tossed the note into his wastebasket and settled down to examine some blueprints before he went over to see Moran.

The era of speakeasies would end soon, Patrick thought as he entered Izzy's, and a whole surreptitious way of life with it. Billions had been made, he mused, out of the Volstead Act. Nobody would have voted for it, he thought, if they had understood Original Sin. He was on time, as was Jack Moran, who came in wearing a camel hair overcoat and a fedora with brim almost as big as a cowboy's. He opened the coat but did not remove it as he sat down with Patrick at a corner table.

"Well, Patty, you're building houses for nuns and schools for the kiddies, I see," he said as he dropped his hat in the seat of an extra chair at the table. Before Patrick could comment, Moran called to a waiter for service and hunched into his confidential position.

"Pat, you remember our last talk. I don't know whether you ever mentioned it to the mayor or not."

"Why would you doubt it?"

Jack looked around as though he was afraid that he might be overheard.

"I wouldn't be talking to you at all if I hadn't known you so long. It's just that we haven't heard anything, not anything encouraging, from your little Bohemian friend. He didn't seem to get the message, as far as the boys can see, even though I told them it went special delivery."

"You know me better than that."

"That's what I figured. Now I've got another message for your friend. The boys are very upset and that's the truth. So he should be very careful."

"Is this a threat, Jack? You should know better than to make threats."

"Only because you're my old friend, I'm telling you what's in the mind of some of the boys."

Their drinks arrived and Patrick studied Moran as he paid the waiter. The little boy had become a real professional, Patrick thought, a rock-hard man who still had some regard for old ties, but whether because of their friendship or because Kinsella might be useful to him, Patrick was not sure. He was quite sure, however, that he wanted to be extremely cautious with Moran, who seemed quirkier and less predictable than he had ever seen him.

"I'm more a contractor now than anything else," Patrick said. "The mayor doesn't need me as much."

"Come on, Pat, you're talking to your old pal. There's a lot riding on having an understanding with the administration here. But I can't tell you what will happen if we don't get some word soon."

"The mayor's been sick. He won't be around."

"He'll get sicker if we don't hear from him."

"Thanks for the drink, Jack," Patrick said calmly. "I've got to get back to work."

Jack said nothing as Kinsella took his own coat and made his way out of Izzy's place. He watched the door close and then turned toward a cluster of other customers and called, "Say, any of you want to hear some Irish songs?"

Patrick was genuinely worried by Moran's statements and decided to call Cermak long-distance and tell him about them. When the mayor got on the line, he sounded tired and irritable.

"What's that, Irisher? If you see him again, and I don't think you should, tell the son of a bitch to get out of town before I have him arrested and close up his business for good. He's nothing but a two-bit pimp. You hear me?"

"Yes, sure," Patrick replied. "I think he's dangerous though."

"Nothing but a fucking pimp."

There was a long pause. "Well, take care of yourself," Patrick finally said.

"I would but I've got to meet Roosevelt, son of a bitch,

tonight. There's a big rally and it's all politics. But we should get the money for the city."

They rang off and Patrick left City Hall to drive out through the stubborn ridges of February snow to a construction site where he and F.X., as he called Maher, would break ground in the spring for a new school. Then he drove back, picked up Mae, and went with Dick Daley and his girl friend, Eleanor, to dinner and a show. Daley was working in the county treasurer's office and still attending law school at night. He and Kinsella seldom talked about politics together any more, but they enjoyed the evening and it was late when Patrick finally returned to his mother's house. She was waiting up for him, standing under the hall light clutching her robe when he opened the front door.

"Pat, it's terrible," she said, grasping his arms. "They've shot the mayor."

Patrick, shocked and confused by this sudden information, brought his mother into the small living room, which he had recently refinished, and tried to get the facts between her sobs of distress.

"Some little foreigner shot him . . . trying to shoot Roosevelt and they shot poor Mayor Cermak . . ."

The phone rang. "Oh, they've been calling for you for an hour now . . ."

Patrick answered. It was Uncle Joe Keenan, who quietly informed him of what he had learned. The mayor was still alive but gravely wounded. The President was all right. Cermak was a hero. A foreigner named Zangara pulled the trigger. Nobody knew if he was a Bolshevik or not.

"But I tell you, Patrick, if I was you I'd get down to the mayor's office and keep an eye on things before the thieves take the floors up, not to mention the records."

Patrick knew that the alderman was right. Even if Cermak survived, he would not be back to town for some time. Anything could disappear in the meanwhile. It had happened before. He called Mae to come over and stay with his mother, got back in the car, and headed through the brutally cold darkness toward City Hall once again.

It was 2 A.M. when he arrived. Everything was quiet around the mayor's office, where the police stood guard, but his own office had been ransacked. His Notre Dame diploma had been torn out of its frame and ripped into shreds. The drawers in his desk had been pulled out and papers and blueprints were scattered all over the floor. Kinsella was angry enough to kill as he viewed the scene. Why, he wondered, pick out my office? He kept little of value there. Nothing in the way of important records. Why had he been the chosen one? He pounded the wall with his fist and kicked at the mound of papers before going back to the mayor's office to stay until dawn.

The mayor hung on for two weeks, a bullet in his spine. A reporter named Dienhart claimed Cermak said to FDR, "I'm glad it was me instead of you." That sounded more like Dienhart than Cermak to Patrick. God sent him no light about why his office had been turned inside out. But he wondered if Moran had anything to do with it.

When Cermak died, so large were the crowds of mourners that they had to hold his funeral in the Chicago Stadium; then fifty thousand people went out on a near-zero day to the Bohemian National Cemetery to see him laid away under a mountain of wreaths and flowers. Patrick and Uncle Joe were chilled to the bone when they got back to the city. Patrick was in his office, going over some plans for the transition that would ensue until another mayor was elected or appointed, when the telephone rang.

"Patty? It's me, Jack!"

"What is it? This isn't a good day for a drink."

"Well, that depends entirely on your point of view. The boys are arranging to have a Mass of thanksgiving said for Zangara . . ."

Patrick remained silent, despite his shock, during the deliberate pause. Jack was clearly intimating that there had been no accident. Cermak had been the target all along. The mob had hired Zangara for the job, at least that was the impression Jack left.

"What's the matter, Pat? I thought you'd be glad to know we're still religious-minded, especially seeing you've got such an interest in Catholic schools . . ."

"Did you tear up my office too? Was that all part of this?"

"We just want you to know where the power is, Pat. We didn't find anything worth mouseshit in your office. We just wanted you to know we could get in if we wanted to. Sorry about your Notre Dame diploma. I'll get Michelangelo to make you a new one."

"Never mind, Jack, it would only remind me of you."

"Now, now, Patty. Don't get sore. We'll all be doing business for a long time."

Patrick headed for Uncle Joe's office. It was an official day of mourning and the Hall was almost ominously quiet. Patrick wanted to talk to somebody about what had happened and, without relinquishing the balance he had introduced into their relationship, he thought Alderman Keenan was the right man. Old George Wharton, the Wise Man of the Loop, was just bidding good-by to the alderman as Patrick passed through the empty reception room. After the door closed Uncle Joe sighed and reached for a cigar.

"Poor George. Kept his money in Insull. I warned him, as you yourself must recall. Well now, what can I do for you on this sad day?" He was momentarily obscured by a cloud of fine Havana cigar smoke.

"Uncle Joe," Patrick said as he slipped into the chair next to the alderman's desk. "You heard about my office, I suppose."

"The night they shot Cermak? Yes, yes, I heard that. Did you lose anything of great value?"

"No, just my Notre Dame diploma. It was a message. From the mobs, letting me know they can get at me when they want to."

"Is that so?" Uncle Joe did not seem surprised, or, for that matter, very sympathetic. He was more the detached observer, holding his cigar like a banker, and narrowing his eyes in that appraising way of his. Patrick felt that the old man already knew all about the incident and that its very occurrence had once more placed the alderman in a superior position to him. Keenan resembled an aged coach waiting for an explanation from a young quarterback who had just been sacked in a big play in the game.

"Joe," Patrick said slowly, "what do you know about this?"

Uncle Joe used the pause as theatrically as possible, tapping ashes off his cigar, coughing, and settling himself more comfortably in his chair.

"Well, I may know something. And then again I may not, as it were. But let me tell you a thing or two, especially seeing we'll be part of the same family come June." Keenan reached for another match, struck it, and held it under the tip of his cigar, making it burst briefly into flame. Then he shook the match out and tossed it into his wastebasket. The old bastard, Patrick thought, he's better than Barrymore.

"Now, Patrick, you have what people would call good luck. I don't have to tell you that. And you take risks, impulsively, I fear, sometimes. The point is, you arrived in Chicago with your diploma and big ideas. I could see that. I wondered what would happen to you, not that I wanted anything bad to happen, mind you, not a'tall. You came to see me and you worked some card games with us. Just a sideline, you know, nothing serious there. Just for the fun of it, as it were. But I could see how you had ambition and I had a feeling that it wasn't just your ma you were worried about when you asked me about the Insull stock. Then, later when I asked you about your money, you didn't exactly level with me, did you?" He paused again to reach for a match but this time he puffed his cigar back to life and held the match in his hand as he continued.

"You were a big man, oh, there was no doubt about it, when you grabbed my hand and stared me down when I asked you some questions. Isn't that so?"

Patrick said nothing but he felt the pressure of Keenan's words. He had underestimated the old man.

"Now, Patrick, I'm sixty-eight years old, and I've seen a lot of fellows come and go in this town. And I've learned one thing. That's why I'm here today smoking this fine cigar. I've learned to save myself. 'Please yourself,' my mother used to say, 'and then you'll be sure somebody's pleased.' My poor brother, Father Ned, he couldn't even do that. Well, of course he died at fifty-four, God rest him, the physic that would have been his cure never having been discovered."

Uncle Joe was dragging it out, Patrick thought, for maximum effect. He shifted in his own chair as he became aware of the fact that he was perspiring.

"So, Patrick, seeing I had a certain affection for you but not as much as that I've kept for myself all these years, I decided to cut you loose. Why do you think I told you to get yourself known independent of me? I knew you couldn't resist that bait if only to show me you could do it. You wanted to owe me nothing. Fine, I thought, let the young man open his own charge account. There was only one way you could learn some hard lessons. And that was on your own." Uncle Joe tamped his cigar out and threw it into the wastebasket.

He put his elbows on the desk and leaned forward like a priest on a pulpit.

"What I thought was this, Patrick: that you were too quick on the draw. Bright and strong and secretly rich, like the stardust had fallen on you, or you were born at the end of the rainbow or something. But pushy, and maybe not thinking things out. Grabbing what you could, as you did in getting in with Cermak nice as you please. And I know how well you've done with the aldermen; it's a wonder City Hall is still standing with them beavers gnawing at it all these years. And your own business building schools. Fine, I say, but old F. X. Maher had better hold on to his hat or he'll be out on his ass from the business he himself started. And who will have pushed him? My own nephew-in-law, soon to be, that is, Patrick Kinsella! Well, I knew you'd go from one thing to another, all the time thinking that something like Cermak's dying could never happen. But that's what happens in politics all the time. A very chancy business, so much riding on nothing unusual happening, like acts of God, sudden deaths, and scandals in the papers. Well, you've had a great lesson. Your patron is gone and Pat Nash'll be getting an Irishman back in City Hall. But you, you've got yourself involved with the mob, the very thing I warned you of. You can't sup with the devil, as the old saying goes, without a long spoon. The trouble with you, Patrick, is you think nothing can go wrong for you. So you play a little footsie with Jack Moran, the biggest pimp in town." The old man's voice had grown angry, and he caught himself, coughed, and moderated his tone.

"I knew you'd do it, I knew you couldn't resist finding out what Moran might say or what he might offer you. That's another reason I cut you loose. I didn't want anybody thinking I was your sponsor, I didn't want Jack Moran tapping at my door. So I left you on your own, except to introduce you to Monsignor Williams, a big favor indeed, and one I was glad to do. Monsignors don't carry guns and building schools and convents for the dear nuns is a nice clean business. Well, the thing of it is that Cermak is dead and the mob has delivered a message to you. Not to me, mind you, but to you. They're saying they want a part of you in the future. They're telling you they can get at you and your family." The old man shook his head, the very image of an old pastor disgusted with his congregation.

"Patrick, Patrick, have you learned anything from all this?"

Kinsella sat erect, attempting to act calmly on the surface even though he felt smitten within. Uncle Joe was right about almost everything he had said. Patrick couldn't defend himself.

"Have you nothing to say, man?" Keenan asked as he leaned back in his big desk chair.

Patrick managed a smile. "I'm throwing myself on the mercy of the court." It was a classic Kinsella reply, a charming sentence delivered with a lilt that was itself a challenge to adversity.

Uncle Joe could not suppress a smile. "G'wan with you, you little mick. Don't be giving me the big blue eyes."

"What shall I do, Uncle Joe?" The question was a surrender, one of the few Patrick would ever make, an admission that his relationship with the alderman would forever remain unequal. Keenan would always have the upper hand.

"Get out of politics. Get out of City Hall. Build things, all kinds of things. You'll still have your contacts but you won't be in the line of fire. You were made to be a wolf, not a lamb. This is no time for you to be holding hands with Jack Moran. Do you follow me?"

Patrick nodded although he said nothing. He could feel a rivulet of perspiration struggling down his spine. It had been quite an afternoon at that, an afternoon filled with lessons.

"Here now," Uncle Joe said, obviously pleased with himself and his restoration of his proper place in relationship to his nephew. "I've a bottle of fine old brandy here in the cabinet. Come have a glass with your dear uncle." With that, Keenan rose from his chair and beckoned Patrick to join him as he placed two snifter glasses on the edge of his desk and poured cognac into them.

"Here's to you and Mae," Uncle Joe said with a wink. "And a long and happy life!"

Patrick, ready to abandon politics, went back to clean out his desk and discovered a wrapped present there for him. It was a perfect reproduction of his college diploma, framed and everything. The card read, "How do you like Michelangelo's work? Jack."

6

1946

They were in P.B.'s downtown offices going over plans for what Monsignor Williams always called a new "plant" on the West Side. By that he meant, of course, a new Church and a grade school with matching rectory and convent.

"This is just fine, Pat," Williams said as he peered down at the blueprints that were spread out on a drafting table in a room off Kinsella's main office. "And, since you've gone into the cement business, I expect you'll be able to give us a good price there too."

Kinsella nodded. He was the sole head of the Kinsella Company, having bought F. X. Maher out several years before, not that Maher had wanted to be bought out exactly but Kinsella had not really given him any choice. There were signs and billboards all over postwar Chicago that read "Who Can? Kinsella Can!" Patrick had gradually acquired businesses related to all the aspects of heavy construction, from making nails to lumberyards, with dealerships in cars and trucks, and a prosperous furniture business as well. Then there was the land, lots of land that got more valuable every day. Patrick had never even touched his original nest egg but he had used the connections he had made in politics and he had become a great donor to the Democratic Party. Part of his success, for he was now a millionaire many times over, was due to his ability to get along with labor leaders, a most unusual talent for an Irish-American capitalist. The other part of his success was due to his good relationship with the Roman Catholic Church and with Monsignor Leo Williams, to whom he had first been introduced by Uncle Joe Keenan back at the Congress Hotel during the Democratic Convention in 1932.

"Well, Leo," P.B. said, "St. Pascal's is all set. And it's a fair price all around. Now, when you're ready to talk about that new high school up on Sedgwick, let me know."

"You've had wind of that, eh, Pat? All in good time. Now I have some news for you." Williams turned his back on the blueprints. "Shall we go into your office?"

Patrick bowed with mock gravity. "Right this way."

They entered the main office of the Kinsella Company. It was in the Field Building on La Salle Street in the heart of downtown Chicago. Large and paneled in light wood, it had a view to the east across a stretch of lower buildings to Lake Michigan. Patrick had family pictures everywhere and a shillelagh was mounted on a plaque on the wall behind his leather desk chair. He motioned Monsignor Williams to one of the easy chairs that faced each other across a coffee table near the windows.

"Now, Monsignor, what's the news? Have you found oil under the Chancery office, or what?" P.B. opened a canister of cigars and offered one to Williams, who took it and put it into his breast pocket.

"I'll save this for His Eminence."

"His Eminence?"

"Yes, the old man is being named a Cardinal. There won't be any announcement for a while but I wanted you to know."

"Well," Patrick said, stripping the cellophane off a cigar as he wondered just what Williams wanted from him in return for this confidence.

"Yes, it's remarkable news. No Cardinals could be named during the war, so this will be a big occasion. New York, Detroit, St. Louis, they'll all get a Cardinal this time." Williams's face glowed as he spoke.

"Now, Leo, we haven't been doing business together for almost fifteen years that I haven't learned a thing or two about you." Patrick paused and lighted his cigar. "What is it?" The glow faded from Williams's face.

"Well, Pat, it's a complicated story and the Archbishop doesn't know anything about it. He knows he's to be named a Cardinal, of course, and that's a great honor for him and for the city. Especially the city. But the official announcement hasn't been made. And it won't be for maybe another three weeks." Williams paused and shifted the way a man does when he's coming to the difficult part of his story.

"What's the matter, Leo, do you think I'll tell Kup?"

"No, no," Williams said, looking out toward the lake. "It's just that there's a delicate matter that has come up. You know these are difficult times, the war just being over, and lots of building to be done by the Church."

"Yes, yes," Patrick said, waving his cigar. "And trucks and cars and furniture to be bought. And land for churches and schools. I understand what you're saying."

"So it's in your interest too that we work this out."

"Work what out? What the hell are you talking about?"

Williams stood up, picked a piece of lint from the sleeve of his black suit, and looked again out the windows.

"It's a hurly-burly city, isn't it, Pat?"

P.B. narrowed his eyes and sat expectantly but said nothing. Williams turned back toward him.

"Pat, if a scandal broke in the archdiocese it might prevent the Archbishop from getting the red hat. It might even hurt our plans for more schools, for the building we have in mind. Not that the Archbishop knows of this. He doesn't know a thing, and hardly anybody else does either. Do you understand?"

"Yes, but I don't know what the hell you're talking about. I need some facts. What's this 'scandal' you're hinting at?"

"It's a hard thing. You have three boys, three healthy little boys. And Mae had some miscarriages before they were born."

"Yes," P.B. said, growing a little impatient. "What's that got to do with it?"

"Family. Family, that's the thing. If one of your boys were to be involved in something suspicious, you'd do everything you could to cover it up, I mean, to see that it was handled properly, wouldn't you?"

"I suppose so."

"Well, this involves the Archbishop's family. He doesn't know it, dear old man that he is. But he gave a job to one of his sister's kids, a job at the Chancery that gave him charge of a lot of money."

There was another pause and, exhaling some cigar smoke, P.B. asked sharply, "How much is missing?"

Williams looked startled. "We don't know if anything is

permanently missing, Pat. But there do seem to be irregularities and not all the cash can be accounted for."

"My question still goes. How much is missing?"

Williams cleared his throat. "Five hundred and sixty thousand."

"Give or take a few special collections," P.B. snorted in disgust. "How the hell did it happen? Doesn't anybody keep the books?"

"He did. That was the problem. He kept them too well. I only discovered it by accident when I had to check up on some cemetery funds we've been holding until the war ended so we could build some mausoleums. Big market for mausoleums, especially among the Italians."

"I know, I know," P.B. said impatiently. "The wops don't like the wet ground. Now, what about this guy? And who is he?"

"You've met him. Everett Casey is his name. Thin fellow, eight kids."

"Yeah, sure, you have to watch those scrawny bastards every time. How'd he do it?"

"I don't know, exactly. There are lots of records missing. I haven't told anybody else about this. It would be all over town by now if I had."

"Smart of you. But that's what's smart about Casey too. He knows your hands are tied. He figures he can walk away from this and you can't touch him. Isn't that right? He knows you can't stand the heat or the publicity or his sweet old uncle won't get the red hat. And you'll get farmed out to some country parish and nobody'll know the difference. And somebody else'll start building schools and churches. Is that it? Is that the way this works?"

"I'm afraid so," Williams replied a little weakly. "If this comes out, it'll affect all of us."

"Is that all there is to it? Have you told me everything?"

"Well, Casey's been spending some money, too. That's not such a secret. That's something we've got to quiet down. He's been living a little high, and not with his wife either. We don't need that kind of scandal, not along with everything else."

"You mean, he's running around, living it up? Is that it?"

"I'm afraid so. Very quietly in the last several months. He's got a secretary from the Chancery, uh, in trouble and she's away at some home now waiting for the kid to be born. He's paying for it, on the side, of course."

"With diocesan funds? Jesus, Leo, who's been minding the store? What a nice bunch of headlines this would make. 'Cardinal's Nephew Builds Love Nest with Sunday Collection.' You sure nobody knows about this?"

"Nobody but you, that is."

"Anything else? This son of a bitch hasn't been making movies for stag parties or anything, has he? Not running anything else on the side?"

"No. Just the women. And maybe a little betting."

"Leo, did you talk to him about this?"

"Yes, that's what got me worried."

"What do you mean, got you worried?"

"Well, he didn't deny anything. He didn't say anything. Just sat looking at me, cleaning his fingernails with a penknife. Then he said, 'Is that all that's on your mind?' And he got up and left."

"When did this happen?"

"This morning."

P.B. got out of his chair and moved swiftly toward his desk. He picked up a telephone that was on a table behind his chair.

"Here, this is a private line. Call the Chancery and see if he's in. Tell him you want him down here right away."

Monsignor Williams dialed the Chancery office and asked for Everett Casey. He listened for a moment after contacting Casey's secretary, thanked her and, turning a glum face to Kinsella, hung the phone up.

"He's not in. He left a message that, if I called, he had to leave town on important business." Williams sighed and looked uncomfortably at P.B., who was slowly clenching and unclenching his right fist.

"Of course, of course," P.B. said. "The son of a bitch is probably over the border by now. Leo, I never knew you had such a trusting side."

"Pat, what can we do about this? We've got to keep it quiet for the sake of the Archbishop."

"Yes, a hell of a lot you care about him in the long run. What about us? That's it, isn't it, Leo? What about the future, mine in a way but yours especially? That's the point, isn't it?"

"Well, I'm not sure I'd put it that way. On the other hand, if this can be handled—shall we say sensitively?—then there will be no disturbance for anyone. You wouldn't want to see the Archbishop not get his red hat, would you?"

P.B. had ground out his cigar in an ashtray on his desk and walked around to the windows. He didn't speak as Williams uneasily walked over to stand gazing at the lake with him.

"Will you see what you can do, Pat?"

P.B. grunted but did not turn as Monsignor Williams moved quietly away and left the office. He was thinking about the half a million dollars and the pale, ascetic-looking Everett Casey who had been screwing everyone, the Archbishop, the diocese, any women he could find, and, most unforgivable sin, P.B. Kinsella himself.

"It was good of you to meet me, Dick, very good."

"Glad to see you, Pat, how's the family?" P.B. and Richard J. Daley were seated in a restaurant not far from City Hall. Daley had gained a little weight and Patrick had some silver hair at his temples but otherwise they did not look very different from the way they had when they double-dated with Mae and Eleanor many years before.

"They're fine. How's Sis and all your gang?"

"Fine, fine, gettin' bigger every day." Daley's eyes twinkled and his mouth broke into a half smile. "What can I do for you, Pat? I've got a meetin' at seven-thirty. I'm runnin' for sheriff, you know."

"I heard. I heard that. I appreciate your taking the time to see me. I need some advice."

Daley's face grew solemn as the two men gazed impassively across the table at each other.

"Dick, suppose you wanted to straighten out a delicate matter, one that involves the archdiocese . . ."

Daley's expression did not change as P.B.'s eyes, blue and deep as an innocent child's, locked on their nearly exact counterparts in his old friend. The eyes of two babes, they were, and not blinking at all.

"I mean," P.B. continued, "suppose there were something that might embarrass the Archbishop if it were to come out. And it had to be handled discreetly without the police and without newspapers."

Daley looked like a man waiting for more information but P.B., as wary as this solemn-looking man across the table from him, decided to leave it at that.

"Well, Pat," Daley said, sipping the coffee he had ordered when he had first sat down, "that could only mean a couple of things."

"That's right," P.B. answered, ignoring his own coffee.

"Well, what would you want to be mixed up in a thing like that for?"

"I don't really. I'm not sure I can avoid it."

"I'd be surprised if a bright fellow like you got himself too mixed up with something like that."

"Sometimes you don't have as many choices as you'd like."

"They say that. But a fellow's always got one choice about something that's trouble that he doesn't have to get into. Don't you think so, Pat?"

It was a classic Daley answer, P.B. thought to himself, because it was no answer at all; it was hardly an acknowledgment of the subject.

"Sometimes these things are a good investment for the future, Dick."

"It depends on what a fellow's looking for. They said stocks were good back in the twenties, you remember that, don't you?" Daley's face crinkled around his eyes and his mouth shaped itself into a grin. He began to laugh, another familiar Daley maneuver that pushed a man off merrily before he knew what had happened. But it was hard not to laugh when Daley did and, almost against his will, Patrick was chuckling too.

"A fellow has enough trouble on his own, that's what my mother used to say. Didn't your mother ever tell you that?" Daley was still laughing as he glanced at his watch and began to get up. "I got to be goin' or I'll be late. It was good to see you, Pat. Give my love to Mae and the kids." In a moment Daley was up and off, moving swiftly away as he always did. Patrick watched him bustle across the restaurant and then he picked up his coffee.

Patrick knew that Daley was right. He would survive and prosper without the archdiocese, without Leo Williams, without ever looking at the plans for another school. Daley was absolutely right but Patrick could not let go of this situation. It had hold of him, gripping him in a mysterious way, as though he had no real choice about it, no matter what his instincts told him, as though the fate that had made him wealthy had committed him to a rescue mission for the archdiocese whether he liked the idea or not. And he knew the reason why. The three hundred thousand dollars that he had taken in a valise from Lane's office at the Lake Terrace Club seventeen years before had been an anchor for his

ambition but a dragging weight as well. He had succeeded
finally without ever spending a dime of it, he had supported
his mother, married Mae, and raised a family without ever
spending a dime of it. He had torn up the old promissory
notes years ago and he had also had the diamonds made into
jewelry for Mae. But something had always kept him from
touching that account again after the day he had cashed in his
Insull stock on the strength of the tip Mae had given him
about the old boy's failing sexual prowess. There was blood
and sex in that money and it had made Pat, who walked under
ladders and tossed his hat on the bed even on Friday the
thirteenth, uneasy. He was trying to face that feeling as he
sipped his coffee on this evening when it had all come back
unexpectedly to bother him again. Five hundred and sixty
thousand dollars. That son of a bitch Casey was a smoothie. It
seemed incredible and eerie to P.B. that five hundred and
sixty thousand was what he had gotten the day he turned the
Insull stock in. It was too much of a coincidence and Patrick
knew that God, in a way that didn't make sense, wanted
Patrick's 1929 nest egg back again.

7
1946

The heads of four Chicago construction companies were
gathered in P.B.'s office. Maurice Hayes was digging for
something in the back of his mouth with a toothpick while
Bob McCann and Michael Senese examined a long sheet of
figures together. They were seated in the easy chairs by the
windows waiting for P.B. and Tom Slota to finish a discussion
they had begun at the luncheon Kinsella had just served for
all of them.

"Wrigley'll never sell the Cubs anyway," P.B. was saying as he and Slota joined the others. Hayes had propped one foot up on the coffee table while he continued to work the toothpick vigorously. P.B. offered the canister of cigars to his companions, who, as far as the public knew, were fierce competitors with one another. In truth, they were conspirators who met regularly to arrange their bidding on any large project that was about to be built in the area. It was an orderly procedure, good business all around, as they saw it, and it allowed them to maintain a virtual monopoly on local construction. It was, like grand and profitable schemes, simple and direct. They took turns on the big jobs and, with co-operation on cost estimates and subcontracting, not only controlled the range of bidding and the margin of profit, but eliminated the bloodthirsty hand-to-hand fighting which would have been disastrous for them all. "Bid fixing" was illegal but that did not make it immoral, not as P.B. saw things, especially at a time when the country was in such dire need of new construction. The arrangement made some rational order out of what would otherwise have been chaotic for them, although less expensive for the city and the corporations which gave them their business.

"Say, Moe," P.B. asked in his deadpan way, "shall I send for an oral surgeon?"

Hayes removed the toothpick and held it delicately between two fingers that had grown slimy in the exploration he had been making.

"That steak was good but it left a lot of traces in my teeth, Pat. I've gotta make sure I can bite to stick in with you sharks." They all laughed as he slipped the toothpick into his vest pocket.

"Anything for justice," P.B. said with a smile. "Are there any details to work out on this courthouse job?"

"Well," Senese said quickly, "I think we gotta work this subcontracting thing a little better. You know besides the construction I got an electric company and, with these vets coming home, I'd like to spread the work around some more."

"Good idea," Slota, a muscular man in a pinstripe suit added. "You could throw my little plumbing sideline some work and give Maurice here a good share of the brick work." McCann nodded emphatically. "We've talked about this before and now's the time to do it. There's a boom coming and we ought to be sure of where we stand with each other. Christ, they'll be building schools and airports, and I don't know what the hell else. What do you think, Pat?"

Hayes interjected, "We could agree on all these things now and save a lot of time and money."

"Interesting notion, gentlemen," P.B. responded, "but this one is my turn and I'll make the decisions about the subcontracting. I'll make them fairly, just as I'll be fair with the unions, but I'll make them. You won't want me telling you how to run your business the next time around. And we've all got arrangements that we have to make, and promises we have to keep." P.B. spoke pleasantly without any hint in his tones of the threat he was clearly implying. Kinsella was glad to co-operate but he was the biggest contractor of all and he had no intention of committing himself too early about matters that could be settled later on and then only on the terms he wanted.

"Pat," Maurice Hayes began in a questioning tone, but Kinsella cut him off immediately.

"Maurice, my old friend, I knew you'd be the first one to agree with me. Of course, I've been a help to you in the past and it's good of you to remember that." P.B. stared evenly at the questioner until Hayes looked down and searched in his vest pocket for the toothpick that had been deposited there a few moments before. P.B. continued to stare at him, like a matador who, by force of will, hypnotizes a bull out of the arena and back into his stall.

Kinsella also understood that the staring treatment, this intense concentration of his resistance to compromise on one member of the group, would prove unsettling for the others as well. Besides, he had solved Hayes's problems with the unions a few months before with just one phone call. P.B. had primal instincts for the preservation of power; a man kept it by using it, by seeming to spend it only to find that he had more of it as a result. In postwar Chicago he was not about to cut a deal that would give the appearance of his being only an equal with these other contractors. "The Kinsella," as the others referred to him, would remain clearly out in front of the pack. He smiled inwardly, remembering Rockne's battered face and the similar tricks he had used in football.

He glanced at Senese, the white-haired lizard, as P.B. always thought of him, because of the way his eyes snapped back and forth in the twisted and veined landscape of his skin.

Kinsella would not give Senese any electrical subcontracting because he did not trust him or the way his men worked. Jesus, he thought to himself, let Senese's men get at the new courthouse and the circuits will blow on the first windy night and the whole building will go up in flames. No, the Senese Construction Company liked to mix a little too much sand with its cement; P.B. wanted nothing to do with buildings that began to crumble and chip when you pulled the scaffolding off them. If Senese did not have such good friends in the Syndicate, Kinsella would have begun the process of running him out of business already.

P.B. turned his steady glance at Slota and McCann, good men and trustworthy, good at their trade too, and he knew that they would yield to him without a fight. They wanted to do business with "The Kinsella" in the future and they would not test their strength against his today.

"Are we all settled then?" P.B. inquired as brightly and innocently as a child asking if Santa Claus were coming to town.

"I guess so," Hayes responded glumly as he began digging at the back of his mouth again.

"Why, Maurice," Kinsella said heartily, "that doesn't sound like the enthusiasm of postwar America to me." He glanced at Senese, who was expressing his frustration by puffing angrily on his cigar.

"And you, Mike, how about you? Everything okay?"

"Yeah, yeah," Senese said between puffs.

The others nodded their heads, Slota and McCann with the slightly forced enthusiasm of men who wanted to remain close to Kinsella at all costs.

"Fine," P.B. said. "Shall we have a drink on it?" He stood up and went back to his desk to press a buzzer for a waiter to return with a bar on wheels. As he did so, his own private phone rang.

"Yes?" he asked quietly as he picked it up.

"Pat, it's Leo. Can I talk to you?"

"Well, not right now, I'm in a meeting."

"This is important. Can you listen at least and get back to me later?"

"Go on."

"We're going to have to cover the shortage somehow. Apparently a large part of the money, maybe a hundred thousand, was taken out of the central account within the last month. We've got mortgage payments due in a few days. We can get some delay but unless we can get that money back the bank is going to move against us. We might be able to get through that but there's the danger somebody'll get suspicious. One thing leads to another."

"So I've heard," P.B. answered coldly.

"This is very hard to contain. It won't be good for any of us if this blows up."

"No, you're right there. Listen, I'll call you back in a little while."

Patrick replaced the phone and forced himself to smile. This petty thief Casey from the Chancery office was one man he did not have under his power at the moment, and, although he had just settled some important business, he experienced that old feeling which rose within when he sensed that someone else had a grip on his soul or his freedom of movement. He could not afford to be boxed in by some cashier who screwed homely girls in the diocesan office after siring almost a baseball team at home. Why, the man was a goddamned menace, P.B. thought to himself, a threat to the Archbishop, to women and the sanctity of the home, and, worst of all, to Patrick Bailey Kinsella himself.

"Here's to the courthouse!" Bob McCann broke Kinsella's reverie by raising a balloon glass of brandy to him.

"Come on, Pat, you don't have a drink yet."

Patrick smiled, but it was his shark smile, the grin that meant he had tasted blood in the water and would not rest until he found its source.

"To good times," he said, raising his brandy. But he only sipped a little and paid hardly any attention to the conversation.

"For Christ's sake, Leo, are you telling me you haven't got any idea where this shitass clerk of yours is, or where he put the half million?"

"None at all," Monsignor Williams replied as he squeaked restlessly in one of the leather chairs by the windows of Kinsella's office. He had come down from the Chancery office in response to the call P.B. had made after the contractors had left. "We don't know where he is and I can't bring anybody in the office into my confidence. I found the discrepancy in the central account myself. It's been a tough thing to untangle."

"Well, Leo, you were always good with the balance sheets. Probably a good thing or you would never have found it," P.B. said in bittersweet tones.

"And we can't call the police."

"Hell, no. What about the mayor? Have you thought of talking to Kelly? Ed's always been a reasonable man."

"I'd do it but the pastor of the Cathedral denounced his administration in a sermon a couple of weeks ago. And Kelly's kid was serving the Mass. The mayor didn't take that too well. I'm not sure he wouldn't be glad if the papers found a little corruption in the Church for a change. It would take the heat off him."

"Well, we may need his help before this is over."

"Our immediate problem is the cash shortage. What can we do about that?"

Kinsella laughed sardonically. "Why don't you sell some of that stuff you've got out at the seminary at Mundelein? Hell, there's a fortune in trinkets out there."

"You know I can't do that. The Archbishop would have to know . . ."

P.B. rose from his chair and walked back toward his desk. He had made a reluctant decision but he understood that some combination of fate and faith had pushed him toward it. His nest egg, which in his imagination had grown over the years into a gigantic charm that dangled like a golden anchor from the great ship of his career, the money that had sprouted from blood and flourished through sex, the half million had been no accident. God Himself entrusted it to Patrick so that he would have it at this very moment to put up bail for the Catholic Church in Chicago. He felt freer than he expected as he turned to look past Monsignor Williams toward the darkening sky over the lake. By this action he was making the money sacred, he thought to himself, and besides, he would be picking up a mortgage on Williams that would only make their business relationship more secure. He sat down and removed a bankbook from a drawer of his desk. P.B. felt, in fact, strangely liberated from the accidental fortune he had acquired just before the market crashed.

"Leo," he said dryly, "I will personally cover the missing money."

Williams looked stunned. He could not believe what he was hearing as he eagerly got up and strode swiftly toward P.B.'s desk. Kinsella held up a hand to him.

"Now, this'll be on my terms, Monsignor." He shifted purposely into more formal language. He wanted to underscore the business nature of the transaction that he was about to arrange and he wanted his conditions made clear.

"I'll arrange to have this transferred to the diocesan account first thing in the morning. Naturally, I'll expect a letter from you, notarized, if you please, that acknowledges that you are getting the use of this money. Don't make a carbon. But have it here at nine tomorrow."

"Of course, of course," Williams responded.

"I don't want you to ask any questions about this. And I want you to leave me free to find your man Everett Casey. And the money. If I need anything from you, just do it without any questions. Do you understand?"

"Yes, of course, any way you want this. I'll see that nobody knows anything. What about repayment?"

"We'll have to think about that, won't we? That's not the point just yet. But I expect to be repaid." Patrick smiled at the thought that the blood money would somehow be cleansed by passing it through the Church accounts and it would come back to him, pure and fresh as the biblical hundredfold of bread cast on the waters. He was beginning to like the idea of squeezing the stains out of this first stake of his. He knew that, even though greatly changed, it would come back to him.

"We'll cover it in the morning."

"Do you think you can find Casey?"

"We'll see," P.B. said like a hunter who is confident that there will be game in the fields the next day. "Just let me look into it. There's more to it than just the money. What about the missing records? We'll have to do something about them too. It's not as easy as just replacing the money. That's just an interim arrangement."

"I see," Monsignor Williams replied. "Yes, it won't do if the auditors come and find a lot of records missing."

"Thoroughness," Patrick said, slipping the bankbook back in the drawer. "You must always remember to be thorough, Leo." P.B. smiled again. If he pulled this off he might be able to run for Archbishop himself.

He felt good after Monsignor Williams left. Williams had practically blubbered his thankfulness and Patrick had warned him only half in jest to pull himself together lest he raise suspicions by his sudden uncharacteristic warmth and kindliness to the other Chancery office workers. Patrick pulled his phone toward him and dialed a number he had not called in years.

"Yeah," a voice answered flatly. "Who is it?"

"It's Pat Kinsella, Jack, the great friend of your carefree youth."

"Patty dear." Jack Moran laughed. "'The Kinsella' they call you now, with your billboards all over the town. It's been a long time, Pat. Tell me about yourself before you tell me what you want."

"I'll tell you both if you can arrange to meet me."

"Too bad the speaks are all gone. Can I come to your place?"

"You know that's not a good idea, Jack. How about a ride in the country together. The car's a nice quiet place to talk. Don't you agree?"

"Fine, fine. I'll pick you up, if that's okay, at the corner of Madison and LaSalle. An hour okay?"

"Fine, but I'll have my car follow us so you won't have to drive me all the way home."

"Just as you say, Patty. See you in an hour."

P.B. knew that he was taking a risk but that was in his nature and, besides, he could hardly wash his money clean unless he patched up the records and discovered Everett Casey too. It was in the way of a bargain with the Almighty. He had made many of those over the years and they had generally worked out. Besides, Jack Moran had acquired a great deal of polish in the last fifteen years even though he was still as wedded to the underside of things as barnacles were to deep-sea pilings. P.B. felt more comfortable in calling on Jack, because Moran had returned as a war hero of sorts; he had been recruited by the Office of Strategic Services for special work in planning the invasion and in follow-up assistance in the liberated cities of Europe, which meant that they needed a man who knew how to deal with the psychopaths and gangsters. Jack had become rehabilitated to some extent and, although discriminating Chicagoans left him off their guest list, he had achieved a certain acceptability in society.

Jack's moustache was touched with gray and his hair had receded slightly but he still had a mischievous Irish smile and Patrick was glad to see him as he climbed into the big black

pre-war Cadillac that Moran still used. P.B. signaled for his
own chauffeur to follow them as they pulled off in the
darkness. Kinsella told the story straight, knowing that Jack
would respect his confidence, even to the point of telling him
that he had supplied substitute funds in order to keep the
archdiocese afloat.

"Jesus, Pat, they'll make you a Knight of Malta or something for that."

"I'm not interested in a plumed hat and a cape. This is my
way of paying back for my good fortune, for the luck I've had
all along."

Jack had a certain residual religion in his bones, the kind
that never left Irish Catholics, and a dose of superstition as
well, and the idea appealed to him. There was a crude
sentimentality in it that affected him. He also felt that Pat was
setting an old record straight with him. If Patrick was willing
to put up so much money to cover the Church's bets, it might
just be coming from that cash he had always suspected that
Kinsella had cleaned out of the Lake Terrace Club the day his
uncle and Lane had their shoot-out. When Patrick proposed
that they split whatever they could recover from the missing
Casey, Jack was sure that Kinsella was putting right something that had troubled him for years. P.B. was making a
subtle deal with him that erased the past and made them some
kind of allies for the future which seemed to open so brightly
before both of them. Patrick could stand a counterforce to
Michael Senese's influence in the Syndicate and Jack was
open to any deals at any time, especially those which added
even more to his war hero respectability.

"Can you find this son of a bitch Casey?" Patrick asked.

"I think so, I think so, Pat. And, if we're going to divide
the spoils, I'd better get somebody on it in a hurry. You know
I picked up a lot of interesting things in the OSS. I'll call you
on it tomorrow."

"Here's my private number. Let's not go through any
switchboards."

"You always were thorough, Pat."

"The other big problem we have to deal with is the records.
This is a delicate matter, Jack, it's like making counterfeit
bills inside the mint."

"Michelangelo still does nice work. Do you still have your
diploma?"

"I thought you might be able to get in touch with him. What's he been doing lately?"

"Well, he was doing two to five at Joliet when I got the government to take him on to work with me in Europe. Jesus, we plastered France with so many fake papers, they'll never get the history books straight." Moran began to laugh. "He's been busy fixing up papers that were lost in the war. And good visas are hard to get. I think he's been giving out some honorable discharges to guys who never earned them. How much can I tell him?"

"As little as possible. We'll have to fake an identification for him so that he can work at the Chancery office without arousing suspicion."

"He's a genius at that. He's liable to show up as the Pope, for God's sake."

"That would not have the subtlety we're looking for," Pat responded with a laugh. He was beginning to enjoy the project he had taken on as a kind of avocation, a calling to carry out an old duty and to make himself eligible for new favors from the Lord.

"We need a name for this. The goddamned Army always had a name for things, like Operation Overlord, and all that."

"You're right, Jack. How about 'Operation Shamrock'? Does that have the right lilt to you?"

"Oh, Patty dear, and did you hear," Jack broke into song, "the song that's goin' round . . . ?"

It seemed for a moment that they were boys again, a couple of innocents at loose in the brightly lighted city of sin, and they sang at the top of their voices until Jack stopped the car and Kinsella's limousine pulled up beside them.

8
1946

P.B. arranged for the transfer of the money the next morning. He took the notarized letter from Monsignor Williams and placed it in his office safe. Williams seemed greatly relieved that the archdiocese would be able to make all its payments on time. P.B. felt that his investment had already paid its first dividend in making Monsignor Williams doubly indebted to him. But he would not play that card until he really needed something special. Right now he was preoccupied about getting Michelangelo into the Chancery office, a sad-looking gray building not much bigger than an old brownstone, on Wabash Avenue a block from the Cathedral. Williams suggested that he arrive as an auditor; the monsignor would explain to everybody that he was arranging for a new bookkeeping system and that the man checking the accounts was a consultant on the proposed changeover. That very afternoon at two-thirty Michelangelo, with a new suit, briefcase, and freshly prepared credentials and business cards, arrived for the first of many visits to the diocesan offices.

Just before noon, P.B. had a call from Mae, who sounded disturbed. "What's the matter, the boys okay?"

"Yes, it's not them, it's Uncle Joe."

"What's wrong, is he dead?" The pessimistic side of Patrick's Irish nature asserted itself whenever there was a hint of tragedy in the air.

"No, but he called here trying to reach you. He said he couldn't get you at the office, your lines have been tied up. He sounded upset to me and he wants you to get in touch with him."

P.B. promised that he would and then had his secretary
trace the old man down. Uncle Joe was in his eighties but he
was still an alderman and he went to the office every day. He
even played cards once in a while, P.B. heard, and he smiled
to himself as he thought of the old man and the lessons he had
learned from him. They had led him to great prosperity, once
he had detached himself from active politics.

He wondered what Uncle Joe wanted and then his secretary buzzed him to say that the alderman was on the line.

"Patrick, is that you? Is this 'The Kinsella' I'm speaking
to?"

"Sure, and it is," Patrick replied with an exaggerated
brogue.

"I've something I want to talk to you about, as it were. If
you have the time, that is. I wouldn't call you if I didn't think
it was important."

"I know that, Joe," Patrick said. "I'll drop over to your
office this afternoon. How would that be?"

"Gracious, that's what it would be, gracious for a big man
like you to come and see an old man like me."

"I'll even bring you some good Havana cigars," Patrick
said before he rang off. He looked forward to a visit with
Uncle Joe. In fact, the old alderman might have some ideas
about how to locate Casey, the philandering diocesan bookkeeper.

At just about the time that Michelangelo, done up in
horn-rimmed glasses and a blue pinstripe suit, was laying his
card, which he had audaciously inscribed "Michael Barnum,
Barnum Associates," on the desk of the Chancery reception-
ist, P.B. was entering the outer office of Alderman Joseph
Keenan. It had changed little. The old secretary was gone but
the room was still packed with the beggars and the seekers. A
young blond woman, who purred rather than talked, ushered
Patrick into the old man's office without any delay. P.B. felt
comfortable and yet a little uneasy as he entered the room in
which he had passed so many hours and learned so much
about life and politics. The pictures, even that of Valentino,
were still in place and Uncle Joe, dry and shriveled, rose
slowly to greet him. The derby lay on the side of the desk and
a spray of thin white hair, like that on a baby's crown, rose
from the top of Keenan's head. Joe's eyes were still a
sparkling blue, twinkling like mirages in his desert dry face.

"Patrick, you look grand, grand indeed, for the busy man

you are." The old man's voice was firm and he seemed as alert as ever. Patrick placed a box of cigars on Uncle Joe's desk and the old man smiled.

"The goddamned doctor has cut me down on these, Pat, but I just might try one, for old times' sake, as it were. Have a seat."

P.B. settled into the chair by the side of the alderman's desk and waited while the old man slowly opened the box, removed a cigar, and carefully lighted it with one of his wooden matches.

"Pat, I'll get to the point. Gettin' to the point gets harder when you get older." He puffed on the cigar. "Grand, Patty, a grand cigar. I suppose you have them shipped special. Well, no mind. You're not here to listen to me talk of cigars. I want to talk to you about the city." The cigar did not seem to be burning just right and Joe struck another match and held it just below it.

"Chicago's a wide-open town. You know that, I'm sure. Ed Kelly's been a good mayor ever since your old friend Cermak died. But he's run an open store, as it were, with everybody, the bookies, the mob, the pimps, all of them getting their share of business. But Kelly's a good fellow, understands human nature. Knows what you have to do for the good of a city. And he's a good Democrat, a good man, even though, like my brother Ned, he has a terrible time with his bowels. You can be sitting in his living room, with him and the missus, and they're all dressed up, the mayor with his pince-nez on, and both of them reading the paper proper as you please, and he'll suddenly hunch up and let a fart that would drive a dog off a gut wagon. And the old lady never so much as rattles her paper, she's so used to it. Well, that's neither here nor there. You know the man, you've given money, lots of it, to the party. That's so, ain't it?"

"Well, yes," P.B. said with a mischievous smile. "But if I had ever known about his scandalous homelife . . ."

"Now, now, you're the same old fellow, I see. The point is, however, that Kelly is more than just a mayor or a machine politician. You know he's been supporting the idea of what they call the Open Housing, the thing Roosevelt and all them fellows were for, the thing that'll let the Negroes move out of the places they have to live in and find housing in better parts of the city."

"Yes," P.B. replied carefully. "A lot of Chicagoans are not taking that idea very well."

"Exactly, Patrick, exactly. They hate the Coloreds, want to keep them in their place, don't want them ruining their good neighborhoods. Now, Patrick"—and Uncle Joe broke off to strike yet another match to his cigar. "Patrick, I'm an old, dried-up man, and I've seen a lot. And on this issue, I'm with the mayor." He paused to let the statement sink in. Patrick was surprised because he thought that old Joe would have been quite upset at the idea of his ward's being opened to the Negroes.

"Kelly understands that the world is changing. And, old as I am, so do I. If you don't do something about the Coloreds now, if you take the short view, you're just postponing trouble for the city."

"That's a different tune from that most politicians play."

"Indeed! That's one of the reasons I want to talk to you. People in the party have been going to Jake Arvey to get him to dump Kelly, to slate somebody else for mayor, somebody like Martin Kennelly, the moving man. Why, the goddamned simpletons! They'll put Kennelly in and the City Council will do everything but sell the sidewalks." Uncle Joe was quite worked up and, as he ran out of breath easily, he had to keep relighting his cigar. "That's why I want your help, Pat. You've got influence in this city. Kelly's been good to you, with all those nice jobs in the Sanitary District and all, and never a bit of trouble. Now, Colonel Arvey says they've taken a survey and the people are against Kelly, the Irish Catholics especially, for being good to the Coloreds, and he's gonna tell Kelly the bad news next week. Goddamn it, Patrick, I want you to do me a favor and talk to Arvey, talk to the committeemen, talk sense to them, as it were. Getting a do-gooder for a mayor while they just put off troubles with the coons, that's the start of terrible things that won't come till I'm buried. But I believe in the party and in the city. People like you, maybe only people like you, can do something about it." Uncle Joe was breathing heavily as he finished these sentences and he began to cough when he drew on his barely lighted cigar.

Patrick was unsure about what to do. His feelings told him that Uncle Joe was right but his mind told him that he could not stop the inevitable. Once a political organization made up its mind, there was nothing that anyone, not even a big contributor, could do to stop it.

"And one other thing, Patrick. It's not just to the pols I think you should talk. There's another organization here in town that's got influence, and that's the Catholic Church. And you know it, and you're in good with them, with Monsignor Fat Ass, what's his name, Williams, the fellow has all the say these days. They can get right to the people who resent the Coloreds, they can reach them on the neighborhood level, the only organization that can do that outside the party. If the Church put up a big enough squawk they could save Kelly. And maybe, and for no virtue even, they could save the city a lot of trouble in the long run. And, seeing they preach love of the Negro, they might just practice some of the same, as it were." Uncle Joe was fiddling with his cigar, tearing away a bit of the outer wrapping. "The goddamned cigars don't draw as good as they used to."

"I must say that you are the compassionate statesman this afternoon," P.B. said, although he was wondering if God was taking him up on the new bargain he had just struck with Him, asking him to play his card of influence with the Church on behalf of Mayor Kelly and the Negro population of Chicago. The ironic possibilities made him smile at the long saga of his original nest egg. It was like a wonderful forward pass, sailing through the air with the sweetest possibilities of victory, and it had arched up high over the span of the last fifteen years to come down now into the complications of Church and state in postwar Chicago. I should have left the goddam bag where it was, P.B. thought to himself as Uncle Joe cleared his throat after a spasm of coughing.

"Patrick, there's no statesmanship, just politics in what I have to say. And politics ain't nothing without some compassion. This is a political judgment, Pat, based on good sense about what's going to happen in the next few years." He coughed again. "I'll be long dead, but this is one political decision that needs the long view, the long view."

"I'll be glad to talk to Colonel Arvey, Uncle Joe, if you think it'll do any good. I don't know what I can do about the Church. I'm not even sure what the Church can do."

"The Church can do plenty. They've lots of votes and they've been part of the city government for as long as I can remember. They've gotten plenty from the city in exchange for their support and for their not interfering in things too much."

P.B. did not like the idea of being an intermediary in these matters and he doubted that he could accomplish very much. He could not, however, shake off the feeling that this mission was part of God's new bargain with him and he did not want to deal lightly or carelessly with that. He wanted blessings for the future and the assurance of the Almighty's continued guidance. Kinsella felt the way he did when the priests at Notre Dame used to try to talk him into the seminary. It was a beautiful idea but it wasn't for him. Did God always ask for things you didn't feel like doing? Was not an entire Catholic ascetic theology based on just such a policy? Patrick shook his head free of the grasp of such thoughts.

"I'll see what I can do, Joe, I really will."

"Good lad, good lad. I've seen the signs: 'Who can? Kinsella Can!' But get going on it. The decision on Kelly's almost made." As Patrick got up, Uncle Joe rose slowly out of his chair, clapped his derby on his head, and walked him to the door.

"I wear it like the Pope wears his hat, you know, for ceremonial occasions more than anything else."

P.B. couldn't quite figure out what was happening. It seemed God expected something of him. He had put his first stake back to work to save the Church financially. That should have taken care of his end of the bargain. Uncle Joe was right about the city, P.B. thought, but he didn't get very far when he called Arvey and some of the others. They told him the people were against Kelly, that it would be a tough election, and that the decision had been made. What they were really saying was that the aldermen wanted to take over running the city again. And the newspapers would end up thinking that the slating of Kennelly was a blow for democracy.

P.B. also talked to Leo Williams. Michelangelo was at work and had been accepted by everyone. He even fooled the Archbishop, dropping to the floor and kissing his ring when he met him in the hallway. Michelangelo would be able to forge the right papers to get into heaven, P.B. thought, and he'll probably be selling them at the Last Judgment. Michelangelo told Williams he could remove all traces of Casey's ever having worked at the Chancery.

P.B. also talked to Williams about the Open Housing but
the monsignor backed off with lots of blather about preserving the neighborhoods and the parishes, and the Church not
wanting to interfere in politics. What bull, P.B. said to
himself, since the Church had been up to its belfry in city
politics from the Year One. Not that it was all bad, not at all,
and Kinsella certainly had not suffered because of it. Williams
went on about timing and how, with the financial problem not
fully covered, it was a sensitive period and the Church didn't
want to draw unnecessary fire, because it would hurt other
programs. "What about the Archbishop?" P.B. asked. "Oh,
he would be for the Negroes one hundred per cent," Williams
said, but he had to restrain him a little. The old man didn't
always appreciate the complexities of things. Timing was
everything. Well, Patrick mused that night, God must understand that if I can't get Monsignor Williams to move on the
Open Housing, that I can't do much more on my own. He had
kept his side of the bargain.

9

1946

A few days passed and, although P.B. and Jack Moran kept in
touch with each other, no word had yet come about Everett
Casey. Kinsella wanted to retrieve what money he could from
the Chancery thief, but, against his will, he had developed a
grudging admiration for the man. Anybody who could spirit
half a million dollars out from under Leo Williams, while he
was screwing the secretaries and being acclaimed as a great
family man at the same time, had the brass, even if a bit
tarnished, that P.B. admired.

"Goddam it, Jack, they ought to name him Father of the Year and have his uncle the Archbishop give him a medal," P.B. said in amused tones.

"We'll have something in a day or two, I'm sure of that. Michelangelo tells me the bastard did a pretty smooth job with the books."

"How is the restoration work going?"

"Fine, no trouble. He says that anybody with a little nerve could take the bank away down there and they'd think it went to the foreign missions or to the poor."

"They're beginning to sound more like Democrats all the time, although I've always suspected bishops of being secret Republicans."

"Say, talk of Democrats, Pat, are you going to Judge Forrest's wake?"

"I'd stop by. I remember him when he worked at City Hall." P.B. knew that Moran did not care about the deceased; he was merely suggesting a public place where they might easily meet without giving the appearance of having arranged it beforehand.

"He used to play cards with the alderman. You did a little of that, didn't you, Pat?"

"I just served the drinks, Jack. Look, I'll probably run into you at Harney's tonight. He sure has laid out a lot of judges in his day, hasn't he?"

"Has a nice touch with them, they say. I think he made a deal with a lot of them while they were still alive. If they helped him in this world, he'd give them a free ride into the next."

The two men rang off and Patrick turned to his next appointment, which was with the head of the Plumbers' Union, Max Kollner. P.B. liked Max, whose broad Slavic face had the slightly drawn expression of a man who had sniffed a thousand sour drains. Max was interested in the courthouse, Patrick knew that, and P.B. was not adverse to giving him control of which plumbing outfits got the work. It was barter on the level of chiefs, quite a few steps up, as Patrick viewed it, from members of the bench making deals with undertakers. Besides, neither Kinsella nor Kollner would make a deal in which they could only collect after death. Max got right to the point, that was another thing that Patrick liked about him.

Max thrust a hand, as large and hard as a king's mace, into Kinsella's, and then both men moved to the leather chairs by the windows.

"Glad you got the courthouse, Pat. Can't always trust those other sons of bitches, especially Senese. I presume we can cut a deal."

Even though Patrick was ready to go along with Kollner, he decided to wait him out. "What do you have in mind?"

"Come on, Pat. This is me, Max, from the old days. I know you're the low bid. And I know there'll be some act of God that'll force you to get a change order to raise your cost twenty per cent . . ."

"Fifteen," Patrick said with a smile.

"Don't kid me. Fifteen? What's the matter? You think you're gonna die or somethin'? You afraid of somethin'?" Then Kollner began to smile. He realized that Kinsella had been kidding him. "How much, Pat? Twenty-five per cent? That's it, isn't it, twenty-five? Jesus, I've got to hand it to you."

"Actually, Max, there hasn't been an act of God yet. Who knows? God was on our side during the war but He may not be now."

"Come on, Pat, you've always been good at arranging acts of God. I never knew anybody like you. You must be well connected."

"The luck of the Irish, Max, and nothing more. Now, how about you? I'm Pat, from the old days, remember? And I know whenever there are so many preliminaries, you're spreading a smoke screen for what you want."

Kollner laughed. "Maybe you're right, Pat." He stroked his chin. "You know, things are hard. Not enough jobs, nothing settled yet from the war. I need to put extra men on, more than we'll need, maybe a lot more."

"Ten a day?" P.B. asked nonchalantly. He was as familiar with such sweetheart deals as he was with his prayers. They were part of every day in the construction business. You let Max, or some other union leader, hire more men than the job required, they got paid, the union prospered, and the fellow who wanted the building settled the bill for it all.

"Ten? Pat, swear to God, I need twenty extra jobs at least. Swear to God, Pat."

"Fifteen," Patrick said with some finality.

"It's a deal," Kollner replied, jumping to his feet to pump

Kinsella's hand once more. "You're a good man to do business with."

"Fifteen, Max, and no fooling around. You understand?"

"Swear to God," Max said, clapping Patrick on the shoulder. "Swear to God."

Harney's was a mock Tudor mansion on the West Side. A large clock, outlined in neon, was set in the broad chimney brick that climbed up by the front door. Harney's taste was such that he considered the timepiece a cultural contribution to the neighborhood, especially the slogan, circular tubing twisted into script lettering to read, "Harney Will Take the Time to Give You the Time Any Time." P.B. shook his head as he glanced up at it. He nudged Mae, who had been picked up by the Kinsella driver and brought to the Cape Cod Room, whose Irish maître d' was a favorite of P.B.'s. The Kinsellas had dinner there before they went to the wake together.

"Make a note, Mae, not to bury me from Harney's."

"I thought I'd give you a Viking funeral anyway when—and if—the time ever comes. I'll just set you out in your boat on the lake and have it set afire." Mae laughed at her own teasing as they entered the main door. They found themselves in a red-carpeted room, its white plaster ceiling laced with dark beams, its paneled walls decorated with pictures of the Harneys, father and sons, as well as the family coat of arms. An artificial log glowed a ghastly orange in the fireplace. The elder Harney, his hair not much different in color from that of his silver-rimmed glasses, stepped out of a grouping of five or six other mourners to greet the Kinsellas.

"Welcome, Mr. and Mrs. Kinsella," he said unctuously. "You'll be here for the judge, I suppose."

"Yes, the bench is your specialty, I understand," P.B. said, the irony flowing over the nodding Harney as though it were a honeyed endorsement.

"We have been pleased to be of service to many justices and magistrates, yes." He turned slightly with the marginally deferential dip of the shoulder that was the specialty of Irish undertakers who had taken on airs. "Judge Forrest is in the Galway Room. Just to your left."

Kinsella winced at the name of the parlor and Mae elbowed him to ward off any further remarks.

"I wonder does he have little leprechauns with tiny paint pots to put the roses in the cheeks of the customers," Patrick whispered as they headed down the hallway. "Shh," Mae responded. They were at the open door of the Galway Room, which was filled with mourners. Some were milling about, while others sat and talked with friends on the couches and hard chairs that filled the room. There was a hubbub and at the far end of the room the judge lay almost forgotten in a bronze casket, surrounded by ribboned baskets and sprays of flowers.

"It's fortunate to die young," Mae said, almost to herself. "Then you have a lot of people to remember you."

"That's one way to look at it," P.B. responded as they made their way through the crowd of people, several of whom waved and said hello to them.

"Keep moving, Mae," P.B. said, "or we'll be here all night."

A group of nuns in trailing black cloaks had just risen from their prayers before the coffin and moved off like a flight of birds. The Kinsellas knelt on the plush prie-dieu, wide enough for four people, that was set out before the casket. Patrick and Mae crossed themselves and bowed their heads in prayer against the noise of the room behind them. As they stood up, a slim woman of about forty, dressed in black, winsome as widows went, smiled sweetly at the last of the line of nuns and turned toward them.

"Mrs. Forrest," P.B. said, taking her hand, "as the Irish say, we're sorry for your troubles."

"Yes, and we'll have a Mass said for the dear man," Mae added.

"Thank you for coming, both of you. The judge often spoke of you, he thought very highly of both of you." The widow began to sniffle and Mae put her arms around her and led her to a chair in a crowd of relatives sitting at the side of the room. P.B. moved away to greet some old friends.

He spotted Alderman Keenan looking up from an armchair at a group of men who looked like they had just come from the racetrack. Tony Panetta, little Tony who used to let himself be thrown out the window at the card games, was telling Keenan a story while the other men listened with the same impassiveness with which they watched the horses enter the gates every afternoon.

"Ah, Patrick," Keenan called out as he looked up. "Tony's been tellin' us of his love life."

"Go on, don't let me interrupt," Patrick said as he nodded,

more a signal of recognition than greeting, to the men standing around.

"H,H,H . . . Hello, Pat," Tony said, "I,I was just telling the alderman how I was sitting in the movies with my new girl friend. And did I have a hold on h,h,her! Wh,Why if I knew the Morse code what a l,l,love story I could have told." The men laughed and Patrick smiled as he regarded Tony, who, despite some new lines in his forehead, still looked in good enough shape to take a dive out a window. Maybe, Patrick thought, he's still doing it for a living. He had never observed Tony doing anything else in all the years he had known him. P.B. smiled, thinking of the camaraderie of these con artists, of the way the con had actually become a way of life for them.

"Tony," Keenan said, "remember with women friends, if you've a mind to be serious, the first question is what does her father do?" Then the alderman gestured and Patrick bent his head down toward him. "I understand you've talked to Arvey, Pat. No dice, that's what I hear."

"No dice, that's what I heard too. Seems like their minds are made up."

"And the Church? Did you talk to them?"

"They don't want any trouble, Joe. They aren't quite ready to lead the Crusade yet."

"Yes," Joe said pensively. "That's been the whole deal. If the city let them have their schools, and filled the public school system with Catholics, teachers and principals, well then, they wouldn't interfere with city business." He shook his head as some noise by the entrance to the parlor indicated that an important person had arrived. It was Mayor Kelly himself, a tall, heavyset man with nose glasses like Roosevelt's set in a patrician Irish face. He wore a camel hair overcoat and touched one hand to his thick shock of wavy hair as he moved toward the casket.

"Do you think he knows?" P.B. asked quietly.

"I'm afraid so. But he's got class, he's not a complainer."

Kelly, with two bodyguards standing just behind him, knelt at the bier, his broad shoulders hunched as he prayed for a moment. It had become quiet when he entered but the conversation had begun to pick up again.

"And to think of it! He hated the son of a bitch," Keenan said out of the side of his mouth to Kinsella. "Why, Kelly gave him his judgeship on my recommendation and Forrest disappointed the mayor many a time."

Patrick's eyes widened in surprise. "Had Forrest become a man of principle?"

Uncle Joe glared up at him. "Not a bit of it. Highest bidder, that's all. That was his nickname, 'High Bid' Forrest. Kelly couldn't move him, so he had to put up with him. The pity of it."

"I never heard that."

"Well, you've been busy building things, Pat. That's why I knew you'd be happier out of politics, as it were. You've missed nothing, really. Forrest double-crossed me a few times too. And he wasn't above a little blackmail when he thought he could get away with it. Threatened me about the card games, told me he kept evidence about them."

"Well, why did you come if that's all true?"

"First of all, I wanted to make sure he was dead, the son of a bitch. And, second, I wanted to tell his widow—there she is thinkin' Kelly's prayin' for her husband's soul when he's really wishin' him a thousand years in purgatory—that, if her husband had told her any stories about me and she expected to ask me for money or anything, that tonight was the night for her to do it. 'It's the best night you'll have,' I told her, 'for the judge was so crooked he won't lie straight in the grave.'"

"You actually said that to her?"

"I did earlier, before the crowd came. Only Harney, the fella'll give you the time any time, he was skulkin' around. And she just looked at me and said, 'I'm better off, and the kids too, now that he's gone.' That was the whole thing, all she said. I do believe she thought he was a son of a bitch too. That's the trouble with these goddamned wakes. It's all splash, the last whitewash, as it were. I'll have none of it when I die, not a bit of it, do you hear me, Patrick?"

"I do," Patrick said, a smile on his face. "What would you like?"

"Call the priest, unless I'm so cold there's no sense to it. Then stick a bone in my ass and put me out so the dogs can carry me away."

P.B. began to laugh as a hush descended on the room and the mayor started to leave, nodding with a smile as he moved along, and stopping to shake P.B.'s hand. "I'm grateful for your efforts, Pat," he said looking directly into Kinsella's eyes. He also bent down and whispered something in the alderman's ear that made Keenan grin. In a moment Mayor Kelly was gone and the slow rhythm of the long evening reasserted itself. P.B. looked back by the door as the mayor exited and saw Jack Moran standing by the rostrumlike desk at which people signed the guest book. He broke away from Keenan, greeted a number of old friends, and finally found himself, the guest book pen in his hand, standing right next to Moran.

"We found him," Jack said quietly.

"Where?"

"He's at the Ambassador West. He's been living there for several months under another name. Hadn't been home in some time. The wife kept it quiet, one of those suffering Irish women, so the Archbishop, her husband's uncle, wouldn't find out. Casey's been living it up, having the women in."

"Does he know you're on to him?"

"No. But I think we'd better move if we're going to get any of the dough back."

"Tonight. After I take Mae home. I'll walk over from our apartment. Got a room number?" Patrick signed his name with a flourish on the guest register.

"Seven-nineteen."

"I'll see you in the hallway there in half an hour." Patrick replaced the pen and turned to go back to where Mae was standing.

Monsignor Williams had arrived and was talking to the widow when P.B. reached Mae's side. He nodded at the monsignor.

"Your good Catholic," Williams was saying, "is your contributing Catholic. And so the judge was, a great user of the envelope system . . ."

As Mae and Pat made their way out of the Galway Room, Kinsella said softly, "I wonder if the judge ever helped count the collection at the Cathedral?"

10

1946

Kinsella hurried through the few streets that separated his apartment on Lake Shore Drive from the hotel in which Everett Casey had been living in fugitive elegance. Jack Moran was just approaching the canopied entrance and P.B. called to him to wait.

"Was it hard to find him?"

"No, shit no, once I got a fix on who we were looking for, it was easy. The son of a bitch left a trail through this ward like a leaky sand wagon. Look, Pat, let's enter and leave separately. I'll meet you up on seven."

P.B. nodded and waited a few moments before climbing the stairs up to the lobby and taking the elevator. Moran was waiting halfway down the hall.

"I'll show you some tricks I learned with the OSS. Or did we teach them to the OSS? It got confusing after a while." With that, Moran took a small flat piece of metal from his side pocket and, within seconds, had slipped the lock and pushed the door to room 719 open. It banged against an inner wall but they could hear no other sound, except that of a shade lifting away and falling back against a half-open window. Moran switched on the lights. The room was empty and in good order.

"As neat as his books," P.B. said as he glanced around.

"It ought to be at the prices they get here," Moran said as he pushed the bathroom door open.

P.B. went back and closed the door to the hotel room. When he returned, Jack was standing next to the desk by the open window.

"Well, he's not hiding in the shithouse. Let's see what we can find here." Moran picked a briefcase up from the floor and flipped it open.

"The Jackpot on the first try. Or part of it anyway." Clumps of currency, some in money wrappers and some bound with rubber bands, spilled onto the desk. P.B. watched as Jack then went through the desk, tossing whatever he found onto the floor. Then Moran went to the closet, dragged out a valise, and tipped it over on the desk. Another jumble of money fell onto the pile.

"Let's count this while we have a few minutes," P.B. said. "It would be nice to know where we stand." They each took a pile of the money and began to sort it out, P.B. at the desk and Moran on the bed. In only a few moments, Kinsella looked up expectantly.

"I make it twenty-two five."

"And I," Jack said, dropping the last wad of bills onto the desk, "count thirty-three. That's fifty-five five. Right?"

"He must have some on him, wherever he is," P.B. said flatly. "This is only ten per cent of what he took, a little less, as a matter of fact."

"Well, let's sit down and wait for him. Maybe he knows where there's some more."

P.B. stacked the money in neat rows on the desk top.

"That reflects my good Catholic upbringing. Be neat, the Sister said, even when you're splitting the swag." Patrick picked up the phone. "I'm going to call Monsignor Williams to tell him we've found the Robin Hood of Rush Street. He robbed from the rich and gave to all the poor bookies and hookers up and down the avenue."

"Don't knock that, Pat. I may get some of the dough back that way, you never know." Moran sprawled on the bed, took a penknife from his vest pocket and began to clean his fingernails very carefully.

"Hello, Leo. Pat. We've found Casey, I mean, we've found where he's staying and we're waiting for him to get back." Kinsella listened for a moment. Jack could only hear the faint crackle of a voice on the line and he could not make out any of what Monsignor Williams was saying.

"Of course, we'll keep it quiet. We're not interested in having a press conference. Do you want to see him or not?" P.B. shook his head slowly as he listened again and, after a brief good-by, hung the phone up.

"The monsignor is playing it close to the collar," P.B. said as he walked over and looked down at Moran, who paused in his nail cleaning to glance up quizzically at Kinsella.

"He played dumb once I told him we had it under control. He was half kidding me but, so help me God, he's suffering from Michelangelo's good work. Your records expert has removed all traces of Casey's ever having worked at the Chancery and Williams is pretending that's the way it is."

"He's afraid the telephone operator is listening."

"Maybe. Besides, there's plenty of witnesses who know that Casey worked there for years. But that's the official line. That's so he won't have to tell the Archbishop and get him all upset. Williams has got his eye on a miter as much as the old man wants a red hat." Kinsella started to laugh. "And I paid the way, I should say, we paid the bill for it all."

"You don't think he'll stiff you, do you?" Moran asked, swinging himself up on the edge of the bed.

"Not with the notarized letter I've got. But I think Williams has got himself in the position where he can pay when and as he wants. He's clear now, the Chancery's out of it, the good name of the Church has been preserved. And we did it, you and me. Can't you see how funny that is? We've been taken, nicely, mind you, but taken nevertheless, by a holy priest." Patrick began to laugh again and Jack joined in until they were almost helpless in their sardonic merriment.

"That's okay, Jack. He'll be surprised how much the next church I build will cost." They were at the point where anything either of them said set them both howling with laughter again.

"The last fucking time I'll try to do good for anybody . . ." Moran called, falling back on the bed again.

P.B. wiped his eyes with a handkerchief. "Right now, Jack, all we can net is what we can recover from the bon vivant who's been shacking up here." They settled down after the outlet the laughter had offered them.

"We'd better quiet down or we'll scare him away," Jack said as he rose from the bed and walked back toward the door of the room.

"I'll put the lights out. It'll be a surprise for him."

Then the old friends took chairs and sat quietly in the darkness to await Casey's return.

"You know, Jack, this story would be funny if it hadn't cost

us so much," P.B. said softly. "I'm beginning to think
Providence has worked this whole thing out."

Jack grunted, "Maybe so, Pat, maybe so."

Then they were silent, each with his own thoughts, although these overlapped considerably. Moran mused on the
fact that the search for Casey had enabled Kinsella to work
out something which had always been lost in a fog of
uncertainty. Moran was almost sure that Kinsella had cleared
out the cash at Lane's place but he had never been absolutely
certain. In a way it didn't matter, for Moran had done very
well, but in another way it had bothered him. It had been like
a sheet with a wrinkle in it; he just hadn't been comfortable.
But now it was being ironed out. Kinsella, without explicitly
mentioning the source of the money with which he had bailed
out the Chancery office, had offered Jack 50 per cent of what
they could recover. That did not look to be much in terms of
cash but Jack felt better, a little more respectable because of
the invisible and unspoken exchange that had taken place
between them. He did not feel warmth for Patrick, he never
really had felt that for anybody, but he did feel a rekindled
camaraderie, born of taking risks, of sharing another adventure together.

P.B. rubbed his jaw as he sat in the darkness. The money
was as good as gone, he thought to himself, and good
riddance. God had let him have it and God had taken it away.
How like God that seemed to be. P.B. felt relieved, freed
from a stake that had become a great burden. And it had
gone back to God through the Church. P.B. frowned at the
thought that he had not been able to deduct it as a charitable
contribution. Well, maybe something could be worked out
there too. Leo Williams wouldn't go on pretending that Casey
had never existed, not face to face with P.B. anyway. Still, it
would be a long time before he got the money back. The hell
with it, he thought, I'll take it out in merchandise. He smiled
inwardly at the many ways in which he could increase his level
of profit here or there in his dealings with the diocese.

He could make out Moran's form in the darkness. This
event had untied an old knot in their relationship too. He was
at least out of the shadow of Jack's suspicions, not that he was
afraid of Jack, not exactly. But there was something wrong
with Moran, something that couldn't be fixed easily, and he
did not expect his old friend to remain a true blue war hero

much longer. Jack would be into everything that was illegal, if he hadn't managed it already. This bizarre adventure had settled something between them and, in the future, P.B. would not have to have anything to do with him. They were free of each other and P.B. thought, Well, maybe it's been cheap at the price.

There was some noise outside and then the sound of a key scratching at the door lock. "Shh," Moran said, slipping out of his chair to take a place just beyond the point where the opening door would touch the wall. There was more noise as the door banged open, the sound of a woman's voice and a man humming to himself. The lights snapped on and Moran moved swiftly to grab the entering man by the arm and to shove the woman ahead of them into the room while kicking the door closed at the same time.

Casey was indeed a scrawny fellow, maybe thirty-five, with a widow's peak of jet black hair above eyes that were popping and rolling in surprise. His right arm stuck out stiffly from the grip Moran had on his elbow and his hand splayed open to release the room key silently onto the carpet. The girl, a redhead of about twenty who was wearing exaggerated makeup, simpered as she pulled herself together in the middle of the room. Moran closed a hand over Casey's mouth and held him tightly, like a commando about to kill a storm trooper. He glared at the girl.

"Get out of here. And breathe a word and I'll find you and break your legs," Moran snapped. The girl did not even glance at Casey as she headed straight for the door. She stopped, hand on the knob, and looked back at the scene. "Gee," she said, "John here ain't paid me nothin' yet."

P.B. took a fifty-dollar bill from a pile on the desk. "Here's something for the wear and tear. Now beat it." The girl took the money, put it in her purse, and slipped out the door. Moran forced Casey toward a chair and pushed him down into it.

"Who the hell are you?" Casey asked, rubbing his elbow as he adjusted himself in the chair. "You're Mr. Kinsella, aren't you?"

"That's right," P.B. said, "and we're here to get the money back that you've been siphoning off from the Chancery office."

Casey looked up cautiously at Moran, who was still standing next to him. "And you, who are you?"

"Skip it. We'll ask the questions, Mr. Casey, or do you prefer your phony name, Parnell? Jesus, what a name for you to take! It made it easier to find you, you dumb bastard."

Casey seemed to regain his composure. Jesus, P.B. thought, he's relieved too. What a comedy. Everybody who's chewed at the wad of money is relieved in some way, Williams, Moran, me, and even this son of a bitch who's been spending it on cheap whores and bad horses. We're all relieved, the money's gone, and everybody feels better about it. He smiled at Casey.

"Where's the rest of the money?"

Casey reached into his breast coat pocket and pulled out a leather wallet. He withdrew a handful of bills and spread them on the arm of the chair. Then he removed some stubs that both Kinsella and Moran recognized as the remains of bets made at the racetrack.

Casey's eyes looked first at Moran and then back at Kinsella. Bookkeeper's eyes, P.B. thought to himself, they're good for detail work.

"This is it," Casey said in a calm, deep radio announcer's voice, another surprise considering his small frame. "There's twelve hundred dollars. There was more before I made these bets, these and a hundred others."

"You mean, with the cash on the desk, that's all there is?" Moran asked more in sadness than anger.

"May I have a cigarette?" Casey asked, stretching himself a little. Moran offered him a cigar. "That's all I've got." Casey took it, bit off the end, spat it out, and then struck a match to light it.

"Actually," Casey began, "I'm a little relieved you're here. I knew somebody would come, someday . . ."

"Where's the money?"

Casey was settled, even a bit expansive, as though he were a desperado whose exploits had somehow placed him on the same plane with Kinsella the builder and Moran the mobster.

"Actually, Mr. Kinsella," he said evenly, "I planned to do this for years. It wasn't too hard, once I was sure just how to do it. Say what you will about priests, they are very trusting fellows. Besides which, they're not too good on reading balance sheets." He puffed his cigar contentedly. "And what more could they have wanted from a trusted worker? A good family man, a lovely wife, eight children, right on time every day, extra work on Saturdays. Nothing was ever too much trouble. That's where they made their mistake. They let me take all the trouble. So they had no idea of what I was really doing."

"What about Monsignor Williams? He's supposed to be good at the books, a real administrator," P.B. asked, noticing as he placed the question that his sympathies were unaccountably shifting toward Casey.

"A shrewd man," Casey responded, "but overrated on the balance sheets. And as for administration, he could fuck up a two-car funeral." Moran and Kinsella both laughed. They liked this strange man who had made off with money they both thought was theirs.

"And he's the one who trusted me most. The Archbishop is a sweet man, a dear man, a southern gentleman who would never want to hurt anyone. But not always in contact. He goes and preaches at a priest's funeral and on the way home invariably asks his secretary, 'What was the name of that priest we buried today?' So I never expected him to check up on me too much. The trouble was, I got tired of being good. And then the plan came to me and, before I knew it, I was clear as to just how to do it. The Archbishop's uncertainty about which priest he was burying gave me the insight. The cemetery accounts. Perfect! And a last swipe at the central fund. All done in less than a month when I finally put my mind to it."

"What the hell did you take it for, to have a good time, was that it?" Moran asked, taking out a cigar for himself.

"No, no, but let me tell you something. I've gone through a lot of money, some on politicians, some on horses, a lot on horses. And women, yes, and wine. And I've enjoyed every goddam cent of it." He took a long draw on his cigar, as though he were Samuel Insull home triumphantly from the financial wars. P.B. could not help smiling at the insouciant little man sitting in front of him, bold as brass, as P.B.'s mother used to say, smoking a whoremaster's cigar.

"No, I didn't plan to do it that way. But I was awfully tired of the wife and the kids and homelife, all of that. I had a deal in mind, something I'd picked up through some friends in one of the handbooks. But I needed capital. Then one day I realized that I had the capital, all I had to do was withdraw it."

"What was the deal?" Kinsella asked.

"Voting machines. The beauty of it. The latest thing. Just right for Chicago. And I had a chance to be in on the ground floor. Control sales and distribution. The coming thing, I tell you. If you've any money, you might keep an eye out for an opening." He paused again. "You know there's some good liquor in that cabinet over there. Shall we have a drink?"

"Let's get on with the story," P.B. said. "It's late."

"As you say," Casey said with a sigh. "Well, I'd put a lot of money down in some handbooks when suddenly Kelly and the police commissioner get the beads in their hands again and put in a slough, a long one. That's because they both got hauled before the grand jury and there was lots of talk about malfeasance and misfeasance and they made them stand the whole time they were questioning them. Burned their asses good, so they cracked down on the joints. That was my first bad luck, just after everything was off to a good start. Then I'm ready to follow through on the voting machines and some of the pols start raising hell. They thought I was a reformer, a threat to the Eberhard Faber votes they were good at on the paper ballots. They thought I was out to end fraud. Isn't that rich? I've just taken half a million and they think I'm out to end fraud. Well, they argued and I passed some money around but I might as well have thrown it in the sewer. So there I was, the bookies closed and the voting machine deal off. I began to feel the fucking money was possessed or something. I couldn't seem to do any good with it. So I decided to enjoy it until something turned up. What turned up, unfortunately, was you two." He sighed. "When do the coppers come?"

Moran shook his head. "Jesus, did anybody ever tell you you're a loser? You're bad luck, for Chrissake. Put you in jail and the goddam place'd fall down."

"There won't be any cops, Casey," P.B. said slowly. "There won't be anybody to sign the complaint. The Archbishop has forgotten your name. What do you want to do, Jack?"

"Get him out of here. Get him out of here, he's like a black cat."

P.B. decided to take charge. Moran seemed struck as though Casey had cast a spell of superstition on him. He didn't even look like he cared about the money any more.

"Take the twelve hundred and get the hell out of here,"

Kinsella said. "The game's over. What bothers me, Casey, is that you don't seem to care about your wife and kids. What are you going to do about them?"

"They may be better off without me," Casey responded, shrugging his shoulders as he spoke. This son of a bitch is a con man too, P.B. thought to himself. He's just like all of them I've ever known. No real feelings for anybody else. Just playing for the thrill. A late-blooming con man, Kinsella thought, who devoured my nest egg for me, a little bastard with a wandering eye who took the blood money down at one gulp. There was no telling about fate or Providence or whatever the hell you wanted to call it.

"I want your wife's address," Kinsella said. "She is better off without you. So are your kids. Now get your stuff and get out."

"Well," Casey replied. "And I thought we were getting to be friends. That's the way it's been these last weeks. Well"— he took a long pull on his cigar—"I enjoyed what I could of it."

While he threw some things into a bag, P.B. drew Moran aside and whispered to him, "Jack, I say the hell with this money. It hasn't been good for anybody. Maybe it's got a curse on it." Jack nodded. "I say, let's send the rest to Casey's wife. Maybe that'll take the bad luck out of it. What do you say?"

Jack was superstitious about the money but, in another way, he wanted to match Patrick's generosity, like an Indian in a potlatch ceremony.

"Okay, Pat. We settled what we had to anyway. Let's get this bum out of here."

It did not take long to send Casey scuttling down the back stairs to avoid paying his hotel bill. Then Moran left and P.B. followed him after a few minutes. He carried the briefcase with the money in it back to his apartment.

"Where've you been?" Mae asked, clasping her robe around her.

"You wouldn't believe it, Mae," P.B. said, placing the briefcase in a closet. "Let's just say, I was balancing the books. Yes, that's it, balancing the books."

But he lay awake next to Mae for a long time, thinking about the money that had come into his life so strangely, passed through it again so sadly, and had finally made its way out, for good, he hoped. It had not been such a bad evening, he decided, and Monsignor Williams still owed him a lot of favors. He felt that his ties with Jack had also been severed and he felt good about that. He would wake Mae early, he thought as he dozed off, and celebrate.

11
1960

"What the hell does Tom mean, he thinks he wants to be a priest?"

"Now, Pat," Mae said soothingly, "it would be a blessing for the Kinsella family to have a priest in it."

"That may be so but what the hell, he's got a great career ahead of him. Those priests at Notre Dame put the net out for these unsuspecting lads, fill them full of notions about saving the world . . ."

"What's wrong with that?"

"You don't save the world by hiding away from it. Goddamn it, Mae, Tom'd have greater influence if he went into business. I should have sent him to Harvard."

Mae looked across the breakfast table at her husband without saying a word. She had done this times beyond counting when the Kinsella temper had flared up over a family matter. She knew that patience was the virtue and silence the response in such circumstances.

"Well, what the hell's the matter, Mae, why don't you say something?"

Mae looked out at the expanse of Lake Michigan that stretched eastward from Lake Shore Drive beneath their apartment windows.

"It was a beautiful sunrise this morning, wasn't it, Patty?"

"Sunrise? Who the hell is talking about the sunrise?"

"Finish your coffee before it gets cold."

A half growl from P.B., who knew when he could make no more headway with his wife. He sipped his coffee and joined her in gazing out at the lake.

"I suppose, if he wants to try it, it's okay by me," he said, trying to sound as though he were not really yielding any points in the discussion.

"Yes, Patty, I was sure you'd feel that way. He's sent his application in already." She paused, knowing that she had to get the next bit in before P.B.'s face clouded over again. "They want a priest to come and visit us, you know, to see about his family background."

"What are you telling me? That some bright-eyed young priest is going to come calling to see if we're fit to have a son a priest?" P.B. fumed. "I won't have it, do you hear? I draw the line at that. Who the hell do they think I am? Don't they know who P. B. Kinsella is?"

"I'm sure they do. Maybe that's why they want to see us." Mae started to laugh. "You know, Patty, you're wonderful when you've got your mad face on . . ."

"Wonderful, my foot!" P.B. said before his eyes met those of his wife. He could never resist her, especially when she was calming him down from a display of anger in which he was taking inordinate pleasure.

"Mae, you're pretty as ever, and almost as filled with blarney as I am."

"Then I'll arrange for the good father to pay us a call."

"Make it when I'm out of town, if you can. You'd enjoy an evening talking about shrines and devotions with some young priest. Maybe you could say the rosary together . . ."

"Enough of that malarkey, Patty. You'll be here if any priest comes calling, and on your best behavior too."

The telephone rang as Mae concluded her admonition, and P.B. lifted the receiver from the extension on the breakfast room wall.

"Yes, this is Pat. Who's this? Why, Jack, I didn't recognize your voice at first." P.B.'s expression changed as he listened intently. Mae rose from the table and edged around behind her husband to get the coffeepot from the stove.

"Well, Jack, I'm sorry to hear that. Yes, yes . . . I'll come by this afternoon. No singing until I get there." P.B. replaced the phone and looked solemnly at Mae, who was pouring him another cup of coffee.

"That was Jack Moran. I haven't heard from him in a long while. He's been sick. Wants me to visit him, wants to talk to me."

"I thought you didn't want any contact with him."

"Well, I haven't had any, not official anyway, for a long while. After all, he's still the King of the Pimps, and into the Syndicate as far as you can get. I sometimes think Jack was behind Mike Senese's killing."

"You never told me that. You just called him some terrible Italian name and sent him a wreath of flowers with 'Good Luck' on it."

P.B. smiled. "Yeah, I always wanted to do that to somebody. Uncle Joe told me that he saw that on a horseshoe of flowers for a hood back in the twenties. I thought old Mike would like it, the dirty bastard. Besides, he needed every bit of luck he could get." Patrick paused and took a sip of the fresh coffee. "This is different somehow. Jack's been a crook. But, hell, we grew up together. And we did some business together a long time ago . . ."

"Patty, I don't think I'll ever understand you. Here you are complaining that your son wants to be a priest and that you don't want some good father visiting us, and then you're ready to run off to see a man you say is a crook."

"It's the Irish in me, Mae, or the Catholic . . ."

"Or the Kinsella," Mae said as she stood up in unison with her husband and left the kitchen for the maid's hands. They walked through the dining room to a long hallway that led to the master bedroom.

"You know, Mae," Pat said, slipping a tie under his collar, "I think I would like to see Jack. Partly out of feeling bad for him. He didn't sound too well."

"Well, I'll pray for him today, you can tell him that, if you will."

"I will," P.B. responded, leaning over to give Mae a kiss. "Now, don't put too much in the poor box today. And don't let any fund-raising priests in while I'm gone."

"Suppose they're Democrats and want to hire you to build their shrine or their new school or something?"

"Ah well," P.B. said in his fake brogue, "that would be different, wouldn't it?"

Jack Moran was living in the Edgewater Beach Hotel, a fading great lady of a place still trailing frills and veils from another age that stood waiting for the inevitable wrecking ball along the lake's edge several miles north of the Kinsella apartment. Since Jack had never married, its room service and restaurants had suited his convenience very well when he was in town. Moran lived in a corner suite that gave him a view of the lake and the lights of the city.

The first thing Patrick noticed was the smell. It reminded him of when he was a boy and had to visit an ancient aunt of his, a great aunt as he recalled, who was dying in a rambling old house that had been converted into a kind of nursing home; she had tubes running out of her and his mother made him wash his hands thoroughly when they got home. Jack didn't have any tubes but he did seem to give off a faint smell the way P.B.'s great aunt had, although, as Kinsella thought, it could have been the rooms, sealed up for years and filled with the odors of every evil Jack had been a part of. Jack looked thinner and there were dark shadows under his eyes. He seemed to move all right, a little slower than usual, of course, but not so bad, P.B. thought as Moran walked across the living room just ahead of him. It was when Moran sat down that he seemed to settle, like a building riding an earth tremor, and his bones and features appeared to drop a fraction of an inch. P.B. half expected to see dust rise as his old friend made himself more comfortable in his chair.

"Patty," Moran said in a husky voice, "it was good of you to come. I think I'm on my way out, Patty . . ."

"Nonsense," P.B. replied, but Jack raised his hand before he could say more.

"One thing about me, Patty, was I could always face the truth." He hunched a little and coughed. "And me, hardly fifty. I'm a wreck, that's what the doctor says. No damn good to me now. Says I've got a number of problems, so many that to treat one would make the others worse. I'm going all rotten inside, Patty." He coughed again and this time P.B. shifted uneasily in his chair. He tried to rid his mind of the image of Moran's insides collapsing like the floors of a tenement gutted by a fire.

"Nothing I've got is catching," Moran said, managing a

chuckle. "It took me a long while to get this way, Pat, I won't be handing it on to you."

"Well, what can I do for you then?" P.B. asked.

"I'm not afraid, Pat, I want you to know that. I'm surprised in a way, because I've had time to think about my life. I'd plan an escape if I could. Over the wall, if there was a wall . . ." He breathed deeply. "But there's no escape from this. So I decided, and here's where you can help me, I decided I want to die in the Church. Hell, you ought to be able to fix that, you've been hand in glove with them. And there's your old friend, the one who's a bishop now . . ."

"Williams," P.B. said. "Auxiliary Bishop Williams."

"He's the fella buried Uncle Joe, as I remember. That was a good funeral, I mean, as funerals go. How old was Joe?"

"Ninety-four and still playing cards," P.B. answered.

Jack started to laugh but it quickly turned into a cough.

"I went to the funeral, do you remember? Stood in the back. Great funeral, with the Irish step dancers, and the Pipers, and all them nuns and priests . . ."

P.B. wondered if religion or superstition were stirring in Moran's soul, or whether they were waging some battle for it before his body collapsed completely. It was hard to tell which had the upper hand with Jack; it always had been.

"You know, Pat, we haven't seen each other too much. I've been able to help you a little. And you've helped me." He coughed and covered his face with a handkerchief. P.B.'s imagination flashed him a view of the gutted tenement again with foam and water dripping down through all the broken places. Jack spat something into the handkerchief and cleared his throat.

"Patty, the thing is, I think you tried to be square with me. You cut me in on that money that thieving bastard Casey lifted from the Chancery, even though I didn't take it and we sent it to his wife. You know that son of a bitch is still around? Lives in Elgin or Joliet or someplace like that. Well, you were square on that and I felt good that you were ready to make a split with me. Fixed a little sore spot between us."

P.B. said nothing. He was not going to rake all that up again. As far as he was concerned, the Lord had given him the money and taken it away again. Blessed be the Name of the Lord. He had made it back from the Church in his own way.

"So, Patty, I figure you'll see if you can't fix me with the

Church. I'd like to go out in style, like Uncle Joe. Not like
that son of a bitch Senese. The Church wouldn't bury him, do
you remember? Said he was a public sinner and couldn't have
a Mass. Had to have the service in a parlor, with some dago
priest they brought in to say a couple of prayers. I hear they
let him in the mausoleum though. He had title to a vault and
they couldn't do a goddam thing about it. Is that so, Pat?"

"That's so. Yes. Mike had an untimely death as I recall."

Jack smiled crookedly. "Yes, cut down in his prime." He
coughed again. "The hell he was. He had it coming for a long
time. Anyway, Pat, I'll be damned if I want to be called a
public sinner and have some fucking Rotarian service out at
Harney's with the organ playin' 'Oh, Promise Me' or some
goddam soap opera music. What do you say? Can you do me
one last favor?"

P.B. looked at Jack, who had grown tired during their
conversation and was busy with his handkerchief again. He
didn't think Jack was exactly contrite but maybe you couldn't
expect much more from Jack. But he had been a public
sinner; that would be hard to deny. The Church was still
pretty tough on public sinners. It looked bad to the people to
be giving these gangsters send-offs at flower-filled Solemn
High Masses, so they had drawn the line years ago. He wasn't
sure if Leo Williams would step across it.

"I'll see what I can do," P.B. said. "You ought to rest
awhile. I'll call you later."

Bishop Williams, it turned out, was at the archdiocesan
seminary more than an hour's drive from the city at Mun-
delein, Illinois, a small town named after the Cardinal
Archbishop who had overseen the seminary's construction.
Set on several hundred acres, with a twenty-seven-hole golf
course and a spread of Georgian brick buildings to shame an
Ivy League campus, it had been envisioned by the old
Cardinal as the Catholic University of the West.

The other bishops never went along with that and rumor
had it that, from the moment of that rejection, not only were
Chicago priests-to-be trained in surroundings that surpassed
their typically humble beginnings in every way, but the old
Cardinal only sent a dollar a year to the annual bishops'
collection for the Catholic University in Washington. Mundelein had died out at the seminary in the bedroom of a building
that, save for its brick exterior, was an exact replica of Mount

Vernon. Nobody ever said the old fellow didn't have class. P.B. knew about but discounted the rumors that Mundelein had been murdered out there. In any case, none of this ever deterred Bishop Williams from moving into the brick house for a week to catch up on paper work, to eavesdrop on the seminary, and to play a little golf.

"Hello, Pat," Williams said into the phone.

"When will you be in the City? I'd like to see you about something."

"Well, Pat, I'd come right in for you, you know that, but I, I . . ."

"You've bought some new oxen and have to try them out."

"No, no, Pat, I have to interview the young men who are going to be ordained this year. The Cardinal has asked me to do it for him."

"That doesn't sound important. What do you think you're going to find out about them now that you shouldn't have known long ago?"

"Well, their files are all in order. It's a requirement of canon law. We have to adhere to that or the Congregation on Seminaries would be all over us. This is a Pontifical Seminary, you know, so we have to be careful."

"It's wonderful, Leo, and I hope you don't get any sick calls while you're there. Do any of those professors ever see any real people?"

"Well, many of them do parish work on weekends . . ."

"Forget it, I'm just giving you the needle. Look, I'll expect to see you tomorrow afternoon. I'll be out at two o'clock. Clear the decks for me for an hour or so."

The bishop hardly had time to agree before P.B. had said a quick good-by and hung up his phone. Kinsella stood up and stretched. He reached down and picked a cigar up from his desk. As he lighted it he smiled at the thought of Jack Moran's wanting a Church funeral. Well, why not, P.B. mused, since many a worse lad had been hauled down the aisle at Holy Name Cathedral and at other places, many of them built by Kinsella himself, throughout the archdiocese. There was old Mooney, P.B. remembered, a whoremaster every bit as much as Moran. What was it they said of him to get him a Mass? He put a lot of girls to work, that was it. P.B. laughed out loud and sat down at his desk again. Even Jack's uncle, the crooked copper who shot it out with Lane, got an inspector's funeral. And it was all coming full circle now,

Kinsella thought; that whole episode at the Lake Terrace Club could be written off forever once he got Jack Moran a Christian burial. It was a last lark with his old friend Moran, a last trick to give Moran the kind of thrill he had lived for, a last con job into consecrated ground. Well, let the poor bastard be. His guts were coming down like the insides of a burnout anyway. God would understand . . .

Bishop Williams met P.B. at the front door of the replica of Mount Vernon. He was dressed as neatly as the carefully tended seminary grounds, wearing his pale red sash, his jeweled pectoral cross, and even a skullcap.

"You look like Bishop Sheen, Leo, are you going on TV?"

"No, it's to set a standard for the seminarians. Everything formal, everything proper; they will either learn their manners here or they never will."

They walked around the house to the lawn from which they could look out on the lake, one of two on the property, and across to the cluster of buildings that spread out from a central chapel that was a reproduction of a New England church. Groups of black-cassocked seminarians could be seen moving along the roads and pathways of the seminary grounds.

"I wish I'd built this place," P.B. said with a grin. Then he turned to Bishop Williams and suggested that they go inside. When they were seated in the living room and were sure that nobody else was in earshot except the nun who brought them a tray of coffee and cake, P.B. explained briefly the reason for his visit. Bishop Williams, carefully spooning some sugar from the silver service into his coffee, looked grave.

"Pat, this is a very unusual set of circumstances. I mean, I don't think I can commit the Church to giving him a Christian burial. There's canon law . . ."

"Yes, Leo, you're very concerned about canon law now that you're a bishop. It's becoming in a clergyman with a promising future." P.B. grinned tightly again. "Surely you must know how to use the law for the advantage of the sheep that was lost."

"But the way you describe him," Williams said uneasily, "there's no indication that he's repentant. I mean, he's lived a life that has given scandal to many." Williams was beginning to sound pompous. "No, Pat, I can't commit the Church on a thing like that. Think of the scandal to the faithful, the publicity. We'd be the laughingstock of the country."

P.B. bit his lower lip as he reached into the inside pocket of his coat.

"You're right, Leo. You're right and you're wrong at the same time. This thing goes two ways, this scandal business, doesn't it? What do you think the papers would do with this?"

He unfolded an old letter, one that was notarized and bore the signature of Leo Williams. It told of the Church's indebtedness to Kinsella for five hundred and sixty thousand dollars.

Williams's mouth fell slightly open and a tic appeared in his left eye as he reached for the letter and read it through for the first time in almost fifteen years.

"Surely, Pat, you wouldn't let this out. I mean . . ."

"Why wouldn't I?"

"Well, for one thing, your name is on it too. You wouldn't want bad publicity either, would you?"

"Why not? I'm the good guy, the one in the white hat. You're the one holding the bag."

"You're forgetting how thorough you were, Pat. Don't you remember how you used to warn me about being thorough? There is no record that Everett Casey ever worked at the Chancery office." Williams had regained his composure and was gazing steadily at Kinsella.

"Touché, Leo, touché. But that won't hold up and you know it."

"It will to the new Archbishop. He'll accept my word and what the records say. You can't really prove that anything happened with this letter." Williams handed it back to Kinsella.

"Well, Leo," P.B. said, standing up to look down on the bishop, "I think we'll just see about that. Casey's kids are around somewhere, and his wife, too . . ."

"She died years ago. The kids were farmed out to orphanages and foster homes."

"You're playing a good hand of cards, Leo, I'll say that for you." P.B. leaned down and looked into the bishop's uplifted gray eyes. They looked as hard as tombstone.

"Leo, I don't give a damn about your canon law. I saved your ass once. Now I'm going to make you into a parish priest again. You're going to visit Jack Moran at the Edgewater

Beach. Hear his confession, anoint him, get him ready for his last journey. You're going to do that because if you don't, I'll take this letter down to the *Sun-Times* and the *Tribune* this afternoon. Then we'll see if they find Casey or any of his kids, or some of the people who remember him like me and Jack Moran. Who the hell found him for you? Jack did. Who arranged for Michelangelo to fix the books and the records? Jack did. Now, goddam it, you're going to take care of Moran. You're going to do it personally. And you're going to make sure he has a first-class wake and funeral."

Kinsella's face was only a few inches from the bishop's. P.B. was breathing heavily. He straightened up and put the letter back into its envelope and slipped it into his pocket.

"You do this right, Leo, and people will think you saved a sinner. You'll be the good shepherd of Chicago. Nothing will stop you then. That's what you've needed, Leo, to complete your image as a bishop, a touch of spiritual concern." P.B. started to leave the room.

"Wait a minute, Pat," Williams called after him, "let's talk about this some more. Let's not be hasty over such a delicate subject."

"There's nothing delicate about a man's insides being eaten out even if by your standards he was a sinner. He saved the Church here—and you too, I might add—a lot of embarrass-ment. If he was leaving you a million dollars, you'd be front and center at the Edgewater Beach."

"Well, Pat, what I mean is that there are other ways this could be handled. His own parish priest could visit him. I could arrange that right now. He'd be there this afternoon."

P.B. shook his head. "That would be nice. Then you wouldn't be involved. I can see your innocent expression now when you end up denying him a funeral anyway, or when you make the pastor have it quietly with no disturbance to anyone."

"Well, surely, it's his soul you're concerned about. What difference does the funeral make as long as he's fortified with the sacraments? It couldn't make any difference to him."

P.B. stepped back toward the bishop, who sat with a bland expression on his face.

"The funeral, the wake, that's what Moran wants as much as anything, maybe more than anything else. He wants to pass out with a little respectability." P.B. patted the coat pocket in which he had placed the letter signed by Williams.

"So, Leo, you're elected. Have a bishop see you off to heaven and you've got one foot on the pearly stairs already. And, if you say the Mass for him, the one thing he wants, he'll get. You might even say a few kind words over him. The trouble, Leo, is that you don't think I'll give this letter to the papers. But you're not sure, are you? You know I might just do it, no matter what publicity comes for either one of us. That's why I know you'll go see Moran. You can't take any chances. That's right, isn't it?"

The bishop looked up at him. His eyes didn't blink but his cheeks began to redden.

"If I go, Pat, it won't be because of that letter. It will be for pastoral concern for a man's soul."

"That's the way to talk. By God, I'm proud of you, Leo. You think it over." P.B. glanced at his wristwatch. "Now, I'm going back to my office. Jack'll be waiting for you. He doesn't go out much anymore."

P.B. turned, casting one last taut smile over his shoulder. "Don't get up, Leo. I can find my way out."

P.B. never spoke to Jack again but he was not surprised, ten days later, to get a call from one of Moran's Syndicate associates telling him that Jack had died early that morning.

"He died hard. But he wanted me to tell you good-by and thanks for everything. Some bishop was here a few days ago and Jack got himself all straightened out with the Church. Seemed to make him happy, like he was waiting for that before he could really die."

P.B. learned that the wake would be at Harney's and that there would be a funeral at the Cathedral with Bishop Williams saying the Mass. Moran's friend didn't quite know what to make of this surprise ending for the old whoremaster. "He's sure going out first-class, ain't he?"

"Yes, first-class," P.B. said with a smile as he hung up his phone. Williams had some guts after all. He would have to call Mae and arrange to go to the wake.

"But, Pat, a Father Squires is coming to see us tonight. You know, about Tom's going to the seminary. We can't very well take him to a mobster's wake. That would hardly make the right impression on him."

"It would be good for him. Besides, otherwise he'll just sit around and talk about turning the Mass into English or some

other fruitcake stuff. We'll take him along and give him a little
pastoral experience."

Father Squires was rather puzzled to be hurried into the
Kinsella limousine right after dinner and transported out to
the West Side funeral home where the neon clock on the
chimney bricks still blinked Harney's promise to take the time
to give the time any time. He was not quite sure what to make
of P. B. Kinsella's spirited recollections of his early years
growing up with Jack Moran. In fact, Father Squires, a
scholarly man who spoke very softly, had no idea who Jack
Moran was and he was extremely polite to the varied group of
mob figures who crowded the new, expanded Galway Room
for the wake. He found it a little difficult making conversation
with some of them especially when they talked about horses
and odds and asked him to say a prayer for the sixth race at
Washington Park the next day.

"I told you it would be good for him," Patrick said to Mae.
"Broadens his horizons, gives him a feel for real life."

The walls of the room were stacked with floral tributes and
bouquets and P.B. smiled when the Irish Pipers arrived and
played some funeral dirges that were sad enough to please the
most melancholy Irishman. They finished up with "Danny
Boy" and "The Minstrel Boy" and then, the colors of their
tartans softened in the muted light, trooped out playing "The
March from Saul." It was everything that Jack could have
wished for. The newspapers were hard on Moran but they
had some words of praise for Bishop Williams, who, according to their accounts, had taken it upon himself to seek out
the sheep that was lost. The bishop even came to the wake
and led the rosary. He dragged it out and P.B. smiled at the
thought that the mobsters in the room had spent more time
on their knees that evening than they had in their whole
previous lifetimes.

P.B. enjoyed the wake immensely. He saw Bishop Williams out to his car and bent to kiss his ring. P.B. smiled as he
looked up at Williams, who seemed very pleased with himself
and the many favorable comments he had received for being
so pastorally zealous for souls.

"I told you you'd like being a priest, Leo."

"Pat, I wish my duties allowed me time for more pastoral
work."

"I'll see if I can dig some more up for you. Good night, Bishop."

Williams glared uneasily at Kinsella as he settled into the back of his automobile. Patrick waved him into the night, his smile giving way to laughter as the car pulled off. There, he said to himself, there, Jack, we're all even now.

PART VII

PART VI

1
October 22, 1983
5:30 A.M.

Well, I don't suppose I ever saw Father Thomas so shaken. He stood looking down at Father Allen for a long terrible moment and then he turned to Coach Finn.

"Call the doctor. Tell him to get here right away. Get Howard Engel, he's the best one in town . . ."

"But . . ."

"He was Jack's doctor. He ought to pronounce him dead. For God's sake, move!" Then he and Finn left the room while I stood there, mumbling some prayers for Allen's soul, not that I felt he needed them, mind you, but it's a wonderful thing, and very Catholic, to be able to do at such awful times. Father Allen was still tilted a little sideways, his eyes staring blindly, and I tried to tug him into an upright position. But he sagged again and I thought, better leave him at peace, when Father Thomas returned with the Holy Oils, as we used to call them, in his hands. He dipped his thumb into the little gold ampule and, his hand shaking slightly, drew a cross on Jack's forehead.

"*Per istam sanctam unctionem et suam piissimam misericordiam,*" he said, surprising me with the Latin, "*indulgeat tibi Dominus quidquid deliquisti in nomine Patris et Filii et Spiritus Sancti.*" Then he knelt down by the side of Jack's chair, closing his eyes as he bowed his head, and prayed silently. Matt Finn came through the door just as he stood up.

"Dr. Engel's on his way."

"Good," Thomas said as he rose to a standing position. He gazed down at his old friend. "I thought you'd like the Latin, Jack," he said softly, as though in a quiet conversation with

419

the dead man. "Like old times." Then he reached over and
closed the lids on Father Allen's eyes. That seemed to put an
end to the mournful proceedings, because he was all business
when he turned back to Finn.

"Thanks, Matt. Now get back to Moreau Seminary with
the football team. I don't want them to start wandering
around at this hour. And you've got a big game today."

"But, Father . . ."

"Later, Matt, right now I want you where you belong. Do
you understand? There'll be plenty of time to talk later on."
Then he turned toward me.

"Austin, I want you to go down and wait for Dr. Engel to
arrive. Then show him up here. No need to tell anybody until
we've got this settled. Jack always hated the way the vultures
gathered when a priest died, ready to take his golf shoes or his
television set." He looked at Jack's body as he said this,
smiling, as if in recollection of so many good times, all now
past.

"And get Monsignor Egan for me. Ask him to come to my
room."

Well, I felt good at my age getting all these important
errands to do, so I bustled out of the door just behind Matt
Finn, leaving Father Thomas to keep watch with his old
friend. I had the feeling that he wanted an interlude of quiet
with Allen, a brief space in a day that he knew would be filled
with tumult and shouting, a few quiet moments for mourning
and pulling himself together. It was a matter of friendship, of
what was demanded by the kind of strong relationship men,
when they are lucky, can sometimes have with each other. I
felt I would have been an intruder if I had stayed.

Finn went one way and I another after we descended the
stairs. Dr. Engel, an outwardly fierce little rooster of a fellow
who, although Jewish, loved Notre Dame dearly, was just
climbing the front stairs as I arrived there. "These goddam
priests," Engel said to me as we went back upstairs. "They
don't take proper care of themselves." It was his way of
cursing the mortality that was the enemy of the physician in
him and of hiding his tenderness but it was clear that he was
as distressed as the rest of us. "They're going to miss him," he
said as he entered the room where Father Kinsella was sitting,
still in a kind of communion with his dead friend.

I withdrew to hunt up Monsignor Egan but I could not help
but think, at this craziest of dawns, of how irreparable the loss

really was for Thomas and for the University. The loonies had just occupied the Lourdes Shrine and were hoping for a television spectacular for their purity revival campaign and Greenie wanted to use that to get a leg up on the presidency; in a few hours thousands of cars and buses would begin to arrive with the full-house crowd Notre Dame drew for every football game; God only knew what Thomas would do about old P.B., who was sleeping innocent as a babe at the Morris Inn, or Archbishop Trafficante and the offer to become Archbishop of Chicago; and what of Maria Moore, who was also on her way to South Bend? And the store of common sense in the world had just been thrown permanently out of balance by the death of Jack Allen. All the more reason to find Monsignor Egan as soon as possible, I thought to myself as I skirted through the trees up above the Lourdes Shrine toward his room in Bronson Hall. As I passed I could hear voices drifting up through the now palely lighted quiet that was the edge of the new day.

"Jesus, Joe," Timothy Duffy whispered to his roommate as they stood at the edge of the stone shrine that was a reasonable facsimile of the famous grotto at Lourdes, "Jesus, Joe, they've got her covered with blankets. Over there, see?"

"Oh, yeah," Joe replied as he craned his neck for a better view.

"They've been hiding her from the campus police."

"They just drove by again. What do you think?" Joe Sclafani wanted to get something to eat and leave the revivalists to themselves.

"Joe, I've got to talk with her." Tim sounded mountain-climber resolute, as though he had to speak to her because she was there.

"Come on, Tim, let's get the hell out of here."

"You go, Joe, if you want to. I've got to stay. I was in at the beginning of this and I could have done something but I didn't. I've got to help end it."

"Tim, who the hell do you think you are—Superstudent? There's no phone booth around here for you to change in."

"You go, Joe, I'm going to talk to her." With that he began to work his way through the crowd, which seemed to be swelling with new recruits drifting toward its edges on the brimming tide of morning. Joe shook his head, then plunged into the throng to stick with his friend Timothy.

At the center of the gathering David Weber was listening to Father Green. They had just pulled the blankets off the girl on the cross, which had been laid out on the ground in front of a bank of vigil candles that had been quickly lighted by one of the sign-carrying students. Against the flickering bed of candles Greenie and Weber looked intense and self-confident, like a couple of young political managers who had just won the first primary for a long shot candidate. In truth, the moonstruck procession had traveled farther than anybody else with sense thought that it could, a point that Father Green was emphasizing.

"I see God's hand in this, David. We have stuck faithfully together through the dark night of abandonment. Now we are ready to share the triumph of resurrection. But we have to secure our base here. The only way we can do that is by increasing the crowd. Our presence must become such a strong and positive thing, such a, yes, such a sign of witness that the world will have to pay attention to us."

"Yes, Father. What do we do? People seem to be coming all the time."

"We cannot leave it to chance. We have to send out the call. People must be called here just as the fishermen were called by Jesus. I want you to get some of the students to fan out through the dorms and some others to start contacting friends in town, in Chicago, anyplace nearby. Let the call go out, do you understand? I want the media here, too. Some-body has got to get in touch with the television crew near the stadium. And the radio stations and the newspapers. Now, while we have a few hours, let's move." Greenie sounded every bit like the zealot whose role he had gladly accepted in the night's strange drama. There was something just a little frightening about him, as though he gave off a fine spray of paranoia as he spoke. Weber, no stranger to dark thoughts and plans himself, pulled back slightly under the pressure of Green's enthusiasm.

"Shouldn't we try to keep this more a private thing?"

"Would St. Paul have used television if he were living today? Let's get moving on this."

Weber turned away without another word to carry out his instructions and Greenie called to the guitarists to start some music.

"All right, everybody," the girl musician said, striking a

chord on her instrument. "Let's all join in 'Gonna Sing, My Lord.'"

Green knelt down by the girl, whose eyes had just opened. "Where am I?" she asked in a feeble voice.

"You're at the shrine, Mary Ann, just as you wanted."

"Who are you? Are you my master?" She seemed very confused.

"No, Mary Ann," Greenie whispered. "We are all pilgrims together."

She tugged at her bonds and a shudder rippled through her body.

"My hands hurt," she said, turning her head up toward the crossbar. "My God, I'm bleeding."

"Hush, now," Green said, glad that the singing was drowning out her comments. "You must be quiet. You are a chosen one."

She strained at the twists that held her firmly in position.

"You mothers are all the same," she said in an irritated tone. "All the same . . ." Then she fainted again as Greenie, on the fine edge of panic, breathed a sigh of relief. No one had heard the exchange. He was glad that he had sent Weber on his recruiting mission. It would never do to have her begin speaking from the cross like that, not at a religious revival. And what else might she be capable of saying? Greenie signaled to a student who lived in the same hall with him.

"Tom," Father Green said urgently. "I want you to go back to the dorm, to my room. In the medicine chest you'll find a small blue box. I want you to bring it back here right away. And bring some water, there's some bottled water there too. Bring one of those back. And as quickly as you can." The student hurried off through the singing crowd like a knight heading for the Holy Grail and Greenie knelt down next to the girl, saying a silent prayer that she would remain asleep until the sedatives arrived.

It was almost six o'clock when Monsignor Egan and I arrived back at Father Thomas's rooms. He and Dr. Engel were standing in the hallway along with a handful of the other priests who had been awakened by the noise. Two burly paramedics were just removing Father Allen's body on a covered stretcher. A special silence hung over the corridor. All that could be heard was the movement of the litter bearers, the rustling of their clothes and the muted padding of their rubber-soled shoes. Father Thomas signaled all of us, Dr. Engel included, to come into his room. He did not sit down and neither did we.

"I've a lot of decisions to make today," Father Thomas said in a firm but reflective tone. "And I'm going to need help from each one of you. I'm going to ride down to the hospital with Howard here. Then I'm personally going to make arrangements with the undertakers. I don't want one of those cardboard coffins they like to bury us in, not for Jack anyway. Then I'm coming back to my office." He turned slightly in the direction of Monsignor Egan, who had taken a small black book from his pocket and was poised to make notes.

"Jack, I want you to contact my father in an hour or so. I should be back, but even so, tell him what happened and that I can't meet him at breakfast. I'll have to see him later. Tell him you'll let him know when. Then I want you to get a fix on what's going on at the Lourdes Shrine. Austin, you can help Monsignor with that. I want you to contact the state police and warn them that we may have heavier than usual traffic today. They're to keep order but not to interfere with this so-called religious demonstration on campus. We don't want anybody taking pictures of troopers driving pilgrims away from a shrine. You're also to contact the media and try to cool this story as much as you can. We don't have to sit still for them moving that TV stuff across our campus. Austin"—he turned back toward me—"Maria Moore will be arriving early. I'm not sure just when. If she's here before I get back, I want you to take care of her. Use my office if you want and don't let any reporters get near her. You understand?"

I nodded, pleased as a schoolboy to have such a significant and pleasant assignment.

"One other thing, Jack. We have a guest here, Archbishop Trafficante. See if you can take him to breakfast, tell him I'll contact him when I get back on campus. And keep him away from table hoppers or nitwits who want to take him to see the Lourdes Shrine." Thomas stopped for a moment, as though he had just been stricken with the remembrance that his best friend had died, and needed to swallow hard before he continued.

"I want you both to meet me at my office about eight A.M., no matter what happens. I should be back by then. There's a lot of business to settle today." With that he put his arm on

Dr. Engel's shoulder and they went out the door and down the corridor together.

At the Lourdes Shrine, the crowd was now kneeling, reciting the rosary that was being led by a middle-aged woman who had a shopping bag filled with leaflets hooked over one arm. David Weber had not returned but Timothy Duffy had made his way to within a few rows of the place where the girl lay below the glittering ramps of candles. Father Green, his bloodstained stole hanging partly off one shoulder, looked nervous as he stood like a guard above the still unconscious girl. The crowd of people was so closely packed in the first lines that Timothy felt he would have to make an end run in order to reach the cross. Just then, however, the crowd parted slightly to make room for the student who had gone for the medicine and the water and Timothy slipped in behind him.

"I'm glad you made it so quick, Tom," Greenie said, taking the box and removing a pill. "Here, let me have the water now." Tim watched as if paralyzed, like a diver who gets to the high board but cannot jump, as Green knelt down and began to speak to the girl.

"Mary Ann, this is Father Green," he said against the rhythmic chant of prayers from the crowd. "Mary Ann, I have something for you." Timothy willed himself to move forward against the revulsion he suddenly felt as he looked down at the girl trussed up on the cross. She looked pitiful rather than commanding as she had the evening before. The girl opened her eyes and tried to focus as Greenie attempted to force a small capsule into her mouth. She resisted, spitting and heaving a little. "What is that?" she asked weakly.

"It's medicine, it'll make you feel better, Mary Ann."

"Where'd you get it? On the street?" Greenie bent lower to prevent her from being overheard. Timothy slipped down beside him. The girl looked very strange and her neck muscles corded out as she attempted to lift her head.

"Who are you—Dr. Feelgood?" she asked, letting her head fall back again. "Dr. Feelgood has the best shit on the street." Then her eyes rolled back and she passed out again. Greenie turned and was shocked to find Timothy kneeling so close to him. He was still holding the bottle of Perrier water and the capsule the girl had refused.

"She's out of her head, poor girl."

Timothy just stared at him, not knowing quite what to answer.

"Did you hear anything she said?" Greenie asked uneasily. "You mustn't pay attention to anything she said. I mean, it's been quite an ordeal for her . . ."

"No," Timothy said, feeling there was no advantage in admitting anything to Father Green, who, with his cassock, his dangling stole, and his hands filled with bottled water and pills, seemed like Father Frankenstein to him. "No, I couldn't hear her."

At that very moment, David Weber, secretly as pleased with himself as a jogger who had just completed his workout, returned. "I've had good luck," he said to Greenie. "The TV should be here in an hour or so . . ."

2

October 22, 1983
6 A.M.

Father Thomas and Dr. Engel walked down the steps together, neither saying much, each, as it seemed, lost in his own thoughts. Father Simmons followed along after a moment's hesitation and overtook them as they reached the main door.

"Can I ride along?" he asked plaintively.

Father Thomas looked at the stricken young man and spoke softly. "Jack would have liked you to be with him, I'm sure."

Engel, his face still troubled at the fact that death had breached the defenses he had tried to erect around his priest patients at Notre Dame, climbed into his car as Fathers Simmons and Kinsella got into the one Thomas usually drove. The ambulance was just pulling away as they started their engines and eased into procession behind it.

"Jack was a great friend of yours, wasn't he?" Kinsella asked the younger man next to him.

"He knew me when I was just a kid," Simmons replied as tears welled up in his eyes once more. "It doesn't seem right." He choked a little as he spoke. "It just doesn't seem fair . . ."

They had looped around the edge of the campus and were passing the Morris Inn. "God needed a good storyteller, I guess," Thomas said with a tone of sentimental reassurance that sounded false even to himself, but he said it gently and it seemed right in a way he did not fully understand. He was, in truth, as sad as young Simmons. Thomas was not only troubled that Jack was gone on a day during which he could have used his strong presence, but he was also depressed, even though he firmly believed that his friend had been warmly received in heaven, that Allen had not been granted one more chance at life, more fair days and good times, a stretch of sunny and untroubled weather for a man who, for all his gruffness, had borne the problems of others with an understanding heart. Thomas wished that he could talk to him one more time.

There was not much traffic although the special routes that were standard procedures in South Bend on the day of a Notre Dame home game had already been blocked off. As state policemen waved them along toward the downtown area, Thomas began to think back on the years that he had known Father Allen. He wondered if all the listening, to distressed priests especially, all the changes, all the troubles of others he seemed to accept and understand with such wry good humor, had not suddenly accumulated beyond the strength of Jack Allen's broad shoulders to bear them. Had Jack died of an infection that ran through a changing Church? Thomas smiled to himself as he remembered Allen's laugh and the Nebraska Plan, and a thousand good times with the kind of friend one seldom found in life.   —

Father Thomas emerged from his reverie when they got to the undertaker's. Father Simmons was still snuffling from his crying as they entered the office to wait for the owner's arrival. Simmons had talked and Thomas had made some kind of answers as they had driven along but Kinsella couldn't remember what he had said; he still had vivid pictures of Father Allen in his mind. Their business with the undertaker did not take long. His name was Shaughnessy and, like many a fat man trying to blend unction and efficiency, he always looked sweaty and was constantly patting his hair down in back.

"Would you like to see the selection of couches?" he asked almost sweetly.

"No," Thomas answered firmly. "And don't try to sell me one with a green silk lining and a border of harps and angels."

"Well, no," Shaughnessy said, backing off a little. "But you might like to see the one with the Notre Dame colors. Very good taste . . ."

"I wouldn't be caught dead in a coffin like that. And neither will Jack Allen. Just give him first-class treatment and we don't want one of those gray boxes they make out of egg carton material. You're burying a man, one who was strong and plain. That's how his coffin should be. Do you understand me?"

"As you wish, Father. It's just that for Notre Dame priests . . ."

"Never mind that, Mr. Shaughnessy. A good, simple coffin. And send me the bill personally. Let me know when you're ready and I'll come back to put the vestments on him. Do you understand?"

"Yes, yes, of course," Shaughnessy said. "Just as you wish. Now there is just a little paper work."

"Later," Thomas said, standing up and gesturing to Father Simmons to follow him. "And one more thing, Mr. Shaughnessy. No roses in the cheeks, and no pancake makeup. He was a very plain man."

"Well, sometimes it's necessary for . . ."

Thomas broke in, "You do understand, don't you?" Then he turned and with Father Simmons at his side walked out of the building to the parking lot.

They were quiet as they drove back toward the University. Once they recognized Father Thomas, the state troopers waved the car along, at a few corners shifting wooden horses that had been put in place for traffic control for the afternoon game.

Thomas decided to swing around and go north on Route 31 to see what he could of the demonstration that had invaded the western edge of the campus at dawn.

"Look at the cars," Andrew Simmons said in surprise as they approached a side entrance road just below the area where Green's army, as Thomas had begun to think of it, had

penetrated the border of the University grounds. Troopers
lined the road and they were attempting to keep cars without
proper indentification from entering the campus. Still, they
seemed slightly harried by the unusually heavy volume of
early morning traffic and by the number of people who were
being dropped from the cars which they had kept from getting
on campus. Crowds of people were also walking along the
shoulders of the road and entering wherever they could; it
was impossible to control all of them.

"My God, this will be a sideshow in a few hours," he said,
more to himself than to Father Simmons. He eased the car
onto the road that cut eastward toward the heart of the
campus and drove slowly as the visitors bound for the
Lourdes Shrine parted to let the car through. Thomas rolled
down the window as they came to the Rockne memorial and
made a left turn onto the road that passed below the shrine as
it looped around the central cluster of University buildings.
Groups of people, perhaps fifty in all, were hurrying along
ahead of the car. Father Kinsella recognized the man in black
pants pedaling a wobbly course on a bike whose handlebars
bore a weight of electronic machinery. An aerial, with a plain
white pennant tied to its top, flopped over the rider's shoulder
like the feather on an old-fashioned hat.

"That's Brother Chrysostym," Father Simmons said as they
passed him. "From that place north of here . . ."

"I wonder if his keeper knows he's out," Thomas said as an
uneasy feeling about the descent of the crazies on the campus
tightened its hold on his stomach. "Is that blood on his face?"

"I think so," Simmons responded, turning back to get a
better look.

"There's Jack," Kinsella said as Monsignor Egan, clutching
his pen and small black book like a reporter, stepped onto the
road about fifty yards ahead of them. Thomas slowed the car
and Jack opened the back door and climbed in.

"How do you read it?" Thomas asked as Egan leaned
forward to put his head between the two priests in the front
seat.

"About five hundred is my guess," Egan said, glancing
down at his notebook. "They're singing now. Listen, you can
hear them." They were silent and, sure enough, a muffled
chorus rode on the morning air: "We gather together to sing
the Lord's praises, To worship the Father through Jesus his
son . . ." Thomas cranked the window back up as they

curved around below the area where the Lourdes Shrine lay hidden by a tree-lined slope.

"Very quiet otherwise. Fifty students, maybe a few more, most of them down front carrying signs and banners. The girl on the cross is propped up below the shrine itself, like the cross was leaning on a box or something. Very hard to see her and she seems to be asleep."

"What about Greenie?"

Egan cleared his throat. "Looks like he's in the middle of it. He's wearing a stole and he seemed to be running the show, such as it is. I didn't see any other priests. Not from here anyway. I think there are a few from other places, maybe a couple of student priests. It's all quiet, although a couple of reporters are back and I understand the television people are raising a squawk because the troopers won't let them move their van."

"They'll have mini-cams out in no time from the city," Thomas said quietly. "Jack, how fast do you think that crowd is growing?"

"Hard to say. I'd guess it will double by eight o'clock."

"How are the campus police doing?"

"Nothing much they can do but keep order. No incidents yet. They're following your orders and there really hasn't been any trouble. We're getting off easy so far, that's how I see it."

"Yes, very easy," Thomas said somewhat sarcastically. "We just have a hysterical girl tied to a cross and a chorus of five hundred being led by one of our vice-presidents. Not to mention sixty thousand more people about to descend on us for a football game."

"It could be worse, Tom," Egan said. "The crowd is at least quiet."

"Yes," Thomas said as he turned into the road that led to the rear of the administration building. "We could have the Penitentes out there, I suppose." He pulled into a space close to the rear entrance.

"Jack, I'd like you to arrange that breakfast with Trafficante and tell my father I'll see him later. I'm going to my office. Andy, why don't you go back and see what you can do to straighten out Jack's room. And don't let any of the wolves in."

Thomas could still hear the singing as he opened the

ground floor door of the building on the top of which the golden dome was beginning to glisten in the first bar of the day's sunlight.

Over at the Lourdes Shrine Father Green was not sure about what to do next. He had been shaken by the statements that Mary Ann had made about Dr. Feelgood and the best shit on the street. That was not exactly the language of a mystic and he briefly entertained the notion that she had become possessed like the girl in *The Exorcist* and he involuntarily pulled back to get out of range in case she started puking green stuff in his direction. Then he shook his head, as if to clear it, rearranged his stole, put the sedative in his pocket, and placed the bottle of Perrier water in the base of a nearby candlestand.

"How is she, Father?" David Weber asked in a voice that had grown detached and mechanical.

"I'm not sure," Greenie answered, suddenly expressing the misgiving that had rooted itself in his soul. "I don't know."

"She's sick," Timothy Duffy said, sensing an opening in a previously tightly defended circle of activity. "We ought to get her to a hospital." Greenie just stared down at the girl, his own mouth slightly open, as though he were mimicking her expression. "No," he said slowly. "She can't be sick. She can't be sick."

"Who are you?" Weber shot at Timothy.

"I'm a student here and I saw Mary Ann last night. She tried to get me in on this." He was anxious to lay a foundation for his own authority. "I mean, I saw her before you guys did. I think she's off the wall."

Weber glared at him. "How can you say that, you doubter!" Weber's eyes flashed and Timothy braced himself against the shove that he felt was coming his way. Instead, Weber merely grabbed Timothy's arm and, bringing his face to within an inch of Duffy's, said, "Why don't you get the hell out of here? You must have some homework to do."

"Let go of me. Look, you guys can stop this, you know that. Let go of me," Timothy said. "Let's do it before this crowd gets any bigger."

"You're a filthy doubter," Weber said, pressing his fingers

into Timothy's arm. "Mind your own business." And with
that, he gave Timothy a push that sent the young man
stumbling over the protruding edge of the cross and down on
his back so that his head was only a foot or so from Mary
Ann's.

"Leave him alone," Greenie said blankly as the crowd,
aware of some violent twitch at the edge of the shrine, surged
forward. Timothy was not hurt but he found himself pinned
in next to the cross by the advancing crowd. He was not
sure that Mary Ann could hear him, but since he could not
get up, he decided to try to speak to her. Because of the
singing and the shuffling, he had to shout to make himself
heard.

"Mary Ann! May Ann! It's me, Timothy Duffy. Remember me? You picked me out to help you. Me, Timothy. Now,
I want to get you home."

Mary Ann's head was tilted at an angle so that as she
opened her eyes she found herself staring right down into
Timothy's face.

"Timothy," she said, although the din of the crowd made it
difficult to hear her. "Dear, sweet Timothy." A dribble of
spittle lowered like a spider on a web from the side of her
mouth and landed on Timothy's chin. "Tim, how would you
like to ball me?"

Timothy strained to get up but the press of the surrounding
crowd made it impossible. He was sure that he had, by
watching her lips, gotten the drift of what she had said and he
was convinced that although the invitation was strangely
tempting, he had to do something to put an end to the
craziness. Mary Ann's eyes closed again and Timothy found
that he could not move. Above him Father Green seemed to
have regained his composure. The priest raised his arms to
quiet the crowd.

"It's time," he said after the singing stopped and the back
and forth surging of the crowd eased up, "it's time to raise the
cross for all to see."

Back at the Morris Inn Patrick B. Kinsella had gotten out
of bed and was shaving. Mae had turned over on her side and
was dozing quietly. Patrick shook his razor out under a
stream of hot water and placed it on the edge of the sink. He
rinsed and then dried his face, tossing the towel casually in

the overhand flip that he had learned from watching Rockne. The old coach had sat in his dreams all night long. He was at one end of a long table and Sam Insull was at the other. In the middle sat a figure in Cardinal's robes. He had not been able to make out exactly who it was. But as that scene dissolved, Rockne's face, like a thrust of limestone, loomed up in the darkness, biting out words like a man in a silent movie. Patrick shook his head and, stripping off his pajama bottoms, climbed back into bed. He reached over and pulled Mae close to him.

"Mae," he whispered, "are you awake?"

"What?" Mae groaned sleepily. She knew it was P.B., and she knew what he wanted. She had been through this times beyond counting in bedrooms all over the world. P.B. would get up and shave so that his face would be very smooth against hers and, in the darkness, he would seem like the young man she had married so many years before. P.B. could be very romantic when he wanted to but Mae also felt that his early morning interest in making love was sometimes related to the business he had to deal with that day. He would always nuzzle her gently and say, "What better way to start the day? Clears out all the cobwebs." But Mae felt that he was also proving something to himself, that, although he loved her, he was also demonstrating that he was still fit to take on the world.

"Oh, Pat," she said, turning to look into his eyes, "you'll never change, will you?"

"I hope not," he said as he moved his hand to touch her right breast. "And you know something, Mae? I don't believe you've changed over all these years either."

She could never resist him, not even when she knew he was reassuring himself, making sure of some mythic source of strength as he began to move over on top of her.

"Just a minute, Patty," she said. "You're in a great hurry today. What are you going to do, try to get in the game?" She pulled out from under him and eased out of the bed. "Your wife is going to the bathroom first."

"It's too bad young people don't know what marriage is really like," P.B. said in mock upset. "If they only knew how much going to the bathroom was involved . . ." But Mae was soon back, out of her gown, and cuddling close to him. She rubbed her face against his smooth-shaven jaw.

"Patty dear, you're an old love." She kissed him on the lips. "But what are you up to today?"

"Nothing, Mae," P.B. answered as he kissed her in return. "What would ever make you think a simple old Irisher like me would be up to something today?"

3
―――
October 22, 1983
6:45 A.M.

P.B. and Mae were lying side by side, as they had on so many mornings before the long, always busy days began. P.B. was restless, however, and for Mae this was another signal which, added to the cues she had already picked up, told her that her husband had some major problems on his mind.

"Has this got to do with Father Tom?"

"What? Has what got to do with Father Tom?"

"Whatever it is you're thinking about. You're a thousand miles away."

P.B. grunted and turned on his side to face away from Mae.

"Come now, my romantic dear, you don't think you can hide anything from me after all these years, do you?"

"Mae, you hiring out as a private detective these days? Or is this part of the mystical Irish earth mother in you?"

"It is about Tom, I can tell that. About Tom and you. That's why you're seeing him alone for breakfast, isn't it? It's got something to do with that investigation they keep talking about."

"Mae, you don't believe what you read in the papers, not after all these years, do you? Do you know that Franklin Roosevelt never read a paper for two weeks before any election?"

"No distracting tales about your old political friends, now, Patty. What are you up to with Tom?"

"Damn it, Mae, what do you want to know? I'm going to confession to him. That's it. Honest to God. I'm going to confess my role in the Patty Hearst kidnapping."

"Stop it, Pat. There's something up and I ought to be able to find out what it is. Don't be mean."

P.B. rolled over and put an arm around Mae. His face was but an inch from hers. He spoke very softly.

"I'm sorry. I don't want to be mean, not to you, not ever. Forgive me."

Then he kissed her gently and held his face close to hers.

"Today could be an important day for the Kinsellas. That's all I can say right now. I have to see Tom, I have to talk to him first. Then I'll tell you everything."

"Promise?"

"I promise." P.B. rolled back slightly away from Mae so that he could look into her face. "Everything after I talk to Tom."

The telephone rang and P.B. reached over and pulled the whole phone into the bed.

"Yes, this is Pat Kinsella. Oh, Monsignor Egan, how are you?"

He pulled himself up and dropped his legs over the side of the bed. Mae propped herself up on one arm. She sensed alarm in her husband's voice.

"What! When?" P.B. turned his head halfway back to Mae. "Jack Allen died this morning." Mae gasped and pulled herself up, clutching the bedclothes around her. "God be good to him," she said automatically. P.B. was still listening intently on the phone.

"What the hell is the matter with this place anyway? Okay, okay. Thanks for calling, Monsignor. I'll see you later."

P.B. replaced the phone on the bedside table and reached down to pick his pajama pants up from the floor and to slip into them. He looked across at Mae, who was already halfway into her robe. She muttered, "Poor dear Jack," half to herself as she stood up.

"Jesus Christ, Mae," P.B. said with a snort. "These crazy sons of bitches who were on campus last night are all over at the Lourdes Shrine with that girl on the cross again." He strode across the room, pulled the drapes open, and tilted the blind so that he could see the broad quadrangle, splotched with autumn colors, that led toward the administration building. Our Lady, Notre Dame herself, had caught the full blaze of dawn on top of the Golden Dome.

"And Tom's tied up. So he can't have breakfast with me. Can't see me till late. How do you like that? He's liable to be the next Cardinal Archbishop of Chicago and he's out burying the dead and breaking up demonstrations . . ." He broke off as he realized that he had said out loud what he had vowed to keep secret from Mae. She stood as though paralyzed by the revelation.

"So that's it, Patty . . ." She went over and sat down. "Why didn't you want to tell me that? Why on earth didn't you want to tell me that?"

The phone rang again and P.B., still naked to the waist, went back and sat at the edge of the bed while Mae followed him with her eyes, unsure of what to say, unsure of what it meant, but strangely wary that a dream she had had for a long time, that Tom would become a bishop, might come true.

"Your Eminence," P.B. said with forced heartiness. "How are you this fine morning? No, no, not a thing. I won't be seeing my son for a while. There's been some disturbance on campus . . . Oh, you just heard about it on the radio . . . Yes, that and also Tom's best friend, a Father Allen, died this morning. No, it's not exactly the way we expected it. But I'm sure it's all set." Patrick listened for a few moments, shifting his position so that he could look over at Mae, who was staring at him steadily. Inwardly she felt that in a way that she could not quite understand she was in a conflict of loyalties between her husband, her son, and her Church. P.B. smiled at her and made a quacking gesture with his free hand to indicate that the Cardinal was talking and was hard to interrupt.

"No, Leo," P.B. said at last, "I wouldn't worry about that. If everything goes as well as I think it will, there won't be anything for any of us to worry about. I'll call you later."

He hung up the phone and went over to stand by Mae. He touched her on the shoulder and she looked up at him as though she were trying to peer deeply inside him.

"Patrick," she said slowly, "you're not getting Tom involved in something. Tell me you're not. Joe and Martin can't be helped. But Thomas is special. A fair child always. Please tell me you're not mixing him up in some deal or other."

"Now, Mae," Patrick said, letting his hand rest on his

wife's shoulder, "there are times when we all have to stick together. That's what being a Kinsella means. Tom can't avoid his responsibilities, no matter who or what he is . . ."

Mae stood up and wordlessly pulled away from her husband. She went into the bathroom and closed the door.

4
October 22, 1983
7 A.M.

Father Thomas entered the administration building, and squinted momentarily as his eyes adjusted to the darkened basement corridor before he headed for the stairs.

"Tom," a voice called out of a little niche to the left in which a small counter served as an information center. Joe Kinsella, dressed in a blue blazer and gray pants, stepped into the hallway like a hit man coming out of an alley.

"Joe," Thomas said in genuine surprise, "what are you doing here?"

"I've been waiting for you, Tom. We need to have a talk."

"Well, this just about makes the day complete. Why didn't you just call me? You knew I'd be seeing you before the game."

"You haven't exactly been easy to reach, Father," Joe said sarcastically. Then he softened his tone. "I'm sorry about Jack Allen."

"Yes, yes," Thomas said, waving his hand as if to cut off any further discussion of his dead friend. "We'll all miss him." He looked into his brother's eyes. "Martin called me last night. Do you want to see me about the same business?"

"Let's say, I want to discuss a family matter."

"Can't it wait? I've got a lot of things to do this morning."

Joe touched his arm. "Tom, this can't wait at all."

Thomas pulled back just slightly. He was amazed at how much Joe looked and sounded like old P.B. He had the feeling that he was looking at P.B., that he had been caught for a fraction of a second in some pinch of time and that he was facing his father of thirty years before. Then its grip loosened and he shook his head.

"Let's go to my office. Austin Kenna's holding the fort for me."

They climbed the wide stairs of the old building, the creaking of the steps about the only noise that could be heard at that hour. They passed down the dark corridor along the walls of which hung the paintings of previous University presidents. They seemed to be watching Thomas even more closely than they had the evening before. He paused and looked up at the handsome face of Theodore Hesburgh gazing down from a gilt-edged frame.

"You know," Thomas said as he got to the door to his outer office, "Ted Hesburgh was lucky. When he had a big problem he could always call Eppie Lederer for some advice." He smiled crookedly at Joe. "Have you thought of calling Ann Landers yourself?"

Joe's eyes, as blue and clear as coral waters, remained fixed on Thomas. There was no light of humor in them. Thomas opened the door and they passed through the drab reception room and into Kinsella's office, where, I must confess, I had nodded off in an easy chair.

"One by land, Austin," Thomas said to me with false heartiness, "and two by sea. Where would our country be if you had been on watch in the Old North Church that night?"

I sputtered up with a start, greeted Joe Kinsella, and explained that there had been no word from Maria as yet. I felt the charge of an Irish standoff in the air and began to shuffle out.

"No need to go, Austin," Thomas said firmly. "We're going to have a family discussion anyway."

Joe looked angry and uneasy; he opened his mouth but, thinking better of it, checked himself and said nothing. I wondered if Thomas wanted me as a cheering section or a witness. Whatever, I sat down again, glad for my ringside seat.

"I suppose it doesn't make any difference," Joe said calmly enough as Thomas moved behind his big desk.

"Well, Joe, what is it?" Thomas said as he sank into his

chair. "I've got lots to do." Father Thomas was hugging the line that ran between control and rage.

"Tom, the family knows all about your chance to become Archbishop. We want you to take it . . ."

"Martin," Thomas said, cutting his brother off, "went through all that with me last night."

"Well, it's more serious than even he understands. We're right on the edge of a big problem."

"You mean this investigation by the U.S. Attorney? I can't believe that P.B. doesn't have a staff of lawyers to handle that. Besides, there can't be anything that bad in the family closet."

"It's bad enough, Tom. There's plenty you don't know about, plenty you've kept your nose out of since you went away to the seminary. What the hell do you think Kinsella Industries is, a charitable organization? And the old man isn't a scoutmaster, you know."

"I was never tempted to think he was."

"Well, believe me, when these bastards want to make a case against you, they don't stop at anything. And it isn't just us. It's other people in construction and paving, lots of big Democrats, lots of them involved in this."

"If this is all political, I expect you'll be able to take care of yourselves without making my career a part of your defense. I've never let you use Notre Dame in any way and I'll be damned if you're going to get me to do it now."

Joe walked over, bent down slightly, and placed the palms of his hands on Thomas's desk top. He looked very grave.

"Nobody's asking you to use Notre Dame. We're just asking you to do the right thing. You don't seem to realize that this investigation could send a lot of people to jail. This attorney's not kidding, he's got ambitions and he's going to use the breaking of the Kinsellas to achieve them. This son of a bitch wants to run for the U. S. Senate waving P.B.'s scalp. Christ, the old man spent all afternoon yesterday before he came here with this bastard Murphy. This situation is worse than you think; it's worse even than Martin thinks." Joe stepped back and walked toward the windows. There was something in his tone that arrested Thomas's attention, that shifted Thomas's tone of response a notch toward sympathy.

"What do you mean, worse than Martin thinks?"

Joe turned around and, dramatically outlined against the tall windows, began to speak swiftly.

"I'm not sure when the last time was that Martin actually did think. But I know what the old man is up to. I know how he thinks. And he thinks about saving himself, that's what he thinks. And that's what he's going to do. And, God help us, he's going to let me and Marty pay the price. Us and several others, old Slota and a lot of his old pals."

"I don't understand what you mean."

"Immunity, Tom, immunity. For Chrissake, Tom, what the hell do you think this U. S. Attorney's built his career on? Evidence? Hell, he's been putting people away by giving immunity to people who've been in on things in exchange for their testimony against others. How the hell do you think they've been so successful in indicting people and putting them in the slammer? He's made his record by immunizing co-conspirators."

There was silence for a moment while Thomas digested what Joe had clearly implied.

"You mean the old man is willing to accept immunity to save himself?"

"What do you want me to do, paint this on the wall in big letters? What the hell do you think he was arranging yesterday? P.B. hasn't survived so long on sentiment, you know, and he's willing to let us take the rap, just so long as he's high on the beach after the wave breaks. Do you understand me now? Marty and I'll go to jail if this investigation goes on. The old man'll get off, sure, but we won't. We're supposed to take a dive. He thinks we're young enough to survive it, he'll keep everything going until we get out. Hell, don't you think he's capable of that?"

Thomas merely closed his eyes as Joe, whose voice had grown harsh, turned back toward the windows again.

"So, Thomas, the only thing that might kill this whole goddam thing is your co-operation. You take the job. Hell, you've always wanted a job like that anyway. Don't tell me you haven't. That's P.B.'s ace in the hole. I think he was buying a little more time by taking the immunity, or promising to. I hope he was anyway. He knows, he knows from Cardinal Williams, that the job is yours. You can have it today. And Murphy, the little bastard, will back off once he knows this is in the works."

Thomas's face looked strained to me, with lines I had never seemed to notice before strung taut across his forehead. He opened his eyes but remained silent.

"You may think I'm kidding, Tom, but I'm not."

"Does Mother know about this?"

"A little. She doesn't know much. I don't think so anyway. P.B. hasn't told much to anybody but me. And some to Martin."

"And you think P.B. has accepted immunity, you really think that?"

"Don't you believe he would?"

Thomas looked up at Joe. He ran a finger around inside his shirt collar.

"Oh, I think he'd do it all right. I just want to be sure. Did he actually tell you that? Do you know that from him?"

"It was about as clear as anything. He talked about it, said he was going to see the U. S. Attorney, that he was ready to do it, and that I had to be ready for anything. Just like that, calm and cool. Hell, I don't know what he said to the attorney. He didn't have many choices, not from his viewpoint anyway. The old man's been all over this week, talking to all kinds of people. I didn't know where he was half the time. You've seen him like that."

"Yes, yes, I certainly have." Thomas formed a pyramid with his fingers as he leaned forward on his elbows. He lapsed into silence again and I must say I noticed how I had pulled myself to attention to hear what was coming next.

"So you want me to go bail for you, is that it?"

"I wouldn't put it that way, Tom. It isn't like we're asking you to go to jail. Hell, this is a big thing for you, a good thing. And I think it would slow U. S. Attorney Finbar Murphy down quite a bit. P.B. wouldn't have to cash in on the immunity. He's counting on you . . ."

"Joe, I don't know what to say about this immunity business. If the old man has decided to do that, then there's no way to stop him. I'd like to think I could without having the question of my becoming Archbishop of Chicago being mixed up in it. But I can't barter with that very freely . . ."

"Tom," Joe said almost fervently, "this is for the family. And you know very well that people have been bartering with archbishoprics all through history. Hell, Cardinal Williams didn't get the job because he recited the rosary in a pure, clear voice. There's a business side to all these things."

"Joe, I don't want to see you and Martin go to jail. I don't want to see our mother heartbroken. And I'm not sure how comfortable P.B. would feel after he let this happen . . ."

"He'd sleep like a baby. And you know it."

Thomas's private phone rang, snapping the tension in the room.

"Hello," Thomas said somewhat stiffly. "Yes, Monsignor, that's fine. Thanks. What's the situation at the grotto?" There was a pause as Monsignor Egan gave Thomas a situation report. "Okay, come over here as soon as you can." Thomas hung up the phone.

"The first tourist bus has just pulled in at the Lourdes Shrine. Monsignor Egan figures there's a thousand or more people there now. Father Green is leading a prayer service beneath the cross." He paused and shook his head. "They're claiming that the girl is bleeding from the hands, that she's a stigmatic." He looked up as his brother sighed, and spoke again.

"Joe, I have to think about what you said. But right now I've got to put an end to the mass hysteria at the grotto."

Father Thomas stood up and looked toward Joe Kinsella, who remained motionless by the windows.

"Joe, I don't know what else I can say to you right now. You're welcome to stay here but things may be a little hectic for a few hours."

"You won't give me an answer?"

"No." Thomas spoke the word softly but definitively. "Not now."

"Remember, Tom, the old man doesn't kid around about things like this. And remember Martin and I have wives and children. There's more to the Kinsella family than 'The Kinsella' himself." Joe was frustrated but there was little more he could say or do. Nothing I had ever observed more resembled the meeting of the irresistible force with the immovable object than two Kinsellas shoulder to shoulder. Joe Kinsella walked swiftly across the room.

"I'll see you at the luncheon." He didn't slam the door but he did leave it open, and with it a tingling challenge hanging in the air. Monsignor Egan came bustling in a few seconds later, looking as though he had come at a jogger's pace across the campus.

"Was that your brother Joe I just passed?" he asked. "He seemed in a hurry."

"Yes," Thomas replied dryly. "Something of a hurry. It's a family characteristic. Now, where do we stand with this crazy business?"

Egan dropped into a chair, still half looking toward the door as though he remained uncertain about whether he had seen Joe Kinsella or a fleeting mirage.

"The traffic is getting very bad and the state troopers can't keep people on foot from entering the campus. They seem to be coming in from all over. They try to keep the traffic flowing but that's getting to be a problem too. And that's bound to get worse as the morning passes. The trouble is, a lot of the buses have the right stickers to get on the campus but they're all anxious to find out what's going on at the shrine. And then there are the people who get here early to walk around the campus and have a tailgate luncheon. Some of them are just curious, but the crowds are getting larger and we'll have to do something dramatic to free things up. You know, it's liable to get dangerous, people might get trampled or hurt. I don't like it right now . . ."

"And Greenie is leading prayers?"

"Yes, but that helps a little. At least it keeps the crowd busy, keeps them from getting restless."

"How about the girl on the cross?"

"She looks out of it, asleep or unconscious. Anyway, she's not saying anything and that keeps the fervor down." He paused. "It could be worse."

"I guess so," Thomas replied. "They could be offering an Aztec sacrifice. Look, Jack, I haven't wanted to get into this. And I won't unless it's absolutely necessary. Get Harry Maxwell and Fred Morgan. They're close to Greenie. Tell them to get down there and to persuade him to break this thing up and get back to his room. It's better if we can have this thing collapse from the inside. But, Jack, we don't have any more time to speculate about this, we've got to get this show closed down within the hour."

"Right away," Monsignor Egan said, halfway out of his chair and on the way to the door. "I'll call back if we need any help."

Thomas smiled at me in the sudden silence that descended after the intense conversation of the last hour.

"Well, Austin, I think I'll just draw up a contingency plan." He reached for his phone. "Just in case."

"Let us all pray," Father Green intoned in a voice that sounded as though it was filled with splinters. "Let us pray for light and truth. Let us pray for a return to religion in our great country."

He was standing on an overturned soft drink case just in front of the cross so that Mary Ann's inert form hung just above his head. The cross had been jammed against the stone altar at the side of the shrine; it was held firmly in position by a number of objects that had been pressed against it, including benches and rocks that had been scooped up from the campus by David Weber and some of the other eager followers. Brother Dingbat's bicycle rested against this ungainly base, its aerial arching up toward one of the crossbars. Brother himself, the blood from his superficial injury congealed on his forehead, was standing just below Father Green, rocking back and forth with the crowd as it thundered out its responses to the invocations, "Let us pray to the Lord."

A mini-cam unit from the CBS affiliate in South Bend had arrived and, at a far edge of the crowd, began to record the morning's events. Reporters also elbowed through the throng of people, trying to get closer to the place where Mary Ann, her white robes slightly disheveled and dirty, hung in a troubled sleep just above the heads of the onlookers. Her head had fallen slightly forward and the early morning sun caught and illumined one side of her face as well as the strands of long brown hair which rose and fell on the intermittent breeze. At the point where the road joined the swelling crowd a blue chartered bus had come to a stop. It was filled with sixty men from a gun club in a Chicago suburb; they had obtained a block of tickets and had organized themselves for a day of masculine camaraderie in the football stands. Even though it was early in the morning, flasks had been passed up and down the aisle of the bus during the two-hour ride to South Bend. A burly man named Frank Trask, who had a seat right behind the driver, led the group in the Notre Dame Victory March, reminding his fellow travelers that POWs had sung it in Vietnam as an expression of Americanism when their captors forbade them to sing patriotic songs. Trask's mood was mellow and lusty as the bus door hissed open and, aching to find a bathroom, he descended the stairs. The fresh morning air surprised him and he tripped on the bottom step and went sprawling into a group of pilgrims at the near rim of the crowd.

"God bless you, brother," a tall man in a turtleneck

sweater said to Trask as he struggled to get to his feet. He blinked his eyes toward the shrine, catching a glimpse of what looked like a real live girl tied to a cross. Something clanged in his subconscious; it was the sound of a closing dungeon door from deep in the repressed layers of Trask's unexplored yearnings. He stared at Mary Ann from a distance of a thousand feet; he felt trapped between the need to find a bathroom and an attraction that burned like a flare somewhere inside him. "Jesus," he said out loud. "Jesus Christ!"

"Praised be the name of the Lord," the tall man said approvingly, then, "God bless you, brother."

Trask looked at him in a dumbfounded way and began to move roughly through the swaying crowd toward the cross.

Fathers Maxwell and Morgan had just arrived from the main part of the campus. They were dressed, at Monsignor Egan's suggestion, in their black shirts and clerical collars. Timothy Duffy, who had been able to get off the ground when the cross was raised, had remained near the front of the crowd, waiting for a chance to intervene again. He noticed Maxwell and Morgan as they joined themselves to the people at the perimeter of the gathering and turning now this way and now that made their way toward Father Green. Duffy decided to join forces with them and, moving sideways, began to snake through the hymn singers.

Father Green was still praying away in his hoarse and failing voice, pumping his arms up and down to maintain the rhythm of the chanted responses. With his eyes he signaled for the young couple with the guitars to come toward him and to take over with an interlude of singing. He stepped down off the box as the last wave of "Let us pray to the Lord" rolled over him. His eyes were filmy and he breathed heavily as he stood looking up at Mary Ann.

A reporter broke out of the throng before him and began to question him as the first notes of the Lourdes Hymn, "Ave, Ave, Ave Maria," were struck on the guitars.

"Father, what did you feel when you first heard of the girl on the cross?"

Green turned toward the reporter who was trying to hold a microphone from a small cassette recorder under his chin.

"I, I," Green began, "I felt wonderful. I felt that God had sent us a sign."

"What kind of a sign?" the reporter shot back quickly.

Another reporter, with yet another cassette recorder, popped out of the crowd in front of Father Green.

"A sign of our need for repentance," Father Green answered weakly. Just then Father Frederick Morgan's large hand grasped Green's arm and Father Maxwell moved around to his other side. Timothy Duffy pulled himself between two plump ladies to the place where the reporters stood with their microphones held out like oxygen tubes toward Father Green.

"No more questions," Morgan said to the reporters.

"I don't mind," Green said in a cracking and uncertain voice.

"That's enough," Father Maxwell said. "Just tell the people to go home now, tell them the prayer service is over."

Father Green, his eyes bulging and bloodshot, looked at Maxwell as though he did not recognize him. "I can't do that, I simply can't do that." Then he swayed and fell forward into Father Morgan's arms. A stir of concern interrupted the singing at the front of the crowd. Timothy leaned forward toward a candlestand, removed the bottle of Perrier water that Green had stowed there earlier, and held it up as the reporters crowded around the collapsing priest. Father Maxwell took it and dashed some of the water in Green's face. He stirred and opened his eyes as the water dripped down his cheeks and his chin. Morgan elbowed the microphone away. "Come on now, you've got to get some rest." With that, he half picked up Green and carried him around the front of the shrine and away from the crowd. The singing began to fracture at this frontal dislocation of the group but the guitarists picked up the refrain once more and the voices fell together again. "Ave, Ave . . ." The blood-streaked stole trailed along on the ground as, followed by a cluster of news reporters, Morgan carried Greenie, his head bobbing against his broad shoulder, up the lawn toward Corby Hall.

Back at the Morris Inn, Patrick B. Kinsella had just adjusted an emerald green tie while Mae tugged at the neckline of a blouse with enough lace at the throat to have choked George Washington. The room was filled with the heavy silence generated by couples temporarily out of sorts with each other. P.B. slipped into a blue sport coat, not unlike the one his son Joe wore, grumbling and grunting as he did so. Mae turned her head away from him as he moved toward her.

"Mae," Kinsella said softly, "it's me, the last of the fighting Irishmen. Are you willing to reopen diplomatic negotiations?"

Mae straightened up and, without a word, walked past him, letting the neckline adjustment go as a bad job. He looked at her back as she searched in her pocketbook for a gold charm bracelet.

"Did I ever tell you, Mae, that you've never lost that graceful line to your back? You know Picasso once said, or somebody, that there was nothing more lovely than the line of a woman's back."

More silence as Mae snapped the bracelet on her wrist and then shook it to sort out the cluster of charms. But now Patrick knew she was prepared to negotiate because she had run out of things to do to get ready for breakfast. He was as familiar with the mechanics of the scene as she was, and neither of them liked the silence.

"You know, Mae, here these minutes are passing away and we'll never get them back this side of the grave. Wouldn't it be awful to regret that we hadn't used them to talk to each other?"

That did it.

"Patrick, will you stop the palaver! You've a great store of charm. And I do love you. But you don't seem to care how I feel when you hide something from me, especially something important, something about Tom . . ."

There was no doubt about her anger, so Patrick did what he always did in desperate situations. He told her the truth. It only took a few moments to outline the situation to her. He left out the part about the immunity.

"Mae, you're right and I'm sorry. But I didn't tell you because I didn't want to hurt you."

"Hurt me? Patrick, not telling me this has hurt me as much as anything you've ever done." She gazed steadily at him. "I'm not fooling. I don't want you to mix Tom up in any of this."

"Mix him up in it? Hell, I can't even get an appointment with him," Patrick answered as he let his best smile spread slowly across his face.

"Patty, what will you do if he says no to this?"

He knew he had been almost forgiven when she called him

Patty, so he took her by the arm and walked her toward the door.

"Well," he said sweetly, "I'll just have to think of something else, won't I?"

Matt Finn had been up most of the night and he was restless during the Mass that was being celebrated for the football team at Moreau Seminary. He had to get back to the main part of the campus, he had to speak to Father Kinsella again. He hadn't had much luck on the last try but, now that the day had begun, he might be able to reach him and help resolve the problem of the girl on the cross. He had walked outside for a while before the Mass had started and thought he could hear snatches of singing across St. Joseph's Lake. Was the demonstration in full swing again? He blessed himself in the careless manner of lifelong Catholics as the priest concluded the liturgy. Then he made his decision. He whispered in the ear of one of the assistant coaches who was kneeling next to him, then he rose, genuflected, and hurried out of the chapel.

Back at the grotto, Timothy found himself without allies as he stood at the front of the crowd that had suddenly been made headless by Father Green's departure. The hymn was just concluding and as he looked to his left he saw that David Weber was approaching with the hurried air of a man who intended to take over the situation before it disintegrated. Behind Timothy Frank Trask had made a crude passage through the crowd, like a boar in the underbrush, so that he was only five feet away. Timothy looked to the right to see Brother Dingbat still swaying even though the music had stopped. He crossed himself, whispered, "Now or never!" and jumped up on the overturned box. He was tall enough by stretching as far as he could to reach the crossbar. He pulled at the ties that held Mary Ann's right arm in place as cries of protest began to go up from the crowd behind him.

Mary Ann's arm flailed down as she sagged slowly toward Timothy's shoulders. Timothy could feel David Weber's hand pulling at the back of his shirt as he strained to bear the weight of the girl's body, which had swung out and down like somebody trying to jump off a train. Her eyes opened as the crowd noise increased.

"Timothy," she said. "Timothy, you little fucker, I knew you'd help me."

Duffy was still trying to balance the partially freed girl and to ward off the assault from David Weber when he felt a sharp blow to his right kidney. Frank Trask, grinning like a triumphant tank commander, struck him again and Timothy had one last view of Brother Dingbat charging toward him before he lost his balance. The crowd shrieked and screamed as the cross, with Mary Ann flopping down over Timothy's shoulder, began to wobble and fall forward. The crossbar caught Brother Dingbat on the forehead, reopening his wound as it knocked him senseless onto the pavement. The top of the vertical plank of the cross cracked sharply on Trask's head and he pitched forward beneath the collapsing bodies of Duffy, Mary Ann, and David Weber. The latter's head grazed a candlestand as it tipped over and he dropped into unconsciousness like a man slipping into a deep and silent sea. Timothy landed on top of Trask, whose body cushioned the fall. Mary Ann fell on top of Timothy as the cross bounced down on them. She was looking directly into his eyes and her body was pressed firmly against his.

"Man," she said. "When you fuck, you sure do fuck."

5

October 22, 1983
8:00 A.M.

Father Thomas had no sooner hung up the phone than it rang again. It was Archbishop Trafficante.

"Did you rest well, Excellency?" Thomas slipped into the old smoothness with no effort. He could sleepwalk through conversations like this.

"No, just a minor disturbance . . . Well, many groups bring religious overtones to their gatherings these days . . . No, I think it's all well in hand. I'm glad you called, because

I've made up my mind about our discussion of last evening . . . Well, many factors, I had to think about many things . . . Well, if you're free right now, I'll come over . . . Fine. I'll come to your rooms in a few minutes."

Thomas gave a closing salutation in Italian and replaced the phone on its cradle. It rang again immediately, but Thomas ignored it. He just sat there looking at me. I, of course, was hoping that he would tell me if and when he was moving to Chicago, and if he could use a wise old man around the Cardinal's house, but he said nothing and his face revealed no more than that. The phone kept ringing in the background.

"Austin," Father Thomas said as he stood up, "I wish Joe hadn't told me about that immunity business." Then he walked to the door as I turned my head to follow him. I didn't know what to say, or whether to wish him good luck or happy landing. I sighed, part from weariness and part from wonder about what he was going to do. He turned as he opened his office door, smiled, sort of like a boy going bravely to the principal's office, and winked at me. I didn't have any clear idea of what he had decided but I had a half vision of old P.B.'s hand on his shoulder as he turned to go. The phone was still ringing, so I went over to answer it.

"No, this is not Father Kinsella, no, he'll be back within the hour, I expect." Then I coughed in some embarrassment. "Oh, Mrs. Kinsella, it's you. Yes, yes, I'm still alive. Would you believe it? . . . All right, I'll leave a note to tell him his mother called." We both laughed a little, although I thought she sounded distraught, and I hung up.

The phone rang again and for an hour I was busy taking messages from all over the country. There were irate alumni wanting to know who the girl on the cross was and how she got there, and there was Jack Allen's brother wanting to know about the funeral arrangements, and there was somebody with a Texas accent who wanted two tickets to the Southern California game that afternoon. Well, it was a busy shift in the president's office and, seeing it was Saturday and his secretary wouldn't be coming in, I was scratching away at the note pad at a great rate. Father Andrew Greeley called wanting to know what was going on, and so did *Time* and *Newsweek,* and a fellow from the New York *Times,* and I don't know how many others. I referred them all to Dick Cummings in public relations, although I was sure he had his hands full already. Then there was a knock on the door and in came Maria Moore and Matt Finn. Big Matt looked a little sheepish, as indeed, having seen him out in the fields before the cross in the middle of the night, I thought he should be.

"Miss Moore's car was just arriving as I came along, so I told her I'd bring her up to Father Kinsella's office."

Maria was in a simple wool suit, a gray one, with a silk scarf tied at her neck. She looked fine, and more than that, but I didn't know exactly what to say, except that I was the official welcoming committee and we were in the proper holding area until Father Thomas reappeared. I got her comfortably seated and asked after Helen Barnes, who had remained back in Chicago. Then I turned back to Finn.

"Father Kinsella's gone to see the visiting Archbishop." Then I put my hand on his arm and looked him in the eye, as though I was a detective in the movies about to unravel some plot twist. "I'd suggest, Matt, that if you've something to tell Father Kinsella that can clear up the trouble we've been having with the loonies, now's the time to do it." I was surprised at my own directness. And Finn was no less surprised as I went on. "Matt, I saw you out there in the fields last night with Mary Ann. It's late but not too late if you can get this thing straightened out." Then, feeling I had said almost enough, I let go of his arm.

"Do you know anything about what's happening now?" Finn asked. "I came directly here. Are they at the shrine?"

"So I'm told." The phone began to ring insistently again. "We're expecting a report from the front at any minute. Excuse me." I went over to the desk and picked up the phone. It was Monsignor Egan.

"Well, there've been a lot of calls, oh, lots of calls. What's that? Well, he's with the Archbishop right now. Yes, I'll tell him if he gets back. Why don't you call him at the guest suite?" I hung up and surveyed Maria and Matt, both of whom looked intensely curious about the latest developments.

"Monsignor Egan says all hell is breaking loose at the grotto."

Maria sighed and Finn's eyes flashed.

"I'm heading over there," the coach said, and was out the door before I could respond. I looked back at Maria Moore. She had taken out a handkerchief and was crying softly, a

development that flustered me completely. I went over next
to her, reached tentatively down toward her shoulder, pulled
my hand back, and cleared my throat.

"Oh, Austin," she said, looking up at me, "you old dear,
I'm sorry, I just can't help it." She sniffed and replaced her
handkerchief in her pocketbook.

But she couldn't, or wouldn't even pretend to put her sad
looks away. What was I to say, even though my head was
swimming with thoughts about her and Father Thomas and of
how much sacrifice had gone into loving him in the strange
long-distance way she had? And I thought of the loonies
parading out on the campus with the poor girl on the cross,
Mary Ann, who had drawn the corruption out of so-called
religious behavior like a poultice pulling the poison out of an
infection. I could only wonder at what Maria was thinking of
these developments, the whole of it stranger than any make-
believe she'd ever known.

"Austin," she asked almost plaintively, "what's Thomas
going to do? Did he tell you what he was going to do?"

Finn went trotting cross-country to the grotto, where things
had indeed gone from bad to worse. More buses had arrived
to disgorge groups of ticket holders, great numbers of whom
were as merry from drinking their way to South Bend as
Frank Trask's gun club had been. Students and other fans,
family groups mostly, had wandered over to see what was
going on, so that over two thousand people were there by the
time Finn arrived. The singing had gone to pieces when the
cross went down but many of the pilgrims had formed
themselves into small clusters within the great swirling mass
around them. Some were singing while others chanted
prayers or said the rosary. Many were pushing and shoving as
though there were lifeboats at the edge of the shrine area and
they were determined to find places in them. Several fistfights
had broken out near the buses and half-drunken men, caught
up in a fantasy that they had at last found the John Wayne
barroom brawl of their dreams, were swinging wildly at each
other, stumbling over benches and trampling shrubs and
falling through hedges. A half dozen men wearing blue
warm-up jackets emblazoned with the words "Cicero A.C."
had begun to fight among themselves and had crossed the
road and circled back on the grass toward a spur of St.
Joseph's Lake. Two of them tumbled to the ground as if in a

dead man's grip with each other and rolled over and over, their jackets picking up the stray weeds of autumn, until, with a great splash, they went, like a barrel off a beer truck, into the water.

The mini-cams were doing their best to record the excitement as their operators and assistants struggled to move toward the place where the cross was still spread out over a tangle of people. Members of the crowd had surged forward to help but they were confused and uncertain of what to do since Green was gone and Weber was out cold. They only added to the confusion as some pulled on the cross and others pushed and Mary Ann, still half strapped to it, yelled, "Will you bastards fuck off!" But she was bouncing up and down on the dazed Timothy and nobody could hear her because of the surrounding clamor.

The wail of a police siren could be heard as reinforcements of state troopers called in to help the campus police tried, largely without success because of the buses that blocked the way, to get close to the area. Finn, as sure as he was when he sent a play in to his quarterback, headed straight for the cross, which, as he glimpsed it when the crowd opened and closed in its tortured and noisy shiftings, was moving almost in slow motion, a dowser's rod for the craziness of the day. Finn dragged David Weber to his feet and handed him off to the guitarists, who had been standing by trying to protect their instruments from harm. Weber, his face almost angelically peaceful, was a dead weight as they attempted to move him away. Then the coach put one hand down to steady the cross and reached with the other to loosen the ties first on Mary Ann's legs and then on her left arm. She fell onto Timothy's chest, groaning as the air was knocked out of her.

Finn shook off another pilgrim who tried to impede his work and, with a quick motion, lifted the cross up and away from Mary Ann's back. He gave it a push and it went upright, tottering for a moment above the heads of the crowd, the loosened ropes and clothes still dangling from the crossbars.

"Catch it, you damn fools!" Finn yelled as the cross began to pitch sideways. Joe Sclafani, who had held back from involvement until that moment, reached out his arms and supported the cross until it could be lowered slowly and propped against the stone pulpit at the side of the shrine.

"Let me get some of the rope as a relic," a wild-eyed devotee cried, trying to climb past the now perspiring coach.

Finn gave the man a sharp elbow in the ribs and he was deflected into the crowds, from which catcalls of derision had begun to rise.

"You!" Finn said sharply to Sclafani. "Give me a hand here."

They pulled Brother Dingbat aside. He was bleeding again, and he looked more seriously hurt than he was, but he was still unconscious, pursuing mystical delights in his own half-lit inner world.

"Stretch him out on the grass over there until a doctor gets here."

Then the coach leaned down and gently lifted Mary Ann off Timothy. As Duffy struggled to get to his feet, Finn knelt down beside the girl, putting a muscular arm around her shoulder and looking at her face under her tousled and bowed head the way he might with an injured player out on the football field.

"There, there," Finn said gently. "It's all over, Mary Ann, it's all over now."

Pilgrims moved in to crowd around the coach and the girl, asking questions, bumping against them, and pinning them into an airless circle.

"Get back," Finn yelled. "She needs air. For God's sake, move back." But the crowd, like any crowd at an accident, had a stubborn and curious mind of its own. Besides that, members of the news media were relentlessly pushing to get a better view and, if possible, an interview, their equivalent of a hunter's kill for the day.

"What's your name, young lady?" a television reporter yelled. "No, hold it, hold it till the camera gets here."

Finn held Mary Ann as though he were a fierce eagle protecting a chick under a great ruffling wing. He turned his head away from the reporters who were crowding in around him.

"Say," one of them called as he pushed a microphone toward Finn, "aren't you the football coach here?"

Monsignor Egan had finally reached Father Kinsella in Archbishop Trafficante's rooms. He had gone there in person and rapped on the door like a policeman routing a dice game. He pushed past the waxen-looking Trafficante and marched across the room to where Thomas, his eyebrows still arched in surprise, was sitting.

Egan bent down and whispered in Father Kinsella's ear, "D-Day, Tom, the crazies just went over the top. You'd better get on this."

Thomas rose, smiled graciously at the Archbishop, and moved to pick up the nearby phone.

"Put Plan B into effect," he said simply, and then turned back to Trafficante. Egan was aware that the tension from the discussion he had interrupted still choked the air like humidity on a summer night.

"Archbishop, would you please excuse me? There is some urgent business I have to take care of." Thomas paused just a fraction of a second. "But I think we see things the same way."

The Archbishop, as calm as a gambler accustomed to having his joint raided, gave an automatic smile. "Yes, Father, that is so."

What the hell were they talking about? Egan wondered. And what had they decided? But Kinsella had him by the arm and they moved swiftly out the door and down the stairs.

"What the hell is Plan B?" Egan asked as they picked up their pace once they got into the air of the October morning. Students were hurrying all around them toward the same destination.

"You'll see shortly," Thomas said.

In a few minutes they were just above the shrine. Kinsella stopped and looked around. He coul' hear the yelling and shouting and see the crowds spreading out in disarray from both sides of the stone grotto. Father Thomas seemed to be looking for someone.

"There he is," he said in an urgent voice as he sighted Father Simmons hurrying toward them with a bullhorn.

"Let's go," Father Kinsella said as Simmons reached them, and the three priests, with the verve of musketeers, scrambled around the edge of the shrine to the place where Matt Finn and the girl were under siege from the reporters and the still curious crowd.

Father Kinsella made an easy jump over the gate and took a position in the inner part of the grotto. Egan made a cautious climb after him and Father Simmons handed over the bullhorn and then joined them. Father Thomas moved as best he could to a central position and then took the horn in his hands.

"This is Father Kinsella speaking," he said clearly to the

crowd that still resisted like an incoming tide. "I want your
attention." He repeated that several times and the milling
crowd, secretly in search of a leader, began to quiet down and
look toward the University president. The reporters quickly
shifted away from Finn and the girl and moved noisily but
quickly to places just below and in front of Kinsella.

He waited a moment while the closest thing to silence the
area had known in several hours began to descend.

"This is Father Kinsella," he began again. "God is grateful
for all those who prayed here sincerely today. Our Lady of
Notre Dame hears your prayers just as she knows your
hearts." He paused again. "None of you wants to harm
anyone else. I know that and you know it. You're all good
people. And now it's time for us to go home. Notre Dame
makes room for everyone, you all know that. But I want you
all to leave here now." He never mentioned the girl, the
cross, or the head football coach who was shielding her just
beyond the reporters in front of him. The crowd shifted and a
voice cried out, "Let us stay, let us stay." It was in the rhythm
of a chant, the kind of singsong phrase that Thomas knew
might catch on if he gave it half a chance. He raised his right
hand. He was at the point where he could win or lose it all and
he knew it. "God bless you all," he called out in a resonant
voice. "And now"—he paused just long enough to tighten his
grasp on their attention. Then, as he let his arm drop, he
called out, "We've got a football game to win today!"

As his arm chopped down through the air, a cymbal
crashed nearby and then the full sound of the Notre Dame
Band welled up as it struck the opening notes of the Victory
March. Kinsella had ordered the band director to assemble all
the musicians in their uniforms in the Sacred Heart Church.
While he had been speaking, they had been gathering under
the cover of the trees and bushes up behind the grotto. And
now, booming away, they were streaming down past the side
of the shrine playing the anthem that was sacred music to
every Notre Dame fan. On and on they went, the rhythms
infecting the crowd with a stirring sweetness, ranks and ranks
of them in blue and tartan uniforms, a tall drum major
leading them down along the side of the crowd toward the
road that arched around the back of the campus. People in
the crowd began to cheer and move in step with the music
that never failed to warm their hearts. Now it had distracted

them from the scene at the shrine; that was already beginning to seem to them like a dream, something that had not really occurred, as they fell behind the band, first in twos or threes, and then in great hurrying masses. The drum major was on the road heading away from the grotto, the band pounding away behind him, and clustering at their sides and in the rear, most of the crowd that just a few moments before had been noisily gathered beneath the statue of the Virgin in the shrine.

Some people remained, of course, but even the newsmen hurried away, taken up by the sudden dramatic appearance of the marching band. Kinsella smiled as he handed the bullhorn back to Simmons. He had won, he had won a gamble of power in that instant in which he dropped his arm and called forth the uniformed legions. He smiled at Jack Egan, who was pumping his hand and laughing. "I'd like to see Plan C some time."

"You may see it sooner than you think," Kinsella said as he vaulted over the fence near the place where the fallen cross was propped against the railing. Joe Sclafani and Timothy Duffy were leaning down toward the coach, who still had his arm around Mary Ann.

"Well, Matt," Thomas asked evenly. "Can you fill us in?"

6

October 22, 1983
9:00 A.M.

"Done like a true Kinsella!" P.B. said, chuckling aloud. He and Mae were back in their room watching the television coverage of the dismissal of the crowds at the grotto. "You know, Mae, there's more of me in him than I thought."

"Now, Patty, don't start taking too much credit. I've always told you there's a touch of the Fagan there too."

The coverage dissolved as the band and the marching pilgrims rounded the bend and there was a switch back to the newsroom for a wrap-up. "This has been a special presentation . . ."

"Pat, you're taking inordinate pleasure in what Father Tom did."

"By God, I'm going to have a cigar on it." P.B. stood up and went to the dresser where a box of Havanas lay unopened. He cracked the seal with his thumbnail, still chuckling to himself. His amusement made Mae wary of whatever plans he had in mind for the rest of the day.

"Patty, just what are you going to ask Tom to do? Or, should I ask, how are you going to ask him to do it?"

P.B. shook out the match with which he had just lighted a cigar.

"Mae, I wouldn't ask him to do anything but his duty, you know that." Then he removed the cigar and smiled again. "But, by God, you've got to admire his style. He can handle any job they want to give him."

"But you're not trying to involve him in any of your tricks, are you? I know you well, Patty. What you liked about the

458

band parading that crowd away was the trick aspect of it.
There's nothing you love more than a good trick."

"Hell, Mae, I'm afraid I've run out of tricks this time
around. But, if Tom takes the job in Chicago, well, we won't
need any tricks, will we?" P.B. tapped his cigar on a standing
ashtray. He tried to look serious but he could not hide his
shark's smile.

"Patty, I'd like to believe you, I really would." Mae sighed.
"And I've gone along with lots of your tricks over the years."
Her voice hardened. "But I'm not on your side if there's any
trick in this, not if you're going to hurt Tom, or use him, or
the Church. I can't do much about Martin and Joe. They're in
business and they wouldn't cross you no matter what . . ."

"I hope you're right," P.B. said, waving his cigar as he
spoke. "But, Mae, there's something you've got to face about
wonderful Thomas. What the hell, do you think he was
conceived without Original Sin? He's a big boy now; what is
he, forty-three? You don't get to be president of Notre Dame
because you were a good altar boy. Hell, Mae, watching Tom
just now I realized something, maybe for the first time. The
reason Tom and I have had our differences is because we're so
much alike. Hell, put a Roman collar on me and I'll run the
Archdiocese of Chicago as well as he could." P.B. laughed
again. It was his exuberance at Thomas's action that increased the level of Mae's distress. She knew when the inmost
core of P.B. Kinsella's soul had been ignited, she knew when
the glow spread all through him, and that when he couldn't
stop chuckling, he was on the verge of something big, that he
was close to getting things the way he wanted them.

"I'll admit, Mae," he said, walking across toward the
windows, "I love a little of the con. How do you think this
University got started?" He pointed in the direction of Father
Sorin's statue in the quadrangle north of the inn. "Father
Sorin was a master of it, with a straight face and an open
pocketbook. Hell, Rock was the greatest con artist I ever
knew. In the war, if you used the con, they called it
psychological warfare. Even the Pope knows how to use the
tricks of the trade, kissing the ground and hugging babies."
He drew on his cigar as he turned around to look at Mae,
whose face had grown more fixed and unrelieved. "And that's
what Tom used, a great con, a con that would have delighted
your Uncle Joe." P.B.'s eyes lighted up as he pointed his cigar

toward Mae. "Hell, Mae, that's where he gets it, from your mother's side of the family." He chuckled again and leaned down to kiss her on the cheek. But she pulled slightly back.

"Patrick," she said, looking up into her husband's eyes, using his full name as a sign of distance and gravity, "I'm glad you're having such a good time, seeing the U. S. Attorney's threatening to throw us all in jail. One thing I know about you, you're still not telling me everything. I've lived with you too long not to know that. I want you to know something, and it's something I never thought I'd say to you. I've been trying to reach Tom on the phone. And when I do, or when I see him, I'm going to warn him, God help me, I'm going to warn him to be careful about you, I'm going to warn him not to trust his own father."

P.B. pulled back but he did not seem too dismayed. Instead he smiled and winked at Mae. "He hasn't trusted me in years."

One of the state police cars had pulled up and Father Thomas had made the coach, the girl, and Monsignor Egan climb in. He turned to Father Simmons. "Make sure the grounds crew gets this place cleaned up right away. And have them get this cross out of here, get it locked up somewhere. Stay here and keep an eye on things. Okay?"

Simmons nodded and Thomas climbed into the front seat of the patrol car. "Drive us to the back of the infirmary building. Dr. Engel should be there by now."

Howard Engel was indeed waiting, when they arrived at the infirmary, scowling a little as Thomas greeted him.

"That brother is all right," Dr. Engel said. "Somebody's coming to pick him up from his community later today. I hope they bring a net."

"How about the others?"

"The student Weber is still out of it. I think we'll keep him in bed a day or so. Father Green is resting. I've got him sedated. And the guy Trask has a head like concrete. He wants to go to the game now that he's come to."

"Then he'll probably sue us," Thomas said unsmilingly. "Any other casualties?"

"I've asked them to bring in the student who tried to get her off the cross. Duffy is his name. I want to look him over."

Thomas nodded and let the doctor take the girl, who

looked dazed and unsteady, down the hall for an examination. Then he turned toward Matt Finn.

"We don't have much time, Matt. You've got a game to coach."

Kinsella, Egan, and the coach went into a small office on the ground floor of the building and closed the door. After they were seated, Finn rubbed his eyes and then looked silently for a moment at Father Thomas.

"You know, Father, I wanted to talk to you earlier today." Then he shifted his glance to Monsignor Egan. "And I tried to tell you why I was out on the golf course last night but you insisted that I get back to the seminary with no ifs, ands, or buts." Egan grunted and Thomas said nothing.

"This all goes back to Philip Ryan," Finn said, "and Fred Peters . . ."

Thomas felt a sudden tremor in his chest. Maybe it was because he had eaten no breakfast, he thought, but he felt that it was more likely caused by Fred Peters reaching out from the grave to squeeze his heart. Was Father Peters going to follow him all through his life, waiting on the far side of even the most innocent-looking experiences? Was there an invisible trail he was following without recognizing or understanding it, one that led him inevitably back to the tortured face of Fred Peters? Was Thomas, with all his successes and good fortune, the one who had chosen the way that turned out to be the path of vanity, leading to the narrow gate through which the rich ones of this world could not pass? And had Fred paid the price of entrance into the Kingdom through suffering and rejection, through a life, like his death, that supposedly wise people thought should be disguised or forgotten? Hadn't Fred known more about religion than the hundreds of people who so quickly turned away from the girl on the cross to follow the Notre Dame Marching Band? Was Fred going to laugh at him from the wings for the rest of his life while Thomas pursued the goals of power?

He shook his head free of these thoughts and found the coach looking at him expectantly, as though he had been waiting for Kinsella to snap out of his reverie.

"Excuse me, Matt, go ahead . . ."

"Well, you remember the place we found Fred the night Philip had been stabbed, that gay club where they were having the party? I have to admit that I'd been there before.

Not that I'm gay, don't get that idea. No way. But Father
Peters had become friendly with me. I liked him and I'd talk
to him about some of my problems, about troubles at home,
and how I used to get high maybe a little too much on the
banquet circuit. Things like that. Then one day he tells me his
problems. He came to my office and he looked pretty bad and
he said he'd been seeing a psychiatrist but he still wanted to
talk to somebody else."

Finn cleared his throat before he went on. "Hell, I'd had
people tell me they were gay before. Even here on campus,
even guys on the team, or they thought they might be because
they liked looking at other guys in the shower or something
like that. Growing pains, that's what most of them had. But
Father Peters was different. He wasn't a college student. And
he was suffering, I could see that. Well, I couldn't tell him
much but to keep seeing his doctor and that I'd do what I
could for him, seeing as he'd been such a help to me. And he
was a priest and all . . .

"Well, maybe a month passed and I got a call that he was
up in Chicago, that he and Philip Ryan were at some hotel.
And I said, Jesus, you're with Philip, I know his old man, he's
a good friend of mine. I didn't want to get into any mess
between them, because I didn't think he had Philip there just
to see the sights. Well, he tells me that Philip is sick, he's
passed out from some bad grass or something like that. I
didn't know what the hell it was. But I did go into the city to
the hotel. And I found Philip, no clothes on, out cold on a
couch, and the room a mess. But no Father Peters. So I
hauled Philip into the shower, ordered some black coffee,
and after a while, he began to come around. He tells me that
Father Peters has probably gone to a party, that he was
supposed to go too, but he got sick . . ."

The coach twisted a little in his chair and lowered his eyes
to look at his hands as he took up his narrative again. "I made
sure Phil was all right, told him I'd be back to get him and
take him home, and then I headed for this 'Green Necktie,'
where the party was, the same place the other one was. Well,
I felt a little funny. They let me in downstairs, some black guy
who gave me the eye, and up we went to this big room where I
couldn't see a hell of a lot at first. Those crazy strobe lights
were going and music and people in all kind of mix. I
remember some guy in gold lamé had an Irish Wolfhound on
a leash, and the leash was covered with lamé too. Well, I felt

uncomfortable, but fascinated too. All I wanted was to get hold of Peters and get everybody the hell back to South Bend. Well, damned if I don't find him sitting at a table way over in the corner. And he's holding hands with a girl, a beautiful girl in not much of a gown that was held together by a chain around her waist.

"It was Mary Ann but she had all this makeup on. She looked different, that's why I wasn't sure last night if it was her or not. Anyway, she was pretty strung out on drugs and Fred, of all things, was telling her he wants to help her and maybe she ought to get out of this life, and he'll do what he can for her. Well, he was good-hearted but it was the blind leading the blind, and I pulled up a chair and I'm trying to get him to leave. And Mary Ann started looking at me, and asking me who the hell I was, and . . ." Finn began to blush. "And would I like to be her master, and she liked discipline, and she liked big men like me . . ." His voice broke off again.

"I'll get some coffee," Monsignor Egan said. "There's a machine in the hall."

"Good idea," Thomas said, glad for the break in the troubled morning.

When they were all sipping from their Styrofoam cups, Finn began to speak in a more tense voice.

"Well, Fred kept talking to her, and I kept saying, 'We've got to go,' and she said, 'Wait,' that she's going to be part of the show. Well, I was pretty anxious, reminding Fred about Philip and how his old man wasn't going to like this if he heard about it, that I knew Maurice from way back and that he's liable to show up with the National Guard. In a few minutes people were pushing back from the floor to the sides of the room, and the rock music stopped and some somber music came on. Mary Ann slipped away from the table in the darkness and I grabbed Fred's hand and said, 'Let's get the hell out of here,' and we got up to go but a spotlight came on and we couldn't move because of the crowd. Then a group of guys dressed like slaves, with little laurel wreaths on their heads and nothing but gold-painted jockstraps on, they come out carrying Mary Ann on their shoulders and they put her down on a throne in the middle of the floor and everybody was applauding and hooting, all good fun at the freak house. Then a fat guy in a tuxedo that was all sequins came bouncing in, laughing a funny kind of laugh, and they were shouting at him and throwing flowers and things at him. And he loved it, it was all a show, a put-on. But he got the floor finally and, like an MC on a game show, he gave this talk about the award they were giving, that it was on behalf of 'Whip and Lash' publications, and it was for Miss Pain and Passion of the year, and here she was, ladies and gentlemen, in person, the one and only Mary Ann. Then some greased-up muscleman came out wearing a Tarzan costume, except he was carrying a whip in one hand and a crown of thorns in the other. And everybody was still hooting and applauding and he stuck the crown on her head and gave her a crack of the whip at the same time. And I was pulling Fred along the wall and all the while he was telling me, 'This is no joke, she's hooked on bondage,' and that he wanted to help her, he was the only one she talked to, but she was into drugs too. Well, this big muscleman was proclaiming he was her master and she was the Queen of his dungeon, and, by God, there was some real blood trickling down her forehead, and she started to slip out of her clothes, and I said to Fred, 'That's it, we're getting the hell out of here!' . . ."

Finn went on with his story of getting Father Peters and Phil Ryan home and of how nervous he was because he felt he should help Philip and he didn't know whether to tell Maurice Ryan or not.

"Well, Fred would slip in and see the girl once in a while when he was in Chicago. He thought he could help her but she was deep into this crazy life, with periods when she would half pull out of it. She was at the Green Necktie the night Philip was cut, and she was at the police station too. You saw her probably. She wanted to help Fred, she hung around to see what she could do. She gave him her cigarette when he needed one . . ."

A picture of the precinct station came back to Father Thomas, along with all the sights and smells of that nightmare Saturday evening. He vaguely remembered the girl, he could see her in his imagination, she had tried to be tender to Fred in his moment of disgrace. Kinsella suddenly felt as though he might cry for all the sadness in the tale that Finn had told. He clenched his fists and closed his eyes.

"When Fred was killed she tried to kill herself. That's what she told me when she was coming out of it just now. But she'd been into drugs for years, and she's had a kid and put it up for adoption, and she's been into every scene. She's no co-ed, you know. She's twenty-nine. I don't know how the hell she ended up here or whether she walked into classes without anybody noticing, or how the hell she rigged this whole thing up. But it was her demonstration for Fred, her memorial service. She was so stoned out, though, she didn't know what she was doing. When I heard about it over at Moreau last night, it hit me that it might be her. So I slipped out. But some of the team saw me go and they were in a playful mood, they wanted a look too, and they followed me. Honest to God, I didn't know they were there until I started to walk through the crowd to try to get a better look at her. Then I didn't know what to do. I was pretty sure who it was but I had the whole damned team over on the golf course. So I let them all kneel down so we could get out of there in an orderly manner. Then"—and he turned to Monsignor Egan, who had stopped taking notes some moments before—"Monsignor here arrived with word from you to get back to Moreau and no mistake about it. I tried to talk to him but after he sent us off I thought the whole thing would break up. Well, I couldn't sleep and I went walking and I followed some students who were hustling out toward the highway. And I decided to try again. But she was out of it, high as a kite . . ."

Thomas let the coach finish his story, thanked him, and told him to get back to the team. He would see him later.

"Jack," he said to Monsignor Egan, "I'm not sure I'll get to the president's lunch on time. Be sure to be there and get somebody to greet everybody for me. I've got to get back to my office for a while."

He felt Fred's ghost again as he left the building and he could not help but wonder how often he would reappear in his life. Poor Fred, he thought, and poor Mary Ann. And poor Father Green. There was a crack across the universe all right and it wasn't so much sin as it was the brokenness of everything. And maybe only those who understood that could be saved. He wondered if Archbishop Trafficante with his smooth talk of "the Holy Father's wishes" and "the Church's call to you" ever thought about such things. And he thought about Cardinal Williams and, most unexpected of sentiments, he felt sorry for him and his problems and, in a strange way, he wished him well.

He thought also of Maria, who must certainly be waiting in his office by now. Maybe she was right, maybe it was time to leave the enterprise to the crazies and to make something at last of life together. Then he thought of his father, old P.B., still cunning in his seventies, and ready to make a good deal to save himself even if some of his sons went under.

Poor Maria. Poor Fred. Poor Cardinal Williams. Poor me.

7
October 22, 1983
10:00 A.M.

The campus was streaming with fans and students on their way to the stadium and Thomas walked slowly, letting the warmth of the October morning heal his spirit. Banners made from bed sheets flapped from dormitory windows, the legend "God Made Us Number One" folding in on itself and then billowing out again in the light breeze. People passed him, greeting him enthusiastically as they hurried along with their Notre Dame pennants and hats and the seat cushions that offered the slightest protection from the hard wooden benches of the football amphitheater. Father Kinsella was preoccupied with his own thoughts and, although he nodded and smiled, the greetings barely registered on him. He was thinking of Maria and of his father when the man in the cowboy hat caught up with him.

"Why, Father Kinsella, don't you recognize an old friend?" This in a drawl in which the honey just barely overpowered the gall. It was Cal McConnery, a wealthy lawyer from the Southwest who had been a generous benefactor, but an all-American bore. He was just the kind of man Thomas did not wish to see at the moment.

"Why, Father, I've got the limousine over by the stadium, got a little bar in the back, and I've got the nicest couple from down home. I told them you'd be glad to come over and have a little bitty drink with us, and a little chat before the game.

What do you say?" He reached his arm around Thomas's shoulder but Kinsella pulled away, smiling as graciously as he could.

"Well, thanks, Cal. But I've had a busy day . . ."

Cal interrupted in tones inflated by condescension.

"Why, I understand you had a little filly tied on a cross. Gosh sake, Father, that's all over now. Come on along, I promised these people."

"No," Kinsella said firmly, "I'd try to do it any other time but it's impossible just now. I'm not even going to get to my own luncheon."

Cal looked crestfallen. "Well, I'm mighty disappointed, that's all I can say, mighty disappointed. But I'll keep an eye out for you . . ." He winked in a leering sort of way, clapped Thomas on the shoulder once more, and started to walk away. "You'all could still come by if you have a chance. You'all could do it for the people who support you."

Thomas just turned and kept walking. The burden of people like McConnery who thought they had bought you because they had contributed to the fund drive was one of the heaviest a University president had to bear. He wished he could summon the band to drum McConnery into his limousine and off the campus. How many people he had smiled at falsely because of their donations to the work of the University! Oh well, he thought, all for the cause. But what about the cause, he asked himself as he climbed the stairs to his office, what exactly was the cause these days and where was his heart?

I, of course, had been sitting with Maria. We had turned on the little television set in the corner of the president's office to watch the clearing of the grotto and Maria, rooting for Thomas all through it, seemed relieved as the crazy parade went trailing out of camera sight. Thomas did not even greet me as he came through the door. He went directly over to Maria as she rose eagerly from her chair. You would have thought he had just come home from the war, which, in a sense, he had.

They embraced and held each other without speaking. Then Thomas, keeping one arm around her shoulder, turned to me.

"Austin, thank you for being so gallant to Maria."

"Nothing, Father Thomas, nothing to it. We were glad to see you get the loonies moving."

"Any messages?"

I held up a sheaf of them. "I referred most everybody to Dick Cummings, except, of course, your mother, who's called a couple of times. She asked me to tell you she was on your side . . ."

"Against Southern California?" Thomas asked, disarming me with a smile. "That's a mother's love for you."

"And your father called."

"Yes?"

"And he said, seeing you were missing your own luncheon, could he count on you to be in your box for the game?"

"You reassured him, I trust?" Thomas said as he sifted through the messages. "I'm sure Dick has taken care of most of these." He dropped them back on the desk.

"Austin, would you see if you can get catering to serve some sandwiches here for Maria and me?"

I nodded, waiting a bit for an invitation to join them. But it was not offered and, with as much dignity as I could summon in order to cover my curiosity, I withdrew to order them lunch.

"Oh, Tom," Maria said without raising her head from Father Kinsella's chest, "I'm so sorry about Jack Allen."

"Yes," Thomas said as he brushed his jaw against her hair. "Jack was a great man. It didn't seem quite right that he didn't have more time . . ."

"Did he die peacefully?"

"Yes, but I think he died of other people's troubles." Thomas raised his head as Maria looked up into his eyes. "Jack Allen died for our sins."

"What do you mean?" Maria asked, still holding close to him like a person seeking shelter against the cold.

"You can only carry so many burdens, listen to so many sad stories. I don't know, I've been tempted to think that the girl on the cross and the reaction to her—the way people, in the name of religion, flocked to her—capped it for him." Thomas shook his head as he and Maria drew apart. He took her by the hand and they moved toward a couch on the book-lined side of the room.

"Jack never could abide phoniness or fakery. He felt—and he said out loud—that what we had last night was reciprocal sexual hysteria wearing the raiment of faith. Break the dam a little and everything that's been pent up comes rushing out."

They sat down side by side. "It was a crazy night. They came out of the trees, out of our own woodwork . . ."

"Poor Tom, you sound surprised that it could have happened."

"I am. We've never had things like that here. We didn't even have a plan. And the more I expected others to handle it, the worse the infection became. And, Maria"—he wrinkled his forehead as he turned to look full face at her—"I seem to be pursued by Fred Peters. His ghost shows up all the time. That's why this girl was here. Poor thing, she was putting on some religious memorial for him. She knew him when he used to visit those bizarre places in Chicago. She had some attachment to him, some crazy need to mourn him and his screwed-up life in her own screwed-up way. She was Queen of the Whips or something like that . . ."

"Maybe, in her own way, she loved him . . ."

"Maybe . . ." Thomas was silent for a few moments, his face as grave as a surgeon's who has just discovered something he can't operate on. "But it's haunting. That whole business with Fred, the poor bastard. And all the other hardship and suffering—and craziness too—that we've covered up, or never really examined. That's what this is all connected with. And everywhere I look I seem to see Fred, not taunting me, but just standing there with that stricken look in his eyes, as though he were saying, 'If you understand what I suffered, and what Philip Ryan went through, if you remember that Mary Ann is human too, you'll do something about it.'"

"Tom, you can't take all this on yourself. Not today anyway."

"No, no, there are other things to settle." He sighed and patted her hand.

"You mean this business about becoming an Archbishop?"

"That, yes. And seeing my father. It's all related."

"Tom, what are you going to do about this? I mean, are you going to accept, are you going to get farther away from me by going to Chicago?"

Thomas rose and walked to the window. He said nothing as he gazed out toward the campus and the crowds that were passing toward the stadium beneath the banked fire of the autumn leaves. Then he turned and looked again at Maria. He was conscious of the clock's ticking on his desk.

"I don't know, I don't know what I'm going to do."

"What did you tell the man from the Vatican, Archbishop whatever his name is?"

"Trafficante. I didn't get to tell him anything. He had just laid out all the details for me. We only talked about the preliminaries, the ground rules about how concerned they are to show proper respect to Cardinal Williams, do it right, and so forth. Then Monsignor Egan came knocking to tell me all hell had broken loose in the grotto."

The telephone rang and Thomas picked it up, listened a moment, murmured a thank-you, and then hung up.

"That was Dr. Engel. He's arranged to hospitalize the girl. Everybody else is okay, or will be. I think we'll have to have Greenie take a long rest, however." Thomas sat down in his desk chair.

"Maria, I don't know what I'm going to do, I honestly don't."

"What has your father got to do with this?"

"Why do you think he's got something to do with it?"

"I know you very well, Thomas. You always get a certain look when your father's on your mind. And you said it was all connected."

"You're right. That's one of the things that bothers me. P.B. wants me to become Archbishop of Chicago, among other reasons, because then the U. S. Attorney won't dare investigate him or Kinsella Industries. Crazy, it gets crazier all the time, doesn't it?"

"Would that really protect him, I mean, would it have that much effect?"

"I don't know. It would delay things, at least, give the old man time to scramble, try an onside kick or something like that. But how can I accept the offer when I know part of what I'm doing is political for my own family?"

"That's not all it means to you, is it?"

"No, of course not. And it would give me a chance to do a lot of good, I know that. It's just that, well, there's a little more to it." Thomas went on to describe his brother Joe's conversation with him a few hours before. "So my father may already have set a deal up. And, if I don't say yes, I'll be letting my brothers run the chance of going to jail. And the troubles for my mother." He shook his head again. "It's a hell of a position to be in."

"Tom, do you want to be the Archbishop of Chicago?

Suppose none of these other things were true. What would you want?"

"I can't imagine they're not true. I'm a priest, a University president. But I'm a Kinsella too."

"How well I know . . ." They lapsed into a momentary silence as Thomas absently sorted through the messages on his desk again. The phone rang and Father Thomas made short work of the call.

"That was Shaughnessy, the undertaker. I've promised to put the vestments on Jack later . . ."

Maria watched Father Thomas for a moment and then spoke in a voice that was a shade more serious than it had been.

"Tom, this may not be the best time. There's no good time. But we have to talk about us."

That's all I need, Thomas thought to himself, because he half dreaded and half welcomed the chance to talk more personally with Maria. But he did not know exactly what to say.

"You're a Kinsella all right. It's good I've had a life and a career of my own. I've often thought that, even if we were married, I might not see you much more than I do now. Being a Kinsella is a full-time job."

"It has its moments," he said. Then he stopped short of being humorous as he felt that Maria's glance ruled out small talk and the distractions he had a talent for raising.

"Tom, I know you've got a lot on your mind. But we have to talk. This is all connected too."

He turned his chair more fully toward her as thoughts about his father and the Cardinal's job were pressed to the edges of his consciousness. His office seemed to grow smaller until everything—books, drapes, windows—all dropped away and he and Maria saw only each other's faces.

"Tom, all this talk about the strange things that came out under the full moon, and all this about your father's being ready to let Martin and Joe take the penalty, if there is one, for him; doesn't it make you think that maybe the price for being a Kinsella is a little high?"

Thomas raised his eyebrows and gave a slight shrug of his shoulders. "It's high enough."

"Tom, I've got to talk to you about the way I feel."

"Yes."

"I'm not asking you for any big decisions, and I'm not

trying to take you away from the Church or the priesthood. You know that. And I'm not trying to tell you what to decide today. But you can't decide any of this without knowing something about what I feel too."

"Yes," Thomas said softly, "I know . . ."

"I'm not sure I can go on, for my sake or for yours, loving you from afar, never really able to have you, always just in the background, just a good friend. I've tried, and I know you've tried, but I can't live just on dreams that someday, somehow we might be able to have a life together. Maybe I'm getting older, maybe I'm losing courage, or faith." She paused a moment. "Maybe *I* need *you* now."

"Maria, I need some time . . ."

"Tom, you'll never have enough time. Do you, can you understand how I feel?"

Thomas was not completely sure how Maria felt but he did experience the weight of expectation which she suddenly pressed against him. He could not blame her but he recognized deep down in himself his own uneasiness at ever being pinned down. Never being pinned down, Father Kinsella knew, was one of the supreme advantages of the clerical life-style. Nobody was ever quite sure whether you were going to show up at the wedding or the party; a cleric could come and go as he pleased, and always claim that he had to leave early in order to say his prayers. Not being pinned down suited Thomas well; it left him as the master of his daily fate. He did not know what to say but he could feel Maria's question in his heart. She was not asking him to tear off his collar and flee the campus that afternoon. No, it was something deeper than that. She wanted to know where and whether, aside from Church rules and regulations, she fit into his life. She wanted to know what he really felt about her.

"Thomas," she asked almost plaintively, "don't you ever desire me?"

He flushed and gritted his teeth slightly.

"I can't have you," he said softly. "We've been through that . . ."

"That's not the point. I don't even feel that you'd take me if you could. Not any more. You don't make me feel like you do want me. I have to know that you really want me, that you still ache for me sometimes just as much as I do for you."

After a long morning, Thomas had not expected this. He

had wanted comfort and he was getting confrontation instead and he couldn't call the band to sweep it away for him.

"Tom, I feel like I'm in some kind of niche in your life. That's what I can't handle anymore. If we love each other, even if we have to keep making sacrifices, I have to know that you still want me, that you love me for myself, that we're not angels and don't have to try to be all the time." Tears welled up in her eyes. "Can't you understand how I feel? Sometimes you don't even seem to understand what bothers me."

"Maria, I do love you. And I have wanted you, believe me, I have. It hasn't been easy for me either. Especially after Rome, especially after that. And the other times too. It isn't easy for me right this minute."

"Tom, I just haven't felt that you have really loved me for myself for a long time. And I don't feel it this minute either. You've been so busy, especially since Rome, that's what you mean. Especially since we've made love. But you've pulled away in the last year or so. I've always been put to one side. Something else has been on your mind, I can feel it. The hard part is always standing by, always being on the outside of what you're really doing. Just as I have been today, just as I have to be when the Church asks if you want to be an Archbishop and a Cardinal. What woman could possibly compete with that?"

Thomas said nothing as Maria took out a handkerchief. She was forcing him to look at things he did not like to examine. What did he believe in and why did he remain celibate, and did he really love her enough to ask himself these questions? "Can't you understand that to love you and not have you is at the center of my life? And I can't do that, even with God's help, unless I feel you're on the other side of this, loving me just as much?" Thomas lowered his eyes. "Oh, Thomas, Thomas, you're funny. You're a Kinsella and you don't know what that does to you. And at the same time then you're an idealist. And you think everybody else can be too. No wonder Fred Peters haunts you. Maybe he was too honest about himself, but that's all he had. Oh, dear Tom, you're like a knight, filled with chivalry. The ideal of chivalry was to love but not to touch. Do you think human love can last like that?"

"No, I suppose not but I do love you. I love you the way any man loves a woman. Don't you think I've been tortured by the fact that we can't live as man and wife? Do you think it's been easy for me?"

"Honestly, Tom, much as I love you, I've sometimes wondered!"

Thomas rose from his chair and walked over to sit beside her again. He put his arm around Maria's shoulder.

"Tom, I don't want to ruin your life, or take you away from the Church." She began to sob and buried her head in his chest again. He sat silently, trying to express his effort to understand by holding her gently.

"Notre Dame is the other woman in your life, Tom, I know that. She always will be." Maria straightened up and Thomas took a crisp handkerchief from his pocket and dabbed at her eyes.

"The real problem is power. You know that don't you, Tom?"

"I don't know what my real problem is," he said quietly.

"It's power, Tom, that's why you're in such conflict about becoming a bishop. I can tell when power begins to pull at you." She paused again, weighing her words carefully. "It's when you pull away from me, when I feel you love me but don't want me, when you want something else more.

"It's power, Tom, that's your mistress."

Thomas felt his heart beating faster. She had struck him from an unexpected angle. He had rehearsed his religious arguments many times; he had, in fact, recited them often, given sermons about them, spoken them to Maria, and he thought he had prayed about them. He pictured himself as a dedicated servant of God who accepted celibacy as a condition of his priesthood. He believed it too. And now Maria had not questioned that and had not allowed him to speak his arguments; she had sidestepped them and focused on the very motive he looked away from. He was shaken as only men with an instinctive feel for power are when someone faces them with the unacknowledged truth about themselves. He loved the power the presidency gave him, not only at Notre Dame but also because of the doors it opened—at the White House, the foundations, everywhere . . .

"You're a Kinsella, Tom. You know how to use power. That's why you could use it so easily at the grotto, that's why you're not shy with Archbishops from the Vatican and why you're not surprised when you're offered the chance to be an Archbishop. That's why Fred Peters haunts you. He was powerless in every way that you're powerful. That's why you were never shy with me. But I can tell—maybe only I can do it—when power is what you're hungry for. Because that's when you're not hungry for me. It's what leaves me feeling cold and on the outside of your life. It makes me feel that you desire it more than you desire me. And maybe you love it more than you love me."

"Maria," Thomas said, "I've never thought of myself as a powerful man, I've never looked on myself that way."

"Oh, Tom, it's all right. You don't have to explain. It's just that I get all filled up and I have to tell you what I feel. And if you don't understand, who ever would? I have to face the facts. I love you. And I know you love me. But I'll never have you and I have to accept that. But I have to face the facts. I can't live unless I do. And you have to face them too."

Thomas did not know what to say. There was, in fact, nothing to say but plenty to think about. It was about this time that I barged in with a man from the catering service and a luncheon tray for Thomas and Maria. And a bite for me. The atmosphere was intense as we made our purposely noisy entrance, and I could tell that Maria had been crying. Father Thomas waved me into a chair, anxious, I thought, to lessen whatever had built up the pressure. Then it was mostly small talk while we munched on roast beef sandwiches and sipped black coffee. But finally Maria put down her cup and looked, a great and tender look it was, at Thomas, and said sweetly, "Thomas, the trouble with you is that you've always thought you were completely different from your father." She smiled, the way a person does sometimes even in the middle of sadness. "But, Tom, your mother was right. What there is of Fagan in you is only a touch."

The president, of course, was conspicuously absent from the luncheon which was held on the lower level of the Center for Continuing Education just across from the entrance of the Morris Inn. Only those with invitations were checked down the stairs of the inn and through the tunnel, hung with pictures from Notre Dame's past, to the area where the meal was served. Monsignor Egan shepherded Archbishop Trafficante around while a squad of vice-presidents greeted distinguished guests and alumni. The Kinsellas had a table near the wall, and P.B. waved greetings to dozens of prosperous Chicago Irish, beefy and pink-cheeked, who were also guests for the pre-game meal. It was one of the old traditions of University life in the fall and, outwardly at least, P.B. seemed to be enjoying it immensely.

"Patty," Mae whispered to him, "you're waving your hand like a policeman. Are you running for election?"

"Anybody could be a juror, Mae," P.B. said out of the side of his mouth. "I'm not taking any chances."

"Don't make jokes about serious things, Patty. I can see you're upset. You haven't eaten a thing. It will be a long time before we get to the lake for dinner."

P.B. picked up half a roast beef sandwich, took a bite, and spoke as he chewed.

"Mae, this is an important day, very important." He swallowed. "I wish to hell your favorite son was here. Where the hell is he anyway?"

"I'm sure he's busy. You've put enough on his mind. I don't blame him."

Patrick took another bite. "What do you make of that ginney Archbishop Monsignor Egan's taking care of? He's probably looking for pasta. What do you think, Mae, can you tell anything from his face? Does he look happy to you?"

"Happier than you do, I'd say that. Why don't you ask him if you're going to be the proud father of the next Archbishop of Chicago? And then ask him if he'd like to have you build something over at the Vatican . . ."

"Mae, Mae," P.B. frowned. "That's not helping things at all." He placed the remains of his sandwich on his plate. "Someday, Mae, you'll thank me for what I'm going to do this afternoon. Someday you'll understand. You have to trust me that I know what's the best for all of us."

"Patty," Mae said edgily, "I've known you too long not to trust you. But I know you better than you know yourself. You like playing the game more than anything else. Sometimes I think you love it more than you love me . . ."

Maria had only eaten a few bites of her sandwich and Father Thomas only about half of his. I, on the other hand, ate heartily, hungry as I was from my night's exertions. And I was alert, too, at the quiet and melancholy mood that had descended on two people I always remembered as laughing in each other's presence.

"Maria," Thomas said as he dropped his napkin back on the tray, "I want to thank you for being so truthful. A man doesn't think about things the way a woman does . . ."

Maria patted her lips with her napkin and held it aloft as she said gently, "Tom, I haven't wanted to hurt you, you know that . . ."

"Yes, I know, I know that."

"And I love you more than anything in this world. You know that too, don't you?"

"Yes," Father Thomas said rather flatly. He was quite preoccupied, drawn back slightly into himself the way he always got in thoughtful moments.

"Maria, I'm going to find out how much I'm like my father this afternoon. Pray that what I'm going to do will be the right thing."

"You know I'll do that."

"And trust me. I have to ask you to trust me, to believe that what I decide will be the best for all of us, for you and me, for the Kinsella family." He looked directly into Maria's eyes. "Whatever I do, Maria, I have to ask you for some more time. I have to ask you to wait while I work things out the best I can."

Maria smiled. "I trust you, Tom, especially when I feel that you're not just playing a game."

"No, no games this afternoon." Then he got up and that wonderful smile rose like a sunrise on his face. "Except with Southern California."

Maria laughed and stood up next to him. The sadness seemed to end like a somber passage in a violin concerto. Lightness and peace, hard-won but peace nonetheless, settled into the room. Still, I was damned if I knew what Father Thomas was going to do.

"Austin, will you go with Maria to the game? Her car has the stickers to park by the stadium." He reached in his desk drawer. "Here are the tickets. You know my box, the whole clan will be there, or nearby . . ."

"My pleasure," I said, taking the tickets and extending my arm to Maria.

Maria moved closer to Thomas. She kissed him gently.

"Tom, whatever you do this afternoon, you'll never love more than you are loved." Then she took my arm and we went out of the office and down the stairs. At my last glimpse of Father Thomas he was picking up his phone and dialing a number.

A telephone rang in the corner of the room where the luncheon was being served. One of the priests took the message, scribbling something on a small pad. He edged through the crowded room that was filled with talk and laughter and the clatter of eating toward Monsignor Egan.

"The switchboard has a message from the president. Father Kinsella would like you to bring the Archbishop to the Morris Inn. He wants to talk to him there right away."

Monsignor Egan nodded and leaned toward the Archbishop, who had been talking to a handsome Irish-looking lady about how wonderful it was that she had ten children.

"Archbishop," Monsignor Egan said, "Father Kinsella has an answer for you . . ."

The young priest continued past Egan's table to the side of the hall. Joe Kinsella, who had been late in arriving for the luncheon, met him a table's distance away from P.B. himself.

"Mr. Kinsella," the priest said to Joe, "there's a call for your father. From Chicago. The switchboard operator said they claimed it was important enough to disturb him."

Joe blanched, blinked slightly, and then regained his composure. "What's the number? Who called?"

"Here's the number," the priest said, handing Joe a slip of paper. Fifteen feet away, P.B. watched the exchange as carefully as he once observed Uncle Joe shuffle cards.

"There was a message from a Mr. Murphy," the priest added as Joe began to turn away. He reversed himself swiftly.

"Murphy? What Mr. Murphy?"

"A Mr. Finbar Murphy. I think he said from the U. S. Attorney's office."

"Yes, yes?" Joe asked, the note beginning to tremble in his hand.

"Something about 'Please call right away,' something like that. They want your father to call back as soon as he can."

Joe felt dazed as he turned to bring the message to P.B. A giant hand seemed to squeeze his body. Was it all over, he wondered, was it all over but the sentencing?

8

October 22, 1983
1:00 P.M.

It was shortly after one o'clock when Maria's driver opened the door of her limousine for us in the parking lot next to the stadium. It was crowded with cars and people, a festive air rising off the crowds that hurried along under the blue October sky, everyone moving toward the brick structure which Rockne had coaxed the University into building so many years before, family groups loaded down with blankets and Notre Dame caps, students dressed like they had just dropped their shovels at the mining site a few moments before, couples of all ages, some of whom had gotten their season tickets through inheritance, and visitors of all kinds. The big television bus was back in its proper place by the playing field wall, with cables trailing up over the rim that was studded with pennants of Notre Dame opponents snapping in the breeze.

Maria put on dark glasses and I took her arm as gallantly as I could. A short fellow dressed as a leprechaun, in green velvet suit and an Irish hat, skipped past us. He was waving a shillelagh with a miniature Irish flag attached to its top. We turned at the sound of band music to see the phalanx of the Notre Dame Marching Band pouring across the lawn on the edge of the parking lot, the drum major strutting like he was heading for the Last Judgment, which, in a way, was the rough equivalent of a Saturday football game at Notre Dame.

It was a true devotion these groups were gathering for, a dip in the green river of their religious and cultural identity, a renewal of the American Irish Catholic spirit that Notre

Dame had come to symbolize every fall. A grand ritual, I
thought to myself, grander than many a Mass I'd been to, as
we made our way along past the stands, where, incongruously
enough, students were selling Polish hot dogs to people
wearing Irish tams and shawls, and past the hawkers of
buttons and pins and glossy programs. And past the hopeful-
looking people, men mostly, holding up placards scrawled
with desperate little pleas: "Need One Ticket," or two, or
whatever.

We went under an arch in the stadium wall into the musty
shadows of the stands themselves. One of the ticket takers, a
brash fellow in a red coat, shouted, "That's Maria Moore
with the old man!" I rapped his knuckles with my cane and
said, "It's none of your business surely," as though I might
have been her aged lover, and we plunged into the throng
pressing up the cement ramp that led to the center section of
the stadium itself.

Half a mile back Father Thomas was just quick-stepping it
down the quadrangle in front of the administration building.
The fresh air felt good as he strode along, acknowledging the
greetings of the crowd hurrying past him, only slightly more
aware of them than he had been earlier. He thought again of
Fred Peters as he moved toward the Morris Inn and his
meeting with the Archbishop. Would he never be free of his
image in his mind, would he be obsessed by his spirit
somehow until he had settled all the business of the day?

"Father! Father Kinsella!" The voice was unmistakable.
Cal McConnery had been lying in wait for him on a bench
under a tree at the side of the path.

"Why, Father, I jus' knew you'all'd find the time to come
along with me. Got these folks in the car and, if my watch is
right, and at twenty-five hundred dollars it ought to be right,
we jus' have time for a quick one before kickoff."

"I'm sorry, Cal," Father Kinsella said with as much good
humor as he could muster, "I'm probably going to be late for
the game as it is."

The lawyer stepped directly in front of Father Kinsella.
"Come on now, padre, I promised these people you'all'd
come by. How am I gonna look if you don't show up?"

"Plead *nolo contendere*," Thomas said, moving around the
lawyer in the ten-gallon hat. McConnery grabbed his arm and
Father Thomas felt a storm blowing up in his Irish soul.

"Ain't no time for lawyer jokes, padre. I mean these people have oil, I mean they could be a big help to you, if you get what I mean."

Thomas grabbed McConnery's hand firmly and pulled it away from his arm.

"Some other time, Cal, I simply can't do it now."

McConnery's face clouded. He was not accustomed to having his requests turned down. "Now listen, Father Kinsella," he said, pushing his cowboy hat back on his head, "just who the goddamned hell do you think you're talking to? I gave you a hundred thousand dollars in the last few years. Now, I expect to have some interest paid on it."

Thomas stopped and looked coldly into McConnery's eyes.

"Mr. McConnery," he began deliberately, "if you're here after the game, come to my office. I'll write you a check for every cent you've given us. Then we'll be even. Good afternoon." Then he turned and marched away, leaving the cowboy lawyer open-mouthed and reddening with anger.

By God, Thomas thought to himself, Maria is right. I'm a lot like my father after all.

"No, Joe," P.B. said in a voice that settled it, "I'll take care of this myself. You stay here with your mother." He leaned across the table. "Martin, you stay here too." He stood up, walked around and kissed his daughters-in-law, circling back behind Mae's chair. He bent down and whispered in her ear.

"Mae darlin', this is the big game. And I don't mean Southern California."

Mae was alarmed and looked up into her husband's lined but handsome face. "Now, Patty," she whispered back, "I expect you to take care of all of us, whatever you're up to. I trust you but I don't want my sons hurt."

P.B. gripped her uplifted hand. "Trust me, Mae." Then he kissed her lightly on the cheek and moved off.

Joe looked nervous and Martin looked puzzled.

"Is Tom ready to take the job?" Martin asked his brother.

"I'm afraid this is about another matter," Joe said, staring glumly down at his plate.

P.B. glanced at his watch as he walked swiftly through the tunnel and back to the Morris Inn. He was playing his last cards in a long game, he mused to himself, but, what the hell, it had been fun most of the way. He glanced up at the walls and Jack Moran's face, prompted by a look-alike in a photo, popped into his mind. Old Jack coughing himself to death at fifty, old Jack, with whom he had helped bail out the Cardinal almost forty years before. Jack had been in his imagination all week, sitting in a dark corner, as he had sat, all breaking down inside, at the Edgewater Beach Hotel a quarter of a century before. And he thought of the money, the fortune that had been a mainstay and a dead weight at the same time, the money that came from nowhere and disappeared, in a good cause, through some Providential disposition. He hoped that Providence had a long memory and played sentimental favorites, like Notre Dame and P. B. Kinsella. Then he saw Rockne's picture and a thousand images spread out like a fan to his inner eye. Rock in the wheelchair at the Pittsburgh game and Rock before his last game, pulling every trick he knew to outwit Southern California. P.B. smiled his old shark smile as he stepped into the elevator on the lower level of the Morris Inn. The doors closed and he thought of Sam Insull and smiled again as he recalled his successful lovemaking with Mae that very morning.

The door opened on the lobby level and in stepped his son Thomas and Archbishop Trafficante. Everyone seemed startled but, after brief introductions, they settled into silence. The door opened on the second floor and Father Thomas and the Archbishop stepped out of the car.

"Can I send a play in from the bench?" P.B. asked, flashing his smile again.

Thomas smiled back. "I think I know what you'd suggest anyway."

P.B. could see the perplexed look on the Archbishop's face as the elevator doors closed once more. He got off on the third floor and began to hum the Notre Dame Victory March as he headed toward his room.

We were soon seated in the president's box, not that it was as elegant as it sounded, for the folding chairs were hard and narrow. The stadium was a bowl of subtle steepness that swept up from the field to the pennanted ridge at the top, and almost every seat was filled already. Great white clouds drifted overhead, their shadows moving across the field to chill us with a reminder that we were deep into the fall. Out on the real grass field the Notre Dame team had been working out and a smattering of applause followed them as they left for the locker room at twenty past one. I pointed out the various sights to Maria, not that there were so many, but she seemed to enjoy my explanations, as though it helped to fill in the time while we waited for Father Thomas to return and tell us of his decision.

The Kinsellas, minus P.B., arrived just as a mellow-toned voice came over the loudspeaker system. "The University of Notre Dame proudly presents its marching band, the oldest in the country, now in its one hundred and thirty-eighth year . . ." We greeted Mae and the others who joined us in our box and the one next to us. Two chairs were left vacant in the front row, one for P.B. and one for Father Thomas. Our comments, most of them pass-the-time-of-day comments anyway, were lost as the members of the band, their tartan sashes swinging smartly from their shoulders, spread across the field, pumping away at an entrance march while they split and divided and shifted as precisely as a chorus line. The fans loved it, especially as the little fellow dressed as a leprechaun went darting out to wave his tiny flag at the multitude. The band wheeled down and across a fifty-yard section of the middle of the field. The leader raised his baton and the first notes of "America" came smoothly out of the woodwinds and the brass. The music softened and the voice on the loud-speaker cut in to read the prologue to the Declaration of Independence. We were in the midst of a great solemn crowd and the two empty seats began to pulse in my imagination, as though they were sending out signals about their absent occupants. Were they signals of distress or what? The band stopped and in the brief pause, Maria asked me, "I wonder where they are."

The mellifluous voice spoke once more on the loudspeaker. "We ask you to join in singing 'America the Beautiful.'" They weren't skipping anything today, I thought to myself, and the music flowed like honey over the contented crowd. "Ladies and gentlemen," the deep voice sounded, "our National Anthem!" With that, of course, we were all on our feet. I helped Maria up and thought she was very tense as we began to sing "The Star-Spangled Banner." It sounded good rising from almost sixty thousand throats. Then we rose swiftly to our feet again as the herald on the loudspeaker announced the Notre Dame Victory March. Well, the crowd exploded as usual as the familiar strains filled the air and the band marched proudly off the field. It would have been a

great moment for the arrival of Father Thomas or P.B. but I
saw no sign of either of them. The announcer began to
introduce the Southern California players.

"You'll notice, Maria," I said as sagaciously as I could,
"there are more Irish on the opposing team than there are on
ours."

At the north end of the field the cheerleaders, a co-ed
crowd for many years by then, held hands just in front of the
entranceway to the tunnel that led to the Notre Dame locker
room. The referees and the team captains were already in the
middle of the field, making the coin toss and selecting the goal
that would be defended by the winner. It all had to do with
the wind and I never got it quite straight. The empty seats
were beginning to look like eyesores to me and I said a prayer
that P.B. and Thomas were not having a hand-wrestle under
the stands. A plane flew just west of the stadium trailing a
sign: "Go Irish, Go Aer Lingus."

The leprechaun charged onto the field and hundreds of
Notre Dame students, whooping and yelling, swept down out
of the stands and began to string themselves out on either side
of the tunnel entrance. Then the announcer's voice sounded
again, "The Fighting Irish of Notre Dame," the band struck
up, and a sad man it would be whose pulse didn't quicken as
the team, led by Matt Finn, charged out onto the field.

Still no Father Thomas or P.B. as the Notre Dame team
lined up to kick off. There was an interlude of quiet, then a
mounting, whirring kind of yell that reached a climax as the
kicker's foot set the ball sailing high into the air; the sound
trailed off as the Southern California receiver took the ball
and was tackled immediately. The game was engaged but the
main players, as far as we were concerned, had not yet
arrived.

The first quarter dragged by and eight minutes of the
second with nothing much happening. It was a seesaw affair.
A quiet settled on the stands, and every once in a while an
interval occurred of perhaps a second's duration in which
there was no sound at all, as if the crowd had become
disconnected from its energy source momentarily and could
only find it again when a new play began. Well, there we
were, growing more tense by the moment when, just as the
crowd roared its approval of a Notre Dame interception, an
usher leaned over the railing of our box. "Miss Moore?" he

asked against the noise of the crowd. It was like trying to talk
at the base of Niagara Falls. "Father Kinsella would like to
see you at your car." Notre Dame made a first down on the
Southern California twelve-yard line as I rose to accompany
Maria through the corridor of deafening noise down the ramp
and out to the parking lot.

We could hear the crowd as we passed out of one of the
arches in the lower portico of the stadium but it sounded
muffled within the amphitheater we had just left. I puffed
along to keep up with Maria and in a few moments we were
back at her car. Father Thomas had been waiting inside but
he got out and opened the door for Maria before her
chauffeur could. The driver stayed outside with me as the
door closed again. I could see Thomas give her a brotherly
kiss of welcome but was distracted as the driver said to me, "I
hear you can get good Polish sausage here." I pointed with
my stick toward a stand by the field and turned back to
observe the scene inside the long black car.

"Tom, Tom, I've been thinking of you every minute."

"I could feel it, I knew you were with me." Thomas patted
her hand. "Maria, I told Archbishop Trafficante I would not
accept the call to go to Chicago."

"You what?"

"I told him no. He was surprised. Maybe you're surprised
too."

"No, I'm not, not really. I know where your heart is. And I
knew you didn't want to leave here."

"That's right. Even though my father wanted me to do it,
even though it might have saved Kinsella Industries from the
U. S. Attorney. But it was the right thing to do. Hard, but
right."

Maria leaned forward and kissed him. Thomas's face grew
serious.

"And, Maria, this is even harder. I have to say no to you,
too. No for now anyway."

Maria put her arms around Thomas's shoulders and leaned
against him. Thomas felt a pressure in his chest that was
almost unbearable. He felt like crying and, try as he would,
he could do nothing to stop himself. A tear fell on Maria's
shoulder.

"Oh, Tom," Maria said. "Poor Tom, it's been hard for you,
hasn't it? Harder than even I imagined." He began to sob and

she held him while the tension of the past several hours—and the past several years—fragmented like a collapsing dam and was washed away by the torrent of his weeping.

"Forgive me, Maria," Thomas said, his face streaked with tears.

"Why? Aren't Kinsellas allowed to cry?" Maria had the calm women are able to restore more quickly than men after a shaking emotional experience.

"I knew you'd say no to me. Otherwise, Tom, you would have asked me to say yes a long time ago." She helped him unfold a handkerchief and dried his face with it. "I understand that. I just needed to know if you understood what you wanted, what you thought about me. I had to know if you understood how I felt."

Thomas had regained control of himself. He did not seem sheepish or ashamed that he had broken down in front of Maria.

"I'm sorry, Maria. And I'm sorry I got you into all this. Sorry I involved you with me, or with the Kinsellas, sorry I can't take you away someplace where we could be alone."

"So am I, Tom, but I never expected that you would. I know you're married to Notre Dame."

He looked at her tenderly, as though having forsaken her for his work, he suddenly loved her more.

"Tom," she said evenly, "your heart is here. And your power is here. And it makes you powerful in other places too. You're not ready to separate, not at all."

"I'm afraid you're right. But I believe in what I'm doing, I believe in Christianity and the meaning of Notre Dame as a Catholic University. God forgive me, I can't help it."

"There's no need to explain all that. I'm a believer too. And right now I believe in you."

"We may not see each other very much."

"We don't really see each other very much now. We're—what was it your friend Father Allen called them?—'a surprising combination.'"

"We are that," Thomas said, managing a smile. "And maybe someday things will be different."

"Do you really think so? Do you think you'll become less involved, less important? Do you think you'll change, Tom, really change enough to do anything but what you're doing?"

Thomas shook his head slowly. "I don't know, I honestly

don't know." He wiped his face with his handkerchief again.
"But I know I'll always love you even if I can't prove that to
you."

"I know that," Maria answered. "I know you love me. It
was important for me to feel that you really did love me, that
you felt for me the way a human does instead of a disembod-
ied spirit. That doesn't clear up our problem. But it gives me
strength to bear it again for a while."

"For a while?"

"For as long as I can, Tom, for as long as I can. You know, I
once played Héloïse in a play about Abelard. Talk about
impossible loves! She entered a convent for him. And after
ten years she wrote him and said, 'I only want one thing from
you: to hear from your own lips the truth about our relationship, to tell me yourself what everybody else says is true
anyway, that you took me out of lust and put me away out of
fear.' She needed the truth from him. But poor Abelard
composed a prayer as a reply, a prayer that God would
forgive them for their sins."

Her voice trailed off and they sat in silence. "Tom, I don't
think you took me out of lust. I think that was love. I know it
was. But I think you might have put me away out of fear.
That's why I had to hear how you felt, from your lips, the way
you really feel, and not some spiritual version of it. That
would have left me with nothing at all."

They sat quietly for a while and I was growing quite restive,
not that I cared about the football game, although the up and
down cheers and groans that came up over the stadium wall
told me that exciting things were going on. I could tell that it
was half-time when the band music floated on the breeze
again and people in search of food or a stretch of the legs
began wandering out of the gate areas.

Thomas and Maria climbed out of the car. They seemed
quiet but peaceful, as though they had come to some deeper
understanding of each other and their relationship. Thomas
wasn't smiling yet and his eyes looked red but he was calm
and purposeful, I could see that. They didn't look happy,
mind you, but they did look peaceful.

"What will your father think?" Maria asked.

"Well, we'll soon find out. That looks like him heading for
the field over there."

Sure enough, about two lines of cars away, just above the

roof levels, I could see P.B.'s head, his wavy white hair blowing in the breeze and his face set like an Indian chief's as he moved swiftly toward the stadium.

"We'd better catch up with him," Father Thomas said, a smile, whose origin puzzled me, beginning to form on his face.

I looked up as we began to walk back to the football field. Another plane was flying over, trailing a different sign: "Pray for Peace—Farley Cadillac." Amen, I thought to myself as we showed our ticket stubs at the gate and passed once more into the cool shadows beneath the stands.

9

October 22, 1983
2:00 P.M.

P.B. was sipping a cup of coffee at the edge of a crowded concession stand. We walked over to him and he flashed a brief smile as he kissed Maria and shook hands with me and Thomas. He raised his cup to his lips, studying us with his eyes as he did so. There was a hubbub as the half-time crowds shifted around us and the voice of the announcer could be heard echoing across the field. "And now the marching band of the University of Notre Dame presents a medley of Irish favorites."

"They're playing my song," P.B. said, a hint of the familiar shark smile playing on his face as the first strains of the music came drifting down the passageways.

"P.B.," Thomas said, "I've made a decision."

"I knew you would. When do I call you 'Your Excellency'?" A passerby jostled P.B.'s shoulder and he almost spilled his drink. "Take it easy, pal," P.B. called after him.

"I'm afraid that's not in the cards. I turned down the offer to go to Chicago."

"You did *what?*" P.B. sounded incredulous.

"I told Archbishop Trafficante I'd rather stay here, that my most important work was right here." Maria was cheering Tom on silently.

"I don't understand you, Tom, I don't understand you at all." P.B. crushed his cup and tossed it into a nearby garbage can. "Don't you know what this means to me? Don't you know what it means to the family? How the hell could you turn down such an offer?"

"I did it because of what it means to me," Tom said, moving closer to his father as the crowd swelled behind him. "I couldn't do something like that just to protect the family from an investigation."

P.B.'s face hardened the way General Patton's must have just before he slapped that soldier.

"Do you know what you're saying?" P.B. asked angrily. He and his son were toe to toe, the elder Kinsella snorting like a dragon. He lunged slightly toward Thomas, raising his arm like a prizefighter. Thomas grabbed his father's forearm. Their faces were just inches apart as they both grimaced, their locked grip causing their arms to stiffen and tremble.

"Don't start something," Thomas said, his face straining.

"If you can't finish it," P.B. said, letting a rush of breath out as they broke free of each other. I would have called it a draw.

P.B.'s eyes were sparking as he looked at his son. They were still very close to each other.

"You were a damned fool to turn that job down. You could have been a Cardinal, like that goddam Taco King, what the hell is his name? Muñoz, that's it. Muñoz."

"Or like your friend, Williams."

"Oh, Leo's not so bad, not bad at all. You have to understand him." A smile played at the corner of P.B.'s lips as he said this. "So you turned it down." He shook his head. The crowd had begun to move back up the ramps toward the seats again. Some bars of "Danny Boy" could be heard above the mumble of the moving people.

"I want to stay here, I believe in this place."

"By God," P.B. said, standing back a few inches to appraise his son freshly, "you may be more like me than I thought." He laughed a little. "No wonder we've had trouble getting along. I couldn't get along with me either, if I were someone else." He turned toward Maria. "What do you think of the Kinsellas, Maria?" Nobody knew what to make of P.B.'s reaction; no all clear had been sounded yet.

"I think he's very much like his father," she said, holding P.B. off with her tone as well as Thomas had held him off in their tense arm struggle a few moments before.

"Yes, yes, he is . . ." P.B. gave us a full smile. "That's why I expected him to turn it down. Oh, I wanted him to take it all right. But I never thought he would."

"You tried hard enough to get me to take it," Thomas said firmly.

"Sure, sure. Hell, it's a good job." P.B. rubbed his chin. "And your mother would have loved it. But, hell, there was never anything but an outside chance you'd take it." He turned toward Maria. "And, if you'll pardon me, Miss Moore, there's never been much chance Tom would run off with you either. I might, but he wouldn't. Not that his mother hasn't worried about it."

Maria and Thomas both blushed. Maria touched Thomas's arm. She looked sad, the way noblewomen look in old paintings.

"No, Tom, I've known you have a mind of your own for a long time. That's why I never counted on you in this, not for a minute."

It was Thomas's turn to be incredulous. "What? You mean you let me think you wanted me to take that job to save the family and you never counted on it?"

"That's right," P.B. said easily. "Now, your brothers were different. Hell, Joe thinks he's like me. Well, he isn't. And Martin is a nice boy, but he is a boy. They've lost faith in their old man, that's their problem. They thought I needed you to save my skin, that they needed you to save their skin." P.B. shook his head.

"Did you turn them in? Is that what you did? Did you take the immunity?" Thomas asked urgently.

P.B. raised his hand. "They were so worried about their asses they couldn't think straight. They kept telling me that everything would be fine if you became the Archbishop. Maybe so. But there were two things wrong with that idea . . ."

The crowds had left the area and the band was winding up on the field. The second half would start in a few minutes.

"What do you mean?" Thomas asked.

"Well, first of all . . ." P.B. pulled us all a little closer. I could tell he was beginning to enjoy himself but I was damned if I knew why. "First of all, Tom, I didn't think it would work. This U. S. Attorney might go ahead and investigate even if you were the Pope. And, secondly, it would have made me depend on you, made me seem to owe it to you, no matter what, if the investigation fell through. I didn't like the odds."

P.B. removed a cigar from his pocket. He went through his regular stage business of lighting and puffing it until he was satisfied with the way it burned.

"Maybe we should go up and join your mother. She'll be worried."

With that, and calm as he could be, P.B. led us up the ramp and down to the presidential box. Mae looked glad to see him, and the other sons and their wives inspected him anxiously. "Relax," he said to them. "It's a long story. And we've got a game to win . . ." He seated himself and Thomas got down next to him. I ended up just behind them as the kickoff signaled the beginning of the second half. Notre Dame received and promptly fumbled the ball, turning it over on their own twenty-four-yard line. "Goddamn it, Tom, what the hell's the matter with this team?" P.B. growled. The score was tied at seven points each and Southern California had just been given a golden opportunity for a touchdown. The crowd groaned and then began spirited shouting all around us.

"P.B., stop enjoying yourself so much. What about the immunity? Is that what you did? Did you take it?"

"Oh, that," P.B. said, moving his head close to Thomas's. "I got to thinking about immunity, that's true. Then I realized it might work both ways . . ."

The United States Attorney for the Northern District of Illinois occupies a corner suite of offices in the Dirksen Federal Building on Dearborn Street in downtown Chicago. P.B. had been summoned there by Finbar Murphy, the crusading holder of the office who had already sent a variety of criminal types to jail, more, according to some, to advance his own career than to rid the city of corruption. Murphy was a tall, slender man of thirty-seven, a reformer and a do-gooder, a twin curse for old-line Chicago politicians. He had brought indictments against a number of aldermen and even some judges. He had jailed some business associates of P. B. Kinsella's. And he had used the same device every time. He would guarantee immunity from prosecution to some co-conspirator, somebody just as guilty as the accused person, in exchange for testimony on behalf of the prosecution.

Now Murphy was prepared to bait the biggest hook he had. If he could get P. B. Kinsella to accept immunity, he could break open two generations of deals and secret arrangements. He could make national headlines with such a performance. And then he could run for the Senate. Who knew what might happen after that? It would be cheap at the price if he could get P.B. to accept the immunity, cheap to let Kinsella Industries off with a slap on the wrist and maybe win suspended sentences for some of the sons. It was Friday and Patrick Bailey Kinsella, "The Kinsella" himself, would arrive in Murphy's carpeted office any moment. His secretary buzzed.

"Mr. Kinsella is here. He has two gentlemen with him."

"I'd like to see Mr. Kinsella alone, please," Murphy said. Probably has his lawyers with him, Murphy thought. Well, there will be time for that later. First he wanted to talk informally with the old man about the arrangements for immunity.

"Ah, Mr. Kinsella," Murphy said as P.B. entered.

"Mr. Murphy," P.B. said grimly.

"Let's just sit over here." Murphy pointed to a sofa and some easy chairs set around a coffee table in the corner.

P.B. remained silent as Murphy offered him a cigar.

"I've got my own," he finally said. "Why don't we get down to business?"

"As you say, Mr. Kinsella. That's why I wanted to talk off the record, just the two of us, before your lawyers get involved."

P.B. arched his eyebrows as though he were going to ask a question. He did not, however; he waited for Murphy to speak again.

The attorney went through a brief technical description of immunity and how it worked in the kinds of cases he had been bringing to court.

"Do you understand, Mr. Kinsella?"

"Not very difficult. You're asking me to turn others in.

Then you'll let me and my businesses go without a mark on them?"

"Well, as I've indicated, we may have to bring some charges. But I can guarantee that your sons will only get suspended sentences."

"Including the one who's president of Notre Dame?"

Murphy smiled uneasily. "Well, no, I mean he has nothing to do with your business."

"How do you know?" Kinsella asked offhandedly.

Murphy looked a little flustered. Score one for the old man.

"Well, it would be unusual if a priest were to hold any active interest in something like Kinsella Industries. It would be very unusual."

"We're an unusual family," P.B. said as he removed a cigar from his coat pocket. "You must know that."

"Well, be that as it may," Murphy said, trying to regain the high ground, "I'm saying that we would offer every assurance that your family's interests would not be treated harshly."

P.B. struck a match and fiddled with it as he held it beneath the tip of his cigar. He loved the small drama of lighting one, a trick he had learned from Uncle Joe Keenan. It always unsettled the other person.

"Very thoughtful of you," P.B. said between puffs. "But I wonder how much you really know about my business. Or my family. Or how they're related."

Murphy did not know exactly what to say. He wanted to ease this big fish in slowly, get his co-operation, and, at this point, not antagonize him. P.B. stood up. He thought of Uncle Joe many years before and of how he wandered around his big office to question the unwary. P.B. walked over to the windows and gazed down at the sprawl of the city.

"Great city, Mr. Murphy. Filled with good people, 'good family men,' as Dick Daley used to say, God rest him."

Murphy sat still. Might as well let him walk around, he thought, there's plenty of time for business, let him reminisce, let him talk about the great old days.

"Mr. Murphy, I've been around this city a long time. I know a lot about it. It is a city of good family people."

"I'm sure it is," Murphy said patiently.

P.B. turned back toward him.

"Mr. Murphy, just a point of interest. How much do you know about your own family?"

Murphy didn't know what to make of the question.

"Well, my father was killed in the war. I didn't have all the advantages your sons have had." Murphy was growing angry. "My mother died when I was two. I was raised in a wonderful home, by wonderful foster-parents."

P.B. waved his cigar and cut in on him.

"So I've heard, Mr. Murphy, so I've heard. Yours is a great story. You're a self-made man, an all-American." P.B. paused. "A fellow like you could grow up and be President some day."

Murphy cleared his throat. "I'd like to get back to the subject."

"I'm on the subject, Mr. Murphy. Or may I call you Finbar? Hell of a name, don't hear it much any more."

"We're talking about immunity, Mr. Kinsella."

"That's right," P.B. said as he strolled over and sat down behind the U. S. Attorney's large desk. "Immunity for you."

"What?" Murphy asked confusedly. "What is this, the Kinsella idea of a joke? Don't try to intimidate me, Mr. Kinsella!" He was openly angry now.

"Why, Finbar," P.B. said calmly. "Why ever would I do a thing like that?" P.B. stood up and moved slowly back toward the couch where the U. S. Attorney was sitting. He looked down at Murphy.

"Now, listen to me, Mr. Murphy. I'm here to make you an offer of immunity. Thoroughness, Mr. Murphy, is an important virtue. And while you have been busy trying to find out about me, I decided to find out a thing or two about you."

There was no sound in the room.

"My life history doesn't have a blemish on it," Murphy said. "You know that."

"Well, now," P.B. said, gesturing again with his cigar. "That's fine. Unless, of course, you don't know any more about your family than you know about mine or the way it's connected with my business. And I don't think you do." P.B. was moving in for the kill as Murphy looked up, puzzled and irritated at the same time.

"Mr. Kinsella, let's stop this playacting."

"Fine, Mr. Murphy, fine. Now let me tell you a thing or two. I've spent a considerable amount of time, and some money, on this, so pay attention." P.B.'s voice was filled with a harsh electricity.

"You think you're the son of a war hero and a mother who died working hard for you when you were two. Well, suppose

I tell you another story. Your father's name was Everett Casey and he worked in the Chancery office of the archdiocese. And your mother was a secretary there he used to screw on his lunch hour, on the couch in the Cardinal's office when he was out of town, that's how I hear it. Your mother had you at a Good Shepherd home in Iowa and you were farmed out to the Murphys early. Go on, call your mother if you want to, see what she can tell you. Ask her about your war hero father. Let me tell you about Everett Casey." P.B. took a breath as Murphy sat, his mouth fallen open, rage building inside him.

"Mr. Kinsella, you can't make accusations like that and get away with them. I'll send all of you, including the president of Notre Dame, to jail!"

"Like hell you will," P.B. said. "Now sit still and listen to me. These are your roots I'm telling you about, the roots nobody knows about and nobody needs to know about." P.B. stepped a few feet to the left and dropped his cigar in an ashtray.

"Your old man, Casey that is, was a crook. Took the archdiocese for five hundred and sixty thousand. Had a wife and a bunch of kids. Took the money and spent most of it on horses and women. That's who your real father was. And who saved his skin, and the archdiocese too? I did, Patrick Bailey Kinsella, that's who. I covered the loss and a pimp named Jack Moran and I traced your old man down, got what was left of the money, and sent it to his wife. Then we sent him packing."

"This can't be true," Murphy said in a stunned tone.

"Well, look at this for openers," P.B. said, removing a yellowed envelope from his coat pocket and handing Murphy the letter with the notarized signature of the then Monsignor Williams attesting to Kinsella's bail-out of the archdiocese.

Murphy read it through. "This says nothing about my father."

"No, no, but it sets the scene doesn't it, Finbar? Fills in the circumstances nicely, the background. You want to know about your father? Call in those men who came with me, those men you were so sure were my lawyers. You shouldn't jump to conclusions, Finbar, not a nice young fellow with a promising career like yours."

Murphy walked stiffly to his desk and asked his secretary to send in the men who were waiting outside.

They were both elderly, around Kinsella's age but not nearly in such good shape. One of them carried a briefcase.

"Mr. Murphy," P.B. intoned, "meet your father, Everett Casey. I traced him down to Joliet the other day. Nice old gentleman, he's been working as an accountant."

Murphy gazed in disbelief at the gray-haired man who walked toward him with his arms out.

"I always wondered what happened to you, son," Casey said in a low voice. "Your mother was a beauty."

Murphy backed away, as though Casey were about to lay unclean hands on him.

"This is preposterous," Murphy said. "Stay where you are."

"So you're my little boy," Casey said a little absently as P.B. brought the man with the briefcase up to the attorney's desk.

"And this is Mr. Barnum. He was hired by the Chancery to study the financial records at the time of the troubles and to remove any evidence that Mr. Casey or your mother ever worked there. Happily, he preserved the original records and would like to show them to you."

Murphy looked aghast as Mr. Barnum, with white curly hair, looking like an ancient Harpo Marx, snapped open the briefcase he had placed on the desk.

"Here, Mr. Murphy, are the records of the employment of both your father and mother. Her name was Priscilla Owens," P.B. growled. The mute Mr. Barnum, in reality the aged but still spry Michelangelo, tossed two packets of papers on the blotter. "Go ahead, look at them," Kinsella said. Then Barnum removed several other documents. P.B. took them one by one and dropped them on the table. "And here are the records from the Good Shepherd home in Des Moines, and here's your birth certificate. Your name is really Lawrence Casey, in case you're interested. And here's letters and records about your being taken in by the Murphys. All quite thorough and proper. Would you like to examine them?"

Murphy was shaking as he picked up the papers and riffled through them. "My God," he said in a whisper. "My God, this can't be true, this can't be true."

"We have other records too," P.B. added. "But we'll leave these for you to look over."

"My little boy," Everett Casey said as he looked down at

Murphy, who was paging through the papers. "Your mother sure was a honey . . ."

P.B. smiled at the bewildered Murphy. "Now, about this immunity, Finbar. I'll be glad to give it to you. You know, if they can show the diocese didn't have the evidence until now, the statute may still be running. Would you like to indict your old man? You just let me know, after you've studied all this . . ."

P.B. paused, his hand on the doorknob. "Good day, Senator," he said. "That has a nice ring, doesn't it?" He looked back at the stunned and open-mouthed Murphy. "There's a mouse on your cape," P.B. said, laughing out loud as he closed the door.

Notre Dame was behind 21–17, by the time P.B. finished telling his story to the small group of people huddled in deepest concentration around him.

"So that was what the call was about. Murphy's backing off. Hell, he must have thought I was Bicycle Irish. And by the way, Tom, you're listed as part owner of everything, you're listed in more things than you know, so you might have gone down with the ship anyway."

Thomas was caught between amusement and wonder. "Did Murphy check the records out? Is that what he did?"

"As many as he could. He's not going to cause us any trouble." P.B. smiled and leaned over to kiss Mae. "I told you to trust me."

"Oh, Patty," she said, nuzzling him as the crowd rose noisily to its feet around us. We were all in a daze from P.B.'s story but he was back cheering for the Irish. At that moment the Notre Dame quarterback, a lithe young black athlete named, so help me, Pat Riley, threw a pass that seemed to float off the end of his hand, the stitching of the ball appearing and disappearing as it spiraled down the field into the end zone to be caught for a touchdown by a husky fellow named Linowitz. The crowd exploded in a roar that soon collapsed when they realized that there had been a flag on the play. "Personal foul against Notre Dame," the announcer's voice informed the crowd. As the referee marched the Irish back fifteen yards, P.B. turned toward Thomas.

"It wasn't easy to find Michelangelo. But he was glad to see me. And Everett Casey, that wasn't so easy either. That's where I was all week when your brothers thought I was making a deal with Murphy."

"Were all those records real?" Thomas asked, remembering countless stories he had heard about Michelangelo and his re-creation of his father's college diploma.

P.B. held a hand up into the hush that fell on the crowd as the Notre Dame team lined up for what would be the last play of the game. The quarterback Riley had good protection and he lofted another pass, this time to a player named Caruso, who bobbled it a moment, then closed his arms on it as he fell under a charge of Southern California tackles in the end zone. The referee signaled a touchdown as time ran out on the clock. Whoops and hollers, and Irish battle cries went up like an offering back to the God the crowd had been praying to.

Programs sailed past our heads and confetti came down as though an Irishman had been elected Pope, and P.B. cheered as enthusiastically as anyone. Then, of course, things began to settle down, and the people started to collect their field glasses and souvenirs and to separate themselves from what they would always remember as a golden afternoon. P.B. turned to Thomas and the rest of us, grinning broadly against the background of the fans who were breaking for the exits.

"I asked you a question, P.B.," Thomas said, a half smile on his face. "Did you fake those records, or some of them?"

P.B. affected a hurt look. Then the outlines of a mischievous smile began to appear on his face as he put one arm around Mae and asked, "Now, what kind of an Irisher would do a thing like that?"

Another plane was just flying across the sky above the rim of the stadium opposite us. It trailed a sign—an answer—in big letters: "WHO CAN? KINSELLA CAN."

Well, we were astounded at what seemed to be a heavenly reply. Then P.B. laughed and Thomas, despite his reservations about his father's tactics, couldn't help himself. And, although her mood was bittersweet, Maria laughed too. Mae and the other sons and their wives joined in and I would have been a spoilsport, wouldn't I, not to laugh heartily myself?

The satisfied crowd was streaming past us, some of its members staring curiously as we laughed and slapped each other on the back like a group of musketeers. I stepped back from the family group to take a look at the pack of them, the Kinsellas and Maria, wiping their eyes and chuckling, as the stadium emptied out around them. They almost had control